Library of America, a nonprofit organization,
champions our nation's cultural heritage
by publishing America's greatest writing in
authoritative new editions and providing resources
for readers to explore this rich, living legacy.

RAY BRADBURY

Ray Bradbury

THE ILLUSTRATED MAN
THE OCTOBER COUNTRY
OTHER STORIES

Jonathan R. Eller, *editor*

THE LIBRARY OF AMERICA

Published in the United States by Library of America,
14 East 60th Street, New York, NY 10022.
Visit our website at www.loa.org.

This paper exceeds the requirements of
ANSI/NISO Z39.48–1992 (Permanence of Paper).

Distributed to the trade in the United States
by Penguin Random House Inc.
and in Canada by Penguin Random House Canada Ltd.

The authorized representative in the EU for product safety and compliance
is eucomply OÜ, Pärnu mnt, 139b-14, 11317 Tallinn, Estonia.
hello@eucompliancepartner.com

Library of Congress Control Number: 2021950350
ISBN 978–1–59853–728–0

Second Printing
The Library of America—360

Manufactured in the United States of America

Contents

THE ILLUSTRATED MAN

This book is for

FATHER, MOTHER, *and* SKIP,

with love.

Contents

PROLOGUE: *The Illustrated Man*

It was a warm afternoon in early September when I first met the Illustrated Man. Walking along an asphalt road, I was on the final leg of a two weeks' walking tour of Wisconsin. Late in the afternoon I stopped, ate some pork, beans, and a doughnut, and was preparing to stretch out and read when the Illustrated Man walked over the hill and stood for a moment against the sky.

I didn't know he was Illustrated then. I only knew that he was tall, once well muscled, but now, for some reason, going to fat. I recall that his arms were long, and the hands thick, but that his face was like a child's, set upon a massive body.

He seemed only to sense my presence, for he didn't look directly at me when he spoke his first words:

"Do you know where I can find a job?"

"I'm afraid not," I said.

"I haven't had a job that's lasted in forty years," he said.

Though it was a hot late afternoon, he wore his wool shirt buttoned tight about his neck. His sleeves were rolled and buttoned down over his thick wrists. Perspiration was streaming from his face, yet he made no move to open his shirt.

"Well," he said at last, "this is as good a place as any to spend the night. Do you mind company?"

"I have some extra food you'd be welcome to," I said.

He sat down heavily, grunting. "You'll be sorry you asked me to stay," he said. "Everyone always is. That's why I'm walking. Here it is, early September, the cream of the Labor Day carnival season. I should be making money hand over fist at any small town side show celebration, but here I am with no prospects."

He took off an immense shoe and peered at it closely. "I usually keep a job about ten days. Then something happens and they fire me. By now every carnival in America won't touch me with a ten-foot pole."

"What seems to be the trouble?" I asked.

For answer, he unbuttoned his tight collar, slowly. With his eyes shut, he put a slow hand to the task of unbuttoning his shirt all the way down. He slipped his fingers in to feel his chest. "Funny," he said, eyes still shut. "You can't feel them but they're there. I always hope that someday I'll look and they'll be gone. I walk in the sun for hours on the hottest days, baking, and hope that my sweat'll wash them off, the sun'll cook them off, but at sundown they're still there." He turned his head slightly toward me and exposed his chest. "Are they still there now?"

After a long while I exhaled. "Yes," I said. "They're still there."

The Illustrations.

"Another reason I keep my collar buttoned up," he said, opening his eyes, "is the children. They follow me along country roads. Everyone wants to see the pictures, and yet nobody wants to see them."

He took his shirt off and wadded it in his hands. He was covered with Illustrations from the blue tattooed ring about his neck to his belt line.

"It keeps right on going," he said, guessing my thought. "All of me is Illustrated. Look." He opened his hand. On his palm was a rose, freshly cut, with drops of crystal water among the soft pink petals. I put my hand out to touch it, but it was only an Illustration.

As for the rest of him, I cannot say how I sat and stared, for he was a riot of rockets and fountains and people, in such intricate detail and color that you could hear the voices murmuring small and muted, from the crowds that inhabited his body. When his flesh twitched, the tiny mouths flickered, the tiny green-and-gold eyes winked, the tiny pink hands gestured. There were yellow meadows and blue rivers and mountains and stars and suns and planets spread in a Milky Way across his chest. The people themselves were in twenty or more odd groups upon his arms, shoulders, back, sides, and wrists, as well as on the flat of his stomach. You found them in forests of hair, lurking among a constellation of freckles, or peering from armpit caverns, diamond eyes aglitter. Each seemed intent upon his own activity; each was a separate gallery portrait.

"Why, they're beautiful!*" I said.*

How can I explain about his Illustrations? If El Greco had painted miniatures in his prime, no bigger than your hand, infinitely detailed, with all his sulphurous color, elongation, and anatomy, perhaps he might have used this man's body for his art. The colors burned in three dimensions. They were windows looking in upon fiery reality. Here, gathered on one wall, were all the finest scenes in the universe; the man was a walking treasure gallery. This wasn't the work of a cheap carnival tattoo man with three colors and whisky on his breath. This was the accomplishment of a living genius, vibrant, clear, and beautiful.

"Oh yes," said the Illustrated Man. "I'm so proud of my Illustrations that I'd like to burn them off. I've tried sandpaper, acid, a knife . . ."

The sun was setting. The moon was already up in the East.

"For, you see," said the Illustrated Man, "these Illustrations predict the future."

I said nothing.

"It's all right in sunlight," he went on. "I could keep a carnival day job. But at night—the pictures move. The pictures change."

I must have smiled. "How long have you been Illustrated?"

"In 1900, when I was twenty years old and working a carnival, I broke my leg. It laid me up; I had to do something to keep my hand in, so I decided to get tattooed."

"But who tattooed you? What happened to the artist?"

"She went back to the future," he said. "I mean it. She was an old woman in a little house in the middle of Wisconsin here somewhere not far from this place. A little old witch who looked a thousand years old one moment and twenty years old the next, but she said she could travel in time. I laughed. Now, I know better."

"How did you happen to meet her?"

He told me. He had seen her painted sign by the road: SKIN ILLUSTRATION! *Illustration instead of tattoo! Artistic! So he had sat all night while her magic needles stung him wasp stings and delicate bee stings. By morning he looked like a man who had fallen into a twenty-color print press and been squeezed out, all bright and picturesque.*

"I've hunted every summer for fifty years," he said, putting his hands out on the air. "When I find that witch I'm going to kill her."

The sun was gone. Now the first stars were shining and the moon had brightened the fields of grass and wheat. Still the Illustrated Man's pictures glowed like charcoals in the half light, like scattered rubies and emeralds, with Rouault colors and Picasso colors and the long, pressed-out El Greco bodies.

"So people fire me when my pictures move. They don't like it when violent things happen in my Illustrations. Each Illustration is a little story. If you watch them, in a few minutes they tell you a tale. In three hours of looking you could see eighteen or twenty stories acted right on my body, you could hear voices and think thoughts. It's all here, just waiting for you to look. But most of all, there's a special spot on my body." He bared his back. "See? There's no special design on my right shoulder blade, just a jumble."

"Yes."

"When I've been around a person long enough, that spot clouds over and fills in. If I'm with a woman, her picture comes there on my back, in an hour, and shows her whole life—how she'll live, how she'll die, what she'll look like when she's sixty. And if it's a man, an hour later his picture's here on my back. It shows him falling off a cliff, or dying under a train. So I'm fired again."

All the time he had been talking his hands had wandered over the Illustrations, as if to adjust their frames, to brush away dust—the motions of a connoisseur, an art patron. Now he lay back, long and full in the moonlight. It was a warm night. There was no breeze and the air was stifling. We both had our shirts off.

"And you've never found the old woman?"

"Never."

"And you think she came from the future?"

"How else could she know these stories she painted on me?"

He shut his eyes tiredly. His voice grew fainter. "Sometimes at night I can feel them, the pictures, like ants, crawling on my skin. Then I know they're doing what they have to do. I never look at them any more. I just try to rest. I don't sleep much. Don't you look at them either, I warn you. Turn the other way when you sleep."

I lay back a few feet from him. He didn't seem violent, and the pictures were beautiful. Otherwise I might have been tempted to get out and away from such babbling. But the Illustrations . . . I let my eyes fill up on them. Any person would go a little mad with such things upon his body.

The night was serene. I could hear the Illustrated Man's breathing in the moonlight. Crickets were stirring gently in the distant ravines. I lay with my body sidewise so I could watch the Illustrations. Perhaps half an hour passed. Whether the

Illustrated Man slept I could not tell, but suddenly I heard him whisper, "They're moving, aren't they?"

I waited a minute.

Then I said, "Yes."

The pictures were moving, each in its turn, each for a brief minute or two. There in the moonlight, with the tiny tinkling thoughts and the distant sea voices, it seemed, each little drama was enacted. Whether it took an hour or three hours for the dramas to finish, it would be hard to say. I only know that I lay fascinated and did not move while the stars wheeled in the sky.

Eighteen Illustrations, eighteen tales. I counted them one by one.

Primarily my eyes focused upon a scene, a large house with two people in it. I saw a flight of vultures on a blazing flesh sky, I saw yellow lions, and I heard voices.

The first Illustration quivered and came to life. . . .

The Veldt

"GEORGE, I WISH you'd look at the nursery."

"What's wrong with it?"

"I don't know."

"Well, then."

"I just want you to look at it, is all, or call a psychologist in to look at it."

"What would a psychologist want with a nursery?"

"You know very well what he'd want." His wife paused in the middle of the kitchen and watched the stove busy humming to itself, making supper for four.

"It's just that the nursery is different now than it was."

"All right, let's have a look."

They walked down the hall of their soundproofed, Happylife Home, which had cost them thirty thousand dollars installed, this house which clothed and fed and rocked them to sleep and played and sang and was good to them. Their approach sensitized a switch somewhere and the nursery light flicked on when they came within ten feet of it. Similarly, behind them, in the halls, lights went on and off as they left them behind, with a soft automaticity.

"Well," said George Hadley.

They stood on the thatched floor of the nursery. It was forty feet across by forty feet long and thirty feet high; it had cost half again as much as the rest of the house. "But nothing's too good for our children," George had said.

The nursery was silent. It was empty as a jungle glade at hot high noon. The walls were blank and two dimensional. Now, as George and Lydia Hadley stood in the center of the room, the walls began to purr and recede into crystalline distance, it seemed, and presently an African veldt appeared, in three dimensions, on all sides, in color, reproduced to the final pebble and bit of straw. The ceiling above them became a deep sky with a hot yellow sun.

George Hadley felt the perspiration start on his brow.

"Let's get out of this sun," he said. "This is a little too real. But I don't see anything wrong."

"Wait a moment, you'll see," said his wife.

Now the hidden odorophonics were beginning to blow a wind of odor at the two people in the middle of the baked veldtland. The hot straw smell of lion grass, the cool green smell of the hidden water hole, the great rusty smell of animals, the smell of dust like a red paprika in the hot air. And now the sounds: the thump of distant antelope feet on grassy sod, the papery rustling of vultures. A shadow passed through the sky. The shadow flickered on George Hadley's upturned, sweating face.

"Filthy creatures," he heard his wife say.

"The vultures."

"You see, there are the lions, far over, that way. Now they're on their way to the water hole. They've just been eating," said Lydia. "I don't know what."

"Some animal." George Hadley put his hand up to shield off the burning light from his squinted eyes. "A zebra or a baby giraffe, maybe."

"Are you sure?" His wife sounded peculiarly tense.

"No, it's a little late to be sure," he said, amused. "Nothing over there I can see but cleaned bone, and the vultures dropping for what's left."

"Did you hear that scream?" she asked.

"No."

"About a minute ago?"

"Sorry, no."

The lions were coming. And again George Hadley was filled with admiration for the mechanical genius who had conceived this room. A miracle of efficiency selling for an absurdly low price. Every home should have one. Oh, occasionally they frightened you with their clinical accuracy, they startled you, gave you a twinge, but most of the time what fun for everyone, not only your own son and daughter, but for yourself when you felt like a quick jaunt to a foreign land, a quick change of scenery. Well, here it was!

And here were the lions now, fifteen feet away, so real, so feverishly and startlingly real that you could feel the prickling fur on your hand, and your mouth was stuffed with the dusty upholstery smell of their heated pelts, and the yellow of them was in your eyes like the yellow of an exquisite French tapestry, the yellows of lions and summer grass, and the sound of the matted lion lungs exhaling on the silent noontide, and the smell of meat from the panting, dripping mouths.

The lions stood looking at George and Lydia Hadley with terrible green-yellow eyes.

"Watch out!" screamed Lydia.

The lions came running at them.

Lydia bolted and ran. Instinctively, George sprang after her. Outside, in the hall, with the door slammed, he was laughing and she was crying, and they both stood appalled at the other's reaction.

"George!"

"Lydia! Oh, my dear poor sweet Lydia!"

"They almost got us!"

"Walls, Lydia, remember; crystal walls, that's all they are. Oh, they look real, I must admit—Africa in your parlor—but it's all dimensional superreactionary, supersensitive color film and mental tape film behind glass screens. It's all odorophonics and sonics, Lydia. Here's my handkerchief."

"I'm afraid." She came to him and put her body against him and cried steadily. "Did you see? Did you *feel*? It's too real."

"Now, Lydia . . ."

"You've got to tell Wendy and Peter not to read any more on Africa."

"Of course—of course." He patted her.

"Promise?"

"Sure."

"And lock the nursery for a few days until I get my nerves settled."

"You know how difficult Peter is about that. When I punished him a month ago by locking the nursery for even a few hours—the tantrum he threw! And Wendy too. They *live* for the nursery."

"It's got to be locked, that's all there is to it."

"All right." Reluctantly he locked the huge door. "You've been working too hard. You need a rest."

"I don't know—I don't know," she said, blowing her nose,

sitting down in a chair that immediately began to rock and comfort her. "Maybe I don't have enough to do. Maybe I have time to think too much. Why don't we shut the whole house off for a few days and take a vacation?"

"You mean you want to fry my eggs for me?"

"Yes." She nodded.

"And darn my socks?"

"Yes." A frantic, watery-eyed nodding.

"And sweep the house?"

"Yes, yes—oh, yes!"

"But I thought that's why we bought this house, so we wouldn't have to do anything?"

"That's just it. I feel like I don't belong here. The house is wife and mother now and nursemaid. Can I compete with an African veldt? Can I give a bath and scrub the children as efficiently or quickly as the automatic scrub bath can? I cannot. And it isn't just me. It's you. You've been awfully nervous lately."

"I suppose I have been smoking too much."

"You look as if you didn't know what to do with yourself in this house, either. You smoke a little more every morning and drink a little more every afternoon and need a little more sedative every night. You're beginning to feel unnecessary too."

"Am I?" He paused and tried to feel into himself to see what was really there.

"Oh, George!" She looked beyond him, at the nursery door. "Those lions can't get out of there, can they?"

He looked at the door and saw it tremble as if something had jumped against it from the other side.

"Of course not," he said.

At dinner they ate alone, for Wendy and Peter were at a special plastic carnival across town and had televised home to say they'd be late, to go ahead eating. So George Hadley, bemused, sat watching the dining-room table produce warm dishes of food from its mechanical interior.

"We forgot the ketchup," he said.

"Sorry," said a small voice within the table, and ketchup appeared.

As for the nursery, thought George Hadley, it won't hurt

for the children to be locked out of it awhile. Too much of anything isn't good for anyone. And it was clearly indicated that the children had been spending a little too much time on Africa. That *sun.* He could feel it on his neck, still, like a hot paw. And the *lions.* And the smell of blood. Remarkable how the nursery caught the telepathic emanations of the children's minds and created life to fill their every desire. The children thought lions, and there were lions. The children thought zebras, and there were zebras. Sun—sun. Giraffes—giraffes. Death and death.

That *last.* He chewed tastelessly on the meat that the table had cut for him. Death thoughts. They were awfully young, Wendy and Peter, for death thoughts. Or, no, you were never too young, really. Long before you knew what death was you were wishing it on someone else. When you were two years old you were shooting people with cap pistols.

But this—the long, hot African veldt—the awful death in the jaws of a lion. And repeated again and again.

"Where are you going?"

He didn't answer Lydia. Preoccupied, he let the lights glow softly on ahead of him, extinguish behind him as he padded to the nursery door. He listened against it. Far away, a lion roared.

He unlocked the door and opened it. Just before he stepped inside, he heard a faraway scream. And then another roar from the lions, which subsided quickly.

He stepped into Africa. How many times in the last year had he opened this door and found Wonderland, Alice, the Mock Turtle, or Aladdin and his Magical Lamp, or Jack Pumpkinhead of Oz, or Dr. Doolittle, or the cow jumping over a very real-appearing moon—all the delightful contraptions of a make-believe world. How often had he seen Pegasus flying in the sky ceiling, or seen fountains of red fireworks, or heard angel voices singing. But now, this yellow hot Africa, this bake oven with murder in the heat. Perhaps Lydia was right. Perhaps they needed a little vacation from the fantasy which was growing a bit too real for ten-year-old children. It was all right to exercise one's mind with gymnastic fantasies, but when the lively child mind settled on one pattern . . . ? It seemed that, at a distance, for the past month, he had heard lions roaring, and smelled their strong odor seeping as far away as his study door. But, being busy, he had paid it no attention.

George Hadley stood on the African grassland alone. The lions looked up from their feeding, watching him. The only flaw to the illusion was the open door through which he could see his wife, far down the dark hall, like a framed picture, eating her dinner abstractedly.

"Go away," he said to the lions.

They did not go.

He knew the principle of the room exactly. You sent out your thoughts. Whatever you thought would appear.

"Let's have Aladdin and his lamp," he snapped.

The veldtland remained; the lions remained.

"Come on, room! I demand Aladdin!" he said.

Nothing happened. The lions mumbled in their baked pelts.

"Aladdin!"

He went back to dinner. "The fool room's out of order," he said. "It won't respond."

"Or——"

"Or what?"

"Or it *can't* respond," said Lydia, "because the children have thought about Africa and lions and killing so many days that the room's in a rut."

"Could be."

"Or Peter's set it to remain that way."

"*Set* it?"

"He may have got into the machinery and fixed something."

"Peter doesn't know machinery."

"He's a wise one for ten. That I.Q. of his——"

"Nevertheless——"

"Hello, Mom. Hello, Dad."

The Hadleys turned. Wendy and Peter were coming in the front door, cheeks like peppermint candy, eyes like bright blue agate marbles, a smell of ozone on their jumpers from their trip in the helicopter.

"You're just in time for supper," said both parents.

"We're full of strawberry ice cream and hot dogs," said the children, holding hands. "But we'll sit and watch."

"Yes, come tell us about the nursery," said George Hadley.

The brother and sister blinked at him and then at each other. "Nursery?"

"All about Africa and everything," said the father with false joviality.

"I don't understand," said Peter.

"Your mother and I were just traveling through Africa with rod and reel; Tom Swift and his Electric Lion," said George Hadley.

"There's no Africa in the nursery," said Peter simply.

"Oh, come now, Peter. We know better."

"I don't remember any Africa," said Peter to Wendy. "Do you?"

"No."

"Run see and come tell."

She obeyed.

"Wendy, come back here!" said George Hadley, but she was gone. The house lights followed her like a flock of fireflies. Too late, he realized he had forgotten to lock the nursery door after his last inspection.

"Wendy'll look and come tell us," said Peter.

"She doesn't have to tell *me*. I've seen it."

"I'm sure you're mistaken, Father."

"I'm not, Peter. Come along now."

But Wendy was back. "It's not Africa," she said breathlessly.

"We'll see about this," said George Hadley, and they all walked down the hall together and opened the nursery door.

There was a green, lovely forest, a lovely river, a purple mountain, high voices singing, and Rima, lovely and mysterious, lurking in the trees with colorful flights of butterflies, like animated bouquets, lingering in her long hair. The African veldtland was gone. The lions were gone. Only Rima was here now, singing a song so beautiful that it brought tears to your eyes.

George Hadley looked in at the changed scene. "Go to bed," he said to the children.

They opened their mouths.

"You heard me," he said.

They went off to the air closet, where a wind sucked them like brown leaves up the flue to their slumber rooms.

George Hadley walked through the singing glade and

picked up something that lay in the corner near where the lions had been. He walked slowly back to his wife.

"What is that?" she asked.

"An old wallet of mine," he said.

He showed it to her. The smell of hot grass was on it and the smell of a lion. There were drops of saliva on it, it had been chewed, and there were blood smears on both sides.

He closed the nursery door and locked it, tight.

In the middle of the night he was still awake and he knew his wife was awake. "Do you think Wendy changed it?" she said at last, in the dark room.

"Of course."

"Made it from a veldt into a forest and put Rima there instead of lions?"

"Yes."

"Why?"

"I don't know. But it's staying locked until I find out."

"How did your wallet get there?"

"I don't know anything," he said, "except that I'm beginning to be sorry we bought that room for the children. If children are neurotic at all, a room like that——"

"It's supposed to help them work off their neuroses in a healthful way."

"I'm starting to wonder." He stared at the ceiling.

"We've given the children everything they ever wanted. Is this our reward—secrecy, disobedience?"

"Who was it said, 'Children are carpets, they should be stepped on occasionally'? We've never lifted a hand. They're insufferable—let's admit it. They come and go when they like; they treat us as if we were offspring. They're spoiled and we're spoiled."

"They've been acting funny ever since you forbade them to take the rocket to New York a few months ago."

"They're not old enough to do that alone, I explained."

"Nevertheless, I've noticed they've been decidedly cool toward us since."

"I think I'll have David McClean come tomorrow morning to have a look at Africa."

"But it's not Africa now, it's Green Mansions country and Rima."

"I have a feeling it'll be Africa again before then."

A moment later they heard the screams.

Two screams. Two people screaming from downstairs. And then a roar of lions.

"Wendy and Peter aren't in their rooms," said his wife.

He lay in his bed with his beating heart. "No," he said. "They've broken into the nursery."

"Those screams—they sound familiar."

"Do they?"

"Yes, awfully."

And although their beds tried very hard, the two adults couldn't be rocked to sleep for another hour. A smell of cats was in the night air.

"Father?" said Peter.

"Yes."

Peter looked at his shoes. He never looked at his father any more, nor at his mother. "You aren't going to lock up the nursery for good, are you?"

"That all depends."

"On what?" snapped Peter.

"On you and your sister. If you intersperse this Africa with a little variety—oh, Sweden perhaps, or Denmark or China——"

"I thought we were free to play as we wished."

"You are, within reasonable bounds."

"What's wrong with Africa, Father?"

"Oh, so now you admit you have been conjuring up Africa, do you?"

"I wouldn't want the nursery locked up," said Peter coldly. "Ever."

"Matter of fact, we're thinking of turning the whole house off for about a month. Live sort of a carefree one-for-all existence."

"That sounds dreadful! Would I have to tie my own shoes instead of letting the shoe tier do it? And brush my own teeth and comb my hair and give myself a bath?"

"It would be fun for a change, don't you think?"

"No, it would be horrid. I didn't like it when you took out the picture painter last month."

"That's because I wanted you to learn to paint all by yourself, son."

"I don't want to do anything but look and listen and smell; what else *is* there to do?"

"All right, go play in Africa."

"Will you shut off the house sometime soon?"

"We're considering it."

"I don't think you'd better consider it any more, Father."

"I won't have any threats from my son!"

"Very well." And Peter strolled off to the nursery.

"Am I on time?" said David McClean.

"Breakfast?" asked George Hadley.

"Thanks, had some. What's the trouble?"

"David, you're a psychologist."

"I should hope so."

"Well, then, have a look at our nursery. You saw it a year ago when you dropped by; did you notice anything peculiar about it then?"

"Can't say I did; the usual violences, a tendency toward a slight paranoia here or there, usual in children because they feel persecuted by parents constantly, but, oh, really nothing."

They walked down the hall. "I locked the nursery up," explained the father, "and the children broke back into it during the night. I let them stay so they could form the patterns for you to see."

There was a terrible screaming from the nursery.

"There it is," said George Hadley. "See what you make of it."

They walked in on the children without rapping.

The screams had faded. The lions were feeding.

"Run outside a moment, children," said George Hadley. "No, don't change the mental combination. Leave the walls as they are. Get!"

With the children gone, the two men stood studying the lions clustered at a distance, eating with great relish whatever it was they had caught.

"I wish I knew what it was," said George Hadley. "Sometimes I can almost see. Do you think if I brought high-powered binoculars here and——"

David McClean laughed dryly. "Hardly." He turned to study all four walls. "How long has this been going on?"

"A little over a month."

"It certainly doesn't *feel* good."

"I want facts, not feelings."

"My dear George, a psychologist never saw a fact in his life. He only hears about feelings; vague things. This doesn't feel good, I tell you. Trust my hunches and my instincts. I have a nose for something bad. This is very bad. My advice to you is to have the whole damn room torn down and your children brought to me every day during the next year for treatment."

"Is it that bad?"

"I'm afraid so. One of the original uses of these nurseries was so that we could study the patterns left on the walls by the child's mind, study at our leisure, and help the child. In this case, however, the room has become a channel toward—destructive thoughts, instead of a release away from them."

"Didn't you sense this before?"

"I sensed only that you had spoiled your children more than most. And now you're letting them down in some way. What way?"

"I wouldn't let them go to New York."

"What else?"

"I've taken a few machines from the house and threatened them, a month ago, with closing up the nursery unless they did their homework. I did close it for a few days to show I meant business."

"Ah, ha!"

"Does that mean anything?"

"Everything. Where before they had a Santa Claus now they have a Scrooge. Children prefer Santas. You've let this room and this house replace you and your wife in your children's affections. This room is their mother and father, far more important in their lives than their real parents. And now you come along and want to shut it off. No wonder there's hatred here. You can feel it coming out of the sky. Feel that sun. George, you'll have to change your life. Like too many others, you've built it around creature comforts. Why, you'd starve tomorrow if something went wrong in your kitchen. You wouldn't know how to tap an egg. Nevertheless, turn everything off. Start new. It'll take time. But we'll make good children out of bad in a year, wait and see."

"But won't the shock be too much for the children, shutting the room up abruptly, for good?"

"I don't want them going any deeper into this, that's all."

The lions were finished with their red feast.

The lions were standing on the edge of the clearing watching the two men.

"Now *I'm* feeling persecuted," said McClean. "Let's get out of here. I never have cared for these damned rooms. Make me nervous."

"The lions look real, don't they?" said George Hadley. "I don't suppose there's any way——"

"What?"

"—that they could *become* real?"

"Not that I know."

"Some flaw in the machinery, a tampering or something?"

"No."

They went to the door.

"I don't imagine the room will like being turned off," said the father.

"Nothing ever likes to die—even a room."

"I wonder if it hates me for wanting to switch it off?"

"Paranoia is thick around here today," said David McClean. "You can follow it like a spoor. Hello." He bent and picked up a bloody scarf. "This yours?"

"No." George Hadley's face was rigid. "It belongs to Lydia."

They went to the fuse box together and threw the switch that killed the nursery.

The two children were in hysterics. They screamed and pranced and threw things. They yelled and sobbed and swore and jumped at the furniture.

"You can't do that to the nursery, you can't!"

"Now, children."

The children flung themselves onto a couch, weeping.

"George," said Lydia Hadley, "turn on the nursery, just for a few moments. You can't be so abrupt."

"No."

"You can't be so cruel."

"Lydia, it's off, and it stays off. And the whole damn house dies as of here and now. The more I see of the mess we've put ourselves in, the more it sickens me. We've been contemplating our mechanical, electronic navels for too long. My God, how we need a breath of honest air!"

And he marched about the house turning off the voice clocks, the stoves, the heaters, the shoe shiners, the shoe lacers, the body scrubbers and swabbers and massagers, and every other machine he could put his hand to.

The house was full of dead bodies, it seemed. It felt like a mechanical cemetery. So silent. None of the humming hidden energy of machines waiting to function at the tap of a button.

"Don't let them do it!" wailed Peter at the ceiling, as if he was talking to the house, the nursery. "Don't let Father kill everything." He turned to his father. "Oh, I hate you!"

"Insults won't get you anywhere."

"I wish you were dead!"

"We were, for a long while. Now we're going to really start living. Instead of being handled and massaged, we're going to *live*."

Wendy was still crying and Peter joined her again. "Just a moment, just one moment, just another moment of nursery," they wailed.

"Oh, George," said the wife, "it can't hurt."

"All right—all right, if they'll only just shut up. One minute, mind you, and then off forever."

"Daddy, Daddy, Daddy!" sang the children, smiling with wet faces.

"And then we're going on a vacation. David McClean is coming back in half an hour to help us move out and get to the airport. I'm going to dress. You turn the nursery on for a minute, Lydia, just a minute, mind you."

And the three of them went babbling off while he let himself be vacuumed upstairs through the air flue and set about dressing himself. A minute later Lydia appeared.

"I'll be glad when we get away," she sighed.

"Did you leave them in the nursery?"

"I wanted to dress too. Oh, that horrid Africa. What can they see in it?"

"Well, in five minutes we'll be on our way to Iowa. Lord, how did we ever get in this house? What prompted us to buy a nightmare?"

"Pride, money, foolishness."

"I think we'd better get downstairs before those kids get engrossed with those damned beasts again."

Just then they heard the children calling, "Daddy, Mommy, come quick—quick!"

They went downstairs in the air flue and ran down the hall. The children were nowhere in sight. "Wendy? Peter!"

They ran into the nursery. The veldtland was empty save for the lions waiting, looking at them. "Peter, Wendy?"

The door slammed.

"Wendy, Peter!"

George Hadley and his wife whirled and ran back to the door.

"Open the door!" cried George Hadley, trying the knob. "Why, they've locked it from the outside! Peter!" He beat at the door. "Open up!"

He heard Peter's voice outside, against the door.

"Don't let them switch off the nursery and the house," he was saying.

Mr. and Mrs. George Hadley beat at the door. "Now, don't be ridiculous, children. It's time to go. Mr. McClean'll be here in a minute and . . ."

And then they heard the sounds.

The lions on three sides of them, in the yellow veldt grass, padding through the dry straw, rumbling and roaring in their throats.

The lions.

Mr. Hadley looked at his wife and they turned and looked back at the beasts edging slowly forward, crouching, tails stiff.

Mr. and Mrs. Hadley screamed.

And suddenly they realized why those other screams had sounded familiar.

"Well, here I am," said David McClean in the nursery doorway. "Oh, hello." He stared at the two children seated in the center of the open glade eating a little picnic lunch. Beyond them was the water hole and the yellow veldtland; above was the hot sun. He began to perspire. “Where are your father and mother?”

The children looked up and smiled. “Oh, they’ll be here directly.”

“Good, we must get going.” At a distance Mr. McClean saw the lions fighting and clawing and then quieting down to feed in silence under the shady trees.

He squinted at the lions with his hand up to his eyes.

Now the lions were done feeding. They moved to the water hole to drink.

A shadow flickered over Mr. McClean’s hot face. Many shadows flickered. The vultures were dropping down the blazing sky.

“A cup of tea?” asked Wendy in the silence.

The Illustrated Man shifted in his sleep. He turned, and each time he turned another picture came to view, coloring his back, his arm, his wrist. He flung a hand over the dry night grass. The fingers uncurled and there upon his palm another Illustration stirred to life. He twisted, and on his chest was an empty space of stars and blackness, deep, deep, and something moving among those stars, something falling in the blackness, falling while I watched. . . .

Kaleidoscope

THE FIRST CONCUSSION cut the rocket up the side with a giant can opener. The men were thrown into space like a dozen wriggling silverfish. They were scattered into a dark sea; and the ship, in a million pieces, went on, a meteor swarm seeking a lost sun.

"Barkley, Barkley, where are you?"

The sound of voices calling like lost children on a cold night.

"Woode, Woode!"

"Captain!"

"Hollis, Hollis, this is Stone."

"Stone, this is Hollis. Where are you?"

"I don't know. How can I? Which way is up? I'm falling. Good God, I'm falling."

They fell. They fell as pebbles fall down wells. They were scattered as jackstones are scattered from a gigantic throw. And now instead of men there were only voices—all kinds of voices, disembodied and impassioned, in varying degrees of terror and resignation.

"We're going away from each other."

This was true. Hollis, swinging head over heels, knew this was true. He knew it with a vague acceptance. They were parting to go their separate ways, and nothing could bring them back. They were wearing their sealed-tight space suits with the glass tubes over their pale faces, but they hadn't had time to lock on their force units. With them they could be small lifeboats in space, saving themselves, saving others, collecting together, finding each other until they were an island of men with some plan. But without the force units snapped to their shoulders they were meteors, senseless, each going to a separate and irrevocable fate.

A period of perhaps ten minutes elapsed while the first terror died and a metallic calm took its place. Space began to weave its strange voices in and out, on a great dark loom, crossing, recrossing, making a final pattern.

"Stone to Hollis. How long can we talk by phone?"

"It depends on how fast you're going your way and I'm going mine."

"An hour, I make it."

"That should do it," said Hollis, abstracted and quiet.

"What happened?" said Hollis a minute later.

"The rocket blew up, that's all. Rockets do blow up."

"Which way are you going?"

"It looks like I'll hit the moon."

"It's Earth for me. Back to old Mother Earth at ten thousand miles per hour. I'll burn like a match." Hollis thought of it with a queer abstraction of mind. He seemed to be removed from his body, watching it fall down and down through space, as objective as he had been in regard to the first falling snowflakes of a winter season long gone.

The others were silent, thinking of the destiny that had brought them to this, falling, falling, and nothing they could do to change it. Even the captain was quiet, for there was no command or plan he knew that could put things back together again.

"Oh, it's a long way down. Oh, it's a long way down, a long, long, long way down," said a voice. "I don't want to die, I don't want to die, it's a long way down."

"Who's that?"

"I don't know."

"Stimson, I think. Stimson, is that you?"

"It's a long, long way and I don't like it. Oh, God, I don't like it."

"Stimson, this is Hollis. Stimson, you hear me?"

A pause while they fell separate from one another.

"Stimson?"

"Yes." He replied at last.

"Stimson, take it easy; we're all in the same fix."

"I don't want to be here. I want to be somewhere else."

"There's a chance we'll be found."

"I must be, I must be," said Stimson. "I don't believe this; I don't believe any of this is happening."

"It's a bad dream," said someone.

"Shut up!" said Hollis.

"Come and make me," said the voice. It was Applegate. He laughed easily, with a similar objectivity. "Come and shut me up."

Hollis for the first time felt the impossibility of his position. A great anger filled him, for he wanted more than anything at this moment to be able to do something to Applegate. He had wanted for many years to do something and now it was too late. Applegate was only a telephonic voice.

Falling, falling, falling . . .

Now, as if they had discovered the horror, two of the men began to scream. In a nightmare Hollis saw one of them float by, very near, screaming and screaming.

"Stop it!" The man was almost at his fingertips, screaming insanely. He would never stop. He would go on screaming for a million miles, as long as he was in radio range, disturbing all of them, making it impossible for them to talk to one another.

Hollis reached out. It was best this way. He made the extra effort and touched the man. He grasped the man's ankle and pulled himself up along the body until he reached the head. The man screamed and clawed frantically, like a drowning swimmer. The screaming filled the universe.

One way or the other, thought Hollis. The moon or Earth or meteors will kill him, so why not now?

He smashed the man's glass mask with his iron fist. The screaming stopped. He pushed off from the body and let it spin away on its own course, falling.

Falling, falling down space Hollis and the rest of them went in the long, endless dropping and whirling of silence.

"Hollis, you still there?"

Hollis did not speak, but felt the rush of heat in his face.

"This is Applegate again."

"All right, Applegate."

"Let's talk. We haven't anything else to do."

The captain cut in. "That's enough of that. We've got to figure a way out of this."

"Captain, why don't you shut up?" said Applegate.

"What!"

"You heard me, Captain. Don't pull your rank on me, you're ten thousand miles away by now, and let's not kid ourselves. As Stimson puts it, it's a long way down."

"See here, Applegate!"

"Can it. This is a mutiny of one. I haven't a damn thing to

lose. Your ship was a bad ship and you were a bad captain and I hope you break when you hit the Moon."

"I'm ordering you to stop!"

"Go on, order me again." Applegate smiled across ten thousand miles. The captain was silent. Applegate continued, "Where were we, Hollis? Oh yes, I remember. I hate you too. But you know that. You've known it for a long time."

Hollis clenched his fists, helplessly.

"I want to tell you something," said Applegate. "Make you happy. I was the one who blackballed you with the Rocket Company five years ago."

A meteor flashed by. Hollis looked down and his left hand was gone. Blood spurted. Suddenly there was no air in his suit. He had enough air in his lungs to move his right hand over and twist a knob at his left elbow, tightening the joint and sealing the leak. It had happened so quickly that he was not surprised. Nothing surprised him any more. The air in the suit came back to normal in an instant now that the leak was sealed. And the blood that had flowed so swiftly was pressured as he fastened the knob yet tighter, until it made a tourniquet.

All of this took place in a terrible silence on his part. And the other men chatted. That one man, Lespere, went on and on with his talk about his wife on Mars, his wife on Venus, his wife on Jupiter, his money, his wondrous times, his drunkenness, his gambling, his happiness. On and on, while they all fell. Lespere reminisced on the past, happy, while he fell to his death.

It was so very odd. Space, thousands of miles of space, and these voices vibrating in the center of it. No one visible at all, and only the radio waves quivering and trying to quicken other men into emotion.

"Are you angry, Hollis?"

"No." And he was not. The abstraction had returned and he was a thing of dull concrete, forever falling nowhere.

"You wanted to get to the top all your life, Hollis. You always wondered what happened. I put the black mark on you just before I was tossed out myself."

"That isn't important," said Hollis. And it was not. It was gone. When life is over it is like a flicker of bright film, an instant on the screen, all of its prejudices and passions condensed and illumined for an instant on space, and before you could cry out, "There was a happy day, there a bad one, there an evil face, there a good one," the film burned to a cinder, the screen went dark.

From this outer edge of his life, looking back, there was only one remorse, and that was only that he wished to go on living. Did all dying people feel this way, as if they had never lived? Did life seem that short, indeed, over and done before you took a breath? Did it seem this abrupt and impossible to everyone, or only to himself, here, now, with a few hours left to him for thought and deliberation?

One of the other men, Lespere, was talking. "Well, I had me a good time: I had a wife on Mars, Venus, and Jupiter. Each of them had money and treated me swell. I got drunk and once I gambled away twenty thousand dollars."

But you're here now, thought Hollis. I didn't have any of those things. When I was living I was jealous of you, Lespere; when I had another day ahead of me I envied you your women and your good times. Women frightened me and I went into space, always wanting them and jealous of you for having them, and money, and as much happiness as you could have in your own wild way. But now, falling here, with everything over, I'm not jealous of you any more, because it's over for you as it is for me, and right now it's like it never was. Hollis craned his face forward and shouted into the telephone.

"It's all over, Lespere!"

Silence.

"It's just as if it never was, Lespere!"

"Who's that?" Lespere's faltering voice.

"This is Hollis."

He was being mean. He felt the meanness, the senseless meanness of dying. Applegate had hurt him; now he wanted to hurt another. Applegate and space had both wounded him.

"You're out here, Lespere. It's all over. It's just as if it had never happened, isn't it?"

"No."

"When anything's over, it's just like it never happened. Where's your life any better than mine, now? Now is what counts. Is it any better? Is it?"

"Yes, it's better!"

"How!"

"Because I got my thoughts, I remember!" cried Lespere, far away, indignant, holding his memories to his chest with both hands.

And he was right. With a feeling of cold water rushing through his head and body, Hollis knew he was right. There were differences between memories and dreams. He had only dreams of things he had wanted to do, while Lespere had memories of things done and accomplished. And this knowledge began to pull Hollis apart, with a slow, quivering precision.

"What good does it do you?" he cried to Lespere. "Now? When a thing's over it's not good any more. You're no better off than me."

"I'm resting easy," said Lespere. "I've had my turn. I'm not getting mean at the end, like you."

"Mean?" Hollis turned the word on his tongue. He had never been mean, as long as he could remember, in his life. He had never dared to be mean. He must have saved it all of these years for such a time as this. "Mean." He rolled the word into the back of his mind. He felt tears start into his eyes and roll down his face. Someone must have heard his gasping voice.

"Take it easy, Hollis."

It was, of course, ridiculous. Only a minute before he had been giving advice to others, to Stimson; he had felt a braveness which he had thought to be the genuine thing, and now he knew that it had been nothing but shock and the objectivity possible in shock. Now he was trying to pack a lifetime of suppressed emotion into an interval of minutes.

"I know how you feel, Hollis," said Lespere, now twenty thousand miles away, his voice fading. "I don't take it personally."

But aren't we equal? he wondered. Lespere and I? Here, now? If a thing's over, it's done, and what good is it? You die anyway. But he knew he was rationalizing, for it was like trying to tell the difference between a live man and a corpse. There was a spark in one, and not in the other—an aura, a mysterious element.

So it was with Lespere and himself; Lespere had lived a good full life, and it made him a different man now, and he, Hollis, had been as good as dead for many years. They came to death by separate paths and, in all likelihood, if there were kinds of death, their kinds would be as different as night from day. The quality of death, like that of life, must be of an infinite variety, and if one has already died once, then what was there to look for in dying for good and all, as he was now?

It was a second later that he discovered his right foot was cut sheer away. It almost made him laugh. The air was gone from his suit again. He bent quickly, and there was blood, and the meteor had taken flesh and suit away to the ankle. Oh, death in space was most humorous. It cut you away, piece by piece, like a black and invisible butcher. He tightened the valve at the knee, his head whirling into pain, fighting to remain aware, and with the valve tightened, the blood retained, the air kept, he straightened up and went on falling, falling, for that was all there was left to do.

"Hollis?"

Hollis nodded sleepily, tired of waiting for death.

"This is Applegate again," said the voice.

"Yes."

"I've had time to think. I listened to you. This isn't good. It makes us bad. This is a bad way to die. It brings all the bile out. You listening, Hollis?"

"Yes."

"I lied. A minute ago. I lied. I didn't blackball you. I don't know why I said that. Guess I wanted to hurt you. You seemed the one to hurt. We've always fought. Guess I'm getting old fast and repenting fast. I guess listening to you be mean made me ashamed. Whatever the reason, I want you to know I was an idiot too. There's not an ounce of truth in what I said. To hell with you."

Hollis felt his heart begin to work again. It seemed as if it hadn't worked for five minutes, but now all of his limbs began to take color and warmth. The shock was over, and the successive shocks of anger and terror and loneliness were passing. He felt like a man emerging from a cold shower in the morning, ready for breakfast and a new day.

"Thanks, Applegate."

"Don't mention it. Up your nose, you bastard."

"Hey," said Stone.

"What?" Hollis called across space; for Stone, of all of them, was a good friend.

"I've got myself into a meteor swarm, some little asteroids."

"Meteors?"

"I think it's the Myrmidone cluster that goes out past Mars and in toward Earth once every five years. I'm right in the middle. It's like a big kaleidoscope. You get all kinds of colors and shapes and sizes. God, it's beautiful, all that metal."

Silence.

"I'm going with them," said Stone. "They're taking me off with them. I'll be damned." He laughed.

Hollis looked to see, but saw nothing. There were only the great diamonds and sapphires and emerald mists and velvet inks of space, with God's voice mingling among the crystal fires. There was a kind of wonder and imagination in the thought of Stone going off in the meteor swarm, out past Mars for years and coming in toward Earth every five years, passing in and out of the planet's ken for the next million centuries, Stone and the Myrmidone cluster eternal and unending, shifting and shaping like the kaleidoscope colors when you were a child and held the long tube to the sun and gave it a twirl.

"So long, Hollis." Stone's voice, very faint now. "So long."

"Good luck," shouted Hollis across thirty thousand miles.

"Don't be funny," said Stone, and was gone.

The stars closed in.

Now all the voices were fading, each on his own trajectory, some to Mars, others into farthest space. And Hollis himself . . . He looked down. He, of all the others, was going back to Earth alone.

"So long."

"Take it easy."

"So long, Hollis." That was Applegate.

The many good-bys. The short farewells. And now the great loose brain was disintegrating. The components of the brain which had worked so beautifully and efficiently in the skull case of the rocket ship firing through space were dying one by one; the meaning of their life together was falling apart. And as a body dies when the brain ceases functioning, so the spirit of the ship and their long time together and what they meant to one another was dying. Applegate was now no more than a finger blown from the parent body, no longer to be despised and worked against. The brain was exploded, and the senseless, useless fragments of it were far scattered. The voices faded and now all of space was silent. Hollis was alone, falling.

They were all alone. Their voices had died like echoes of the words of God spoken and vibrating in the starred deep. There went the captain to the Moon; there Stone with the meteor swarm; there Stimson; there Applegate toward Pluto; there Smith and Turner and Underwood and all the rest, the shards of the kaleidoscope that had formed a thinking pattern for so long, hurled apart.

And I? thought Hollis. What can I do? Is there anything I can do now to make up for a terrible and empty life? If only I could do one good thing to make up for the meanness I collected all these years and didn't even know was in me! But there's no one here but myself, and how can you do good all alone? You can't. Tomorrow night I'll hit Earth's atmosphere.

I'll burn, he thought, and be scattered in ashes all over the continental lands. I'll be put to use. Just a little bit, but ashes are ashes and they'll add to the land.

He fell swiftly, like a bullet, like a pebble, like an iron weight, objective, objective all of the time now, not sad or happy or anything, but only wishing he could do a good thing now that everything was gone, a good thing for just himself to know about.

When I hit the atmosphere, I'll burn like a meteor.

"I wonder," he said, "if anyone'll see me?"

The small boy on the country road looked up and screamed. "Look, Mom, look! A falling star!"

The blazing white star fell down the sky of dusk in Illinois.

"Make a wish," said his mother. "Make a wish."

The Illustrated Man turned in the moonlight. He turned again . . . and again . . . and again. . . .

The Other Foot

WHEN THEY HEARD the news they came out of the restaurants and cafés and hotels and looked at the sky. They lifted their dark hands over their upturned white eyes. Their mouths hung wide. In the hot noon for thousands of miles there were little towns where the dark people stood with their shadows under them, looking up.

In her kitchen Hattie Johnson covered the boiling soup, wiped her thin fingers on a cloth, and walked carefully to the back porch.

"Come on, Ma! Hey, Ma, come on—you'll miss it!"

"Hey, Mom!"

Three little Negro boys danced around in the dusty yard, yelling. Now and then they looked at the house frantically.

"I'm coming," said Hattie, and opened the screen door. "Where you hear this rumor?"

"Up at Jones's, Ma. They say a rocket's coming, first one in twenty years, with a white man in it!"

"What's a white man? I never seen one."

"You'll find out," said Hattie. "Yes indeed, you'll find out."

"Tell us about one, Ma. Tell like you did."

Hattie frowned. "Well, it's been a long time. I was a little girl, you see. That was back in 1965."

"Tell us about a white man, Mom!"

She came and stood in the yard, looking up at the blue clear Martian sky with the thin white Martian clouds, and in the distance the Martian hills broiling in the heat. She said at last, "Well, first of all, they got white hands."

"White hands!" The boys joked, slapping each other.

"And they got white arms."

"White arms!" hooted the boys.

"And white faces."

"White faces! *Really?*"

"White like this, Mom?" The smallest threw dust on his face, sneezing. "This way?"

"Whiter than that," she said gravely, and turned to the sky

again. There was a troubled thing in her eyes, as if she was looking for a thundershower up high, and not seeing it made her worry. "Maybe you better go inside."

"Oh, Mom!" They stared at her in disbelief. "We got to watch, we just got to. Nothing's going to happen, is it?"

"I don't know. I got a feeling, is all."

"We just want to see the ship and maybe run down to the port and see that white man. What's he like, huh, Mom?"

"I don't know. I just don't know," she mused, shaking her head.

"Tell us some more!"

"Well, the white people live on Earth, which is where we all come from, twenty years ago. We just up and walked away and came to Mars and set down and built towns and here we are. Now we're Martians instead of Earth people. And no white men've come up here in all that time. That's the story."

"Why didn't they come up, Mom?"

"Well, 'cause. Right after we got up here, Earth got in an atom war. They blew each other up terribly. They forgot us. When they finished fighting, after years, they didn't have any rockets. Took them until recently to build more. So here they come now, twenty years later, to visit." She gazed at her children numbly and then began to walk. "You wait here. I'm going down the line to Elizabeth Brown's house. You promise to stay?"

"We don't want to but we will."

"All right, then." And she ran off down the road.

At the Browns' she arrived in time to see everybody packed into the family car. "Hey there, Hattie! Come on along!"

"Where you going?" she said, breathlessly running up.

"To see the white man!"

"That's right," said Mr. Brown seriously. He waved at his load. "These children never saw one, and *I* almost forgot."

"What you going to do with that white man?" asked Hattie.

"Do?" said everyone. "Why—just *look* at him, is all."

"You sure?"

"What else *can* we do?"

"I don't know," said Hattie. "I just thought there might be trouble."

"What kind of trouble?"

"You *know*," said Hattie vaguely, embarrassed. "You ain't going to lynch him?"

"Lynch him?" Everyone laughed. Mr. Brown slapped his knee. "Why, bless you, child, no! We're going to shake his hand. Ain't we, everyone?"

"Sure, sure!"

Another car drove up from another direction and Hattie gave a cry. "Willie!"

"What you doing 'way down here? Where're the kids?" shouted her husband angrily. He glared at the others. "You going down like a bunch of fools to see that man come in?"

"That appears to be just right," agreed Mr. Brown, nodding and smiling.

"Well, take your guns along," said Willie. "I'm on my way home for mine right now!"

"Willie!"

"You get in this car, Hattie." He held the door open firmly, looking at her until she obeyed. Without another word to the others he roared the car down the dusty road.

"Willie, not so fast!"

"Not so fast, huh? We'll see about that." He watched the road tear under the car. "What right they got coming up here this late? Why don't they leave us in peace? Why didn't they blow themselves up on that old world and let us be?"

"Willie, that ain't no Christian way to talk."

"I'm not feeling Christian," he said savagely, gripping the wheel. "I'm just feeling mean. After all them years of doing what they did to our folks—my mom and dad, and your mom and dad—— You remember? You remember how they hung my father on Knockwood Hill and shot my mother? You remember? Or you got a memory that's short like the others?"

"I remember," she said.

"You remember Dr. Phillips and Mr. Burton and their big houses, and my mother's washing shack, and Dad working when he was old, and the thanks he got was being hung by Dr. Phillips and Mr. Burton. Well," said Willie, "the shoe's on the other foot now. We'll see who gets laws passed against him, who gets lynched, who rides the back of streetcars, who gets segregated in shows. We'll just wait and see."

"Oh, Willie, you're talking trouble."

"Everybody's talking. Everybody's thought on this day, thinking it'd never be. Thinking, What kind of day would it be if the white man ever came up here to Mars? But here's the day, and we can't run away."

"Ain't you going to let the white people live up here?"

"Sure." He smiled, but it was a wide, mean smile, and his eyes were mad. "They can come up and live and work here; why, certainly. All they got to do to deserve it is live in their own small part of town, the slums, and shine our shoes for us, and mop up our trash, and sit in the last row in the balcony. That's all we ask. And once a week we hang one or two of them. Simple."

"You don't sound human, and I don't like it."

"You'll have to get used to it," he said. He braked the car to a stop before the house and jumped out. "Find my guns and some rope. We'll do this right."

"Oh, Willie," she wailed, and just sat there in the car while he ran up the steps and slammed the front door.

She went along. She didn't want to go along, but he rattled around in the attic, cursing like a crazy man until he found four guns. She saw the brutal metal of them glittering in the black attic, and she couldn't see him at all, he was so dark; she heard only his swearing, and at last his long legs came climbing down from the attic in a shower of dust, and he stacked up bunches of brass shells and blew out the gun chambers and clicked shells into them, his face stern and heavy and folded in upon the gnawing bitterness there. "Leave us alone," he kept muttering, his hands flying away from him suddenly, uncontrolled. "Leave us blame alone, why don't they?"

"Willie, Willie."

"You too—you too." And he gave her the same look, and a pressure of his hatred touched her mind.

Outside the window the boys gabbled to each other. "White as milk, she said. White as milk."

"White as this old flower, you *see*?"

"White as a stone, like chalk you write with."

Willie plunged out of the house. "You children come inside, I'm locking you up. You ain't seeing no white man, you ain't talking about them, you ain't doing nothing. Come on now."

"But, Daddy——"

He shoved them through the door and went and fetched a bucket of paint and a stencil and from the garage a long thick hairy rope coil into which he fashioned a hangman's knot, very carefully watching the sky while his hands felt their way at their task.

And then they were in the car, leaving bolls of dust behind them down the road. "Slow up, Willie."

"This is no slowing-up time," he said. "This is a hurrying time, and I'm hurrying."

All along the road people were looking up in the sky, or climbing in their cars, or riding in cars, and guns were sticking up out of some cars like telescopes sighting all the evils of a world coming to an end.

She looked at the guns. "You been talking," she accused her husband.

"That's what I been doing," he grunted, nodding. He watched the road, fiercely. "I stopped at every house and I told them what to do, to get their guns, to get paint, to bring rope and be ready. And here we all are, the welcoming committee, to give them the key to the city. Yes, sir!"

She pressed her thin dark hands together to push away the terror growing in her now, and she felt the car bucket and lurch around other cars. She heard the voices yelling, Hey, Willie, look! and hands holding up ropes and guns as they rushed by! and mouths smiling at them in the swift rushing.

"Here we are," said Willie, and braked the car into dusty halting and silence. He kicked the door open with a big foot and, laden with weapons, stepped out, lugging them across the airport meadow.

"Have you *thought*, Willie?"

"That's all I done for twenty years. I was sixteen when I left Earth, and I was glad to leave," he said. "There wasn't anything there for me or you or anybody like us. I've never been sorry I left. We've had peace here, the first time we ever drew a solid breath. Now, come on."

He pushed through the dark crowd which came to meet him.

"Willie, Willie, what we gonna do?" they said.

"Here's a gun," he said. "Here's a gun. Here's another." He passed them out with savage jabs of his arms. "Here's a pistol. Here's a shotgun."

The people were so close together it looked like one dark body with a thousand arms reaching out to take the weapons.

"Willie, Willie."

His wife stood tall and silent by him, her fluted lips pressed shut, and her large eyes wet and tragic. "Bring the paint," he said to her. And she lugged a gallon can of yellow paint across the field to where, at that moment, a trolley car was pulling up, with a fresh-painted sign on its front, TO THE WHITE MAN'S LANDING, full of talking people who got off and ran across the meadow, stumbling, looking up. Women with picnic boxes, men with straw hats, in shirt sleeves. The streetcar stood humming and empty. Willie climbed up, set the paint cans down, opened them, stirred the paint, tested a brush, drew forth a stencil, and climbed up on a seat.

"Hey, there!" The conductor came around behind him, his coin changer jangling. "What you think you're doing? Get down off there!"

"You see what I'm doing. Keep your shirt on."

And Willie began the stenciling in yellow paint. He dabbed on an *F* and an *O* and an *R* with terrible pride in his work. And when he finished it the conductor squinted up and read the fresh glinting yellow words: FOR WHITES: REAR SECTION. He read it again. FOR WHITES. He blinked. REAR SECTION. The conductor looked at Willie and began to smile.

"Does that suit you?" asked Willie, stepping down.

Said the conductor, "That suits me just fine, sir."

Hattie was looking at the sign from outside, and holding her hands over her breasts.

Willie returned to the crowd, which was growing now, taking size from every auto that groaned to a halt, and every new trolley car which squealed around the bend from the nearby town.

Willie climbed up on a packing box. "Let's have a delegation to paint every streetcar in the next hour. Volunteers?"

Hands leapt up.

"Get going!"

They went.

"Let's have a delegation to fix theater seats, roped off, the last two rows for whites."

More hands.

"Go on!"

They ran off.

Willie peered around, bubbled with perspiration, panting with exertion, proud of his energy, his hand on his wife's shoulder who stood under him looking at the ground with her downcast eyes. "Let's see now," he declared. "Oh yes. We got to pass a law this afternoon; no intermarriages!"

"That's right," said a lot of people.

"All shoeshine boys quit their jobs today."

"Quittin' right now!" Some men threw down the rags they carried, in their excitement, all across town.

"Got to pass a minimum wage law, don't we?"

"Sure!"

"Pay them white folks at least ten cents an hour."

"That's right!"

The mayor of the town hurried up. "Now look here, Willie Johnson. Get down off that box!"

"Mayor, I can't be made to do nothing like that."

"You're making a mob, Willie Johnson."

"That's the idea."

"The same thing you always hated when you were a kid. You're no better than some of those white men you yell about!"

"This is the other shoe, Mayor, and the other foot," said Willie, not even looking at the mayor, looking at the faces beneath him, some of them smiling, some of them doubtful, others bewildered, some of them reluctant and drawing away, fearful.

"You'll be sorry," said the mayor.

"We'll have an election and get a new mayor," said Willie. And he glanced off at the town where up and down the streets signs were being hung, fresh-painted: LIMITED CLIENTELE: *Right to serve customer revokable at any time.* He grinned and slapped his hands. Lord! And streetcars were being halted and sections being painted white in back, to suggest their future inhabitants. And theaters were being invaded and roped off by chuckling men, while their wives stood wondering on the curbs and children were spanked into houses to be hid away from this awful time.

"Are we all ready?" called Willie Johnson, the rope in his hands with the noose tied and neat.

"Ready!" shouted half the crowd. The other half murmured

and moved like figures in a nightmare in which they wished no participation.

"Here it comes!" called a small boy.

Like marionette heads on a single string, the heads of the crowd turned upward.

Across the sky, very high and beautiful, a rocket burned on a sweep of orange fire. It circled and came down, causing all to gasp. It landed, setting the meadow afire here and there; the fire burned out, the rocket lay a moment in quiet, and then, as the silent crowd watched, a great door in the side of the vessel whispered out a breath of oxygen, the door slid back and an old man stepped out.

"A white man, a white man, a white man . . ." The words traveled back in the expectant crowd, the children speaking in each other's ears, whispering, butting each other, the words moving in ripples to where the crowd stopped and the streetcars stood in the windy sunlight, the smell of paint coming out their opened windows. The whispering wore itself away and it was gone.

No one moved.

The white man was tall and straight, but a deep weariness was in his face. He had not shaved this day, and his eyes were as old as the eyes of a man can be and still be alive. His eyes were colorless; almost white and sightless with things he had seen in the passing years. He was as thin as a winter bush. His hands trembled and he had to lean against the portway of the ship as he looked out over the crowd.

He put out a hand and half smiled, but drew his hand back.

No one moved.

He looked down into their faces, and perhaps he saw but did not see the guns and the ropes, and perhaps he smelled the paint. No one ever asked him. He began to talk. He started very quietly and slowly, expecting no interruptions, and receiving none, and his voice was very tired and old and pale.

"It doesn't matter who I am," he said. "I'd be just a name to you, anyhow. I don't know your names, either. That'll come later." He paused, closed his eyes for a moment, and then continued:

"Twenty years ago you left Earth. That's a long, long time. It's more like twenty centuries, so much has happened. After you left, the War came." He nodded slowly. "Yes, the *big* one. The Third One. It went on for a long time. Until last year. We bombed all of the cities of the world. We destroyed New York and London and Moscow and Paris and Shanghai and Bombay and Alexandria. We ruined it all. And when we finished with the big cities we went to the little cities and atom-bombed and burned them."

Now he began to name cities and places, and streets. And as he named them, a murmur rose up in his audience.

"We destroyed Natchez . . ."

A murmur.

"And Columbus, Georgia . . ."

Another murmur.

"We burned New Orleans . . ."

A sigh.

"And Atlanta . . ."

Still another.

"And there was nothing left of Greenwater, Alabama."

Willie Johnson jerked his head and his mouth opened. Hattie saw this gesture, and the recognition coming into his dark eyes.

"Nothing was left," said the old man in the port, speaking slowly. "Cotton fields, burned."

Oh, said everyone.

"Cotton mills bombed out——"

"Oh."

"And the factories, radioactive; everything radioactive. All the roads and the farms and the foods, radioactive. Everything." He named more names of towns and villages.

"Tampa."

"That's my town," someone whispered.

"Fulton."

"That's mine," someone else said.

"Memphis."

"Memphis. Did they burn *Memphis*?" A shocked query.

"Memphis, blown up."

"*Fourth* Street in Memphis?"

"All of it," said the old man.

It was stirring them now. After twenty years it was rushing back. The towns and the places, the trees and the brick buildings, the signs and the churches and the familiar stores, all of it was coming to the surface among the gathered people. Each name touched memory, and there was no one present without a thought of another day. They were all old enough for that, save the children.

"Laredo."

"I remember Laredo."

"New York City."

"I had a store in Harlem."

"Harlem, bombed out."

The ominous words. The familiar, remembered places. The struggle to imagine all of those places in ruins.

Willie Johnson murmured the words, "Greenwater, Alabama. That's where I was born. I remember."

Gone. All of it gone. The man said so.

The man continued, "So we destroyed everything and ruined everything, like the fools that we were and the fools that we are. We killed millions. I don't think there are more than five hundred thousand people left in the world, all kinds and types. And out of all the wreckage we salvaged enough metal to build this one rocket, and we came to Mars in it this month to seek your help."

He hesitated and looked down among the faces to see what could be found there, but he was uncertain.

Hattie Johnson felt her husband's arm tense, saw his fingers grip the rope.

"We've been fools," said the old man quietly. "We've brought the Earth and civilization down about our heads. None of the cities are worth saving—they'll be radioactive for a century. Earth is over and done with. Its age is through. You have rockets here which you haven't tried to use to return to Earth in twenty years. Now I've come to ask you to use them. To come to Earth, to pick up the survivors and bring them back to Mars. To help us go on at this time. We've been stupid. Before God we admit our stupidity and our evilness. All the Chinese and the Indians and the Russians and the British and the Americans. We're asking to be taken in. Your Martian soil has lain fallow for numberless centuries; there's room for everyone; it's good soil—I've seen your fields from above. We'll come and work it *for* you. Yes, we'll even do that. We deserve anything you want to do to us, but don't shut us out. We can't force you to act now. If you want I'll get into my ship and go back and that will be all there is to it. We won't bother you again. But we'll come here and we'll work for you and do the things you did for us—clean your houses, cook your meals, shine your shoes, and humble ourselves in the sight of God for the things we have done over the centuries to ourselves, to others, to you."

He was finished.

There was a silence of silences. A silence you could hold in your hand and a silence that came down like a pressure of a distant storm over the crowd. Their long arms hung like dark pendulums in the sunlight, and their eyes were upon the old man and he did not move now, but waited.

Willie Johnson held the rope in his hands. Those around him watched to see what he might do. His wife Hattie waited, clutching his arm.

She wanted to get at the hate of them all, to pry at it and work at it until she found a little chink, and then pull out a pebble or a stone or a brick and then a part of the wall, and, once started, the whole edifice might roar down and be done away with. It was teetering now. But which was the keystone, and how to get at it? How to touch them and get a thing started in all of them to make a ruin of their hate?

She looked at Willie there in the strong silence and the only thing she knew about the situation was him and his life and what had happened to him, and suddenly he was the keystone; suddenly she knew that if he could be pried loose, then the thing in all of them might be loosened and torn away.

"Mister——" She stepped forward. She didn't even know the first words to say. The crowd stared at her back; she felt them staring. "Mister——"

The man turned to her with a tired smile.

"Mister," she said, "do you know Knockwood Hill in Greenwater, Alabama?"

The old man spoke over his shoulder to someone within the ship. A moment later a photographic map was handed out and the man held it, waiting.

"You know the big oak on top of that hill, mister?"

The big oak. The place where Willie's father was shot and hung and found swinging in the morning wind.

"Yes."

"Is that still there?" asked Hattie.

"It's gone," said the old man. "Blown up. The hill's all gone, and the oak tree too. You see?" He touched the photograph.

"Let me see that," said Willie, jerking forward and looking at the map.

Hattie blinked at the white man, heart pounding.

"Tell me about Greenwater," she said quickly.

"What do you want to know?"

"About Dr. Phillips. Is he still alive?"

A moment in which the information was found in a clicking machine within the rocket . . .

"Killed in the war."

"And his son?"

"Dead."

"What about their house?"

"Burned. Like all the other houses."

"What about that other big tree on Knockwood Hill?"

"All the trees went—burned."

"*That* tree went, you're sure?" said Willie.

"Yes."

Willie's body loosened somewhat.

"And what about that Mr. Burton's house and Mr. Burton?"

"No houses at all left, no people."

"You know Mrs. Johnson's washing shack, my mother's place?"

The place where she was shot.

"That's gone too. Everything's gone. Here are the pictures, you can see for yourself."

The pictures were there to be held and looked at and thought about. The rocket was full of pictures and answers to questions. Any town, any building, any place.

Willie stood with the rope in his hands.

He was remembering Earth, the green Earth and the green town where he was born and raised, and he was thinking now of that town, gone to pieces, to ruin, blown up and scattered, all of the landmarks with it, all of the supposed or certain evil scattered with it, all of the hard men gone, the stables, the ironsmiths, the curio shops, the soda founts, the gin mills, the river bridges, the lynching trees, the buckshot-covered hills, the roads, the cows, the mimosas, and his own house as well as those big-pillared houses down near the long river, those white mortuaries where the women as delicate as moths fluttered in the autumn light, distant, far away. Those houses where the cold men rocked, with glasses of drink in their hands, guns leaned against the porch newels, sniffing the autumn airs and considering death. Gone, all gone; gone and never coming back. Now, for certain, all of that civilization ripped into confetti and strewn at their feet. Nothing, nothing of it left to hate—not an empty brass gun shell, or a twisted hemp, or a tree, or even a hill of it to hate. Nothing but some alien people in a rocket, people who might shine his shoes and ride in the back of trolleys or sit far up in midnight theaters . . .

"You won't have to do that," said Willie Johnson.

His wife glanced at his big hands.

His fingers were opening.

The rope, released, fell and coiled upon itself along the ground.

They ran through the streets of their town and tore down the new signs so quickly made, and painted out the fresh yellow signs on streetcars, and they cut down the ropes in the theater balconies, and unloaded their guns and stacked their ropes away.

"A new start for everyone," said Hattie, on the way home in their car.

"Yes," said Willie at last. "The Lord's let us come through, a few here and a few there. And what happens next is up to all of us. The time for being fools is over. We got to be something else except fools. I knew that when he talked. I knew then that now the white man's as lonely as we've always been. He's got no home now, just like we didn't have one for so long. Now everything's even. We can start all over again, on the same level."

He stopped the car and sat in it, not moving, while Hattie went to let the children out. They ran down to see their father. "You see the white man? You see him?" they cried.

"Yes, sir," said Willie, sitting behind the wheel, rubbing his face with his slow fingers. "Seems like for the first time today I really seen the white man—I really seen him clear."

The Highway

THE COOLING AFTERNOON rain had come over the valley, touching the corn in the tilled mountain fields, tapping on the dry grass roof of the hut. In the rainy darkness the woman ground corn between cakes of lava rock, working steadily. In the wet lightlessness, somewhere, a baby cried.

Hernando stood waiting for the rain to cease so he might take the wooden plow into the field again. Below, the river boiled brown and thickened in its course. The concrete highway, another river, did not flow at all; it lay shining, empty. A car had not come along it in an hour. This was, in itself, of unusual interest. Over the years there had not been an hour when a car had not pulled up, someone shouting, "Hey there, can we take your picture?" Someone with a box that clicked, and a coin in his hand. If he walked slowly across the field without his hat, sometimes they called, "Oh, we want you with your hat on!" And they waved their hands, rich with gold things that told time, or identified them, or did nothing at all but winked like spider's eyes in the sun. So he would turn and go back to get his hat.

His wife spoke. "Something is wrong, Hernando?"

"Sí. The road. Something big has happened. Something big to make the road so empty this way."

He walked from the hut slowly and easily, the rain washing over the twined shoes of grass and thick tire rubber he wore. He remembered very well the incident of this pair of shoes. The tire had come into the hut with violence one night, exploding the chickens and the pots apart! It had come alone, rolling swiftly. The car, off which it had come, had rushed on, as far as the curve, and hung a moment, headlights reflected, before plunging into the river. The car was still there. One might see it on a good day, when the river ran slow and the mud cleared. Deep under, shining its metal, long and low and very rich, lay the car. But then the mud came in again and you saw nothing.

The following day he had carved the shoe soles from the tire rubber.

He reached the highway now, and stood upon it, listening to the small sounds it made in the rain.

Then, suddenly, as if at a signal, the cars came. Hundreds of them, miles of them, rushing and rushing as he stood, by and by him. The big long black cars heading north toward the United States, roaring, taking the curves at too great a speed. With a ceaseless blowing and honking. And there was something about the faces of the people packed into the cars, something which dropped him into a deep silence. He stood back to let the cars roar on. He counted them until he tired. Five hundred, a thousand cars passed, and there was something in the faces of all of them. But they moved too swiftly for him to tell what this thing was.

Finally the silence and emptiness returned. The swift long low convertible cars were gone. He heard the last horn fade.

The road was empty again.

It had been like a funeral cortege. But a wild one, racing, hair out, screaming to some ceremony ever northward. Why? He could only shake his head and rub his fingers softly, at his sides.

Now, all alone, a final car. There was something very, very final about it. Down the mountain road in the thin cool rain, fuming up great clouds of steam, came an old Ford. It was traveling as swiftly as it might. He expected it to break apart any instant. When this ancient Ford saw Hernando it pulled up, caked with mud and rusted, the radiator bubbling angrily.

"May we have some water, please, señor!"

A young man, perhaps twenty-one, was driving. He wore a yellow sweater, an open-collared white shirt and gray pants. In the topless car the rain fell upon him and five young women packed so they could not move in the interior. They were all very pretty and they were keeping the rain from themselves and the driver with old newspapers. But the rain got through to them, soaking their bright dresses, soaking the young man. His hair was plastered with rain. But they did not seem to care. None complained, and this was unusual. Always before they complained; of rain, of heat, of time, of cold, of distance.

Hernando nodded. "I'll bring you water."

"Oh, please hurry!" one of the girls cried. She sounded very high and afraid. There was no impatience in her, only an asking out of fear. For the first time Hernando ran when a tourist asked; always before he had walked slower at such requests.

He returned with a hub lid full of water. This, too, had been a gift from the highway. One afternoon it had sailed like a flung coin into his field, round and glittering. The car to which it belonged had slid on, oblivious to the fact that it had lost a silver eye. Until now, he and his wife had used it for washing and cooking; it made a fine bowl.

As he poured the water into the boiling radiator, Hernando looked up at their stricken faces. "Oh, thank you, thank you," said one of the girls. "You don't know what this means."

Hernando smiled. "So much traffic in this hour. It all goes one way. North."

He did not mean to say anything to hurt them. But when he looked up again there all of them sat, in the rain, and they were crying. They were crying very hard. And the young man was trying to stop them by laying his hands on their shoulders and shaking them gently, one at a time, but they held their papers over their heads and their mouths moved and their eyes were shut and their faces changed color and they cried, some loud, some soft.

Hernando stood with the half-empty lid in his fingers. "I did not mean to say anything, señor," he apologized.

"That's all right," said the driver.

"What is wrong, señor?"

"Haven't you heard?" replied the young man, turning, holding tightly to the wheel with one hand, leaning forward. "It's happened."

This was bad. The others, at this, cried still harder, holding onto each other, forgetting the newspapers, letting the rain fall and mingle with their tears.

Hernando stiffened. He put the rest of the water into the radiator. He looked at the sky, which was black with storm. He looked at the river rushing. He felt the asphalt under his shoes.

He came to the side of the car. The young man took his hand and gave him a peso. "No." Hernando gave it back. "It is my pleasure."

"Thank you, you're so kind," said one of the girls, still

sobbing. “Oh, Mama, Papa. Oh, I want to be home, I want to be home. Oh, Mama, Dad.” And others held her.

“I did not hear, señor,” said Hernando quietly.

“The war!” shouted the young man as if no one could hear. “It’s come, the atom war, the end of the world!”

“Señor, señor,” said Hernando.

“Thank you, thank you for your help. Good-by,” said the young man.

“Good-by,” they all said in the rain, not seeing him.

He stood while the car engaged its gears and rattled off down, fading away, through the valley. Finally it was gone, with the young women in it, the last car, the newspapers held and fluttered over their heads.

Hernando did not move for a long time. The rain ran very cold down his cheeks and along his fingers and into the woven garment on his legs. He held his breath, waiting, tight and tensed.

He watched the highway, but it did not move again. He doubted that it would move much for a very long time.

The rain stopped. The sky broke through the clouds. In ten minutes the storm was gone, like a bad breath. A sweet wind blew the smell of the jungle up to him. He could hear the river moving gently and easily on its way. The jungle was very green; everything was fresh. He walked down through the field to his house and picked up his plow. With his hands on it he looked at the sky beginning to burn hot with the sun.

His wife called out from her work. “What happened, Hernando?”

“It is nothing,” he replied.

He set the plow in the furrow, he called sharply to his burro, “Burrrrrrr-o!” And they walked together through the rich field, under the clearing sky, on their tilled land by the deep river.

“What do they mean, ‘the world’?” he said.

The Man

CAPTAIN HART STOOD in the door of the rocket. "Why don't they come?" he said.

"Who knows?" said Martin, his lieutenant. "Do I know, Captain?"

"What kind of a place is this, anyway?" The captain lighted a cigar. He tossed the match out into the glittering meadow. The grass started to burn.

Martin moved to stamp it out with his boot.

"No," ordered Captain Hart, "let it burn. Maybe they'll come see what's happening then, the ignorant fools."

Martin shrugged and withdrew his foot from the spreading fire.

Captain Hart examined his watch. "An hour ago we landed here, and does the welcoming committee rush out with a brass band to shake our hands? No indeed! Here we ride millions of miles through space and the fine citizens of some silly town on some unknown planet ignore us!" He snorted, tapping his watch. "Well, I'll just give them five more minutes, and then——"

"And then what?" asked Martin, ever so politely, watching the captain's jowls shake.

"We'll fly over their damned city again and scare hell out of them." His voice grew quieter. "Do you think, Martin, maybe they didn't see us land?"

"They saw us. They looked up as we flew over."

"Then why aren't they running across the field? Are they hiding? Are they yellow?"

Martin shook his head. "No. Take these binoculars, sir. See for yourself. Everybody's walking around. They're not frightened. They—well, they just don't seem to care."

Captain Hart placed the binoculars to his tired eyes. Martin looked up and had time to observe the lines and the grooves of irritation, tiredness, nervousness there. Hart looked a million years old; he never slept, he ate little, and drove himself on, on. Now his mouth moved, aged and drear, but sharp, under the held binoculars.

"Really, Martin, I don't know why we bother. We build rockets, we go to all the trouble of crossing space, searching for them, and this is what we get. Neglect. Look at those idiots wander about in there. Don't they realize how big this is? The first space flight to touch their provincial land. How many times does that happen? Are they that blasé?"

Martin didn't know.

Captain Hart gave him back the binoculars wearily. "Why do we do it, Martin? This space travel, I mean. Always on the go. Always searching. Our insides always tight, never any rest."

"Maybe we're looking for peace and quiet. Certainly there's none on Earth," said Martin.

"No, there's not, is there?" Captain Hart was thoughtful, the fire damped down. "Not since Darwin, eh? Not since everything went by the board, everything we used to believe in, eh? Divine power and all that. And so you think maybe that's why we're going out to the stars, eh, Martin? Looking for our lost souls, is that it? Trying to get away from our evil planet to a good one?"

"Perhaps, sir. Certainly we're looking for something."

Captain Hart cleared his throat and tightened back into sharpness. "Well, right now we're looking for the mayor of that city there. Run in, tell them who we are, the first rocket expedition to Planet Forty-three in Star System Three. Captain Hart sends his salutations and desires to meet the mayor. On the double!"

"Yes, sir." Martin walked slowly across the meadow.

"Hurry!" snapped the captain.

"Yes, sir!" Martin trotted away. Then he walked again, smiling to himself.

The captain had smoked two cigars before Martin returned.

Martin stopped and looked up into the door of the rocket, swaying, seemingly unable to focus his eyes or think.

"Well?" snapped Hart. "What happened? Are they coming to welcome us?"

"No." Martin had to lean dizzily against the ship.

"Why not?"

"It's not important," said Martin. "Give me a cigarette, please, Captain." His fingers groped blindly at the rising pack, for he was looking at the golden city and blinking. He lighted one and smoked quietly for a long time.

"Say something!" cried the captain. "Aren't they interested in our rocket?"

Martin said, "What? Oh. The rocket?" He inspected his cigarette. "No, they're not interested. Seems we came at an inopportune time."

"Inopportune time!"

Martin was patient. "Captain, listen. Something big happened yesterday in that city. It's so big, so important that we're second-rate—second fiddle. I've got to sit down." He lost his balance and sat heavily, gasping for air.

The captain chewed his cigar angrily. "What happened?"

Martin lifted his head, smoke from the burning cigarette in his fingers, blowing in the wind. "Sir, yesterday, in that city, a remarkable man appeared—good, intelligent, compassionate, and infinitely wise!"

The captain glared at his lieutenant. "What's that to do with us?"

"It's hard to explain. But he was a man for whom they'd waited a long time—a million years maybe. And yesterday he walked into their city. That's why today, sir, our rocket landing means nothing."

The captain sat down violently. "Who was it? Not Ashley? He didn't arrive in his rocket before us and steal my glory, did he?" He seized Martin's arm. His face was pale and dismayed.

"Not Ashley, sir."

"Then it was Burton! I knew it. Burton stole in ahead of us and ruined my landing! You can't trust anyone any more."

"Not Burton, either, sir," said Martin quietly.

The captain was incredulous. "There were only three rockets. We were in the lead. This man who got here ahead of us? What was his name!"

"He didn't have a name. He doesn't need one. It would be different on every planet, sir."

The captain stared at his lieutenant with hard, cynical eyes.

"Well, what did he do that was so wonderful that nobody even looks at our ship?"

"For one thing," said Martin steadily, "he healed the sick and comforted the poor. He fought hypocrisy and dirty politics and sat among the people, talking, through the day."

"Is that so wonderful?"

"Yes, Captain."

"I don't get this." The captain confronted Martin, peered into his face and eyes. "You been drinking, eh?" He was suspicious. He backed away. "I don't understand."

Martin looked at the city. "Captain, if you don't understand, there's no way of telling you."

The captain followed his gaze. The city was quiet and beautiful and a great peace lay over it. The captain stepped forward, taking his cigar from his lips. He squinted first at Martin, then at the golden spires of the buildings.

"You don't mean—you *can't* mean—— That man you're talking about couldn't be——"

Martin nodded. "That's what I mean, sir."

The captain stood silently, not moving. He drew himself up. "I don't believe it," he said at last.

At high noon Captain Hart walked briskly into the city, accompanied by Lieutenant Martin and an assistant who was carrying some electrical equipment. Every once in a while the captain laughed loudly, put his hands on his hips and shook his head.

The mayor of the town confronted him. Martin set up a tripod, screwed a box onto it, and switched on the batteries.

"Are you the mayor?" The captain jabbed a finger out.

"I am," said the mayor.

The delicate apparatus stood between them, controlled and adjusted by Martin and the assistant. Instantaneous translations from any language were made by the box. The words sounded crisply on the mild air of the city.

"About this occurrence yesterday," said the captain. "It occurred?"

"It did."

"You have witnesses?"

"We have."

"May we talk to them?"

"Talk to any of us," said the mayor. "We are all witnesses."

In an aside to Martin the captain said, "Mass hallucination." To the mayor, "What did this man—this stranger—look like?"

"That would be hard to say," said the mayor, smiling a little.

"Why would it?"

"Opinions might differ slightly."

"I'd like your opinion, sir, anyway," said the captain. "Record this," he snapped to Martin over his shoulder. The lieutenant pressed the button of a hand recorder.

"Well," said the mayor of the city, "he was a very gentle and kind man. He was of a great and knowing intelligence."

"Yes—yes, I know, I know." The captain waved his fingers. "Generalizations. I want something specific. What did he look like?"

"I don't believe that is important," replied the mayor.

"It's very important," said the captain sternly. "I want a description of this fellow. If I can't get it from you, I'll get it from others." To Martin, "I'm sure it must have been Burton, pulling one of his practical jokes."

Martin would not look him in the face. Martin was coldly silent.

The captain snapped his fingers. "There was something or other—a healing?"

"Many healings," said the mayor.

"May I see one?"

"You may," said the mayor. "My son." He nodded at a small boy who stepped forward. "He was afflicted with a withered arm. Now, look upon it."

At this the captain laughed tolerantly. "Yes, yes. This isn't even circumstantial evidence, you know. I didn't see the boy's withered arm. I see only his arm whole and well. That's no proof. What proof have you that the boy's arm was withered yesterday and today is well?"

"My word is my proof," said the mayor simply.

"My dear man!" cried the captain. "You don't expect me to go on hearsay, do you? Oh no!"

"I'm sorry," said the mayor, looking upon the captain with what appeared to be curiosity and pity.

"Do you have any pictures of the boy before today?" asked the captain.

After a moment a large oil portrait was carried forth, showing the son with a withered arm.

"My dear fellow!" The captain waved it away. "Anybody can paint a picture. Paintings lie. I want a photograph of the boy."

There was no photograph. Photography was not a known art in their society.

"Well," sighed the captain, face twitching, "let me talk to a few other citizens. We're getting nowhere." He pointed at a woman. "You." She hesitated. "Yes, you; come here," ordered the captain. "Tell me about this *wonderful* man you saw yesterday."

The woman looked steadily at the captain. "He walked among us and was very fine and good."

"What color were his eyes?"

"The color of the sun, the color of the sea, the color of a flower, the color of the mountains, the color of the night."

"That'll do." The captain threw up his hands. "See, Martin? Absolutely nothing. Some charlatan wanders through whispering sweet nothings in their ears and——"

"Please, stop it," said Martin.

The captain stepped back. "What?"

"You heard what I said," said Martin. "I like these people. I believe what they say. You're entitled to your opinion, but keep it to yourself, sir."

"You can't talk to me this way," shouted the captain.

"I've had enough of your highhandedness," replied Martin. "Leave these people alone. They've got something good and decent, and you come and foul up the nest and sneer at it. Well, I've talked to them too. I've gone through the city and seen their faces, and they've got something you'll never have—a little simple faith, and they'll move mountains with it. You, you're boiled because someone stole your act, got here ahead and made you unimportant!"

"I'll give you five seconds to finish," remarked the captain. "I understand. You've been under a strain, Martin. Months of traveling in space, nostalgia, loneliness. And now, with this thing happening, I sympathize, Martin. I overlook your petty insubordination."

"I don't overlook your petty tyranny," replied Martin. "I'm stepping out. I'm staying here."

"You can't do that!"

"Can't I? Try and stop me. This is what I came looking for. I didn't know it, but this is it. This is for me. Take your filth somewhere else and foul up other nests with your doubt and your—scientific method!" He looked swiftly about. "These people have had an experience, and you can't seem to get it through your head that it's really happened and we were lucky enough to almost arrive in time to be in on it.

"People on Earth have talked about this man for twenty centuries after he walked through the old world. We've all wanted to see him and hear him, and never had the chance. And now, today, we just missed seeing him by a few hours."

Captain Hart looked at Martin's cheeks. "You're crying like a baby. Stop it."

"I don't care."

"Well, I do. In front of these natives we're to keep up a front. You're overwrought. As I said, I forgive you."

"I don't want your forgiveness."

"You idiot. Can't you see this is one of Burton's tricks, to fool these people, to bilk them, to establish his oil and mineral concerns under a religious guise! You fool, Martin. You absolute fool! You should know Earthmen by now. They'll do anything—blaspheme, lie, cheat, steal, kill, to get their ends. Anything is fine if it works; the true pragmatist, that's Burton. You know him!"

The captain scoffed heavily. "Come off it, Martin, admit it; this is the sort of scaly thing Burton might carry off, polish up these citizens and pluck them when they're ripe."

"No," said Martin, thinking of it.

The captain put his hand up. "That's Burton. That's him. That's his dirt, that's his criminal way. I have to admire the old dragon. Flaming in here in a blaze and a halo and a soft word and a loving touch, with a medicated salve here and a healing ray there. That's Burton all right!"

"No." Martin's voice was dazed. He covered his eyes. "No, I won't believe it."

"You don't want to believe." Captain Hart kept at it. "Admit it now. Admit it! It's just the thing Burton would do. Stop day-dreaming, Martin. Wake up! It's morning. This is a real world and we're real, dirty people—Burton the dirtiest of us all!"

Martin turned away.

"There, there, Martin," said Hart, mechanically patting the man's back. "I understand. Quite a shock for you. I know. A rotten shame, and all that. That Burton is a rascal. You go take it easy. Let me handle this."

Martin walked off slowly toward the rocket.

Captain Hart watched him go. Then, taking a deep breath, he turned to the woman he had been questioning. "Well. Tell me some more about this man. As you were saying, madam?"

Later the officers of the rocket ship ate supper on card tables outside. The captain correlated his data to a silent Martin who sat red-eyed and brooding over his meal.

"Interviewed three dozen people, all of them full of the same milk and hogwash," said the captain. "It's Burton's work all right, I'm positive. He'll be spilling back in here tomorrow or next week to consolidate his miracles and beat us out in our contracts. I think I'll stick on and spoil it for him."

Martin glanced up sullenly. "I'll kill him," he said.

"Now, now, Martin! There, there, boy."

"I'll kill him—so help me, I will."

"We'll put an anchor on his wagon. You have to admit he's clever. Unethical but clever."

"He's dirty."

"You must promise not to do anything violent." Captain Hart checked his figures. "According to this, there were thirty miracles of healing performed, a blind man restored to vision, a leper cured. Oh, Burton's efficient, give him that."

A gong sounded. A moment later a man ran up. "Captain, sir. A report! Burton's ship is coming down. Also the Ashley ship, sir!"

"See!" Captain Hart beat the table. "Here come the jackals to the harvest! They can't wait to feed. Wait till I confront them. I'll make them cut me in on this feast—I will!"

Martin looked sick. He stared at the captain.

"Business, my dear boy, business," said the captain.

Everybody looked up. Two rockets swung down out of the sky.

When the rockets landed they almost crashed.

"What's wrong with those fools?" cried the captain, jumping

up. The men ran across the meadowlands to the steaming ships. The captain arrived. The airlock door popped open on Burton's ship.

A man fell out into their arms.

"What's wrong?" cried Captain Hart.

The man lay on the ground. They bent over him and he was burned, badly burned. His body was covered with wounds and scars and tissue that was inflamed and smoking. He looked up out of puffed eyes and his thick tongue moved in his split lips.

"What happened?" demanded the captain, kneeling down, shaking the man's arm.

"Sir, sir," whispered the dying man. "Forty-eight hours ago, back in Space Sector Seventy-nine DFS, off Planet One in this system, our ship, and Ashley's ship, ran into a cosmic storm, sir." Liquid ran gray from the man's nostrils. Blood trickled from his mouth. "Wiped out. All crew. Burton dead. Ashley died an hour ago. Only three survivals."

"Listen to me!" shouted Hart, bending over the bleeding man. "You didn't come to this planet before this very hour?"

Silence.

"Answer me!" cried Hart.

The dying man said, "No. Storm. Burton dead two days ago. This first landing on any world in six months."

"Are you sure?" shouted Hart, shaking violently, gripping the man in his hands. "Are you sure?"

"Sure, sure," mouthed the dying man.

"Burton died two days ago? You're positive?"

"Yes, yes," whispered the man. His head fell forward. The man was dead.

The captain knelt beside the silent body. The captain's face twitched, the muscles jerking involuntarily. The other members of the crew stood back of him looking down. Martin waited. The captain asked to be helped to his feet, finally, and this was done. They stood looking at the city. "That means——"

"That means?" said Martin.

"We're the only ones who've been here," whispered Captain Hart. "And that man——"

"What about that man, Captain?" asked Martin.

The captain's face twitched senselessly. He looked very old

indeed, and gray. His eyes were glazed. He moved forward in the dry grass.

"Come along, Martin. Come along. Hold me up; for my sake, hold me. I'm afraid I'll fall. And hurry. We can't waste time——"

They moved, stumbling, toward the city, in the long dry grass, in the blowing wind.

Several hours later they were sitting in the mayor's auditorium. A thousand people had come and talked and gone. The captain had remained seated, his face haggard, listening, listening. There was so much light in the faces of those who came and testified and talked he could not bear to see them. And all the while his hands traveled, on his knees, together; on his belt, jerking and quivering.

When it was over, Captain Hart turned to the mayor and with strange eyes said:

"But you must know where he went?"

"He didn't say where he was going," replied the mayor.

"To one of the other nearby worlds?" demanded the captain.

"I don't know."

"You must know."

"Do you see him?" asked the mayor, indicating the crowd.

The captain looked. "No."

"Then he is probably gone," said the mayor.

"Probably, probably!" cried the captain weakly. "I've made a horrible mistake, and I want to see him now. Why, it just came to me, this is a most unusual thing in history. To be in on something like this. Why, the chances are one in billions we'd arrived at one certain planet among millions of planets the day after *he* came! You must know where he's gone!"

"Each finds him in his own way," replied the mayor gently.

"You're hiding him." The captain's face grew slowly ugly. Some of the old hardness returned in stages. He began to stand up.

"No," said the mayor.

"You know where he is then?" The captain's fingers twitched at the leather holster on his right side.

"I couldn't tell you where he is, exactly," said the mayor.

"I advise you to start talking," and the captain took out a small steel gun.

"There's no way," said the mayor, "to tell you anything."

"Liar!"

An expression of pity came into the mayor's face as he looked at Hart.

"You're very tired," he said. "You've traveled a long way and you belong to a tired people who've been without faith a long time, and you want to believe so much now that you're interfering with yourself. You'll only make it harder if you kill. You'll never find him that way."

"Where'd he go? He told you; you know. Come on, tell me!" The captain waved the gun.

The mayor shook his head.

"Tell me! Tell me!"

The gun cracked once, twice. The mayor fell, his arm wounded.

Martin leaped forward. "Captain!"

The gun flashed at Martin. "Don't interfere."

On the floor, holding his wounded arm, the mayor looked up. "Put down your gun. You're hurting yourself. You've never believed, and now that you think you believe, you hurt people because of it."

"I don't need you," said Hart, standing over him. "If I missed him by one day here, I'll go on to another world. And another and another. I'll miss him by half a day on the next planet, maybe, and a quarter of a day on the third planet, and two hours on the next, and an hour on the next, and half an hour on the next, and a minute on the next. But after that, one day I'll catch up with him! Do you hear that?" He was shouting now, leaning wearily over the man on the floor. He staggered with exhaustion. "Come along, Martin." He let the gun hang in his hand.

"No," said Martin. "I'm staying here."

"You're a fool. Stay if you like. But I'm going on, with the others, as far as I can go."

The mayor looked up at Martin. "I'll be all right. Leave me. Others will tend my wounds."

"I'll be back," said Martin. "I'll walk as far as the rocket."

They walked with vicious speed through the city. One could see with what effort the captain struggled to show all the old iron, to keep himself going. When he reached the rocket he slapped the side of it with a trembling hand. He holstered his gun. He looked at Martin.

"Well, Martin?"

Martin looked at him. "Well, Captain?"

The captain's eyes were on the sky. "Sure you won't—come with—with me, eh?"

"No, sir."

"It'll be a great adventure, by God. I know I'll find him."

"You are set on it now, aren't you, sir?" asked Martin.

The captain's face quivered and his eyes closed. "Yes."

"There's one thing I'd like to know."

"What?"

"Sir, when you find him—*if* you find him," asked Martin, "what will you ask of him?"

"Why——" The captain faltered, opening his eyes. His hands clenched and unclenched. He puzzled a moment and then broke into a strange smile. "Why, I'll ask him for a little—peace and quiet." He touched the rocket. "It's been a long time, a long, long time since—since I relaxed."

"Did you ever just try, Captain?"

"I don't understand," said Hart.

"Never mind. So long, Captain."

"Good-by, Mr. Martin."

The crew stood by the port. Out of their number only three were going on with Hart. Seven others were remaining behind, they said, with Martin.

Captain Hart surveyed them and uttered his verdict: "Fools!"

He, last of all, climbed into the airlock, gave a brisk salute, laughed sharply. The door slammed.

The rocket lifted into the sky on a pillar of fire.

Martin watched it go far away and vanish.

At the meadow's edge the mayor, supported by several men, beckoned.

"He's gone," said Martin, walking up.

"Yes, poor man, he's gone," said the mayor. "And he'll go on, planet after planet, seeking and seeking, and always and always he will be an hour late, or a half hour late, or ten minutes late, or a minute late. And finally he will miss out by only a few seconds. And when he has visited three hundred worlds and is seventy or eighty years old he will miss out by only a fraction of a second, and then a smaller fraction of a second. And he will go on and on, thinking to find that very thing which he left behind here, on this planet, in this city——"

Martin looked steadily at the mayor.

The mayor put out his hand. "Was there ever any doubt of it?" He beckoned to the others and turned. "Come along now. We mustn't keep him waiting."

They walked into the city.

The Long Rain

The rain continued. It was a hard rain, a perpetual rain, a sweating and steaming rain; it was a mizzle, a downpour, a fountain, a whipping at the eyes, an undertow at the ankles; it was a rain to drown all rains and the memory of rains. It came by the pound and the ton, it hacked at the jungle and cut the trees like scissors and shaved the grass and tunneled the soil and molted the bushes. It shrank men's hands into the hands of wrinkled apes; it rained a solid glassy rain, and it never stopped.

"How much farther, Lieutenant?"

"I don't know. A mile, ten miles, a thousand."

"Aren't you sure?"

"How can I be sure?"

"I don't like this rain. If we only knew how far it is to the Sun Dome, I'd feel better."

"Another hour or two from here."

"You really think so, Lieutenant?"

"Of course."

"Or are you lying to keep us happy?"

"I'm lying to keep you happy. Shut up!"

The two men sat together in the rain. Behind them sat two other men who were wet and tired and slumped like clay that was melting.

The lieutenant looked up. He had a face that once had been brown and now the rain had washed it pale, and the rain had washed the color from his eyes and they were white, as were his teeth, and as was his hair. He was all white. Even his uniform was beginning to turn white, and perhaps a little green with fungus.

The lieutenant felt the rain on his cheeks. "How many million years since the rain stopped raining here on Venus?"

"Don't be crazy," said one of the two other men. "It never stops raining on Venus. It just goes on and on. I've lived here for ten years and I never saw a minute, or even a second, when it wasn't pouring."

"It's like living under water," said the lieutenant, and rose up, shrugging his guns into place. "Well, we'd better get going. We'll find that Sun Dome yet."

"Or we won't find it," said the cynic.

"It's an hour or so."

"Now you're lying to me, Lieutenant."

"No, now I'm lying to myself. This is one of those times when you've got to lie. I can't take much more of this."

They walked down the jungle trail, now and then looking at their compasses. There was no direction anywhere, only what the compass said. There was a gray sky and rain falling and jungle and a path, and, far back behind them somewhere, a rocket in which they had ridden and fallen. A rocket in which lay two of their friends, dead and dripping rain.

They walked in single file, not speaking. They came to a river which lay wide and flat and brown, flowing down to the great Single Sea. The surface of it was stippled in a billion places by the rain.

"All right, Simmons."

The lieutenant nodded and Simmons took a small packet from his back which, with a pressure of hidden chemical, inflated into a large boat. The lieutenant directed the cutting of wood and the quick making of paddles and they set out into the river, paddling swiftly across the smooth surface in the rain.

The lieutenant felt the cold rain on his cheeks and on his neck and on his moving arms. The cold was beginning to seep into his lungs. He felt the rain on his ears, on his eyes, on his legs.

"I didn't sleep last night," he said.

"Who could? Who has? When? How many nights *have* we slept? Thirty nights, thirty days! Who can sleep with rain slamming their head, banging away. . . . I'd give anything for a hat. Anything at all, just so it wouldn't hit my head any more. I get headaches. My head is sore; it hurts all the time."

"I'm sorry I came to China," said one of the others.

"First time *I* ever heard Venus called China."

"Sure, China. Chinese water cure. Remember the old torture? Rope you against a wall. Drop one drop of water on your head every half-hour. You go crazy waiting for the next one. Well, that's Venus, but on a big scale. We're not made for water. You can't sleep, you can't breathe right, and you're crazy from just being soggy. If we'd been ready for a crash, we'd have brought waterproofed uniforms and hats. It's this beating rain on your head gets you, most of all. It's so heavy. It's like BB shot. I don't know how long I can take it."

"Boy, me for the Sun Dome! The man who thought *them* up, thought of something."

They crossed the river, and in crossing they thought of the Sun Dome, somewhere ahead of them, shining in the jungle rain. A yellow house, round and bright as the sun. A house fifteen feet high by one hundred feet in diameter, in which was warmth and quiet and hot food and freedom from rain. And in the center of the Sun Dome, of course, was a sun. A small floating free globe of yellow fire, drifting in a space at the top of the building where you could look at it from where you sat, smoking or reading a book or drinking your hot chocolate crowned with marshmallow dollops. There it would be, the yellow sun, just the size of the Earth sun, and it was warm and continuous, and the rain world of Venus would be forgotten as long as they stayed in that house and idled their time.

The lieutenant turned and looked back at the three men using their oars and gritting their teeth. They were as white as mushrooms, as white as he was. Venus bleached everything away in a few months. Even the jungle was an immense cartoon nightmare, for how could the jungle be green with no sun, with always rain falling and always dusk? The white, white jungle with the pale cheese-colored leaves, and the earth carved of wet Camembert, and the tree boles like immense toadstools—everything black and white. And how often could you see the soil itself? Wasn't it mostly a creek, a stream, a puddle, a pool, a lake, a river, and then, at last, the sea?

"Here we are!"

They leaped out on the farthest shore, splashing and sending up showers. The boat was deflated and stored in a cigarette packet. Then, standing on the rainy shore, they tried to light up a few smokes for themselves, and it was five minutes or so before, shuddering, they worked the inverted lighter and, cupping their hands, managed a few drags upon cigarettes that all too quickly were limp and beaten away from their lips by a sudden slap of rain.

They walked on.

"Wait just a moment," said the lieutenant. "I thought I saw something ahead."

"The Sun Dome?"

"I'm not sure. The rain closed in again."

Simmons began to run. "The Sun Dome!"

"Come back, Simmons!"

"The Sun Dome!"

Simmons vanished in the rain. The others ran after him.

They found him in a little clearing, and they stopped and looked at him and what he had discovered.

The rocket ship.

It was lying where they had left it. Somehow they had circled back and were where they had started. In the ruin of the ship green fungus was growing up out of the mouths of the two dead men. As they watched, the fungus took flower, the petals broke away in the rain, and the fungus died.

"How did we do it?"

"An electrical storm must be nearby. Threw our compasses off. That explains it."

"You're right."

"What'll we do now?"

"Start out again."

"Good lord, we're not any closer to anywhere!"

"Let's try to keep calm about it, Simmons."

"Calm, calm! This rain's driving me wild!"

"We've enough food for another two days if we're careful."

The rain danced on their skin, on their wet uniforms; the rain streamed from their noses and ears, from their fingers and knees. They looked like stone fountains frozen in the jungle, issuing forth water from every pore.

And, as they stood, from a distance they heard a roar.

And the monster came out of the rain.

The monster was supported upon a thousand electric blue legs. It walked swiftly and terribly. It struck down a leg with a driving blow. Everywhere a leg struck a tree fell and burned. Great whiffs of ozone filled the rainy air, and smoke blew away and was broken up by the rain. The monster was a half mile wide and a mile high and it felt of the ground like a great blind thing. Sometimes, for a moment, it had no legs at all.

And then, in an instant, a thousand whips would fall out of its belly, white-blue whips, to sting the jungle.

"There's the electrical storm," said one of the men. "There's the thing ruined our compasses. And it's coming this way."

"Lie down, everyone," said the lieutenant.

"Run!" cried Simmons.

"Don't be a fool. Lie down. It hits the highest points. We may get through unhurt. Lie down about fifty feet from the rocket. It may very well spend its force there and leave us be. Get down!"

The men flopped.

"Is it coming?" they asked each other, after a moment.

"Coming."

"Is it nearer?"

"Two hundred yards off."

"Nearer?"

"Here she is!"

The monster came and stood over them. It dropped down ten blue bolts of lightning which struck the rocket. The rocket flashed like a beaten gong and gave off a metal ringing. The monster let down fifteen more bolts which danced about in a ridiculous pantomime, feeling of the jungle and the watery soil.

"No, no!" One of the men jumped up.

"Get down, you fool!" said the lieutenant.

"No!"

The lightning struck the rocket another dozen times. The lieutenant turned his head on his arm and saw the blue blazing flashes. He saw trees split and crumple into ruin. He saw the monstrous dark cloud turn like a black disk overhead and hurl down a hundred other poles of electricity.

The man who had leaped up was now running, like someone in a great hall of pillars. He ran and dodged between the pillars and then at last a dozen of the pillars slammed down and there was the sound a fly makes when landing upon the grill wires of an exterminator. The lieutenant remembered this from his childhood on a farm. And there was a smell of a man burned to a cinder.

The lieutenant lowered his head. "Don't look up," he told the others. He was afraid that he too might run at any moment.

The storm above them flashed down another series of bolts and then moved on away. Once again there was only the rain, which rapidly cleared the air of the charred smell, and in a moment the three remaining men were sitting and waiting for the beat of their hearts to subside into quiet once more.

They walked over to the body, thinking that perhaps they could still save the man's life. They couldn't believe that there wasn't some way to help the man. It was the natural act of men who have not accepted death until they have touched it and turned it over and made plans to bury it or leave it there for the jungle to bury in an hour of quick growth.

The body was twisted steel, wrapped in burned leather. It looked like a wax dummy that had been thrown into an incinerator and pulled out after the wax had sunk to the charcoal skeleton. Only the teeth were white, and they shone like a strange white bracelet dropped half through a clenched black fist.

"He shouldn't have jumped up." They said it almost at the same time.

Even as they stood over the body it began to vanish, for the vegetation was edging in upon it, little vines and ivy and creepers, and even flowers for the dead.

At a distance the storm walked off on blue bolts of lightning and was gone.

They crossed a river and a creek and a stream and a dozen other rivers and creeks and streams. Before their eyes rivers appeared, rushing, new rivers, while old rivers changed their courses—rivers the color of mercury, rivers the color of silver and milk.

They came to the sea.

The Single Sea. There was only one continent on Venus. This land was three thousand miles long by a thousand miles wide, and about this island was the Single Sea, which covered the entire raining planet. The Single Sea, which lay upon the pallid shore with little motion . . .

"This way." The lieutenant nodded south. "I'm sure there are two Sun Domes down that way."

"While they were at it, why didn't they build a hundred more?"

"There're a hundred and twenty of them now, aren't there?"

"One hundred and twenty-six, as of last month. They tried to push a bill through Congress back on Earth a year ago to provide for a couple dozen more, but oh no, you know how *that* is. They'd rather a few men went crazy with the rain."

They started south.

The lieutenant and Simmons and the third man, Pickard, walked in the rain, in the rain that fell heavily and lightly, heavily and lightly; in the rain that poured and hammered and did not stop falling upon the land and the sea and the walking people.

Simmons saw it first. "There it is!"

"There's what?"

"The Sun Dome!"

The lieutenant blinked the water from his eyes and raised his hands to ward off the stinging blows of the rain.

At a distance there was a yellow glow on the edge of the jungle, by the sea. It was, indeed, the Sun Dome.

The men smiled at each other.

"Looks like you were right, Lieutenant."

"Luck."

"Brother, that puts muscle in me, just seeing it. Come on! Last one there's a son-of-a-bitch!" Simmons began to trot. The others automatically fell in with this, gasping, tired, but keeping pace.

"A big pot of coffee for me," panted Simmons, smiling. "And a pan of cinnamon buns, by God! And just lie there and let the old sun hit you. The guy that invented the Sun Domes, he should have got a medal!"

They ran faster. The yellow glow grew brighter.

"Guess a lot of men went crazy before they figured out the cure. Think it'd be obvious! Right off." Simmons panted the words in cadence to his running. "Rain, rain! Years ago. Found a friend. Of mine. Out in the jungle. Wandering around. In the rain. Saying over and over, 'Don't know enough, to come in, outta the rain. Don't know enough, to come in, outta the rain. Don't know enough——' On and on. Like that. Poor crazy bastard."

"Save your breath!"

They ran.

They all laughed. They reached the door of the Sun Dome, laughing.

Simmons yanked the door wide. "Hey!" he yelled. "Bring on the coffee and buns!"

There was no reply.

They stepped through the door.

The Sun Dome was empty and dark. There was no synthetic yellow sun floating in a high gaseous whisper at the center of the blue ceiling. There was no food waiting. It was cold as a vault. And through a thousand holes which had been newly punctured in the ceiling water streamed, the rain fell down, soaking into the thick rugs and the heavy modern furniture and splashing on the glass tables. The jungle was growing up like a moss in the room, on top of the bookcases and the divans. The rain slashed through the holes and fell upon the three men's faces.

Pickard began to laugh quietly.

"Shut up, Pickard!"

"Ye gods, look what's here for us—no food, no sun, nothing. The Venusians—they did it! Of course!"

Simmons nodded, with the rain funneling down on his face. The water ran in his silvered hair and on his white eyebrows. "Every once in a while the Venusians come up out of the sea and attack a Sun Dome. They know if they ruin the Sun Domes they can ruin us."

"But aren't the Sun Domes protected with guns?"

"Sure." Simmons stepped aside to a place that was relatively dry. "But it's been five years since the Venusians tried anything. Defense relaxes. They caught this Dome unaware."

"Where are the bodies?"

"The Venusians took them all down into the sea. I hear they have a delightful way of drowning you. It takes about eight hours to drown the way they work it. Really delightful."

"I bet there isn't any food here at all." Pickard laughed.

The lieutenant frowned at him, nodded at him so Simmons could see. Simmons shook his head and went back to a room at one side of the oval chamber. The kitchen was strewn with soggy loaves of bread, and meat that had grown a faint green fur. Rain came through a hundred holes in the kitchen roof.

"Brilliant." The lieutenant glanced up at the holes. "I don't suppose we can plug up all those holes and get snug here."

"Without food, sir?" Simmons snorted. "I notice the sun machine's torn apart. Our best bet is to make our way to the next Sun Dome. How far is that from here?"

"Not far. As I recall, they built two rather close together here. Perhaps if we waited here, a rescue mission from the other might——"

"It's probably been here and gone already, some days ago. They'll send a crew to repair this place in about six months, when they get the money from Congress. I don't think we'd better wait."

"All right then, we'll eat what's left of our rations and get on to the next Dome."

Pickard said, "If only the rain wouldn't hit my head, just for a few minutes. If I could only remember what it's like not to be bothered." He put his hands on his skull and held it tight. "I remember when I was in school a bully used to sit in back of me and pinch me and pinch me and pinch me every five minutes, all day long. He did that for weeks and months. My arms were sore and black and blue all the time. And I thought I'd go crazy from being pinched. One day I must have gone a little mad from being hurt and hurt, and I turned around and took a metal trisquare I used in mechanical drawing and I almost killed that bastard. I almost cut his lousy head off. I almost took his eye out before they dragged me out of the room, and I kept yelling, 'Why don't he leave me alone? why don't he leave me alone?' Brother!" His hands clenched the bone of his head, shaking, tightening, his eyes shut. "But what do I do now? Who do I hit, who do I tell to lay off, stop bothering me, this damn rain, like the pinching, always on you, that's all you hear, that's all you feel!"

"We'll be at the other Sun Dome by four this afternoon."

"Sun Dome? Look at this one! What if all the Sun Domes on Venus are gone? What then? What if there are holes in all the ceilings, and the rain coming in!"

"We'll have to chance it."

"I'm tired of chancing it. All I want is a roof and some quiet. I want to be alone."

"That's only eight hours off, if you hold on."

"Don't worry, I'll hold on all right." And Pickard laughed, not looking at them.

"Let's eat," said Simmons, watching him.

They set off down the coast, southward again. After four hours they had to cut inland to go around a river that was a mile wide and so swift it was not navigable by boat. They had to walk inland six miles to a place where the river boiled out of the earth, suddenly, like a mortal wound. In the rain, they walked on solid ground and returned to the sea.

"I've got to sleep," said Pickard at last. He slumped. "Haven't slept in four weeks. Tried, but couldn't. Sleep here."

The sky was getting darker. The night of Venus was setting in and it was so completely black that it was dangerous to move. Simmons and the lieutenant fell to their knees also, and the lieutenant said, "All right, we'll see what we can do. We've tried it before, but I don't know. Sleep doesn't seem one of the things you can get in this weather."

They lay out full, propping their heads up so the water wouldn't come to their mouths, and they closed their eyes.

The lieutenant twitched.

He did not sleep.

There were things that crawled on his skin. Things grew upon him in layers. Drops fell and touched other drops and they became streams that trickled over his body, and while these moved down his flesh, the small growths of the forest took root in his clothing. He felt the ivy cling and make a second garment over him; he felt the small flowers bud and open and petal away, and still the rain pattered on his body and on his head. In the luminous night—for the vegetation glowed in the darkness—he could see the other two men outlined, like logs that had fallen and taken upon themselves velvet coverings of grass and flowers. The rain hit his face. He covered his face with his hands. The rain hit his neck. He turned over on his stomach in the mud, on the rubbery plants, and the rain hit his back and hit his legs.

Suddenly he leaped up and began to brush the water from himself. A thousand hands were touching him and he no longer wanted to be touched. He no longer could stand being touched. He floundered and struck something else and knew that it was

Simmons, standing up in the rain, sneezing moisture, coughing and choking. And then Pickard was up, shouting, running about.

"Wait a minute, Pickard!"

"Stop it, stop it!" Pickard screamed. He fired off his gun six times at the night sky. In the flashes of powdery illumination they could see armies of raindrops, suspended as in a vast motionless amber, for an instant, hesitating as if shocked by the explosion, fifteen billion droplets, fifteen billion tears, fifteen billion ornaments, jewels standing out against a white velvet viewing board. And then, with the light gone, the drops which had waited to have their pictures taken, which had suspended their downward rush, fell upon them, stinging, in an insect cloud of coldness and pain.

"Stop it! Stop it!"

"Pickard!"

But Pickard was only standing now, alone. When the lieutenant switched on a small hand lamp and played it over Pickard's wet face, the eyes of the man were dilated, and his mouth was open, his face turned up, so the water hit and splashed on his tongue, and hit and drowned the wide eyes, and bubbled in a whispering froth on the nostrils.

"Pickard!"

The man would not reply. He simply stood there for a long while with the bubbles of rain breaking out in his whitened hair and manacles of rain jewels dripping from his wrists and his neck.

"Pickard! We're leaving. We're going on. Follow us."

The rain dripped from Pickard's ears.

"Do you hear me, Pickard!"

It was like shouting down a well.

"Pickard!"

"Leave him alone," said Simmons.

"We can't go on without him."

"What'll we do, carry him?" Simmons spat. "He's no good to us or himself. You know what he'll do? He'll just stand here and drown."

"What?"

"You ought to know that by now. Don't you know the story? He'll just stand here with his head up and let the rain come in his nostrils and his mouth. He'll breathe the water."

"No."

"That's how they found General Mendt that time. Sitting on a rock with his head back, breathing the rain. His lungs were full of water."

The lieutenant turned the light back to the unblinking face. Pickard's nostrils gave off a tiny whispering wet sound.

"Pickard!" The lieutenant slapped the face.

"He can't even feel you," said Simmons. "A few days in this rain and you don't have any face or any legs or hands."

The lieutenant looked at his own hand in horror. He could no longer feel it.

"But we can't leave Pickard here."

"I'll show you what we can do." Simmons fired his gun.

Pickard fell into the raining earth.

Simmons said, "Don't move, Lieutenant. I've got my gun ready for you too. Think it over; he would only have stood or sat there and drowned. It's quicker this way."

The lieutenant blinked at the body. "But you killed him."

"Yes, because he'd have killed us by being a burden. You saw his face. Insane."

After a moment the lieutenant nodded. "All right."

They walked off into the rain.

It was dark and their hand lamps threw a beam that pierced the rain for only a few feet. After a half hour they had to stop and sit through the rest of the night, aching with hunger, waiting for the dawn to come; when it did come it was gray and continually raining as before, and they began to walk again.

"We've miscalculated," said Simmons.

"No. Another hour."

"Speak louder. I can't hear you." Simmons stopped and smiled. "By Christ," he said, and touched his ears. "My ears. They've gone out on me. All the rain pouring finally numbed me right down to the bone."

"Can't you hear anything?" said the lieutenant.

"What?" Simmons's eyes were puzzled.

"Nothing. Come on."

"I think I'll wait here. You go on ahead."

"You can't do that."

"I can't hear you. You go on. I'm tired. I don't think the

Sun Dome is down this way. And, if it is, it's probably got holes in the roof, like the last one. I think I'll just sit here."

"Get up from there!"

"So long, Lieutenant."

"You can't give up now."

"I've got a gun here that says I'm staying. I just don't give a damn any more. I'm not crazy yet, but I'm the next thing to it. I don't want to go out that way. As soon as you get out of sight I'm going to use this gun on myself."

"Simmons!"

"You said my name. I can read that much off your lips."

"Simmons."

"Look, it's a matter of time. Either I die now or in a few hours. Wait'll you get to that next Dome, if you ever get there, and find rain coming in through the roof. Won't that be nice?"

The lieutenant waited and then splashed off in the rain. He turned and called back once, but Simmons was only sitting there with the gun in his hands, waiting for him to get out of sight. He shook his head and waved the lieutenant on.

The lieutenant didn't even hear the sound of the gun.

He began to eat the flowers as he walked. They stayed down for a time, and weren't poisonous; neither were they particularly sustaining, and he vomited them up, sickly, a minute or so later.

Once he took some leaves and tried to make himself a hat, but he had tried that before; the rain melted the leaves from his head. Once picked, the vegetation rotted quickly and fell away into gray masses in his fingers.

"Another five minutes," he told himself. "Another five minutes and then I'll walk into the sea and keep walking. We weren't made for this; no Earthman was or ever will be able to take it. Your nerves, your nerves."

He floundered his way through a sea of slush and foliage and came to a small hill.

At a distance there was a faint yellow smudge in the cold veils of water.

The next Sun Dome.

Through the trees, a long round yellow building, far away. For a moment he only stood, swaying, looking at it.

He began to run and then he slowed down, for he was

afraid. He didn't call out. What if it's the same one? What if it's the dead Sun Dome, with no sun in it? he thought.

He slipped and fell. Lie here, he thought; it's the wrong one. Lie here. It's no use. Drink all you want.

But he managed to climb to his feet again and crossed several creeks, and the yellow light grew very bright, and he began to run again, his feet crashing into mirrors and glass, his arms flailing at diamonds and precious stones.

He stood before the yellow door. The printed letters over it said THE SUN DOME. He put his numb hand up to feel it. Then he twisted the doorknob and stumbled in.

He stood for a moment looking about. Behind him the rain whirled at the door. Ahead of him, upon a low table, stood a silver pot of hot chocolate, steaming, and a cup, full, with a marshmallow in it. And beside that, on another tray, stood thick sandwiches of rich chicken meat and fresh-cut tomatoes and green onions. And on a rod just before his eyes was a great thick green Turkish towel, and a bin in which to throw wet clothes, and, to his right, a small cubicle in which heat rays might dry you instantly. And upon a chair, a fresh change of uniform, waiting for anyone—himself, or any lost one—to make use of it. And farther over, coffee in steaming copper urns, and a phonograph from which music was playing quietly, and books bound in red and brown leather. And near the books a cot, a soft deep cot upon which one might lie, exposed and bare, to drink in the rays of the one great bright thing which dominated the long room.

He put his hands to his eyes. He saw other men moving toward him, but said nothing to them. He waited, and opened his eyes, and looked. The water from his uniform pooled at his feet, and he felt it drying from his hair and his face and his chest and his arms and his legs.

He was looking at the sun.

It hung in the center of the room, large and yellow and warm. It made not a sound, and there was no sound in the room. The door was shut and the rain only a memory to his tingling body. The sun hung high in the blue sky of the room, warm, hot, yellow, and very fine.

He walked forward, tearing off his clothes as he went.

The Rocket Man

THE ELECTRICAL FIREFLIES were hovering above Mother's dark hair to light her path. She stood in her bedroom door looking out at me as I passed in the silent hall. "You *will* help me keep him here this time, won't you?" she asked.

"I guess so," I said.

"Please." The fireflies cast moving bits of light on her white face. "This time he mustn't go away again."

"All right," I said, after standing there a moment. "But it won't do any good; it's no use."

She went away, and the fireflies, on their electric circuits, fluttered after her like an errant constellation, showing her how to walk in darkness. I heard her say, faintly, "We've got to try, anyway."

Other fireflies followed me to my room. When the weight of my body cut a circuit in the bed, the fireflies winked out. It was midnight, and my mother and I waited, our rooms separated by darkness, in bed. The bed began to rock me and sing to me. I touched a switch; the singing and rocking stopped. I didn't want to sleep. I didn't want to sleep at all.

This night was no different from a thousand others in our time. We would wake nights and feel the cool air turn hot, feel the fire in the wind, or see the walls burned a bright color for an instant, and then we knew *his* rocket was over our house—his rocket, and the oak trees swaying from the concussion. And I would lie there, eyes wide, panting, and mother in her room. Her voice would come to me over the interroom radio:

"Did you feel it?"

And I would answer, "That was him, all right."

That was my father's ship passing over our town, a small town where *space* rockets never came, and we would lie awake for the next two hours, thinking, "Now Dad's landed in Springfield, now he's on the tarmac, now he's signing the papers, now he's in the helicopter, now he's over the river, now the hills, now he's settling the helicopter in at the little airport at Green Village here. . . ." And the night would be half over when, in our separate cool beds, Mother and I would be listening, listening. "Now he's walking down Bell Street. He always walks . . . never takes a cab . . . now across the park, now turning the corner of Oakhurst and *now* . . ."

I lifted my head from my pillow. Far down the street, coming closer and closer, smartly, quickly, briskly—footsteps. Now turning in at our house, up the porch steps. And we were both smiling in the cool darkness, Mom and I, when we heard the front door open in recognition, speak a quiet word of welcome, and shut, downstairs. . . .

Three hours later I turned the brass knob to their room quietly, holding my breath, balancing in a darkness as big as the space between the planets, my hand out to reach the small black case at the foot of my parents' sleeping bed. Taking it, I ran silently to my room, thinking, He won't tell me, he doesn't want me to *know.*

And from the opened case spilled his black uniform, like a black nebula, stars glittering here or there, distantly, in the material. I kneaded the dark stuff in my warm hands; I smelled the planet Mars, an iron smell, and the planet Venus, a green ivy smell, and the planet Mercury, a scent of sulphur and fire; and I could smell the milky moon and the hardness of stars. I pushed the uniform into a centrifuge machine I'd built in my ninth-grade shop that year, set it whirling. Soon a fine powder precipitated into a retort. This I slid under a microscope. And while my parents slept unaware, and while our house was asleep, all the automatic bakers and servers and robot cleaners in an electric slumber, I stared down upon brilliant motes of meteor dust, comet tail, and loam from far Jupiter glistening like worlds themselves which drew me down the tube a billion miles into space, at terrific accelerations.

At dawn, exhausted with my journey and fearful of discovery, I returned the boxed uniform to their sleeping room.

Then I slept, only to waken at the sound of the horn of the dry-cleaning car which stopped in the yard below. They took the black uniform box with them. It's good I didn't wait, I thought. For the uniform would be back in an hour, clean of all its destiny and travel.

I slept again, with the little vial of magical dust in my pajama pocket, over my beating heart.

When I came downstairs, there was Dad at the breakfast table, biting into his toast. "Sleep good, Doug?" he said, as if he had been here all the time, and hadn't been gone for three months.

"All right," I said.

"Toast?"

He pressed a button and the breakfast table made me four pieces, golden brown.

I remember my father that afternoon, digging and digging in the garden, like an animal after something, it seemed. There he was with his long dark arms moving swiftly, planting, tamping, fixing, cutting, pruning, his dark face always down to the soil, his eyes always down to what he was doing, never up to the sky, never looking at me, or Mother, even, unless we knelt with him to feel the earth soak up through the overalls at our knees, to put our hands into the black dirt and not look at the bright, crazy sky. Then he would glance to either side, to Mother or me, and give us a gentle wink, and go on, bent down, face down, the sky staring at his back.

That night we sat on the mechanical porch swing which swung us and blew a wind upon us and sang to us. It was summer and moonlight and we had lemonade to drink, and we held the cold glasses in our hands, and Dad read the stereo-newspapers inserted into the special hat you put on your head and which turned the microscopic page in front of the magnifying lens if you blinked three times in succession. Dad smoked cigarettes and told me about how it was when he was a boy in the year 1997. After a while he said, as he had always said, "Why aren't you out playing kick-the-can, Doug?"

I didn't say anything, but Mom said, "He does, on nights when you're not here."

Dad looked at me and then, for the first time that day, at the sky. Mother always watched him when he glanced at the stars. The first day and night when he got home he wouldn't look at the sky much. I thought about him gardening and gardening so furiously, his face almost driven into the earth. But the second night he looked at the stars a little more. Mother wasn't afraid of the sky in the day so much, but it was the night stars that she wanted to turn off, and sometimes I could almost see her reaching for a switch in her mind, but never finding it. And by the third night maybe Dad'd be out here on the porch until 'way after we were all ready for bed, and then I'd hear Mom call him in, almost like she called me from the street at times. And then I would hear Dad fitting the electric-eye door lock in place, with a sigh. And the next morning at breakfast I'd glance down and see his little black case near his feet as he buttered his toast and Mother slept late.

"Well, be seeing you, Doug," he'd say, and we'd shake hands.

"In about three months?"

"Right."

And he'd walk away down the street, not taking a helicopter or beetle or bus, just walking with his uniform hidden in his small underarm case; he didn't want anyone to think he was vain about being a Rocket Man.

Mother would come out to eat breakfast, one piece of dry toast, about an hour later.

But now it was tonight, the first night, the good night, and he wasn't looking at the stars much at all.

"Let's go to the television carnival," I said.

"Fine," said Dad.

Mother smiled at me.

And we rushed off to town in a helicopter and took Dad through a thousand exhibits, to keep his face and head down with us and not looking anywhere else. And as we laughed at the funny things and looked serious at the serious ones, I thought, My father goes to Saturn and Neptune and Pluto, but he never brings me presents. Other boys whose fathers go into space bring back bits of ore from Callisto and hunks of black meteor or blue sand. But I have to get my own collection, trading from other boys, the Martian rocks and Mercurian sands which filled my room, but about which Dad would never comment.

On occasion, I remembered, he brought something for Mother. He planted some Martian sunflowers once in our yard, but after he was gone a month and the sunflowers grew large, Mom ran out one day and cut them all down.

Without thinking, as we paused at one of the three-dimensional exhibits, I asked Dad the question I always asked:

"What's it like, out in space?"

Mother shot me a frightened glance. It was too late.

Dad stood there for a full half minute trying to find an answer, then he shrugged.

"It's the best thing in a lifetime of best things." Then he caught himself. "Oh, it's really nothing at all. Routine. You wouldn't like it." He looked at me, apprehensively.

"But *you* always go back."

"Habit."

"Where're you going next?"

"I haven't decided yet. I'll think it over."

He always thought it over. In those days rocket pilots were rare and he could pick and choose, work when he liked. On the third night of his homecoming you could see him picking and choosing among the stars.

"Come on," said Mother, "let's go home."

It was still early when we got home. I wanted Dad to put on his uniform. I shouldn't have asked—it always made Mother unhappy—but I could not help myself. I kept at him, though he had always refused. I had never seen him in it, and at last he said, "Oh, all right."

We waited in the parlor while he went upstairs in the air flue. Mother looked at me dully, as if she couldn't believe that her own son could do this to her. I glanced away. "I'm sorry," I said.

"You're not helping at all," she said. "At all."

There was a whisper in the air flue a moment later.

"Here I am," said Dad quietly.

We looked at him in his uniform.

It was glossy black with silver buttons and silver rims to the heels of the black boots, and it looked as if someone had cut the arms and legs and body from a dark nebula, with little faint stars glowing through it. It fit as close as a glove fits to a slender long hand, and it smelled like cool air and metal and space. It smelled of fire and time.

Father stood, smiling awkwardly, in the center of the room.

"Turn around," said Mother.

Her eyes were remote, looking at him.

When he was gone, she never talked of him. She never said

anything about anything but the weather or the condition of my neck and the need of a washcloth for it, or the fact that she didn't sleep nights. Once she said the light was too strong at night.

"But there's no moon this week," I said.

"There's starlight," she said.

I went to the store and bought her some darker, greener shades. As I lay in bed at night, I could hear her pull them down tight to the bottom of the windows. It made a long rustling noise.

Once I tried to mow the lawn.

"No." Mom stood in the door. "Put the mower away."

So the grass went three months at a time without cutting. Dad cut it when he came home.

She wouldn't let me do anything else either, like repairing the electrical breakfast maker or the mechanical book reader. She saved everything up, as if for Christmas. And then I would see Dad hammering or tinkering, and always smiling at his work, and Mother smiling over him, happy.

No, she never talked of him when he was gone. And as for Dad, he never did anything to make a contact across the millions of miles. He said once, "If I called you, I'd want to be with you. I wouldn't be happy."

Once Dad said to me, "Your mother treats me, sometimes, as if I weren't here—as if I were invisible."

I had seen her do it. She would look just beyond him, over his shoulder, at his chin or hands, but never into his eyes. If she did look at his eyes, her eyes were covered with a film, like an animal going to sleep. She said yes at the right times, and smiled, but always a half second later than expected.

"I'm not there for her," said Dad.

But other days she would be there and he would be there for her, and they would hold hands and walk around the block, or take rides, with Mom's hair flying like a girl's behind her, and she would cut off all the mechanical devices in the kitchen and bake him incredible cakes and pies and cookies, looking deep into his face, her smile a real smile. But at the end of such days when he was there to her, she would always cry. And Dad would stand helpless, gazing about the room as if to find the answer, but never finding it.

Dad turned slowly, in his uniform, for us to see.

"Turn around again," said Mom.

The next morning Dad came rushing into the house with handfuls of tickets. Pink rocket tickets for California, blue tickets for Mexico.

"Come on!" he said. "We'll buy disposable clothes and burn them when they're soiled. Look, we take the noon rocket to L.A., the two-o'clock helicopter to Santa Barbara, the nine-o'clock plane to Ensenada, sleep overnight!"

And we went to California and up and down the Pacific Coast for a day and a half, settling at last on the sands of Malibu to cook wieners at night. Dad was always listening or singing or watching things on all sides of him, holding onto things as if the world were a centrifuge going so swiftly that he might be flung off away from us at any instant.

The last afternoon at Malibu Mom was up in the hotel room. Dad lay on the sand beside me for a long time in the hot sun. "Ah," he sighed, "this is it." His eyes were gently closed; he lay on his back, drinking the sun. "You *miss* this," he said.

He meant "on the rocket," of course. But he never said "the rocket" or mentioned the rocket and all the things you couldn't have on the rocket. You couldn't have a salt wind on the rocket or a blue sky or a yellow sun or Mom's cooking. You couldn't talk to your fourteen-year-old boy on a rocket.

"Let's hear it," he said at last.

And I knew that now we would talk, as we had always talked, for three hours straight. All afternoon we would murmur back and forth in the lazy sun about my school grades, how high I could jump, how fast I could swim.

Dad nodded each time I spoke and smiled and slapped my chest lightly in approval. We talked. We did not talk of rockets or space, but we talked of Mexico, where we had driven once in an ancient car, and of the butterflies we had caught in the rain forests of green warm Mexico at noon, seeing the hundred butterflies sucked to our radiator, dying there, beating their blue and crimson wings, twitching, beautiful, and sad. We talked of such things instead of the things I wanted to talk about. And he listened to me. That was the thing he did, as if he was trying to fill himself up with all the sounds he could hear. He listened to the wind and the falling ocean and my voice, always with a rapt attention, a concentration that almost excluded physical bodies themselves and kept only the sounds. He shut his eyes to listen. I would see him listening to the lawn mower as he cut the grass by hand instead of using the remote-control device, and I would see him smelling the cut grass as it sprayed up at him behind the mower in a green fount.

"Doug," he said, about five in the afternoon, as we were picking up our towels and heading back along the beach near the surf, "I want you to promise me something."

"What?"

"Don't ever be a Rocket Man."

I stopped.

"I mean it," he said. "Because when you're out there you want to be here, and when you're here you want to be out there. Don't start that. Don't let it get hold of you."

"But——"

"You don't know what it is. Every time I'm out there I think, If I ever get back to Earth I'll stay there; I'll never go out again. But I go out, and I guess I'll always go out."

"I've thought about being a Rocket Man for a long time," I said.

He didn't hear me. "I *try* to stay here. Last Saturday when I got home I started trying so damned hard to *stay* here."

I remembered him in the garden, sweating, and all the traveling and doing and listening, and I knew that he did this to convince himself that the sea and the towns and the land and his family were the only real things and the good things. But I knew where he would be tonight: looking at the jewelry in Orion from our front porch.

"Promise me you won't be like me," he said.

I hesitated awhile. "Okay," I said.

He shook my hand. "Good boy," he said.

The dinner was fine that night. Mom had run about the kitchen with handfuls of cinnamon and dough and pots and pans tinkling, and now a great turkey fumed on the table, with dressing, cranberry sauce, peas, and pumpkin pie.

"In the middle of August?" said Dad, amazed.

"You won't be here for Thanksgiving."

"So I won't."

He sniffed it. He lifted each lid from each tureen and let the flavor steam over his sunburned face. He said "Ah" to each. He looked at the room and his hands. He gazed at the pictures on the wall, the chairs, the table, me, and Mom. He cleared his throat. I saw him make up his mind. "Lilly?"

"Yes?" Mom looked across her table which she had set like a wonderful silver trap, a miraculous gravy pit into which, like a struggling beast of the past caught in a tar pool, her husband might at last be caught and held, gazing out through a jail of wishbones, safe forever. Her eyes sparkled.

"Lilly," said Dad.

Go on, I thought crazily. Say it, quick; say you'll stay home this time, for good, and never go away; *say* it!

Just then a passing helicopter jarred the room and the windowpane shook with a crystal sound. Dad glanced at the window.

The blue stars of evening were there, and the red planet Mars was rising in the East.

Dad looked at Mars a full minute. Then he put his hand out blindly toward me. "May I have some peas," he said.

"Excuse me," said Mother. "I'm going to get some bread." She rushed out into the kitchen.

"But there's bread on the table," I said.

Dad didn't look at me as he began his meal.

I couldn't sleep that night. I came downstairs at one in the morning and the moonlight was like ice on all the housetops, and dew glittered in a snow field on our grass. I stood in the doorway in my pajamas, feeling the warm night wind, and then I knew that Dad was sitting in the mechanical porch swing, gliding gently. I could see his profile tilted back, and he was watching the stars wheel over the sky. His eyes were like gray crystal there, the moon in each one.

I went out and sat beside him.

We glided awhile in the swing.

At last I said, "How many ways are there to die in space?"

"A million."

"Name some."

"The meteors hit you. The air goes out of your rocket. Or

comets take you along with them. Concussion. Strangulation. Explosion. Centrifugal force. Too much acceleration. Too little. The heat, the cold, the sun, the moon, the stars, the planets, the asteroids, the planetoids, radiation . . ."

"And do they bury you?"

"They never find you."

"Where do you go?"

"A billion miles away. Traveling graves, they call them. You become a meteor or a planetoid traveling forever through space."

I said nothing.

"One thing," he said later, "it's quick in space. Death. It's over like that. You don't linger. Most of the time you don't even know it. You're dead and that's it."

We went up to bed.

It was morning.

Standing in the doorway, Dad listened to the yellow canary singing in its golden cage.

"Well, I've decided," he said. "Next time I come home, I'm home to stay."

"Dad!" I said.

"Tell your mother that when she gets up," he said.

"You *mean* it!"

He nodded gravely. "See you in about three months."

And there he went off down the street, carrying his uniform in its secret box, whistling and looking at the tall green trees and picking chinaberries off the chinaberry bush as he brushed by, tossing them ahead of him as he walked away into the bright shade of early morning. . . .

I asked Mother about a few things that morning after Father had been gone a number of hours. "Dad said that sometimes you don't act as if you hear or see him," I said.

And then she explained everything to me quietly.

"When he went off into space ten years ago, I said to myself, 'He's dead.' Or as good as dead. So think of him dead. And when he comes back, three or four times a year, it's not him at all, it's only a pleasant little memory or a dream. And if a memory stops or a dream stops, it can't hurt half as much. So most of the time I think of him dead——"

"But other times——"

"Other times I can't help myself. I bake pies and treat him as if he were alive, and then it hurts. No, it's better to think he hasn't been here for ten years and I'll never see him again. It doesn't hurt as much."

"Didn't he say next time he'd settle down."

She shook her head slowly. "No, he's dead. I'm very sure of that."

"He'll come alive again, then," I said.

"Ten years ago," said Mother, "I thought, What if he dies on Venus? Then we'll never be able to see Venus again. What if he dies on Mars? We'll never be able to look at Mars again, all red in the sky, without wanting to go in and lock the door. Or what if he died on Jupiter or Saturn or Neptune? On those nights when those planets were high in the sky, we wouldn't want to have anything to do with the stars."

"I guess not," I said.

The message came the next day.

The messenger gave it to me and I read it standing on the porch. The sun was setting. Mom stood in the screen door behind me, watching me fold the message and put it in my pocket.

"Mom," I said.

"Don't tell me anything I don't already know," she said.

She didn't cry.

Well, it wasn't Mars, and it wasn't Venus, and it wasn't Jupiter or Saturn that killed him. We wouldn't have to think of him every time Jupiter or Saturn or Mars lit up the evening sky.

This was different.

His ship had fallen into the sun.

And the sun was big and fiery and merciless, and it was always in the sky and you couldn't get away from it.

So for a long time after my father died my mother slept through the days and wouldn't go out. We had breakfast at midnight and lunch at three in the morning, and dinner at the cold dim hour of 6 A.M. We went to all-night shows and went to bed at sunrise.

And, for a long while, the only days we ever went out to walk were the days when it was raining and there was no sun.

The Fire Balloons

FIRE EXPLODED OVER summer night lawns. You saw sparkling faces of uncles and aunts. Skyrockets fell up in the brown shining eyes of cousins on the porch, and the cold charred sticks thumped down in dry meadows far away.

The Very Reverend Father Joseph Daniel Peregrine opened his eyes. What a dream: he and his cousins with their fiery play at his grandfather's ancient Ohio home so many years ago!

He lay listening to the great hollow of the church, the other cells where other Fathers lay. Had they, too, on the eve of the flight of the rocket *Crucifix*, lain with memories of the Fourth of July? Yes. This was like those breathless Independence dawns when you waited for the first concussion and rushed out on the dewy sidewalks, your hands full of loud miracles.

So here they were, the Episcopal Fathers, in the breathing dawn before they pinwheeled off to Mars, leaving their incense through the velvet cathedral of space.

"Should we go at all?" whispered Father Peregrine. "Shouldn't we solve our own sins on Earth? Aren't we running from our lives here?"

He arose, his fleshy body, with its rich look of strawberries, milk, and steak, moving heavily.

"Or is it sloth?" he wondered. "Do I dread the journey?"

He stepped into the needle-spray shower.

"But I shall take you to Mars, body." He addressed himself. "Leaving old sins here. And on to Mars to find *new* sins?" A delightful thought, almost. Sins no one had ever thought of. Oh, he himself had written a little book: *The Problem of Sin on Other Worlds*, ignored as somehow not serious enough by his Episcopal brethren.

Only last night, over a final cigar, he and Father Stone had talked of it.

"On Mars sin might appear as virtue. We must guard against virtuous acts there that, later, might be found to be sins!" said Father Peregrine, beaming. "How exciting! It's been centuries since so much adventure has accompanied the prospect of being a missionary!"

"*I* will recognize sin," said Father Stone bluntly, "even on Mars."

"Oh, we priests pride ourselves on being litmus paper, changing color in sin's presence," retorted Father Peregrine, "but what if Martian chemistry is such we do not color *at all*! If there are new senses on Mars, you must admit the possibility of unrecognizable sin."

"If there is no malice aforethought, there is no sin or punishment for same—the Lord assures us that," Father Stone replied.

"On Earth, yes. But perhaps a Martian sin might inform the subconscious of its evil, telepathically, leaving the conscious mind of man free to act, seemingly without malice! What *then*?"

"What *could* there be in the way of new sins?"

Father Peregrine leaned heavily forward. "Adam *alone* did not sin. Add Eve and you add temptation. Add a second man and you make adultery possible. With the addition of sex or people, you add sin. If men were armless they could not strangle with their hands. You would not have that particular sin of murder. Add arms, and you add the possibility of a new violence. Amoebas cannot sin because they reproduce by fission. They do not covet wives or murder each other. Add sex to amoebas, add arms and legs, and you would have murder and adultery. Add an arm or leg or person, or take away each, and you add or subtract possible evil. On Mars, what if there are five new senses, organs, invisible limbs we can't conceive of—then mightn't there be five *new sins*?"

Father Stone gasped. "I think you *enjoy* this sort of thing!"

"I keep my mind alive, Father; just alive, is all."

"Your mind's always juggling, isn't it?—mirrors, torches, plates."

"Yes. Because sometimes the Church seems like those posed circus tableaus where the curtain lifts and men, white, zinc-oxide, talcum-powder statues, freeze to represent abstract Beauty. Very wonderful. But I hope there will always be room for me to dart about among the statues, don't you, Father Stone?"

Father Stone had moved away. "I think we'd better go to

bed. In a few hours we'll be jumping up to see your *new* sins, Father Peregrine."

The rocket stood ready for the firing.

The Fathers walked from their devotions in the chilly morning, many a fine priest from New York or Chicago or Los Angeles—the Church was sending its best—walking across town to the frosty field. Walking, Father Peregrine remembered the Bishop's words:

"Father Peregrine, you will captain the missionaries, with Father Stone at your side. Having chosen you for this serious task, I find my reasons deplorably obscure, Father, but your pamphlet on planetary sin did not go unread. You are a flexible man. And Mars is like that uncleaned closet we have neglected for millenniums. Sin has collected there like bric-a-brac. Mars is twice Earth's age and has had double the number of Saturday nights, liquor baths, and eye-poppings at women as naked as white seals. When we open that closet door, things will fall on us. We need a quick, flexible man—one whose mind can dodge. Anyone a little too dogmatic might break in two. I feel you'll be resilient. Father, the job is yours."

The Bishop and the Fathers knelt.

The blessing was said and the rocket given a little shower of holy water. Arising, the Bishop addressed them:

"I know you will go with God, to prepare the Martians for the reception of His Truth. I wish you all a *thoughtful* journey."

They filed past the Bishop, twenty men, robes whispering, to deliver their hands into his kind hands before passing into the cleansed projectile.

"I wonder," said Father Peregrine, at the last moment, "if Mars is hell? Only waiting for our arrival before it bursts into brimstone and fire."

"Lord, be with us," said Father Stone.

The rocket moved.

Coming out of space was like coming out of the most beautiful cathedral they had ever seen. Touching Mars was like touching the ordinary pavement outside the church five minutes after having *really* known your love for God.

The Fathers stepped gingerly from the steaming rocket and knelt upon Martian sand while Father Peregrine gave thanks.

"Lord, we thank Thee for the journey through Thy rooms. And, Lord, we have reached a new land, so we must have new eyes. We shall hear new sounds and must needs have new ears. And there will be new sins, for which we ask the gift of better and firmer and purer hearts. Amen."

They arose.

And here was Mars like a sea under which they trudged in the guise of submarine biologists, seeking life. Here the territory of hidden sin. Oh, how carefully they must all balance, like gray feathers, in this new element, afraid that walking *itself* might be sinful; or breathing, or simple fasting!

And here was the mayor of First Town come to meet them with outstretched hand. "What can I do for you, Father Peregrine?"

"We'd like to know about the Martians. For only if we know about them can we plan our church intelligently. Are they ten feet tall? We will build large doors. Are their skins blue or red or green? We must know when we put human figures in the stained glass so we may use the right skin color. Are they heavy? We will build sturdy seats for them."

"Father," said the mayor, "I don't think you should worry about the Martians. There are two races. One of them is pretty well dead. A few are in hiding. And the second race—well, they're not quite human."

"Oh?" Father Peregrine's heart quickened.

"They're round luminous globes of light, Father, living in those hills. Man or beast, who can say? But they act intelligently, I hear." The mayor shrugged. "Of course, they're not men, so I don't think you'll care——"

"On the contrary," said Father Peregrine swiftly. "Intelligent, you say?"

"There's a story. A prospector broke his leg in those hills and would have died there. The blue spheres of light came at him. When he woke, he was down on a highway and didn't know how he got there."

"Drunk," said Father Stone.

"That's the story," said the mayor. "Father Peregrine, with most of the Martians dead, and only these blue spheres, I frankly think you'd be better off in First City. Mars is opening up. It's a frontier now, like in the old days on Earth, out West, and in Alaska. Men are pouring up here. There're a couple thousand black Irish mechanics and miners and day laborers in First Town who need saving, because there're too many wicked women came with them, and too much ten-century-old Martian wine——"

Father Peregrine was gazing into the soft blue hills.

Father Stone cleared his throat. "Well, Father?"

Father Peregrine did not hear. "Spheres of blue *fire*?"

"Yes, Father."

"Ah," Father Peregrine sighed.

"Blue balloons." Father Stone shook his head. "A circus!"

Father Peregrine felt his wrists pounding. He saw the little frontier town with raw, fresh-built sin, and he saw the hills, old with the oldest and yet perhaps an even newer (to him) sin.

"Mayor, could your black Irish laborers cook one more day in hellfire?"

"I'd turn and baste them for you, Father."

Father Peregrine nodded to the hills. "Then that's where we'll go."

There was a murmur from everyone.

"It would be so simple," explained Father Peregrine, "to go into town. I prefer to think that if the Lord walked here and people said, 'Here is the beaten path,' He would reply, 'Show me the weeds. I will *make* a path.'"

"But——"

"Father Stone, think how it would weigh upon us if we passed sinners by and did not extend our hands."

"But globes of fire!"

"I imagine man looked funny to other animals when we first appeared. Yet he has a soul, for all his homeliness. Until we prove otherwise, let us assume that these fiery spheres have souls."

"All right," agreed the mayor, "but you'll be back to town."

"We'll see. First, some breakfast. Then you and I, Father Stone, will walk alone into the hills. I don't want to frighten those fiery Martians with machines or crowds. Shall we have breakfast?"

The Fathers ate in silence.

At nightfall Father Peregrine and Father Stone were high in the hills. They stopped and sat upon a rock to enjoy a moment of relaxation and waiting. The Martians had not as yet appeared and they both felt vaguely disappointed.

"I wonder——" Father Peregrine mopped his face. "Do you think if we called 'Hello!' they might answer?"

"Father Peregrine, won't you ever be serious?"

"Not until the good Lord is. Oh, don't look so terribly shocked, please. The Lord is not serious. In fact, it is a little hard to know just what else He is except loving. And love has to do with humor, doesn't it? For you cannot love someone unless you put up with him, can you? And you cannot put up with someone constantly unless you can laugh at him. Isn't that true? And certainly we are ridiculous little animals wallowing in the fudge bowl, and God must love us all the more because we appeal to His humor."

"*I* never thought of God as humorous," said Father Stone.

"The Creator of the platypus, the camel, the ostrich, and man? Oh, come now!" Father Peregrine laughed.

But at this instant, from among the twilight hills, like a series of blue lamps lit to guide their way, came the Martians.

Father Stone saw them first. "Look!"

Father Peregrine turned and the laughter stopped in his mouth.

The round blue globes of fire hovered among the twinkling stars, distantly trembling.

"Monsters!" Father Stone leaped up. But Father Peregrine caught him. "Wait!"

"We should've gone to town!"

"No, listen, look!" pleaded Father Peregrine.

"I'm afraid!"

"Don't be. This is God's work!"

"The devil's!"

"No, now, quiet!" Father Peregrine gentled him and they crouched with the soft blue light on their upturned faces as the fiery orbs drew near.

And again, Independence Night, thought Father Peregrine, tremoring. He felt like a child back in those July Fourth evenings, the sky blowing apart, breaking into powdery stars and burning sound, the concussions jingling house windows like the ice on a thousand thin ponds. The aunts, uncles, cousins crying, "Ah!" as to some celestial physician. The summer sky colors. And the Fire Balloons, lit by an indulgent grandfather, steadied in his massively tender hands. Oh, the memory of those lovely Fire Balloons, softly lighted, warmly billowed bits of tissue, like insect wings, lying like folded wasps in boxes and, last of all, after the day of riot and fury, at long last from their boxes, delicately unfolded, blue, red, white, patriotic—the Fire Balloons! He saw the dim faces of dear relatives long dead and mantled with moss as Grandfather lit the tiny candle and let the warm air breathe up to form the balloon plumply luminous in his hands, a shining vision which they held, reluctant to let it go; for, once released, it was yet another year gone from life, another Fourth, another bit of Beauty vanished. And then up, up, still up through the warm summer night constellations, the Fire Balloons had drifted, while red-white-and-blue eyes followed them, wordless, from family porches. Away into deep Illinois country, over night rivers and sleeping mansions the Fire Balloons dwindled, forever gone. . . .

Father Peregrine felt tears in his eyes. Above him the Martians, not one but a *thousand* whispering Fire Balloons, it seemed, hovered. Any moment he might find his long-dead and blessed grandfather at his elbow, staring up at Beauty.

But it was Father Stone.

"Let's go, please, Father!"

"I must speak to them." Father Peregrine rustled forward, not knowing what to say, for what had he ever said to the Fire Balloons of time past except with his mind: *you are beautiful, you are beautiful*, and that was not enough now. He could only lift his heavy arms and call upward, as he had often wished to call after the enchanted Fire Balloons, "Hello!"

But the fiery spheres only burned like images in a dark mirror. They seemed fixed, gaseous, miraculous, forever.

"We come with God," said Father Peregrine to the sky.

"Silly, silly, silly." Father Stone chewed the back of his hand. "In the name of God, Father Peregrine, stop!"

But now the phosphorescent spheres blew away into the hills. In a moment they were gone.

Father Peregrine called again, and the echo of his last cry shook the hills above. Turning, he saw an avalanche shake out dust, pause, and then, with a thunder of stone wheels, crash down the mountain upon them.

"Look what you've done!" cried Father Stone.

Father Peregrine was almost fascinated, then horrified. He turned, knowing they could run only a few feet before the rocks crushed them into ruins. He had time to whisper, *Oh, Lord!* and the rocks fell!

"Father!"

They were separated like chaff from wheat. There was a blue shimmering of globes, a shift of cold stars, a roar, and then they stood upon a ledge two hundred feet away watching the spot where their bodies should have been buried under tons of stone.

The blue light evaporated.

The two Fathers clutched each other. "What happened?"

"The blue fires lifted us!"

"We ran, *that* was it!"

"No, the globes saved us."

"They couldn't!"

"They *did*."

The sky was empty. There was a feel as if a great bell had just stopped tolling. Reverberations lingered in their teeth and marrows.

"Let's get away from here. You'll have us killed."

"I haven't feared death for a good many years, Father Stone."

"We've proved nothing. Those blue lights ran off at the first cry. It's useless."

"No." Father Peregrine was suffused with a stubborn wonder. "Somehow, they saved us. That proves they have souls."

"It proves only that they *might* have saved us. Everything was confused. We might have escaped, ourselves."

"They are not animals, Father Stone. Animals do not save lives, especially of strangers. There is mercy and compassion here. Perhaps, tomorrow, we may prove more."

"Prove what? How?" Father Stone was immensely tired

now; the outrage to his mind and body showed on his stiff face. "Follow them in helicopters, reading chapter and verse? They're not human. They haven't eyes or ears or bodies like ours."

"But I feel something about them," replied Father Peregrine. "I know a great revelation is at hand. They saved us. They *think*. They had a choice; let us live or die. That proves free will!"

Father Stone set to work building a fire, glaring at the sticks in his hands, choking on the gray smoke. "I myself will open a convent for nursling geese, a monastery for sainted swine, and I shall build a miniature apse in a microscope so that paramecium can attend services and tell their beads with their flagella."

"Oh, Father Stone."

"I'm sorry." Father Stone blinked redly across the fire. "But this is like blessing a crocodile before he chews you up. You're risking the entire missionary expedition. We belong in First Town, washing liquor from men's throats and perfume off their hands!"

"Can't you recognize the human in the inhuman?"

"I'd much rather recognize the inhuman in the human."

"But if I prove these things sin, know sin, know a moral life, have free will and intellect, Father Stone?"

"That will take much convincing."

The night grew rapidly cold and they peered into the fire to find their wildest thoughts, while eating biscuits and berries, and soon they were bundled for sleep under the chiming stars. And just before turning over one last time Father Stone, who had been thinking for many minutes to find something to bother Father Peregrine about, stared into the soft pink charcoal bed and said, "No Adam and Eve on Mars. No original sin. Maybe the Martians live in a state of God's grace. Then we can go back down to town and start work on the Earthmen."

Father Peregrine reminded himself to say a little prayer for Father Stone, who got so mad and who was now being vindictive, God help him. "Yes, Father Stone, but the Martians killed some of our settlers. That's sinful. There must have been an Original Sin and a Martian Adam and Eve. We'll find them.

Men are men, unfortunately, no matter what their shape, and inclined to sin."

But Father Stone was pretending sleep.

Father Peregrine did not shut his eyes.

Of course they couldn't let these Martians go to hell, could they? With a compromise to their consciences, could they go back to the new colonial towns, those towns so full of sinful gullets and women with scintilla eyes and white oyster bodies rollicking in beds with lonely laborers? Wasn't that the place for the Fathers? Wasn't this trek into the hills merely a personal whim? Was he really thinking of God's Church, or was he quenching the thirst of a spongelike curiosity? Those blue round globes of St. Anthony's fire—how they burned in his mind! What a challenge, to find the man behind the mask, the human behind the inhuman. Wouldn't he be proud if he could say, even to his secret self, that he had converted a rolling huge pool table full of fiery spheres! What a sin of pride! Worth doing penance for! But then one did many prideful things out of Love, and he loved the Lord so much and was so happy at it that he wanted everyone else to be happy too.

The last thing he saw before sleep was the return of the blue fires, like a flight of burning angels silently singing him to his worried rest.

The blue round dreams were still there in the sky when Father Peregrine awoke in the early morning.

Father Stone slept like a stiff bundle, quietly. Father Peregrine watched the Martians floating and watching him. They were human—he *knew* it. But he must prove it or face a dry-mouthed, dry-eyed Bishop telling him kindly to step aside.

But how to prove humanity if they hid in the high vaults of the sky? How to bring them nearer and provide answers to the many questions?

"They saved us from the avalanche."

Father Peregrine arose, moved off among the rocks, and began to climb the nearest hill until he came to a place where a cliff dropped sheerly to a floor two hundred feet below. He was choking from his vigorous climb in the frosty air. He stood, getting his breath.

"If I fell from here, it would surely kill me."

He let a pebble drop. Moments later it clicked on the rocks below.

"The Lord would never forgive me."

He tossed another pebble.

"It wouldn't be suicide, would it, if I did it out of Love . . . ?"

He lifted his gaze to the blue spheres. "But first, another try." He called to them: "Hello, hello!"

The echoes tumbled upon each other, but the blue fires did not blink or move.

He talked to them for five minutes. When he stopped, he peered down and saw Father Stone, still indignantly asleep, below in the little camp.

"I must prove everything." Father Peregrine stepped to the cliff rim. "I am an old man. I am not afraid. Surely the Lord will understand that I am doing this for Him?"

He drew a deep breath. All his life swam through his eyes and he thought, In a moment shall I die? I am afraid that I love living much too much. But I love other things more.

And, thinking thus, he stepped off the cliff.

He fell.

"Fool!" he cried. He tumbled end over end. "You were wrong!" The rocks rushed up at him and he saw himself dashed on them and sent to glory. "Why did I do this thing?" But he knew the answer, and an instant later was calm as he fell. The wind roared around him and the rocks hurtled to meet him.

And then there was a shift of stars, a glimmering of blue light, and he felt himself surrounded by blueness and suspended. A moment later he was deposited, with a gentle bump, upon the rocks, where he sat a full moment, alive, and touching himself, and looking up at those blue lights that had withdrawn instantly.

"You saved me!" he whispered. "You wouldn't let me die. You knew it was wrong."

He rushed over to Father Stone, who still lay quietly asleep. "Father, Father, wake up!" He shook him and brought him round. "Father, they saved me!"

"Who saved you?" Father Stone blinked and sat up.

Father Peregrine related his experience.

"A dream, a nightmare; go back to sleep," said Father Stone irritably. "You and your circus balloons."

"But I was awake!"

"Now, now, Father, calm yourself. There now."

"You don't believe me? Have you a gun? Yes, there, let me have it."

"What are you going to do?" Father Stone handed over the small pistol they had brought along for protection against snakes or other similar and unpredictable animals.

Father Peregrine seized the pistol. "I'll prove it!"

He pointed the pistol at his own hand and fired.

"Stop!"

There was a shimmer of light, and before their eyes the bullet stood upon the air, poised an inch from his open palm. It hung for a moment, surrounded by a blue phosphorescence. Then it fell, hissing, into the dust.

Father Peregrine fired the gun three times—at his hand, at his leg, at his body. The three bullets hovered, glittering, and, like dead insects, fell at their feet.

"You see?" said Father Peregrine, letting his arm fall, and allowing the pistol to drop after the bullets. "They know. They understand. They are not animals. They think and judge and live in a moral climate. What animal would save me from myself like this? There is no animal would do that. Only another man, Father. Now, do you believe?"

Father Stone was watching the sky and the blue lights, and now, silently, he dropped to one knee and picked up the warm bullets and cupped them in his hand. He closed his hand tight.

The sun was rising behind them.

"I think we had better go down to the others and tell them of this and bring them back up here," said Father Peregrine.

By the time the sun was up, they were well on their way back to the rocket.

Father Peregrine drew the round circle in the center of the blackboard.

"This is Christ, the son of the Father."

He pretended not to hear the other Fathers' sharp intake of breath.

"This is Christ, in all his Glory," he continued.

"It looks like a geometry problem," observed Father Stone.

"A fortunate comparison, for we deal with symbols here. Christ is no less Christ, you must admit, in being represented by a circle or a square. For centuries the cross has symbolized his love and agony. So this circle will be the Martian Christ. This is how we shall bring Him to Mars."

The Fathers stirred fretfully and looked at each other.

"You, Brother Mathias, will create, in glass, a replica of this circle, a globe, filled with bright fire. It will stand upon the altar."

"A cheap magic trick," muttered Father Stone.

Father Peregrine went on patiently: "On the contrary. We are giving them God in an understandable image. If Christ had come to us on Earth as an octopus, would we have accepted him readily?" He spread his hands. "Was it then a cheap magic trick of the Lord's to bring us Christ through Jesus, in man's shape? After we bless the church we build here and sanctify its altar and this symbol, do you think Christ would refuse to inhabit the shape before us? You know in your hearts He would not refuse."

"But the body of a soulless animal," said Brother Mathias.

"We've already gone over that, many times since we returned this morning, Brother Mathias. These creatures saved us from the avalanche. They realized that self-destruction was sinful, and prevented it, time after time. Therefore we must build a church in the hills, live with them, to find their own special ways of sinning, the alien ways, and help them to discover God."

The Fathers did not seem pleased at the prospect.

"Is it because they are so odd to the eye?" wondered Father Peregrine. "But what is a shape? Only a cup for the blazing soul that God provides us all. If tomorrow I found that sea lions suddenly possessed free will, intellect, knew when not to sin, knew what life was and tempered justice with mercy and life with love, then I would build an undersea cathedral. And if the sparrows should, miraculously, with God's will, gain everlasting souls tomorrow, I would freight a church with helium and take after them, for all souls, in any shape, if they have free will and are aware of their sins, will burn in hell unless given their rightful communions. I would not let a Martian sphere burn in hell, either, for it is a sphere only in mine eyes. When

I close my eyes it stands before me, an intelligence, a love, a soul—and I must not deny it."

"But that glass globe you wish placed on the altar," protested Father Stone.

"Consider the Chinese," replied Father Peregrine imperturbably. "What sort of Christ do Christian Chinese worship? An oriental Christ, naturally. You've all seen oriental Nativity scenes. How is Christ dressed? In Eastern robes. Where does He walk? In Chinese settings of bamboo and misty mountain and crooked tree. His eyelids taper, his cheekbones rise. Each country, each race adds something to Our Lord. I am reminded of the Virgin of Guadalupe, to whom all Mexico pays its love. Her skin? Have you noticed the paintings of her? A dark skin, like that of her worshipers. Is this blasphemy? Not at all. It is not logical that men should accept a God, no matter how real, of another color. I often wonder why our missionaries do well in Africa, with a snow-white Christ. Perhaps because white is a sacred color, in albino, or any other form, to the African tribes. Given time, mightn't Christ darken there too? The form does not matter. Content is everything. We cannot expect these Martians to accept an alien form. We shall give them Christ in their own image."

"There's a flaw in your reasoning, Father," said Father Stone. "Won't the Martians suspect us of hypocrisy? They will realize that we don't worship a round, globular Christ, but a man with limbs and a head. How do we explain the difference?"

"By showing there is none. Christ will fill any vessel that is offered. Bodies or globes, he is there, and each will worship the same thing in a different guise. What is more, we must *believe* in this globe we give the Martians. We must believe in a shape which is meaningless to us as to form. This spheroid *will* be Christ. And we must remember that we ourselves, and the shape of our Earth Christ, would be meaningless, ridiculous, a squander of material to these Martians."

Father Peregrine laid aside his chalk. "Now let us go into the hills and build our church."

The Fathers began to pack their equipment.

The church was not a church but an area cleared of rocks, a plateau on one of the low mountains, its soil smoothed and brushed, and an altar established whereon Brother Mathias placed the fiery globe he had constructed.

At the end of six days of work the "church" was ready.

"What shall we do with this?" Father Stone tapped an iron bell they had brought along. "What does a bell mean to *them*?"

"I imagine I brought it for our own comfort," admitted Father Peregrine. "We need a few familiarities. This church seems so little like a church. And we feel somewhat absurd here—even I; for it is something new, this business of converting the creatures of another world. I feel like a ridiculous play actor at times. And then I pray to God to lend me strength."

"Many of the Fathers are unhappy. Some of them joke about all this, Father Peregrine."

"I know. We'll put this bell in a small tower, for their comfort, anyway."

"What about the organ?"

"We'll play it at the first service, tomorrow."

"But, the Martians——"

"I know. But again, I suppose, for our own comfort, our own music. Later we may discover theirs."

They arose very early on Sunday morning and moved through the coldness like pale phantoms, rime tinkling on their habits; covered with chimes they were, shaking down showers of silver water.

"I wonder if it *is* Sunday here on Mars?" mused Father Peregrine, but seeing Father Stone wince, he hastened on, "It might be Tuesday or Thursday—who knows? But no matter. My idle fancy. It's Sunday to *us*. Come."

The Fathers walked into the flat wide area of the "church" and knelt, shivering and blue-lipped.

Father Peregrine said a little prayer and put his cold fingers to the organ keys. The music went up like a flight of pretty birds. He touched the keys like a man moving his hands among the weeds of a wild garden, startling up great soarings of beauty into the hills.

The music calmed the air. It smelled the fresh smell of morning. The music drifted into the mountains and shook down mineral powders in a dusty rain.

The Fathers waited.

"Well, Father Peregrine." Father Stone eyed the empty sky where the sun was rising, furnace-red. "I don't see our friends."

"Let me try again." Father Peregrine was perspiring.

He built an architecture of Bach, stone by exquisite stone, raising a music cathedral so vast that its furthest chancels were in Nineveh, its furthest dome at St. Peter's left hand. The music stayed and did not crash in ruin when it was over, but partook of a series of white clouds and was carried away among other lands.

The sky was still empty.

"They'll come!" But Father Peregrine felt the panic in his chest, very small, growing. "Let us pray. Let us ask them to come. They read minds; they *know*."

The Fathers lowered themselves yet again, in rustlings and whispers. They prayed.

And to the East, out of the icy mountains of seven o'clock on Sunday morning or perhaps Thursday morning or maybe Monday morning on Mars, came the soft fiery globes.

They hovered and sank and filled the area around the shivering priests. "Thank you; oh, thank you, Lord." Father Peregrine shut his eyes tight and played the music, and when it was done he turned and gazed upon his wondrous congregation.

And a voice touched his mind, and the voice said:

"We have come for a little while."

"You may stay," said Father Peregrine.

"For a little while only," said the voice quietly. "We have come to tell you certain things. We should have spoken sooner. But we had hoped that you might go on your way if left alone."

Father Peregrine started to speak, but the voice hushed him.

"We are the Old Ones," the voice said, and it entered him like a blue gaseous flare and burned in the chambers of his head. "We are the old Martians, who left our marble cities and went into the hills, forsaking the material life we had lived. So very long ago we became these things that we now are. Once we were men, with bodies and legs and arms such as yours. The legend has it that one of us, a good man, discovered a way to free man's soul and intellect, to free him of bodily ills and melancholies, of deaths and transfigurations, of ill humors and senilities, and so we took on the look of lightning and blue fire and have lived in the winds and skies and hills forever after that, neither prideful nor arrogant, neither rich nor poor, passionate nor cold. We have lived apart from those we left behind, those other men of this world, and how we came to be has been forgotten, the process lost; but we shall never die, nor do harm. We have put away the sins of the body and live in God's grace. We covet no other property; we have no property. We do not steal, nor kill, nor lust, nor hate. We live in happiness. We cannot reproduce; we do not eat or drink or make war. All the sensualities and childishnesses and sins of the body were stripped away when our bodies were put aside. We have left sin behind, Father Peregrine, and it is burned like the leaves in the autumn, and it is gone like the soiled snow of an evil winter, and it is gone like the sexual flowers of a red-and-yellow spring, and it is gone like the panting nights of hottest summer, and our season is temperate and our clime is rich in thought."

Father Peregrine was standing now, for the voice touched him at such a pitch that it almost shook him from his senses. It was an ecstasy and a fire washing through him.

"We wish to tell you that we appreciate your building this place for us, but we have no need of it, for each of us is a temple unto himself and needs no place wherein to cleanse himself. Forgive us for not coming to you sooner, but we are separate and apart and have talked to no one for ten thousand years, nor have we interfered in any way with the life of this planet. It has come into your mind now that we are the lilies of the field; we toil not, neither do we spin. You are right. And so we suggest that you take the parts of this temple into your own new cities and there cleanse others. For, rest assured, we are happy and at peace."

The Fathers were on their knees in the vast blue light, and Father Peregrine was down, too, and they were weeping, and it did not matter that their time had been wasted; it did not matter to them at all.

The blue spheres murmured and began to rise once more, on a breath of cool air.

"May I"—cried Father Peregrine, not daring to ask, eyes closed—"may I come again, someday, that I may learn from you?"

The blue fires blazed. The air trembled.

Yes. Someday he might come again. Someday.

And then the Fire Balloons blew away and were gone, and he was like a child, on his knees, tears streaming from his eyes, crying to himself, "Come back, come back!" And at any moment Grandfather might lift him and carry him upstairs to his bedroom in a long-gone Ohio town. . . .

They filed down out of the hills at sunset. Looking back, Father Peregrine saw the blue fires burning. No, he thought, we couldn't build a church for the likes of you. You're Beauty itself. What church could compete with the fireworks of the pure soul?

Father Stone moved in silence beside him. And at last he spoke:

"The way I see it is there's a Truth on every planet. All parts of the Big Truth. On a certain day they'll all fit together like the pieces of a jigsaw. This has been a shaking experience. I'll never doubt again, Father Peregrine. For this Truth here is as true as Earth's Truth, and they lie side by side. And we'll go on to other worlds, adding the sum of the parts of the Truth until one day the whole Total will stand before us like the light of a new day."

"That's a lot, coming from you, Father Stone."

"I'm sorry now, in a way, we're going down to the town to handle our own kind. Those blue lights now. When they settled about us, and that *voice* . . ." Father Stone shivered.

Father Peregrine reached out to take the other's arm. They walked together.

"And you know," said Father Stone finally, fixing his eyes on Brother Mathias, who strode ahead with the glass sphere tenderly carried in his arms, that glass sphere with the blue phosphorous light glowing forever inside it, "you know, Father Peregrine, that globe there——"

"Yes?"

"It's Him. It *is* Him, after all."

Father Peregrine smiled, and they walked down out of the hills toward the new town.

The Last Night of the World

"WHAT WOULD YOU do if you knew that this was the last night of the world?"

"What would I do? You mean seriously?"

"Yes, seriously."

"I don't know. I hadn't thought."

He poured some coffee. In the background the two girls were playing blocks on the parlor rug in the light of the green hurricane lamps. There was an easy, clean aroma of the brewed coffee in the evening air.

"Well, better start thinking about it," he said.

"You don't mean it!"

He nodded.

"A war?"

He shook his head.

"Not the hydrogen or atom bomb?"

"No."

"Or germ warfare?"

"None of those at all," he said, stirring his coffee slowly. "But just, let's say, the closing of a book."

"I don't think I understand."

"No, nor do I, really; it's just a feeling. Sometimes it frightens me, sometimes I'm not frightened at all but at peace." He glanced in at the girls and their yellow hair shining in the lamplight. "I didn't say anything to you. It first happened about four nights ago."

"What?"

"A dream I had. I dreamed that it was all going to be over, and a voice said it was; not any kind of voice I can remember, but a voice anyway, and it said things would stop here on Earth. I didn't think too much about it the next day, but then I went to the office and caught Stan Willis looking out the window in the middle of the afternoon, and I said a penny for your thoughts, Stan, and he said, I had a dream last night, and before he even told me the dream I knew what it was. I could have told him, but he told me and I listened to him."

"It was the same dream?"

"The same. I told Stan I had dreamed it too. He didn't seem surprised. He relaxed, in fact. Then we started walking through the office, for the hell of it. It wasn't planned. We didn't say, 'Let's walk around.' We just walked on our own, and everywhere we saw people looking at their desks or their hands or out windows. I talked to a few. So did Stan."

"And they all had dreamed?"

"All of them. The same dream, with no difference."

"Do you believe in it?"

"Yes. I've never been more certain."

"And when will it stop? The world, I mean."

"Sometime during the night for us, and then as the night goes on around the world, that'll go too. It'll take twenty-four hours for it all to go."

They sat awhile not touching their coffee. Then they lifted it slowly and drank, looking at each other.

"Do we deserve this?" she said.

"It's not a matter of deserving; it's just that things didn't work out. I notice you didn't even argue about this. Why not?"

"I guess I've a reason," she said.

"The same one everyone at the office had?"

She nodded slowly. "I didn't want to say anything. It happened last night. And the women on the block talked about it, among themselves, today. They dreamed. I thought it was only a coincidence." She picked up the evening paper. "There's nothing in the paper about it."

"Everyone knows, so there's no need."

He sat back in his chair, watching her. "Are you afraid?"

"No. I always thought I would be, but I'm not."

"Where's that spirit called self-preservation they talk so much about?"

"I don't know. You don't get too excited when you feel things are logical. This is logical. Nothing else but this could have happened from the way we've lived."

"We haven't been too bad, have we?"

"No, nor enormously good. I suppose that's the trouble—we haven't been very much of anything except us, while a big part of the world was busy being lots of quite awful things."

The girls were laughing in the parlor.

"I always thought people would be screaming in the streets at a time like this."

"I guess not. You don't scream about the real thing."

"Do you know, I won't miss anything but you and the girls. I never liked cities or my work or anything except you three. I won't miss a thing except perhaps the change in the weather, and a glass of ice water when it's hot, and I might miss sleeping. How can we sit here and talk this way?"

"Because there's nothing else to do."

"That's it, of course; for if there were, we'd be doing it. I suppose this is the first time in the history of the world that everyone has known just what they were going to do during the night."

"I wonder what everyone else will do now, this evening, for the next few hours."

"Go to a show, listen to the radio, watch television, play cards, put the children to bed, go to bed themselves, like always."

"In a way that's something to be proud of—like always."

They sat a moment and then he poured himself another coffee. "Why do you suppose it's tonight?"

"Because."

"Why not some other night in the last century, or five centuries ago, or ten?"

"Maybe it's because it was never October 19, 1969, ever before in history, and now it is and that's it; because this date means more than any other date ever meant; because it's the year when things are as they are all over the world and that's why it's the end."

"There are bombers on their schedules both ways across the ocean tonight that'll never see land."

"That's part of the reason why."

"Well," he said, getting up, "what shall it be? Wash the dishes?"

They washed the dishes and stacked them away with special neatness. At eight-thirty the girls were put to bed and kissed good night and the little lights by their beds turned on and the door left open just a trifle.

"I wonder," said the husband, coming from the bedroom and glancing back, standing there with his pipe for a moment.

"What?"

"If the door will be shut all the way, or if it'll be left just a little ajar so some light comes in."

"I wonder if the children know."

"No, of course not."

They sat and read the papers and talked and listened to some radio music and then sat together by the fireplace watching the charcoal embers as the clock struck ten-thirty and eleven and eleven-thirty. They thought of all the other people in the world who had spent their evening, each in his own special way.

"Well," he said at last.

He kissed his wife for a long time.

"We've been good for each other, anyway."

"Do you want to cry?" he asked.

"I don't think so."

They moved through the house and turned out the lights and went into the bedroom and stood in the night cool darkness undressing and pushing back the covers. "The sheets are so clean and nice."

"I'm tired."

"We're *all* tired."

They got into bed and lay back.

"Just a moment," she said.

He heard her get out of bed and go into the kitchen. A moment later, she returned. "I left the water running in the sink," she said.

Something about this was so very funny that he had to laugh.

She laughed with him, knowing what it was that she had done that was funny. They stopped laughing at last and lay in their cool night bed, their hands clasped, their heads together.

"Good night," he said, after a moment.

"Good night," she said.

The Exiles

THEIR EYES WERE fire and the breath flamed out the witches' mouths as they bent to probe the caldron with greasy stick and bony finger.

> "When shall we three meet again
> In thunder, lightning, or in rain?"

They danced drunkenly on the shore of an empty sea, fouling the air with their three tongues, and burning it with their cats' eyes malevolently aglitter:

> "Round about the cauldron go;
> In the poison'd entrails throw. . . .
> Double, double, toil and trouble;
> Fire burn, and cauldron bubble!"

They paused and cast a glance about. "Where's the crystal? Where the needles?"

"Here!"

"Good!"

"Is the yellow wax thickened?"

"Yes!"

"Pour it in the iron mold!"

"Is the wax figure done?" They shaped it like molasses adrip on their green hands.

"Shove the needle through the heart!"

"The crystal, the crystal; fetch it from the tarot bag. Dust it off; have a look!"

They bent to the crystal, their faces white.

> "See, see, see . . ."

A rocket ship moved through space from the planet Earth to the planet Mars. On the rocket ship men were dying.

The captain raised his head, tiredly. "We'll have to use the morphine."

"But, Captain——"

"You see yourself this man's condition." The captain lifted the wool blanket and the man restrained beneath the wet sheet moved and groaned. The air was full of sulphurous thunder.

"I saw it—I saw it." The man opened his eyes and stared at the port where there were only black spaces, reeling stars, Earth far removed, and the planet Mars rising large and red. "I saw it—a bat, a huge thing, a bat with a man's face, spread over the front port. Fluttering and fluttering, fluttering and fluttering."

"Pulse?" asked the captain.

The orderly measured it. "One hundred and thirty."

"He can't go on with that. Use the morphine. Come along, Smith."

They moved away. Suddenly the floor plates were laced with bone and white skulls that screamed. The captain did not dare look down, and over the screaming he said, "Is this where Perse is?" turning in at a hatch.

A white-smocked surgeon stepped away from a body. "I just don't understand it."

"How did Perse die?"

"We don't know, Captain. It wasn't his heart, his brain, or shock. He just—died."

The captain felt the doctor's wrist, which changed to a hissing snake and bit him. The captain did not flinch. "Take care of yourself. You've a pulse too."

The doctor nodded. "Perse complained of pains—needles, he said—in his wrists and legs. Said he felt like wax, melting. He fell. I helped him up. He cried like a child. Said he had a silver needle in his heart. He died. Here he is. We can repeat the autopsy for you. Everything's physically normal."

"That's impossible! He died of *something*!"

The captain walked to a port. He smelled of menthol and iodine and green soap on his polished and manicured hands. His white teeth were dentifriced, and his ears scoured to a pinkness, as were his cheeks. His uniform was the color of new salt, and his boots were black mirrors shining below him. His crisp crew-cut hair smelled of sharp alcohol. Even his breath was sharp and new and clean. There was no spot to him. He was a fresh instrument, honed and ready, still hot from the surgeon's oven.

The men with him were from the same mold. One expected huge brass keys spiraling slowly from their backs. They were expensive, talented, well-oiled toys, obedient and quick.

The captain watched the planet Mars grow very large in space.

"We'll be landing in an hour on that damned place. Smith, did you see any bats, or have other nightmares?"

"Yes, sir. The month before our rocket took off from New York, sir. White rats biting my neck, drinking my blood. I didn't tell. I was afraid you wouldn't let me come on this trip."

"Never mind," sighed the captain. "I had dreams too. In all of my fifty years I never had a dream until that week before we took off from Earth. And then every night I dreamed I was a white wolf. Caught on a snowy hill. Shot with a silver bullet. Buried with a stake in my heart." He moved his head toward Mars. "Do you think, Smith, *they* know we're coming?"

"We don't know if there *are* Martian people, sir."

"Don't we? They began frightening us off eight weeks ago, before we started. They've killed Perse and Reynolds now. Yesterday they made Grenville go blind. How? I don't know. Bats, needles, dreams, men dying for no reason. I'd call it witchcraft in another day. But this is the year 2120, Smith. We're rational men. This all can't be happening. But it is! Whoever they are, with their needles and their bats, they'll try to finish us all." He swung about. "Smith, fetch those books from my file. I want them when we land."

Two hundred books were piled on the rocket deck.

"Thank you, Smith. Have you glanced at them? Think I'm insane? Perhaps. It's a crazy hunch. At that last moment I ordered these books from the Historical Museum. Because of my dreams. Twenty nights I was stabbed, butchered, a screaming bat pinned to a surgical mat, a thing rotting underground in a black box; bad, wicked dreams. Our whole crew dreamed of witch-things and were-things, vampires and phantoms, things they *couldn't* know anything about. Why? Because books on such ghastly subjects were destroyed a century ago. By law. Forbidden for anyone to own the grisly volumes. These books you see here are the *last* copies, kept for historical purposes in the locked museum vaults."

Smith bent to read the dusty titles:

"*Tales of Mystery and Imagination*, by Edgar Allan Poe. *Dracula*, by Bram Stoker. *Frankenstein*, by Mary Shelley. *The Turn of the Screw*, by Henry James. *The Legend of Sleepy Hollow*, by Washington Irving. *Rappaccini's Daughter*, by Nathaniel Hawthorne. *An Occurrence at Owl Creek Bridge*, by Ambrose Bierce. *Alice in Wonderland*, by Lewis Carroll. *The Willows*, by Algernon Blackwood. *The Wizard of Oz*, by L. Frank Baum. *The Weird Shadow Over Innsmouth*, by H. P. Lovecraft. And more! Books by Walter de la Mare, Wakefield, Harvey, Wells, Asquith, Huxley—all forbidden authors. All burned in the same year that Halloween was outlawed and Christmas was banned! But, sir, what good are these to us on the rocket?"

"I don't know," sighed the captain, "yet."

The three hags lifted the crystal where the captain's image flickered, his tiny voice tinkling out of the glass:

"I don't know," sighed the captain, "yet."

The three witches glared redly into one another's faces.

"We haven't much time," said one.

"Better warn *Them* in the City."

"They'll want to know about the books. It doesn't look good. That fool of a captain!"

"In an hour they'll land their rocket."

The three hags shuddered and blinked up at the Emerald City by the edge of the dry Martian sea. In its highest window a small man held a blood-red drape aside. He watched the wastelands where the three witches fed their caldron and shaped the waxes. Farther along, ten thousand other blue fires and laurel incenses, black tobacco smokes and fir weeds, cinnamons and bone dusts rose soft as moths through the Martian night. The man counted the angry, magical fires. Then, as the three witches stared, he turned. The crimson drape, released, fell, causing the distant portal to wink, like a yellow eye.

Mr. Edgar Allan Poe stood in the tower window, a faint vapor of spirits upon his breath. "Hecate's friends are busy tonight," he said, seeing the witches, far below.

A voice behind him said, "I saw Will Shakespeare at the shore, earlier, whipping them on. All along the sea Shakespeare's army alone, tonight, numbers thousands: the three witches, Oberon, Hamlet's father, Puck—all, all of them—thousands! Good lord, a regular sea of people."

"Good William." Poe turned. He let the crimson drape fall shut. He stood for a moment to observe the raw stone room, the black-timbered table, the candle flame, the other man, Mr. Ambrose Bierce, sitting very idly there, lighting matches and watching them burn down, whistling under his breath, now and then laughing to himself.

"We'll have to tell Mr. Dickens now," said Mr. Poe. "We've put it off too long. It's a matter of hours. Will you go down to his home with me, Bierce?"

Bierce glanced up merrily. "I've just been thinking—what'll happen to us?"

"If we can't kill the rocket men off, frighten them away, then we'll have to leave, of course. We'll go on to Jupiter, and when they come to Jupiter, we'll go on to Saturn, and when they come to Saturn, we'll go to Uranus, or Neptune, and then on out to Pluto——"

"Where then?"

Mr. Poe's face was weary; there were fire coals remaining, fading, in his eyes, and a sad wildness in the way he talked, and a uselessness of his hands and the way his hair fell lankly over his amazing white brow. He was like a satan of some lost dark cause, a general arrived from a derelict invasion. His silky, soft, black mustache was worn away by his musing lips. He was so small his brow seemed to float, vast and phosphorescent, by itself, in the dark room.

"We have the advantages of superior forms of travel," he said. "We can always hope for one of their atomic wars, dissolution, the dark ages come again. The return of superstition. We could go back then to Earth, all of us, in one night." Mr. Poe's black eyes brooded under his round and luminant brow. He gazed at the ceiling. "So they're coming to ruin *this* world too? They won't leave *anything* undefiled, will they?"

"Does a wolf pack stop until it's killed its prey and eaten the guts? It should be quite a war. I shall sit on the side lines and be the scorekeeper. So many Earthmen boiled in oil, so many

Mss. Found in Bottles burnt, so many Earthmen stabbed with needles, so many Red Deaths put to flight by a battery of hypodermic syringes—ha!"

Poe swayed angrily, faintly drunk with wine. "What did we do? Be *with* us, Bierce, in the name of God! Did we have a fair trial before a company of literary critics? No! Our books were plucked up by neat, sterile, surgeon's pliers, and flung into vats, to boil, to be killed of all their mortuary germs. Damn them all!"

"I find our situation amusing," said Bierce.

They were interrupted by a hysterical shout from the tower stair.

"Mr. Poe! Mr. Bierce!"

"Yes, yes, we're coming!" Poe and Bierce descended to find a man gasping against the stone passage wall.

"Have you heard the news?" he cried immediately, clawing at them like a man about to fall over a cliff. "In an hour they'll land! They're bringing books with them—*old* books, the witches said! What're you doing in the tower at a time like this? Why aren't you acting?"

Poe said: "We're doing everything we can, Blackwood. You're new to all this. Come along, we're going to Mr. Charles Dickens' place——"

"—to contemplate our doom, our black doom," said Mr. Bierce, with a wink.

They moved down the echoing throats of the castle, level after dim green level, down into mustiness and decay and spiders and dreamlike webbing. "Don't worry," said Poe, his brow like a huge white lamp before them, descending, sinking. "All along the dead sea tonight I've called the others. Your friends and mine, Blackwood—Bierce. They're all there. The animals and the old women and the tall men with the sharp white teeth. The traps are waiting; the pits, yes, and the pendulums. The Red Death." Here he laughed quietly. "Yes, even the Red Death. I never thought—no, I never thought the time would come when a thing like the Red Death would actually *be*. But *they* asked for it, and they shall have it!"

"But are we strong enough?" wondered Blackwood.

"How strong is strong? They won't be prepared for us, at

least. They haven't the imagination. Those clean young rocket men with their antiseptic bloomers and fish-bowl helmets, with their new religion. About their necks, on gold chains, scalpels. Upon their heads, a diadem of microscopes. In their holy fingers, steaming incense urns which in reality are only germicidal ovens for steaming out superstition. The names of Poe, Bierce, Hawthorne, Blackwood—blasphemy to their clean lips."

Outside the castle they advanced through a watery space, a tarn that was not a tarn, which misted before them like the stuff of nightmares. The air filled with wing sounds and a whirring, a motion of winds and blacknesses. Voices changed, figures swayed at campfires. Mr. Poe watched the needles knitting, knitting, knitting, in the firelight; knitting pain and misery, knitting wickedness into wax marionettes, clay puppets. The caldron smells of wild garlic and cayenne and saffron hissed up to fill the night with evil pungency.

"Get on with it!" said Poe. "I'll be back!"

All down the empty seashore black figures spindled and waned, grew up and blew into black smoke on the sky. Bells rang in mountain towers and licorice ravens spilled out with the bronze sounds and spun away to ashes.

Over a lonely moor and into a small valley Poe and Bierce hurried, and found themselves quite suddenly on a cobbled street, in cold, bleak, biting weather, with people stomping up and down stony courtyards to warm their feet; foggy withal, and candles flaring in the windows of offices and shops where hung the Yuletide turkeys. At a distance some boys, all bundled up, snorting their pale breaths on the wintry air, were trilling, "God Rest Ye Merry, Gentlemen," while the immense tones of a great clock continuously sounded midnight. Children dashed by from the baker's with dinners all asteam in their grubby fists, on trays and under silver bowls.

At a sign which read SCROOGE, MARLEY AND DICKENS, Poe gave the Marley-faced knocker a rap, and from within, as the door popped open a few inches, a sudden gust of music almost swept them into a dance. And there, beyond the shoulder of the man who was sticking a trim goatee and mustaches at them, was Mr. Fezziwig clapping his hands, and Mrs.

Fezziwig, one vast substantial smile, dancing and colliding with other merrymakers, while the fiddle chirped and laughter ran about a table like chandelier crystals given a sudden push of wind. The large table was heaped with brawn and turkey and holly and geese; with mince pies, suckling pigs, wreaths of sausages, oranges and apples; and there was Bob Cratchit and Little Dorrit and Tiny Tim and Mr. Fagin himself, and a man who looked as if he might be an undigested bit of beef, a blot of mustard, a crumb of cheese, a fragment of an underdone potato—who else but Mr. Marley, chains and all, while the wine poured and the brown turkeys did their excellent best to steam!

"What do you want?" demanded Mr. Charles Dickens.

"We've come to plead with you again, Charles; we need your help," said Poe.

"Help? Do you think I would help you fight against those good men coming in the rocket? I don't belong here, anyway. My books were burned by mistake. I'm no supernaturalist, no writer of horrors and terrors like you, Poe; you, Bierce, or the others. I'll have nothing to do with you terrible people!"

"You are a persuasive talker," reasoned Poe. "You could go to meet the rocket men, lull them, lull their suspicions and then—then we would take care of them."

Mr. Dickens eyed the folds of the black cape which hid Poe's hands. From it, smiling, Poe drew forth a black cat. "For *one* of our visitors."

"And for the others?"

Poe smiled again, well pleased. "The Premature Burial?"

"You are a grim man, Mr. Poe."

"I am a frightened and an angry man. I am a god, Mr. Dickens, even as you are a god, even as we all are gods, and our inventions—our people, if you wish—have not only been threatened, but banished and burned, torn up and censored, ruined and done away with. The worlds we created are falling into ruin. Even gods must fight!"

"So?" Mr. Dickens tilted his head, impatient to return to the party, the music, the food. "Perhaps you can explain why we are here? How did we come here?"

"War begets war. Destruction begets destruction. On Earth, a century ago, in the year 2020 they outlawed our books. Oh, what a horrible thing—to destroy our literary creations that way! It summoned us out of—what? Death? The Beyond? I don't like abstract things. I don't know. I only know that our worlds and our creations called us and we tried to save them, and the only saving thing we could do was wait out the century here on Mars, hoping Earth might overweight itself with these scientists and their doubtings; but now they're coming to clean us out of here, us and our dark things, and all the alchemists, witches, vampires, and were-things that, one by one, retreated across space as science made inroads through every country on Earth and finally left no alternative at all but exodus. You must help us. You have a good speaking manner. We need you."

"I repeat, I am not of you, I don't approve of you and the others," cried Dickens angrily. "I was no player with witches and vampires and midnight things."

"What of *A Christmas Carol*?"

"Ridiculous! *One* story. Oh, I wrote a few others about ghosts, perhaps, but what of that? My basic works had none of that nonsense!"

"Mistaken or not, they grouped you with us. They destroyed your books—your worlds too. You must hate them, Mr. Dickens!"

"I admit they are stupid and rude, but that is all. Good day!"

"Let Mr. Marley come, at least!"

"*No!*"

The door slammed. As Poe turned away, down the street, skimming over the frosty ground, the coachman playing a lively air on a bugle, came a great coach, out of which, cherry-red, laughing and singing, piled the Pickwickians, banging on the door, shouting Merry Christmas good and loud, when the door was opened by the fat boy.

Mr. Poe hurried along the midnight shore of the dry sea. By fires and smoke he hesitated, to shout orders, to check the bubbling caldrons, the poisons and the chalked pentagrams. "Good!" he said, and ran on. "Fine!" he shouted, and ran again. People joined him and ran with him. Here were Mr. Coppard and Mr. Machen running with him now. And there were hating serpents and angry demons and fiery bronze dragons and spitting vipers and trembling witches like the barbs and nettles and thorns and all the vile flotsam and jetsam of the retreating sea of imagination, left on the melancholy shore, whining and frothing and spitting.

Mr. Machen stopped. He sat like a child on the cold sand. He began to sob. They tried to soothe him, but he would not listen. "I just thought," he said. "What happens to us on the day when the *last* copies of our books are destroyed?"

The air whirled.

"Don't speak of it!"

"We must," wailed Mr. Machen. "Now, now, as the rocket comes down, you, Mr. Poe; you, Coppard; you, Bierce—all of you grow faint. Like wood smoke. Blowing away. Your faces melt—"

"Death! *Real* death for all of us."

"We exist only through Earth's sufferance. If a final edict tonight destroyed our last few works we'd be like lights put out."

Coppard brooded gently. "I wonder who I am. In what Earth mind tonight do I exist? In some African hut? Some hermit, reading my tales? Is he the lonely candle in the wind of time and science? The flickering orb sustaining me here in rebellious exile? Is it him? Or some boy in a discarded attic, finding me, only just in time! Oh, last night I felt ill, ill, ill to the marrows of me, for there is a body of the soul as well as a body of the body, and this soul body ached in all of its glowing parts, and last night I felt myself a candle, guttering. When suddenly I sprang up, given new light! As some child, sneezing with dust, in some yellow garret on Earth once more found a worn, time-specked copy of me! And so I'm given a short respite!"

A door banged wide in a little hut by the shore. A thin short man, with flesh hanging from him in folds, stepped out and, paying no attention to the others, sat down and stared into his clenched fists.

"There's the one I'm sorry for," whispered Blackwood. "Look at him, dying away. He was once more real than we, who were men. They took him, a skeleton thought, and clothed him in centuries of pink flesh and snow beard and red velvet suit and black boot; made him reindeers, tinsel, holly.

And after centuries of manufacturing him they drowned him in a vat of Lysol, you might say."

The men were silent.

"What must it be on Earth?" wondered Poe. "Without Christmas? No hot chestnuts, no tree, no ornaments or drums or candles—nothing; nothing but the snow and wind and the lonely, factual people. . . ."

They all looked at the thin little old man with the scraggly beard and faded red velvet suit.

"Have you heard his story?"

"I can imagine it. The glitter-eyed psychiatrist, the clever sociologist, the resentful, froth-mouthed educationalist, the antiseptic parents——"

"A regrettable situation," said Bierce, smiling, "for the Yuletide merchants who, toward the last there, as I recall, were beginning to put up holly and sing Noel the day before Halloween. With any luck at all this year they might have started on Labor Day!"

Bierce did not continue. He fell forward with a sigh. As he lay upon the ground he had time to say only, "How interesting." And then, as they all watched, horrified, his body burned into blue dust and charred bone, the ashes of which fled through the air in black tatters.

"Bierce, Bierce!"

"Gone!"

"His last book gone. Someone on Earth just now burned it."

"God rest him. Nothing of him left now. For what are we but books, and when those are gone, nothing's to be seen."

A rushing sound filled the sky.

They cried out, terrified, and looked up. In the sky, dazzling it with sizzling fire clouds, was the rocket! Around the men on the seashore lanterns bobbed; there was a squealing and a bubbling and an odor of cooked spells. Candle-eyed pumpkins lifted into the cold clear air. Thin fingers clenched into fists and a witch screamed from her withered mouth:

"Ship, ship, break, fall!
Ship, ship, burn all!
Crack, flake, shake, melt!
Mummy dust, cat pelt!"

"Time to go," murmured Blackwood. "On to Jupiter, on to Saturn or Pluto."

"Run away?" shouted Poe in the wind. "Never!"

"I'm a tired old man!"

Poe gazed into the old man's face and believed him. He climbed atop a huge boulder and faced the ten thousand gray shadows and green lights and yellow eyes on the hissing wind.

"The powders!" he shouted.

A thick hot smell of bitter almond, civet, cumin, wormseed and orris!

The rocket came down—steadily down, with the shriek of a damned spirit! Poe raged at it! He flung his fists up and the orchestra of heat and smell and hatred answered in symphony! Like stripped tree fragments, bats flew upward! Burning hearts, flung like missiles, burst in bloody fireworks on the singed air. Down, down, relentlessly down, like a pendulum the rocket came. And Poe howled, furiously, and shrank back with every sweep and sweep of the rocket cutting and ravening the air! All the dead sea seemed a pit in which, trapped, they waited the sinking of the dread machinery, the glistening ax; they were people under the avalanche!

"The snakes!" screamed Poe.

And luminous serpentines of undulant green hurtled toward the rocket. But it came down, a sweep, a fire, a motion, and it lay panting out exhaustions of red plumage on the sand, a mile away.

"At it!" shrieked Poe. "The plan's changed! Only one chance! Run! At it! At it! Drown them with our bodies! Kill them!"

And as if he had commanded a violent sea to change its course, to suck itself free from primeval beds, the whirls and savage gouts of fire spread and ran like wind and rain and stark lightning over the sea sands, down empty river deltas, shadowing and screaming, whistling and whining, sputtering and coalescing toward the rocket which, extinguished, lay like a clean metal torch in the farthest hollow. As if a great charred caldron of sparkling lava had been overturned, the boiling people and snapping animals churned down the dry fathoms.

"Kill them!" screamed Poe, running.

The rocket men leaped out of their ship, guns ready. They stalked about, sniffing the air like hounds. They saw nothing. They relaxed.

The captain stepped forth last. He gave sharp commands. Wood was gathered, kindled, and a fire leapt up in an instant. The captain beckoned his men into a half circle about him.

"A new world," he said, forcing himself to speak deliberately, though he glanced nervously, now and again, over his shoulder at the empty sea. "The old world left behind. A new start. What more symbolic than that we here dedicate ourselves all the more firmly to science and progress." He nodded crisply to his lieutenant. "The books."

Firelight limned the faded gilt titles: *The Willows*, *The Outsider*, *Behold*, *The Dreamer*, *Dr. Jekyll and Mr. Hyde*, *The Land of Oz*, *Pellucidar*, *The Land That Time Forgot*, *A Midsummer Night's Dream*, and the monstrous names of Machen and Edgar Allan Poe and Cabell and Dunsany and Blackwood and Lewis Carroll; the names, the old names, the evil names.

"A new world. With a gesture, we burn the last of the old."

The captain ripped pages from the books. Leaf by seared leaf, he fed them into the fire.

A scream!

Leaping back, the men stared beyond the firelight at the edges of the encroaching and uninhabited sea.

Another scream! A high and wailing thing, like the death of a dragon and the thrashing of a bronzed whale left gasping when the waters of a leviathan's sea drain down the shingles and evaporate.

It was the sound of air rushing in to fill a vacuum, where, a moment before, there had been *something*!

The captain neatly disposed of the last book by putting it into the fire.

The air stopped quivering.

Silence!

The rocket men leaned and listened.

"Captain, did you hear it?"

"No."

"Like a wave, sir. On the sea bottom! I thought I saw something. Over there. A black wave. Big. Running at us."

"You were mistaken."

"There, sir!"

"What?"

"See it? There! The city! Way over! That green city near the lake! It's splitting in half. It's falling!"

The men squinted and shuffled forward.

Smith stood trembling among them. He put his hand to his head as if to find a thought there. "I remember. Yes, now I do. A long time back. When I was a child. A book I read. A story. Oz, I think it was. Yes, Oz. *The Emerald City of Oz* . . ."

"Oz? Never heard of it."

"Yes, Oz, that's what it was. I saw it just now, like in the story. I saw it fall."

"Smith!"

"Yes, sir?"

"Report for psychoanalysis tomorrow."

"Yes, sir!" A brisk salute.

"Be careful."

The men tiptoed, guns alert, beyond the ship's aseptic light to gaze at the long sea and the low hills.

"Why," whispered Smith, disappointed, "there's no one here at all, is there? No one here at all."

The wind blew sand over his shoes, whining.

No Particular Night or Morning

HE HAD SMOKED a packet of cigarettes in two hours.

"How far out in space are we?"

"A billion miles."

"A billion miles from where?" said Hitchcock.

"It all depends," said Clemens, not smoking at all. "A billion miles from home, you might say."

"Then say it."

"Home. Earth. New York. Chicago. Wherever you were from."

"I don't even remember," said Hitchcock. "I don't even believe there is an Earth now, do you?"

"Yes," said Clemens. "I dreamt about it this morning."

"There is no morning in space."

"During the night then."

"It's always night," said Hitchcock quietly. "Which night do you mean?"

"Shut up," said Clemens irritably. "Let me finish."

Hitchcock lit another cigarette. His hand did not shake, but it looked as if, inside the sunburned flesh, it might be tremoring all to itself, a small tremor in each hand and a large invisible tremor in his body. The two men sat on the observation corridor floor, looking out at the stars. Clemens's eyes flashed, but Hitchcock's eyes focused on nothing; they were blank and puzzled.

"I woke up at 0500 hours myself," said Hitchcock, as if he were talking to his right hand. "And I heard myself screaming, 'Where am I? where am I?' And the answer was 'Nowhere!' And I said, 'Where've I been?' And I said, 'Earth!' 'What's Earth?' I wondered. 'Where I was born,' I said. But it was nothing and worse than nothing. I don't believe in anything I can't see or hear or touch. I can't see Earth, so why should I believe in it? It's safer this way, not to believe."

"There's Earth." Clemens pointed, smiling. "That point of light there."

"That's not Earth; that's our sun. You can't see Earth from here."

"I can see it. I have a good memory."

"It's not the same, you fool," said Hitchcock suddenly. There was a touch of anger in his voice. "I mean see it. I've always been that way. When I'm in Boston, New York is dead. When I'm in New York, Boston is dead. When I don't see a man for a day, he's dead. When he comes walking down the street, my God, it's a resurrection. I do a dance, almost, I'm so glad to see him. I used to, anyway. I don't dance any more. I just look. And when the man walks off, he's dead again."

Clemens laughed. "It's simply that your mind works on a primitive level. You can't hold to things. You've got no imagination, Hitchcock old man. You've got to learn to hold on."

"Why should I hold onto things I can't use?" said Hitchcock, his eyes wide, still staring into space. "I'm practical. If Earth isn't here for me to walk on, you want me to walk on a memory? That *hurts.* Memories, as my father once said, are porcupines. To hell with them! Stay away from them. They make you unhappy. They ruin your work. They make you cry."

"I'm walking on Earth right now," said Clemens, squinting to himself, blowing smoke.

"You're kicking porcupines. Later in the day you won't be able to eat lunch, and you'll wonder why," said Hitchcock in a dead voice. "And it'll be because you've got a footful of quills aching in you. To hell with it! If I can't drink it, pinch it, punch it, or lie on it, then I say drop it in the sun. I'm dead to Earth. It's dead to me. There's no one in New York weeping for me tonight. Shove New York. There isn't any season here; winter and summer are gone. So is spring, and autumn. It isn't any particular night or morning; it's space and space. The only thing right now is you and me and this rocket ship. And the only thing I'm positive of is *me.* That's all of it."

Clemens ignored this. "I'm putting a nickel in the phone slot right now," he said, pantomiming it with a slow smile. "And calling my girl in Evanston. Hello, Barbara!"

The rocket sailed on through space.

The lunch bell rang at 1305 hours. The men ran by on soft rubber sneakers and sat at the cushioned tables.

Clemens wasn't hungry.

"See, what did I tell you!" said Hitchcock. "You and your damned porcupines! Leave them alone, like I told you. Look at me, shoveling away food." He said this with a mechanical, slow, and unhumorous voice. "Watch me." He put a big piece of pie in his mouth and felt it with his tongue. He looked at the pie on his plate as if to see the texture. He moved it with his fork. He felt the fork handle. He mashed the lemon filling and watched it jet up between the tines. Then he touched a bottle of milk all over and poured out half a quart into a glass, listening to it. He looked at the milk as if to make it whiter. He drank the milk so swiftly that he couldn't have tasted it. He had eaten his entire lunch in a few minutes, cramming it in feverishly, and now he looked around for more, but it was gone. He gazed out the window of the rocket, blankly. "Those aren't real, either," he said.

"What?" asked Clemens.

"The stars. Who's ever touched one? I can see them, sure, but what's the use of seeing a thing that's a million or a billion miles away? Anything that far off isn't worth bothering with."

"Why did you come on this trip?" asked Clemens suddenly.

Hitchcock peered into his amazingly empty milk glass and clenched it tight, then relaxed his hand and clenched it again. "I don't know." He ran his tongue on the glass rim. "I just had to, is all. How do you know why you do anything in this life?"

"You liked the idea of space travel? Going places?"

"I don't know. Yes. No. It wasn't going places. It was being *between*." Hitchcock for the first time tried to focus his eyes upon something, but it was so nebulous and far off that his eyes couldn't make the adjustment, though he worked his face and hands. "Mostly it was space. So much space. I liked the idea of nothing on top, nothing on the bottom, and a lot of nothing in between, and me in the middle of the nothing."

"I never heard it put that way before."

"*I* just put it that way; I hope you listened."

Hitchcock took out his cigarettes and lit up and began to suck and blow the smoke, again and again.

Clemens said, "What sort of childhood did you have, Hitchcock?"

"I was never young. Whoever I was then is dead. That's

more of your quills. I don't want a hide full, thanks. I've always figured it that you die each day and each day is a box, you see, all numbered and neat; but never go back and lift the lids, because you've died a couple of thousand times in your life, and that's a lot of corpses, each dead a different way, each with a worse expression. Each of those days is a different you, somebody you don't know or understand or want to understand."

"You're cutting yourself off, that way."

"Why should I have anything to do with that younger Hitchcock? He was a fool, and he was yanked around and taken advantage of and used. His father was no good, and he was glad when his mother died, because she was the same. Should I go back and see his face on that day and gloat over it? He was a fool."

"We're all fools," said Clemens, "all the time. It's just we're a different kind each day. We think, I'm not a fool today. I've learned my lesson. I was a fool yesterday but not this morning. Then tomorrow we find out that, yes, we were a fool today too. I think the only way we can grow and get on in this world is to accept the fact we're not perfect and live accordingly."

"I don't want to remember imperfect things," said Hitchcock. "I can't shake hands with that younger Hitchcock, can I? Where is he? Can you find him for me? He's dead, so to hell with him! I won't shape what I do tomorrow by some lousy thing I did yesterday."

"You've got it wrong."

"Let me have it then." Hitchcock sat, finished with his meal, looking out the port. The other men glanced at him.

"Do meteors exist?" asked Hitchcock.

"You know damn well they do."

"In our radar machines—yes, as streaks of light in space. No, I don't believe in anything that doesn't exist and act in my presence. Sometimes"—he nodded at the men finishing their food—"sometimes I don't believe in anyone or anything but me." He sat up. "Is there an upstairs to this ship?"

"Yes."

"I've got to see it immediately."

"Don't get excited."

"You wait here; I'll be right back." Hitchcock walked out swiftly. The other men sat nibbling their food slowly. A moment passed. One of the men raised his head. "How long's this been going on? I mean Hitchcock."

"Just today."

"He acted funny the other day too."

"Yes, but it's worse today."

"Has anyone told the psychiatrist?"

"We thought he'd come out of it. Everyone has a little touch of space the first time out. I've had it. You get wildly philosophical, then frightened. You break into a sweat, then you doubt your parentage, you don't believe in Earth, you get drunk, wake up with a hang-over, and that's it."

"But Hitchcock don't get drunk," said someone. "I wish he would."

"How'd he ever get past the examining board?"

"How'd we all get past? They need men. Space scares the hell out of most people. So the board lets a lot of borderlines through."

"That man isn't a borderline," said someone. "He's a fall-off-a-cliff-and-no-bottom-to-hit."

They waited for five minutes. Hitchcock didn't come back.

Clemens finally got up and went out and climbed the circular stair to the flight deck above. Hitchcock was there, touching the wall tenderly.

"It's here," he said.

"Of course it is."

"I was afraid it might not be." Hitchcock peered at Clemens. "And you're alive."

"I have been for a long time."

"No," said Hitchcock. "Now, just *now*, this *instant*, while you're here with me, you're alive. A moment ago you weren't anything."

"I was to me," said the other.

"That's not important. You weren't here with me," said Hitchcock. "Only that's important. Is the crew down below?"

"Yes."

"Can you prove it?"

"Look, Hitchcock, you'd better see Dr. Edwards. I think you need a little servicing."

"No, I'm all right. Who's the doctor, anyway? Can you prove he's on this ship?"

"I can. All I have to do is call him."

"No. I mean, standing here, in this instant, you can't prove he's here, can you?"

"Not without moving, I can't."

"You see. You have no mental evidence. That's what I want, a mental evidence I can *feel*. I don't want physical evidence, proof you have to go out and drag in. I want evidence that you can carry in your mind and always touch and smell and feel. But there's no way to do that. In order to believe in a thing you've got to carry it with you. You can't carry the Earth, or a man, in your pocket. I want a way to do that, carry things with me always, so I can believe in them. How clumsy to have to go to all the trouble of going out and bringing in something terribly physical to prove something. I hate physical things because they can be left behind and become impossible to believe in then."

"Those are the rules of the game."

"I want to change them. Wouldn't it be fine if we could *prove* things with our mind, and know for certain that things are always in their place. I'd like to know what a place is *like* when I'm *not there*. I'd like to be *sure*."

"That's not possible."

"You know," said Hitchcock, "I first got the idea of coming out into space about five years ago. About the time I lost my job. Did you know I wanted to be a writer? Oh yes, one of those men who always talk about writing but rarely write. And too much temper. So I lost my good job and left the editorial business and couldn't get another job and went on down hill. Then my wife died. You see, nothing stays where you put it—you can't trust material things. I had to put my boy in an aunt's trust, and things got worse; then one day I had a story published with my name on it, but it wasn't me."

"I don't get you."

Hitchcock's face was pale and sweating.

"I can only say that I looked at the page with my name under the title. By Joseph Hitchcock. But it was some other man. There was no way to *prove*—actually *prove*, *really* prove—that that man was me. The story was familiar—I knew I had written it—but that name on the paper still was not me. It was a symbol, a name. It was alien. And then I realized that even if I did become successful at writing, it would never mean a thing to me, because I couldn't identify myself with that name. It would be soot and ashes. So I didn't write any more. I was never sure, anyway, that the stories I had in my desk a few days later were mine, though I remembered typing them. There was always that gap of proof. That gap between doing and having done. What is done is dead and is not proof, for it is not an action. Only actions are important. And pieces of paper were remains of actions done and over and now unseen. The proof of doing was over and done. Nothing but memory remained, and I didn't trust my memory. Could I actually *prove* I'd written these stories? No. Can *any* author? I mean *proof.* I mean action as proof. No. Not really. Not unless someone sits in the room while you type, and then maybe you're doing it from memory. And once a thing is accomplished there is no proof, only memory. So then I began to find gaps between everything. I doubted I was married or had a child or ever had a job in my life. I doubted that I had been born in Illinois and had a drunken father and swinish mother. I couldn't prove anything. Oh yes, people could say, 'You are thus and so and such and such,' but that was nothing."

"You should get your mind off stuff like that," said Clemens.

"I can't. All the gaps and spaces. And that's how I got to thinking about the stars. I thought how I'd like to be in a rocket ship, in space, in nothing, in *nothing*, going on into nothing, with just a thin something, a thin eggshell of metal holding me, going on away from all the somethings with gaps in them that couldn't prove themselves. I knew then that the only happiness for me was space. When I get to Aldebaran II I'll sign up to return on the five-year journey to Earth and so go back and forth like a shuttlecock all the rest of my life."

"Have you talked about this to the psychiatrist?"

"So he could try to mortar up the gaps for me, fill in the gulfs with noise and warm water and words and hands touching me, and all that? No, thanks." Hitchcock stopped. "I'm getting worse, aren't I? I thought so. This morning when I woke up I thought, I'm getting worse. Or is it better?" He paused again and cocked an eye at Clemens. "Are you there? Are you *really* there? Go on, prove it."

Clemens slapped him on the arm, hard.

"Yes," said Hitchcock, rubbing his arm, looking at it very thoroughly, wonderingly, massaging it. "You were there. For a brief fraction of an instant. But I wonder if you are—*now*."

"See you later," said Clemens. He was on his way to find the doctor. He walked away.

A bell rang. Two bells, three bells rang. The ship rocked as if a hand had slapped it. There was a sucking sound, the sound of a vacuum cleaner turned on. Clemens heard the screams and felt the air thin. The air hissed away about his ears. Suddenly there was nothing in his nose or lungs. He stumbled and then the hissing stopped.

He heard someone cry, "A meteor." Another said, "It's patched!" And this was true. The ship's emergency spider, running over the outside of the hull, had slapped a hot patch on the hole in the metal and welded it tight.

Someone was talking and talking and then beginning to shout at a distance. Clemens ran along the corridor through the freshening, thickening air. As he turned in at a bulkhead he saw the hole in the steel wall, freshly sealed; he saw the meteor fragments lying about the room like bits of a toy. He saw the captain and the members of the crew and a man lying on the floor. It was Hitchcock. His eyes were closed and he was crying. "It tried to kill me," he said, over and over. "It tried to kill me." They got him on his feet. "It can't do that," said Hitchcock. "That's not how it should be. Things like that can't happen, can they? It came in after me. Why did it do that?"

"All right, all right, Hitchcock," said the captain.

The doctor was bandaging a small cut on Hitchcock's arm. Hitchcock looked up, his face pale, and saw Clemens there looking at him. "It tried to *kill* me," he said.

"I know," said Clemens.

Seventeen hours passed. The ship moved on in space.

Clemens stepped through a bulkhead and waited. The psychiatrist and the captain were there. Hitchcock sat on the floor with his legs drawn up to his chest, arms wrapped tight about them.

"Hitchcock," said the captain.

No answer.

"Hitchcock, listen to me," said the psychiatrist.

They turned to Clemens. "You're his friend?"

"Yes."

"Do you want to help us?"

"If I can."

"It was that damned meteor," said the captain. "This might not have happened if it hadn't been for that."

"It would've come anyway, sooner or later," said the doctor. To Clemens: "You might talk to him."

Clemens walked quietly over and crouched by Hitchcock and began to shake his arm gently, calling in a low voice, "Hey there, Hitchcock."

No reply.

"Hey, it's me. Me, Clemens," said Clemens. "Look, I'm here." He gave the arm a little slap. He massaged the rigid neck, gently, and the back of the bent-down head. He glanced at the psychiatrist, who sighed very softly. The captain shrugged.

"Shock treatment, Doctor?"

The psychiatrist nodded. "We'll start within the hour."

Yes, thought Clemens, shock treatment. Play a dozen jazz records for him, wave a bottle of fresh green chlorophyll and dandelions under his nose, put grass under his feet, squirt Chanel on the air, cut his hair, clip his fingernails, bring him a woman, shout, bang and crash at him, fry him with electricity, fill the gap and the gulf, but where's your proof? You can't keep proving to him forever. You can't entertain a baby with rattles and sirens all night every night for the next thirty years. Sometime you've got to stop. When you do that, he's lost again. That is, if he pays any attention to you at all.

"Hitchcock!" he cried, as loud as he could, almost frantically, as if he himself were falling over a cliff. "It's me. It's your pal! Hey!"

Clemens turned and walked away out of the silent room.

Twelve hours later another alarm bell rang.

After all of the running had died down, the captain explained: "Hitchcock snapped out of it for a minute or so. He was alone. He climbed into a space suit. He opened an airlock. Then he walked out into space—alone."

Clemens blinked through the immense glass port, where

there was a blur of stars and distant blackness. "He's out there now?"

"Yes. A million miles behind us. We'd never find him. First time I knew he was outside the ship was when his helmet radio came in on our control-room beam. I heard him talking to himself."

"What did he say?"

"Something like 'No more space ship now. Never was any. No people. No people in all the universe. Never were any. No planets. No stars.' That's what he said. And then he said something about his hands and feet and legs. 'No hands,' he said. 'I haven't any hands any more. Never had any. No feet. Never had any. Can't prove it. No body. Never had any. No lips. No face. No head. Nothing. Only space. Only space. Only the gap.'"

The men turned quietly to look from the glass port out into the remote and cold stars.

Space, thought Clemens. The space that Hitchcock loved so well. Space, with nothing on top, nothing on the bottom, a lot of empty nothings between, and Hitchcock falling in the middle of the nothing, on his way to no particular night and no particular morning. . . .

The Fox and the Forest

THERE WERE FIREWORKS the very first night, things that you should be afraid of perhaps, for they might remind you of other more horrible things, but these were beautiful, rockets that ascended into the ancient soft air of Mexico and shook the stars apart in blue and white fragments. Everything was good and sweet, the air was that blend of the dead and the living, of the rains and the dusts, of the incense from the church, and the brass smell of the tubas on the bandstand which pulsed out vast rhythms of "La Paloma." The church doors were thrown wide and it seemed as if a giant yellow constellation had fallen from the October sky and lay breathing fire upon the church walls; a million candles sent their color and fumes about. Newer and better fireworks scurried like tight-rope walking comets across the cool-tiled square, banged against adobe café walls, then rushed on hot wires to bash the high church tower, in which boys' naked feet alone could be seen kicking and re-kicking, clanging and tilting and re-tilting the monster bells into monstrous music. A flaming bull blundered about the plaza chasing laughing men and screaming children.

"The year is 1938," said William Travis, standing by his wife on the edge of the yelling crowd, smiling. "A good year."

The bull rushed upon them. Ducking, the couple ran, with fire balls pelting them, past the music and riot, the church, the band, under the stars, clutching each other, laughing. The bull passed, carried lightly on the shoulders of a charging Mexican, a framework of bamboo and sulphurous gunpowder.

"I've never enjoyed myself so much in my life." Susan Travis had stopped for her breath.

"It's amazing," said William.

"It will go on, won't it?"

"All night."

"No, I mean our trip."

He frowned and patted his breast pocket. "I've enough traveler's checks for a lifetime. Enjoy yourself. Forget it. They'll never find us."

"Never?"

"Never."

Now someone was setting off giant crackers, hurling them from the great bell-tolling tower of the church in a sputter of smoke, while the crowd below fell back under the threat and the crackers exploded in wonderful concussions among their dancing feet and flailing bodies. A wondrous smell of frying tortillas hung all about, and in the cafés men sat at tables looking out, mugs of beer in their brown hands.

The bull was dead. The fire was out of the bamboo tubes and he was expended. The laborer lifted the framework from his shoulders. Little boys clustered to touch the magnificent papier-mâché head, the real horns.

"Let's examine the bull," said William.

As they walked past the café entrance Susan saw the man looking out at them, a white man in a salt-white suit, with a blue tie and blue shirt, and a thin, sunburned face. His hair was blond and straight and his eyes were blue, and he watched them as they walked.

She would never have noticed him if it had not been for the bottles at his immaculate elbow; a fat bottle of crème de menthe, a clear bottle of vermouth, a flagon of cognac, and seven other bottles of assorted liqueurs, and, at his finger tips, ten small half-filled glasses from which, without taking his eyes off the street, he sipped, occasionally squinting, pressing his thin mouth shut upon the savor. In his free hand a thin Havana cigar smoked, and on a chair stood twenty cartons of Turkish cigarettes, six boxes of cigars, and some packaged colognes.

"Bill——" whispered Susan.

"Take it easy," he said. "He's nobody."

"I saw him in the plaza this morning."

"Don't look back, keep walking. Examine the papier-mâché bull here. That's it, ask questions."

"Do you think he's from the Searchers?"

"They couldn't follow us!"

"They might!"

"What a nice bull," said William to the man who owned it.

"He couldn't have followed us back through two hundred years, could he?"

"Watch yourself, for God's sake," said William.

She swayed. He crushed her elbow tightly, steering her away.

"Don't faint." He smiled, to make it look good. "You'll be all right. Let's go right in that café, drink in front of him, so if he *is* what we think he is, he won't suspect."

"No, I couldn't."

"We've *got* to. Come on now. And so I said to David, that's ridiculous!" This last in a loud voice as they went up the café steps.

We are here, thought Susan. Who are we? Where are we going? What do we fear? Start at the beginning, she told herself, holding to her sanity, as she felt the adobe floor underfoot.

My name is Ann Kristen; my husband's name is Roger. We were born in the year 2155 A.D. And we lived in a world that was evil. A world that was like a great black ship pulling away from the shore of sanity and civilization, roaring its black horn in the night, taking two billion people with it, whether they wanted to go or not, to death, to fall over the edge of the earth and the sea into radioactive flame and madness.

They walked into the café. The man was staring at them.

A phone rang.

The phone startled Susan. She remembered a phone ringing two hundred years in the future, on that blue April morning in 2155, and herself answering it:

"Ann, this is Rene! Have you heard? I mean about Travel in Time, Incorporated? Trips to Rome in 21 B.C., trips to Napoleon's Waterloo—any time, any place!"

"Rene, you're joking."

"No. Clinton Smith left this morning for Philadelphia in 1776. Travel in Time, Inc., arranges everything. Costs money. But, *think*—to actually *see* the burning of Rome, Kubla Khan, Moses and the Red Sea! You've probably got an ad in your tube mail now."

She had opened the suction mail tube and there was the metal foil advertisement:

> ROME AND THE BORGIAS!
> THE WRIGHT BROTHERS AT KITTY HAWK!
> Travel in Time, Inc., can costume you, put you in a crowd during the assassination of Lincoln or Caesar! We guarantee to teach you any language you need to move freely in any civilization, in any year, without friction. Latin, Greek, ancient American colloquial. Take your vacation in *Time* as well as Place!

Rene's voice was buzzing on the phone. "Tom and I leave for 1492 tomorrow. They're arranging for Tom to sail with Columbus. Isn't it amazing!"

"Yes," murmured Ann, stunned. "What does the Government say about this Time Machine company?"

"Oh, the police have an eye on it. Afraid people might evade the draft, run off and hide in the Past. Everyone has to leave a security bond behind, his house and belongings, to guarantee return. After all, the war's on."

"Yes, the war," murmured Ann. "The war."

Standing there, holding the phone, she had thought, Here is the chance my husband and I have talked and prayed over for so many years. We don't like this world of 2155. We want to run away from his work at the bomb factory, I from my position with disease-culture units. Perhaps there is a chance for us to escape, to run for centuries into a wild country of years where they will never find and bring us back to burn our books, censor our thoughts, scald our minds with fear, march us, scream at us with radios . . .

They were in Mexico in the year 1938.

She looked at the stained café wall.

Good workers for the Future State were allowed vacations into the Past to escape fatigue. And so she and her husband had moved back into 1938, a room in New York City, and enjoyed the theaters and the Statue of Liberty which still stood green in the harbor. And on the third day they had changed their clothes, their names, and had flown off to hide in Mexico!

"It *must* be him," whispered Susan, looking at the stranger seated at the table. "Those cigarettes, the cigars, the liquor. They give him away. Remember our first night in the Past?"

A month ago, their first night in New York, before their flight, drinking all the strange drinks, savoring and buying odd foods, perfumes, cigarettes of ten dozen rare brands, for they were rare in the Future, where war was everything. So they had made fools of themselves, rushing in and out of stores, salons, tobacconists, going up to their room to get wonderfully ill.

And now here was this stranger doing likewise, doing a

thing that only a man from the Future would do who had been starved for liquors and cigarettes for many years.

Susan and William sat and ordered a drink.

The stranger was examining their clothes, their hair, their jewelry—the way they walked and sat.

"Sit easily," said William under his breath. "Look as if you've worn this clothing style all your life."

"We should never have tried to escape."

"My God!" said William, "he's coming over. Let me do the talking."

The stranger bowed before them. There was the faintest tap of heels knocking together. Susan stiffened. That military sound!—unmistakable as that certain ugly rap on your door at midnight.

"Mr. Roger Kristen," said the stranger, "you did not pull up your pant legs when you sat down."

William froze. He looked at his hands lying on either leg, innocently. Susan's heart was beating swiftly.

"You've got the wrong person," said William quickly. "My name's not Krisler."

"Kristen," corrected the stranger.

"I'm William Travis," said William. "And I don't see what my pant legs have to do with you!"

"Sorry." The stranger pulled up a chair. "Let us say I thought I knew you because you did *not* pull your trousers up. *Everyone* does. If they don't, the trousers bag quickly. I am a long way from home, Mr.—Travis, and in need of company. My name is Simms."

"Mr. Simms, we appreciate your loneliness, but we're tired. We're leaving for Acapulco tomorrow."

"A charming spot. I was just there, looking for some friends of mine. They are somewhere. I shall find them yet. Oh, is the lady a bit sick?"

"Good night, Mr. Simms."

They started out the door, William holding Susan's arm firmly. They did not look back when Mr. Simms called, "Oh, just one other thing." He paused and then slowly spoke the words:

"2155 A.D."

Susan shut her eyes and felt the earth falter under her. She kept going, into the fiery plaza, seeing nothing.

They locked the door of their hotel room. And then she was crying and they were standing in the dark, and the room tilted under them. Far away firecrackers exploded, and there was laughter in the plaza.

"What a damned, loud nerve," said William. "Him sitting there, looking us up and down like animals, smoking his damn cigarettes, drinking his drinks. I should have killed him then!" His voice was nearly hysterical. "He even had the nerve to use his real name to us. The Chief of the Searchers. And the thing about my pant legs. My God, I should have pulled them up when I sat. It's an automatic gesture of this day and age. When I didn't do it, it set me off from the others; it made *him* think, Here's a man who never wore pants, a man used to breech uniforms and future styles. I could kill myself for giving us away!"

"No, no, it was my walk—these high heels—that did it. Our haircuts—so new, so fresh. Everything about us odd and uneasy."

He turned on the light. "He's still testing us. He's not positive of us—not completely. We can't run out on him, then. We can't make him certain. We'll go to Acapulco leisurely."

"Maybe he *is* sure of us, but is just playing."

"I wouldn't put it past him. He's got all the time in the world. He can dally here if he wants, and bring us back to the Future sixty seconds after we left it. He might keep us wondering for days, laughing at us."

Susan sat on the bed, wiping the tears from her face, smelling the old smell of charcoal and incense.

"They won't make a scene, will they?"

"They won't dare. They'll have to get us alone to put us in that Time Machine and send us back."

"There's a solution then," she said. "We'll never be alone; we'll always be in crowds. We'll make a million friends, visit markets, sleep in the Official Palaces in each town, pay the Chief of Police to guard us until we find a way to kill Simms and escape, disguise ourselves in new clothes, perhaps as Mexicans."

Footsteps sounded outside their locked door.

They turned out the light and undressed in silence. The footsteps went away. A door closed.

Susan stood by the window looking down at the plaza in the darkness. "So that building there is a church?"

"Yes."

"I've often wondered what a church looked like. It's been so long since anyone saw one. Can we visit it tomorrow?"

"Of course. Come to bed."

They lay in the dark room.

Half an hour later their phone rang. She lifted the receiver. "Hello?"

"The rabbits may hide in the forest," said a voice, "but a fox can always find them."

She replaced the receiver and lay back straight and cold in the bed.

Outside, in the year 1938, a man played three tunes upon a guitar, one following another.

During the night she put her hand out and almost touched the year 2155. She felt her fingers slide over cool spaces of time, as over a corrugated surface, and she heard the insistent thump of marching feet, a million bands playing a million military tunes, and she saw the fifty thousand rows of disease cultures in their aseptic glass tubes, her hand reaching out to them at her work in that huge factory in the Future; the tubes of leprosy, bubonic, typhoid, tuberculosis, and then the great explosion. She saw her hand burned to a wrinkled plum, felt it recoil from a concussion so immense that the world was lifted and let fall and all the buildings broke and people hemorrhaged and lay silent. Great volcanoes, machines, winds, avalanches slid down to silence and she awoke, sobbing, in the bed, in Mexico, many years away. . . .

In the early morning, drugged with the single hour's sleep they had finally been able to obtain, they awoke to the sound of loud automobiles in the street. Susan peered down from the iron balcony at a small crowd of eight people only now emerging, chattering, yelling, from trucks and cars with red lettering on them. A crowd of Mexicans had followed the trucks.

"*Qué pasa?*" Susan called to a little boy.

The boy replied.

Susan turned back to her husband. "An American motion-picture company, here on location."

"Sounds interesting." William was in the shower. "Let's watch them. I don't think we'd better leave today. We'll try to lull Simms. Watch the films being made. They say the primitive film making was something. Get our minds off ourselves."

Ourselves, thought Susan. For a moment, in the bright sun, she had forgotten that somewhere in the hotel, waiting, was a man smoking a thousand cigarettes, it seemed. She saw the eight loud happy Americans below and wanted to call to them: "Save me, hide me, help me! Color my hair, my eyes; clothe me in strange clothes. I need your help. I'm from the year 2155!"

But the words stayed in her throat. The functionaries of Travel in Time, Inc., were not foolish. In your brain, before you left on your trip, they placed a psychological bloc. You could tell no one your true time or birthplace, nor could you reveal any of the Future to those in the Past. The Past and the Future must be protected from each other. Only with this psychological bloc were people allowed to travel unguarded through the ages. The Future must be protected from any change brought about by her people traveling in the Past. Even if she wanted to with all her heart, she could not tell any of those happy people below in the plaza who she was, or what her predicament had become.

"What about breakfast?" said William.

Breakfast was being served in the immense dining room. Ham and eggs for everyone. The place was full of tourists. The film people entered, all eight of them—six men and two women, giggling, shoving chairs about. And Susan sat near them, feeling the warmth and protection they offered, even when Mr. Simms came down the lobby stairs, smoking his Turkish cigarette with great intensity. He nodded at them from a distance, and Susan nodded back, smiling, because he couldn't do anything to them here, in front of eight film people and twenty other tourists.

"Those actors," said William. "Perhaps I could hire two of them, say it was a joke, dress them in our clothes, have them drive off in our car when Simms is in such a spot where he can't see their faces. If two people pretending to be us could lure him off for a few hours, we might make it to Mexico City. It'd take him years to find us there!"

"Hey!"

A fat man, with liquor on his breath, leaned on their table.

"American tourists!" he cried. "I'm so sick of seeing Mexicans, I could kiss you!" He shook their hands. "Come on, eat with us. Misery loves company. I'm Misery, this is Miss Gloom, and Mr. and Mrs. Do-We-Hate-Mexico! We all hate it. But we're here for some preliminary shots for a damn film. The rest of the crew arrives tomorrow. My name's Joe Melton. I'm a director. And if this ain't a hell of a country! Funerals in the streets, people dying. Come on, move over. Join the party; cheer us up!"

Susan and William were both laughing.

"Am I funny?" Mr. Melton asked the immediate world.

"Wonderful!" Susan moved over.

Mr. Simms was glaring across the dining room at them.

She made a face at him.

Mr. Simms advanced among the tables.

"Mr. and Mrs. Travis," he called. "I thought we were breakfasting together, alone."

"Sorry," said William.

"Sit down, pal," said Mr. Melton. "Any friend of theirs is a pal of mine."

Mr. Simms sat. The film people talked loudly, and while they talked, Mr. Simms said quietly, "I hope you slept well."

"Did you?"

"I'm not used to spring mattresses," replied Mr. Simms wryly. "But there are compensations. I stayed up half the night trying new cigarettes and foods. Odd, fascinating. A whole new spectrum of sensation, these ancient vices."

"We don't know what you're talking about," said Susan.

"Always the play acting." Simms laughed. "It's no use. Nor is this stratagem of crowds. I'll get you alone soon enough. I'm immensely patient."

"Say," Mr. Melton broke in, his face flushed, "is this guy giving you any trouble?"

"It's all right."

"Say the word and I'll give him the bum's rush."

Melton turned back to yell at his associates. In the laughter, Mr. Simms went on: "Let us come to the point. It took me a month of tracing you through towns and cities to find you, and all of yesterday to be sure of you. If you come with me quietly, I might be able to get you off with no punishment, if you agree to go back to work on the hydrogen-plus bomb."

"Science this guy talks at breakfast!" observed Mr. Melton, half listening.

Simms went on, imperturbably. "Think it over. You can't escape. If you kill me, others will follow you."

"We don't know what you're talking about."

"Stop it!" cried Simms irritably. "Use your intelligence! You know we can't let you get away with this escape. Other people in the year 2155 might get the same idea and do what you've done. We need people."

"To fight your wars," said William at last.

"Bill!"

"It's all right, Susan. We'll talk on his terms now. We can't escape."

"Excellent," said Simms. "Really, you've both been incredibly romantic, running away from your responsibilities."

"Running away from horror."

"Nonsense. Only a war."

"What are you guys talking about?" asked Mr. Melton.

Susan wanted to tell him. But you could only speak in generalities. The psychological bloc in your mind allowed that. Generalities, such as Simms and William were now discussing.

"Only *the* war," said William. "Half the world dead of leprosy bombs!"

"Nevertheless," Simms pointed out, "the inhabitants of the Future resent you two hiding on a tropical isle, as it were, while they drop off the cliff into hell. Death loves death, not life. Dying people love to know that others die with them. It is a comfort to learn you are not alone in the kiln, in the grave. I am the guardian of their collective resentment against you two."

"Look at the guardian of resentments!" said Mr. Melton to his companions.

"The longer you keep me waiting, the harder it will go for you. We need you on the bomb project, Mr. Travis. Return now—no torture. Later, we'll force you to work, and after you've finished the bomb, we'll try a number of complicated new devices on you, sir."

"I've a proposition," said William. "I'll come back with you if my wife stays here alive, safe, away from that war."

Mr. Simms considered it. "All right. Meet me in the plaza in ten minutes. Pick me up in your car. Drive me to a deserted country spot. I'll have the Travel Machine pick us up there."

"Bill!" Susan held his arm tightly.

"Don't argue." He looked over at her. "It's settled." To Simms: "One thing. Last night you could have gotten in our room and kidnaped us. Why didn't you?"

"Shall we say that I was enjoying myself?" replied Mr. Simms languidly, sucking his new cigar. "I hate giving up this wonderful atmosphere, this sun, this vacation. I regret leaving behind the wine and the cigarettes. Oh, how I regret it. The plaza then, in ten minutes. Your wife will be protected and may stay here as long as she wishes. Say your good-bys."

Mr. Simms arose and walked out.

"There goes Mr. Big Talk!" yelled Mr. Melton at the departing gentleman. He turned and looked at Susan. "Hey. Someone's crying. Breakfast's no time for people to cry. Now *is* it?"

At nine-fifteen Susan stood on the balcony of their room, gazing down at the plaza. Mr. Simms was seated there, his neat legs crossed, on a delicate bronze bench. Biting the tip from a cigar, he lit it tenderly.

Susan heard the throb of a motor, and far up the street, out of a garage and down the cobbled hill, slowly, came William in his car.

The car picked up speed. Thirty, now forty, now fifty miles an hour. Chickens scattered before it.

Mr. Simms took off his white panama hat and mopped his pink forehead, put his hat back on, and then saw the car.

It was rushing sixty miles an hour, straight on for the plaza.

"William!" screamed Susan.

The car hit the low plaza curb, thundering; it jumped up, sped across the tiles toward the green bench where Mr. Simms now dropped his cigar, shrieked, flailed his hands, and was hit by the car. His body flew up and up in the air, and down and down, crazily, into the street.

On the far side of the plaza, one front wheel broken, the car stopped. People were running.

Susan went in and closed the balcony doors.

They came down the Official Palace steps together, arm in arm, their faces pale, at twelve noon.

"*Adiós, señor,*" said the mayor behind them. "*Señora.*"

They stood in the plaza where the crowd was pointing at the blood.

"Will they want to see you again?" asked Susan.

"No, we went over and over it. It was an accident. I lost control of the car. I wept for them. God knows I had to get my relief out somewhere. I *felt* like weeping. I hated to kill him. I've never wanted to do anything like that in my life."

"They won't prosecute you?"

"They talked about it, but no. I talked faster. They believe me. It was an accident. It's over."

"Where will we go? Mexico City? Uruapan?"

"The car's in the repair shop. It'll be ready at four this afternoon. Then we'll get the hell out."

"Will we be followed? Was Simms working alone?"

"I don't know. We'll have a little head start on them, I think."

The film people were coming out of the hotel as they approached. Mr. Melton hurried up, scowling. "Hey I heard what happened. Too bad. Everything okay now? Want to get your minds off it? We're doing some preliminary shots up the street. You want to watch, you're welcome. Come on, do you good."

They went.

They stood on the cobbled street while the film camera was being set up. Susan looked at the road leading down and away, and the highway going to Acapulco and the sea, past pyramids and ruins and little adobe towns with yellow walls, blue walls, purple walls and flaming bougainvillea, and she thought, We shall take the roads, travel in clusters and crowds, in markets, in lobbies, bribe police to sleep near, keep double locks, but always the crowds, never alone again, always afraid the next person who passes may be another Simms. Never knowing if we've tricked and lost the Searchers. And always up ahead, in the Future, they'll wait for us to be brought back, waiting with their bombs to burn us and disease to rot us, and their police to tell us to roll over, turn around, jump through the hoop! And so we'll keep running through the forest, and we'll never ever stop or sleep well again in our lives.

A crowd gathered to watch the film being made. And Susan watched the crowd and the streets.

"Seen anyone suspicious?"

"No. What time is it?"

"Three o'clock. The car should be almost ready."

The test film was finished at three forty-five. They all walked down to the hotel, talking. William paused at the garage. "The car'll be ready at six," he said, coming out, worried.

"But no later than that?"

"It'll be ready, don't worry."

In the hotel lobby they looked around for other men traveling alone, men who resembled Mr. Simms, men with new haircuts and too much cigarette smoke and cologne smell about them, but the lobby was empty. Going up the stairs, Mr. Melton said, "Well, it's been a long hard day. Who'd like to put a header on it? You folks? Martini? Beer?"

"Maybe one."

The whole crowd pushed into Mr. Melton's room and the drinking began.

"Watch the time," said William.

Time, thought Susan. If only they had time. All she wanted was to sit in the plaza all of a long bright day in October, with not a worry or a thought, with the sun on her face and arms, her eyes closed, smiling at the warmth, and never move. Just sleep in the Mexican sun, and sleep warmly and easily and slowly and happily for many, many days. . . .

Mr. Melton opened the champagne.

"To a very beautiful lady, lovely enough for films," he said, toasting Susan. "I might even give you a test."

She laughed.

"I mean it," said Melton. "You're very nice. I could make you a movie star."

"And take me to Hollywood?" cried Susan.

"Get the hell out of Mexico, sure!"

Susan glanced at William and he lifted an eyebrow and

nodded. It would be a change of scene, clothing, locale, name, perhaps; and they would be traveling with eight other people, a good shield against any interference from the Future.

"It sounds wonderful," said Susan.

She was feeling the champagne now. The afternoon was slipping by; the party was whirling about her. She felt safe and good and alive and truly happy for the first time in many years.

"What kind of film would my wife be good for?" asked William, refilling his glass.

Melton appraised Susan. The party stopped laughing and listened.

"Well, I'd like to do a story of suspense," said Melton. "A story of a man and wife, like yourselves."

"Go on."

"Sort of a war story, maybe," said the director, examining the color of his drink against the sunlight.

Susan and William waited.

"A story about a man and wife who live in a little house on a little street in the year 2155, maybe," said Melton. "This is ad lib, understand. But this man and wife are faced with a terrible war, super-plus hydrogen bombs, censorship, death in that year, and—here's the gimmick—they escape into the Past, followed by a man who they think is evil, but who is only trying to show them what their duty is."

William dropped his glass to the floor.

Mr. Melton continued: "And this couple take refuge with a group of film people whom they learn to trust. Safety in numbers, they say to themselves."

Susan felt herself slip down into a chair. Everyone was watching the director. He took a little sip of wine. "Ah, that's a fine wine. Well, this man and woman, it seems, don't realize how important they are to the Future. The man, especially, is the keystone to a new bomb metal. So the Searchers, let's call them, spare no trouble or expense to find, capture, and take home the man and wife, once they get them totally alone, in a hotel room, where no one can see. Strategy. The Searchers work alone, or in groups of eight. One trick or another will do it. Don't you think it would make a wonderful film, Susan? Don't you, Bill?" He finished his drink.

Susan sat with her eyes straight ahead of her.

"Have a drink?" said Mr. Melton.

William's gun was out and fired three times, and one of the men fell, and the others ran forward. Susan screamed. A hand was clamped to her mouth. Now the gun was on the floor and William was struggling, held.

Mr. Melton said, "Please," standing there where he had stood, blood showing on his fingers. "Let's not make matters worse."

Someone pounded on the hall door.

"Let me in!"

"The manager," said Mr. Melton dryly. He jerked his head. "Everyone, let's move!"

"Let me in! I'll call the police!"

Susan and William looked at each other quickly, and then at the door.

"The manager wishes to come in," said Mr. Melton. "Quick!"

A camera was carried forward. From it shot a blue light which encompassed the room instantly. It widened out and the people of the party vanished, one by one.

"Quickly!"

Outside the window, in the instant before she vanished, Susan saw the green land and the purple and yellow and blue and crimson walls and the cobbles flowing down like a river, a man upon a burro riding into the warm hills, a boy drinking Orange Crush, she could feel the sweet liquid in her throat, a man standing under a cool plaza tree with a guitar, she could feel her hand upon the strings, and, far away, the sea, the blue and tender sea, she could feel it roll her over and take her in.

And then she was gone. Her husband was gone.

The door burst wide open. The manager and his staff rushed in.

The room was empty.

"But they were just here! I saw them come in, and now—gone!" cried the manager. "The windows are covered with iron grating. They couldn't get out that way!"

In the late afternoon the priest was summoned and they opened the room again and aired it out, and had him sprinkle holy water through each corner and give it his blessing.

"What shall we do with these?" asked the charwoman.

She pointed to the closet, where there were 67 bottles of chartreuse, cognac, *crème de cacao*, absinthe, vermouth, tequila, 106 cartons of Turkish cigarettes, and 198 yellow boxes of fifty-cent pure Havana-filler cigars. . . .

The Visitor

SAUL WILLIAMS AWOKE to the still morning. He looked wearily out of his tent and thought about how far away Earth was. Millions of miles, he thought. But then what could you do about it? Your lungs were full of the "blood rust." You coughed all the time.

Saul arose this particular morning at seven o'clock. He was a tall man, lean, thinned by his illness. It was a quiet morning on Mars, with the dead sea bottom-flat and silent—no wind on it. The sun was clear and cool in the empty sky. He washed his face and ate breakfast.

After that he wanted very much to be back on Earth. During the day he tried every way that it was possible to be in New York City. Sometimes, if he sat right and held his hands a certain way, he did it. He could almost smell New York. Most of the time, though, it was impossible.

Later in the morning Saul tried to die. He lay on the sand and told his heart to stop. It continued beating. He imagined himself leaping from a cliff or cutting his wrists, but laughed to himself—he knew he lacked the nerve for either act.

Maybe if I squeeze tight and think about it enough, I'll just sleep and never wake, he thought. He tried it. An hour later he awoke with a mouth full of blood. He got up and spat it out and felt very sorry for himself. This blood rust—it filled your mouth and your nose; it ran from your ears, your fingernails; and it took a year to kill you. The only cure was shoving you in a rocket and shooting you out to exile on Mars. There was no known cure on Earth, and remaining there would contaminate and kill others. So here he was, bleeding all the time, and lonely.

Saul's eyes narrowed. In the distance, by an ancient city ruin, he saw another man lying on a filthy blanket.

When Saul walked up, the man on the blanket stirred weakly.

"Hello, Saul," he said.

"Another morning," said Saul. "Christ, I'm lonely!"

"It is an affliction of the rusted ones," said the man on the blanket, not moving, very pale and as if he might vanish if you touched him.

"I wish to God," said Saul, looking down at the man, "that you could at least talk. Why is it that intellectuals never get the blood rust and come up here?"

"It is a conspiracy against you, Saul," said the man, shutting his eyes, too weary to keep them open. "Once I had the strength to be an intellectual. Now, it is a job to think."

"If only we could talk," said Saul Williams.

The other man merely shrugged indifferently.

"Come tomorrow. Perhaps I'll have enough strength to talk about Aristotle then. I'll try. Really I will." The man sank down under the worn tree. He opened one eye. "Remember, once we did talk on Aristotle, six months ago, on that good day I had."

"I remember," said Saul, not listening. He looked at the dead sea. "I wish I were as sick as you, then maybe I wouldn't worry about being an intellectual. Then maybe I'd get some peace."

"You'll get just as bad as I am now in about six months," said the dying man. "Then you won't care about anything but sleep and more sleep. Sleep will be like a woman to you. You'll always go back to her, because she's fresh and good and faithful and she always treats you kindly and the same. You only wake up so you can think about going back to sleep. It's a nice thought." The man's voice was a bare whisper. Now it stopped and a light breathing took over.

Saul walked off.

Along the shores of the dead sea, like so many emptied bottles flung up by some long-gone wave, were the huddled bodies of sleeping men. Saul could see them all down the curve of the empty sea. One, two, three—all of them sleeping alone, most of them worse off than he, each with his little cache of food, each grown into himself, because social converse was weakening and sleep was good.

At first there had been a few nights around mutual campfires. And they had all talked about Earth. That was the only thing they talked about. Earth and the way the waters ran in town creeks and what homemade strawberry pie tasted like and how New York looked in the early morning coming over on the Jersey ferry in the salt wind.

I want Earth, thought Saul. I want it so bad it hurts. I want something I can never have again. And they all want it and it hurts them not to have it. More than food or a woman or anything, I just want Earth. This sickness puts women away forever; they're not things to be wanted. But Earth, yes. That's a thing for the mind and not the weak body.

The bright metal flashed on the sky.

Saul looked up.

The bright metal flashed again.

A minute later the rocket landed on the sea bottom. A valve opened, a man stepped out, carrying his luggage with him. Two other men, in protective germicide suits, accompanied him, bringing out vast cases of food, setting up a tent for him.

Another minute and the rocket returned to the sky. The exile stood alone.

Saul began to run. He hadn't run in weeks, and it was very tiring, but he ran and yelled.

"Hello, hello!"

The young man looked Saul up and down when he arrived.

"Hello. So this is Mars. My name's Leonard Mark."

"I'm Saul Williams."

They shook hands. Leonard Mark was very young—only eighteen; very blond, pink-faced, blue-eyed and fresh in spite of his illness.

"How are things in New York?" said Saul.

"Like this," said Leonard Mark. And he looked at Saul.

New York grew up out of the desert, made of stone and filled with March winds. Neons exploded in electric color. Yellow taxis glided in a still night. Bridges rose and tugs chanted in the midnight harbors. Curtains rose on spangled musicals.

Saul put his hands to his head, violently.

"Hold on, hold on!" he cried. "What's happening to me? What's wrong with me? I'm going crazy!"

Leaves sprouted from trees in Central Park, green and new. On the pathway Saul strolled along, smelling the air.

"Stop it, stop it, you fool!" Saul shouted at himself. He pressed his forehead with his hands. "This can't be!"

"It is," said Leonard Mark.

The New York towers faded. Mars returned. Saul stood on the empty sea bottom, staring limply at the young newcomer.

"You," he said, putting his hand out to Leonard Mark. "You did it. You did it with your mind."

"Yes," said Leonard Mark.

Silently they stood facing each other. Finally, trembling, Saul seized the other exile's hand and wrung it again and again, saying, "Oh, but I'm glad you're here. You can't know how glad I am!"

They drank their rich brown coffee from the tin cups.

It was high noon. They had been talking all through the warm morning time.

"And this ability of yours?" said Saul over his cup, looking steadily at the young Leonard Mark.

"It's just something I was born with," said Mark, looking into his drink. "My mother was in the blowup of London back in '57. I was born ten months later. I don't know what you'd call my ability. Telepathy and thought transference, I suppose. I used to have an act. I traveled all around the world. Leonard Mark, the mental marvel, they said on the billboards. I was pretty well off. Most people thought I was a charlatan. You know what people think of theatrical folks. Only I knew I was really genuine, but I didn't let anybody know. It was safer not to let it get around too much. Oh, a few of my close friends knew about my real ability. I had a lot of talents that will come in handy now that I'm here on Mars."

"You sure scared the hell out of me," said Saul, his cup rigid in his hand. "When New York came right up out of the ground that way, I thought I was insane."

"It's a form of hypnotism which affects all of the sensual organs at once—eyes, ears, nose, mouth, skin—all of them. What would you like to be doing now most of all?"

Saul put down his cup. He tried to hold his hands very steady. He wet his lips. "I'd like to be in a little creek I used to swim in in Mellin Town, Illinois, when I was a kid. I'd like to be stark-naked and swimming."

"Well," said Leonard Mark and moved his head ever so little.

Saul fell back on the sand, his eyes shut.

Leonard Mark sat watching him.

Saul lay on the sand. From time to time his hands moved, twitched excitedly. His mouth spasmed open; sounds issued from his tightening and relaxing throat.

Saul began to make slow movements of his arms, out and back, out and back, gasping with his head to one side, his arms going and coming slowly on the warm air, stirring the yellow sand under him, his body turning slowly over.

Leonard Mark quietly finished his coffee. While he drank he kept his eyes on the moving, whispering Saul lying there on the dead sea bottom.

"All right," said Leonard Mark.

Saul sat up, rubbing his face.

After a moment he told Leonard Mark, "I *saw* the creek. I ran along the bank and I took off my clothes," he said breathlessly, his smile incredulous. "And I *dived in* and swam around!"

"I'm pleased," said Leonard Mark.

"Here!" Saul reached into his pocket and drew forth his last bar of chocolate. "This is for you."

"What's this?" Leonard Mark looked at the gift. "Chocolate? Nonsense, I'm not doing this for pay. I'm doing it because it makes you happy. Put that thing back in your pocket before I turn it into a rattlesnake and it bites you."

"Thank you, thank you!" Saul put it away. "You don't know how good that water was." He fetched the coffeepot. "More?"

Pouring the coffee, Saul shut his eyes a moment.

I've got Socrates here, he thought; Socrates and Plato, and Nietzsche and Schopenhauer. This man, by his talk, is a genius. By his talent, he's incredible! Think of the long, easy days and the cool nights of talk we'll have. It won't be a bad year at all. Not half.

He spilled the coffee.

"What's wrong?"

"Nothing." Saul himself was confused, startled.

We'll be in Greece, he thought. In Athens. We'll be in Rome, if we want, when we study the Roman writers. We'll stand in the Parthenon and the Acropolis. It won't be just talk, but it'll be a place to be, besides. This man can do it. He has the power to do it. When we talk the plays of Racine, he can make a stage and players and all of it for me. By Christ, this is better than life ever was! How much better to be sick and here than well on Earth without these abilities! How many people have ever seen a Greek drama played in a Greek amphitheater in the year 31 B.C.?

And if I ask, quietly and earnestly, will this man take on the aspect of Schopenhauer and Darwin and Bergson and all the other thoughtful men of the ages . . . ? Yes, why not? To sit and talk with Nietzsche in person, with Plato himself . . . !

There was only one thing wrong. Saul felt himself swaying.

The other men. The other sick ones along the bottom of this dead sea.

In the distance men were moving, walking toward them. They had seen the rocket flash, land, dislodge a passenger. Now they were coming, slowly, painfully, to greet the new arrival.

Saul was cold. "Look," he said. "Mark, I think we'd better head for the mountains."

"Why?"

"See those men coming? Some of them are insane."

"Really?"

"Yes."

"Isolation and all make them that way?"

"Yes, that's it. We'd better get going."

"They don't look very dangerous. They move slowly."

"You'd be surprised."

Mark looked at Saul. "You're trembling. Why's that?"

"There's no time to talk," said Saul, getting up swiftly. "Come on. Don't you realize what'll happen once they discover your talent? They'll fight over you. They'll kill each other—kill you—for the right to own you."

"Oh, but I don't belong to anybody," said Leonard Mark. He looked at Saul. "No. Not even you."

Saul jerked his head. "I didn't even think of that."

"Didn't you now?" Mark laughed.

"We haven't time to argue," answered Saul, eyes blinking, cheeks blazing. "Come on!"

"I don't want to. I'm going to sit right here until those men show up. You're a little too possessive. My life's my own."

Saul felt an ugliness in himself. His face began to twist. "You *heard* what I said."

"How very quickly you changed from a friend to an enemy," observed Mark.

Saul hit at him. It was a neat quick blow, coming down.

Mark ducked aside, laughing. "No, you don't!"

They were in the center of Times Square. Cars roared, hooting, upon them. Buildings plunged up, hot, into the blue air.

"It's a lie!" cried Saul, staggering under the visual impact. "For God's sake, don't, Mark! The men are coming. You'll be killed!"

Mark sat there on the pavement, laughing at his joke. "Let them come. I can fool them all!"

New York distracted Saul. It was meant to distract—meant to keep his attention with its unholy beauty, after so many months away from it. Instead of attacking Mark he could only stand, drinking in the alien but familiar scene.

He shut his eyes. "No." And fell forward, dragging Mark with him. Horns screamed in his ears. Brakes hissed and caught violently. He smashed at Mark's chin.

Silence.

Mark lay on the sea bottom.

Taking the unconscious man in his arms, Saul began to run, heavily.

New York was gone. There was only the wide soundlessness of the dead sea. The men were closing in around him. He headed for the hills with his precious cargo, with New York and green country and fresh springs and old friends held in his arms. He fell once and struggled up. He did not stop running.

Night filled the cave. The wind wandered in and out, tugging at the small fire, scattering ashes.

Mark opened his eyes. He was tied with ropes and leaning against the dry wall of the cave, facing the fire.

Saul put another stick on the fire, glancing now and again with a catlike nervousness at the cave entrance.

"You're a fool."

Saul started.

"Yes," said Mark, "you're a fool. They'll find us. If they have to hunt for six months they'll find us. They saw New York, at a distance, like a mirage. And us in the center of it. It's too much to think they won't be curious and follow our trail."

"I'll move on with you then," said Saul, staring into the fire.

"And they'll come after."

"Shut up!"

Mark smiled. "Is that the way to speak to your wife?"

"You heard me!"

"Oh, a fine marriage this is—your greed and my mental ability. What do you want to see now? Shall I show you a few more of your childhood scenes?"

Saul felt the sweat coming out on his brow. He didn't know if the man was joking or not. "Yes," he said.

"All right," said Mark, "watch!"

Flame gushed out of the rocks. Sulphur choked him. Pits of brimstone exploded, concussions rocked the cave. Heaving up, Saul coughed and blundered, burned, withered by hell!

Hell went away. The cave returned.

Mark was laughing.

Saul stood over him. "You," he said coldly, bending down.

"What else do you expect?" cried Mark. "To be tied up, toted off, made the intellectual bride of a man insane with loneliness—do you think I enjoy this?"

"I'll untie you if you promise not to run away."

"I couldn't promise that. I'm a free agent. I don't belong to anybody."

Saul got down on his knees. "But you've *got* to belong, do you hear? You've *got* to belong. I can't let you go away!"

"My dear fellow, the more you say things like that, the more remote I am. If you'd had any sense and done things intelligently, we'd have been friends. I'd have been glad to do you these little hypnotic favors. After all, they're no trouble for me to conjure up. Fun, really. But you've botched it. You wanted me all to yourself. You were afraid the others would take me away from you. Oh, how mistaken you were. I have enough power to keep them all happy. You could have shared me, like a community kitchen. I'd have felt quite like a god among children, being kind, doing favors, in return for which you might bring me little gifts, special tidbits of food."

"I'm sorry, I'm sorry!" Saul cried. "But I know those men too well."

"Are you any different? Hardly! Go out and see if they're coming. I thought I heard a noise."

Saul ran. In the cave entrance he cupped his hands, peering down into the night-filled gully. Dim shapes stirred. Was it only the wind blowing the roving clumps of weeds? He began to tremble—a fine, aching tremble.

"I don't see anything." He came back into an empty cave.

He stared at the fireplace. "Mark!"

Mark was gone.

There was nothing but the cave, filled with boulders, stones, pebbles, the lonely fire flickering, the wind sighing. And Saul standing there, incredulous and numb.

"Mark! Mark! Come back!"

The man had worked free of his bonds, slowly, carefully, and using the ruse of imagining he heard other men approaching, had gone—where?

The cave was deep, but ended in a blank wall. And Mark could not have slipped past him into the night. How then?

Saul stepped around the fire. He drew his knife and approached a large boulder that stood against the cave wall. Smiling, he pressed the knife against the boulder. Smiling, he tapped the knife there. Then he drew his knife back to plunge it into the boulder.

"Stop!" shouted Mark.

The boulder vanished. Mark was there.

Saul suspended his knife. The fire played on his cheeks. His eyes were quite insane.

"It didn't work," he whispered. He reached down and put his hands on Mark's throat and closed his fingers. Mark said nothing, but moved uneasily in the grip, his eyes ironic, telling things to Saul that Saul knew.

If you kill me, the eyes said, where will all your dreams be? If you kill me, where will all the streams and brook trout be? Kill me, kill Plato, kill Aristotle, kill Einstein; yes, kill all of us! Go ahead, strangle me. I dare you.

Saul's fingers released the throat.

Shadows moved into the cave mouth.

Both men turned their heads.

The other men were there. Five of them, haggard with travel, panting, waiting in the outer rim of light.

"Good evening," called Mark, laughing. "Come in, come in, gentlemen!"

By dawn the arguments and ferocities still continued. Mark sat among the glaring men, rubbing his wrists, newly released from his bonds. He created a mahogany-paneled conference hall and a marble table at which they all sat, ridiculously bearded, evil-smelling, sweating and greedy men, eyes bent upon their treasure.

"The way to settle it," said Mark at last, "is for each of you to have certain hours of certain days for appointments with me. I'll treat you all equally. I'll be city property, free to come and go. That's fair enough. As for Saul here, he's on probation. When he's proved he can be a civil person once more, I'll give him a treatment or two. Until that time, I'll have nothing more to do with him."

The other exiles grinned at Saul.

"I'm sorry," Saul said. "I didn't know what I was doing. I'm all right now."

"We'll see," said Mark. "Let's give ourselves a month, shall we?"

The other men grinned at Saul.

Saul said nothing. He sat staring at the floor of the cave.

"Let's see now," said Mark. "On Mondays it's your day, Smith."

Smith nodded.

"On Tuesdays I'll take Peter there, for an hour or so."

Peter nodded.

"On Wednesdays I'll finish up with Johnson, Holtzman, and Jim, here."

The last three men looked at each other.

"The rest of the week I'm to be left strictly alone, do you hear?" Mark told them. "A little should be better than nothing. If you don't obey, I won't perform at all."

"Maybe we'll *make* you perform," said Johnson. He caught the other men's eye. "Look, we're five against his one. We can make him do anything we want. If we co-operate, we've got a great thing here."

"Don't be idiots," Mark warned the other men.

"Let me talk," said Johnson. "He's telling *us* what he'll do.

Why don't we tell *him*! Are we bigger than him, or not? And him threatening not to perform! Well, just let me get a sliver of wood under his toenails and maybe burn his fingers a bit with a steel file, and we'll see if he performs! Why shouldn't we have performances, I want to know, every night in the week?"

"Don't listen to him!" said Mark. "He's crazy. He can't be depended on. You know what he'll do, don't you? He'll get you all off guard, one by one, and kill you; yes, kill all of you, so that when he's done, he'll be alone—just him and me! That's his sort."

The listening men blinked. First at Mark, then at Johnson.

"For that matter," observed Mark, "none of you can trust the others. This is a fool's conference. The minute your back is turned one of the other men will murder you. I dare say, at the week's end, you'll all be dead or dying."

A cold wind blew into the mahogany room. It began to dissolve and became a cave once more. Mark was tired of his joke. The marble table splashed and rained and evaporated.

The men gazed suspiciously at each other with little bright animal eyes. What was spoken was true. They saw each other in the days to come, surprising one another, killing—until that last lucky one remained to enjoy the intellectual treasure that walked among them.

Saul watched them and felt alone and disquieted. Once you have made a mistake, how hard to admit your wrongness, to go back, start fresh. They were *all* wrong. They had been lost a long time. Now they were worse than lost.

"And to make matters very bad," said Mark at last, "one of you has a gun. All the rest of you have only knives. But one of you, I know, has a gun."

Everybody jumped up. "Search!" said Mark. "Find the one with the gun or you're all dead!"

That did it. The men plunged wildly about, not knowing whom to search first. Their hands grappled, they cried out, and Mark watched them in contempt.

Johnson fell back, feeling in his jacket. "All right," he said. "We might as well have it over now! Here, you, Smith."

And he shot Smith through the chest. Smith fell. The other men yelled. They broke apart. Johnson aimed and fired twice more.

"Stop!" cried Mark.

New York soared up around them, out of rock and cave and sky. Sun glinted on high towers. The elevated thundered; tugs blew in the harbor. The green lady stared across the bay, a torch in her hand.

"Look, you fools!" said Mark. Central Park broke out constellations of spring blossoms. The wind blew fresh-cut lawn smells over them in a wave.

And in the center of New York, bewildered, the men stumbled. Johnson fired his gun three times more. Saul ran forward. He crashed against Johnson, bore him down, wrenched the gun away. It fired again.

The men stopped milling.

They stood. Saul lay across Johnson. They ceased struggling.

There was a terrible silence. The men stood watching. New York sank down into the sea. With a hissing, bubbling, sighing; with a cry of ruined metal and old time, the great structures leaned, warped, flowed, collapsed.

Mark stood among the buildings. Then, like a building, a neat red hole drilled into his chest, wordless, he fell.

Saul lay staring at the men, at the body.

He got up, the gun in his hand.

Johnson did not move—was afraid to move.

They all shut their eyes and opened them again, thinking that by so doing they might reanimate the man who lay before them.

The cave was cold.

Saul stood up and looked, remotely, at the gun in his hand. He took it and threw it far out over the valley and did not watch it fall.

They looked down at the body as if they could not believe it. Saul bent down and took hold of the limp hand. "Leonard!" he said softly. "Leonard?" He shook the hand. "Leonard!"

Leonard Mark did not move. His eyes were shut; his chest had ceased going up and down. He was getting cold.

Saul got up. "We've killed him," he said, not looking at the men. His mouth was filling with a raw liquor now. "The only one we didn't want to kill, we killed." He put his shaking hand to his eyes. The other men stood waiting.

"Get a spade," said Saul. "Bury him." He turned away. "I'll have nothing to do with you."

Somebody walked off to find a spade.

Saul was so weak he couldn't move. His legs were grown into the earth, with roots feeding deep of loneliness and fear and the cold of the night. The fire had almost died out and now there was only the double moonlight riding over the blue mountains.

There was the sound of someone digging in the earth with a spade.

"We don't need him anyhow," said somebody, much too loudly.

The sound of digging went on. Saul walked off slowly and let himself slide down the side of a dark tree until he reached and was sitting blankly on the sand, his hands blindly in his lap.

Sleep, he thought. We'll all go to sleep now. We have that much, anyway. Go to sleep and try to dream of New York and all the rest.

He closed his eyes wearily, the blood gathering in his nose and his mouth and in his quivering eyes.

"How did he do it?" he asked in a tired voice. His head fell forward on his chest. "How did he bring New York up here and make us walk around in it? Let's try. It shouldn't be too hard. Think! Think of New York," he whispered, falling down into sleep. "New York and Central Park and then Illinois in the spring, apple blossoms and green grass."

It didn't work. It wasn't the same. New York was gone and nothing he could do would bring it back. He would rise every morning and walk on the dead sea looking for it, and walk forever around Mars, looking for it, and never find it. And finally lie, too tired to walk, trying to find New York in his head, but not finding it.

The last thing he heard before he slept was the spade rising and falling and digging a hole into which, with a tremendous crash of metal and golden mist and odor and color and sound, New York collapsed, fell, and was buried.

He cried all night in his sleep.

The Concrete Mixer

HE LISTENED TO the dry-grass rustle of the old witches' voices beneath his open window:

"Ettil, the coward! Ettil, the refuser! Ettil, who will not wage the glorious war of Mars against Earth!"

"Speak on, witches!" he cried.

The voices dropped to a murmur like that of water in the long canals under the Martian sky.

"Ettil, the father of a son who must grow up in the shadow of this horrid knowledge!" said the old wrinkled women. They knocked their sly-eyed heads gently together. "Shame, shame!"

His wife was crying on the other side of the room. Her tears were as rain, numerous and cool on the tiles. "Oh, Ettil, how can you think this way?"

Ettil laid aside his metal book which, at his beckoning, had been singing him a story all morning from its thin golden-wired frame.

"I've tried to explain," he said. "This is a foolish thing, Mars invading Earth. We'll be destroyed, utterly."

Outside, a banging, crashing boom, a surge of brass, a drum, a cry, marching feet, pennants and songs. Through the stone streets the army, fire weapons to shoulder, stamped. Children skipped after. Old women waved dirty flags.

"I shall remain on Mars and read a book," said Ettil.

A blunt knock on the door. Tylla answered. Father-in-law stormed in. "What's this I hear about my son-in-law? A traitor?"

"Yes, Father."

"You're not fighting in the Martian Army?"

"No, Father."

"Gods!" The old father turned very red. "A plague on your name! You'll be shot."

"Shoot me, then, and have it over."

"Who ever heard of a Martian *not* invading? Who!"

"Nobody. It is, I admit, quite incredible."

"Incredible," husked the witch voices under the window.

"Father, can't you reason with him?" demanded Tylla.

"Reason with a dung heap," cried Father, eyes blazing. He came and stood over Ettil. "Bands playing, a fine day, women weeping, children jumping, everything right, men marching bravely, and you sit here! Oh, shame!"

"Shame," sobbed the faraway voices in the hedge.

"Get the devil out of my house with your inane chatter," said Ettil, exploding. "Take your medals and your drums and run!"

He shoved Father-in-law past a screaming wife, only to have the door thrown wide at this moment, as a military detail entered.

A voice shouted, "Ettil Vrye?"

"Yes!"

"You are under arrest!"

"Good-by, my dear wife. I am off to the wars with these fools!" shouted Ettil, dragged through the door by the men in bronze mesh.

"Good-by, good-by," said the town witches, fading away. . . .

The cell was neat and clean. Without a book, Ettil was nervous. He gripped the bars and watched the rockets shoot up into the night air. The stars were cold and numerous; they seemed to scatter when every rocket blasted up among them.

"Fools," whispered Ettil. "Fools!"

The cell door opened. One man with a kind of vehicle entered, full of books; books here, there, everywhere in the chambers of the vehicle. Behind him the Military Assignor loomed.

"Ettil Vrye, we want to know why you had these illegal Earth books in your house. These copies of *Wonder Stories*, *Scientific Tales*, *Fantastic Stories*. Explain." The man gripped Ettil's wrist.

Ettil shook him free. "If you're going to shoot me, shoot me. That literature, from Earth, is the very reason why I won't try to invade them. It's the reason why your invasion will fail."

"How so?" The assignor scowled and turned to the yellowed magazines.

"Pick any copy," said Ettil. "Any one at all. Nine out of ten stories in the years 1929, '30 to '50, Earth calendar, have every Martian invasion successfully invading Earth."

"Ah!" The assignor smiled, nodded.

"And then," said Ettil, "failing."

"That's treason! Owning such literature!"

"So be it, if you wish. But let me draw a few conclusions. Invariably, each invasion is thwarted by a young man, usually lean, usually Irish, usually alone, named Mick or Rick or Jick or Bannon, who destroys the Martians."

"You don't believe that!"

"No, I don't believe Earthmen can actually do that—no. But they have a background, understand, Assignor, of generations of children reading just such fiction, absorbing it. They have nothing but a literature of invasions successfully thwarted. Can you say the same for Martian literature?"

"Well——"

"No."

"I guess not."

"You know not. We never wrote stories of such a fantastic nature. Now we rebel, we attack, and we shall die."

"I don't see your reasoning on that. Where does this tie in with the magazine stories?"

"Morale. A big thing. The Earthmen know they can't fail. It is in them like blood beating in their veins. They cannot fail. They will repel each invasion, no matter how well organized. Their youth of reading just such fiction as this has given them a faith we cannot equal. We Martians? We are uncertain; we know that we might fail. Our morale is low, in spite of the banged drums and tooted horns."

"I won't listen to this treason," cried the assignor. "This fiction will be burned, as you will be, within the next ten minutes. You have a choice, Ettil Vrye. Join the Legion of War, or burn."

"It is a choice of deaths. I choose to burn."

"Men!"

He was hustled out into the courtyard. There he saw his carefully hoarded reading matter set to the torch. A special pit was prepared, with oil five feet deep in it. This, with a great thunder, was set afire. Into this, in a minute, he would be pushed.

On the far side of the courtyard, in shadow, he noticed the solemn figure of his son standing alone, his great yellow eyes luminous with sorrow and fear. He did not put out his hand or speak, but only looked at his father like some dying animal, a wordless animal seeking rescue.

Ettil looked at the flaming pit. He felt the rough hands seize him, strip him, push him forward to the hot perimeter of death. Only then did Ettil swallow and cry out, "Wait!"

The assignor's face, bright with the orange fire, pushed forward in the trembling air. "What is it?"

"I will join the Legion of War," replied Ettil.

"Good! Release him!"

The hands fell away.

As he turned he saw his son standing far across the court, waiting. His son was not smiling, only waiting. In the sky a bronze rocket leaped across the stars, ablaze. . . .

"And now we bid good-by to these stalwart warriors," said the assignor. The band thumped and the wind blew a fine sweet rain of tears gently upon the sweating army. The children cavorted. In the chaos Ettil saw his wife weeping with pride, his son solemn and silent at her side.

They marched into the ship, everybody laughing and brave. They buckled themselves into their spiderwebs. All through the tense ship the spiderwebs were filled with lounging, lazy men. They chewed on bits of food and waited. A great lid slammed shut. A valve hissed.

"Off to Earth and destruction," whispered Ettil.

"What?" asked someone.

"Off to glorious victory," said Ettil, grimacing.

The rocket jumped.

Space, thought Ettil. Here we are banging across black inks and pink lights of space in a brass kettle. Here we are, a celebratory rocket heaved out to fill the Earthmen's eyes with fear flames as they look up to the sky. What is it like, being far, far away from your home, your wife, your child, here and now?

He tried to analyze his trembling. It was like tying your most secret inward working organs to Mars and then jumping out a million miles. Your heart was still on Mars, pumping, glowing. Your brain was still on Mars, thinking, crenulated, like an abandoned torch. Your stomach was still on Mars, somnolent, trying to digest the final dinner. Your lungs were still in the cool blue wine air of Mars, a soft folded bellows screaming for release, one part of you longing for the rest.

For here you were, a meshless, cogless automaton, a body upon which officials had performed clinical autopsy and left all of you that counted back upon the empty seas and strewn over the darkened hills. Here you were, bottle-empty, fireless, chill, with only your hands to give death to Earthmen. A pair of hands is all you are now, he thought in cold remoteness.

Here you lie in the tremendous web. Others are about you, but they are whole—whole hearts and bodies. But all of you that lives is back there walking the desolate seas in evening winds. This thing here, this cold clay thing, is already dead.

"Attack stations, attack stations, attack!"

"Ready, ready, ready!"

"Up!"

"Out of the webs, quick!"

Ettil moved. Somewhere before him his two cold hands moved.

How swift it has all been, he thought. A year ago one Earth rocket reached Mars. Our scientists, with their incredible telepathic ability, copied it; our workers, with their incredible plants, reproduced it a hundredfold. No other Earth ship has reached Mars since then, and yet we know their language perfectly, all of us. We know their culture, their logic. And we shall pay the price of our brilliance. . . .

"Guns on the ready!"

"Right!"

"Sights!"

"Reading by miles?"

"Ten thousand!"

"Attack!"

A humming silence. A silence of insects throbbing in the walls of the rocket. The insect singing of tiny bobbins and levers and whirls of wheels. Silence of waiting men. Silence of glands emitting the slow steady pulse of sweat under arm, on brow, under staring pale eyes!

"Wait! Ready!"

Ettil hung onto his sanity with his fingernails, hung hard and long.

Silence, silence, silence. Waiting.

Teeee-e-ee!

"What's that?"

"Earth radio!"

"Cut them in!"

"They're trying to reach us, call us. Cut them in!"

Eee-e-e!

"Here they are! Listen!"

"Calling Martian invasion fleet!"

The listening silence, the insect hum pulling back to let the sharp Earth voice crack in upon the rooms of waiting men.

"This is Earth calling. This is William Sommers, president of the Association of United American Producers!"

Ettil held tight to his station, bent forward, eyes shut.

"Welcome to Earth."

"What?" the men in the rocket roared. "What did he say?"

"Yes, welcome to Earth."

"It's a trick!"

Ettil shivered, opened his eyes to stare in bewilderment at the unseen voice from the ceiling source.

"Welcome! Welcome to green, industrial Earth!" declared the friendly voice. "With open arms we welcome you, to turn a bloody invasion into a time of friendships that will last through all of Time."

"A trick!"

"Hush, listen!"

"Many years ago we of Earth renounced war, destroyed our atom bombs. Now, unprepared as we are, there is nothing for us but to welcome you. The planet is yours. We ask only mercy from you good and merciful invaders."

"It can't be true!" a voice whispered.

"It must be a trick!"

"Land and be welcomed, all of you," said Mr. William Sommers of Earth. "Land anywhere. Earth is yours; we are all brothers!"

Ettil began to laugh. Everyone in the room turned to see him. The other Martians blinked. "He's gone mad!"

He did not stop laughing until they hit him.

The tiny fat man in the center of the hot rocket tarmac at Green Town, California, jerked out a clean white handkerchief and touched it to his wet brow. He squinted blindly from the fresh plank platform at the fifty thousand people restrained behind a fence of policemen, arm to arm. Everybody looked at the sky.

"There they are!"

A gasp.

"No, just sea gulls!"

A disappointed grumble.

"I'm beginning to think it would have been better to have declared war on them," whispered the mayor. "Then we could all go home."

"*Sh-h!*" said his wife.

"There!" The crowd roared.

Out of the sun came the Martian rockets.

"Everybody ready?" The mayor glanced nervously about.

"Yes, sir," said Miss California 1965.

"Yes," said Miss America 1940, who had come rushing up at the last minute as a substitute for Miss America 1966, who was ill at home.

"Yes siree," said Mr. Biggest Grapefruit in San Fernando Valley 1956, eagerly.

"Ready, band?"

The band poised its brass like so many guns.

"Ready!"

The rockets landed. "Go!"

The band played "California, Here I Come" ten times.

From noon until one o'clock the mayor made a speech, shaking his hands in the direction of the silent, apprehensive rockets.

At one-fifteen the seals of the rockets opened.

The band played "Oh, You Golden State" three times.

Ettil and fifty other Martians leaped out, guns at the ready.

The mayor ran forward with the key to Earth in his hands.

The band played "Santa Claus Is Coming to Town," and a

full chorus of singers imported from Long Beach sang different words to it, something about "Martians Are Coming to Town."

Seeing no weapons about, the Martians relaxed, but kept their guns out.

From one-thirty until two-fifteen the mayor made the same speech over for the benefit of the Martians.

At two-thirty Miss America of 1940 volunteered to kiss all the Martians if they lined up.

At two-thirty and ten seconds the band played "How Do You Do, Everybody," to cover up the confusion caused by Miss America's suggestion.

At two thirty-five Mr. Biggest Grapefruit presented the Martians with a two-ton truck full of grapefruit.

At two thirty-seven the mayor gave them all free passes to the Elite and Majestic theaters, combining this gesture with another speech which lasted until after three.

The band played, and the fifty thousand people sang, "For They Are Jolly Good Fellows."

It was over at four o'clock.

Ettil sat down in the shadow of the rocket, two of his fellows with him. "So this is Earth!"

"I say kill the filthy rats," said one Martian. "I don't trust them. They're sneaky. What's their motive for treating us this way?" He held up a box of something that rustled. "What's this stuff they gave me? A sample, they said." He read the label. BLIX, *the new sudsy soap.*

The crowd had drifted about, was mingling with the Martians like a carnival throng. Everywhere was the buzzing murmur of people fingering the rockets, asking questions.

Ettil was cold. He was beginning to tremble even more now. "Don't you feel it?" he whispered. "The tenseness, the evilness of all this. Something's going to happen to us. They have some plan. Something subtle and horrible. They're going to do something to us—I know."

"I say kill every one of them!"

"How can you kill people who call you 'pal' and 'buddy'?" asked another Martian.

Ettil shook his head. "They're sincere. And yet I feel as if we were in a big acid vat melting away, away. I'm frightened."

He put his mind out to touch among the crowd. "Yes, they're really friendly, hail-fellows-well-met (one of their terms). One huge mass of common men, loving dogs and cats and Martians equally. And yet—and yet——"

The band played "Roll Out the Barrel." Free beer was being distributed through the courtesy of Hagenback Beer, Fresno, California.

The sickness came.

The men poured out fountains of slush from their mouths. The sound of sickness filled the land.

Gagging, Ettil sat beneath a sycamore tree. "A plot, a plot—a horrible plot," he groaned, holding his stomach.

"What did you eat?" The assignor stood over him.

"Something that they called popcorn," groaned Ettil.

"And?"

"And some sort of long meat on a bun, and some yellow liquid in an iced vat, and some sort of fish and something called pastrami," sighed Ettil, eyelids flickering.

The moans of the Martian invaders sounded all about.

"Kill the plotting snakes!" somebody cried weakly.

"Hold on," said the assignor. "It's merely hospitality. They overdid it. Up on your feet now, men. Into the town. We've got to place small garrisons of men about to make sure all is well. Other ships are landing in other cities. We've our job to do here."

The men gained their feet and stood blinking stupidly about.

"Forward, march!"

One, two, three, *four*! One, two, three, *four*! . . .

The white stores of the little town lay dreaming in shimmering heat. Heat emanated from everything—poles, concrete, metal, awnings, roofs, tar paper—everything.

The sound of Martian feet sounded on the asphalt.

"Careful, men!" whispered the assignor.

They walked past a beauty shop.

From inside, a furtive giggle.

"Look!"

A coppery head bobbed and vanished like a doll in the window. A blue eye glinted and winked at a keyhole.

"It's a plot," whispered Ettil. "A plot, I tell you!"

The odors of perfume were fanned out on the summer air by the whirling vents of the grottoes where the women hid like undersea creatures, under electric cones, their hair curled into wild whorls and peaks, their eyes shrewd and glassy, animal and sly, their mouths painted a neon red. Fans were whirring, the perfumed wind issuing upon the stillness, moving among green trees, creeping among the amazed Martians.

"For God's sake!" screamed Ettil, his nerves suddenly breaking loose. "Let's get in our rockets—go home! They'll get us! Those horrid things in there. See them? Those evil undersea things, those women in their cool little caverns of artificial rock!"

"Shut up!"

Look at them in there, he thought, drifting their dresses like cool green gills over their pillar legs. He shouted.

"Someone shut his mouth!"

"They'll rush out on us, hurling chocolate boxes and copies of *Kleig Love* and *Holly Pick-ture*, shrieking with their red greasy mouths! Inundate us with banality, destroy our sensibilities! Look at them, being electrocuted by devices, their voices like hums and chants and murmurs! Do you dare go in there?"

"Why not?" asked the other Martians.

"They'll fry you, bleach you, change you! Crack you, flake you away until you're nothing but a husband, a working man, the one with the money who pays so they can come sit in there devouring their evil chocolates! Do you think you could control them?"

"Yes, by the gods!"

From a distance a voice drifted, a high and shrill voice, a woman's voice saying, "Ain't that middle one there cute?"

"Martians ain't so bad after all. Gee, they're just men," said another, fading.

"Hey, there. *Yoo-hoo!* Martians! Hey!"

Yelling, Ettil ran. . . .

He sat in a park and trembled steadily. He remembered what he had seen. Looking up at the dark night sky, he felt so far from home, so deserted. Even now, as he sat among the still trees, in the distance he could see Martian warriors walking the streets with the Earth women, vanishing into the phantom darknesses of the little emotion palaces to hear the ghastly sounds of white things moving on gray screens, with little frizz-haired women beside them, wads of gelatinous gum working in their jaws, other wads under the seats, hardening with the fossil imprints of the women's tiny cat teeth forever imbedded therein. The cave of winds—the cinema.

"Hello."

He jerked his head in terror.

A woman sat on the bench beside him, chewing gum lazily.

"Don't run off; I don't bite," she said.

"Oh," he said.

"Like to go to the pictures?" she said.

"No."

"Aw, come on," she said. "Everybody else is."

"No," he said. "Is that all you do in this world?"

"All? Ain't that enough?" Her blue eyes widened suspiciously. "What you want me to do—sit home, read a book? Ha, ha! That's rich."

Ettil stared at her a moment before asking a question.

"Do you do anything else?" he asked.

"Ride in cars. You got a car? You oughta get you a big new convertible Podler Six. Gee, they're fancy! Any man with a Podler Six can go out with any gal, you bet!" she said, blinking at him. "I bet you got all kinds of money—you come from Mars and all. I bet if you really wanted you could get a Podler Six and travel everywhere."

"To the show maybe?"

"What's wrong with 'at?"

"Nothing—nothing."

"You know what you talk like, mister?" she said. "A Communist! Yes, sir, that's the kinda talk nobody stands for, by gosh. Nothing wrong with our little old system. We was good enough to let you Martians invade, and we never raised even our bitty finger, did we?"

"That's what I've been trying to understand," said Ettil. "Why did you let us?"

"'Cause we're bighearted, mister; that's why! Just remember that, bighearted." She walked off to look for someone else.

Gathering courage to himself, Ettil began to write a letter to his wife, moving the pen carefully over the paper on his knee.

"Dear Tylla——"

But again he was interrupted. A small-little-girl-of-an-old-woman, with a pale round wrinkled little face, shook her tambourine in front of his nose, forcing him to glance up.

"Brother," she cried, eyes blazing. "Have you been saved?"

"Am I in danger?" Ettil dropped his pen, jumping.

"Terrible danger!" she wailed, clanking her tambourine, gazing at the sky. "You need to be saved, brother, in the worst way!"

"I'm inclined to agree," he said, trembling.

"We saved lots already today. I saved three myself, of you Mars people. Ain't that nice?" She grinned at him.

"I guess so."

She was acutely suspicious. She leaned forward with her secret whisper. "Brother," she wanted to know, "you been baptized?"

"I don't know," he whispered back.

"You don't know?" she cried, flinging up hand and tambourine.

"Is it like being shot?" he asked.

"Brother," she said, "you are in a bad and sinful condition. I blame it on your ignorant bringing up. I bet those schools on Mars are terrible—don't teach you no truth at all. Just a pack of made-up lies. Brother, you got to be baptized if you want to be happy."

"Will it make me happy even in this world here?" he said.

"Don't ask for everything on your platter," she said. "Be satisfied with a wrinkled pea, for there's another world we're all going to that's better than this one."

"I know that world," he said.

"It's peaceful," she said.

"Yes."

"There's quiet," she said.

"Yes."

"There's milk and honey flowing."

"Why, yes," he said.

"And everybody's laughing."

"I can see it now," he said.

"A better world," she said.

"Far better," he said. "Yes, Mars is a great planet."

"Mister," she said, tightening up and almost flinging the tambourine in his face, "you been joking with me?"

"Why, no." He was embarrassed and bewildered. "I thought you were talking about——"

"Not about mean old nasty Mars, I tell you, mister! It's your type that is going to boil for years, and suffer and break out in black pimples and be tortured——"

"I must admit Earth isn't very nice. You've described it beautifully."

"Mister, you're funning me again!" she cried angrily.

"No, no—please. I plead ignorance."

"Well," she said, "you're a heathen, and heathens are improper. Here's a paper. Come to this address tomorrow night and be baptized and be happy. We shouts and we stomps and we talk in voices, so if you want to hear our all-cornet, all-brass band, you come, won't you now?"

"I'll try," he said hesitantly.

Down the street she went, patting her tambourine, singing at the top of her voice, "Happy Am I, I'm Always Happy."

Dazed, Ettil returned to his letter.

"Dear Tylla: To think that in my naïveté I imagined that the Earthmen would have to counterattack with guns and bombs. No, no. I was sadly wrong. There is no Rick or Mick or Jick or Bannon—those lever fellows who save worlds. No.

"There are blond robots with pink rubber bodies, real, but somehow unreal, alive but somehow automatic in all responses, living in caves all of their lives. Their derrières are incredible in girth. Their eyes are fixed and motionless from an endless time of staring at picture screens. The only muscles they have occur in their jaws from their ceaseless chewing of gum.

"And it is not only these, my dear Tylla, but the entire civilization into which we have been dropped like a shovelful of seeds into a large concrete mixer. Nothing of us will survive. We will be killed not by the gun but by the glad-hand. We will be destroyed not by the rocket but by the automobile . . ."

Somebody screamed. A crash, another crash. Silence.

Ettil leaped up from his letter. Outside, on the street,

two cars had crashed. One full of Martians, another with Earthmen. Ettil returned to his letter:

"Dear, dear Tylla, a few statistics if you will allow. Forty-five thousand people killed every year on this continent of America; made into jelly right in the can, as it were, in the automobiles. Red blood jelly, with white marrow bones like sudden thoughts, ridiculous horror thoughts, transfixed in the immutable jelly. The cars roll up in tight neat sardine rolls—all sauce, all silence.

"Blood manure for green buzzing summer flies, all over the highways. Faces made into Halloween masks by sudden stops. Halloween is one of their holidays. I think they worship the automobile on that night—something to do with death, anyway.

"You look out your window and see two people lying atop each other in friendly fashion who, a moment ago, had never met before, dead. I foresee our army mashed, diseased, trapped in cinemas by witches and gum. Sometime in the next day I shall try to escape back to Mars before it is too late.

"Somewhere on Earth tonight, my Tylla, there is a Man with a Lever, which, when he pulls it, Will Save the World. The man is now unemployed. His switch gathers dust. He himself plays pinochle.

"The women of this evil planet are drowning us in a tide of banal sentimentality, misplaced romance, and one last fling before the makers of glycerin boil them down for usage. Good night, Tylla. Wish me well, for I shall probably die trying to escape. My love to our child."

Weeping silently, he folded the letter and reminded himself to mail it later at the rocket post.

He left the park. What was there to do? Escape? But how? Return to the post late tonight, steal one of the rockets alone and go back to Mars? Would it be possible? He shook his head. He was much too confused.

All that he really knew was that if he stayed here he would soon be the property of a lot of things that buzzed and snorted and hissed, that gave off fumes or stenches. In six months he would be the owner of a large pink, trained ulcer, a blood pressure of algebraic dimensions, a myopia this side of blindness, and nightmares as deep as oceans and infested with improbable lengths of dream intestines through which he must violently force his way each night. No, no.

He looked at the haunted faces of the Earthmen drifting violently along in their mechanical death boxes. Soon—yes, very soon—they would invent an auto with six silver handles on it!

"Hey, there!"

An auto horn. A large long hearse of a car, black and ominous pulled to the curb. A man leaned out.

"You a Martian?"

"Yes."

"Just the man I gotta see. Hop in quick—the chance of a lifetime. Hop in. Take you to a real nice joint where we can talk. Come on—don't stand there."

As if hypnotized, Ettil opened the door of the car, got in.

They drove off.

"What'll it be, E.V.? How about a manhattan? Two manhattans, waiter. Okay, E.V. This is my treat. This is on me and Big Studios! Don't even touch your wallet. Pleased to meet you, E.V. My name's R. R. Van Plank. Maybe you hearda me? No? Well, shake anyhow."

Ettil felt his hand massaged and dropped. They were in a dark hole with music and waiters drifting about. Two drinks were set down. It had all happened so swiftly. Now Van Plank, hands crossed on his chest, was surveying his Martian discovery.

"What I want you for, E.V., is this. It's the most magnanimous idea I ever got in my life. I don't know how it came to me, just in a flash. I was sitting home tonight and I thought to myself, My God, what a picture it would make! *Invasion of Earth by Mars.* So what I got to do? I got to find an adviser for the film. So I climbed in my car and found you and here we are. Drink up! Here's to your health and our future. *Skoal!*"

"But——" said Ettil.

"Now, I know, you'll want money. Well, we got plenty of that. Besides, I got a li'l black book full of peaches I can lend you."

"I don't like most of your Earth fruit and——"

"You're a card, mac, really. Well, here's how I get the picture in my mind—listen." He leaned forward excitedly. "We got a flash scene of the Martians at a big powwow, drummin' drums, gettin' stewed on Mars. In the background are huge silver cities——"

"But that's not the way Martian cities are——"

"We got to have color, kid. Color. Let your pappy fix this. Anyway, there are all the Martians doing a dance around a fire——"

"We don't dance around fires——"

"In *this* film you got a fire and you dance," declared Van Plank, eyes shut, proud of his certainty. He nodded, dreaming it over on his tongue. "Then we got a beautiful Martian woman, tall and blond."

"Martian women are dark——"

"Look, I don't see how we're going to be happy, E.V. By the way, son, you ought to change your name. What was it again?"

"Ettil."

"That's a woman's name. I'll give you a better one. Call you Joe. Okay, Joe. As I was saying, our Martian women are gonna be blond, because, see, just because. Or else your poppa won't be happy. You got any suggestions?"

"I thought that——"

"And another thing we gotta have is a scene, very tearful, where the Martian woman saves the whole ship of Martian men from dying when a meteor or something hits the ship. That'll make a whackeroo of a scene. You know, I'm glad I found you, Joe. You're going to have a good deal with us, I tell you."

Ettil reached out and held the man's wrist tight. "Just a minute. There's something I want to ask you."

"Sure, Joe, shoot."

"Why are you being so nice to us? We invade your planet, and you welcome us—everybody—like long-lost children. Why?"

"They sure grow 'em green on Mars, don't they? You're a naïve-type guy—I can see from way over here. Mac, look at it this way. We're all Little People, ain't we?" He waved a small tan hand garnished with emeralds.

"We're all common as dirt, ain't we? Well, here on Earth, we're proud of that. This is the century of the Common Man, Bill, and we're proud we're small. Billy, you're looking at a planet full of Saroyans. Yes, sir. A great big fat family of friendly Saroyans—everybody loving everybody. We understand you Martians, Joe, and we know why you invaded Earth. We know how lonely you were up on that little cold planet Mars, how you envied us our cities——"

"Our civilization is much older than yours——"

"Please, Joe, you make me unhappy when you interrupt. Let me finish my theory and then you talk all you want. As I was saying, you was lonely up there, and down you came to see our cities and our women and all, and we welcomed you in, because you're our brothers, Common Men like all of us.

"And then, as a kind of side incident, Roscoe, there's a certain little small profit to be had from this invasion. I mean for instance this picture I plan, which will net us, neat, a billion dollars, I bet. Next week we start putting out a special Martian doll at thirty bucks a throw. Think of the millions there. I also got a contract to make a Martian game to sell for five bucks. There's all sorts of angles."

"I see," said Ettil, drawing back.

"And then of course there's that whole nice new market. Think of all the depilatories and gum and shoeshine we can sell to you Martians."

"Wait. Another question."

"Shoot."

"What's your first name? What's the R.R. stand for?"

"Richard Robert."

Ettil looked at the ceiling. "Do they sometimes, perhaps, on occasion, once in a while, by accident, call you—Rick?"

"How'd you guess, mac? Rick, sure."

Ettil sighed and began to laugh and laugh. He put out his hand. "So you're Rick? Rick! So you're Rick!"

"What's the joke, laughing boy? Let Poppa in!"

"You wouldn't understand—a private joke. Ha, ha!" Tears ran down his cheeks and into his open mouth. He pounded the table again and again. "So you're Rick. Oh, how different, how funny. No bulging muscles, no lean jaw, no gun. Only a wallet full of money and an emerald ring and a big middle!"

"Hey, watch the language! I may not be no Apollo, but——"

"Shake hands, Rick. I've wanted to meet you. You're the man who'll conquer Mars, with cocktail shakers and foot arches and poker chips and riding crops and leather boots and checkered caps and rum collinses."

"I'm only a humble businessman," said Van Plank, eyes slyly down. "I do my work and take my humble little piece of money pie. But, as I was saying, Mort, I been thinking of the market on Mars for Uncle Wiggily games and Dick Tracy comics; all new. A big wide field never even heard of cartoons, right? Right! So we just toss a great big bunch of stuff on the Martians' heads. They'll fight for it, kid, fight! Who wouldn't, for perfumes and Paris dresses and Oshkosh overalls, eh? And nice new shoes——"

"We don't wear shoes."

"What have I got here?" R.R. asked of the ceiling. "A planet full of Okies? Look, Joe, we'll take care of that. We'll shame everyone into wearing shoes. Then we sell them the polish!"

"Oh."

He slapped Ettil's arm. "Is it a deal? Will you be technical director on my film? You'll get two hundred a week to start, a five-hundred top. What you say?"

"I'm sick," said Ettil. He had drunk the manhattan and was now turning blue.

"Say, I'm sorry. I didn't know it would do that to you. Let's get some fresh air."

In the open air Ettil felt better. He swayed. "So that's why Earth took us in?"

"Sure, son. Any time an Earthman can turn an honest dollar, watch him steam. The customer is always right. No hard feelings. Here's my card. Be at the studio in Hollywood tomorrow morning at nine o'clock. They'll show you your office. I'll arrive at eleven and see you then. Be sure you get there at nine o'clock. It's a strict rule."

"Why?"

"Gallagher, you're a queer oyster, but I love you. Good night. Happy invasion!"

The car drove off.

Ettil blinked after it, incredulous. Then, rubbing his brow with the palm of his hand, he walked slowly along the street toward the rocket port.

"Well, what are you going to do?" he asked himself, aloud.

The rockets lay gleaming in the moonlight, silent. From

the city came the sounds of distant revelry. In the medical compound an extreme case of nervous breakdown was being tended to: a young Martian who, by his screams, had seen too much, drunk too much, heard too many songs on the little red-and-yellow boxes in the drinking places, and had been chased around innumerable tables by a large elephant-like woman. He kept murmuring:

"Can't breathe . . . crushed, trapped."

The sobbing faded. Ettil came out of the shadows and moved on across a wide avenue toward the ships. Far over, he could see the guards lying about drunkenly. He listened. From the vast city came the faint sounds of cars and music and sirens. And he imagined other sounds too: the insidious whir of malt machines stirring malts to fatten the warriors and make them lazy and forgetful, the narcotic voices of the cinema caverns lulling and lulling the Martians fast, fast into a slumber through which, all of their remaining lives, they would sleepwalk.

A year from now, how many Martians dead of cirrhosis of the liver, bad kidneys, high blood pressure, suicide?

He stood in the middle of the empty avenue. Two blocks away a car was rushing toward him.

He had a choice: stay here, take the studio job, report for work each morning as adviser on a picture, and, in time, come to agree with the producer that, yes indeed, there were massacres on Mars; yes, the women were tall and blond; yes, there were tribal dances and sacrifices; yes, yes, yes. Or he could walk over and get into a rocket ship and, alone, return to Mars.

"But what about next year?" he said.

The Blue Canal Night Club brought to Mars. The Ancient City Gambling Casino, Built Right Inside. Yes, Right Inside a Real Martian Ancient City! Neons, racing forms blowing in the old cities, picnic lunches in the ancestral graveyards—all of it, all of it.

But not quite yet. In a few days he could be home. Tylla would be waiting with their son, and then for the last few years of gentle life he might sit with his wife in the blowing weather on the edge of the canal reading his good, gentle books, sipping a rare and light wine, talking and living out their short time until the neon bewilderment fell from the sky.

And then perhaps he and Tylla might move into the blue mountains and hide for another year or two until the tourists came to snap their cameras and say how quaint things were.

He knew just what he would say to Tylla. "War is a bad thing, but peace can be a living horror."

He stood in the middle of the wide avenue.

Turning, it was with no surprise that he saw a car bearing down upon him, a car full of screaming children. These boys and girls, none older than sixteen, were swerving and ricocheting their open-top car down the avenue. He saw them point at him and yell. He heard the motor roar louder. The car sped forward at sixty miles an hour.

He began to run.

Yes, yes, he thought tiredly, with the car upon him, how strange, how sad. It sounds so much like . . . a concrete mixer.

Marionettes, Inc.

THEY WALKED SLOWLY down the street at about ten in the evening, talking calmly. They were both about thirty-five, both eminently sober.

"But why so early?" said Smith.

"Because," said Braling.

"Your first night out in years and you go home at ten o'clock."

"Nerves, I suppose."

"What I wonder is how you ever managed it. I've been trying to get you out for ten years for a quiet drink. And now, on the one night, you insist on turning in early."

"Mustn't crowd my luck," said Braling.

"What did you do, put sleeping powder in your wife's coffee?"

"No, that would be unethical. You'll see soon enough."

They turned a corner. "Honestly, Braling, I hate to say this, but you *have* been patient with her. You may not admit it to me, but marriage has been awful for you, hasn't it?"

"I wouldn't say that."

"It's got around, anyway, here and there, how she got you to marry her. That time back in 1979 when you were going to Rio——"

"Dear Rio. I never *did* see it after all my plans."

"And how she tore her clothes and rumpled her hair and threatened to call the police unless you married her."

"She always was nervous, Smith, understand."

"It was more than unfair. You didn't love her. You told her as much, didn't you?"

"I recall that I was quite firm on the subject."

"But you married her anyhow."

"I had my business to think of, as well as my mother and father. A thing like that would have killed them."

"And it's been ten years."

"Yes," said Braling, his gray eyes steady. "But I think perhaps it might change now. I think what I've waited for has come about. Look here."

He drew forth a long blue ticket.

"Why, it's a ticket for Rio on the Thursday rocket!"

"Yes, I'm finally going to make it."

"But how wonderful! You *do* deserve it! But won't *she* object? Cause trouble?"

Braling smiled nervously. "She won't know I'm gone. I'll be back in a month and no one the wiser, except you."

Smith sighed. "I wish I were going with you."

"Poor Smith, *your* marriage hasn't exactly been roses, has it?"

"Not exactly, married to a woman who overdoes it. I mean, after all, when you've been married ten years, you don't expect a woman to sit on your lap for two hours every evening, call you at work twelve times a day and talk baby talk. And it seems to me that in the last month she's gotten worse. I wonder if perhaps she isn't just a little simple-minded?"

"Ah, Smith, always the conservative. Well, here's my house. Now, would you like to know my secret? How I made it out this evening?"

"Will you really tell?"

"Look up, there!" said Braling.

They both stared up through the dark air.

In the window above them, on the second floor, a shade was raised. A man about thirty-five years old, with a touch of gray at either temple, sad gray eyes, and a small thin mustache looked down at them.

"Why, that's you!" cried Smith.

"Sh-h-h, not so loud!" Braling waved upward. The man in the window gestured significantly and vanished.

"I must be insane," said Smith.

"Hold on a moment."

They waited.

The street door of the apartment opened and the tall spare gentleman with the mustache and the grieved eyes came out to meet them.

"Hello, Braling," he said.

"Hello, Braling," said Braling.

They were identical.

Smith stared. "Is this your twin brother? I never knew——"

"No, no," said Braling quietly. "Bend close. Put your ear to Braling Two's chest."

Smith hesitated and then leaned forward to place his head against the uncomplaining ribs.

Tick-tick-tick-tick-tick-tick-tick-tick.

"Oh no! It *can't* be!"

"It is."

"Let me listen again."

Tick-tick-tick-tick-tick-tick-tick-tick.

Smith staggered back and fluttered his eyelids, appalled. He reached out and touched the warm hands and the cheeks of the thing.

"Where'd you get him?"

"Isn't he excellently fashioned?"

"Incredible. Where?"

"Give the man your card, Braling Two."

Braling Two did a magic trick and produced a white card:

MARIONETTES, INC.

Duplicate self or friends; new humanoid plastic 1990 models, guaranteed against all physical wear. From $7,600 to our $15,000 de luxe model.

"No," said Smith.

"Yes," said Braling.

"Naturally," said Braling Two.

"How long has this gone on?"

"I've had him for a month. I keep him in the cellar in a toolbox. My wife never goes downstairs, and I have the only lock and key to that box. Tonight I said I wished to take a walk to buy a cigar. I went down cellar and took Braling Two out of his box and sent him back up to sit with my wife while I came on out to see you, Smith."

"Wonderful! He even *smells* like you: Bond Street and Melachrinos!"

"It may be splitting hairs, but I think it highly ethical. After all, what my wife wants most of all is *me*. This marionette *is* me to the hairiest detail. I've been home all evening. I shall be home with her for the next month. In the meantime another gentleman will be in Rio after ten years of waiting. When I return from Rio, Braling Two here will go back in his box."

Smith thought that over a minute or two. "Will he walk around without sustenance for a month?" he finally asked.

"For six months if necessary. And he's built to do everything—eat, sleep, perspire—everything, natural as natural is. You'll take good care of my wife, won't you, Braling Two?"

"Your wife is rather nice," said Braling Two. "I've grown rather fond of her."

Smith was beginning to tremble. "How long has Marionettes, Inc., been in business?"

"Secretly, for two years."

"Could I—I mean, is there a possibility——" Smith took his friend's elbow earnestly. "Can you tell me where I can get one, a robot, a marionette, for myself? You *will* give me the address, won't you?"

"Here you are."

Smith took the card and turned it round and round. "Thank you," he said. "You don't know what this means. Just a little respite. A night or so, once a month even. My wife loves me so much she can't bear to have me gone an hour. I love her dearly, you know, but remember the old poem: 'Love will fly if held too lightly, love will die if held too tightly.' I just want her to relax her grip a little bit."

"You're lucky, at least, that your wife loves you. Hate's my problem. Not so easy."

"Oh, Nettie loves me madly. It will be my task to make her love me comfortably."

"Good luck to you, Smith. Do drop around while I'm in Rio. It will seem strange, if you suddenly stop calling by, to my wife. You're to treat Braling Two, here, just like me."

"Right! Good-by. And thank you."

Smith went smiling down the street. Braling and Braling Two turned and walked into the apartment hall.

On the crosstown bus Smith whistled softly, turning the white card in his fingers:

> Clients must be pledged to secrecy, for while an act is pending in Congress to legalize Marionettes, Inc., it is still a felony, if caught, to use one.

"Well," said Smith.

> Clients must have a mold made of their body and a color index check of their eyes, lips, hair, skin, etc. Clients must expect to wait for two months until their model is finished.

Not so long, thought Smith. Two months from now my ribs will have a chance to mend from the crushing they've taken. Two months from now my hand will heal from being so constantly held. Two months from now my bruised underlip will begin to reshape itself. I don't mean to sound *ungrateful* . . . He flipped the card over.

> Marionettes, Inc., is two years old and has a fine record of satisfied customers behind it. Our motto is "No Strings Attached." Address: 43 South Wesley Drive.

The bus pulled to his stop; he alighted, and while humming up the stairs he thought, Nettie and I have fifteen thousand in our joint bank account. I'll just slip eight thousand out as a business venture, you might say. The marionette will probably pay back my money, with interest, in many ways. Nettie needn't know. He unlocked the door and in a minute was in the bedroom. There lay Nettie, pale, huge, and piously asleep.

"Dear Nettie." He was almost overwhelmed with remorse at her innocent face there in the semidarkness. "If you were awake you would smother me with kisses and coo in my ear. Really, you make me feel like a criminal. You have been such a good, loving wife. Sometimes it is impossible for me to believe you married me instead of that Bud Chapman you once liked. It seems that in the last month you have loved me more wildly than *ever* before."

Tears came to his eyes. Suddenly he wished to kiss her, confess his love, tear up the card, forget the whole business. But as he moved to do this, his hand ached and his ribs cracked and groaned. He stopped, with a pained look in his eyes, and turned away. He moved out into the hall and through the dark rooms. Humming, he opened the kidney desk in the library and filched the bankbook. "Just take eight thousand dollars is all," he said. "No more than that." He stopped. "Wait a minute."

He rechecked the bankbook frantically. "Hold on here!" he cried. "Ten thousand dollars is missing!" He leaped up. "There's only five thousand left! What's she done? What's Nettie done with it? More hats, more clothes, more perfume! Or, wait—I know! She bought that little house on the Hudson she's been talking about for months, without so much as a by your leave!"

He stormed into the bedroom, righteous and indignant. What did she mean, taking their money like this? He bent over her. "Nettie!" he shouted. "Nettie, wake up!"

She did not stir. "What've you done with my money!" he bellowed.

She stirred fitfully. The light from the street flushed over her beautiful cheeks.

There was something about her. His heart throbbed violently. His tongue dried. He shivered. His knees suddenly turned to water. He collapsed. "Nettie, Nettie!" he cried. "What've you done with my money!"

And then, the horrid thought. And then the terror and the loneliness engulfed him. And then the fever and disillusionment. For, without desiring to do so, he bent forward and yet forward again until his fevered ear was resting firmly and irrevocably upon her round pink bosom. "Nettie!" he cried.

Tick-tick-tick-tick-tick-tick-tick-tick-tick-tick-tick.

As Smith walked away down the avenue in the night, Braling and Braling Two turned in at the door to the apartment. "I'm glad he'll be happy too," said Braling.

"Yes," said Braling Two abstractedly.

"Well, it's the cellar box for you, B-Two." Braling guided the other creature's elbow down the stairs to the cellar.

"That's what I want to talk to you about," said Braling Two, as they reached the concrete floor and walked across it. "The cellar. I don't like it. I don't like that toolbox."

"I'll try and fix up something more comfortable."

"Marionettes are made to move, not lie still. How would you like to lie in a box most of the time?"

"Well——"

"You wouldn't like it at all. I keep running. There's no way to shut me off. I'm perfectly alive and I have feelings."

"It'll only be a few days now. I'll be off to Rio and you won't have to stay in the box. You can live upstairs."

Braling Two gestured irritably. "And when you come back from having a good time, back in the box I go."

Braling said, "They didn't tell me at the marionette shop that I'd get a difficult specimen."

"There's a lot they don't know about us," said Braling Two. "We're pretty new. And we're sensitive. I hate the idea of you going off and laughing and lying in the sun in Rio while we're stuck here in the cold."

"But I've wanted that trip all my life," said Braling quietly.

He squinted his eyes and could see the sea and the mountains and the yellow sand. The sound of the waves was good to his inward mind. The sun was fine on his bared shoulders. The wine was most excellent.

"*I'll* never get to go to Rio," said the other man. "Have you thought of that?"

"No, I——"

"And another thing. Your wife."

"What about her?" asked Braling, beginning to edge toward the door.

"I've grown quite fond of her."

"I'm glad you're enjoying your employment." Braling licked his lips nervously.

"I'm afraid you don't understand. I think—I'm in love with her."

Braling took another step and froze. "You're *what*?"

"And I've been thinking," said Braling Two, "how nice it is in Rio and how I'll never get there, and I've thought about your wife and—I think we could be very happy."

"T-that's nice." Braling strolled as casually as he could to the cellar door. "You won't mind waiting a moment, will you? I have to make a phone call."

"To whom?" Braling Two frowned.

"No one important."

"To Marionettes, Incorporated? To tell them to come get me?"

"No, no—nothing like that!" He tried to rush out the door.

A metal-firm grip seized his wrists. "Don't run!"

"Take your hands off!"

"No."

"Did my wife put you up to this?"

"No."

"Did she guess? Did she talk to you? Does she know? Is *that* it?" He screamed. A hand clapped over his mouth.

"You'll never know, will you?" Braling Two smiled delicately. "You'll never know."

Braling struggled. "She *must* have guessed; she *must* have affected you!"

Braling Two said, "I'm going to put you in the box, lock it, and lose the key. Then I'll buy another Rio ticket for your wife."

"Now, now, wait a minute. Hold on. Don't be rash. Let's talk this over!"

"Good-by, Braling."

Braling stiffened. "What do you mean, 'good-by'?"

Ten minutes later Mrs. Braling awoke. She put her hand to her cheek. Someone had just kissed it. She shivered and looked up. "Why—you haven't done that in years," she murmured.

"We'll see what we can do about that," someone said.

The City

THE CITY WAITED twenty thousand years.

The planet moved through space and the flowers of the fields grew up and fell away, and still the city waited; and the rivers of the planet rose and waned and turned to dust. Still the city waited. The winds that had been young and wild grew old and serene, and the clouds of the sky that had been ripped and torn were left alone to drift in idle whitenesses. Still the city waited.

The city waited with its windows and its black obsidian walls and its sky towers and its unpennanted turrets, with its untrod streets and its untouched doorknobs, with not a scrap of paper or a fingerprint upon it. The city waited while the planet arced in space, following its orbit about a blue-white sun, and the seasons passed from ice to fire and back to ice and then to green fields and yellow summer meadows.

It was on a summer afternoon in the middle of the twenty thousandth year that the city ceased waiting.

In the sky a rocket appeared.

The rocket soared over, turned, came back, and landed in the shale meadow fifty yards from the obsidian wall.

There were booted footsteps in the thin grass and calling voices from men within the rocket to men without.

"Ready?"

"All right, men. Careful! Into the city. Jensen, you and Hutchinson patrol ahead. Keep a sharp eye."

The city opened secret nostrils in its black walls and a steady suction vent deep in the body of the city drew storms of air back through channels, through thistle filters and dust collectors, to a fine and tremblingly delicate series of coils and webs which glowed with silver light. Again and again the immense suctions occurred; again and again the odors from the meadow were borne upon warm winds into the city.

"Fire odor, the scent of a fallen meteor, hot metal. A ship has come from another world. The brass smell, the dusty fire smell of burned powder, sulphur, and rocket brimstone."

This information, stamped on tapes which sprocketed into slots, slid down through yellow cogs into further machines.

Click-chakk-chakk-chakk.

A calculator made the sound of a metronome. Five, six, seven, eight, nine. Nine men! An instantaneous typewriter inked this message on tape which slithered and vanished.

Clickety-click-chakk-chakk.

The city awaited the soft tread of their rubberoid boots.

The great city nostrils dilated again.

The smell of butter. In the city air, from the stalking men, faintly, the aura which wafted to the great Nose broke down into memories of milk, cheese, ice cream, butter, the effluvium of a dairy economy.

Click-click.

"Careful, men!"

"Jones, get your gun out. Don't be a fool!"

"The city's dead; why worry?"

"You can't tell."

Now, at the barking talk, the Ears awoke. After centuries of listening to winds that blew small and faint, of hearing leaves strip from trees and grass grow softly in the time of melting snows, now the Ears oiled themselves in a self-lubrication, drew taut, great drums upon which the heartbeat of the invaders might pummel and thud delicately as the tremor of a gnat's wing. The Ears listened and the Nose siphoned up great chambers of odor.

The perspiration of frightened men arose. There were islands of sweat under their arms, and sweat in their hands as they held their guns.

The Nose sifted and worried this air, like a connoisseur busy with an ancient vintage.

Chikk-chikk-chakk-click.

Information rotated down on parallel check tapes. Perspiration; chlorides such and such per cent; sulphates so-and-so; urea nitrogen, ammonia nitrogen, *thus*: creatinine, sugar, lactic acid, *there*!

Bells rang. Small totals jumped up.

The Nose whispered, expelling the tested air. The great Ears listened:

"I think we should go back to the rocket, Captain."

"I give the orders, Mr. Smith!"

"Yes, sir."

"You, up there! Patrol! See anything?"

"Nothing, sir. Looks like it's been dead a long time!"

"You see, Smith? Nothing to fear."

"I don't like it. I don't know why. You ever feel you've seen a place before? Well, this city's too familiar."

"Nonsense. This planetary system's billions of miles from Earth; we couldn't possibly've been here ever before. Ours is the only light-year rocket in existence."

"That's how I feel, anyway, sir. I think we should get out."

The footsteps faltered. There was only the sound of the intruder's breath on the still air.

The Ear heard and quickened. Rotors glided, liquids glittered in small creeks through valves and blowers. A formula and a concoction—one followed another. Moments later, responding to the summons of the Ear and Nose, through giant holes in the city walls a fresh vapor blew out over the invaders.

"Smell *that*, Smith? Ahh. Green grass. Ever smell anything better? By God, I just like to stand here and smell it."

Invisible chlorophyll blew among the standing men.

"*Ahh!*"

The footsteps continued.

"Nothing wrong with *that*, eh, Smith? Come on!"

The Ear and Nose relaxed a billionth of a fraction. The countermove had succeeded. The pawns were proceeding forward.

Now the cloudy Eyes of the city moved out of fog and mist.

"Captain, the windows!"

"What?"

"Those house windows, there! I saw them move!"

"*I* didn't see it."

"They shifted. They changed color. From dark to light."

"Look like ordinary square windows to me."

Blurred objects focused. In the mechanical ravines of the city oiled shafts plunged, balance wheels dipped over into green oil pools. The window frames flexed. The windows gleamed.

Below, in the street, walked two men, a patrol, followed, at a safe interval, by seven more. Their uniforms were white, their faces as pink as if they had been slapped; their eyes were blue.

They walked upright, upon hind legs, carrying metal weapons. Their feet were booted. They were males, with eyes, ears, mouths, noses.

The windows trembled. The windows thinned. They dilated imperceptibly, like the irises of numberless eyes.

"I tell you, Captain, it's the windows!"

"Get along."

"I'm going back, sir."

"What?"

"I'm going back to the rocket."

"Mr. Smith!"

"I'm not falling into any trap!"

"Afraid of an empty city?"

The others laughed, uneasily.

"Go on, laugh!"

The street was stone-cobbled, each stone three inches wide, six inches long. With a move unrecognizable as such, the street settled. It weighed the invaders.

In a machine cellar a red wand touched a numeral: 178 pounds . . . 210, 154, 201, 198—each man weighed, registered and the record spooled down into a correlative darkness.

Now the city was fully awake!

Now the vents sucked and blew air, the tobacco odor from the invaders' mouths, the green soap scent from their hands. Even their eyeballs had a delicate odor. The city detected it, and this information formed totals which scurried down to total other totals. The crystal windows glittered, the Ear tautened and skinned the drum of its hearing tight, tighter—all of the senses of the city swarming like a fall of unseen snow, counting the respiration and the dim hidden heartbeats of the men, listening, watching, tasting.

For the streets were like tongues, and where the men passed, the taste of their heels ebbed down through stone pores to be calculated on litmus. This chemical totality, so subtly collected, was appended to the now increasing sums waiting the final calculation among the whirling wheels and whispering spokes.

Footsteps. Running.

"Come back! Smith!"

"No, blast you!"

"Get him, men!"

Footsteps rushing.

A final test. The city, having listened, watched, tasted, felt, weighed, and balanced, must perform a final task.

A trap flung wide in the street. The captain, unseen to the others, running, vanished.

Hung by his feet, a razor drawn across his throat, another down his chest, his carcass instantly emptied of its entrails, exposed upon a table under the street, in a hidden cell, the captain died. Great crystal microscopes stared at the red twines of muscle; bodiless fingers probed the still pulsing heart. The flaps of his sliced skin were pinned to the table while hands shifted parts of his body like a quick and curious player of chess, using the red pawns and the red pieces.

Above on the street the men ran. Smith ran, men shouted. Smith shouted, and below in this curious room blood flowed into capsules, was shaken, spun, shoved on smear slides under further microscopes, counts made, temperatures taken, heart cut in seventeen sections, liver and kidneys expertly halved. Brain was drilled and scooped from bone socket, nerves pulled forth like the dead wires of a switchboard, muscles plucked for elasticity, while in the electric subterrene of the city the Mind at last totaled out its grandest total and all of the machinery ground to a monstrous and momentary halt.

The total.

These *are* men. These *are* men from a far world, a *certain* planet, and they have certain eyes, certain ears, and they walk upon legs in a specified way and carry weapons and think and fight, and they have particular hearts and all such organs as are recorded from long ago.

Above, men ran down the street toward the rocket.

Smith ran.

The total.

These are our enemies. These are the ones we have waited for twenty thousand years to see again. These are the men upon whom we waited to visit revenge. Everything totals. These are the men of a planet called Earth, who declared war upon Taollan twenty thousand years ago, who kept us in slavery and ruined us and destroyed us with a great disease. Then they went off to live in another galaxy to escape that disease which they visited upon us after ransacking our world. They have forgotten that war and that time, and they have forgotten us. But we have not forgotten them. These are our enemies. This is certain. Our waiting is done.

"Smith, come back!"

Quickly. Upon the red table, with the spread-eagled captain's body empty, new hands began a fight of motion. Into the wet interior were placed organs of copper, brass, silver, aluminum, rubber and silk; spiders spun gold web which was stung into the skin; a heart was attached, and into the skull case was fitted a platinum brain which hummed and fluttered small sparkles of blue fire, and the wires led down through the body to the arms and legs. In a moment the body was sewn tight, the incisions waxed, healed at neck and throat and about the skull—perfect, fresh, new.

The captain sat up and flexed his arms.

"Stop!"

On the street the captain reappeared, raised his gun and fired.

Smith fell, a bullet in his heart.

The other men turned.

The captain ran to them.

"That fool! Afraid of a city!"

They looked at the body of Smith at their feet.

They looked at their captain, and their eyes widened and narrowed.

"Listen to me," said the captain. "I have something important to tell you."

Now the city, which had weighed and tasted and smelled them, which had used all its powers save one, prepared to use its final ability, the power of speech. It did not speak with the rage and hostility of its massed walls or towers, nor with the bulk of its cobbled avenues and fortresses of machinery. It spoke with the quiet voice of one man.

"I am no longer your captain," he said. "Nor am I a man."

The men moved back.

"I am the city," he said, and smiled.

"I've waited two hundred centuries," he said. "I've waited for the sons of the sons of the sons to return."

"Captain, sir!"

"Let me continue. Who built me? The city. The men who died built me. The old race who once lived here. The people whom the Earthmen left to die of a terrible disease, a form of leprosy with no cure. And the men of that old race, dreaming of the day when Earthmen might return, built this city, and the name of this city was and is Revenge, upon the planet of Darkness, near the shore of the Sea of Centuries, by the Mountains of the Dead; all very poetic. This city was to be a balancing machine, a litmus, an antenna to test all future space travelers. In twenty thousand years only two other rockets landed here. One from a distant galaxy called Ennt, and the inhabitants of that craft were tested, weighed, found wanting, and let free, unscathed, from the city. As were the visitors in the second ship. But today! At long last, you've come! The revenge will be carried out to the last detail. Those men have been dead two hundred centuries, but they left a city here to welcome you."

"Captain, sir, you're not feeling well. Perhaps you'd better come back to the ship, sir."

The city trembled.

The pavements opened and the men fell, screaming. Falling, they saw bright razors flash to meet them!

Time passed. Soon came the call:

"Smith?"

"Here!"

"Jensen?"

"Here!"

"Jones, Hutchinson, Springer?"

"Here, here, here!"

They stood by the door of the rocket.

"We return to Earth immediately."

"Yes, sir!"

The incisions on their necks were invisible, as were their hidden brass hearts and silver organs and the fine golden wire of their nerves. There was a faint electric hum from their heads.

"On the double!"

Nine men hurried the golden bombs of disease culture into the rocket.

"These are to be dropped on Earth."

"Right, sir!"

The rocket valve slammed. The rocket jumped into the sky.

As the thunder faded, the city lay upon the summer meadow. Its glass eyes were dulled over. The Ear relaxed, the great nostril vents stopped, the streets no longer weighed or balanced, and the hidden machinery paused in its bath of oil.

In the sky the rocket dwindled.

Slowly, pleasurably, the city enjoyed the luxury of dying.

Zero Hour

OH, IT WAS to be so jolly! What a game! Such excitement they hadn't known in years. The children catapulted this way and that across the green lawns, shouting at each other, holding hands, flying in circles, climbing trees, laughing. Overhead the rockets flew, and beetle cars whispered by on the streets, but the children played on. Such fun, such tremulous joy, such tumbling and hearty screaming.

Mink ran into the house, all dirt and sweat. For her seven years she was loud and strong and definite. Her mother, Mrs. Morris, hardly saw her as she yanked out drawers and rattled pans and tools into a large sack.

"Heavens, Mink, what's going on?"

"The most exciting game ever!" gasped Mink, pink-faced.

"Stop and get your breath," said the mother.

"No, I'm all right," gasped Mink. "Okay I take these things, Mom?"

"But don't dent them," said Mrs. Morris.

"Thank you, thank you!" cried Mink, and boom! she was gone, like a rocket.

Mrs. Morris surveyed the fleeing tot. "What's the name of the game?"

"Invasion!" said Mink. The door slammed.

In every yard on the street children brought out knives and forks and pokers and old stovepipes and can openers.

It was an interesting fact that this fury and bustle occurred only among the younger children. The older ones, those ten years and more, disdained the affair and marched scornfully off on hikes or played a more dignified version of hide-and-seek on their own.

Meanwhile, parents came and went in chromium beetles. Repairmen came to repair the vacuum elevators in houses, to fix fluttering television sets or hammer upon stubborn food-delivery tubes. The adult civilization passed and repassed the busy youngsters, jealous of the fierce energy of the wild tots, tolerantly amused at their flourishings, longing to join in themselves.

"This and this and *this*," said Mink, instructing the others with their assorted spoons and wrenches. "Do that, and bring *that* over here. No! *Here*, ninny! Right. Now, get back while I fix this." Tongue in teeth, face wrinkled in thought. "Like that. See?"

"Yayyyy!" shouted the kids.

Twelve-year-old Joseph Connors ran up.

"Go away," said Mink straight at him.

"I wanna play," said Joseph.

"Can't!" said Mink.

"Why not?"

"You'd just make fun of us."

"Honest, I wouldn't."

"No. We know you. Go away or we'll kick you."

Another twelve-year-old boy whirred by on little motor skates. "Hey, Joe! Come on! Let them sissies play!"

Joseph showed reluctance and a certain wistfulness. "I *want* to play," he said.

"You're old," said Mink firmly.

"Not *that* old," said Joe sensibly.

"You'd only laugh and spoil the Invasion."

The boy on the motor skates made a rude lip noise. "Come on, Joe! Them and their fairies! Nuts!"

Joseph walked off slowly. He kept looking back, all down the block.

Mink was already busy again. She made a kind of apparatus with her gathered equipment. She had appointed another little girl with a pad and pencil to take down notes in painful slow scribbles. Their voices rose and fell in the warm sunlight.

All around them the city hummed. The streets were lined with good green and peaceful trees. Only the wind made a conflict across the city, across the country, across the continent. In a thousand other cities there were trees and children and avenues, businessmen in their quiet offices taping their voices, or watching televisors. Rockets hovered like darning needles in the blue sky. There was the universal, quiet conceit and easiness of men accustomed to peace, quite certain there would never be trouble again. Arm in arm, men all over earth were a united front. The perfect weapons were held in equal trust by all nations. A situation of incredibly beautiful balance had been brought about. There were no traitors among men, no unhappy ones, no disgruntled ones; therefore the world was based upon a stable ground. Sunlight illumined half the world and the trees drowsed in a tide of warm air.

Mink's mother, from her upstairs window, gazed down.

The children. She looked upon them and shook her head. Well, they'd eat well, sleep well, and be in school on Monday. Bless their vigorous little bodies. She listened.

Mink talked earnestly to someone near the rose bush—though there was no one there.

These odd children. And the little girl, what was her name? Anna? Anna took notes on a pad. First, Mink asked the rose bush a question, then called the answer to Anna.

"Triangle," said Mink.

"What's a tri," said Anna with difficulty, "angle?"

"Never mind," said Mink.

"How you spell it?" asked Anna.

"T-r-i——" spelled Mink slowly, then snapped, "Oh, spell it yourself!" She went on to other words. "Beam," she said.

"I haven't got tri," said Anna, "angle down yet!"

"Well, hurry, hurry!" cried Mink.

Mink's mother leaned out the upstairs window. "A-n-g-l-e," she spelled down at Anna.

"Oh, thanks, Mrs. Morris," said Anna.

"Certainly," said Mink's mother and withdrew, laughing, to dust the hall with an electro-duster magnet.

The voices wavered on the shimmery air. "Beam," said Anna. Fading.

"Four-nine-seven-A-and-B-and-X," said Mink, far away, seriously. "And a fork and a string and a—hex-hex-agony—hexagon*al*!"

At lunch Mink gulped milk at one toss and was at the door. Her mother slapped the table.

"You sit right back down," commanded Mrs. Morris. "Hot soup in a minute." She poked a red button on the kitchen butler, and ten seconds later something landed with a bump in the rubber receiver. Mrs. Morris opened it, took out a can with a pair of aluminum holders, unsealed it with a flick, and poured hot soup into a bowl.

During all this Mink fidgeted. "Hurry, Mom! This is a matter of life and death! Aw——"

"I was the same way at your age. Always life and death. I know."

Mink banged away at the soup.

"Slow down," said Mom.

"Can't," said Mink. "Drill's waiting for me."

"Who's Drill? What a peculiar name," said Mom.

"You don't know him," said Mink.

"A new boy in the neighborhood?" asked Mom.

"He's new all right," said Mink. She started on her second bowl.

"Which one is Drill?" asked Mom.

"He's around," said Mink evasively. "You'll make fun. Everybody pokes fun. Gee, darn."

"Is Drill shy?"

"Yes. No. In a way. Gosh, Mom, I got to run if we want to have the Invasion!"

"Who's invading what?"

"Martians invading Earth. Well, not exactly Martians. They're—I don't know. From up." She pointed with her spoon.

"And *inside*," said Mom, touching Mink's feverish brow.

Mink rebelled. "You're laughing! You'll kill Drill and everybody."

"I didn't mean to," said Mom. "Drill's a Martian?"

"No. He's—well—maybe from Jupiter or Saturn or Venus. Anyway, he's had a hard time."

"I imagine." Mrs. Morris hid her mouth behind her hand.

"They couldn't figure a way to attack Earth."

"We're impregnable," said Mom in mock seriousness.

"That's the word Drill used! Impreg—— That was the word, Mom."

"My, my, Drill's a brilliant little boy. Two-bit words."

"They couldn't figure a way to attack, Mom. Drill says—he says in order to make a good fight you got to have a new way of surprising people. That way you win. And he says also you got to have help from your enemy."

"A fifth column," said Mom.

"Yeah. That's what Drill said. And they couldn't figure a way to surprise Earth or get help."

"No wonder. We're pretty darn strong." Mom laughed, cleaning up. Mink sat there, staring at the table, seeing what she was talking about.

"Until, one day," whispered Mink melodramatically, "they thought of children!"

"*Well!*" said Mrs. Morris brightly.

"And they thought of how grownups are so busy they never look under rosebushes or on lawns!"

"Only for snails and fungus."

"And then there's something about dim-dims."

"Dim-dims?"

"Dimens-shuns."

"Dimensions?"

"Four of 'em! And there's something about kids under nine and imagination. It's real funny to hear Drill talk."

Mrs. Morris was tired. "Well, it must be funny. You're keeping Drill waiting now. It's getting late in the day and, if you want to have your Invasion before your supper bath, you'd better jump."

"Do I have to take a bath?" growled Mink.

"You do. Why is it children hate water? No matter what age you live in children hate water behind the ears!"

"Drill says I won't have to take baths," said Mink.

"Oh, he does, does he?"

"He told all the kids that. No more baths. And we can stay up till ten o'clock and go to two televisor shows on Saturday 'stead of one!"

"Well, Mr. Drill better mind his p's and q's. I'll call up his mother and——"

Mink went to the door. "We're having trouble with guys like Pete Britz and Dale Jerrick. They're growing up. They make fun. They're worse than parents. They just won't believe in Drill. They're so snooty, 'cause they're growing up. You'd think they'd know better. They were little only a coupla years ago. I hate them worst. We'll kill them *first*."

"Your father and I last?"

"Drill says you're dangerous. Know why? 'Cause you don't

believe in Martians! They're going to let us run the world. Well, not just us, but the kids over in the next block, too. I might be queen." She opened the door.

"Mom?"

"Yes?"

"What's lodge-ick?"

"Logic? Why, dear, logic is knowing what things are true and not true."

"He *mentioned* that," said Mink. "And what's im-pres-sion-able?" It took her a minute to say it.

"Why, it means——" Her mother looked at the floor, laughing gently. "It means—to be a child, dear."

"Thanks for lunch!" Mink ran out, then stuck her head back in. "Mom, I'll be sure you won't be hurt much, really!"

"Well, thanks," said Mom.

Slam went the door.

At four o'clock the audio-visor buzzed. Mrs. Morris flipped the tab. "Hello, Helen!" she said in welcome.

"Hello, Mary. How are things in New York?"

"Fine. How are things in Scranton? You look tired."

"So do you. The children. Underfoot," said Helen.

Mrs. Morris sighed. "My Mink too. The super-Invasion."

Helen laughed. "Are your kids playing that game too?"

"Lord, yes. Tomorrow it'll be geometrical jacks and motorized hopscotch. Were we this bad when we were kids in '48?"

"Worse. Japs and Nazis. Don't know how my parents put up with me. Tomboy."

"Parents learn to shut their ears."

A silence.

"What's wrong, Mary?" asked Helen.

Mrs. Morris's eyes were half closed; her tongue slid slowly, thoughtfully, over her lower lip. "Eh?" She jerked. "Oh, nothing. Just thought about *that.* Shutting ears and such. Never mind. Where were we?"

"My boy Tim's got a crush on some guy named—*Drill*, I think it was."

"Must be a new password. Mink likes him too."

"Didn't know it had got as far as New York. Word of mouth, I imagine. Looks like a scrap drive. I talked to Josephine and she said her kids—that's in Boston—are wild on this new game. It's sweeping the country."

At this moment Mink trotted into the kitchen to gulp a glass of water. Mrs. Morris turned. "How're things going?"

"Almost finished," said Mink.

"Swell," said Mrs. Morris. "What's *that*?"

"A yo-yo," said Mink. "Watch."

She flung the yo-yo down its string. Reaching the end it—

It vanished.

"See?" said Mink. "Ope!" Dibbling her finger, she made the yo-yo reappear and zip up the string.

"Do that again," said her mother.

"Can't. Zero hour's five o'clock! 'By." Mink exited, zipping her yo-yo.

On the audio-visor, Helen laughed. "Tim brought one of those yo-yos in this morning, but when I got curious he said he wouldn't show it to me, and when I tried to work it, finally, it wouldn't work."

"You're not *impressionable*," said Mrs. Morris.

"What?"

"Never mind. Something I thought of. Can I help you, Helen?"

"I wanted to get that black-and-white cake recipe——"

The hour drowsed by. The day waned. The sun lowered in the peaceful blue sky. Shadows lengthened on the green lawns. The laughter and excitement continued. One little girl ran away, crying. Mrs. Morris came out the front door.

"Mink, was that Peggy Ann crying?"

Mink was bent over in the yard, near the rosebush. "Yeah. She's a scarebaby. We won't let her play, now. She's getting too old to play. I guess she grew up all of a sudden."

"Is that why she cried? Nonsense. Give me a civil answer, young lady, or inside you come!"

Mink whirled in consternation, mixed with irritation. "I can't quit now. It's almost time. I'll be good. I'm sorry."

"Did you hit Peggy Ann?"

"No, honest. You ask her. It was something—well, she's just a scaredy pants."

The ring of children drew in around Mink where she

scowled at her work with spoons and a kind of square-shaped arrangement of hammers and pipes. "There and there," murmured Mink.

"What's wrong?" said Mrs. Morris.

"Drill's stuck. Halfway. If we could only get him all the way through, it'd be easier. Then all the others could come through after him."

"Can I help?"

"No'm, thanks. I'll fix it."

"All right. I'll call you for your bath in half an hour. I'm tired of watching you."

She went in and sat in the electric relaxing chair, sipping a little beer from a half-empty glass. The chair massaged her back. Children, children. Children and love and hate, side by side. Sometimes children loved you, hated you—all in half a second. Strange children, did they ever forget or forgive the whippings and the harsh, strict words of command? She wondered. How can you ever forget or forgive those over and above you, those tall and silly dictators?

Time passed. A curious, waiting silence came upon the street, deepening.

Five o'clock. A clock sang softly somewhere in the house in a quiet, musical voice: "Five o'clock—five o'clock. Time's a-wasting. Five o'clock," and purred away into silence.

Zero hour.

Mrs. Morris chuckled in her throat. Zero hour.

A beetle car hummed into the driveway. Mr. Morris. Mrs. Morris smiled. Mr. Morris got out of the beetle, locked it, and called hello to Mink at her work. Mink ignored him. He laughed and stood for a moment watching the children. Then he walked up the front steps.

"Hello, darling."

"Hello, Henry."

She strained forward on the edge of the chair, listening. The children were silent. Too silent.

He emptied his pipe, refilled it. "Swell day. Makes you glad to be alive."

Buzz.

"What's that?" asked Henry.

"I don't know." She got up suddenly, her eyes widening. She

was going to say something. She stopped it. Ridiculous. Her nerves jumped. "Those children haven't anything dangerous out there, have they?" she said.

"Nothing but pipes and hammers. Why?"

"Nothing electrical?"

"Heck, no," said Henry. "I looked."

She walked to the kitchen. The buzzing continued. "Just the same, you'd better go tell them to quit. It's after five. Tell them——" Her eyes widened and narrowed. "Tell them to put off their Invasion until tomorrow." She laughed, nervously.

The buzzing grew louder.

"What are they up to? I'd better go look, all right."

The explosion!

The house shook with dull sound. There were other explosions in other yards on other streets.

Involuntarily, Mrs. Morris screamed. "Up this way!" she cried senselessly, knowing no sense, no reason. Perhaps she saw something from the corners of her eyes; perhaps she smelled a new odor or heard a new noise. There was no time to argue with Henry to convince him. Let him think her insane. Yes, insane! Shrieking, she ran upstairs. He ran after her to see what she was up to. "In the attic!" she screamed. "That's where it is!" It was only a poor excuse to get him in the attic in time. Oh, God—in time!

Another explosion outside. The children screamed with delight, as if at a great fireworks display.

"It's not in the attic!" cried Henry. "It's outside!"

"No, no!" Wheezing, gasping, she fumbled at the attic door. "I'll show you. Hurry! I'll show you!"

They tumbled into the attic. She slammed the door, locked it, took the key, threw it into a far, cluttered corner.

She was babbling wild stuff now. It came out of her. All the subconscious suspicion and fear that had gathered secretly all afternoon and fermented like a wine in her. All the little revelations and knowledges and sense that had bothered her all day and which she had logically and carefully and sensibly rejected and censored. Now it exploded in her and shook her to bits.

"There, there," she said, sobbing against the door. "We're safe until tonight. Maybe we can sneak out. Maybe we can escape!"

Henry blew up too, but for another reason. "Are you crazy? Why'd you throw that key away? Damn it, honey!"

"Yes, yes, I'm crazy, if it helps, but stay here with me!"

"I don't know how in hell I *can* get out!"

"Quiet. They'll hear us. Oh, God, they'll find us soon enough——"

Below them, Mink's voice. The husband stopped. There was a great universal humming and sizzling, a screaming and giggling. Downstairs the audio-televisor buzzed and buzzed insistently, alarmingly, violently. *Is that Helen calling?* thought Mrs. Morris. *And is she calling about what I think she's calling about?*

Footsteps came into the house. Heavy footsteps.

"Who's coming in my house?" demanded Henry angrily. "Who's tramping around down there?"

Heavy feet. Twenty, thirty, forty, fifty of them. Fifty persons crowding into the house. The humming. The giggling of the children. "This way!" cried Mink, below.

"Who's downstairs?" roared Henry. "Who's there!"

"Hush. Oh, nonononononono!" said his wife weakly, holding him. "Please, be quiet. They might go away."

"Mom?" called Mink. "Dad?" A pause. "Where are you?"

Heavy footsteps, heavy, heavy, *very heavy* footsteps, came up the stairs. Mink leading them.

"Mom?" A hesitation. "Dad?" A waiting, a silence.

Humming. Footsteps toward the attic. Mink's first.

They trembled together in silence in the attic, Mr. and Mrs. Morris. For some reason the electric humming, the queer cold light suddenly visible under the door crack, the strange odor and the alien sound of eagerness in Mink's voice finally got through to Henry Morris too. He stood, shivering, in the dark silence, his wife beside him.

"Mom! Dad!"

Footsteps. A little humming sound. The attic lock melted. The door opened. Mink peered inside, tall blue shadows behind her.

"Peekaboo," said Mink.

The Rocket

MANY NIGHTS FIORELLO Bodoni would awaken to hear the rockets sighing in the dark sky. He would tiptoe from bed, certain that his kind wife was dreaming, to let himself out into the night air. For a few moments he would be free of the smells of old food in the small house by the river. For a silent moment he would let his heart soar alone into space, following the rockets.

Now, this very night, he stood half naked in the darkness, watching the fire fountains murmuring in the air. The rockets on their long wild way to Mars and Saturn and Venus!

"Well, well, Bodoni."

Bodoni started.

On a milk crate, by the silent river, sat an old man who also watched the rockets through the midnight hush.

"Oh, it's you, Bramante!"

"Do you come out every night, Bodoni?"

"Only for the air."

"So? I prefer the rockets myself," said old Bramante. "I was a boy when they started. Eighty years ago, and I've never been on one yet."

"I will ride up in one someday," said Bodoni.

"Fool!" cried Bramante. "You'll never go. This is a rich man's world." He shook his gray head, remembering. "When I was young they wrote it in fiery letters: THE WORLD OF THE FUTURE! Science, Comfort, and New Things for All! Ha! Eighty years. The Future becomes Now! Do we fly rockets? No! We live in shacks like our ancestors before us."

"Perhaps my *sons*——" said Bodoni.

"No, nor *their* sons!" the old man shouted. "It's the rich who have dreams and rockets!"

Bodoni hesitated. "Old man, I've saved three thousand dollars. It took me six years to save it. For my business, to invest in machinery. But every night for a month now I've been awake. I hear the rockets. I think. And tonight I've made up my mind. One of us will fly to Mars!" His eyes were shining and dark.

"Idiot," snapped Bramante. "How will you choose? Who will go? If you go, your wife will hate you, for you will be just a bit nearer God, in space. When you tell your amazing trip to her, over the years, won't bitterness gnaw at her?"

"No, no!"

"Yes! And your children? Will their lives be filled with the memory of Papa, who flew to Mars while they stayed here? What a senseless task you will set your boys. They will think of the rocket all their lives. They will lie awake. They will be sick with wanting it. Just as you are sick now. They will want to die if they cannot go. Don't set that goal, I warn you. Let them be content with being poor. Turn their eyes down to their hands and to your junk yard, not up to the stars."

"But——"

"Suppose your wife went? How would you feel, knowing she had seen and you had not? She would become holy. You would think of throwing her in the river. No, Bodoni, buy a new wrecking machine, which you need, and pull your dreams apart with it, and smash them to pieces."

The old man subsided, gazing at the river in which, drowned, images of rockets burned down the sky.

"Good night," said Bodoni.

"Sleep well," said the other.

When the toast jumped from its silver box, Bodoni almost screamed. The night had been sleepless. Among his nervous children, beside his mountainous wife, Bodoni had twisted and stared at nothing. Bramante was right. Better to invest the money. Why save it when only one of the family could ride the rocket, while the others remained to melt in frustration?

"Fiorello, eat your toast," said his wife, Maria.

"My throat is shriveled," said Bodoni.

The children rushed in, the three boys fighting over a toy rocket, the two girls carrying dolls which duplicated the inhabitants of Mars, Venus, and Neptune, green mannequins with three yellow eyes and twelve fingers.

"I saw the Venus rocket!" cried Paolo.

"It took off, *whoosh!*" hissed Antonello.

"Children!" shouted Bodoni, hands to his ears.

They stared at him. He seldom shouted.

Bodoni arose. "Listen, all of you," he said. "I have enough money to take one of us on the Mars rocket."

Everyone yelled.

"You understand?" he asked. "Only *one* of us. Who?"

"Me, me, me!" cried the children.

"You," said Maria.

"You," said Bodoni to her.

They all fell silent.

The children reconsidered. "Let Lorenzo go—he's oldest."

"Let Miriamne go—she's a girl!"

"Think what you would see," said Bodoni's wife to him. But her eyes were strange. Her voice shook. "The meteors, like fish. The universe. The Moon. Someone should go who could tell it well on returning. You have a way with words."

"Nonsense. So have you," he objected.

Everyone trembled.

"Here," said Bodoni unhappily. From a broom he broke straws of various lengths. "The short straw wins." He held out his tight fist. "Choose."

Solemnly each took his turn.

"Long straw."

"Long straw."

Another.

"Long straw."

The children finished. The room was quiet.

Two straws remained. Bodoni felt his heart ache in him. "Now," he whispered. "Maria."

She drew.

"The short straw," she said.

"Ah," sighed Lorenzo, half happy, half sad. "Mama goes to Mars."

Bodoni tried to smile. "Congratulations. I will buy your ticket today."

"Wait, Fiorello——"

"You can leave next week," he murmured.

She saw the sad eyes of her children upon her, with the smiles beneath their straight, large noses. She returned the straw slowly to her husband. "I cannot go to Mars."

"But why not?"

"I will be busy with another child."

"What!"

She would not look at him. "It wouldn't do for me to travel in my condition."

He took her elbow. "Is this the truth?"

"Draw again. Start over."

"Why didn't you tell me before?" he said incredulously.

"I didn't remember."

"Maria, Maria," he whispered, patting her face. He turned to the children. "Draw again."

Paolo immediately drew the short straw.

"I go to Mars!" He danced wildly. "Thank you, Father!"

The other children edged away. "That's swell, Paolo."

Paolo stopped smiling to examine his parents and his brothers and sisters. "I *can* go, can't I?" he asked uncertainly.

"Yes."

"And you'll *like* me when I come back?"

"Of course."

Paolo studied the precious broomstraw on his trembling hand and shook his head. He threw it away. "I forgot. School starts. I can't go. Draw again."

But none would draw. A full sadness lay on them.

"None of us will go," said Lorenzo.

"That's best," said Maria.

"Bramante was right," said Bodoni.

With his breakfast curdled within him, Fiorello Bodoni worked in his junk yard, ripping metal, melting it, pouring out usable ingots. His equipment flaked apart; competition had kept him on the insane edge of poverty for twenty years. It was a very bad morning.

In the afternoon a man entered the junk yard and called up to Bodoni on his wrecking machine. "Hey, Bodoni, I got some metal for you!"

"What is it, Mr. Mathews?" asked Bodoni, listlessly.

"A rocket ship. What's wrong? Don't you want it?"

"Yes, yes!" He seized the man's arm, and stopped, bewildered.

"Of course," said Mathews, "it's only a mockup. You know. When they plan a rocket they build a full-scale model first, of aluminum. You might make a small profit boiling her down. Let you have her for two thousand——"

Bodoni dropped his hand. "I haven't the money."

"Sorry. Thought I'd help you. Last time we talked you said how everyone outbid you on junk. Thought I'd slip this to you on the q.t. Well——"

"I need new equipment. I saved money for that."

"I understand."

"If I bought your rocket, I wouldn't even be able to melt it down. My aluminum furnace broke down last week——"

"Sure."

"I couldn't possibly use the rocket if I bought it from you."

"I know."

Bodoni blinked and shut his eyes. He opened them and looked at Mr. Mathews. "But I am a great fool. I will take my money from the bank and give it to you."

"But if you can't melt the rocket down——"

"Deliver it," said Bodoni.

"All right, if you say so. Tonight?"

"Tonight," said Bodoni, "would be fine. Yes, I would like to have a rocket ship tonight."

There was a moon. The rocket was white and big in the junk yard. It held the whiteness of the moon and the blueness of the stars. Bodoni looked at it and loved all of it. He wanted to pet it and lie against it, pressing it with his cheek, telling it all the secret wants of his heart.

He stared up at it. "You are all mine," he said. "Even if you never move or spit fire, and just sit there and rust for fifty years, you are mine."

The rocket smelled of time and distance. It was like walking into a clock. It was finished with Swiss delicacy. One might wear it on one's watch fob. "I might even sleep here tonight," Bodoni whispered excitedly.

He sat in the pilot's seat.

He touched a lever.

He hummed in his shut mouth, his eyes closed.

The humming grew louder, louder, higher, higher, wilder, stranger, more exhilarating, trembling in him and leaning him forward and pulling him and the ship in a roaring silence and in a kind of metal screaming, while his fists flew over the controls, and his shut eyes quivered, and the sound grew and grew until it was a fire, a strength, a lifting and a pushing of power that threatened to tear him in half. He gasped. He hummed again and again, and did not stop, for it could not be stopped, it could only go on, his eyes tighter, his heart furious. "Taking off!" he screamed. *The jolting concussion! The thunder!* "The Moon!" he cried, eyes blind, tight. "The meteors!" *The silent rush in volcanic light.* "Mars. Oh, God, Mars! Mars!"

He fell back, exhausted and panting. His shaking hands came loose of the controls and his head tilted back wildly. He sat for a long time, breathing out and in, his heart slowing.

Slowly, slowly, he opened his eyes.

The junk yard was still there.

He sat motionless. He looked at the heaped piles of metal for a minute, his eyes never leaving them. Then, leaping up, he kicked the levers. "Take off, damn you!"

The ship was silent.

"I'll show you!" he cried.

Out in the night air, stumbling, he started the fierce motor of his terrible wrecking machine and advanced upon the rocket. He maneuvered the massive weights into the moonlit sky. He readied his trembling hands to plunge the weights, to smash, to rip apart this insolently false dream, this silly thing for which he had paid his money, which would not move, which would not do his bidding. "I'll teach you!" he shouted.

But his hand stayed.

The silver rocket lay in the light of the moon. And beyond the rocket stood the yellow lights of his home, a block away, burning warmly. He heard the family radio playing some distant music. He sat for half an hour considering the rocket and the house lights, and his eyes narrowed and grew wide. He stepped down from the wrecking machine and began to walk, and as he walked he began to laugh, and when he reached the back door of his house he took a deep breath and called, "Maria, Maria, start packing. We're going to Mars!"

"Oh!"

"Ah!"

"I can't *believe* it!"

"You will, you will."

The children balanced in the windy yard, under the glowing rocket, not touching it yet. They started to cry.

Maria looked at her husband. "What have you done?" she said. "Taken our money for this? It will never fly."

"It will fly," he said, looking at it.

"Rocket ships cost millions. Have you millions?"

"It will fly," he repeated steadily. "Now, go to the house, all of you. I have phone calls to make, work to do. Tomorrow we leave! Tell no one, understand? It is a secret."

The children edged off from the rocket, stumbling. He saw their small, feverish faces in the house windows, far away.

Maria had not moved. "You have ruined us," she said. "Our money used for this—this thing. When it should have been spent on equipment."

"You will see," he said.

Without a word she turned away.

"God help me," he whispered, and started to work.

Through the midnight hours trucks arrived, packages were delivered, and Bodoni, smiling, exhausted his bank account. With blowtorch and metal stripping he assaulted the rocket, added, took away, worked fiery magics and secret insults upon it. He bolted nine ancient automobile motors into the rocket's empty engine room. Then he welded the engine room shut, so none could see his hidden labor.

At dawn he entered the kitchen. "Maria," he said, "I'm ready for breakfast."

She would not speak to him.

At sunset he called to the children. "We're ready! Come on!" The house was silent.

"I've locked them in the closet," said Maria.

"What do you mean?" he demanded.

"You'll be killed in that rocket," she said. "What kind of rocket can you buy for two thousand dollars? A bad one!"

"Listen to me, Maria."

"It will blow up. Anyway, you are no pilot."

"Nevertheless, I can fly *this* ship. I have fixed it."

"You have gone mad," she said.

"Where is the key to the closet?"

"I have it here."

He put out his hand. "Give it to me."

She handed it to him. "You will kill them."

"No, no."

"Yes, you will. I *feel* it."

He stood before her. "You won't come along?"

"I'll stay here," she said.

"You will understand; you will see then," he said, and smiled. He unlocked the closet. "Come, children. Follow your father."

"Good-by, good-by, Mama!"

She stayed in the kitchen window, looking out at them, very straight and silent.

At the door of the rocket the father said, "Children, we will be gone a week. You must come back to school, and I to my business." He took each of their hands in turn. "Listen. This rocket is very old and will fly only *one* more journey. It will not fly again. This will be the one trip of your life. Keep your eyes wide."

"Yes, Papa."

"Listen, keep your ears clean. Smell the smells of a rocket. *Feel. Remember.* So when you return you will talk of it all the rest of your lives."

"Yes, Papa."

The ship was quiet as a stopped clock. The airlock hissed shut behind them. He strapped them all, like tiny mummies, into rubber hammocks. "Ready?" he called.

"Ready!" all replied.

"Take-off!" He jerked ten switches. The rocket thundered and leaped. The children danced in their hammocks, screaming.

"Here comes the Moon!"

The moon dreamed by. Meteors broke into fireworks. Time flowed away in a serpentine of gas. The children shouted. Released from their hammocks, hours later, they peered from the ports. "There's Earth!" "There's Mars!"

The rocket dropped pink petals of fire while the hour dials spun; the child eyes dropped shut. At last they hung like drunken moths in their cocoon hammocks.

"Good," whispered Bodoni, alone.

He tiptoed from the control room to stand for a long moment, fearful, at the airlock door.

He pressed a button. The airlock door swung wide. He stepped out. Into space? Into inky tides of meteor and gaseous torch? Into swift mileages and infinite dimensions?

No. Bodoni smiled.

All about the quivering rocket lay the junk yard.

Rusting, unchanged, there stood the padlocked junk-yard gate, the little silent house by the river, the kitchen window lighted, and the river going down to the same sea. And in the center of the junk yard, manufacturing a magic dream, lay the quivering, purring rocket. Shaking and roaring, bouncing the netted children like flies in a web.

Maria stood in the kitchen window.

He waved to her and smiled.

He could not see if she waved or not. A small wave, perhaps. A small smile.

The sun was rising.

Bodoni withdrew hastily into the rocket. Silence. All still slept. He breathed easily. Tying himself into a hammock, he closed his eyes. To himself he prayed, Oh, let nothing happen to the illusion in the next six days. Let all of space come and go, and red Mars come up under our ship, and the moons of Mars, and let there be no flaws in the color film. Let there be three dimensions; let nothing go wrong with the hidden mirrors and screens that mold the fine illusion. Let time pass without crisis.

He awoke.

Red Mars floated near the rocket.

"Papa!" The children thrashed to be free.

Bodoni looked and saw red Mars and it was good and there was no flaw in it and he was very happy.

At sunset on the seventh day the rocket stopped shuddering. "We are home," said Bodoni.

They walked across the junk yard from the open door of the rocket, their blood singing, their faces glowing.

"I have ham and eggs for all of you," said Maria, at the kitchen door.

"Mama, Mama, you should have come, to see it, to see Mars, Mama, and meteors, and everything!"

"Yes," she said.

At bedtime the children gathered before Bodoni. "We want to thank you, Papa."

"It was nothing."

"We will remember it for always, Papa. We will never forget."

Very late in the night Bodoni opened his eyes. He sensed that his wife was lying beside him, watching him. She did not move for a very long time, and then suddenly she kissed his cheeks and his forehead. "What's this?" he cried.

"You're the best father in the world," she whispered.

"Why?"

"Now I see," she said. "I understand."

She lay back and closed her eyes, holding his hand. "Is it a very lovely journey?" she asked.

"Yes," he said.

"Perhaps," she said, "perhaps, some night, you might take me on just a little trip, do you think?"

"Just a little one, perhaps," he said.

"Thank you," she said. "Good night."

"Good night," said Fiorello Bodoni.

Epilogue

It was almost midnight. The moon was high in the sky now. The Illustrated Man lay motionless. I had seen what there was to see. The stories were told; they were over and done.

There remained only that empty space upon the Illustrated Man's back, that area of jumbled colors and shapes.

Now, as I watched, the vague patch began to assemble itself, in slow dissolvings from one shape to another and still another. And at last a face formed itself there, a face that gazed out at me from the colored flesh, a face with a familiar nose and mouth, familiar eyes.

It was very hazy. I saw only enough of the Illustration to make me leap up. I stood there in the moonlight, afraid that the wind or the stars might move and wake the monstrous gallery at my feet. But he slept on, quietly.

The picture on his back showed the Illustrated Man himself, with his fingers about my neck, choking me to death. I didn't wait for it to become clear and sharp and a definite picture.

I ran down the road in the moonlight. I didn't look back. A small town lay ahead, dark and asleep. I knew that, long before morning, I would reach the town. . . .

THE OCTOBER COUNTRY

Illustrated

by Joseph Mugnaini

Contents

For who else but

August Derleth

OCTOBER COUNTRY

. . . that country where it is always turning late in the year. That country where the hills are fog and the rivers are mist; where noons go quickly, dusks and twilights linger, and midnights stay. That country composed in the main of cellars, sub-cellars, coal-bins, closets, attics, and pantries faced away from the sun. That country whose people are autumn people, thinking only autumn thoughts. Whose people passing at night on the empty walks sound like rain. . . .

The Dwarf

AIMEE WATCHED THE sky, quietly.

Tonight was one of those motionless hot summer nights. The concrete pier empty, the strung red, white, yellow bulbs burning like insects in the air above the wooden emptiness. The managers of the various carnival pitches stood, like melting wax dummies, eyes staring blindly, not talking, all down the line.

Two customers had passed through an hour before. Those two lonely people were now in the roller coaster, screaming murderously as it plummeted down the blazing night, around one emptiness after another.

Aimee moved slowly across the strand, a few worn wooden hoopla rings sticking to her wet hands. She stopped behind the ticket booth that fronted the MIRROR MAZE. She saw herself grossly misrepresented in three rippled mirrors outside the Maze. A thousand tired replicas of herself dissolved in the corridor beyond, hot images among so much clear coolness.

She stepped inside the ticket booth and stood looking a long while at Ralph Banghart's thin neck. He clenched an unlit cigar between his long uneven yellow teeth as he laid out a battered game of solitaire on the ticket shelf.

When the roller coaster wailed and fell in its terrible avalanche again, she was reminded to speak.

"What kind of people go up in roller coasters?"

Ralph Banghart worked his cigar a full thirty seconds. "People wanna die. That rollie coaster's the handiest thing to dying there is." He sat listening to the faint sound of rifle shots from the shooting gallery. "This whole damn carny business's crazy. For instance, that dwarf. You seen him? Every night, pays his dime, runs in the Mirror Maze all the way back through to Screwy Louie's Room. You should see this little runt head back there. My God!"

"Oh, yes," said Aimee, remembering. "I always wonder what it's like to be a dwarf. I always feel sorry when I see him."

"I could play him like an accordion."

"Don't say that!"

"My Lord." Ralph patted her thigh with a free hand. "The way you carry on about guys you never even met." He shook his head and chuckled. "Him and his secret. Only he don't know I know, see? Boy howdy!"

"It's a hot night." She twitched the large wooden hoops nervously on her damp fingers.

"Don't change the subject. He'll be here, rain or shine."

Aimee shifted her weight.

Ralph seized her elbow. "Hey! You ain't mad? You wanna see that dwarf, don't you? Sh!" Ralph turned. "Here he comes now!"

The Dwarf's hand, hairy and dark, appeared all by itself reaching up into the booth window with a silver dime. An invisible person called, "One!" in a high, child's voice.

Involuntarily, Aimee bent forward.

The Dwarf looked up at her, resembling nothing more than a dark-eyed, dark-haired, ugly man who has been locked in a winepress, squeezed and wadded down and down, fold on fold, agony on agony, until a bleached, outraged mass is left, the face bloated shapelessly, a face you know must stare wide-eyed and awake at two and three and four o'clock in the morning, lying flat in bed, only the body asleep.

Ralph tore a yellow ticket in half. "One!"

The Dwarf, as if frightened by an approaching storm, pulled his black coat-lapels tightly about his throat and waddled swiftly. A moment later, ten thousand lost and wandering dwarfs wriggled between the mirror flats, like frantic dark beetles, and vanished.

"Quick!"

Ralph squeezed Aimee along a dark passage behind the mirrors. She felt him pat her all the way back through the tunnel to a thin partition with a peekhole.

"This is rich," he chuckled. "Go on—look."

Aimee hesitated, then put her face to the partition.

"You *see* him?" Ralph whispered.

Aimee felt her heart beating. A full minute passed.

There stood the Dwarf in the middle of the small blue room. His eyes were shut. He wasn't ready to open them yet. Now, now he opened his eyelids and looked at a large mirror set before him. And what he saw in the mirror made him smile. He winked, he pirouetted, he stood sidewise, he waved, he bowed, he did a little clumsy dance.

And the mirror repeated each motion with long, thin arms, with a tall, tall body, with a huge wink and an enormous repetition of the dance, ending in a gigantic bow!

"Every night the same thing," whispered Ralph in Aimee's ear. "Ain't that rich?"

Aimee turned her head and looked at Ralph steadily out of her motionless face, for a long time, and she said nothing. Then, as if she could not help herself, she moved her head slowly and very slowly back to stare once more through the opening. She held her breath. She felt her eyes begin to water.

Ralph nudged her, whispering.

"Hey, what's the little gink doin' *now*?"

They were drinking coffee and not looking at each other in the ticket booth half an hour later, when the Dwarf came out of the mirrors. He took his hat off and started to approach the booth, when he saw Aimee and hurried away.

"He wanted something," said Aimee.

"Yeah." Ralph squashed out his cigarette, idly. "I know what, too. But he hasn't got the nerve to ask. One night in this squeaky little voice he says, 'I bet those mirrors are expensive.' Well, I played dumb. I said yeah they were. He sort of looked at me, waiting, and when I didn't say any more, he went home, but next night he said, 'I bet those mirrors cost fifty, a hundred bucks.' I bet they do, I said. I laid me out a hand of solitaire."

"Ralph," she said.

He glanced up. "Why you look at me that way?"

"Ralph," she said, "why don't you sell him one of your extra ones?"

"Look, Aimee, do I tell you how to run your hoop circus?"

"How much do those mirrors cost?"

"I can get 'em secondhand for thirty-five bucks."

"Why don't you tell him where he can buy one, then?"

"Aimee, you're not smart." He laid his hand on her knee. She moved her knee away. "Even if I told him where to go, you think he'd buy one? Not on your life. And why? He's self-conscious. Why, if he even knew I knew he was flirtin' around in front of that mirror in Screwy Louie's Room, he'd never come back. He plays like he's goin' through the Maze to get lost, like everybody else. Pretends like he don't care about that special room. Always waits for business to turn bad, late nights, so he has that room to himself. What he does for entertainment on nights when business is good, God knows. No, sir, he wouldn't dare go buy a mirror anywhere. He ain't got no friends, and even if he did he couldn't ask them to buy him a thing like that. Pride, by God, pride. Only reason he even mentioned it to me is I'm practically the only guy he knows. Besides, look at him—he ain't got enough to buy a mirror like those. He might be savin' up, but where in hell in the world today can a dwarf work? Dime a dozen, drug on the market, outside of circuses."

"I feel awful. I feel sad." Aimee sat staring at the empty boardwalk. "Where does he live?"

"Flytrap down on the waterfront. The Ganghes Arms. Why?"

"I'm madly in love with him, if you must know."

He grinned around his cigar. "Aimee," he said. "You and your very funny jokes."

A warm night, a hot morning, and a blazing noon. The sea was a sheet of burning tinsel and glass.

Aimee came walking, in the locked-up carnival alleys out over the warm sea, keeping in the shade, half a dozen sun-bleached magazines under her arm. She opened a flaking door and called into hot darkness. "Ralph?" She picked her way through the black hall behind the mirrors, her heels tacking the wooden floor. "Ralph?"

Someone stirred sluggishly on the canvas cot. "Aimee?"

He sat up and screwed a dim light bulb into the dressing table socket. He squinted at her, half blinded. "Hey, you look like the cat swallowed a canary."

"Ralph, I came about the midget!"

"Dwarf, Aimee honey, dwarf. A midget is in the cells, born that way. A dwarf is in the glands. . . ."

"Ralph! I just found out the most wonderful thing about him!"

"Honest to God," he said to his hands, holding them out as witnesses to his disbelief. "This woman! Who in hell gives two cents for some ugly little——"

"Ralph!" She held out the magazines, her eyes shining. "He's a writer! Think of that!"

"It's a pretty hot day for thinking." He lay back and examined her, smiling faintly.

"I just happened to pass the Ganghes Arms, and saw Mr. Greeley, the manager. He says the typewriter runs all night in Mr. Big's room!"

"Is *that* his name?" Ralph began to roar with laughter.

"Writes just enough pulp detective stories to live. I found one of his stories in the secondhand magazine place, and, Ralph, guess what?"

"I'm tired, Aimee."

"This little guy's got a soul as big as all outdoors; he's got *everything* in his head!"

"Why ain't he writin' for the big magazines, then, I ask you?"

"Because maybe he's afraid—maybe he doesn't know he can do it. That happens. People don't believe in themselves. But if he only tried, I bet he could sell stories anywhere in the world."

"Why ain't he rich, I wonder?"

"Maybe because ideas come slow because he's down in the dumps. Who wouldn't be? So small that way? I bet it's hard to think of anything except being so small and living in a one-room cheap apartment."

"Hell!" snorted Ralph. "You talk like Florence Nightingale's grandma."

She held up the magazine. "I'll read you part of his crime story. It's got all the guns and tough people, but it's told by a dwarf. I bet the editors never guessed the author knew what he was writing about. Oh, please don't sit there like that, Ralph! Listen."

And she began to read aloud.

"I am a dwarf and I am a murderer. The two things cannot be separated. One is the cause of the other.

"The man I murdered used to stop me on the street when I was twenty-one, pick me up in his arms, kiss my brow, croon wildly to me, sing Rock-a-bye Baby, haul me into meat markets, toss me on the scales and cry, 'Watch it. Don't weigh your thumb, there, butcher!'

"Do you *see* how our lives moved toward murder? This fool, this persecutor of my flesh and soul!

"As for my childhood: my parents were small people, not quite dwarfs, not quite. My father's inheritance kept us in a doll's house, an amazing thing like a white-scrolled wedding cake—little rooms, little chairs, miniature paintings, cameos, ambers with insects caught inside, everything tiny, tiny, tiny! The world of Giants far away, an ugly rumor beyond the garden wall. Poor mama, papa! They meant only the best for me. They kept me, like a porcelain vase, small and treasured, to themselves, in our ant world, our beehive rooms, our microscopic library, our land of beetle-sized doors and moth windows. Only now do I see the magnificent size of my parents' psychosis! They must have dreamed they would live forever, keeping me like a butterfly under glass. But first father died, and then fire ate up the little house, the wasp's nest, and every postage-stamp mirror and saltcellar closet within. Mama, too, gone! And myself alone, watching the fallen embers, tossed out into a world of Monsters and Titans, caught in a landslide of reality, rushed, rolled, and smashed to the bottom of the cliff!

"It took me a year to adjust. A job with a sideshow was unthinkable. There seemed no place for me in the world. And then, a month ago, the Persecutor came into my life, clapped a bonnet on my unsuspecting head, and cried to friends, 'I want you to meet the little woman!'"

Aimee stopped reading. Her eyes were unsteady and the magazine shook as she handed it to Ralph. "You finish it. The rest is a murder story. It's all right. But don't you see? That little man. That little man."

Ralph tossed the magazine aside and lit a cigarette lazily. "I like Westerns better."

"Ralph, you got to read it. He needs someone to tell him how good he is and keep him writing."

Ralph looked at her, his head to one side. "And guess who's going to do it? Well, well, ain't we just the Saviour's right hand?"

"I won't listen!"

"Use your head, damn it! You go busting in on him he'll think you're handing him pity. He'll chase you screamin' outa his room."

She sat down, thinking about it slowly, trying to turn it over and see it from every side. "I don't know. Maybe you're right. Oh, it's not just pity, Ralph, honest. But maybe it'd look like it to him. I've got to be awful careful."

He shook her shoulder back and forth, pinching softly, with his fingers. "Hell, hell, lay off him, is all I ask; you'll get nothing but trouble for your dough. God, Aimee, I never *seen* you so hepped on anything. Look, you and me, let's make it a day, take a lunch, get us some gas, and just drive on down the coast as far as we can drive; swim, have supper, see a good show in some little town—to hell with the carnival, how about it? A damn nice day and no worries. I been savin' a coupla bucks."

"It's because I know he's different," she said, looking off into darkness. "It's because he's something we can never be—you and me and all the rest of us here on the pier. It's so funny, so funny. Life fixed him so he's good for nothing but carny shows, yet there he is on the land. And life made us so we wouldn't have to work in the carny shows, but here we are, anyway, way out here at sea on the pier. Sometimes it seems a million miles to shore. How come, Ralph, that we got the bodies, but he's got the brains and can think things we'll never even guess?"

"You haven't even been listening to me!" said Ralph.

She sat with him standing over her, his voice far away. Her eyes were half shut and her hands were in her lap, twitching.

"I don't like that shrewd look you're getting on," he said, finally.

She opened her purse slowly and took out a small roll of bills and started counting. "Thirty-five, forty dollars. There. I'm going to phone Billie Fine and have him send out one of those tall-type mirrors to Mr. Bigelow at the Ganghes Arms. Yes, I am!"

"What!"

"Think how wonderful for him, Ralph, having one in his own room any time he wants it. Can I use your phone?"

"Go ahead, *be* nutty."

Ralph turned quickly and walked off down the tunnel. A door slammed.

Aimee waited, then after a while put her hands to the phone and began to dial, with painful slowness. She paused between numbers, holding her breath, shutting her eyes, thinking how it might seem to be small in the world, and then one day someone sends a special mirror by. A mirror for your room where you can hide away with the big reflection of yourself, shining, and write stories and stories, never going out into the world unless you had to. How might it be then, alone, with the wonderful illusion all in one piece in the room. Would it make you happy or sad, would it help your writing or hurt it? She shook her head back and forth, back and forth. At least this way there would be no one to look down at you. Night after night, perhaps rising secretly at three in the cold morning, you could wink and dance around and smile and wave at yourself, so tall, so tall, so very fine and tall in the bright looking-glass.

A telephone voice said, "Billie Fine's."

"Oh, *Billie*!" she cried.

Night came in over the pier. The ocean lay dark and loud under the planks. Ralph sat cold and waxen in his glass coffin, laying out the cards, his eyes fixed, his mouth stiff. At his elbow, a growing pyramid of burnt cigarette butts grew larger. When Aimee walked along under the hot red and blue bulbs, smiling, waving, he did not stop setting the cards down slow and very slow. "Hi, Ralph!" she said.

"How's the love affair?" he asked, drinking from a dirty glass of iced water. "How's Charlie Boyer, or is it Cary Grant?"

"I just went and bought me a new hat," she said, smiling. "Gosh, I feel *good*! You know why? Billie Fine's sending a mirror out tomorrow! Can't you just see the nice little guy's face?"

"I'm not so hot at imagining."

"Oh, Lord, you'd think I was going to marry him or something."

"Why not? Carry him around in a suitcase. People say, Where's your husband? all you do is open your bag, yell, Here he is! Like a silver cornet. Take him outa his case any old hour, play a tune, stash him away. Keep a little sandbox for him on the back porch."

"I was feeling so good," she said.

"Benevolent is the word." Ralph did not look at her, his mouth tight. "Ben-ev-o-*lent*. I suppose this all comes from me watching him through that knothole, getting my kicks? That why you sent the mirror? People like you run around with tambourines, taking the joy out of my life."

"Remind me not to come to your place for drinks any more. I'd rather go with no people at all than mean people."

Ralph exhaled a deep breath. "Aimee, Aimee. Don't you know you can't help that guy? He's bats. And this crazy thing of yours is like saying, Go ahead, *be* batty, I'll help you, pal."

"Once in a lifetime anyway, it's nice to make a mistake if you think it'll do somebody some good," she said.

"God deliver me from do-gooders, Aimee."

"Shut up, shut up!" she cried, and then said nothing more.

He let the silence lie awhile, and then got up, putting his finger-printed glass aside. "Mind the booth for me?"

"Sure. Why?"

She saw ten thousand cold white images of him stalking down the glassy corridors, between mirrors, his mouth straight and his fingers working themselves.

She sat in the booth for a full minute and then suddenly shivered. A small clock ticked in the booth and she turned the deck of cards over, one by one, waiting. She heard a hammer pounding and knocking and pounding again, far away inside the Maze; a silence, more waiting, and then ten thousand images folding and refolding and dissolving, Ralph striding, looking out at ten thousand images of her in the booth. She heard his quiet laughter as he came down the ramp.

"Well, what's put you in such a good mood?" she asked, suspiciously.

"Aimee," he said, carelessly, "we shouldn't quarrel. You say tomorrow Billie's sending that mirror to Mr. Big's?"

"You're not going to try anything funny?"

"Me?" He moved her out of the booth and took over the cards, humming, his eyes bright. "Not me, oh no, not me." He did not look at her, but started quickly to slap out the cards. She stood behind him. Her right eye began to twitch a little. She folded and unfolded her arms. A minute ticked by. The only sound was the ocean under the night pier, Ralph breathing in the heat, the soft ruffle of the cards. The sky over the pier was hot and thick with clouds. Out at sea, faint glows of lightning were beginning to show.

"Ralph," she said at last.

"Relax, Aimee," he said.

"About that trip you wanted to take down the coast——"

"Tomorrow," he said. "Maybe next month. Maybe next year. Old Ralph Banghart's a patient guy. I'm not worried, Aimee. Look." He held up a hand. "I'm calm."

She waited for a roll of thunder at sea to fade away.

"I just don't want you mad, is all. I just don't want anything bad to happen, promise me."

The wind, now warm, now cool, blew along the pier. There was a smell of rain in the wind. The clock ticked. Aimee began to perspire heavily, watching the cards move and move. Distantly, you could hear targets being hit and the sound of the pistols at the shooting gallery.

And then, there he was.

Waddling along the lonely concourse, under the insect bulbs, his face twisted and dark, every movement an effort. From a long way down the pier he came, with Aimee watching. She wanted to say to him, This is your last night, the last time you'll have to embarrass yourself by coming here, the last time you'll have to put up with being watched by Ralph, even in secret. She wished she could cry out and laugh and say it right in front of Ralph. But she said nothing.

"Hello, hello!" shouted Ralph. "It's free, on the house, tonight! Special for old customers!"

The Dwarf looked up, startled, his little black eyes darting and swimming in confusion. His mouth formed the word thanks and he turned, one hand to his neck, pulling his tiny lapels tight up about his convulsing throat, the other hand clenching the silver dime secretly. Looking back, he gave a little nod, and then scores of dozens of compressed and tortured faces, burnt a strange dark color by the lights, wandered in the glass corridors.

"Ralph," Aimee took his elbow. "What's going on?"

He grinned. "I'm being benevolent, Aimee, benevolent.

"Ralph," she said.

"Sh," he said. "*Listen.*"

They waited in the booth in the long warm silence.

Then, a long way off, muffled, there was a scream.

"Ralph!" said Aimee.

"Listen, listen!" he said.

There was another scream, and another and still another, and a threshing and a pounding and a breaking, a rushing around and through the maze. There, there, wildly colliding and ricocheting, from mirror to mirror, shrieking hysterically and sobbing, tears on his face, mouth gasped open, came Mr. Bigelow. He fell out in the blazing night air, glanced about wildly, wailed, and ran off down the pier.

"Ralph, what happened?"

Ralph sat laughing and slapping at his thighs.

She slapped his face. "What'd you *do*?"

He didn't quite stop laughing. "Come on. I'll show you!"

And then she was in the maze, rushed from white-hot mirror to mirror, seeing her lipstick all red fire a thousand times repeated on down a burning silver cavern where strange hysterical women much like herself followed a quick-moving, smiling man. "Come on!" he cried. And they broke free into a dust-smelling tiny room.

"Ralph!" she said.

They both stood on the threshold of the little room where the Dwarf had come every night for a year. They both stood where the Dwarf had stood each night, before opening his eyes to see the miraculous image in front of him.

Aimee shuffled slowly, one hand out, into the dim room.

The mirror had been changed.

This new mirror made even normal people small, small, small; it made even tall people little and dark and twisted smaller as you moved forward.

And Aimee stood before it thinking and thinking that if it made big people small, standing here, God, what would it do to a dwarf, a tiny dwarf, a dark dwarf, a startled and lonely dwarf?

She turned and almost fell. Ralph stood looking at her. "Ralph," she said. "God, why did you do it?"

"Aimee, come back!"

She ran out through the mirrors, crying. Staring with blurred eyes, it was hard to find the way, but she found it.

She stood blinking at the empty pier, started to run one way, then another, then still another, then stopped. Ralph came up behind her, talking, but it was like a voice heard behind a wall late at night, remote and foreign.

"Don't talk to me," she said.

Someone came running up the pier. It was Mr. Kelly from the shooting gallery. "Hey, any you see a little guy just now? Little stiff swiped a pistol from my place, loaded, run off before I'd get a hand on him! You help me find him?"

And Kelly was gone, sprinting, turning his head to search between all the canvas sheds, on away under the hot blue and red and yellow strung bulbs.

Aimee rocked back and forth and took a step.

"Aimee, where you going?"

She looked at Ralph as if they had just turned a corner, strangers passing, and bumped into each other. "I guess," she said, "I'm going to help search."

"You won't be able to do nothing."

"I got to try, anyway. Oh God, Ralph, this is all my fault! I shouldn't have phoned Billie Fine! I shouldn't've ordered a mirror and got you so mad you did this! It's *me* should've gone to Mr. Big, not a crazy thing like I bought! I'm going to find him if it's the last thing I ever do in my life."

Swinging about slowly, her cheeks wet, she saw the quivery mirrors that stood in front of the Maze, Ralph's reflection was in one of them. She could not take her eyes away from the image; it held her in a cool and trembling fascination, with her mouth open.

"Aimee, what's wrong? What're you——"

He sensed where she was looking and twisted about to see what was going on. His eyes widened.

He scowled at the blazing mirror.

A horrid, ugly little man, two feet high, with a pale, squashed face under an ancient straw hat, scowled back at him. Ralph stood there glaring at himself, his hands at his sides.

Aimee walked slowly and then began to walk fast and then began to run. She ran down the empty pier and the wind blew warm and it blew large drops of hot rain out of the sky on her all the time she was running.

The Next in Line

IT WAS A little caricature of a town square. In it were the following fresh ingredients: a candy-box of a bandstand where men stood on Thursday and Sunday nights exploding music; fine, green-patinated bronze-copper benches all scrolled and flourished; fine blue and pink tiled walks—blue as women's newly lacquered eyes, pink as women's hidden wonders; and fine French-clipped trees in the shapes of exact hatboxes. The whole, from your hotel window, had the fresh ingratiation and unbelievable fantasy one might expect of a French villa in the nineties. But no, this was Mexico! and this a plaza in a small colonial Mexican town, with a fine State Opera House (in which movies were shown for two pesos admission: *Rasputin and the Empress*, *The Big House*, *Madame Curie*, *Love Affair*, *Mama Loves Papa*).

Joseph came out on the sun-heated balcony in the morning and knelt by the grille, pointing his little box Brownie. Behind him, in the bath, the water was running and Marie's voice came out:

"What're you doing?"

He muttered "—a picture." She asked again. He clicked the shutter, stood up, wound the spool inside, squinting, and said, "Took a picture of the town square. God, didn't those men shout last night? I didn't sleep until two-thirty. We would have to arrive when the local Rotary's having its whingding."

"What're our plans for today?" she asked.

"We're going to see the mummies," he said.

"Oh," she said. There was a long silence.

He came in, set the camera down, and lit himself a cigarette.

"I'll go up and see them alone," he said, "if you'd rather."

"No," she said, not very loud. "I'll go along. But I wish we could forget the whole thing. It's such a lovely little town."

"Look here!" he cried, catching a movement from the corner of his eyes. He hurried to the balcony, stood there, his cigarette smoking and forgotten in his fingers. "Come quick, Marie!"

"I'm drying myself," she said.

"Please, hurry," he said, fascinated, looking down into the street.

There was movement behind him, and then the odor of soap and water-rinsed flesh, wet towel, fresh cologne; Marie was at his elbow. "Stay right there," she cautioned him, "so I can look without exposing myself. I'm stark. What *is* it?"

"Look!" he cried.

A procession traveled along the street. One man led it, with a package on his head. Behind him came women in black rebozos, chewing away the peels of oranges and spitting them on the cobbles; little children at their elbows, men ahead of them. Some ate sugar cane, gnawing away at the outer bark until it split down and they pulled it off in great hunks to get at the succulent pulp, and the juicy sinews on which to suck. In all, there were fifty people.

"Joe," said Marie behind him, holding his arm.

It was no ordinary package the first man in the procession carried on his head, balanced delicately as a chicken-plume. It was covered with silver satin and silver fringe and silver rosettes. And he held it gently with one brown hand, the other hand swinging free.

This was a funeral and the little package was a coffin.

Joseph glanced at his wife.

She was the color of fine, fresh milk. The pink color of the bath was gone. Her heart had sucked it all down to some hidden vacuum in her. She held fast to the french doorway and watched the traveling people go, watched them eat fruit, heard them talk gently, laugh gently. She forgot she was naked.

He said, "Some little girl or boy gone to a happier place."

"Where are they taking—her?"

She did not think it unusual, her choice of the feminine pronoun. Already she had identified herself with that tiny fragment parceled like an unripe variety of fruit. Now, in this moment, she was being carried up the hill within compressing darkness, a stone in a peach, silent and terrified, the touch of the father against the coffin material outside; gentle and noiseless and firm inside.

"To the graveyard, naturally; that's where they're taking

her," he said, the cigarette making a filter of smoke across his casual face.

"Not *the* graveyard?"

"There's only one cemetery in these towns, you know that. They usually hurry it. That little girl had probably been dead only a few hours."

"A few hours——"

She turned away, quite ridiculous, quite naked, with only the towel supported by her limp, untrying hands. She walked toward the bed. "A few hours ago she was alive, and now——"

He went on, "Now they're hurrying her up the hill. The climate isn't kind to the dead. It's hot, there's no embalming. They have to finish it quickly."

"But to *that* graveyard, that horrible place," she said, with a voice from a dream.

"Oh, the mummies," he said. "Don't let that bother you."

She sat on the bed, again and again stroking the towel laid across her lap. Her eyes were blind as the brown paps of her breasts. She did not see him or the room. She knew that if he snapped his fingers or coughed, she wouldn't even look up.

"They were eating fruit at her funeral, and laughing," she said.

"It's a long climb to the cemetery."

She shuddered, a convulsive motion, like a fish trying to free itself from a deep-swallowed hook. She lay back and he looked at her as one examines a poor sculpture; all criticism, all quiet and easy and uncaring. She wondered idly just how much his hands had had to do with the broadening and flattening and changement of her body. Certainly this was not the body he'd started with. It was past saving now. Like clay which the sculptor has carelessly impregnated with water, it was impossible to shape again. In order to shape clay you warm it with your hands, evaporate the moisture with heat. But there was no more of that fine summer weather between them. There was no warmth to bake away the aging moisture that collected and made pendant now her breasts and body. When the heat is gone, it is marvelous and unsettling to see how quickly a vessel stores self-destroying water in its cells.

"I don't feel well," she said. She lay there, thinking it over. "I don't feel well," she said again, when he made no response.

After another minute or two she lifted herself. "Let's not stay here another night, Joe."

"But it's a wonderful town."

"Yes, but we've seen everything." She got up. She knew what came next. Gayness, blitheness, encouragement, everything quite false and hopeful. "We could go on to Patzcuaro. Make it in no time. You won't have to pack, I'll do it all myself, darling! We can get a room at the Don Posada there. They say it's a beautiful little town—"

"This," he remarked, "is a beautiful little town."

"Bougainvillea climb all over the buildings—" she said.

"These—" he pointed to some flowers at the window "—are bougainvillea."

"—and we'd fish, you like fishing," she said in bright haste. "And I'd fish, too, I'd learn, yes I would, I've always *wanted* to learn! And they say the Tarascan Indians there are almost Mongoloid in feature, and don't speak much Spanish, and from there we could go to Paricutin, that's near Uruapan, and they have some of the finest lacquered boxes there, oh, it'll be fun, Joe. I'll pack. You just take it easy, and—"

"Marie."

He stopped her with one word as she ran to the bathroom door.

"Yes?"

"I thought you said you didn't feel well?"

"I didn't. I don't. But, thinking of all those swell places—"

"We haven't seen one-tenth of this town," he explained logically. "There's that statue of Morelos on the hill, I want a shot of that, and some of that French architecture up the street . . . we've traveled three hundred miles and we've been here one day and now want to rush off somewhere else. I've already paid the rent for another night. . . ."

"You can get it back," she said.

"Why do you want to run away?" he said, looking at her with an attentive simplicity. "Don't you like the town?"

"I simply adore it," she said, her cheeks white, smiling. "It's so green and pretty."

"Well, then," he said. "Another day. You'll love it. That's settled."

She started to speak.

"Yes?" he asked.

"Nothing."

She closed the bathroom door. Behind it she rattled open a medicine box. Water rushed into a tumbler. She was taking something for her stomach.

He came to the bathroom door.

"Marie, the mummies don't bother you, do they?"

"Unh-unh," she said.

"Was it the funeral, then?"

"Unh."

"Because, if you were really afraid, I'd pack in a moment, you know that, darling."

He waited.

"No, I'm not afraid," she said.

"Good girl," he said.

The graveyard was enclosed by a thick adobe wall, and at its four corners small stone angels tilted out on stony wings, their grimy heads capped with bird droppings, their hands gifted with amulets of the same substance, their faces unquestionably freckled.

In the warm smooth flow of sunlight which was like a depthless, tideless river, Joseph and Marie climbed up the hill, their shadows slanting blue behind them. Helping one another, they made the cemetery gate, swung back the Spanish blue iron grille and entered.

It was several mornings after the celebratory fiesta of El Dia de Muerte, the Day of the Dead, and ribbons and ravels of tissue and sparkle-tape still clung like insane hair to the raised stones, to the hand-carved, love-polished crucifixes, and to the above-ground tombs which resembled marble jewel-cases. There were statues frozen in angelic postures over gravel mounds, and intricately carved stones tall as men with angels spilling all down their rims, and tombs as big and ridiculous as beds put out to dry in the sun after some nocturnal accident. And within the four walls of the yard, inserted into square mouths and slots, were coffins, walled in, plated in by marble plates and plaster, upon which names were struck and upon which hung tin pictures, cheap peso portraits of the inserted dead. Thumb-tacked to the different pictures were trinkets they'd loved in life, silver charms, silver arms, legs, bodies, silver cups, silver dogs, silver church medallions, bits of red crape and blue ribbon. On some places were painted slats of tin showing the dead rising to heaven in oil-tinted angels' arms.

Looking at the graves again, they saw the remnants of the death fiesta. The little tablets of tallow splashed over the stones by the lighted festive candles, the wilted orchid blossoms lying like crushed red-purple tarantulas against the milky stones, some of them looking horridly sexual, limp and withered. There were loop-frames of cactus leaves, bamboo, reeds, and wild, dead morning-glories. There were circles of gardenias and sprigs of bougainvillea, desiccated. The entire floor of the yard seemed a ballroom after a wild dancing, from which the participants have fled; the tables askew, confetti, candles, ribbons and deep dreams left behind.

They stood, Marie and Joseph, in the warm silent yard, among the stones, between the walls. Far over in one corner a little man with high cheekbones, the milk color of the Spanish infiltration, thick glasses, a black coat, a gray hat and gray, unpressed pants and neatly laced shoes, moved about among the stones, supervising something or other that another man in overalls was doing to a grave with a shovel. The little man with glasses carried a thrice folded newspaper under his left arm and had his hands in his pockets.

"*Buenos diaz, senora y senor!*" he said, when he finally noticed Joseph and Marie and came to see them.

"Is this the place of *las mommias*?" asked Joseph. "They do exist, do they not?"

"*Si*, the mummies," said the man. "They exist and are here. In the catacombs."

"*Por favor*," said Joseph. "*Yo quiero veo las mommias, si?*"

"*Si, senor.*"

"*Me Espanol es mucho estupido, es muy malo*," apologized Joseph.

"No, no, *senor*. You speak well! This way, please."

He led between the flowered stones to a tomb near the wall shadows. It was a large flat tomb, flush with the gravel, with a thin kindling door flat on it, padlocked. It was unlocked and the wooden door flung back rattling to one side. Revealed was a round hole the circled interior of which contained steps which screwed into the earth.

Before Joseph could move, his wife had set her foot on the first step. "Here," he said. "Me first."

"No. That's all right," she said, and went down and around in a darkening spiral until the earth vanished her. She moved carefully, for the steps were hardly enough to contain a child's feet. It got dark and she heard the caretaker stepping after her, at her ears, and then it got light again. They stepped out into a long whitewashed hall twenty feet under the earth, dimly lit by a few small gothic windows high in the arched ceiling. The hall was fifty yards long, ending on the left in a double door in which were set tall crystal panes and a sign forbidding entrance. On the right end of the hall was a large stack of white rods and round white stones.

"The soldiers who fought for Father Morelos," said the caretaker.

They walked to the vast pile. They were neatly put in place, bone on bone, like firewood, and on top was a mound of a thousand dry skulls.

"I don't mind skulls and bones," said Marie. "There's nothing even vaguely human to them. I'm not scared of skulls and bones. They're like something insectile. If a child was raised and didn't know he had a skeleton in him, he wouldn't think anything of bones, would he? That's how it is with me. Everything human has been scraped off *these.* There's nothing familiar left to be horrible. In order for a thing to be horrible it has to suffer a change you can recognize. This isn't changed. They're still skeletons, like they always were. The part that changed is gone, and so there's nothing to show for it. Isn't that interesting?"

Joseph nodded.

She was quite brave now.

"Well," she said, "let's see the mummies."

"Here, *senora,*" said the caretaker.

He took them far down the hall away from the stack of bones and when Joseph paid him a peso he unlocked the forbidden crystal doors and opened them wide and they looked into an even longer, dimly lighted hall in which stood the people.

They waited inside the door in a long line under the arch-roofed ceiling, fifty-five of them against one wall, on the left, fifty-five of them against the right wall, and five of them way down at the very end.

"Mister Interlocutor!" said Joseph, briskly.

They resembled nothing more than those preliminary erections of a sculptor, the wire frame, the first tendons of clay, the muscles, and a thin lacquer of skin. They were unfinished, all one hundred and fifteen of them.

They were parchment-colored and the skin was stretched as if to dry, from bone to bone. The bodies were intact, only the watery humors had evaporated from them.

"The climate," said the caretaker. "It preserves them. Very dry."

"How long have they been here?" asked Joseph.

"Some one year, some five, *senor*, some ten, some seventy."

There was an embarrassment of horror. You started with the first man on your right, hooked and wired upright against the wall, and he was not good to look upon, and you went on to the woman next to him who was unbelievable and then to a man who was horrendous and then to a woman who was very sorry she was dead and in such a place as this.

"What are they doing here?" said Joseph.

"Their relatives did not pay the rent upon their graves."

"Is there a rent?"

"*Si, senor.* Twenty pesos a year. Or, if they desire the permanent interment, one hundred seventy pesos. But our people, they are very poor, as you must know, and one hundred seventy pesos is as much as many of them make in two years. So they carry their dead here and place them into the earth for one year, and the twenty pesos are paid, with fine intentions of paying each year and each year, but each year and each year after the first year they have a burro to buy or a new mouth to feed, or maybe three new mouths, and the dead, after all, are not hungry, and the dead, after all, can pull no ploughs; or there is a new wife or there is a roof in need of mending, and the dead, remember, can be in no beds with a man, and the dead, you understand, can keep no rain off one, and so it is that the dead are not paid up upon their rent."

"*Then* what happens? Are you listening, Marie?" said Joseph.

Marie counted the bodies. One, two, three, four, five, six, seven, eight, "What?" she said, quietly.

"Are you listening?"

"I think so. What? Oh, yes! I'm listening."

Eight, nine, ten, eleven, twelve, thirteen.

"Well, then," said the little man. "I call a *trabajador* and with his delicate shovel at the end of the first year he does dig and dig and dig down. How deep do you think we dig, *senor*?"

"Six feet. That's the usual depth."

"Ah, no, ah, no. There, *senor*, you would be wrong. Knowing that after the first year the rent is liable not to be paid, we bury the poorest two feet down. It is less work, you understand? Of course, we must judge by the family who own a body. Some of them we bury sometimes three, sometimes four feet deep, sometimes five, sometimes six, depending on how rich the family is, depending on what the chances are we won't have to dig him from out his place a year later. And, let me tell you, *senor*, when we bury a man the whole six feet deep we are very certain of his staying. We have never dug up a six-foot-buried one yet, that is the accuracy with which we know the money of the people."

Twenty-one, twenty-two, twenty-three. Marie's lips moved with a small whisper.

"And the bodies which are dug up are placed down here against the wall, with the other *compañeros*."

"Do the relatives know the bodies are here?"

"*Si*." The small man pointed. "This one, *yo veo*? It is new. It has been here but one year. His *madre y padre* know him to be here. But have they money? Ah, no."

"Isn't that rather gruesome for his parents?"

The little man was earnest. "They never think of it," he said.

"Did you hear that, Marie?"

"What?" Thirty, thirty-one, thirty-two, thirty-three, thirty-four. "Yes. They never think of it."

"What if the rent is paid again, after a lapse?" inquired Joseph.

"In that time," said the caretaker, "the bodies are reburied for as many years as are paid."

"Sounds like blackmail," said Joseph.

The little man shrugged, hands in pockets. "We must live."

"You are certain no one can pay the one hundred seventy pesos all at once," said Joseph. "So in this way you get them for twenty pesos a year, year after year, for maybe thirty years. If they don't pay, you threaten to stand *mamacita* or little *nino* in the catacomb."

"We must live," said the little man.

Fifty-one, fifty-two, fifty-three.

Marie counted in the center of the long corridor, the standing dead on all sides of her.

They were screaming.

They looked as if they had leaped, snapped upright in their graves, clutched hands over their shriveled bosoms and screamed, jaws wide, tongues out, nostrils flared.

And been frozen that way.

All of them had open mouths. Theirs was a perpetual screaming. They were dead and they knew it. In every raw fiber and evaporated organ they knew it.

She stood listening to them scream.

They say dogs hear sounds humans never hear, sounds so many decibels higher than normal hearing that they seem nonexistent.

The corridor swarmed with screams. Screams poured from terror-yawned lips and dry tongues, screams you couldn't hear because they were so high.

Joseph walked up to one standing body.

"Say 'ah,'" he said.

Sixty-five, sixty-six, sixty-seven, counted Marie, among the screams.

"Here is an interesting one," said the proprietor.

They saw a woman with arms flung to her head, mouth wide, teeth intact, whose hair was wildly flourished, long and shimmery on her head. Her eyes were small pale white-blue eggs in her skull.

"Sometimes, this happens. This woman, she is a cataleptic. One day she falls down upon the earth, but is really not dead, for, deep in her, the little drum of her heart beats and beats, so dim one cannot hear. So she was buried in the graveyard in a fine inexpensive box. . . ."

"Didn't you know she was cataleptic?"

"Her sisters knew. But this time they thought her at last dead. And funerals are hasty things in this warm town."

"She was buried a few hours after her 'death'?"

"*Si*, the same. All of this, as you see her here, we would never have known, if a year later her sisters, having other things to buy, had not refused the rent on her burial. So we dug very quietly down and loosed the box and took it up and opened the top of her box and laid it aside and looked in upon her——"

Marie stared.

This woman had wakened under the earth. She had torn, shrieked, clubbed at the box-lid with fists, died of suffocation, in this attitude, hands flung over her gaping face, horror-eyed, hair wild.

"Be pleased, *senor*, to find that difference between *her* hands and these other ones," said the caretaker. "Their peaceful fingers at their hips, quiet as little roses. Hers? Ah, hers! are jumped up, very wildly, as if to pound the lid free!"

"Couldn't rigor mortis do that?"

"Believe me, *senor*, rigor mortis pounds upon no lids. Rigor mortis screams not like this, nor twists nor wrestles to rip free nails, *senor*, or prise boards loose hunting for air, *senor*. All these others are open of mouth, *si*, because they were not injected with the fluids of embalming, but theirs is a simple screaming of muscles, *senor*. This *senorita*, here, hers is the *muerte horrible*."

Marie walked, scuffling her shoes, turning first this way, then that. Naked bodies. Long ago the clothes had whispered away. The fat women's breasts were lumps of yeasty dough left in the dust. The men's loins were indrawn, withered orchids.

"Mr. Grimace and Mr. Gape," said Joseph.

He pointed his camera at two men who seemed in conversation, mouths in mid-sentence, hands gesticulant and stiffened over some long-dissolved gossip.

Joseph clicked the shutter, rolled the film, focused the camera on another body, clicked the shutter, rolled the film, walked on to another.

Eighty-one, eighty-two, eighty-three. Jaws down, tongues out like jeering children, eyes pale brown-irised in upclenched sockets. Hairs, waxed and prickled by sunlight, each sharp as quills embedded on the lips, the cheeks, the eyelids, the brows. Little beards on chins and bosoms and loins. Flesh like drumheads and manuscripts and crisp bread dough. The women, huge ill-shaped tallow things, death-melted. The insane hair of them, like nests made and unmade and remade. Teeth, each single, each fine, each perfect, in jaw. Eighty-six, eighty-seven, eighty-eight. A rushing of Marie's eyes. Down the corridor, flicking. Counting, rushing, never stopping. On! Quick! Ninety-one, ninety-two, ninety-three! Here was a man, his stomach open, like a tree hollow where you dropped your child love letters when you were eleven! Her eyes entered the hole in the space under his ribs. She peeked in. He looked like an Erector set inside. The spine, the pelvic plates. The rest was tendon, parchment, bone, eye, beardy jaw, ear, stupefied nostril. And this ragged eaten cincture in his navel into which a pudding might be spooned. Ninety-seven, ninety-eight! Names, places, dates, things!

"This woman died in childbirth!"

Like a little hungry doll, the prematurely born child was wired, dangling, to her wrist.

"This was a soldier. His uniform still half on him——"

Marie's eyes slammed the furthest wall after a back-forth, back-forth swinging from horror to horror, from skull to skull, beating from rib to rib, staring with hypnotic fascination at paralyzed, loveless, fleshless loins, at men made into women by evaporation, at women made into dugged swine. The fearful ricochet of vision, growing, growing, taking impetus from swollen breast to raving mouth, wall to wall, wall to wall, again, again, like a ball hurled in a game, caught in the incredible teeth, spat in a scream across the corridor to be caught in claws, lodged between thin teats, the whole standing chorus invisibly chanting the game on, on, the wild game of sight recoiling, rebounding, reshuttling on down the inconceivable procession, through a montage of erected horrors that ended finally and for all time when vision crashed against the corridor ending with one last scream from all present!

Marie turned and shot her vision far down to where the spiral steps walked up into sunlight. How talented was death. How many expressions and manipulations of hand, face, body, no two alike. They stood like the naked pipes of a vast derelict calliope, their mouths cut into frantic vents. And now the great hand of mania descended upon all keys at once, and the long calliope screamed upon one hundred-throated, unending scream.

Click went the camera and Joseph rolled the film. Click went the camera and Joseph rolled the film.

Moreno, Morelos, Cantine, Gomez, Gutierrez, Villanousul, Ureta, Licon, Navarro, Iturbi; Jorge, Filomena, Nena, Manuel, Jose, Tomas, Ramona. This man walked and this man sang and this man had three wives; and this man died of this, and that of that, and the third from another thing, and the fourth was shot, and the fifth was stabbed and the sixth fell straight down dead; and the seventh drank deep and died dead, and the eighth died in love, and the ninth fell from his horse, and the tenth coughed blood, and the eleventh stopped his heart, and the twelfth used to laugh much, and the thirteenth was a dancing one, and the fourteenth was most beautiful of all, the fifteenth had ten children and the sixteenth is one of those children as is the seventeenth; and the eighteenth was Tomas and did well with his guitar; the next three cut maize in their fields, had three lovers each; the twenty-second was never loved; the twenty-third sold tortillas, patting and shaping them each at the curb before the Opera House with her little charcoal stove; and the twenty-fourth beat his wife and now she walks proudly in the town and is merry with new men and here he stands bewildered by this unfair thing, and the twenty-fifth drank several quarts of river with his lungs and was pulled forth in a net, and the twenty-sixth was a great thinker and his brain now sleeps like a burnt plum in his skull.

"I'd like a color shot of each, and his or her name and how he or she died," said Joseph. "It would be an amazing, an ironical book to publish. The more you think, the more it grows on you. Their life histories and then a picture of each of them standing here."

He tapped each chest, softly. They gave off hollow sounds, like someone rapping on a door.

Marie pushed her way through screams that hung netwise across her path. She walked evenly, in the corridor center, not slow, but not too fast, toward the spiral stair, not looking to either side. Click went the camera behind her.

"You have room down here for more?" said Joseph.

"*Si, senor.* Many more."

"Wouldn't want to be next in line, next on your waiting list."

"Ah, no, *senor*, one would not wish to be next."

"How are chances of buying one of these?"

"Oh, no, no, *senor*. Oh, no, no. Oh no, *senor*."

"I'll pay you fifty pesos."

"Oh, no, *senor*, no, no, *senor*."

In the market, the remainder of candy skulls from the Death Fiesta were sold from flimsy little tables. Women hung with black rebozos sat quietly, now and then speaking one word to each other, the sweet sugar skeletons, the saccharine corpses and white candy skulls at their elbows. Each skull had a name on top in gold candy curlicue; Jose or Carmen or Ramon or Tena or Guiermo or Rosa. They sold cheap. The Death Festival was gone. Joseph paid a peso and got two candy skulls.

Marie stood in the narrow street. She saw the candy skulls and Joseph and the dark ladies who put the skulls in a bag.

"Not *really*," said Marie.

"Why not?" said Joseph.

"Not after just *now*," she said.

"In the catacombs?"

She nodded.

He said, "But these are good."

"They look poisonous."

"Just because they're skull-shaped?"

"No. The sugar itself looks raw, how do you know what kind of people made them, they might have the colic."

"My dear Marie, all people in Mexico have colic," he said.

"You can eat them both," she said.

"Alas, poor Yorick," he said, peeking into the bag.

They walked along a street that was held between high buildings in which were yellow window frames and pink iron grilles and the smell of tamales came from them and the sound of lost fountains splashing on hidden tiles and little birds clustering and peeping in bamboo cages and someone playing Chopin on a piano.

"Chopin, here," said Joseph. "How strange and swell." He looked up. "I like that bridge. Hold this." He handed her the candy bag while he clicked a picture of a red bridge spanning two white buildings with a man walking on it, a red serape on his shoulder. "Fine," said Joseph.

Marie walked looking at Joseph, looking away from him and then back at him, her lips moving but not speaking, her eyes fluttering, a little neck muscle under her chin like a wire, a little nerve in her brow ticking. She passed the candy bag from one hand to the other. She stepped up a curb, leaned back somehow, gestured, said something to restore balance, and dropped the bag.

"For Christ's sake." Joseph snatched up the bag. "Look what you've done! Clumsy!"

"I should have broken my ankle," she said, "I suppose."

"These were the best skulls; both of them smashed; I wanted to save them for friends up home."

"I'm sorry," she said, vaguely.

"For God's sake, oh, damn it to hell." He scowled into the bag. "I might not find any more good as these. Oh, I don't know, I give up!"

The wind blew and they were alone in the street, he staring down into the shattered debris in the bag, she with the street shadows all around her, sun on the other side of the street, nobody about, and the world far away, the two of them alone, two thousand miles from anywhere, on a street in a false town behind which was nothing and around which was nothing but blank desert and circled hawks. On top the State Opera House, a block down, the golden Greek statues stood sun-bright and high, and in a beer place a shouting phonograph cried AY, MARIMBA . . . *corazon* . . . and all kinds of alien words which the wind stirred away.

Joseph twisted the bag shut, stuck it furiously in his pocket.

They walked back to the two-thirty lunch at the hotel.

He sat at the table with Marie, sipping Albondigas soup from his moving spoon, silently. Twice she commented cheerfully upon the wall murals and he looked at her steadily and sipped. The bag of cracked skulls lay on the table. . . .

"*Senora* . . ."

The soup plates were cleared by a brown hand. A large plate of *enchiladas* was set down.

Marie looked at the plate.

There were sixteen *enchiladas.*

She put her fork and knife out to take one and stopped. She put her fork and knife down at each side of her plate. She glanced at the walls and then at her husband and then at the sixteen *enchiladas.*

Sixteen. One by one. A long row of them, crowded together.

She counted them.

One, two, three, four, five, six.

Joseph took one on his plate and ate it.

Six, seven, eight, nine, ten, eleven.

She put her hands on her lap.

Twelve, thirteen, fourteen, fifteen, sixteen. She finished counting.

"I'm not hungry," she said.

He placed another *enchilada* before himself. It had an interior clothed in a papyrus of corn *tortilla.* It was slender and it was one of many he cut and placed in his mouth and she chewed it for him in her mind's mouth, and squeezed her eyes tight.

"Eh?" he asked.

"Nothing," she said.

Thirteen *enchiladas* remained, like tiny bundles, like scrolls.

He ate five more.

"I don't feel well," she said.

"Feel better if you ate," he said.

"No."

He finished, then opened the sack and took out one of the half-demolished skulls.

"Not *here*?" she said.

"Why not?" And he put one sugar socket to his lips, chewing. "Not bad," he said, thinking the taste. He popped in another section of skull. "Not bad at all."

She looked at the name on the skull he was eating.

Marie, it said.

It was tremendous, the way she helped him pack. In those newsreels you see men leap off diving-boards into pools, only, a moment later when the reel is reversed, to jump back up in airy fantasy to alight once more safe on the diving-board. Now, as Joseph watched, the suits and dresses flew into their boxes and cases, the hats were like birds darting, clapped into round, bright hatboxes, the shoes seemed to run across the floor like mice to leap into valises. The suitcases banged shut, the hasps clicked, the keys turned.

"There!" she cried. "All packed! Oh, Joe, I'm so glad you let me change your mind."

She started for the door.

"Here, let me help," he said.

"They're not heavy," she said.

"But you never carry suitcases. You never have. I'll call a boy."

"Nonsense," she said, breathless with the weight of the valises.

A boy seized the cases outside the door. "*Senora, por favor!*"

"Have we forgotten anything?" He looked under the two beds, he went out on the balcony and gazed at the plaza, came in, went to the bathroom, looked in the cabinet and on the washbowl. "Here," he said, coming out and handing her something. "You forgot your wrist watch."

"Did I?" She put it on and went out the door.

"I don't know," he said. "It's damn late in the day to be moving out."

"It's only three-thirty," she said. "Only three-thirty."

"I don't know," he said, doubtfully.

He looked around the room, stepped out, closed the door, locked it, went downstairs, jingling the keys.

She was outside in the car already, settled in, her coat folded on her lap, her gloved hands folded on the coat. He came out, supervised the loading of what luggage remained into the trunk receptacle, came to the front door and tapped on the window. She unlocked it and let him in.

"Well, here we *go*!" She cried with a laugh, her face rosy, her eyes frantically bright. She was leaning forward as if by this movement she might set the car rolling merrily down the hill. "Thank you, darling, for letting me get the refund on the money you paid for our room tonight. I'm sure we'll like it much better in Guadalajara tonight. Thank you!"

"Yeah," he said.

Inserting the ignition keys he stepped on the starter.

Nothing happened.

He stepped on the starter again. Her mouth twitched.

"It needs warming," she said. "It was a cold night last night."

He tried it again. Nothing.

Marie's hands tumbled on her lap.

He tried it six more times. "Well," he said, lying back, ceasing.

"Try it again, next time it'll work," she said.

"It's no use," he said. "Something's wrong."

"Well, you've got to try it once more."

He tried it once more.

"It'll work, I'm sure," she said. "Is the ignition on?"

"Is the ignition on," he said. "Yes, it's *on*."

"It doesn't look like it's on," she said.

"It's on." He showed her by twisting the key.

"*Now*, try it," she said.

"There," he said, when nothing happened. "I *told* you."

"You're not doing it right; it almost caught that time," she cried.

"I'll wear out the battery, and God knows where you can buy a battery here."

"Wear it out, then. I'm sure it'll start next time!"

"Well, if you're so good, you try it." He slipped from the car and beckoned her over behind the wheel. "Go ahead!"

She bit her lips and settled behind the wheel. She did things with her hands that were like a little mystic ceremony; with moves of hands and body she was trying to overcome gravity, friction and every other natural law. She patted the starter with her toeless shoe. The car remained solemnly quiet. A little squeak came out of Marie's tightened lips. She rammed the starter home and there was a clear smell in the air as she fluttered the choke.

"You've flooded it," he said. "Fine! Get back over on your side, will you?"

He got three boys to push and they started the car downhill. He jumped in to steer. The car rolled swiftly, bumping and rattling. Marie's face glowed expectantly. "This'll start it!" she said.

Nothing started. They rolled quietly into the filling station at the bottom of the hill, bumping softly on the cobbles, and stopped by the tanks.

She sat there, saying nothing, and when the attendant came from the station her door was locked, the window up, and he had to come around on the husband's side to make his query.

The mechanic arose from the car engine, scowled at Joseph and they spoke together in Spanish, quietly.

She rolled the window down and listened.

"What's he say?" she demanded.

The two men talked on.

"What does he say?" she asked.

The dark mechanic waved at the engine. Joseph nodded and they conversed.

"What's wrong?" Marie wanted to know.

Joseph frowned over at her. "Wait a moment, will you? I can't listen to both of you."

The mechanic took Joseph's elbow. They said many words.

"What's he saying now?" she asked.

"He says—" said Joseph, and was lost as the Mexican took him over to the engine and bent him down in earnest discovery.

"How much will it cost?" she cried, out the window, around at their bent backs.

The mechanic spoke to Joseph.

"Fifty pesos," said Joseph.

"How long will it take?" cried his wife.

Joseph asked the mechanic. The man shrugged and they argued for five minutes.

"How long will it take?" said Marie.

The discussion continued.

The sun went down the sky. She looked at the sun upon the trees that stood high by the cemetery yard. The shadows rose and rose until the valley was enclosed and only the sky was clear and untouched and blue.

"Two days, maybe three," said Joseph, turning to Marie.

"Two days! Can't he fix it so we can just go on to the next town and have the rest done there?"

Joseph asked the man. The man replied.

Joseph said to his wife. "No, he'll have to do the entire job."

"Why, that's silly, it's so silly, he doesn't either, he doesn't really have to do it all, you tell him that, Joe, tell him that, he can hurry and fix it——"

The two men ignored her. They were talking earnestly again.

This time it was all in very slow motion. The unpacking of the suitcases. He did his own, she left hers by the door.

"I don't need anything," she said, leaving it locked.

"You'll need your nightgown," he said.

"I'll sleep naked," she said.

"Well, it isn't my fault," he said. "That damned car."

"You can go down and watch them work on it, later," she said. She sat on the edge of the bed. They were in a new room. She had refused to return to their old room. She said she couldn't stand it. She wanted a new room so it would seem they were in a new hotel in a new city. So this was a new room, with a view of the alley and the sewer system instead of the plaza and the drum-box trees. "You go down and supervise the work, Joe. If you don't, you know they'll take weeks!" She looked at him. "You should be down there now, instead of standing around."

"I'll go down," he said.

"I'll go down with you. I want to buy some magazines."

"You won't find any American magazines in a town like this."

"I can look, can't I?"

"Besides, we haven't much money," he said. "I don't want to have to wire my bank. It takes a god-awful time and it's not worth the bother."

"I can at least have my magazines," she said.

"Maybe one or two," he said.

"As many as I want," she said, feverishly, on the bed.

"For God's sake, you've got a million magazines in the car now, *Posts*, *Collier's*, *Mercury*, *Atlantic Monthlys*, *Barnaby*, *Superman*! You haven't read half of the articles."

"But they're not new," she said. "They're not new, I've *looked* at them and after you've looked at a thing, I don't know——"

"Try reading them instead of looking at them," he said.

As they came downstairs night was in the plaza.

"Give me a few pesos," she said, and he gave her some. "Teach me to say about magazines in Spanish," she said.

"*Quiero una publicacion Americano*," he said, walking swiftly.

She repeated it, stumblingly, and laughed. "Thanks."

He went on ahead to the mechanic's shop, and she turned in at the nearest *Farmacia Botica*, and all the magazines racked before her there were alien colors and alien names. She read the titles with swift moves of her eyes and looked at the old man behind the counter. "Do you have American magazines?" she asked in English, embarrassed to use the Spanish words.

The old man stared at her.

"*Habla Ingles?*" she asked.

"No, *senorita.*"

She tried to think of the right words. "*Quiero*—no!" She stopped. She started again. "*Americano—uh—magg-ah-zeen-as?*"

"Oh, no, *senorita*!"

Her hands opened wide at her waist, then closed, like mouths. Her mouth opened and closed. The shop had a veil over it, in her eyes. Here she was and here were these small baked adobe people to whom she could say nothing and from whom she could get no words she understood, and she was in a town of people who said no words to her and she said no words to them except in blushing confusion and bewilderment. And the town was circled by desert and time, and home was far away, far away in another life.

She whirled and fled.

Shop following shop she found no magazines save those giving bullfights in blood on their covers or murdered people or lace-confection priests. But at last three poor copies of the *Post* were bought with much display and loud laughter and she gave the vendor of this small shop a handsome tip.

Rushing out with the *Posts* eagerly on her bosom in both hands she hurried along the narrow walk, took a skip over the gutter, ran across the street, sang la-la, jumped onto the further walk, made another little scamper with her feet, smiled an inside smile, moving along swiftly, pressing the magazines tightly to her, half-closing her eyes, breathing the charcoal evening air, feeling the wind watering past her ears.

Starlight tinkled in golden nuclei off the highly perched Greek figures atop the State theatre. A man shambled by in the shadow, balancing upon his head a basket. The basket contained bread loaves.

She saw the man and the balanced basket and suddenly she did not move and there was no inside smile, nor did her hands clasp tight the magazines. She watched the man walk, with one hand of his gently poised up to tap the basket any time it unbalanced, and down the street he dwindled, while the magazines slipped from Marie's fingers and scattered on the walk.

Snatching them up, she ran into the hotel and almost fell going upstairs.

She sat in the room. The magazines were piled on each side of her and in a circle at her feet. She had made a little castle with portcullises of words and into this she was withdrawn. All about her were the magazines she had bought and bought and looked at and looked at on other days, and these were the outer barrier, and upon the inside of the barrier, upon her lap, as yet unopened, but her hands were trembling to open them and read and read and read again with hungry eyes, were the three battered *Post* magazines. She opened the first page. She would go through them page by page, line by line, she decided. Not a line would go unnoticed, a comma unread, every little ad and every color would be fixed by her. And—she smiled with discovery—in those other magazines at her feet were still advertisements and cartoons she had neglected—there would be little morsels of stuff for her to reclaim and utilize later.

She would read this first *Post* tonight, yes tonight she would read this first delicious *Post*. Page on page she would eat it and tomorrow night, if there was going to be a tomorrow night, but maybe there wouldn't be a tomorrow night here, maybe the motor would start and there'd be odors of exhaust and round hum of rubber tire on road and wind riding in the window and pennanting her hair—but, suppose, just suppose there would BE a tomorrow night here, in this room. Well, then, there would be two more *Posts*, one for tomorrow night, and the next for the next night. How neatly she said it to herself with her mind's tongue. She turned the first page.

She turned the second page. Her eyes moved over it and over it and her fingers unknown to her slipped under the next page and flickered it in preparation for turning, and the watch ticked on her wrist, and time passed and she sat turning pages, turning pages, hungrily seeing the framed people in the pictures, people who lived in another land in another world where neons bravely held off the night with crimson bars and the smells were home smells and the people talked good fine words and here she was turning the pages, and all the lines went across and down and the pages flew under her hands, making a fan. She threw down the first *Post*, seized on and riffled through the second in half an hour, threw that down, took up the third, threw that down a good fifteen minutes later and found herself breathing, breathing stiffly and swiftly in her body and out of her mouth. She put her hand up to the back of her neck.

Somewhere, a soft breeze was blowing.

The hairs along the back of her neck slowly stood upright.

She touched them with one pale hand as one touches the nape of a dandelion.

Outside, in the plaza, the street lights rocked like crazy flashlights on a wind. Papers ran through the gutters in sheep flocks. Shadows penciled and slashed under the bucketing lamps now this way, now that, here a shadow one instant, there a shadow next, now no shadows, all cold light, now no light, all cold blue-black shadow. The lamps creaked on their high metal hasps.

In the room her hands began to tremble. She saw them tremble. Her body began to tremble. Under the bright bright print of the brightest, loudest skirt she could find to put on especially for tonight, in which she had whirled and cavorted feverishly before the coffin-sized mirror, beneath the rayon skirt the body was all wire and tendon and excitation. Her teeth chattered and fused and chattered. Her lipstick smeared, one lip crushing another.

Joseph knocked on the door.

They got ready for bed. He had returned with the news that something had been done to the car and it would take time, he'd go watch them tomorrow.

"But don't knock on the door," she said, standing before the mirror as she undressed.

"Leave it unlocked then," he said.

"I want it locked. But don't rap. Call."

"What's wrong with rapping?" he said.

"It sounds funny," she said.

"What do you mean, funny?"

She wouldn't say. She was looking at herself in the mirror and she was naked, with her hands at her sides, and there were her breasts and her hips and her entire body, and it moved, it felt the floor under it and the walls and air around it, and the breasts could know hands if hands were put there, and the stomach would make no hollow echo if touched.

"For God's sake," he said, "don't stand there admiring yourself." He was in bed. "What are you doing?" he said. "What're you putting your hands up that way for, over your face?"

He put the lights out.

She could not speak to him for she knew no words that he knew and he said nothing to her that she understood, and she walked to her bed and slipped into it and he lay with his back to her in his bed and he was like one of these brown-baked people of this far-away town upon the moon, and the real earth was off somewhere where it would take a star-flight to reach it. If only he could speak with her and she to him tonight, how good the night might be, and how easy to breathe and how lax the vessels of blood in her ankles and in her wrists and the under-arms, but there was no speaking and the night was ten thousand tickings and ten thousand twistings of the blankets, and the pillow was like a tiny white warm stove under-cheek, and the blackness of the room was a mosquito netting draped all about so that a turn entangled her in it. If only there was one word, one word between them. But there was no word and the veins did not rest easy in the wrists and the heart was a bellows forever blowing upon a little coal of fear, forever illumining and making it into a cherry light, again, pulse, and again, an ingrown light which her inner eyes stared upon with unwanting fascination. The lungs did not rest but were exercised as if she were a drowned person and she herself performing artificial respiration to keep the last life going. And all of these things were lubricated by the sweat of her glowing body, and she was glued fast between the heavy blankets like something pressed, smashed, redolently moist between the white pages of a heavy book.

And as she lay this way the long hours of midnight came when again she was a child. She lay, now and again thumping her heart in tambourine hysteria, then, quieting, the slow sad thoughts of bronze childhood when everything was sun on green trees and sun on water and sun on blond child hair. Faces flowed by on merry-go-rounds of memory, a face rushing to meet her, facing her, and away to the right; another, whirling in from the left, a quick fragment of lost conversation, and out to the right. Around and round. Oh, the night was very long. She consoled herself by thinking of the car starting tomorrow, the throttling sound and the power sound and the road moving under, and she smiled in the dark with pleasure. But then, suppose the car did *not* start? She crumpled in the dark, like a burning, withering paper. All the folds and corners of her clenched in about her and tick tick tick went the wrist-watch, tick tick tick and another tick to wither on. . . .

Morning. She looked at her husband lying straight and easy on his bed. She let her hand laze down at the cool space between the beds. All night her hand had hung in that cold empty interval between. Once she had put her hand out toward him, stretching, but the space was just a little too long, she couldn't reach him. She had snapped her hand back, hoping he hadn't heard the movement of her silent reaching.

There he lay now. His eyes gently closed, the lashes softly interlocked like clasped fingers. Breathing so quietly you could scarce see his ribs move. As usual, by this time of morning, he had worked out of his pajamas. His naked chest was revealed from the waist up. The rest of him lay under cover. His head lay on the pillow, in thoughtful profile.

There was a beard stubble on his chin.

The morning light showed the white of her eyes. They were the only things in the room in motion, in slow starts and stops, tracing the anatomy of the man across from her.

Each little hair was perfect on the chin and cheeks. A tiny hole of sunlight from the window-shade lay on his chin and picked out, like the spikes of a music-box cylinder, each little hair on his face.

His wrists on either side of him had little curly black hairs, each perfect, each separate and shiny and glittering.

The hair on his head was intact, strand by dark strand, down to the roots. The ears were beautifully carved. The teeth were intact behind the lips.

"Joseph!" she screamed.

"Joseph!" she screamed again, flailing up in terror.

Bong! Bong! Bong! went the bell thunder across the street, from the great tiled cathedral!

Pigeons rose in a papery white whirl, like so many magazines fluttered past the window! The pigeons circled the plaza, spiraling up. Bong! went the bells! Honk went a taxi horn! Far away down an alley a music box played "Cielito Lindo."

All these faded into the dripping of the faucet in the bath sink.

Joseph opened his eyes.

His wife sat on her bed, staring at him.

"I thought—" he said. He blinked. "No." He shut his eyes and shook his head. "Just the bells." A sigh. "What time is it?"

"I don't know. Yes, I do. Eight o'clock."

"Good God," he murmured, turning over. "We can sleep three more hours."

"You've got to get up!" she cried.

"Nobody's up. They won't be to work at the garage until ten, you know that, you can't rush these people; keep quiet now."

"But you've got to get up," she said.

He half-turned. Sunlight prickled black hairs into bronze on his upper lip. "*Why*? Why, in Christ's name, do I *have* to get up?"

"You need a shave!" she almost screamed.

He moaned. "So I have to get up and lather myself at eight in the morning because I need a shave."

"Well, you do need one."

"I'm not shaving again till we reach Texas."

"You can't go around looking like a tramp!"

"I can and will. I've shaved every morning for thirty goddamn mornings and put on a tie and had a crease in my pants. From now on, no pants, no ties, no shaving, no nothing."

He yanked the covers over his ears so violently that he pulled the blankets off one of his naked legs.

The leg hung upon the rim of the bed, warm white in the sunlight, each little black hair—perfect.

Her eyes widened, focused, stared upon it.

She put her hand over her mouth, tight.

He went in and out of the hotel all day. He did not shave. He walked along the plaza tiles below. He walked so slowly she wanted to throw a lightning bolt out of the window and hit him. He paused and talked to the hotel manager below, under a drum-cut tree, shifting his shoes on the pale blue plaza tiles. He looked at birds on trees and saw how the State Theatre statues were dressed in fresh morning gilt, and stood on the corner, watching the traffic carefully. There was no traffic! He was standing there on purpose, taking his time, not looking back at her. Why didn't he run, lope down the alley, down the hill to the garage, pound on the doors, threaten the mechanics, lift them by their pants, shove them into the car motor! He stood instead, watching the ridiculous traffic pass. A hobbled swine, a man on a bike, a 1927 Ford, and three half-nude children. Go, go, go, she screamed silently, and almost smashed the window.

He sauntered across the street. He went around the corner. All the way down to the garage he'd stop at windows, read signs, look at pictures, handle pottery. Maybe he'd stop in for a beer. God, yes, a beer.

She walked in the plaza, took the sun, hunted for more magazines. She cleaned her fingernails, burnished them, took a bath, walked again in the plaza, ate very little, and returned to the room to feed upon her magazines.

She did not lie down. She was afraid to. Each time she did she fell into a half-dream, half-drowse in which all her childhood was revealed in a helpless melancholy. Old friends, children she hadn't seen or thought of in twenty years filled her mind. And she thought of things she wanted to do and had never done. She had meant to call Lila Holdridge for the past eight years since college, but somehow she never had. What friends they had been! Dear Lila! She thought, when lying down, of all the books, the fine new and old books, she had meant to buy and might never buy now and read. How she loved books and the smell of books. She thought of a thousand old sad things. She'd wanted to own the Oz books all her life, yet had never bought them. Why *not*? while yet there was life! The first thing she'd do would be to buy them when she got back to New York! And she'd call Lila immediately! And she'd see Bert and Jimmy and Helen and Louise, and go back to Illinois and walk around in her childhood place and see the things to be seen there. If she got back to the States. If. Her heart beat painfully in her, paused, held on to itself, and beat again. *If* she ever got back.

She lay listening to her heart, critically.

Thud and a thud and a thud. Pause. Thud and a thud and a thud. Pause.

What if it should stop while she was listening?

There!

Silence inside her.

"Joseph!"

She leaped up. She grabbed at her breasts as if to squeeze, to pump to start the silent heart again!

It opened in her, closed, rattled and beat nervously, twenty rapid, shot-like times!

She sank on to the bed. What if it should stop again and not start? What would she think? What would there be to do? She'd die of fright, that's what. A joke; it was very humorous. Die of fright if you heard your heart stop. She would have to listen to it, keep it beating. She wanted to go home and see Lila and buy the books and dance again and walk in Central Park and—listen—

Thud and a thud and a thud. Pause.

Joseph knocked on the door. Joseph knocked on the door and the car was not repaired and there would be another night, and Joseph did not shave and each little hair was perfect on his chin, and the magazine shops were closed and there were no more magazines, and they ate supper, a little bit anyway for her, and he went out in the evening to walk in the town.

She sat once more in the chair and slow erections of hair rose as if a magnet were passed over her neck. She was very weak and could not move from the chair, and she had no body, she was only a heart-beat, a huge pulsation of warmth and ache between four walls of the room. Her eyes were hot and pregnant, swollen with child of terror behind the bellied, tautened lids.

Deeply inside herself, she felt the first little cog slip. Another night, another night, another night, she thought. And this will be longer than the last. The first little cog slipped, the pendulum missed a stroke. Followed by the second and third interrelated cogs. The cogs interlocked, a small with a little larger one, the little larger one with a bit larger one, the bit larger one with a large one, the large one with a huge one, the huge one with an immense one, the immense one with a titanic one. . . .

A red ganglion, no bigger than a scarlet thread, snapped and quivered; a nerve, no greater than a red linen fiber twisted. Deep in her one little mech was gone and the entire machine, imbalanced, was about to steadily shake itself to bits.

She didn't fight it. She let it quake and terrorize her and knock the sweat off her brow and jolt down her spine and flood her mouth with horrible wine. She felt as if a broken gyro tilted now this way, now that and blundered and trembled and whined in her. The color fell from her face like light leaving a clicked-off bulb, the crystal cheeks of the bulb vessel showing veins and filaments all colorless. . . .

Joseph was in the room, he had come in, but she didn't even hear him. He was in the room but it made no difference, he changed nothing with his coming. He was getting ready for bed and said nothing as he moved about and she said nothing but fell into the bed while he moved around in a smoke-filled space beyond her and once he spoke but she didn't hear him.

She timed it. Every five minutes she looked at her watch and the watch shook and time shook and the five fingers were fifteen moving, reassembling into five. The shaking never stopped. She called for water. She turned and turned upon the bed. The wind blew outside, cocking the lights and spilling bursts of illumination that hit buildings glancing sidelong blows, causing windows to glitter like opened eyes and shut swiftly as the light tilted in yet another direction. Downstairs, all was quiet after the dinner, no sounds came up into their silent room. He handed her a water glass.

"I'm cold, Joseph," she said, lying deep in folds of cover.

"You're all right," he said.

"No, I'm not. I'm not well. I'm afraid."

"There's nothing to be afraid of."

"I want to get on the train for the United States."

"There's a train in Leon, but none here," he said, lighting a new cigarette.

"Let's drive there."

"In these taxis, with these drivers, and leave our car here?"

"Yes. I want to go."

"You'll be all right in the morning."

"I know I won't be. I'm not well."

He said, "It would cost hundreds of dollars to have the car shipped home."

"I don't care. I have two hundred dollars in the bank at home. I'll pay for it. But, please, let's go home."

"When the sun shines tomorrow you'll feel better, it's just that the sun's gone now."

"Yes, the sun's gone and the wind's blowing," she whispered, closing her eyes, turning her head, listening. "Oh, what a lonely wind. Mexico's a strange land. All the jungles and deserts and lonely stretches, and here and there a little town, like this, with a few lights burning you could put out with a snap of your fingers . . ."

"It's a pretty big country," he said.

"Don't these people ever get lonely?"

"They're used to it this way."

"Don't they get afraid, then?"

"They have a religion for that."

"I wish *I* had a religion."

"The minute you get a religion you stop thinking," he said. "Believe in one thing too much and you have no room for new ideas."

"Tonight," she said, faintly. "I'd like nothing more than to have no more room for new ideas, to stop thinking, to believe in one thing so much it leaves me no time to be afraid."

"You're not afraid," he said.

"If I had a religion," she said, ignoring him, "I'd have a lever with which to lift myself. But I haven't a lever now and I don't know how to lift myself."

"Oh, for God's—" he mumbled to himself, sitting down.

"I used to have a religion," she said.

"Baptist."

"No, that was when I was twelve. I got over that. I mean—*later*."

"You never told me."

"You should have known," she said.

"What religion? Plaster saints in the sacristy? Any special saint you liked to tell your beads to?"

"Yes."

"And did he answer your prayers?"

"For a little while. Lately, no, never. Never any more. Not for years now. But I keep praying."

"Which saint is this?"

"Saint Joseph."

"Saint Joseph." He got up and poured himself a glass of water from the glass pitcher, and it was a lonely trickling sound in the room. "My name."

"Coincidence," she said.

They looked at one another for a few moments.

He looked away. "Plaster saints," he said, drinking the water down.

After a while she said, "Joseph?" He said, "Yes?" and she said, "Come hold my hand, will you?" "Women," he sighed. He came and held her hand. After a minute she drew her hand away, hid it under the blanket, leaving his hand empty behind. With her eyes closed she trembled the words, "Never mind. It's not as nice as I can imagine it. It's really nice the way I can make you hold my hand in my mind." "Gods," he said, and went into the bathroom. She turned off the light. Only the small crack of light under the bathroom door showed. She listened to her heart. It beat one hundred and fifty times a minute, steadily, and the little whining tremor was still in her marrow, as if each bone of her body had a blue-bottle fly imprisoned in it, hovering, buzzing, shaking, quivering deep, deep, deep. Her eyes reversed into herself, to watch the secret heart of herself pounding itself to pieces against the side of her chest.

Water ran in the bathroom. She heard him washing his teeth.

"Joseph!"

"Yes," he said, behind the shut door.

"Come here."

"What do you want?"

"I want you to promise me something, please, oh, please."

"What is it?"

"Open the door, first."

"What *is* it?" he demanded, behind the closed door.

"Promise me," she said, and stopped.

"Promise you what?" he asked, after a long pause.

"Promise me," she said, and couldn't go on. She lay there. He said nothing. She heard the watch and her heart pounding together. A lantern creaked on the hotel exterior. "Promise me, if anything—happens," she heard herself say, muffled and paralyzed, as if she were on one of the surrounding hills talking at him from the distance, "—if anything happens to me, you won't let me be buried here in the graveyard over those terrible catacombs!"

"Don't be foolish," he said, behind the door.

"Promise me?" she said, eyes wide in the dark.

"Of all the foolish things to talk about."

"Promise, *please* promise?"

"You'll be all right in the morning," he said.

"Promise so I can sleep. I can sleep if only you'd say you wouldn't let me be put there. I don't want to be put there."

"Honestly," he said, out of patience.

"Please," she said.

"Why should I promise anything so ridiculous?" he said. "You'll be fine tomorrow. And besides, if you died, you'd look very pretty in the catacomb standing between Mr. Grimace and Mr. Gape, with a sprig of morning-glory in your hair." And he laughed sincerely.

Silence. She lay there in the dark.

"Don't you think you'll look pretty there?" he asked, laughingly, behind the door.

She said nothing in the dark room.

"*Don't* you?" he said.

Somebody walked down below in the plaza, faintly, fading away.

"Eh?" he asked her, brushing his teeth.

She lay there, staring up at the ceiling, her breast rising and falling faster, faster, faster, the air going in and out, in and out her nostrils, a little trickle of blood coming from her clenched lips. Her eyes were very wide, her hands blindly constricted the bedclothes.

"Eh?" he said again behind the door.

She said nothing.

"Sure," he talked to himself. "Pretty as hell," he murmured, under the flow of tap water. He rinsed his mouth. "Sure," he said.

Nothing from her in the bed.

"Women are funny," he said to himself in the mirror.

She lay in the bed.

"Sure," he said. He gargled with some antiseptic, spat it down the drain. "You'll be all right in the morning," he said.

Not a word from her.

"We'll get the car fixed."

She didn't say anything.

"Be morning before you know it." He was screwing caps on things now, putting freshener on his face. "And the car fixed tomorrow, maybe, at the very latest the next day. You won't mind another night here, will you?"

She didn't answer.

"*Will* you?" he asked.

No reply.

The light blinked out under the bathroom door.

"Marie?"

He opened the door.

"Asleep?"

She lay with eyes wide, breasts moving up and down.

"Asleep," he said. "Well, good night, lady."

He climbed into his bed. "Tired," he said.

No reply.

"Tired," he said.

The wind tossed the lights outside; the room was oblong and black and he was in his bed dozing already.

She lay, eyes wide, the watch ticking on her wrist, breasts moving up and down.

It was a fine day coming through the Tropic of Cancer. The automobile pushed along the turning road leaving the jungle country behind, heading for the United States, roaring between the green hills, taking every turn, leaving behind a faint vanishing trail of exhaust smoke. And inside the shiny automobile sat Joseph with his pink, healthy face and his Panama hat, and a little camera cradled on his lap as he drove; a swathe of black silk pinned around the left upper arm of his tan coat. He watched the country slide by and absent-mindedly made a gesture to the seat beside him, and stopped. He broke into a little sheepish smile and turned once more to the window of his car, humming a tuneless tune, his right hand slowly reaching over to touch the seat beside him . . .

Which was empty.

The Watchful Poker Chip of H. Matisse

WHEN FIRST WE meet George Garvey he is nothing at all. Later he'll wear a white poker chip monocle, with a blue eye painted on it by Matisse himself. Later, a golden bird cage might trill within George Garvey's false leg, and his good left hand might possibly be fashioned of shimmering copper and jade.

But at the beginning—gaze upon a terrifyingly ordinary man.

"Financial section, dear?"

The newspapers rattle in his evening apartment.

"Weatherman says 'rain tomorrow.'"

The tiny black hairs in his nostrils breathe in, breathe out, softly, softly, hour after hour.

"Time for bed."

By his look, quite obviously born of several 1907 wax window dummies. And with the trick, much admired by magicians, of sitting in a green velour chair and—vanishing! Turn your head and you forgot his face. Vanilla pudding.

Yet the merest accident made him the nucleus for the wildest avant-garde literary movement in history!

Garvey and his wife had lived enormously alone for twenty years. She was a lovely carnation, but the hazard of meeting *him* pretty well kept visitors off. Neither husband nor wife suspected Garvey's talent for mummifying people instantaneously. Both claimed they were satisfied sitting alone nights after a brisk day at the office. Both worked at anonymous jobs. And sometimes even they could not recall the name of the colorless company which used them like white paint on white paint.

Enter the avant-garde! Enter The Cellar Septet!

These odd souls had flourished in Parisian basements listening to a rather sluggish variety of jazz, preserved a highly volatile relationship six months or more, and, returning to the United States on the point of clamorous disintegration, stumbled into Mr. George Garvey.

"My God!" cried Alexander Pape, erstwhile potentate of the clique. "I met the most astounding bore. You simply must see him! At Bill Timmins' apartment house last night, a note said he'd return in an hour. In the hall this Garvey chap asked if I'd like to wait in his apartment. There we sat, Garvey, his wife, myself! Incredible! He's a monstrous Ennui, produced by our materialistic society. He knows a billion ways to paralyze you! Absolutely rococo with the talent to induce stupor, deep slumber, or stoppage of the heart. What a case study. Let's *all* go visit!"

They swarmed like vultures! Life flowed to Garvey's door, life sat in his parlor. The Cellar Septet perched on his fringed sofa, eyeing their prey.

Garvey fidgeted.

"Anyone wants to smoke——" He smiled faintly. "Why—go right ahead—*smoke.*"

Silence.

The instructions were: "Mum's the word. Put him on the spot. That's the only way to see what a colossal *norm* he is. American culture at absolute zero!"

After three minutes of unblinking quiet, Mr. Garvey leaned forward. "Eh," he said, "what's *your* business. Mr. . . . ?"

"Crabtree. The poet."

Garvey mused over this.

"How's," he said, "business?"

Not a sound.

Here lay a typical Garvey silence. Here sat the largest manufacturer and deliverer of silences in the world; name one, he could provide it packaged and tied with throat-clearings and whispers. Embarrassed, pained, calm, serene, indifferent, blessed, golden, or nervous silences; Garvey was *in* there.

Well, The Cellar Septet simply wallowed in this particular evening's silence. Later, in their cold-water flat, over a bottle of "adequate little red wine" (they were experiencing a phase which led them to contact *real* reality) they tore this silence to bits and worried it.

"Did you *see* how he fingered his collar! Ho!"

"By God, though, I must admit he's almost 'cool.' Mention Muggsy Spanier and Bix Beiderbecke. Notice his expression. *Very* cool. I wish *I* could look so uncaring, so unemotional."

Ready for bed, George Garvey, reflecting upon this extraordinary evening, realized that when situations got out of hand, when strange books or music were discussed, he panicked, he froze.

This hadn't seemed to cause undue concern among his rather oblique guests. In fact, on the way out, they had shaken his hand vigorously, thanked him for a splendid time!

"What a really expert A-number-1 bore!" cried Alexander Pape, across town.

"Perhaps he's secretly laughing at us," said Smith, the minor poet, who never agreed with Pape if he was awake.

"Let's fetch Minnie and Tom; they'd love Garvey. A rare night. We'll talk of it for months!"

"Did you notice?" asked Smith, the minor poet, eyes closed smugly. "When you turn the taps in their bathroom?" He paused dramatically. "*Hot* water."

Everyone stared irritably at Smith.

They hadn't thought to *try*.

The clique, an incredible yeast, soon burst doors and windows, growing.

"You haven't met the Garveys? My God! lie back down in your coffin! Garvey *must* rehearse. No one's *that* boorish without Stanislavsky!" Here the speaker, Alexander Pape, who depressed the entire group because he did perfect imitations, now aped Garvey's slow, self-conscious delivery:

"'*Ulysses*? Wasn't that the book about the Greek, the ship, and the one-eyed monster! Beg pardon?'" A pause. "'Oh.'" Another pause. "'I see.'" A sitting back. "'*Ulysses* was written by *James Joyce*? Odd. I could *swear* I remember, years ago, in school . . .'"

In spite of everyone *hating* Alexander Pape for his brilliant imitations, they roared as he went on:

"'Tennessee Williams? Is he the man who wrote that hillbilly "Waltz?"'"

"Quick! What's Garvey's home address?" everyone cried.

"My," observed Mr. Garvey to his wife, "life is fun these days."

"It's you," replied his wife. "Notice, they hang on your every word."

"Their attention is rapt," said Mr. Garvey, "to the point of hysteria. The least thing I say absolutely explodes them. Odd.

My jokes at the office always met a stony wall. Tonight, for instance, I wasn't trying to be funny at all. I suppose it's an unconscious little stream of wit that flows quietly under everything I do or say. Nice to know I have it in reserve. Ah, there's the bell. Here we go!"

"He's especially rare if you get him out of bed at four A.M.," said Alexander Pape. "The combination of exhaustion and *fin de siècle* morality is a regular salad!"

Everyone was pretty miffed at Pape for being first to think of seeing Garvey at dawn. Nevertheless, interest ran high after midnight in late October.

Mr. Garvey's subconscious told him in utmost secrecy that he was the opener of a theatrical season, his success dependent upon the staying power of the ennui he inspired in others. Enjoying himself, he nevertheless guessed why these lemmings thronged to his private sea. Underneath, Garvey was a surprisingly brilliant man, but his unimaginative parents had crushed him in the Terribly Strange Bed of their environment. From there he had been thrown to a larger lemon-squeezer: his Office, his Factory, his Wife. The result: a man whose potentialities were a time bomb in his own parlor. The Garveys' repressed subconscious half recognized that the avant-gardists had never met anyone like him, or rather had met millions like him but had never considered studying one before.

So here he was, the first of autumn's celebrities. Next month it might be some abstractionist from Allentown who worked on a twelve-foot ladder shooting house-paint, in two colors only, blue and cloud-gray, from cake-decorators and insecticide-sprayers on canvas covered with layers of mucilage and coffee grounds, who simply needed appreciation to grow! or a Chicago tin-cutter of mobiles, aged fifteen, already ancient with knowledge. Mr. Garvey's shrewd subconscious grew even more suspicious when he made the terrible mistake of reading the avant-garde's favorite magazine, *Nucleus.*

"This article on Dante, now," said Garvey. "Fascinating. Especially where it discusses the spatial metaphors conveyed in the foothills of the *Antipurgatorio* and the *Paradiso Terrestre* on top of the Mountain. The bit about Cantos XV–XVIII, the so-called 'doctrinal cantos' is brilliant!"

How did the Cellar Septet react?

Stunned, all of them!

There was a noticeable chill.

They departed in short order when instead of being a delightfully mass-minded, keep-up-with-the-Joneses, machine-dominated chap leading a wishy-washy life of quiet desperation, Garvey enraged them with opinions on *Does Existentialism Still Exist, or Is Kraft-Ebbing?* They didn't want opinions on alchemy and symbolism given in a piccolo voice, Garvey's subconscious warned him. They only wanted Garvey's good old-fashioned plain white bread and churned country butter, to be chewed on later at a dim bar, exclaiming how priceless!

Garvey retreated.

Next night he was his old precious self. Dale Carnegie? Splendid religious leader! Hart Schaffner & Marx? Better than Bond Street! Member of the After-Shave Club? That was Garvey! Latest Book-of-the-Month? Here on the table! Had they ever tried Elinor Glyn?

The Cellar Septet was horrified, delighted. They let themselves be bludgeoned into watching Milton Berle. Garvey laughed at everything Berle said. It was arranged for neighbors to tape-record various daytime soap operas which Garvey replayed evenings with religious awe, while the Cellar Septet analyzed his face and his complete devotion to *Ma Perkins* and *John's Other Wife*.

Oh, Garvey was getting sly. His inner self observed: You're on top. Stay there! Please your public! Tomorrow, play the Two Black Crows records! Mind your step! Bonnie Baker, now . . . that's it! They'll shudder, incredulous that you really like her singing. What about Guy Lombardo? That's the ticket!

The mob-mind, said his subconscious. You're symbolic of the crowd. They came to study the dreadful vulgarity of this imaginary Mass Man they pretend to hate. But they're fascinated with the snake-pit.

Guessing his thought, his wife objected. "They *like* you."

"In a frightening sort of way," he said. "I've lain awake figuring why they should come see me! Always hated and bored myself. Stupid, tattletale-gray man. Not an original thought in my mind. All I know now is: I love company. I've always wanted to be gregarious, never had the chance. It's been a ball these last months! But their interest is dying. I want company forever! What shall I do?"

His subconscious provided shopping lists.

Beer. It's unimaginative.

Pretzels. Delightfully "passé."

Stop by Mother's. Pick up Maxfield Parrish painting, the fly-specked, sunburnt one. Lecture on same tonight.

By December Mr. Garvey was really frightened.

The Cellar Septet was now quite accustomed to Milton Berle and Guy Lombardo. In fact, they had rationalized themselves into a position where they acclaimed Berle as really too *rare* for the American public, and Lombardo was twenty years ahead of his time; the nastiest people liked him for the commonest reasons.

Garvey's empire trembled.

Suddenly he was just another person, no longer diverting the tastes of friends, but frantically pursuing them as they seized at Nora Bayes, the 1917 Knickerbocker Quartette, Al Jolson singing "Where Did Robinson Crusoe Go With Friday on Saturday Night," and Shep Fields and his Rippling Rhythm. Maxfield Parrish's rediscovery left Mr. Garvey in the north pasture. Overnight, everyone agreed, "Beer's intellectual. What a shame so many *idiots* drink it."

In short, his friends vanished. Alexander Pape, it was rumored, for a lark, was even considering hot water for his cold-water flat. This ugly canard was quashed, but not before Alexander Pape suffered a comedown among the *cognoscenti*.

Garvey sweated to anticipate the shifting taste! He increased the free food output, foresaw the swing back to the Roaring Twenties by wearing hairy knickers and displaying his wife in a tube dress and boyish bob long before anyone else.

But, the vultures came, ate, and ran. Now that this frightful Giant, TV, strode the world, they were busily re-embracing radio. Bootlegged 1935 transcriptions of *Vic and Sade* and *Pepper Young's Family* were fought over at intellectual galas.

At long last, Garvey was forced to turn to a series of miraculous tours de force, conceived and carried out by his panic-stricken inner self.

The first accident was a slammed car door.

Mr. Garvey's little fingertip was neatly cut off!

In the resultant chaos, hopping about, Garvey stepped on, then kicked the fingertip into a street drain. By the time they fished it out, no doctor would bother sewing it back on.

A happy accident! Next day, strolling by an oriental shop, Garvey spied a beautiful *objet d'art.* His peppy old subconscious, considering his steadily declining box office and his poor audience-rating among the avant-garde, forced him into the shop and dragged out his wallet.

"Have you seen Garvey lately!" screamed Alexander Pape on the phone. "My God, go see!"

"What's *that*?"

Everyone stared.

"Mandarin's finger-guard." Garvey waved his hand casually. "Oriental antique. Mandarins used them to protect the five-inch nails they cultivated." He drank his beer, the gold-thimbled little finger cocked. "Everyone hates cripples, the sight of things missing. It was sad losing my finger. But I'm happier with this gold thing-amajig."

"It's a much nicer finger now than any of us can *ever* have." His wife dished them all a little green salad. "And George has the *right* to use it."

Garvey was shocked and charmed as his dwindling popularity returned. Ah, art! Ah, life! The pendulum swinging back and forth, from complex to simple, again to complex. From romantic to realistic, back to romantic. The clever man could sense intellectual perihelions, and prepare for the violent new orbits. Garvey's subconscious brilliance sat up, began to eat a bit, and some days dared to walk about, trying its unused limbs. It caught fire!

"How unimaginative the world is," his long-neglected other self said, using his tongue. "If somehow my leg were severed accidentally I wouldn't wear a wooden leg, no! I'd have a gold leg crusted with precious stones made, and part of the leg would be a golden cage in which a bluebird would sing as I walked or sat talking to friends. And if my arm were cut off I'd have a new arm made of copper and jade, all hollow inside, a section for dry ice in it. And five other compartments, one for each finger. Drink, anyone? I'd cry. Sherry? Brandy? Dubonnet? Then I'd twist each finger calmly over the glasses.

From five fingers, five cool streams, five liqueurs or wines. I'd tap the golden faucets shut. 'Bottoms up!' I'd cry.

"But, most of all, one almost wishes that one's eye would offend one. Pluck it out, the Bible says. It *was* the Bible, wasn't it? If that happened to me, I'd use no grisly glass eyes, by God. None of those black, pirate's patches. Know what I'd do? I'd mail a poker chip to your friend in France, *what's* his name? *Matisse!* I'd say, 'Enclosed find poker chip, and personal check. Please paint on this chip one beautiful blue human eye. Yrs., sincerely. G. Garvey!'"

Well, Garvey had always abhorred his body, found his eyes pale, weak, lacking character. So he was not surprised a month later (when his Gallup ran low again) to see his right eye water, fester, and then pull a complete blank!

Garvey was absolutely bombed!

But—equally—secretly pleased.

With the Cellar Septet smiling like a jury of gargoyles at his elbow, he airmailed the poker chip to France with a check for fifty dollars.

The check returned, uncashed, a week later.

In the next mail came the poker chip.

H. Matisse had painted a rare, beautiful blue eye on it, delicately lashed and browed. H. Matisse had tucked this chip in a green-plush jeweler's box, quite obviously as delighted as was Garvey with the entire enterprise.

Harper's Bazaar published a picture of Garvey, wearing the Matisse poker-chip eye, and yet another of Matisse, himself, painting the monocle after considerable experimentation with three dozen chips!

H. Matisse had had the uncommon good sense to summon a photographer to Leica the affair for posterity. He was quoted. "After I had thrown away twenty-seven eyes, I finally got the very one I wanted. It flies posthaste to Monsieur Garvey!"

Reproduced in six colors, the eye rested balefully in its green-plush box. Duplicates were struck off for sales by the Museum of Modern Art. The Friends of the Cellar Septet played poker, using red chips with blue eyes, white chips with red eyes, and blue chips with white eyes.

But there was only *one* man in New York who wore the original Matisse monocle and that was Mr. Garvey.

"I'm *still* a nerve-wracking bore," he told his wife, "but now they'll never know what a dreadful ox I am underneath the monocle and the Mandarin's finger. And if their interest should happen to dwindle again, one can always arrange to lose an arm or leg. No doubt of it. I've thrown up a wondrous facade; no one will ever find the ancient boor again."

And as his wife put it only the other afternoon: "I hardly think of him as the old George Garvey any more. He's changed his name. Giulio, he wants to be called. Sometimes, at night, I look over at him and call, 'George,' but there's no answer. There he is, that mandarin's thimble on his little finger, the white and blue Matisse Poker-Chip monocle in his eye. I wake up and look at him often. And do you know? Sometimes that incredible Matisse Poker Chip seems to give out with a *monstrous* wink."

Skeleton

IT WAS PAST time for him to see the doctor again. Mr. Harris turned palely in at the stair well, and on his way up the flight saw Dr. Burleigh's name gilded over a pointing arrow. Would Dr. Burleigh sigh when he walked in? After all, this would make the tenth trip so far this year. But Burleigh shouldn't complain; he was paid for the examinations!

The nurse looked Mr. Harris over and smiled, a bit amusedly, as she tiptoed to the glazed glass door, opened it, and put her head in. Harris thought he heard her say, "Guess who's here, Doctor." And didn't the doctor's voice reply, faintly, "Oh, my God, *again*?" Harris swallowed uneasily.

When Harris walked in, Dr. Burleigh snorted. "Aches in your bones again! Ah!!" He scowled and adjusted his glasses. "My dear Harris, you've been curried with the finest-tooth combs and bacteria-brushes known to science. You're just nervous. Let's see your fingers. Too many cigarettes. Let's smell your breath. Too much protein. Let's see your eyes. Not enough sleep. My response? Go to bed, stop the protein, no smoking. Ten dollars, please."

Harris stood sulking.

The doctor glanced up from his papers. "*You* still here? You're a hypochondriac! That's *eleven* dollars, now."

"But why should my bones ache?" asked Harris.

Dr. Burleigh spoke as to a child. "You ever had a sore muscle, and kept irritating it, fussing with it, rubbing it? It gets worse, the more you bother it. Then you leave it alone and the pain vanishes. You realize you caused most of the soreness, yourself. Well, son, that's what's with you. Leave yourself alone. Take a dose of salts. Get out of here and take that trip to Phoenix you've stewed about for months. Do you good to travel!"

Five minutes later, Mr. Harris riffled through a classified phone directory at the corner druggist's. A fine lot of sympathy one got from blind fools like Burleigh! He passed his finger down a list of BONE SPECIALISTS, found one named M. Munigant. Munigant lacked an M.D., or any other academic lettering behind his name, but his office was conveniently near. Three blocks down, one block over. . . .

M. Munigant, like his office, was small and dark. Like his office, he smelled of iodoform, iodine, and other odd things. He was a good listener, though, and listened with eager shiny moves of his eyes, and when he talked to Harris, his accent was such that he softly whistled each word; undoubtedly because of imperfect dentures.

Harris told all.

M. Munigant nodded. He had seen cases like this before. The bones of the body. Man was not aware of his bones. Ah, yes, the bones. The skeleton. Most difficult. Something concerning an imbalance, an unsympathetic coordination between soul, flesh, and skeleton. Very complicated, softly whistled M. Munigant. Harris listened, fascinated. Now, *here* was a doctor who understood his illness! Psychological, said M. Munigant. He moved swiftly, delicately to a dingy wall and slashed down half a dozen X-rays to haunt the room with their look of things found floating in an ancient tide. Here, here! The skeleton surprised! Here luminous portraits of the long, the short, the large, the small bones. Mr. Harris must be aware of his position, his problem! M. Munigant's hand tapped, rattled, whispered, scratched at faint nebulae of flesh in which hung ghosts of cranium, spinal-cord, pelvis, lime, calcium, marrow, here, there, this, that, these, those, and others! Look!

Harris shuddered. The X-rays and the paintings blew in a green and phosphorescent wind from a land peopled by the monsters of Dali and Fuseli.

M. Munigant whistled quietly. Did Mr. Harris wish his bones—treated?

"That depends," said Harris.

Well, M. Munigant could not help Harris unless Harris was in the proper mood. Psychologically, one had to *need* help, or the doctor was useless. But (shrugging) M. Munigant would "try."

Harris lay on a table with his mouth open. The lights were

switched off, the shades drawn. M. Munigant approached his patient.

Something touched Harris's tongue.

He felt his jawbones forced out. They creaked and made faint cracking noises. One of those skeleton charts on the dim wall seemed to quiver and jump. A violent shudder seized Harris. Involuntarily, his mouth snapped shut.

M. Munigant shouted. His nose had almost been bitten off! No use, no use! Now was not the time! M. Munigant whispered the shades up, dreadfully disappointed. When Mr. Harris felt he could cooperate psychologically, when Mr. Harris really *needed* help and trusted M. Munigant to help him, then maybe something could be done. M. Munigant held out his little hand. In the meantime, the fee was only two dollars. Mr. Harris must begin to think. Here was a sketch for Mr. Harris to take home and study. It would acquaint him with his body. He must be tremblingly aware of himself. He must be on guard. Skeletons were strange, unwieldy things. M. Munigant's eyes glittered. Good day to Mr. Harris. Oh, and would he care for a breadstick? M. Munigant proffered a jar of long hard salty breadsticks to Harris, taking one himself, saying that chewing breadsticks kept him in—ah—practice. Good day, good day, to Mr. Harris! Mr. Harris went home.

The next day, Sunday, Mr. Harris discovered innumerable fresh aches and pains in his body. He spent the morning, his eyes fixed staring with new interest at the small, anatomically perfect painting of a skeleton M. Munigant had given him.

His wife, Clarisse, startled him at dinner when she cracked her exquisitely thin knuckles, one by one, until he clapped his hands to his ears and cried, "Stop!"

The rest of the afternoon he quarantined himself in his room. Clarisse played bridge in the parlor laughing and chatting with three other ladies while Harris, hidden away, fingered and weighed the limbs of his body with growing curiosity. After an hour he suddenly rose and called:

"Clarisse!"

She had a way of dancing into any room, her body doing all sorts of soft, agreeable things to keep her feet from ever quite touching the nap of a rug. She excused herself from her friends and came to see him now, brightly. She found him re-seated in a far corner and she saw that he was staring at the anatomical sketch. "Are you still brooding, sweet?" she asked. "Please don't." She sat upon his knees.

Her beauty could not distract him now in his absorption. He juggled her lightness, he touched her kneecap, suspiciously. It seemed to move under her pale, glowing skin. "Is it supposed to do that?" he asked, sucking in his breath.

"Is what supposed to do what?" she laughed. "You mean my kneecap?"

"Is it supposed to run around on top your knee that way?"

She experimented. "So it *does*," she marveled.

"I'm glad yours slithers, too," he sighed. "I was beginning to worry."

"About what?"

He patted his ribs. "My ribs don't go all the way down, they stop *here*. And I found some confounded ones that dangle in mid-air!"

Beneath the curve of her small breasts, Clarisse clasped her hands.

"Of course, silly, everybody's ribs stop at a given point. And those funny short ones are floating ribs."

"I hope they don't float around too much." The joke was most uneasy. Now, above all, he wished to be alone. Further discoveries, newer and stranger archaeological diggings, lay within reach of his trembling hands, and he did not wish to be laughed at.

"Thanks for coming in, dear," he said.

"Any time." She rubbed her small nose softly against his.

"Wait! Here, now . . ." He put his finger to touch his nose and hers. "Did you realize? The nose-bone grows down only *this* far. From there on a lot of gristly tissue fills out the rest!"

She wrinkled hers. "Of course, darling!" And she danced from the room.

Now, sitting alone, he felt the perspiration rise from the pools and hollows of his face, to flow in a thin tide down his cheeks. He licked his lips and shut his eyes. Now . . . now . . . next on the agenda, what . . . ? The spinal cord, yes. Here. Slowly, he examined it, in the same way he operated the many push-buttons in his office, thrusting them to summon secretaries, messengers. But now, in these pushings of his spinal column, fears and terrors answered, rushed from a million doors in his mind to confront and shake him! His spine felt horribly—unfamiliar. Like the brittle shards of a fish, freshly eaten, its bones left strewn on a cold china platter. He seized the little rounded knobbins. "Lord! Lord!"

His teeth began to chatter. God All-Mighty! he thought, why haven't I realized it all these years? All these years I've gone around with a—SKELETON—inside me! How is it we take ourselves for granted? How is it we never question our bodies and our being?

A skeleton. One of those jointed, snowy, hard things, one of those foul, dry, brittle, gouge-eyed, skull-faced, shake-fingered, rattling things that sway from neck-chains in abandoned webbed closets, one of those things found on the desert all long and scattered like dice!

He stood upright, because he could not bear to remain seated. Inside me now, he grasped his stomach, his head, inside my head is a—skull. One of those curved carapaces which holds my brain like an electrical jelly, one of those cracked shells with the holes in front like two holes shot through it by a double-barreled shotgun! With its grottoes and caverns of bone, its revetments and placements for my flesh, my smelling, my seeing, my hearing, my thinking! A skull, encompassing my brain, allowing it exit through its brittle windows to see the outside world!

He wanted to dash into the bridge party, upset it, a fox in a chickenyard, the cards fluttering all around like chicken feathers burst upward in clouds! He stopped himself only with a violent, trembling effort. Now, now, man, control yourself. This is a revelation, take it for what it's worth, understand it, savor it. BUT A SKELETON! screamed his subconscious. I won't stand for it. It's vulgar, it's terrible, it's frightening. Skeletons are horrors; they clink and tinkle and rattle in old castles, hung from oaken beams, making long, indolently rustling pendulums on the wind. . . .

"Darling, will you come meet the ladies?" His wife's clear, sweet voice called from far away.

Mr. Harris stood. His SKELETON held him up! This thing inside, this invader, this horror, was supporting his arms, legs, and head! It was like feeling someone just behind you who shouldn't be there. With every step, he realized how dependent he was on this other Thing.

"Darling, I'll be with you in a moment," he called weakly. To himself he said, Come on, brace up! You've got to go back to work tomorrow. Friday you must make that trip to Phoenix. It's a long drive. Hundreds of miles. Must be in shape for that trip or you won't get Mr. Creldon to invest in your ceramics business. Chin up, now!

A moment later he stood among the ladies, being introduced to Mrs. Withers, Mrs. Abblematt, and Miss Kirthy, all of whom had skeletons inside them, but took it very calmly, because nature had carefully clothed the bare nudity of clavicle, tibia, and femur with breasts, thighs, calves, with coiffure and eyebrow satanic, with bee-stung lips and—LORD! shouted Mr. Harris inwardly—when they talk or eat, part of their skeleton shows—their *teeth*! I never thought of that. "Excuse me," he gasped, and ran from the room only in time to drop his lunch among the petunias over the garden balustrade.

That night, seated on the bed as his wife undressed, he pared his toenails and fingernails scrupulously. These parts, too, were where his skeleton was shoving, indignantly growing out. He must have muttered part of this theory, because next thing he knew his wife, in negligee, was on the bed, her arms about his neck, yawning, "Oh, my darling, fingernails are *not* bone, they're only hardened epidermis!"

He threw the scissors down. "Are you certain? I hope so. I'd feel better." He looked at the curve of her body, marveling. "I hope all people are made the same way."

"If you aren't the darndest hypochondriac!" She held him at arm's length. "Come on. What's wrong? Tell mama."

"Something inside me," he said. "Something—I ate."

The next morning and all afternoon at his downtown office, Mr. Harris sorted out the sizes, shapes, and construction of various bones in his body with displeasure. At ten A.M. he asked to feel Mr. Smith's elbow one moment. Mr. Smith obliged, but scowled suspiciously. And after lunch Mr. Harris asked to touch Miss Laurel's shoulder blade and she immediately pushed herself back against him, purring like a kitten and shutting her eyes.

"Miss Laurel!" he snapped. "Stop that!"

Alone, he pondered his neuroses. The war was just over, the pressure of his work, the uncertainty of the future, probably had much to do with his mental outlook. He wanted to leave the office, get into business for himself. He had more than a little talent for ceramics and sculpture. As soon as possible he'd head for Arizona, borrow that money from Mr. Creldon, build a kiln and set up shop. It was a worry. What a case he was. But luckily he had contacted M. Munigant, who seemed eager to understand and help him. He would fight it out with himself, not go back to either Munigant or Dr. Burleigh unless he was forced to. The alien feeling would pass. He sat staring into space.

The alien feeling did not pass. It grew.

On Tuesday and Wednesday it bothered him terrifically that his epidermis, hair and other appendages were of a high disorder, while his integumented skeleton of himself was a slick clean structure of efficient organization. Sometimes, in certain lights with his lips drawn morosely down, weighted with melancholy, he imagined he saw his skull grinning at him behind the flesh.

Let go! he cried. Let go of me! My lungs! Stop!

He gasped convulsively, as if his ribs were crushing the breath from him.

My brain—stop squeezing it!

And terrifying headaches burnt his brain to a blind cinder.

My insides, let them be, for God's sake! Stay away from my heart!

His heart cringed from the fanning motion of ribs like pale spiders crouched and fiddling with their prey.

Drenched with sweat, he lay upon the bed one night while

Clarisse was out attending a Red Cross meeting. He tried to gather his wits but only grew more aware of the conflict between his dirty exterior and this beautiful cool clean calcimed thing inside.

His complexion: wasn't it oily and lined with worry?

Observe the flawless, snow-white perfection of the skull.

His nose: wasn't it too large?

Then observe the tiny bones of the skull's nose before that monstrous nasal cartilage begins forming the lopsided proboscis.

His body: wasn't it plump?

Well, consider the skeleton; slender, svelte, economical of line and contour. Exquisitely carved oriental ivory! Perfect, thin as a white praying mantis!

His eyes: weren't they protuberant, ordinary, numb-looking?

Be so kind as to note the eye-sockets of the skull; so deep and rounded, somber, quiet pools, all-knowing, eternal. Gaze deep and you never touch the bottom of their dark understanding. All irony, all life, all everything is there in the cupped darkness.

Compare. Compare. Compare.

He raged for hours. And the skeleton, ever the frail and solemn philosopher, hung quietly inside, saying not a word, suspended like a delicate insect within a chrysalis, waiting and waiting.

Harris sat slowly up.

"Wait a minute. Hold on!" he exclaimed. "You're helpless, too. I've got you, too. I can make you do anything I want! You can't prevent it! I say move your carpales, metacarpales, and phalanges and—sswtt—up they go, as I wave to someone!" He laughed. "I order the fibula and femur to locomote and *Hunn* two three four, *Hunn* two three four—we walk around the block. There!"

Harris grinned.

"It's a fifty-fifty fight. Even-Stephen. And we'll fight it out, we two! After all, I'm the part that *thinks*! Yes, by God! yes. Even if I didn't have you, I could still think!"

Instantly, a tiger's jaw snapped shut, chewing his brain in half. Harris screamed. The bones of his skull grabbed hold and gave him nightmares. Then slowly, while he shrieked, nuzzled and ate the nightmares one by one, until the last one was gone and the light went out. . . .

At the end of the week he postponed the Phoenix trip because of his health. Weighing himself on a penny scale he saw the slow gliding red arrow point to: 165.

He groaned. Why, I've weighed 175 for years. I can't have lost ten pounds! He examined his cheeks in the fly-dotted mirror. Cold, primitive fear rushed over him in odd little shivers. You, you! I know what you're about, *you*!

He shook his fist at his bony face, particularly addressing his remarks to his superior maxillary, his inferior maxillary, to his cranium and to his cervical vertebrae.

"You damn thing, you! Think you can starve me, make me lose weight, eh? Peel the flesh off, leave nothing, but skin on bone. Trying to ditch me, so you can be supreme, ah? No, no!"

He fled into a cafeteria.

Turkey, dressing, creamed potatoes, four vegetables, three desserts, he could eat none of it, he was sick to his stomach. He forced himself. His teeth began to ache. Bad teeth, is it? he thought angrily. I'll eat in spite of every tooth clanging and banging and rattling so they fall in my gravy.

His head blazed, his breath jerked in and out of a constricted chest, his teeth raged with pain, but he knew one small victory. He was about to drink milk when he stopped and poured it into a vase of nasturtiums. No calcium for you, my boy, no calcium for you. Never again shall I eat foods with calcium or other bone-fortifying minerals. I'll eat for one of us, not both, my lad.

"One hundred and fifty pounds," he said, the following week to his wife. "Do you *see* how I've changed?"

"For the better," said Clarisse. "You were always a little plump for your height, darling." She stroked his chin. "I like your face. It's so much nicer; the lines of it are so firm and strong now."

"They're not *my* lines, they're his, damn him! You mean to say you like him better than you like me?"

"Him? Who's '*him*'?"

In the parlor mirror, beyond Clarisse, his skull smiled back at him behind his fleshy grimace of hatred and despair.

Fuming, he popped malt tablets into his mouth. This was one way of gaining weight when you couldn't keep other foods down. Clarisse noticed the malt pellets.

"But, darling, really, you don't have to regain the weight for me," she said.

Oh, shut up! he felt like saying.

She made him lie with his head in her lap. "Darling," she said, "I've watched you lately. You're so—badly off. You don't say anything, but you look—hunted. You toss in bed at night. Maybe you should go to a psychiatrist. But I think I can tell you everything he would say. I've put it all together from hints you've let escape you. I can tell you that you and your skeleton are one and the same, 'one nation, indivisible, with liberty and justice for all.' United you stand, divided you fall. If you two fellows can't get along like an old married couple in the future, go back and see Dr. Burleigh. But, first, relax. You're in a vicious circle; the more you worry, the more your bones stick out, the more you worry. After all, who picked this fight—you or that anonymous entity you claim is lurking around behind your alimentary canal?"

He closed his eyes. "I did. I guess I did. Go on Clarisse, keep talking."

"You rest now," she said softly. "Rest and forget."

Mr. Harris felt buoyed up for half a day, then he began to sag. It was all very well to blame his imagination, but this particular skeleton, by God, was fighting back.

Harris set out for M. Munigant's office late in the day. Walking for half an hour until he found the address, he caught sight of the name "M. Munigant" initialed in ancient, flaking gold on a glass plate outside the building. Then, his bones seemed to explode from their moorings, blasted and erupted with pain. Blinded, he staggered away. When he opened his eyes again he had rounded a corner. M. Munigant's office was out of sight.

The pains ceased.

M. Munigant was the man to help him. If the sight of his name could cause so titanic a reaction of course M. Munigant *must* be just the man.

But, not today. Each time he tried to return to that office, the terrible pains took hold. Perspiring, he had to give up and swayed into a cocktail bar.

Moving across the dim lounge, he wondered briefly if a

lot of blame couldn't be put on M. Munigant's shoulders. After all, it was Munigant who'd first drawn specific attention to his skeleton, and let the psychological impact of it slam home! Could M. Munigant be using him for some nefarious purpose? But what purpose? Silly to suspect him. Just a little doctor. Trying to be helpful. Munigant and his jar of breadsticks. Ridiculous. M. Munigant was okay, okay . . .

There was a sight within the cocktail lounge to give him hope. A large, fat man, round as a butterball, stood drinking consecutive beers at the bar. Now *there* was a successful man. Harris repressed a desire to go up, clap the fat man's shoulder, and inquire as to how he'd gone about impounding his bones. Yes, the fat man's skeleton was luxuriously closeted. There were pillows of fat here, resilient bulges of it there, with several round chandeliers of fat under his chin. The poor skeleton was lost; it could never fight clear of that blubber. It might have tried once—but not now, overwhelmed, not a bony echo of the fat man's supporter remained.

Not without envy, Harris approached the fat man as one might cut across the bow of an ocean liner. Harris ordered a drink, drank it, and then dared to address the fat man:

"Glands?"

"You talking to me?" asked the fat man.

"Or is there a special diet?" wondered Harris. "I beg your pardon, but, as you see, I'm down. Can't seem to put on any weight. I'd like a stomach like that one of yours. Did you grow it because you were afraid of something?"

"You," announced the fat man, "are drunk. But—I like drunkards." He ordered more drinks. "Listen close, I'll tell you. Layer by layer," said the fat man, "twenty years, man and boy, I built this." He held his vast stomach like a globe of the world, teaching his audience its gastronomical geography. "It was no overnight circus. The tent was not raised before dawn on the wonders installed within. I have cultivated my inner organs as if they were thoroughbred dogs, cats, and other animals. My stomach is a fat pink Persian tom slumbering, rousing at intervals to purr, mew, growl, and cry for chocolate titbits. I feed it well, it will 'most sit up for me. And, my dear fellow, my intestines are the rarest pure-bred Indian anacondas you ever viewed in the sleekest, coiled, fine and ruddy health. Keep 'em in prime, I do, all my pets. For fear of something? Perhaps."

This called for another drink for everyone.

"Gain weight?" The fat man savored the words on his tongue. "Here's what you do: get yourself a quarreling bird of a wife, a baker's dozen of relatives who can flush a covey of troubles out from behind the veriest molehill. Add to these a sprinkling of business associates whose prime motivation is snatching your last lonely quid, and you are well on your way to getting fat. How so? In no time you'll begin subconsciously building fat betwixt yourself and them. A buffer epidermal state, a cellular wall. You'll soon find that eating is the only fun on earth. But one needs to be bothered by outside sources. Too many people in this world haven't enough to worry about, then they begin picking on themselves, and they lose weight. Meet all of the vile, terrible people you can possibly meet, and pretty soon you'll be adding the good old fat!"

And with that advice, the fat man launched himself out into the dark tide of night, swaying mightily and wheezing.

"That's exactly what Dr. Burleigh told me, slightly changed," said Harris thoughtfully. "Perhaps that trip to Phoenix, now, at this time——"

The trip from Los Angeles to Phoenix was a sweltering one, crossing, as it did, the Mojave desert on a broiling yellow day. Traffic was thin and inconstant, and for long stretches there would not be a car on the road for miles ahead or behind. Harris twitched his fingers on the steering wheel. Whether or not Creldon, in Phoenix, lent him the money he needed to start his business, it was still a good thing to get away, to put distance behind.

The car moved in the hot sluice of desert wind. The one Mr. H. sat inside the other Mr. H. Perhaps both perspired. Perhaps both were miserable.

On a curve, the inside Mr. H. suddenly constricted the outer flesh, causing him to jerk forward on the hot steering wheel.

The car plunged off the road into boiling sand and turned half over.

Night came, a wind rose, the road was lonely and silent. The few cars that passed went swiftly on their way, their view obstructed. Mr. Harris lay unconscious, until very late he heard a wind rising out of the desert, felt the sting of little sand needles on his cheeks, and opened his eyes.

Morning found him gritty-eyed and wandering in thoughtless senseless circles, having, in his delirium, got away from the road. At noon he sprawled in the poor shade of a bush. The sun struck him with a keen sword edge, cutting through to his—bones. A vulture circled.

Harris' parched lips cracked open. "So that's it?" he whispered, red-eyed, bristle-cheeked. "One way or another you'll walk me, starve me, thirst me, kill me." He swallowed dry burrs of dust. "Sun cook off my flesh so you can peek out. Vultures lunch off me, and there you'll lie, grinning. Grinning with victory. Like a bleached xylophone strewn and played by vultures with an ear for odd music. You'd like that. Freedom."

He walked on through a landscape that shivered and bubbled in the direct pour of sunlight; stumbling, falling flat, lying to feed himself little mouths of fire. The air was blue alcohol flame, and vultures roasted and steamed and glittered as they flew in glides and circles. Phoenix. The road. Car. Water. Safety.

"Hey!"

Someone called from way off in the blue alcohol flame.

Mr. Harris propped himself up.

"Hey!"

The call was repeated. A crunching of footsteps, quick.

With a cry of unbelievable relief, Harris rose, only to collapse again into the arms of someone in a uniform with a badge.

The car tediously hauled, repaired, Phoenix reached, Harris found himself in such an unholy state of mind that the business transaction was a numb pantomime. Even when he got the loan and held the money in his hand, it meant nothing. This Thing within him like a hard white sword in a scabbard tainted his business, his eating, colored his love for Clarisse, made it unsafe to trust an automobile; all in all this Thing had to be put in its place. The desert incident had brushed too close. Too near the bone, one might say with an ironic twist of one's mouth. Harris heard himself thanking Mr. Creldon, dimly, for the money. Then he turned his car and motored back across the long miles, this time cutting across to San Diego, so he would miss that desert stretch between El Centro and Beaumont. He drove north along the coast. He didn't trust that desert. But—careful! Salt waves boomed, hissing on the beach outside Laguna. Sand, fish and crustacea would cleanse his bones as swiftly as vultures. Slow down on the curves over the surf.

Damn, he was sick!

Where to turn? Clarisse? Burleigh? Munigant? Bone specialist. Munigant. Well?

"Darling!" Clarisse kissed him. He winced at the solidness of the teeth and jaw behind the passionate exchange.

"Darling," he said, slowly, wiping his lips with his wrist, trembling.

"You look thinner; oh, darling, the business deal——?"

"It went through. I guess. Yes, it did."

She kissed him again. They ate a slow, falsely cheerful dinner, with Clarisse laughing and encouraging him. He studied the phone; several times he picked it up indecisively, then laid it down.

His wife walked in, putting on her coat and hat. "Well, sorry, but I have to leave." She pinched him on the cheek. "Come on now, cheer up! I'll be back from Red Cross in three hours. You lie around and snooze. I simply *have* to go."

When Clarisse was gone, Harris dialed the phone, nervously.

"M. Munigant?"

The explosions and the sickness in his body after he set the phone down were unbelievable. His bones were racked with every kind of pain, cold and hot, he had ever thought of or experienced in wildest nightmare. He swallowed all the aspirin he could find, in an effort to stave off the assault; but when the doorbell finally rang an hour later, he could not move; he lay weak and exhausted, panting, tears streaming down his cheeks.

"Come in! Come in, for God's sake!"

M. Munigant came in. Thank God the door was unlocked.

Oh, but Mr. Harris looked terrible. M. Munigant stood in the center of the living room, small and dark. Harris nodded. The pains rushed through him, hitting him with large iron hammers and hooks. M. Munigant's eyes glittered as he saw Harris' protuberant bones. Ah, he saw that Mr. Harris was now psychologically prepared for aid. Was it not so? Harris nodded again, feebly, sobbing. M. Munigant still whistled when he talked; something about his tongue and the whistling. No matter. Through his shimmering eyes Harris seemed to see M. Munigant shrink, get smaller. Imagination, of course. Harris sobbed out his story of the Phoenix trip. M. Munigant sympathized. This skeleton was a—a traitor! They would fix him for once and for all!

"Mr. Munigant," sighed Harris, faintly, "I—I never noticed before. Your tongue. Round, tube-like. Hollow? My eyes. Delirious. What do I do?"

M. Munigant whistled softly, appreciatively, coming closer. If Mr. Harris would relax in his chair, and open his mouth? The lights were switched off. M. Munigant peered into Harris' dropped jaw. Wider, please? It had been so hard, that first visit, to help Harris, with both body and bone in revolt. Now, he had cooperation from the flesh of the man, anyway, even if the skeleton protested. In the darkness, M. Munigant's voice got small, small, tiny, tiny. The whistling became high and shrill. Now. Relax, Mr. Harris. NOW!

Harris felt his jaw pressed violently in all directions, his tongue depressed as with a spoon, his throat clogged. He gasped for breath. Whistle. He couldn't breathe! Something squirmed, corkscrewed his cheeks out, bursting his jaws. Like a hot-water douche, something squirted into his sinuses, his ears clanged! "Ahhhh!" shrieked Harris, gagging. His head, its carapaces riven, shattered, hung loose. Agony shot fire through his lungs.

Harris could breathe again, momentarily. His watery eyes sprang wide. He shouted. His ribs, like sticks picked up and bundled, were loosened in him. Pain! He fell to the floor, wheezing out his hot breath.

Lights flickered in his senseless eyeballs, he felt his limbs swiftly cast loose and free. Through streaming eyes he saw the parlor.

The room was empty.

"M. Munigant? In God's name, where are you, M. Munigant? Come help me!"

M. Munigant was gone.

"Help!"

Then he heard it.

Deep down in the subterranean fissures of his body, the minute, unbelievable noises; little smackings and twistings and little dry chippings and grindings and nuzzling sounds—like a tiny hungry mouse down in the red-blooded dimness, gnawing ever so earnestly and expertly at what might have been, but was not, a submerged timber . . . !

Clarisse, walking along the sidewalk, held her head high and marched straight toward her house on Saint James Place. She was thinking of the Red Cross as she turned the corner and almost ran into this little dark man who smelled of iodine.

Clarisse would have ignored him if it were not for the fact that as she passed, he took something long, white and oddly familiar from his coat and proceeded to chew on it, as on a peppermint stick. Its end devoured, his extraordinary tongue darted within the white confection, sucking out the filling, making contented noises. He was still crunching his goody as she proceeded up the sidewalk to her house, turned the doorknob and walked in.

"Darling?" she called, smiling around. "Darling, where are you?" She shut the door, walked down the hall and into the living room. "Darling . . ."

She stared at the floor for twenty seconds, trying to understand.

She screamed.

Outside in the sycamore darkness, the little man pierced a long white stick with intermittent holes; then, softly, sighing, his lips puckered, played a little sad tune upon the improvised instrument to accompany the shrill and awful singing of Clarisse's voice as she stood in the living room.

Many times as a little girl Clarisse had run on the beach

sands, stepped on a jellyfish and screamed. It was not so bad, finding an intact, gelatin-skinned jellyfish in one's living room. One could step back from it.

It was when the jellyfish *called you by name* . . .

The Jar

IT WAS ONE of those things they keep in a jar in the tent of a sideshow on the outskirts of a little, drowsy town. One of those pale things drifting in alcohol plasma, forever dreaming and circling, with its peeled, dead eyes staring out at you and never seeing you. It went with the noiselessness of late night, and only the crickets chirping, the frogs sobbing off in the moist swampland. One of those things in a big jar that makes your stomach jump as it does when you see a preserved arm in a laboratory vat.

Charlie stared back at it for a long time.

A long time, his big, raw hands, hairy on the roofs of them, clenching the rope that kept back curious people. He had paid his dime and now he stared.

It was getting late. The merry-go-round drowsed down to a lazy mechanical tinkle. Tent-peggers back of a canvas smoked and cursed over a poker game. Lights switched out, putting a summer gloom over the carnival. People streamed homeward in cliques and queues. Somewhere, a radio flared up, then cut, leaving Louisiana sky wide and silent with stars.

There was nothing in the world for Charlie but that pale thing sealed in its universe of serum. Charlie's loose mouth hung open in a pink weal, teeth showing; his eyes were puzzled, admiring, wondering.

Someone walked in the shadows behind him, small beside Charlie's gaunt tallness. "Oh," said the shadow, coming into the light-bulb glare. "You still here, bud?"

"Yeah," said Charlie, like a man in his sleep.

The carny-boss appreciated Charlie's curiosity. He nodded at his old acquaintance in the jar. "Everybody likes it; in a peculiar kinda way, I mean."

Charlie rubbed his long jaw-bone. "You—uh—ever consider selling it?"

The carny-boss's eyes dilated, then closed. He snorted.

"Naw. It brings customers. They like seeing stuff like that. Sure."

Charlie made a disappointed, "oh."

"Well," considered the carny-boss, "if a guy had money, maybe——"

"How much money?"

"If a guy had——" the carny-boss estimated, counting fingers, watching Charlie as he tacked it out one finger after another. "If a guy had three, four, say, maybe seven or eight——"

Charlie nodded with each motion, expectantly. Seeing this, the carny-boss raised his total, "—maybe ten dollars, or maybe fifteen——"

Charlie scowled, worried. The carny-boss retreated. "Say a guy has *twelve* dollars——" Charlie grinned. "Why he could buy that thing in that jar," concluded the carny-boss.

"Funny thing," said Charlie, "I got just twelve bucks in my denims. And I been reckoning how looked-up-to I'd be back down at Wilder's Hollow if I brung home something like this to set on my shelf over the table. The folks would sure look up to me then, I bet."

"*Well*, now, listen here——" said the carny-boss.

The sale was completed with the jar put on the back seat of Charlie's wagon. The horse skittered his hoofs when he saw the jar, and whinnied.

The carny-boss glanced up with an expression of, almost, relief. "I was tired of seeing that damn thing around, anyway. Don't thank me. Lately I been thinking things about it, funny things——but, hell, I'm a big-mouthed so-and-so. S'long, farmer!"

Charlie drove off. The naked blue light bulbs withdrew like dying stars, the open, dark country night of Louisiana swept in around wagon and horse. There was just Charlie, the horse timing his gray hoofs, and the crickets.

And the jar behind the high seat.

It sloshed back and forth, back and forth. Sloshed wet. And the cold gray thing drowsily slumped against the glass, looking out, looking out, but seeing nothing, nothing.

Charlie leaned back to pet the lid. Smelling of strange liquor his hand returned, changed and cold and trembling, excited. *Yes, sir!* he thought to himself, *Yes, sir!*

Slosh, slosh, slosh. . . .

In the Hollow, numerous grass-green and blood-red lanterns tossed dusty light over men huddled, murmuring, spitting, sitting on General Store property.

They knew the creak-bumble of Charlie's wagon and did not shift their raw, drab-haired skulls as he rocked to a halt. Their cigars were glowworms, their voices were frog mutterings on summer nights.

Charlie leaned down eagerly. "Hi, Clem! Hi, Milt!"

"Lo, Charlie. Lo, Charlie," they murmured. The political conflict continued. Charlie cut it down the seam:

"I got somethin' here. I got somethin' you might wanna see!"

Tom Carmody's eyes glinted, green in the lamplight, from the General Store porch. It seemed to Charlie that Tom Carmody was forever installed under porches in shadow, or under trees in shadow, or if in a room, then in the farthest niche shining his eyes out at you from the dark. You never knew what his face was doing, and his eyes were always funning you. And every time they looked at you they laughed a different way.

"You ain't got nothin' we wants to see, baby-doll."

Charlie made a fist and looked at it. "Somethin' in a jar," he went on. "Looks kine a like a brain, kine a like a pickled jellyfish, kine a like—well, come see yourself!"

Someone snicked a cigar into a fall of pink ash and ambled over to look. Charlie grandly elevated the jar lid, and in the uncertain lantern light the man's face changed. "Hey, now, what in hell *is* this——?"

It was the first thaw of the evening. Others shifted lazily upright, leaned forward; gravity pulled them into walking. They made no effort, except to put one shoe before the other to keep from collapsing upon their unusual faces. They circled the jar and contents. And Charlie for the first time in his life, seized on some hidden strategy and crashed the glass lid shut.

"You want to see more, drop aroun' my house! It'll be there," he declared, generously.

Tom Carmody spat from out his porch eyrie. "Ha!"

"Lemme see that again!" cried Gramps Medknowe. "Is it a octopus?"

Charlie flapped the reins; the horse stumbled into action.

"Come on aroun'! You're welcome!"

"What'll your wife say?"

"She'll kick the tar off'n our heels!"

But Charlie and wagon were gone over the hill. The men stood, all of them, chewing their tongues, squinting up the road in the dark. Tom Carmody swore softly from the porch. . . .

Charlie climbed the steps of his shack and carried the jar to its throne in the living room, thinking that from now on this lean-to would be a palace, with an "emperor"—that was the word! "emperor"—all cold and white and quiet drifting in his private pool, raised, elevated upon a shelf over a ramshackle table.

The jar, as he watched, burnt off the cold mist that hung over this place on the rim of the swamp.

"What you got there?"

Thedy's thin soprano turned him from his awe. She stood in the bedroom door glaring out, her thin body clothed in faded blue gingham, her hair drawn to a drab knot behind red ears. Her eyes were faded like the gingham. "Well," she repeated. "What is it?"

"What's it look like to you, Thedy?"

She took a thin step forward, making a slow, indolent pendulum of hips, her eyes intent upon the jar, her lips drawn back to show feline milk teeth.

The dead pale thing hung in its serum.

Thedy snapped a dull-blue glance at Charlie, then back to the jar, once more at Charlie, once more to the jar, then she whirled quickly.

"It—it looks—looks just like *you*, Charlie!" she cried.

The bedroom door slammed.

The reverberation did not disturb the jar's contents. But Charlie stood there, longing after his wife, heart pounding frantically. Much later, when his heart slowed, he talked to the thing in the jar.

"I work the bottom land to the butt-bone every year, and she grabs the money and runs off down home visitin' her folks nine weeks at a stretch. I can't keep hold of her. Her and the men from the store, they make fun of me. I can't help it if I don't know a way to hold onto her! Damn, but I *try*!"

Philosophically, the contents of the jar gave no advice.

"Charlie?"

Someone stood in the front-yard door.

Charlie turned, startled, then broke out a grin.

It was some of the men from the General Store.

"Uh—Charlie—we—we thought—well—we came up to have a look at that—stuff—you got in that there jar——"

July passed warm and it was August.

For the first time in years, Charlie was happy as tall corn growing after a drought. It was gratifying of an evening to hear boots shushing through the tall grass, the sound of men spitting into the ditch prior to setting foot on the porch, the sound of heavy bodies creaking the boards, and the groan of the house as yet another shoulder leaned against its frame door and another voice said, as a hairy wrist wiped a mouth clean:

"Kin I come in?"

With elaborate casualness, Charlie'd invite the arrivals in. There'd be chairs, soapboxes for all, or at least carpets to squat on. And by the time crickets were itching their legs into a summertime humming and frogs were throat-swollen like ladies with goiters shouting in the great night, the room would be full to bursting with people from all the bottom lands.

At first nobody would say anything. The first half-hour of such an evening, while people came in and got settled, was spent in carefully rolling cigarettes. Putting tobacco neatly into the rut of brown paper, loading it, tamping it, as they loaded and tamped and rolled their thoughts and fears and amazement for the evening. It gave them time to think. You could see their brains working behind their eyes as they fingered the cigarettes into smoking order.

It was kind of a rude church gathering. They sat, squatted,

leaned on plaster walls, and one by one, with reverent awe, they stared at the jar upon its shelf.

They wouldn't stare sudden-like. No, they kind of did it slow, casual, as if they were glancing around the room—letting their eyes fumble over just *any* old object that happened into their consciousness.

And—just by accident, of course—the focus of their wandering eyes would occur always at the same place. After a while all eyes in the room would be fastened to it, like pins stuck in some incredible pincushion. And the only sound would be someone sucking a corncob. Or the children's barefooted scurry on the porch planks outside. Maybe some woman's voice would come, "You kids git away, now! Git!" And with a giggle like soft, quick water, the bare feet would rush off to scare the bullfrogs.

Charlie would be up front, naturally, on his rocking chair, a plaid pillow under his lean rump, rocking slow, enjoying the fame and looked-up-to-ness that came with keeping the jar.

Thedy, she'd be seen way back of the room with the womenfolk in a bunch, all gray and quiet, abiding their men.

Thedy looked like she was ripe for jealous screaming. But she said nothing, just watched men tromp into her living room and sit at the feet of Charlie, staring at this here Holy Grail–like thing, and her lips were set cold and hard and she spoke not a civil word to anybody.

After a period of proper silence, someone, maybe old Gramps Medknowe from Crick Road, would clear the phlegm from a deep cave somewhere inside himself, lean forward, blinking, wet his lips, maybe, and there'd be a curious tremble in his calloused fingers.

This would cue everyone to get ready for the talking to come. Ears were primed. People settled like sows in the warm mud after a rain.

Gramps looked a long while, measured his lips with a lizard tongue, then settled back and said, like always, in a high, thin old-man's tenor:

"Wonder what it is? Wonder if it's a he or a she or just a plain old *it*? Sometimes I wake up nights, twist on my corn-matting, think about that jar settin' here in the long dark. Think about it hangin' in liquid, peaceful and pale like an animal oyster. Sometimes I wake Maw and we both think on it. . . ."

While talking, Gramps moved his fingers in a quavering pantomime. Everybody watched his thick thumb weave, and the other heavy-nailed fingers undulate.

". . . we both lay there, thinkin'. And we shivers. May be a hot night, trees sweatin', mosquitoes too hot to fly, but we shivers jest the same, and turn over, tryin' to sleep. . . ."

Gramps lapsed back into silence, as if his speech was enough from him, let some other voice talk the wonder, awe, and strangeness.

Juke Marmer, from Willow Sump, wiped sweat off his palms on the round of his knees and softly said:

"I remember when I was a runnel-nosed kid. We had a cat who was all the time makin' kittens. Lordamighty, she'd a litter any time she jumped around and skipped a fence——" Juke spoke in a kind of holy softness, benevolent. "Well, we give the kittens away, but when this one particular litter busted out, everybody within walkin' distance had one-two our cats by gift, already.

"So Ma busied on the back porch with a big two-gallon glass jar, fillin' it to the top with water. Ma said, 'Juke, you drown them kittens!' I 'member I stood there; the kittens mewed, runnin' 'round, blind, small, helpless, and funny—just beginnin' to get their eyes open. I looked at Ma, I said, 'Not *me*, Ma! *You* do it!' But Ma turned pale and said it had to be done and I was the only one handy. And she went off to stir gravy and fix chicken. I—I picked up one—kitten. I held it. It was warm. It made a mewin' sound, I felt like runnin' away, not ever comin' back."

Juke nodded his head now, eyes bright, young, seeing into the past, making it new, shaping it with words, smoothing it with his tongue.

"I dropped the kitten in the water. The kitten closed his eyes, opened his mouth, tryin' for air. I 'member how the little white fangs showed, the pink tongue came out, and bubbles with it, in a line to the top of the water!

"I know to this day the way that kitten floated after it was all over, driftin' aroun', slow and not worryin', lookin' out at me, not condemnin' me for what I done. But not likin' me, neither. Ahhhh. . . ."

Hearts jumped quick. Eyes swiveled from Juke to the shelved jar, back down, up again apprehensively.

A pause.

Jahdoo, the black man from Heron Swamp, tossed his ivory eyeballs, like a dusky juggler, in his head. His dark knuckles knotted and flexed—grasshoppers alive.

"You know what that is? You know, you *know*? I tells you. That be the center of Life, sure 'nuff! Lord believe me, it so!"

Swaying in a tree-like rhythm, Jahdoo was blown by a swamp wind no one could see, hear or feel, save himself. His eyeballs went around again, as if cut free to wander. His voice needled a dark thread pattern, picking up each person by the lobes of their ears and sewing them into one unbreathing design:

"From that, lyin' back in the Middibamboo Sump, all sort o' thing crawl. It put out hand, it put out feet, it put out tongue an' horn an' it grow. Little bitty amoeba, perhap. Then a frog with a bulge-throat fit ta bust! Yah!" He cracked knuckles. "It slobber on up to its gummy joints and it—it AM HUMAN! That am the center of creation! That am Middibamboo Mama, from which we all come ten thousand year ago. Believe it!"

"Ten thousand year ago!" whispered Granny Carnation.

"It am old! Looky it! It donn worra no more. It know betta. It hang like pork chop in fryin' fat. It got eye to see with, but it donn blink 'em, they donn look fretted, does they? No, man! It know betta. It know that we done come *from* it, and we is goin' back *to* it."

"What color eyes it got?"

"Gray."

"Naw, *green*!"

"What color hair? Brown?"

"Black!"

"Red!"

"No, *gray*!"

Then, Charlie would give his drawling opinion. Some nights he'd say the same thing, some nights not. It didn't matter. When you said the same thing night after night in the deep summer, it always sounded different. The crickets changed it. The frogs changed it. The thing in the jar changed it. Charlie said:

"What if an old man went back into the swamp, or maybe a young kid, and wandered aroun' for years and years lost in all that drippin', on the trails and gullies, in them old wet ravines in the nights, skin a turnin' pale, and makin' cold and shrivelin' up. Bein' away from the sun he'd keep witherin' away up and up and finally sink into a muck-hole and lay in a kind of—scum—like the maggot 'skeeters sleepin' in sump-water. Why, why—for all we can tell, this might be someone we *know*! Someone we passed words with once on a time. For all we know——"

A hissing from among the womenfolk back in the shadow. One woman standing, eyes shining black, fumbled for words. Her name was Mrs. Tridden, and she murmured:

"Lots of little kids run stark naked to the swamp ever' year. They runs around and never comes back. I almost got lost maself. I—I lost my little boy, Foley, that way. You—you DON'T SUPPOSE ! ! !"

Breath was snatched through nostrils, constricted, tightened. Mouths turned down at corners, bent by hard, clinching muscle. Heads turned on celery-stalk necks, and eyes read her horror and hope. It was in Mrs. Tridden's body, wire-taut, holding to the wall back of her with straight fingers stiff.

"My baby," she whispered. She breathed it out. "My baby. My Foley. Foley! Foley, is that you? Foley! Foley, tell me, baby, is that YOU!"

Everybody held their breath, turning to see the jar.

The thing in the jar said nothing. It just stared blind-white out upon the multitude. And deep in rawboned bodies a secret fear juice ran like a spring thaw, and their resolute calmness and belief and easy humbleness was gnawed and eaten by that juice and melted away in a torrent! Someone screamed.

"It moved!"

"No, no, it didn' move. Just your eyes playin' tricks!"

"Hones' ta God!" cried Juke. "I saw it shift slow like a dead kitten!"

"Hush up, now. It's been dead a long, long time. Maybe since before you was born!"

"He made a sign!" screamed Mrs. Tridden. "That's my Foley! My baby you got there! Three-year-old he was! My baby lost and gone in the swamp!"

The sobbing broke from her.

"Now, Mrs. Tridden. There now. Set yourself down, stop shakin'. Ain't no more your child'n mine. There, there."

One of the womenfolk held her and faded out the sobbing into jerked breathing and a fluttering of her lips in butterfly quickness as the breath stroked over them, afraid.

When all was quiet again, Granny Carnation, with a withered pink flower in her shoulder-length gray hair, sucked the pipe in her trap mouth and talked around it, shaking her head to make the hair dance in the light:

"All this talkin' and shovin' words. Like as not we'll never find out, never know what it is. Like as not if we found out we wouldn't *want* to know. It's like magic tricks magicians do at shows. Once you find the fake, ain't no more fun'n the innards of a jackbob. We come collectin' around here every ten nights or so, talkin', social-like, with somethin', always somethin', to talk about. Stands to reason if we spied out what the damn thing is there'd be nothin' to chew about, so there!"

"Well, damn it to hell!" rumbled a bull voice. "I don't think it's nothin'!"

Tom Carmody.

Tom Carmody standing, as always, in shadow. Out on the porch, just his eyes staring in, his lips laughing at you dimly, mocking. His laughter got inside Charlie like a hornet sting. Thedy had put him up to it. Thedy was trying to kill Charlie's new life, she was!

"Nothin'," repeated Carmody, harshly, "in that jar but a bunch of old jellyfish from Sea Cove, a rottin' and stinkin' fit to whelp!"

"You mightn't be jealous, Cousin Carmody?" asked Charlie, slow.

"Haw!" snorted Carmody. "I just come aroun' ta watch you dumb fools jaw about nuthin'. You notice I never set foot inside or took part. I'm goin' home right now. Anybody wanna come along with me?"

He got no offer of company. He laughed again, as if this were a bigger joke, how so many people could be so far gone, and Thedy was raking her palms with her fingernails away back in a corner of the room. Charlie saw her mouth twitch and was cold and could not speak.

Carmody, still laughing, rapped off the porch with his high-heeled boots and the sound of crickets took him away.

Granny Carnation gummed her pipe. "Like I was sayin' before the storm: that thing on the shelf, why couldn't it be sort of—all things? Lots of things. All kinds of life—death—I don't know. Mix rain and sun and muck and jelly, all that together. Grass and snakes and children and mist and all the nights and days in the dead canebrake. Why's it have to be *one* thing? Maybe it's *lots*."

And the talking ran soft for another hour, and Thedy slipped away into the night on the track of Tom Carmody, and Charlie began to sweat. They were up to something, those two. They were planning something. Charlie sweated warm all the rest of the evening. . . .

The meeting broke up late, and Charlie bedded down with mixed emotions. The meeting had gone off well, but what about Thedy and Tom?

Very late, with certain star coveys shuttled down the sky marking the time as after midnight, Charlie heard the shushing of the tall grass parted by her penduluming hips. Her heels tacked soft across the porch, into the house, into the bedroom.

She lay soundlessly in bed, cat eyes staring at him. He couldn't see them, but he could feel them staring.

"Charlie?"

He waited.

Then he said, "I'm awake."

Then she waited.

"Charlie?"

"What?"

"Bet you don't know where I been; bet you don't know where I been." It was a faint, derisive singsong in the night.

He waited.

She waited again. She couldn't bear waiting long, though, and continued:

"I been to the carnival over in Cape City. Tom Carmody drove me. We—we talked to the carny-boss, Charlie, we did, we did, we *sure* did!" And she sort of giggled to herself, secretly.

Charlie was ice-cold. He stirred upright on an elbow.

She said, "We found out what it is in your jar, Charlie——" insinuatingly.

Charlie flumped over, hands to ears. "I don't wanna hear!"

"Oh, but you gotta hear, Charlie. It's a good joke. Oh, it's rare, Charlie," she hissed.

"Go away," he said.

"Unh-unh! No, no, sir, Charlie. Why, no, Charlie—Honey. Not until I tell!"

"Git!" he said.

"Let me tell! We talked to that carny-boss, and he—he liked to die laughin'. He said he sold that jar and what was in it to some, some—hick—for twelve bucks. And it ain't worth more'n two bucks at most!"

Laughter bloomed in the dark, right out of her mouth, an awful kind of laughter.

She finished it, quick:

"It's just junk, Charlie! Rubber, papier-mache, silk, cotton, boric-acid! That's all! Got a metal frame inside! That's all it is, Charlie. That's all!" she shrilled.

"No, no!"

He sat up swiftly, ripping sheets apart in big fingers, roaring.

"I don't wanna hear! Don't wanna hear!" he bellowed over and over.

She said, "Wait'll everyone hears how fake it is! Won't they laugh! Won't they flap their lungs!"

He caught her wrists. "You ain't gonna tell them?"

"Wouldn't wan me known as a liar, would you, Charlie?"

He flung her off and away.

"Whyncha leave me alone? You dirty! Dirty jealous mean of ever'thing I do. I took shine off your nose when I brung the jar home. You didn' sleep right 'til you ruined things!"

She laughed. "Then I won't tell anybody," she said.

He stared at her. "You spoiled *my* fun. That's all that counted. It don't matter if you tell the rest. *I* know. And I'll never have no more fun. You and that Tom Carmody. I wish I could stop him laughin'. He's been laughin' for years at me! Well, you just go tell the rest, the other people, now—might as well have your fun——!"

He strode angrily, grabbed the jar so it sloshed, and would have flung it on the floor, but he stopped trembling, and let it down softly on the spindly table. He leaned over it, sobbing. If he lost this, the world was gone. And he was losing Thedy, too. Every month that passed she danced further away, sneering at him, funning him. For too many years her hips had been the pendulum by which he reckoned the time of his living. But other men, Tom Carmody, for one, were reckoning time from the same source.

Thedy stood waiting for him to smash the jar. Instead, he petted and stroked and gradually quieted himself over it. He thought of the long, good evenings in the past month, those rich evenings of friends and talk, moving about the room. That, at least, was good, if nothing else.

He turned slowly to Thedy. She was lost forever to him.

"Thedy, you didn't go to the carnival."

"Yes, I did."

"You're lyin'," he said, quietly.

"No, I'm not!"

"This—this jar *has* to have somethin' in it. Somethin' besides the junk you say. Too many people believe there's somethin' in it. Thedy. You can't change that. The carny-boss, if you talked with him, he lied." Charlie took a deep breath and then said, "Come here, Thedy."

"What you want?" she asked, sullenly.

"Come over here."

He took a step toward her. "Come here."

"Keep away from me, Charlie."

"Just want to show you something, Thedy." His voice was soft, low, and insistent. "Here, kittie. Here, kittie, kittie, kittie—HERE KITTIE!"

It was another night, about a week later. Gramps Medknowe and Granny Carnation came, followed by young Juke and Mrs. Tridden and Jahdoo, the colored man. Followed by all the others, young and old, sweet and sour, creaking into chairs, each with his or her thought, hope, fear, and wonder in mind. Each not looking at the shrine, but saying hello softly to Charlie.

They waited for the others to gather. From the shine of their eyes one could see that each saw something different in the jar, something of the life and the pale life after life, and the life in death and the death in life, each with his story, his cue, his lines, familiar, old but new.

Charlie sat alone.

"Hello, Charlie." Somebody peered into the empty bedroom. "Your wife gone off again to visit her folks?"

"Yeah, she run for Tennessee. Be back in a couple weeks. She's the darndest one for runnin'. You know Thedy."

"Great one for jumpin' around, that woman."

Soft voices talking, getting settled, and then, quite suddenly, walking on the dark porch and shining his eyes in at the people—Tom Carmody.

Tom Carmody standing outside the door, knees sagging and trembling, arms hanging and shaking at his side, staring into the room. Tom Carmody not daring to enter. Tom Carmody with his mouth open, but not smiling. His lips wet and slack, not smiling. His face pale as chalk, as if it had been sick for a long time.

Gramps looked up at the jar, cleared his throat and said, "Why, I never noticed so definite before. It's got *blue* eyes."

"It always had blue eyes," said Granny Carnation.

"No," whined Gramps. "No, it didn't. They was brown last time we was here." He blinked upward. "And another thing—it's got brown hair. Didn't have brown hair *before*!"

"Yes, yes, it did," sighed Mrs. Tridden.

"No, it didn't!"

"Yes, it did!"

Tom Carmody, shivering in the summer night, staring in at the jar. Charlie, glancing up at it, rolling a cigarette, casually, all peace and calm, very certain of his life and thoughts. Tom Carmody, alone, seeing things about the jar he never saw before. *Everybody* seeing what they wanted to see; all thoughts running in a fall of quick rain:

"My baby. My little baby," thought Mrs. Tridden.

"A brain!" thought Gramps.

The colored man jigged his fingers. "Middibamboo Mama!"

A fisherman pursed his lips. "Jellyfish!"

"Kitten! Here kittie, kittie, kittie!" the thoughts drowned clawing in Juke's eyes. "Kitten!"

"Everything and anything!" shrilled Granny's weazened

thought. "The night, the swamp, death, the pale things, the wet things from the sea!"

Silence. And then Gramps whispered, "I wonder. Wonder if it's a he—or a she—or just a plain old *it*?"

Charlie glanced up, satisfied, tamping his cigarette, shaping it to his mouth. Then he looked at Tom Carmody, who would never smile again, in the door. "I reckon we'll never know. Yeah, I reckon we won't." Charlie shook his head slowly and settled down with his guests, looking, looking.

It was just one of those things they keep in a jar in the tent of a sideshow on the outskirts of a little, drowsy town. One of those pale things drifting in alcohol plasma, forever dreaming and circling, with its peeled dead eyes staring out at you and never seeing you. . . .

The Lake

THE WAVE SHUT me off from the world, from the birds in the sky, the children on the beach, my mother on the shore. There was a moment of green silence. Then the wave gave me back to the sky, the sand, the children yelling. I came out of the lake and the world was waiting for me, having hardly moved since I went away.

I ran up on the beach.

Mama swabbed me with a furry towel. "Stand there and dry," she said.

I stood there, watching the sun take away the water beads on my arms. I replaced them with goose-pimples.

"My, there's a wind," said Mama. "Put on your sweater."

"Wait'll I watch my goose-bumps," I said.

"Harold," said Mama.

I put the sweater on and watched the waves come up and fall down on the beach. But not clumsily. On purpose, with a green sort of elegance. Even a drunken man could not collapse with such elegance as those waves.

It was September. In the last days when things are getting sad for no reason. The beach was so long and lonely with only about six people on it. The kids quit bouncing the ball because somehow the wind made them sad, too, whistling the way it did, and the kids sat down and felt autumn come along the endless shore.

All of the hot-dog stands were boarded up with strips of golden planking, sealing in all the mustard, onion, meat odors of the long, joyful summer. It was like nailing summer into a series of coffins. One by one the places slammed their covers down, padlocked their doors, and the wind came and touched the sand, blowing away all of the million footprints of July and August. It got so that now, in September, there was nothing but the mark of my rubber tennis shoes and Donald and Delaus Arnold's feet, down by the water curve.

Sand blew up in curtains on the sidewalks, and the merry-go-round was hidden with canvas, all of the horses frozen in mid-air on their brass poles, showing teeth, galloping on. With only the wind for music, slipping through canvas.

I stood there. Everyone else was in school. I was not. Tomorrow I would be on my way west across the United States on a train. Mom and I had come to the beach for one last brief moment.

There was something about the loneliness that made me want to get away by myself. "Mama, I want to run up the beach a ways," I said.

"All right, but hurry back, and don't go near the water."

I ran. Sand spun under me and the wind lifted me. You know how it is, running, arms out so you feel veils from your fingers, caused by wind. Like wings.

Mama withdrew into the distance, sitting. Soon she was only a brown speck and I was all alone.

Being alone is a newness to a twelve-year-old child. He is so used to people about. The only way he can be alone is in his mind. There are so many real people around, telling children what and how to do, that a boy has to run off down a beach, even if it's only in his head, to get by himself in his own world.

So now I was really alone.

I went down to the water and let it cool up to my stomach. Always before, with the crowd, I hadn't dared to look, to come to this spot and search around in the water and call a certain name. But now——

Water is like a magician. Sawing you in half. It feels as if you were cut in two, part of you, the lower part, sugar, melting, dissolving away. Cool water, and once in a while a very elegantly stumbling wave that fell with a flourish of lace.

I called her name. A dozen times I called it.

"Tally! Tally! Oh, Tally!"

You really expect answers to your calling when you are young. You feel that whatever you may think can be real. And some times maybe that is not so wrong.

I thought of Tally, swimming out into the water last May, with her pigtails trailing, blond. She went laughing, and the sun was on her small twelve-year-old shoulders. I thought of the water settling quiet, of the life guard leaping into it, of Tally's mother screaming, and of how Tally never came out. . . .

The life guard tried to persuade her to come out, but she

did not. He came back with only bits of water-weed in his big-knuckled fingers, and Tally was gone. She would not sit across from me at school any longer, or chase indoor balls on the brick streets on summer nights. She had gone too far out, and the lake would not let her return.

And now in the lonely autumn when the sky was huge and the water was huge and the beach was so very long, I had come down for the last time, alone.

I called her name again and again. Tally, oh, Tally!

The wind blew so very softly over my ears, the way wind blows over the mouths of sea-shells to set them whispering. The water rose, embraced my chest, then my knees, up and down, one way and another, sucking under my heels.

"Tally! Come back, Tally!"

I was only twelve. But I know how much I loved her. It was that love that comes before all significance of body and morals. It was that love that is no more bad than wind and sea and sand lying side by side forever. It was made of all the warm long days together at the beach, and the humming quiet days of droning education at the school. All the long autumn days of the years past when I had carried her books home from school.

Tally!

I called her name for the last time. I shivered. I felt water on my face and did not know how it got there. The waves had not splashed that high.

Turning, I retreated to the sand and stood there for half an hour, hoping for one glimpse, one sign, one little bit of Tally to remember. Then, I knelt and built a sand castle, shaping it fine, building it as Tally and I had often built so many of them. But this time, I only built half of it. Then I got up.

"Tally, if you hear me, come in and build the rest."

I walked off toward that far-away speck that was Mama. The water came in, blended the sand-castle circle by circle, mashing it down little by little into the original smoothness.

Silently, I walked along the shore.

Far away, a merry-go-round jangled faintly, but it was only the wind.

The next day, I went away on the train.

A train has a poor memory; it soon puts all behind it. It forgets the cornlands of Illinois, the rivers of childhood, the bridges, the lakes, the valleys, the cottages, the hurts and the joys. It spreads them out behind and they drop back of a horizon.

I lengthened my bones, put flesh on them, changed my young mind for an older one, threw away clothes as they no longer fitted, shifted from grammar to high-school, to college. And then there was a young woman in Sacramento. I knew her for a time, and we were married. By the time I was twenty-two, I had almost forgotten what the East was like.

Margaret suggested that our delayed honeymoon be taken back in that direction.

Like a memory, a train works both ways. A train can bring rushing back all those things you left behind so many years before.

Lake Bluff, population 10,000, came up over the sky. Margaret looked so handsome in her fine new clothes. She watched me as I felt my old world gather me back into its living. She held my arm as the train slid into Bluff Station and our baggage was escorted out.

So many years, and the things they do to people's faces and bodies. When we walked through the town together I saw no one I recognized. There were faces with echoes in them. Echoes of hikes on ravine trails. Faces with small laughter in them from closed grammar schools and swinging on metal-linked swings and going up and down on teeter-totters. But I didn't speak. I walked and looked and filled up inside with all those memories, like leaves stacked for autumn burning.

We stayed on two weeks in all, revisiting all the places together. The days were happy. I thought I loved Margaret well. At least I thought I did.

It was on one of the last days that we walked down by the shore. It was not quite as late in the year as that day so many years before, but the first evidences of desertion were coming upon the beach. People were thinning out, several of the hot-dog stands had been shuttered and nailed, and the wind, as always, waited there to sing for us.

I almost saw Mama sitting on the sand as she used to sit. I had that feeling again of wanting to be alone. But I could not force myself to speak of this to Margaret. I only held onto her and waited.

It got late in the day. Most of the children had gone home and only a few men and women remained basking in the windy sun.

The life-guard boat pulled up on the shore. The life guard stepped out of it, slowly, with something in his arms.

I froze there. I held my breath and I felt small, only twelve years old, very little, very infinitesimal and afraid. The wind howled. I could not see Margaret. I could see only the beach, the life guard slowly emerging from the boat with a gray sack in his hands, not very heavy, and his face almost as gray and lined.

"Stay here, Margaret," I said. I don't know why I said it.

"But, why?"

"Just stay here, that's all——"

I walked slowly down the sand to where the life guard stood. He looked at me.

"What is it?" I asked.

The life guard kept looking at me for a long time and he couldn't speak. He put the gray sack on the sand, and water whispered wet up around it and went back.

"What is it?" I insisted.

"Strange," said the life guard, quietly.

I waited.

"Strange," he said, softly. "Strangest thing I ever saw. She's been dead a long time."

I repeated his words.

He nodded. "Ten years, I'd say. There haven't been any children drowned here this year. There were twelve children drowned here since 1933, but we found all of them before a few hours had passed. All except one, I remember. This body here, why it must be ten years in the water. It's not—pleasant."

I stared at the gray sack in his arms. "Open it," I said. I don't know why I said it. The wind was louder.

He fumbled with the sack.

"Hurry, man, open it!" I cried.

"I better not do that," he said. Then perhaps he saw the way my face must have looked. "She was such a *little* girl——"

He opened it only part way. That was enough.

The beach was deserted. There was only the sky and the

wind and the water and the autumn coming on lonely. I looked down at her there.

I said something over and over. A name. The life guard looked at me. "Where did you find her?" I asked.

"Down the beach, that way, in the shallow water. It's a long, long time for her, isn't it?"

I shook my head.

"Yes, it is. Oh God, yes it is."

I thought: people grow. I have grown. But she has not changed. She is still small. She is still young. Death does not permit growth or change. She still has golden hair. She will be forever young and I will love her forever, oh God, I will love her forever.

The life guard tied up the sack again.

Down the beach, a few moments later, I walked by myself. I stopped, and looked down at something. This is where the life guard found her, I said to myself.

There, at the water's edge, lay a sand castle, only half-built. Just like Tally and I used to build them. She half and I half.

I looked at it. I knelt beside the sand castle and saw the small prints of feet coming in from the lake and going back out to the lake again and not returning.

Then—I knew.

"I'll help you finish it," I said.

I did. I built the rest of it up very slowly, then I arose and turned away and walked off, so as not to watch it crumble in the waves, as all things crumble.

I walked back up the beach to where a strange woman named Margaret was waiting for me, smiling. . . .

The Emissary

MARTIN KNEW IT was autumn again, for Dog ran into the house bringing wind and frost and a smell of apples turned to cider under trees. In dark clock-springs of hair, Dog fetched goldenrod, dust of farewell-summer, acorn-husk, hair of squirrel, feather of departed robin, sawdust from fresh-cut cordwood, and leaves like charcoals shaken from a blaze of maple trees. Dog jumped. Showers of brittle fern, blackberry vine, marsh-grass sprang over the bed where Martin shouted. No doubt, no doubt of it at all, this incredible beast was October!

"Here, boy, here!"

And Dog settled to warm Martin's body with all the bonfires and subtle burnings of the season, to fill the room with soft or heavy, wet or dry odors of far-traveling. In spring, he smelled of lilac, iris, lawn-mowered grass; in summer, ice-cream-mustached, he came pungent with firecracker, Roman candle, pinwheel, baked by the sun. But autumn! Autumn!

"Dog, what's it like outside?"

And lying there, Dog told as he always told. Lying there, Martin found autumn as in the old days before sickness bleached him white on his bed. Here was his contact, his carry-all, the quick-moving part of himself he sent with a yell to run and return, circle and scent, collect and deliver the time and texture of worlds in town, country, by creek, river, lake, down-cellar, up-attic, in closet or coal-bin. Ten dozen times a day he was gifted with sunflower seed, cinder-path, milkweed, horse-chestnut, or full flame-smell of pumpkin. Through the loomings of the universe Dog shuttled; the design was hid in his pelt. Put out your hand, it was there. . . .

"And where did you go this morning?"

But he knew without hearing where Dog had rattled down hills where autumn lay in cereal crispness, where children lay in funeral pyres, in rustling heaps, the leaf-buried but watchful dead, as Dog and the world blew by. Martin trembled his fingers, searched the thick fur, read the long journey. Through stubbled fields, over glitters of ravine creek, down marbled spread of cemetery yard, into woods. In the great season of spices and rare incense, now Martin ran through his emissary, around, about, and home!

The bedroom door opened.

"That dog of yours is in trouble again."

Mother brought in a tray of fruit salad, cocoa, and toast, her blue eyes snapping.

"Mother . . ."

"Always digging places. Dug a hole in Miss Tarkin's garden this morning. She's spittin' mad. That's the fourth hole he's dug there this week."

"Maybe he's looking for something."

"Fiddlesticks, he's too darned curious. If he doesn't behave he'll be locked up."

Martin looked at this woman as if she were a stranger. "Oh, you wouldn't do that! How would I learn anything? How would I find things out if Dog didn't tell me?"

Mom's voice was quieter. "Is that what he does—tell you things?"

"There's nothing I don't know when he goes out and around and back, *nothing* I can't find out from him!"

They both sat looking at Dog and the dry strewings of mold and seed over the quilt.

"Well, if he'll just stop digging where he shouldn't, he can run all he wants," said Mother.

"Here, boy, here!"

And Martin snapped a tin note to the dog's collar:

MY OWNER IS MARTIN SMITH—TEN YEARS OLD—SICK IN BED—VISITORS WELCOME.

Dog barked. Mother opened the downstairs door and let him out.

Martin sat listening.

Far off and away you could hear Dog run in the quiet autumn rain that was falling now. You could hear the barking-jingling fade, rise, fade again as he cut down alley, over lawn, to fetch back Mr. Holloway and the oiled metallic smell of the delicate snowflake-interiored watches he repaired in his home shop. Or maybe he would bring Mr. Jacobs, the grocer, whose clothes were rich with lettuce, celery, tomatoes, and the secret tinned and hidden smell of the red demons stamped on cans of deviled ham. Mr. Jacobs and his unseen pink-meat devils waved often from the yard below. Or Dog brought Mr. Jackson, Mrs. Gillespie, Mr. Smith, Mrs. Holmes, *any* friend or near-friend, encountered, cornered, begged, worried, and at last shepherded home for lunch, or tea-and-biscuits.

Now, listening, Martin heard Dog below, with footsteps moving in a light rain behind him. The downstairs bell rang, Mom opened the door, light voices murmured. Martin sat forward, face shining. The stair treads creaked. A young woman's voice laughed quietly. Miss Haight, of course, his teacher from school!

The bedroom door sprang open.

Martin had company.

Morning, afternoon, evening, dawn and dusk, sun and moon circled with Dog, who faithfully reported temperatures of turf and air, color of earth and tree, consistency of mist or rain, but—most important of all—brought back again and again and again—Miss Haight.

On Saturday, Sunday and Monday she baked Martin orange-iced cupcakes, brought him library books about dinosaurs and cavemen. On Tuesday, Wednesday and Thursday somehow he beat her at dominoes, somehow she lost at checkers, and soon, she cried, he'd defeat her handsomely at chess. On Friday, Saturday and Sunday they talked and never stopped talking, and she was so young and laughing and handsome and her hair was a soft, shining brown like the season outside the window, and she walked clear, clean and quick, a heartbeat warm in the bitter afternoon when he heard it. Above all, she had the secret of signs, and could read and interpret Dog and the symbols she searched out and plucked forth from his coat with her miraculous fingers. Eyes shut, softly laughing, in a gypsy's voice, she divined the world from the treasures in her hands.

And on Monday afternoon, Miss Haight was dead.

Martin sat up in bed, slowly.

"Dead?" he whispered.

Dead, said his mother, yes, dead, killed in an auto accident a mile out of town. Dead, yes, dead, which meant cold to Martin, which meant silence and whiteness and winter come long before its time. Dead, silent, cold, white. The thoughts circled round, blew down, and settled in whispers.

Martin held Dog, thinking; turned to the wall. The lady with the autumn-colored hair. The lady with the laughter that was very gentle and never made fun and the eyes that watched your mouth to see everything you ever said. The-other-half-of-autumn-lady, who told what was left untold by Dog, about the world. The heartbeat at the still center of gray afternoon. The heartbeat fading . . .

"Mom? What do they do in the graveyard, Mom, under the ground? Just lay there?"

"*Lie* there."

"Lie there? Is that *all* they do? It doesn't sound like much fun."

"For goodness sake, it's not made out to be fun."

"Why don't they jump up and run around once in a while if they get tired lying there? God's pretty silly——"

"Martin!"

"Well, you'd think He'd treat people better than to tell them to lie still for keeps. That's impossible. Nobody can do it! I tried once. Dog tries. I tell him, 'dead Dog!' He plays dead awhile, then gets sick and tired and wags his tail or opens one eye and looks at me, bored. Boy, I bet sometimes those graveyard people do the same, huh, Dog?"

Dog barked.

"Be still with that kind of talk!" said Mother.

Martin looked off into space.

"Bet that's exactly what they do," he said.

Autumn burnt the trees bare and ran Dog still farther around, fording creek, prowling graveyard as was his custom, and back in the dusk to fire off volleys of barking that shook windows wherever he turned.

In the late last days of October, Dog began to act as if the wind had changed and blew from a strange country. He stood quivering on the porch below. He whined, his eyes fixed at the empty land beyond town. He brought no visitors for Martin. He stood for hours each day, as if leashed, trembling, then shot away straight, as if someone had called. Each night he returned later, with no one following. Each night, Martin sank deeper and deeper in his pillow.

"Well, people are busy," said Mother. "They haven't time to notice the tag Dog carries. Or they mean to come visit, but forget."

But there was more to it than that. There was the fevered shining in Dog's eyes, and his whimpering tic late at night, in some private dream. His shivering in the dark, under the bed. The way he sometimes stood half the night, looking at Martin as if some great and impossible secret was his and he knew no way to tell it save by savagely thumping his tail, or turning in endless circles, never to lie down, spinning and spinning again.

On October thirtieth, Dog ran out and didn't come back at all, even when after supper Martin heard his parents call and call. The hour grew late, the streets and sidewalks stood empty, the air moved cold about the house and there was nothing, nothing.

Long after midnight, Martin lay watching the world beyond the cool, clear glass windows. Now there was not even autumn, for there was no Dog to fetch it in. There would be no winter, for who could bring the snow to melt in your hands? Father, Mother? No, not the same. They couldn't play the game with its special secrets and rules, its sounds and pantomimes. No more seasons. No more time. The go-between, the emissary, was lost to the wild throngings of civilization, poisoned, stolen, hit by a car, left somewhere in a culvert. . . .

Sobbing, Martin turned his face to his pillow. The world was a picture under glass, untouchable. The world was dead.

Martin twisted in bed and in three days the last Hallowe'en pumpkins were rotting in trash cans, papier-mache skulls and witches were burnt on bonfires, and ghosts were stacked on shelves with other linens until next year.

To Martin, Hallowe'en had been nothing more than one evening when tin horns cried off in the cold autumn stars, children blew like goblin leaves along the flinty walks, flinging their heads, or cabbages, at porches, soap-writing names or similar magic symbols on icy windows. All of it as distant, unfathomable, and nightmarish as a puppet show seen from so many miles away that there is no sound or meaning.

For three days in November, Martin watched alternate light and shadow sift across his ceiling. The fire-pageant was over forever; autumn lay in cold ashes. Martin sank deeper, yet deeper in white marble layers of bed, motionless, listening always listening. . . .

Friday evening, his parents kissed him good-night and walked out of the house into the hushed cathedral weather toward a motion-picture show. Miss Tarkins from next door stayed on in the parlor below until Martin called down he was sleepy, then took her knitting off home.

In silence, Martin lay following the great move of stars down a clear and moonlit sky, remembering nights such as this when he'd spanned the town with Dog ahead, behind, around about, tracking the green-plush ravine, lapping slumbrous streams gone milky with the fullness of the moon, leaping cemetery tombstones while whispering the marble names; on, quickly on, through shaved meadows where the only motion was the off-on quivering of stars, to streets where shadows would not stand aside for you but crowded all the sidewalks for mile on mile. Run now run! chasing, being chased by bitter smoke, fog, mist, wind, ghost of mind, fright of memory; home, safe, sound, snug-warm, asleep. . . .

Nine o'clock.

Chime. The drowsy clock in the deep stairwell below. Chime.

Dog, come home, and run the world with you. Dog, bring a thistle with frost on it, or bring nothing else but the wind. Dog, where *are* you? Oh, listen, now, I'll call.

Martin held his breath.

Way off somewhere—a sound.

Martin rose up, trembling.

There, again—the sound.

So small a sound, like a sharp needle-point brushing the sky long miles and many miles away.

The dreamy echo of a dog—barking.

The sound of a dog crossing fields and farms, dirt roads and rabbit paths, running, running, letting out great barks of steam, cracking the night. The sound of a circling dog which came and went, lifted and faded, opened up, shut in, moved forward, went back, as if the animal were kept by someone on a fantastically long chain. As if the dog were running and someone whistled under the chestnut trees, in mold-shadow, tar-shadow, moon-shadow, walking, and the dog circled back and sprang out again toward home.

Dog! Martin thought, oh Dog, come home, boy! Listen, oh, listen, where you *been*? Come on, boy, make tracks!

Five, ten, fifteen minutes; near, very near, the bark, the sound. Martin cried out, thrust his feet from the bed, leaned to the window. Dog! Listen, boy! Dog! Dog! He said it over and over. Dog! Dog! Wicked Dog, run off and gone all these days! Bad Dog, good Dog, home, boy, hurry, and bring what you can!

Near now, near, up the street, barking, to knock clapboard housefronts with sound, whirl iron cocks on rooftops in the moon, firing off volleys—Dog! now at the door below. . . .

Martin shivered.

Should he run—let Dog in, or wait for Mom and Dad? Wait? Oh, God, wait? But what if Dog ran off again? No, he'd go down, snatch the door wide, yell, grab Dog in, and run upstairs so fast, laughing, crying, holding tight, that . . .

Dog stopped barking.

Hey! Martin almost broke the window, jerking to it.

Silence. As if someone had told Dog to hush now, hush, hush.

A full minute passed. Martin clenched his fists.

Below, a faint whimpering.

Then, slowly, the downstairs front door opened. Someone was kind enough to have opened the door for Dog. Of course! Dog had brought Mr. Jacobs or Mr. Gillespie or Miss Tarkins, or . . .

The downstairs door shut.

Dog raced upstairs, whining, flung himself on the bed.

"Dog, Dog, where've you *been*, what've you *done*! Dog, Dog!"

And he crushed Dog hard and long to himself, weeping. Dog, Dog. He laughed and shouted. Dog! But after a moment he stopped laughing and crying, suddenly.

He pulled back away. He held the animal and looked at him, eyes widening.

The odor coming from Dog was different.

It was a smell of strange earth. It was a smell of night within night, the smell of digging down deep in shadow through earth that had lain cheek by jowl with things that were long hidden and decayed. A stinking and rancid soil fell away in clods of dissolution from Dog's muzzle and paws. He had dug deep. He had dug very deep indeed. That *was* it, wasn't it? wasn't it? *wasn't* it!

What kind of message was this from Dog? What could such a message mean? The stench—the ripe and awful cemetery earth.

Dog was a bad dog, digging where he shouldn't. Dog was a good dog, always making friends. Dog loved people. Dog brought them home.

And now, moving up the dark hall stairs, at intervals, came the sound of feet, one foot dragged after the other, painfully, slowly, slowly, slowly.

Dog shivered. A rain of strange night earth fell seething on the bed.

Dog turned.

The bedroom door whispered in.

Martin had company.

UN
FA
POST

Touched with Fire

THEY STOOD IN the blazing sunlight for a long while, looking at the bright faces of their old-fashioned railroad watches, while the shadows tilted beneath them, swaying, and the perspiration ran out under their porous summer hats. When they uncovered their heads to mop their lined and pinkened brows, their hair was white and soaked through, like something that had been out of the light for years. One of the men commented that his shoes felt like two loaves of baked bread and then, sighing warmly, added:

"Are you positive this is the right tenement?"

The second old man, Foxe by name, nodded, as if any quick motion might make him catch fire by friction alone. "I saw this woman every day for three days. She'll show up. If she's still alive, that is. Wait till you *see* her, Shaw. Lord! what a case."

"Such an odd business," said Shaw. "If people knew they'd think us Peeping Toms, doddering old fools. Lord, I feel self-conscious standing here."

Foxe leaned on his cane. "Let me do all the talking if—hold on! There she is!" He lowered his voice. "Take a slow look as she comes out."

The tenement front door slammed viciously. A dumpy woman stood at the top of the thirteen porch steps glancing this way and that with angry jerkings of her eyes. Jamming a plump hand in her purse, she seized some crumpled dollar bills, plunged down the steps brutally, and set off down the street in a charge. Behind her, several heads peered from apartment windows above, summoned by her crashing of the door.

"Come on," whispered Foxe. "Here we go to the butcher's."

The woman flung open a butchershop door, rushed in. The two old men had a glimpse of a mouth sticky with raw lipstick. Her eyebrows were like mustaches over her squinting, always suspicious eyes. Abreast of the butchershop, they heard her voice already screaming inside.

"I want a good cut of meat. Let's see what you got hidden to take home for yourself!"

The butcher stood silently in his bloody-fingerprinted frock, his hands empty. The two old men entered behind the woman and pretended to admire a pink loaf of fresh-ground sirloin.

"Them lambchops look sickly!" cried the woman. "What's the price on brains?"

The butcher told her in a low dry voice.

"Well, weigh me a pound of liver!" said the woman. "Keep your thumbs off!"

The butcher weighed it out, slowly.

"Hurry up!" snapped the woman.

The butcher now stood with his hands out of sight below the counter.

"Look," whispered Foxe. Shaw leaned back a trifle to peer below the case.

In one of the butcher's bloody hands, empty before, a silvery meat ax was now clenched tightly, relaxed, clenched tightly, relaxed. The butcher's eyes were blue and dangerously serene above the white porcelain counter while the woman yelled into those eyes and that pink self-contained face.

"Now do you believe?" whispered Foxe. "She really needs our help."

They stared at the raw red cube-steaks for a long time, noticing all the little dents and marks where it had been hit, ten dozen times, by a steel mallet.

The braying continued at the grocer's and the dime store, with the two old men following at a respectful distance.

"Mrs. Death-Wish," said Mr. Foxe quietly. "It's like watching a two-year-old run out on a battlefield. Any moment, you say, she'll hit a mine; bang! Get the temperature just right, too much humidity, everyone itching, sweating, irritable. Along'll come this fine lady, whining, shrieking. And so good-by. Well, Shaw, do we start business?"

"You mean just walk up to her?" Shaw was stunned by his own suggestion. "Oh, but we're not really going to do this, are we? I thought it was sort of a hobby. People, habits, customs, et cetera. It's been fun. But actually mixing in——? We've better things to do."

"Have we?" Foxe nodded down the street to where the woman ran out in front of cars, making them stop with a great squall of brakes, horn-blowing, and cursing. "Are we Christians? Do we let her feed herself subconsciously to the lions? Or do we convert her?"

"Convert her?"

"To love, to serenity, to a longer life. Look at her. Doesn't want to live any more. Deliberately aggravates people. One day soon, someone'll favor her, with a hammer, or strychnine. She's been going down for the third time a long while now. When you're drowning, you get nasty, grab at people, scream. Let's have lunch and lend a hand, eh? Otherwise, our victim will run on until she finds her murderer."

Shaw stood with the sun driving him into the boiling white sidewalk, and it seemed for a moment the street tilted vertically, became a cliff down which the woman fell toward a blazing sky. At last he shook his head.

"You're right," he said. "I wouldn't want her on my conscience."

The sun burnt the paint from the tenement fronts, bleached the air raw and turned the gutter-waters to vapor by midafternoon when the old men, numbed and evaporated, stood in the inner passageways of a house that funneled bakery air from front to back in a searing torrent. When they spoke it was the submerged, muffled talk of men in steam rooms, preposterously tired and remote.

The front door opened. Foxe stopped a boy who carried a well-mangled loaf of bread. "Son, we're looking for the woman who gives the door an *awful* slam when she goes out."

"Oh, *her*?" The boy ran upstairs, calling back. "Mrs. Shrike!"

Foxe grabbed Shaw's arm. "Lord, Lord! It can't be true!"

"I want to go home," said Shaw.

"But there it is!" said Foxe, incredulous, tapping his cane on the room-index in the lobby. "Mr. and Mrs. Alfred Shrike, 331 upstairs! Husband's a longshoreman, big hulking brute, comes home dirty. Saw them out on Sunday, her jabbering, him never speaking, never looking at her. Oh, come *on*, Shaw."

"It's no use," said Shaw. "You can't help people like her

unless they want to be helped. That's the first law of mental health. You know it, I know it. If you get in her way, she'll trample you. Don't be a fool."

"But who's to speak for her—and people like her? Her husband? Her friends? The grocer, the butcher? They'd sing at her wake! Will they tell her she needs a psychiatrist? Does she know it? No. Who knows it? We do. Well, then, you don't keep vital information like that from the victim, do you?"

Shaw took off his sopping hat and gazed bleakly into it. "Once, in biology class, long ago, our teacher asked if we thought we could remove a frog's nervous system, intact, with a scalpel. Take out the whole delicate antennalike structure, with all its little pink thistles and half-invisible ganglions. Impossible, of course. The nervous system's so much a part of the frog there's no way to pull it like a hand from a green glove. You'd destroy the frog, doing it. Well, that's Mrs. Shrike. There's no way to operate on a souring ganglion. Bile is in the vitreous humor of her mad little elephant eyes. You might as well try to get all the saliva out of her mouth forever. It's very sad. But I think we've gone too far already."

"True," said Foxe patiently, earnestly, nodding. "But all I want to do is post a warning. Drop a little seed in her subconscious. Tell her, 'You're a murderee, a victim looking for a place to happen.' One tiny seed I want to plant in her head and hope it'll sprout and flower. A very faint, very poor hope that before it's too late, she'll gather her courage and go see a psychiatrist!"

"It's too hot to talk."

"All the more reason to act! More murders are committed at ninety-two degrees Fahrenheit than any other temperature. Over one hundred, it's too hot to move. Under ninety, cool enough to survive. But right *at* ninety-two degrees lies the apex of irritability, everything is itches and hair and sweat and cooked pork. The brain becomes a rat rushing around a red-hot maze. The least thing, a word, a look, a sound, the drop of a hair and—irritable murder. *Irritable murder*, there's a pretty and terrifying phrase for you. Look at that hall thermometer, eighty-nine degrees. Crawling up toward ninety, itching up toward ninety-one, sweating toward ninety-two an hour, two hours from now. Here's the first flight of stairs. We can rest on each landing. Up we *go*!"

The two old men moved in the third-floor darkness.

"Don't check the numbers," said Foxe. "Let's guess which apartment is hers."

Behind the last door a radio exploded, the ancient paint shuddered and flaked softly onto the worn carpet at their feet. The men watched the entire door jitter with vibration in its grooves.

They looked at each other and nodded grimly.

Another sound cut like an ax through the paneling; a woman, shrieking to someone across town on a telephone.

"No phone necessary. She should just open her window and yell."

Foxe rapped.

The radio blasted out the rest of its song, the voice bellowed. Foxe rapped again, and tested the knob. To his horror the door got free of his grasp and floated swiftly inward, leaving them like actors trapped on-stage when a curtain rises too soon.

"Oh, no!" cried Shaw.

They were buried in a flood of sound. It was like standing in the spillway of a dam and pulling the gate-lever. Instinctively, the old men raised their hands, wincing as if the sound were pure blazing sunlight that burnt their eyes.

The woman (it was indeed Mrs. Shrike!) stood at a wall phone, saliva flying from her mouth at an incredible rate. She showed all of her large white teeth, chunking off her monologue, nostrils flared, a vein in her wet forehead ridged up, pumping, her free hand flexing and unflexing itself. Her eyes were clenched shut as she yelled:

"Tell that damned son-in-law of mine I won't see him, he's a lazy bum!"

Suddenly the woman snapped her eyes wide, some animal instinct having felt rather than heard or seen an intrusion. She continued yelling into the phone, meanwhile piercing her visitors with a glance forged of the coldest steel. She yelled for a full minute longer, then slammed down the receiver and said, without taking a breath: "Well?"

The two men moved together for protection. Their lips moved.

"Speak up!" cried the woman.

"Would you mind," said Foxe, "turning the radio down?"

She caught the word "radio" by lip reading. Still glaring at them out of her sunburnt face, she slapped the radio without looking at it, as one slaps a child that cries all day every day and has become an unseen pattern in life. The radio subsided.

"I'm not buyin' anything!"

She ripped a dog-eared packet of cheap cigarettes like it was a bone with meat on it, snapped one of the cigarettes in her smeared mouth and lit it, sucking greedily on the smoke, jetting it through her thin nostrils until she was a feverish dragon confronting them in a fire-clouded room. "I got work to do. Make your pitch!"

They looked at the magazines spilled like great catches of bright-colored fish on the linoleum floor, the unwashed coffee cup near the broken rocking chair, the tilted, greasy thumb-marked lamps, the smudged windowpanes, the dishes piled in the sink under a steadily dripping, dripping faucet, the cobwebs floating like dead skin in the ceiling corners, and over all of it the thickened smell of life lived too much, too long, with the window down.

They saw the wall thermometer.

Temperature: ninety degrees Fahrenheit.

They gave each other a half-startled look.

"I'm Mr. Foxe, this is Mr. Shaw. We're retired insurance salesmen. We still sell occasionally, to supplement our retirement fund. Most of the time, however, we're taking it easy and——"

"You tryin' to sell me insurance!" She cocked her head at them through the cigarette smoke.

"There's no money connected with this, no."

"Keep talking," she said.

"I hardly know how to begin. May we sit down?" He looked about and decided there wasn't a thing in the room he would trust himself to sit on. "Never mind." He saw she was about to bellow again, so went on swiftly. "We retired after forty years of seeing people from nursery to cemetery gate, you might say. In that time we'd formulated certain opinions. Last year, sitting in the park talking, we put two and two together. We realized that many people didn't have to die so young. With the correct investigation, a new type of Customer's Information might be provided as a sideline by insurance companies . . ."

"I'm not sick," said the woman.

"Oh, but you *are*!" cried Mr. Foxe, and then put two fingers to his mouth in dismay.

"Don't tell *me* what I am!" she cried.

Foxe plunged headlong. "Let me make it clear. People die every day, psychologically speaking. Some part of them gets tired. And that small part tries to kill off the entire person. For example——" He looked about and seized on his first evidence with what amounted to a vast relief. "There! That light bulb in your bathroom, hung right over the tub on frayed wire. Someday you'll slip, make a grab and—pfft!"

Mrs. Albert J. Shrike squinted at the light bulb in the bathroom. "So?"

"People," Mr. Foxe warmed to his subject, while Mr. Shaw fidgeted, his face now flushed, now dreadfully pale, edged toward the door, "people, like cars, need their brakes checked; their emotional brakes, do you see? Their lights, their batteries, their approaches and responses to life."

Mrs. Shrike snorted. "Your two minutes are up. I haven't learned a damned thing."

Mr. Foxe blinked, first at her, then at the sun burning mercilessly through the dusty windowpanes. Perspiration was running in the soft lines of his face. He chanced a look at the wall thermometer.

"Ninety-one," he said.

"What's eatin' you, pop?" asked Mrs. Shrike.

"I beg your pardon." He stared in fascination at the red-hot line of mercury firing up the small glass vent across the room. "Sometimes—sometimes we all make wrong turnings. Our choice of marriage partners. A wrong job. No money. Illness. Migraine headaches. Glandular deficiencies. Dozens of little prickly, irritable things. Before you know it, you're taking it out on everyone everywhere."

She was watching his mouth as if he were talking a foreign language; she scowled, she squinted, she tilted her head, her cigarette smoldering in one plump hand.

"We run about screaming, making enemies." Foxe swallowed and glanced away from her. "We make people want to see us—gone—sick—dead, even. People want to hit us, knock us down, shoot us. It's all unconscious, though. You *see*?"

God, it's hot in here, he thought. If there were only one window open. Just one. Just one window open.

Mrs. Shrike's eyes were widening, as if to allow in everything he said.

"Some people are not only accident-prones, which means they want to punish themselves physically, for some crime, usually a petty immorality they think they've long forgotten. But their subconscious puts them in dangerous situations, makes them jaywalk, makes them——" He hesitated and the sweat dripped from his chin. "Makes them ignore frayed electric cords over bathtubs—— They're potential victims. It is marked on their faces, hidden like—like tattoos, you might say, on the inner rather than the outer skin. A murderer passing one of these accident-prones, these wishers-after-death, would see the invisible markings, turn, and follow them, instinctively, to the nearest alley. With luck, a potential victim might not happen to cross the tracks of a potential murderer for fifty years. Then—one afternoon—fate! These people, these death-prones, touch all the wrong nerves in passing strangers; they brush the murder in all our breasts."

Mrs. Shrike mashed her cigarette in a dirty saucer, very slowly.

Foxe shifted his cane from one trembling hand to the other. "So it was that a year ago we decided to try to find people who needed help. These are always the people who don't even know they need help, who'd never dream of going to a psychiatrist. At first, I said, we'll make dry-runs. Shaw was always against it, save as a hobby, a harmless little quiet thing between ourselves. I suppose you'd say I'm a fool. Well, we've just completed a year of dry-runs. We watched two men, studied their environmental factors, their work, marriages, at a discreet distance. None of our business, you say? But each time, the men came to a bad end. One killed in a bar-room. Another pushed out a window. A woman we studied, run down by a streetcar. Coincidence? What about that old man accidentally poisoned? Didn't turn on the bathroom light one night. What was there in his mind that wouldn't let him turn the light on? What made him move in the dark and drink medicine in the dark and die in the hospital next day, protesting he wanted nothing but to live? Evidence, evidence, we have it, we have it. Two dozen cases. Coffins nailed to a good half of them in that little time. No more dry-runs; it's time for action, preventative use of data. Time to work *with* people, make friends before the undertaker slips in the side door."

Mrs. Shrike stood as if he had struck her on the head, quite suddenly, with a large weight. Then just her blurred lips moved. "And you came *here*?"

"Well——"

"You've been watching *me*?"

"We only——"

"Following *me*?"

"In order to——"

"Get out!" she said.

"We can——"

"Get out!" she said.

"If you'll only listen——"

"Oh, I *said* this would happen," whispered Shaw, shutting his eyes.

"Dirty old men, get out!" she shouted.

"There's no money involved."

"I'll throw you out, I'll throw you out!" she shrieked, clenching her fists, gritting her teeth. Her face colored insanely. "Who are you, dirty old grandmas, coming here, spying, you old cranks!" she yelled. She seized the straw hat from Mr. Foxe's head; he cried out; she tore the lining from it, cursing. "Get out, get out, get out, get out!" She hurled it to the floor. She crunched one heel through the middle. She kicked it. "Get out, get out!"

"Oh, but you *need* us!" Foxe stared in dismay at the hat as she swore at him in a language that turned corners, blazing, that flew in the air like great searing torches. The woman knew every language and every word in every language. She spoke with fire and alcohol and smoke.

"Who do you think you are? God? God and the Holy Ghost, passing on people, snooping, prying, you old jerks, you old dirty-minded grandmas! You, you——" She gave them further names, names that forced them toward the door in shock, recoiling. She gave them a long vile list of names without pausing for breath. Then she stopped, gasped, trembled, heaved in a great suction of air, and started a further list of ten dozen even viler names.

"See here!" said Foxe, stiffening.

Shaw was out the door, pleading with his partner to come along, it was over and done, it was as he expected, they were fools, they were everything she said they were, oh, how embarrassing!

"Old maid!" shouted the woman.

"I'll thank you to keep a civil tongue."

"Old maid, old maid!"

Somehow this was worse than all the really vile names.

Foxe swayed, his mouth clapped open, shut, open, shut.

"Old woman!" she cried. "Woman, woman, woman!"

He was in a blazing yellow jungle. The room was drowned in fire, it clenched upon him, the furniture seemed to shift and whirl about, the sunlight shot through the rammed-shut windows, firing the dust, which leaped up from the rug in angry sparks when a fly buzzed a crazy spiral from nowhere; her mouth, a feral red thing, licked the air with all the obscenities collected just behind it in a lifetime, and beyond her on the baked brown wallpaper the thermometer said ninety-two, and he looked again and it said ninety-two, and still the woman screamed like the wheels of a train scraping around a vast iron curve of track; fingernails down a blackboard, and steel across marble. "Old maid! Old maid! Old maid!"

Foxe drew his arm back, cane clenched in fist, very high, and struck.

"No!" cried Shaw in the doorway.

But the woman had slipped and fallen aside, gibbering, clawing the floor. Foxe stood over her with a look of positive disbelief on his face. He looked at his arm and his wrist and his hand and his fingers, each in turn, through a great invisible glaring hot wall of crystal that enclosed him. He looked at the cane as if it was an easily seen and incredible exclamation point come out of nowhere to the center of the room. His mouth stayed open, the dust fell in silent embers, dead. He felt the blood drop from his face as if a small door had banged wide into his stomach. "I——"

She frothed.

Scrabbling about, every part of her seemed a separate animal. Her arms and legs, her hands, her head, each was a lopped-off bit of some creature wild to return to itself, but blind to the proper way of making that return. Her mouth still gushed out her sickness with words and sounds that were not even faintly words. It had been in her a long time, a long long time. Foxe looked upon her, in a state of shock, himself. Before today, she had spat her venom out, here, there, another place. Now he had loosed the flood of a lifetime and he felt in danger of drowning here. He sensed someone pulling him by his coat. He saw the door sills pass on either side. He heard the cane fall and rattle like a thin bone far away from his hand, which seemed to have been stung by some terrible unseen wasp. And then he was out, walking mechanically, down through the burning tenement, between the scorched walls. Her voice crashed like a guillotine down the stair. "Get out! Get out! Get *out*!"

Fading like the wail of a person dropped down an open well into darkness.

At the bottom of the last flight, near the street door, Foxe turned himself loose from this other man here, and for a long moment leaned against the wall, his eyes wet, able to do nothing but moan. His hands, while he did this, moved in the air to find the lost cane, moved on his head, touched at his moist eyelids, amazed, and fluttered away. They sat on the bottom hall step for ten minutes in silence, drawing sanity into their lungs with every shuddering breath. Finally Mr. Foxe looked over at Mr. Shaw, who had been staring at him in wonder and fright for the full ten minutes.

"Did you *see* what I did? Oh, oh, that was close. Close. Close." He shook his head. "I'm a fool. That poor, poor woman. She was right."

"There's nothing to be done."

"I see that now. It had to fall on me."

"Here, wipe your face. That's better."

"Do you think she'll tell Mr. Shrike about us?"

"No, no."

"Do you think we could——"

"Talk to *him*?"

They considered this and shook their heads. They opened the front door to a gush of furnace heat and were almost knocked down by a huge man who strode between them.

"Look where you're going!" he cried.

They turned and watched the man move ponderously, in fiery darkness, one step at a time, up into the tenement house, a creature with the ribs of a mastodon and the head of an unshorn lion, with great beefed arms, irritably hairy, painfully sunburnt. The face they had seen briefly as he shouldered past was a sweating, raw, sunblistered pork face, salt droplets under the red eyes, dripping from the chin; great smears of perspiration stained the man's armpits, coloring his tee-shirt to the waist.

They shut the tenement door gently.

"That's him," said Mr. Foxe. "That's the husband."

They stood in the little store across from the tenement. It was five-thirty, the sun tilting down the sky, the shadows the color of hot summer grapes under the rare few trees and in the alleys.

"What was it, hanging out of the husband's back pocket?"

"Longshoreman's hook. Steel. Sharp, heavy-looking. Like those claws one-armed men used to wear on the end of their stumps, years ago."

Mr. Foxe did not speak.

"What's the temperature?" asked Mr. Foxe, a minute later, as if he were too tired to turn his head to look.

"Store thermometer still reads ninety-two. Ninety-two right on the nose."

Foxe sat on a packing crate, making the least motion to hold an orange soda bottle in his fingers. "Cool off," he said. "Yes, I need an orange pop very much, right now."

They sat there in the furnace, looking up at one special tenement window for a long time, waiting, waiting . . .

The Small Assassin

JUST WHEN THE idea occurred to her that she was being murdered she could not tell. There had been little subtle signs, little suspicions for the past month; things as deep as sea tides in her, like looking at a perfectly calm stretch of tropic water, wanting to bathe in it and finding, just as the tide takes your body, that monsters dwell just under the surface, things unseen, bloated, many-armed, sharp-finned, malignant and inescapable.

A room floated around her in an effluvium of hysteria. Sharp instruments hovered and there were voices, and people in sterile white masks.

My name, she thought, what is it?

Alice Leiber. It came to her. David Leiber's wife. But it gave her no comfort. She was alone with these silent, whispering white people and there was great pain and nausea and death-fear in her.

I am being murdered before their eyes. These doctors, these nurses don't realize what hidden thing has happened to me. David doesn't know. Nobody knows except me and—the killer, the little murderer, the small assassin.

I am dying and I can't tell them now. They'd laugh and call me one in delirium. They'll see the murderer and hold him and never think him responsible for my death. But here I am, in front of God and man, dying, no one to believe my story, everyone to doubt me, comfort me with lies, bury me in ignorance, mourn me and salvage my destroyer.

Where is David? she wondered. In the waiting room, smoking one cigarette after another, listening to the long tickings of the very slow clock?

Sweat exploded from all of her body at once, and with it an agonized cry. Now. Now! Try and kill me, she screamed. Try, try, but I won't die! I won't!

There was a hollowness. A vacuum. Suddenly the pain fell away. Exhaustion, and dusk came around. It was over. Oh, God! She plummeted down and struck a black nothingness which gave way to nothingness and nothingness and another and still another. . . .

Footsteps. Gentle, approaching footsteps.

Far away, a voice said, "She's asleep. Don't disturb her."

An odor of tweeds, a pipe, a certain shaving lotion. David was standing over her. And beyond him the immaculate smell of Dr. Jeffers.

She did not open her eyes. "I'm awake," she said, quietly. It was a surprise, a relief to be able to speak, to not be dead.

"Alice," someone said, and it was David beyond her closed eyes, holding her tired hands.

Would you like to meet the murderer, David? she thought. I hear your voice asking to see him, so there's nothing but for me to point him out to you.

David stood over her. She opened her eyes. The room came into focus. Moving a weak hand, she pulled aside a coverlet.

The murderer looked up at David Leiber with a small, red-faced, blue-eyed calm. Its eyes were deep and sparkling.

"Why!" cried David Leiber, smiling. "He's a *fine* baby!"

Dr. Jeffers was waiting for David Leiber the day he came to take his wife and new child home. He motioned Leiber to a chair in his office, gave him a cigar, lit one for himself, sat on the edge of his desk, puffing solemnly for a long moment. Then he cleared his throat, looked David Leiber straight on and said, "Your wife doesn't like her child, Dave."

"What!"

"It's been a hard thing for her. She'll need a lot of love this next year. I didn't say much at the time, but she was hysterical in the delivery room. The strange things she said—I won't repeat them. All I'll say is that she feels alien to the child. Now, this may simply be a thing we can clear up with one or two questions." He sucked on his cigar another moment, then said, "Is this child a 'wanted' child, Dave?"

"Why do you ask?"

"It's vital."

"Yes. Yes, it is a 'wanted' child. We planned it together. Alice was so happy, a year ago, when——"

"Mmmm—— That makes it more difficult. Because if the child was unplanned, it would be a simple case of a woman hating the idea of motherhood. That doesn't fit Alice." Dr. Jeffers took his cigar from his lips, rubbed his hand across his jaw. "It must be something else, then. Perhaps something buried in her childhood that's coming out now. Or it might be the simple temporary doubt and distrust of any mother who's gone through the unusual pain and near-death that Alice has. If so, then a little time should heal that. I thought I'd tell you, though, Dave. It'll help you be easy and tolerant with her if she says anything about—well—about wishing the child had been born dead. And if things don't go well, the three of you drop in on me. I'm always glad to see old friends, eh? Here, take another cigar along for—ah—for the baby."

It was a bright spring afternoon. Their car hummed along wide, tree-lined boulevards. Blue sky, flowers, a warm wind. Dave talked a lot, lit his cigar, talked some more. Alice answered directly, softly, relaxing a bit more as the trip progressed. But she held the baby not tightly or warmly or motherly enough to satisfy the queer ache in Dave's mind. She seemed to be merely carrying a porcelain figurine.

"Well," he said, at last, smiling. "What'll we name him?"

Alice Leiber watched green trees slide by. "Let's not decide yet. I'd rather wait until we get an exceptional name for him. Don't blow smoke in his face." Her sentences ran together with no change of tone. The last statement held no motherly reproof, no interest, no irritation. She just mouthed it and it was said.

The husband, disquieted, dropped the cigar from the window. "Sorry," he said.

The baby rested in the crook of his mother's arm, shadows of sun and tree changing his face. His blue eyes opened like fresh blue spring flowers. Moist noises came from the tiny, pink, elastic mouth.

Alice gave her baby a quick glance. Her husband felt her shiver against him.

"Cold?" he asked.

"A chill. Better raise the window, David."

It was more than a chill. He rolled the window slowly up.

Suppertime.

Dave had brought the child from the nursery, propped him at a tiny, bewildered angle, supported by many pillows, in a newly purchased high chair.

Alice watched her knife and fork move. "He's not high-chair size," she said.

"Fun having him here, anyway," said Dave, feeling fine. "Everything's fun. At the office, too. Orders up to my nose. If I don't watch myself I'll make another fifteen thousand this year. Hey, look at Junior, will you? Drooling all down his chin!" He reached over to wipe the baby's mouth with his napkin. From the corner of his eye he realized that Alice wasn't even watching. He finished the job.

"I guess it wasn't very interesting," he said, back again at his food. "But one would think a mother'd take some interest in her own child!"

Alice jerked her chin up. "Don't speak that way! Not in front of him! Later, if you must."

"Later?" he cried. "In front of, in back of, what's the difference?" He quieted suddenly, swallowed, was sorry. "All right. Okay. I know how it is."

After dinner she let him carry the baby upstairs. She didn't tell him to; she *let* him.

Coming down, he found her standing by the radio, listening to music she didn't hear. Her eyes were closed, her whole attitude one of wondering, self-questioning. She started when he appeared.

Suddenly, she was at him, against him, soft, quick; the same. Her lips found him, kept him. He was stunned. Now that the baby was gone, upstairs, out of the room, she began to breathe again, live again. She was free. She was whispering, rapidly, endlessly.

"Thank you, thank you, darling. For being yourself, always. Dependable, so very dependable!"

He had to laugh. "My father told me, 'Son, provide for your family!'"

Wearily, she rested her dark, shining hair against his neck.

"You've overdone it. Sometimes I wish we were just the way we were when we were first married. No responsibilities, nothing but ourselves. No—no babies."

She crushed his hand in hers, a supernatural whiteness in her face.

"Oh, Dave, once it was just you and me. We protected each other, and now we protect the baby, but get no protection from it. Do you understand? Lying in the hospital I had time to think a lot of things. The world is evil——"

"Is it?"

"Yes. It is. But laws protect us from it. And when there aren't laws, then love does the protecting. You're protected from my hurting you, by my love. You're vulnerable to me, of all people, but love shields you. I feel no fear of you, because love cushions all your irritations, unnatural instincts, hatreds and immaturities. But—what about the baby? It's too young to know love, or a law of love, or anything, until we teach it. And in the meantime be vulnerable to it."

"Vulnerable to a baby?" He held her away and laughed gently.

"Does a baby know the difference between right and wrong?" she asked.

"No. But it'll learn."

"But a baby is so new, so amoral, so conscience-free." She stopped. Her arms dropped from him and she turned swiftly. "That noise? What was it?"

Leiber looked around the room. "I didn't hear——"

She stared at the library door. "In there," she said, slowly.

Leiber crossed the room, opened the door and switched the library lights on and off. "Not a thing." He came back to her. "You're worn out. To bed with you—right now."

Turning out the lights together, they walked slowly up the soundless hall stairs, not speaking. At the top she apologized. "My wild talk, darling. Forgive me. I'm exhausted."

He understood, and said so.

She paused, undecided, by the nursery door. Then she fingered the brass knob sharply, walked in. He watched her approach the crib much too carefully, look down, and stiffen as if she'd been struck in the face. "David!"

Leiber stepped forward, reached the crib.

The baby's face was bright red and very moist; his small pink mouth opened and shut, opened and shut; his eyes were a fiery blue. His hands leapt about on the air.

"Oh," said Dave, "he's just been crying."

"Has he?" Alice Leiber seized the crib-railing to balance herself. "I didn't hear him."

"The door was closed."

"Is that why he breathes so hard, why his face is red?"

"Sure. Poor little guy. Crying all alone in the dark. He can sleep in our room tonight, just in case he cries."

"You'll spoil him," his wife said.

Leiber felt her eyes follow as he rolled the crib into their bedroom. He undressed silently, sat on the edge of the bed. Suddenly he lifted his head, swore under his breath, snapped his fingers. "Damn it! Forgot to tell you. I must fly to Chicago Friday."

"Oh, David." Her voice was lost in the room.

"I've put this trip off for two months, and now it's so critical I just *have* to go."

"I'm afraid to be alone."

"We'll have the new cook by Friday. She'll be here all the time. I'll only be gone a few days."

"I'm afraid. I don't know of what. You wouldn't believe me if I told you. I guess I'm crazy."

He was in bed now. She darkened the room; he heard her walk around the bed, throw back the cover, slide in. He smelled the warm woman-smell of her next to him. He said, "If you want me to wait a few days, perhaps I could——"

"No," she said, unconvinced. "You go. I know it's important. It's just that I keep thinking about what I told you. Laws and love and protection. Love protects you from me. But, the baby——" She took a breath. "What protects you from him, David?"

Before he could answer, before he could tell her how silly it was, speaking of infants, she switched on the bed light, abruptly.

"Look," she said, pointing.

The baby lay wide-awake in its crib, staring straight at him, with deep, sharp blue eyes.

The lights went out again. She trembled against him.

"It's not nice being afraid of the thing you birthed." Her whisper lowered, became harsh, fierce, swift. "He tried to kill me! He lies there, listens to us talking, waiting for you to go away so he can try to kill me again! I swear it!" Sobs broke from her.

"Please," he kept saying, soothing her. "Stop it, stop it. Please."

She cried in the dark for a long time. Very late she relaxed, shakingly, against him. Her breathing came soft, warm, regular, her body twitched its worn reflexes and she slept.

He drowsed.

And just before his eyes lidded wearily down, sinking him into deeper and yet deeper tides, he heard a strange little sound of awareness and awakeness in the room.

The sound of small, moist, pinkly elastic lips.

The baby.

And then—sleep.

In the morning, the sun blazed. Alice smiled.

David Leiber dangled his watch over the crib. "See, baby? Something bright. Something pretty. Sure. Sure. Something bright. Something pretty."

Alice smiled. She told him to go ahead, fly to Chicago, she'd be very brave, no need to worry. She'd take care of baby. Oh, yes, she'd take care of him, all right.

The airplane went east. There was a lot of sky, a lot of sun and clouds and Chicago running over the horizon. Dave was dropped into the rush of ordering, planning, banqueting, telephoning, arguing in conference. But he wrote letters each day and sent telegrams to Alice and the baby.

On the evening of his sixth day away from home he received the long-distance phone call. Los Angeles.

"Alice?"

"No, Dave. This is Jeffers speaking."

"Doctor!"

"Hold onto yourself, son. Alice is sick. You'd better get the next plane home. It's pneumonia. I'll do everything I can, boy. If only it wasn't so soon after the baby. She needs strength."

Leiber dropped the phone into its cradle. He got up, with

no feet under him, and no hands and no body. The hotel room blurred and fell apart.

"Alice," he said, blindly, starting for the door.

The propellers spun about, whirled, fluttered, stopped; time and space were put behind. Under his hand, David felt the doorknob turn; under his feet the floor assumed reality, around him flowed the walls of a bedroom, and in the late-afternoon sunlight Dr. Jeffers stood, turning from a window, as Alice lay waiting in her bed, something carved from a fall of winter snow. Then Dr. Jeffers was talking, talking continuously, gently, the sound rising and falling through the lamp-light, a soft flutter, a white murmur of voice.

"Your wife's too good a mother, Dave. She worried more about the baby than herself. . . ."

Somewhere in the paleness of Alice's face, there was a sudden constriction which smoothed itself out before it was realized. Then, slowly, half-smiling, she began to talk and she talked as a mother should about this, that and the other thing, the telling detail, the minute-by-minute and hour-by-hour report of a mother concerned with a dollhouse world and the miniature life of that world. But she could not stop; the spring was wound tight, and her voice rushed on to anger, fear and the faintest touch of revulsion, which did not change Dr. Jeffers' expression, but caused Dave's heart to match the rhythm of this talk that quickened and could not stop:

"The baby wouldn't sleep. I thought he was sick. He just lay, staring, in his crib, and late at night he'd cry. So loud, he'd cry, and he'd cry all night and all night. I couldn't quiet him, and I couldn't rest."

Dr. Jeffers' head nodded slowly, slowly. "Tired herself right into pneumonia. But she's full of sulfa now and on the safe side of the whole damn thing."

David felt ill. "The baby, what about the baby?"

"Fit as a fiddle; cock of the walk!"

"Thanks, Doctor."

The doctor walked off away and down the stairs, opened the front door faintly, and was gone.

"David!"

He turned to her frightened whisper.

"It was the baby again." She clutched his hand. "I try to lie to myself and say that I'm a fool, but the baby knew I was weak from the hospital, so he cried all night every night, and when he wasn't crying he'd be much too quiet. I knew if I switched on the light he'd be there, staring up at me."

David felt his body close in on itself like a fist. He remembered seeing the baby, feeling the baby, awake in the dark, awake very late at night when babies should be asleep. Awake and lying there, silent as thought, not crying, but watching from its crib. He thrust the thought aside. It was insane.

Alice went on. "I was going to kill the baby. Yes, I was. When you'd been gone only a day on your trip I went to his room and put my hands about his neck; and I stood there, for a long time, thinking, afraid. Then I put the covers up over his face and turned him over on his face and pressed him down and left him that way and ran out of the room."

He tried to stop her.

"No, let me finish," she said, hoarsely, looking at the wall. "When I left his room I thought, It's simple. Babies smother every day. No one'll ever know. But when I came back to see him dead, David, he was alive! Yes, alive, turned over on his back, alive and smiling and breathing. And I couldn't touch him again after that. I left him there and I didn't come back, not to feed him or look at him or do anything. Perhaps the cook tended to him. I don't know. All I know is that his crying kept me awake, and I thought all through the night, and walked around the rooms and now I'm sick." She was almost finished now. "The baby lies there and thinks of ways to kill me. Simple ways. Because he knows I know so much about him. I have no love for him; there is no protection between us; there never will be."

She was through. She collapsed inward on herself and finally slept. David Leiber stood for a long time over her, not able to move. His blood was frozen in his body, not a cell stirred anywhere, anywhere at all.

The next morning there was only one thing to do. He did it. He walked into Dr. Jeffers' office and told him the whole thing, and listened to Jeffers' tolerant replies:

"Let's take this thing slowly, son. It's quite natural for

mothers to hate their children, sometimes. We have a label for it—ambivalence. The ability to hate, while loving. Lovers hate each other, frequently. Children detest their mothers——"

Leiber interrupted. "I never hated my mother."

"You won't admit it, naturally. People don't enjoy admitting hatred for their loved ones."

"So Alice hates her baby."

"Better say she has an obsession. She's gone a step further than plain, ordinary ambivalence. A Caesarian operation brought the child into the world and almost took Alice out of it. She blames the child for her near-death and her pneumonia. She's projecting her troubles, blaming them on the handiest object she can use as a source of blame. We *all* do it. We stumble into a chair and curse the furniture, not our own clumsiness. We miss a golf-stroke and damn the turf or our club, or the make of ball. If our business fails we blame the gods, the weather, our luck. All I can tell you is what I told you before. Love her. Finest medicine in the world. Find little ways of showing your affection, give her security. Find ways of showing her how harmless and innocent the child is. Make her feel that the baby was worth the risk. After awhile, she'll settle down, forget about death, and begin to love the child. If she doesn't come around in the next month or so, ask me. I'll recommend a good psychiatrist. Go on along now, and take that look off your face."

When summer came, things seemed to settle, become easier. Dave worked, immersed himself in office detail, but found much time for his wife. She, in turn, took long walks, gained strength, played an occasional light game of badminton. She rarely burst out any more. She seemed to have rid herself of her fears.

Except on one certain midnight when a sudden summer wind swept around the house, warm and swift, shaking the trees like so many shining tambourines. Alice wakened, trembling, and slid over into her husband's arms, and let him console her, and ask her what was wrong.

She said, "Something's here in the room, watching us."

He switched on the light. "Dreaming again," he said.

"You're better, though. Haven't been troubled for a long time."

She sighed as he clicked off the light again, and suddenly she slept. He held her, considering what a sweet, weird creature she was, for about half an hour.

He heard the bedroom door sway open a few inches.

There was nobody at the door. No reason for it to come open. The wind had died.

He waited. It seemed like an hour he lay silently, in the dark.

Then, far away, wailing like some small meteor dying in the vast inky gulf of space, the baby began to cry in his nursery.

It was a small, lonely sound in the middle of the stars and the dark and the breathing of this woman in his arms and the wind beginning to sweep through the trees again.

Leiber counted to one hundred, slowly. The crying continued.

Carefully disengaging Alice's arm he slipped from bed, put on his slippers, robe, and moved quietly from the room.

He'd go downstairs, he thought, fix some warm milk, bring it up, and——

The blackness dropped out from under him. His foot slipped and plunged. Slipped on something soft. Plunged into nothingness.

He thrust his hands out, caught frantically at the railing. His body stopped falling. He held. He cursed.

The "something soft" that had caused his feet to slip, rustled and thumped down a few steps. His head rang. His heart hammered at the base of his throat, thick and shot with pain.

Why do careless people leave things strewn about a house? He groped carefully with his fingers for the object that had almost spilled him headlong down the stairs.

His hand froze, startled. His breath went in. His heart held one or two beats.

The thing he held in his hand was a toy. A large cumbersome, patchwork doll he had bought as a joke, for——

For the baby.

Alice drove him to work the next day.

She slowed the car halfway downtown; pulled to the curb

and stopped it. Then she turned on the seat and looked at her husband.

"I want to go away on a vacation. I don't know if you can make it now, darling, but if not, please let me go alone. We can get someone to take care of the baby, I'm sure. But I just have to get away. I thought I was growing out of this—this *feeling*. But I haven't. I can't stand being in the room with him. He looks up at me as if he hates me, too. I can't put my finger on it; all I know is I want to get away before something happens."

He got out on his side of the car, came around, motioned to her to move over, got in. "The only thing you're going to do is see a good psychiatrist. And if he suggests a vacation, well, okay. But this can't go on; my stomach's in knots all the time." He started the car. "I'll drive the rest of the way."

Her head was down; she was trying to keep back tears. She looked up when they reached his office building. "All right. Make the appointment. I'll go talk to anyone you want, David."

He kissed her. "Now, you're talking sense, lady. Think you can drive home okay?"

"Of course, silly."

"See you at supper, then. Drive carefully."

"Don't I always? 'Bye."

He stood on the curb, watching her drive off, the wind taking hold of her long, dark, shining hair. Upstairs, a minute later, he phoned Jeffers and arranged an appointment with a reliable neuropsychiatrist.

The day's work went uneasily. Things fogged over; and in the fog he kept seeing Alice lost and calling his name. So much of her fear had come over to him. She actually had him convinced that the child was in some ways not quite natural.

He dictated long, uninspired letters. He checked some shipments downstairs. Assistants had to be questioned, and kept going. At the end of the day he was exhausted, his head throbbed, and he was very glad to go home.

On the way down in the elevator he wondered, What if I told Alice about the toy—that patchwork doll—I slipped on on the stairs last night? Lord, wouldn't *that* back her off? No, I won't ever tell her. Accidents are, after all, accidents.

Daylight lingered in the sky as he drove home in a taxi. In

front of the house he paid the driver and walked slowly up the cement walk, enjoying the light that was still in the sky and the trees. The white colonial front of the house looked unnaturally silent and uninhabited, and then, quietly, he remembered this was Thursday, and the hired help they were able to obtain from time to time were all gone for the day.

He took a deep breath of air. A bird sang behind the house. Traffic moved on the boulevard a block away. He twisted the key in the door. The knob turned under his fingers, oiled, silent.

The door opened. He stepped in, put his hat on the chair with his briefcase, started to shrug out of his coat, when he looked up.

Late sunlight streamed down the stairwell from the window near the top of the hall. Where the sunlight touched it took on the bright color of the patchwork doll sprawled at the bottom of the stairs.

But he paid no attention to the toy.

He could only look, and not move, and look again at Alice.

Alice lay in a broken, grotesque, pallid gesturing and angling of her thin body, at the bottom of the stairs, like a crumpled doll that doesn't want to play any more, ever.

Alice was dead.

The house remained quiet, except for the sound of his heart.

She was dead.

He held her head in his hands, he felt her fingers. He held her body. But she wouldn't live. She wouldn't even try to live. He said her name, out loud, many times, and he tried, once again, by holding her to him, to give her back some of the warmth she had lost, but that didn't help.

He stood up. He must have made a phone call. He didn't remember. He found himself, suddenly, upstairs. He opened the nursery door and walked inside and stared blankly at the crib. His stomach was sick. He couldn't see very well.

The baby's eyes were closed, but his face was red, moist with perspiration, as if he'd been crying long and hard.

"She's dead," said Leiber to the baby. "She's dead."

Then he started laughing low and soft and continuously for a long time until Dr. Jeffers walked in out of the night and slapped him again and again across his face.

"Snap out of it! Pull yourself together!"

"She fell down the stairs, doctor. She tripped on a patchwork doll and fell. I almost slipped on it the other night, myself. And now——"

The doctor shook him.

"Doc, Doc, Doc," said Dave, hazily. "Funny thing. Funny. I—I finally thought of a name for the baby.

The doctor said nothing.

Leiber put his head back in his trembling hands and spoke the words. "I'm going to have him christened next Sunday. Know what name I'm giving him? I'm going to call him Lucifer."

It was eleven at night. A lot of strange people had come and gone through the house, taking the essential flame with them—Alice.

David Leiber sat across from the doctor in the library.

"Alice wasn't crazy," he said, slowly. "She had good reason to fear the baby."

Jeffers exhaled. "Don't follow after her! She blamed the child for her sickness, now you blame it for her death. She stumbled on a toy, remember that. You can't blame the child."

"You mean Lucifer?"

"Stop calling him that!"

Leiber shook his head. "Alice heard things at night, moving in the halls. You want to know what made those noises, Doctor? They were made by the baby. Four months old, moving in the dark, listening to us talk. Listening to every word!" He held to the sides of the chair. "And if I turned the lights on, a baby is so small. It can hide behind furniture, a door, against a wall—below eye-level."

"I want you to stop this!" said Jeffers.

"Let me say what I think or I'll go crazy. When I went to Chicago, who was it kept Alice awake, tiring her into pneumonia? The baby! And when Alice didn't die, then he tried killing me. It was simple; leave a toy on the stairs, cry in the night until your father goes downstairs to fetch your milk, and stumbles. A crude trick, but effective. It didn't get me. But it killed Alice dead."

David Leiber stopped long enough to light a cigarette. "I

should have caught on. I'd turn on the lights in the middle of the night, many nights, and the baby'd be lying there, eyes wide. Most babies sleep all the time. Not this one. He stayed awake, thinking."

"Babies don't think."

"He stayed awake doing whatever he *could* do with his brain, then. What in hell do we know about a baby's mind? He had every reason to hate Alice; she suspected him for what he was—certainly not a normal child. Something—different. What do you know of babies, doctor? The general run, yes. You know, of course, how babies kill their mothers at birth. Why? Could it be resentment at being forced into a lousy world like this one?"

Leiber leaned toward the doctor, tiredly. "It all ties up. Suppose that a few babies out of all the millions born are instantaneously able to move, see, hear, think, like many animals and insects can. Insects are born self-sufficient. In a few weeks most mammals and birds adjust. But children take years to speak and learn to stumble around on their weak legs.

"But suppose one child in a billion is—strange? Born perfectly aware, able to think, instinctively. Wouldn't it be a perfect setup, a perfect blind for anything the baby might want to do? He could pretend to be ordinary, weak, crying, ignorant. With just a *little* expenditure of energy he could crawl about a darkened house, listening. And how easy to place obstacles at the top of stairs. How easy to cry all night and tire a mother into pneumonia. How easy, right at birth, to be so close to the mother that *a few deft maneuvers might cause peritonitis*!"

"For God's sake!" Jeffers was on his feet. "That's a repulsive thing to say!"

"It's a repulsive thing I'm speaking of. How many mothers have died at the birth of their children? How many have suckled strange little improbabilities who cause death one way or another? Strange, red little creatures with brains that work in a bloody darkness we can't even guess at. Elemental little brains, aswarm with racial memory, hatred, and raw cruelty, with no more thought than self-preservation. And self-preservation in this case consisted of eliminating a mother who realized what a horror she had birthed. I ask you, doctor, what is there in the world more selfish than a baby? Nothing!"

Jeffers scowled and shook his head, helplessly.

Leiber dropped his cigarette down. "I'm not claiming any great strength for the child. Just enough to crawl around a little, a few months ahead of schedule. Just enough to listen all the time. Just enough to cry late at night. That's enough, more than enough."

Jeffers tried ridicule. "Call it murder, then. But murder must be motivated. What motive had the child?"

Leiber was ready with the answer. "What is more at peace, more dreamfully content, at ease, at rest, fed, comforted, unbothered, than an unborn child? Nothing. It floats in a sleepy, timeless wonder of nourishment and silence. Then, suddenly, it is asked to give up its berth, is forced to vacate, rushed out into a noisy, uncaring, selfish world where it is asked to shift for itself, to hunt, to feed from the hunting, to seek after a vanishing love that once was its unquestionable right, to meet confusion instead of inner silence and conservative slumber! And the child *resents* it! Resents the cold air, the huge spaces, the sudden departure from familiar things. And in the tiny filament of brain the only thing the child knows is selfishness and hatred because the spell has been rudely shattered. Who is responsible for this disenchantment, this rude breaking of the spell? The mother. So here the new child has someone to hate with all its unreasoning mind. The mother has cast it out, rejected it. And the father is no better, kill him, too! He's responsible in *his* way!"

Jeffers interrupted. "If what you say is true, then every woman in the world would have to look on her baby as something to dread, something to wonder about."

"And why not? Hasn't the child a perfect alibi? A thousand years of accepted medical belief protects him. By all natural accounts he is helpless, not responsible. The child is born hating. And things grow worse, instead of better. At first the baby gets a certain amount of attention and mothering. But then as time passes, things change. When very new, a baby has the power to make parents do silly things when it cries or sneezes, jump when it makes a noise. As the years pass, the baby feels even that small power slip rapidly, forever away, never to return. Why shouldn't it grasp all the power it can have? Why shouldn't it jockey for position while it has all the advantages?

In later years it would be too late to express its hatred. *Now* would be the time to strike."

Leiber's voice was very soft, very low.

"My little boy baby, lying in his crib nights, his face moist and red and out of breath. From crying? No. From climbing slowly out of his crib, from crawling long distances through darkened hallways. My little boy baby. I want to kill him."

The doctor handed him a water glass and some pills. "You're not killing anyone. You're going to sleep for twenty-four hours. Sleep'll change your mind. Take this."

Leiber drank down the pills and let himself be led upstairs to his bedroom, crying, and felt himself being put to bed. The doctor waited until he was moving deep into sleep, then left the house.

Leiber, alone, drifted down, down.

He heard a noise. "What's—what's *that*?" he demanded, feebly.

Something moved in the hall.

David Leiber slept.

Very early the next morning, Dr. Jeffers drove up to the house. It was a good morning, and he was here to drive Leiber to the country for a rest. Leiber would still be asleep upstairs. Jeffers had given him enough sedative to knock him out for at least fifteen hours.

He rang the doorbell. No answer. The servants were probably not up. Jeffers tried the front door, found it open, stepped in. He put his medical kit on the nearest chair.

Something white moved out of sight at the top of the stairs. Just a suggestion of a movement. Jeffers hardly noticed it.

The smell of gas was in the house.

Jeffers ran upstairs, crashed into Leiber's bedroom.

Leiber lay motionless on the bed, and the room billowed with gas, which hissed from a released jet at the base of the wall near the door. Jeffers twisted it off, then forced up all the windows and ran back to Leiber's body.

The body was cold. It had been dead quite a few hours.

Coughing violently, the doctor hurried from the room, eyes watering. Leiber hadn't turned on the gas himself. He *couldn't* have. Those sedatives had knocked him out, he wouldn't have wakened until noon. It wasn't suicide. Or was there the faintest possibility?

Jeffers stood in the hall for five minutes. Then he walked to the door of the nursery. It was shut. He opened it. He walked inside and to the crib.

The crib was empty.

He stood swaying by the crib for half a minute, then he said something to nobody in particular.

"The nursery door blew shut. You couldn't get back into your crib where it was safe. You didn't plan on the door blowing shut. A little thing like a slammed door can ruin the best of plans. I'll find you somewhere in the house, hiding, pretending to be something you are not." The doctor looked dazed. He put his hand to his head and smiled palely. "Now I'm talking like Alice and David talked. But, I can't take any chances. I'm not sure of anything, but I can't take any chances."

He walked downstairs, opened his medical bag on the chair, took something out of it and held it in his hands.

Something rustled down the hall. Something very small and very quiet. Jeffers turned rapidly.

I had to operate to bring you into this world, he thought. Now I guess I can operate to take you out of it. . . .

He took half-a-dozen slow, sure steps forward into the hall. He raised his hand into the sunlight.

"See, baby! Something bright—something pretty!"

A scalpel.

The Crowd

MR. SPALLNER PUT his hands over his face.

There was the feeling of movement in space, the beautifully tortured scream, the impact and tumbling of the car with wall, through wall, over and down like a toy, and him hurled out of it. Then—silence.

The crowd came running. Faintly, where he lay, he heard them running. He could tell their ages and their sizes by the sound of their numerous feet over the summer grass and on the lined pavement, and over the asphalt street, and picking through the cluttered bricks to where his car hung half into the night sky, still spinning its wheels with a senseless centrifuge.

Where the crowd came from he didn't know. He struggled to remain aware and then the crowd faces hemmed in upon him, hung over him like the large glowing leaves of down-bent trees. They were a ring of shifting, compressing, changing faces over him, looking down, looking down, reading the time of his life or death by his face, making his face into a moon-dial, where the moon cast a shadow from his nose out upon his cheek to tell the time of breathing or not breathing any more ever.

How swiftly a crowd comes, he thought, like the iris of an eye compressing in out of nowhere.

A siren. A police voice. Movement. Blood trickled from his lips and he was being moved into an ambulance. Someone said, "Is he dead?" And someone else said, "No, he's not dead." And a third person said, "He won't die, he's not going to die." And he saw the faces of the crowd beyond him in the night, and he knew by their expressions that he wouldn't die. And that was strange. He saw a man's face, thin, bright, pale; the man swallowed and bit his lips, very sick. There was a small woman, too, with red hair and too much red on her cheeks and lips. And a little boy with a freckled face. Others' faces. An old man with a wrinkled upper lip, an old woman, with a mole upon her chin. They had all come from—where? Houses, cars, alleys, from the immediate and the accident-shocked world.

Out of alleys and out of hotels and out of streetcars and seemingly out of nothing they came.

The crowd looked at him and he looked back at them and did not like them at all. There was a vast wrongness to them. He couldn't put his finger on it. They were far worse than this machine-made thing that happened to him now.

The ambulance doors slammed. Through the windows he saw the crowd looking in, looking in. That crowd that always came so fast, so strangely fast, to form a circle, to peer down, to probe, to gawk, to question, to point, to disturb, to spoil the privacy of a man's agony by their frank curiosity.

The ambulance drove off. He sank back and their faces still stared into his face, even with his eyes shut.

The car wheels spun in his mind for days. One wheel, four wheels, spinning, spinning, and whirring, around and around.

He knew it was wrong. Something wrong with the wheels and the whole accident and the running of feet and the curiosity. The crowd faces mixed and spun into the wild rotation of the wheels.

He awoke.

Sunlight, a hospital room, a hand taking his pulse.

"How do you feel?" asked the doctor.

The wheels faded away. Mr. Spallner looked around.

"Fine—I guess."

He tried to find words. About the accident. "Doctor?"

"Yes?"

"That crowd—was it last night?"

"Two days ago. You've been here since Thursday. You're all right, though. You're doing fine. Don't try and get up."

"That crowd. Something about wheels, too. Do accidents make people, well, a—little off?"

"Temporarily, sometimes."

He lay staring up at the doctor. "Does it hurt your time sense?"

"Panic sometimes does."

"Makes a minute seem like an hour, or maybe an hour seem like a minute?"

"Yes."

"Let me tell you then." He felt the bed under him, the

sunlight on his face. "You'll think I'm crazy. I was driving too fast, I know. I'm sorry now. I jumped the curb and hit that wall. I was hurt and numb, I know, but I still remember things. Mostly—the crowd." He waited a moment and then decided to go on, for he suddenly knew what it was that bothered him. "The crowd got there too quickly. Thirty seconds after the smash they were all standing over me and staring at me . . . it's not right they should run that fast, so late at night. . . ."

"You only think it was thirty seconds," said the doctor. "It was probably three or four minutes. Your senses——"

"Yeah, I know—my senses, the accident. But I was conscious! I remember one thing that puts it all together and makes it funny, God, so damned funny. The wheels of my car, upside down. The wheels were still spinning when the crowd got there!"

The doctor smiled.

The man in bed went on. "I'm positive! The wheels were spinning and spinning fast—the front wheels! Wheels don't spin very long, friction cuts them down. And these were really spinning!"

"You're confused," said the doctor.

"I'm not confused. That street was empty. Not a soul in sight. And then the accident and the wheels still spinning and all those faces over me, quick, in no time. And the way they looked down at me, I *knew* I wouldn't die. . . ."

"Simple shock," said the doctor, walking away into the sunlight.

They released him from the hospital two weeks later. He rode home in a taxi. People had come to visit him during his two weeks on his back, and to all of them he had told his story, the accident, the spinning wheels, the crowd. They had all laughed with him concerning it, and passed it off.

He leaned forward and tapped on the taxi window.

"What's wrong?"

The cabbie looked back. "Sorry, boss. This is one helluva town to drive in. Got an accident up ahead. Want me to detour?"

"Yes. No. No! Wait. Go ahead. Let's—let's take a look."

The cab moved forward, honking.

"Funny damn thing," said the cabbie. "Hey, *you*! Get that fleatrap out the way!" Quieter, "Funny thing—more damn people. Nosy people."

Mr. Spallner looked down and watched his fingers tremble on his knee. "You noticed that, too?"

"Sure," said the cabbie. "All the time. There's always a crowd. You'd think it was their own mother got killed."

"They come running awfully fast," said the man in the back of the cab.

"Same way with a fire or an explosion. Nobody around. Boom. Lotsa people around. I dunno."

"Ever seen an accident—at night?"

The cabbie nodded. "Sure. Don't make no difference. There's always a crowd."

The wreck came in view. A body lay on the pavement. You knew there was a body even if you couldn't see it. Because of the crowd. The crowd with its back toward him as he sat in the rear of the cab. With its back toward him. He opened the window and almost started to yell. But he didn't have the nerve. If he yelled they might turn around.

And he was afraid to see their faces.

"I seem to have a penchant for accidents," he said, in his office. It was late afternoon. His friend sat across the desk from him, listening. "I got out of the hospital this morning and first thing on the way home, we detoured around a wreck."

"Things run in cycles," said Morgan.

"Let me tell you about my accident."

"I've heard it. Heard it all."

"But it was funny, you must admit."

"I must admit. Now how about a drink?"

They talked on for half an hour or more. All the while they talked, at the back of Spallner's brain a small watch ticked, a watch that never needed winding. It was the memory of a few little things. Wheels and faces.

At about five-thirty there was a hard metal noise in the street. Morgan nodded and looked out and down. "What'd I tell you? Cycles. A truck and a cream-colored Cadillac. Yes, yes."

Spallner walked to the window. He was very cold and as he

stood there, he looked at his watch, at the small minute hand. One two three four five seconds—people running—eight nine ten eleven twelve—from all over, people came running—fifteen sixteen seventeen eighteen seconds—more people, more cars, more horns blowing. Curiously distant, Spallner looked upon the scene as an explosion in reverse, the fragments of the detonation sucked back to the point of impulsion. Nineteen, twenty, twenty-one seconds and the crowd was there. Spallner made a gesture down at them, wordless.

The crowd had gathered so fast.

He saw a woman's body a moment before the crowd swallowed it up.

Morgan said, "You look lousy. Here. Finish your drink."

"I'm all right, I'm all right. Let me alone. I'm all right. Can you see those people? Can you see any of them? I wish we could see them closer."

Morgan cried out, "Where in hell are you going?"

Spallner was out the door, Morgan after him, and down the stairs, as rapidly as possible. "Come along, and hurry."

"Take it easy, you're not a well man!"

They walked out on to the street. Spallner pushed his way forward. He thought he saw a red-haired woman with too much red color on her cheeks and lips.

"There!" He turned wildly to Morgan. "Did you see her?"

"See *who*?"

"Damn it; she's gone. The crowd closed in!"

The crowd was all around, breathing and looking and shuffling and mixing and mumbling and getting in the way when he tried to shove through. Evidently the red-haired woman had seen him coming and run off.

He saw another familiar face! A little freckled boy. But there are many freckled boys in the world. And, anyway, it was no use, before Spallner reached him, this little boy ran away and vanished among the people.

"Is she dead?" a voice asked. "Is she dead?"

"She's dying," someone else replied. "She'll be dead before the ambulance arrives. They shouldn't have moved her. They shouldn't have moved her."

All the crowd faces—familiar, yet unfamiliar, bending over, looking down, looking down.

"Hey, mister, stop pushing."

"Who you shovin', buddy?"

Spallner came back out, and Morgan caught hold of him before he fell. "You damned fool. You're still sick. Why in hell'd you have to come down here?" Morgan demanded.

"I don't know, I really don't. They moved her, Morgan, someone moved her. You should never move a traffic victim. It kills them. It kills them."

"Yeah. That's the way with people. The idiots."

Spallner arranged the newspaper clippings carefully.

Morgan looked at them. "What's the idea? Ever since your accident you think every traffic scramble is part of you. What are these?"

"Clippings of motor-car crackups, and photos. Look at them. Not at the cars," said Spallner, "but at the crowds around the cars." He pointed. "Here. Compare this photo of a wreck in the Wilshire District with one in Westwood. No resemblance. But now take this Westwood picture and align it with one taken in the Westwood District ten years ago." Again he motioned. "This woman is in both pictures."

"Coincidence. The woman happened to be there once in 1936, again in 1946."

"A coincidence once, maybe. But twelve times over a period of ten years, when the accidents occurred as much as three miles from one another, no. Here." He dealt out a dozen photographs. "She's in *all* of these!"

"Maybe she's perverted."

"She's more than that. How does she *happen* to be there so quickly after each accident? And why does she wear the same clothes in pictures taken over a period of a decade?"

"I'll be damned, so she does."

"And, last of all, why was she standing over *me* the night of my accident, two weeks ago!"

They had a drink. Morgan went over the files. "What'd you do, hire a clipping service while you were in the hospital to go back through the newspapers for you?" Spallner nodded. Morgan sipped his drink. It was getting late. The street lights were coming on in the streets below the office. "What does all this add up to?"

"I don't know," said Spallner, "except that there's a universal law about accidents. *Crowds gather.* They always gather. And like you and me, people have wondered year after year, why they gathered so quickly, and how? I know the answer. Here it is!"

He flung the clippings down. "It frightens me."

"These people—mightn't they be thrill-hunters, perverted sensationalists with a carnal lust for blood and morbidity?"

Spallner shrugged. "Does that explain their being at all the accidents? Notice, they stick to certain territories. A Brentwood accident will bring out one group. A Huntington Park another. But there's a norm for faces, a certain percentage appear at each wreck."

Morgan said, "They're not *all* the same faces, are they?"

"Naturally not. Accidents draw normal people, too, in the course of time. But these, I find, are always the *first* ones there."

"Who are they? What do they want? You keep hinting and never telling. Good Lord, you must have some idea. You've scared yourself and now you've got me jumping."

"I've tried getting to them, but someone always trips me up, I'm always too late. They slip into the crowd and vanish. The crowd seems to offer protection to some of its members. They see me coming."

"Sounds like some sort of clique."

"They have one thing in common, they always show up together. At a fire or an explosion or on the sidelines of a war, at any public demonstration of this thing called death. Vultures, hyenas or saints, I don't know which they are, I just don't know. But I'm going to the police with it, this evening. It's gone on long enough. One of them shifted that woman's body today. They shouldn't have touched her. It killed her."

He placed the clippings in a briefcase. Morgan got up and slipped into his coat. Spallner clicked the briefcase shut. "Or, I just happened to think . . ."

"What?"

"Maybe they *wanted* her dead."

"Why?"

"Who knows. Come along?"

"Sorry. It's late. See you tomorrow. Luck." They went out

together. "Give my regards to the cops. Think they'll believe you?"

"Oh, they'll believe me all right. Good night."

Spallner took it slow driving downtown.

"I want to get there," he told himself, "alive."

He was rather shocked, but not surprised, somehow, when the truck came rolling out of an alley straight at him. He was just congratulating himself on his keen sense of observation and talking out what he would say to the police in his mind, when the truck smashed into his car. It wasn't really his car, that was the disheartening thing about it. In a preoccupied mood he was tossed first this way and then that way, while he thought, what a shame, Morgan has gone and lent me his extra car for a few days until my other car is fixed, and now here I go again. The windshield hammered back into his face. He was forced back and forth in several lightning jerks. Then all motion stopped and all noise stopped and only pain filled him up.

He heard their feet running and running and running. He fumbled with the car door. It clicked. He fell out upon the pavement drunkenly and lay, ear to the asphalt, listening to them coming. It was like a great rainstorm, with many drops, heavy and light and medium, touching the earth. He waited a few seconds and listened to their coming and their arrival. Then, weakly, expectantly, he rolled his head up and looked.

The crowd was there.

He could smell their breaths, the mingled odors of many people sucking and sucking on the air a man needs to live by. They crowded and jostled and sucked and sucked all the air up from around his gasping face until he tried to tell them to move back, they were making him live in a vacuum. His head was bleeding very badly. He tried to move and he realized something was wrong with his spine. He hadn't felt much at the impact, but his spine was hurt. He didn't dare move.

He couldn't speak. Opening his mouth, nothing came out but a gagging.

Someone said, "Give me a hand. We'll roll him over and lift him into a more comfortable position."

Spallner's brain burst apart.

No! Don't move me!

"We'll move him," said the voice, casually.

You idiots, you'll kill me, don't!

But he could not say any of this out loud. He could only think it.

Hands took hold of him. They started to lift him. He cried out and nausea choked him up. They straightened him out into a ramrod of agony. Two men did it. One of them was thin, bright, pale, alert, a young man. The other man was very old and had a wrinkled upper lip.

He had seen their faces before.

A familiar voice said, "Is—is he dead?"

Another voice, a memorable voice, responded, "No. Not yet. But he will be dead before the ambulance arrives."

It was all a very silly, mad plot. Like every accident. He squealed hysterically at the solid wall of faces. They were all around him, these judges and jurors with the faces he had seen before. Through his pain he counted their faces.

The freckled boy. The old man with the wrinkled upper lip.

The red-haired, red-cheeked woman. An old woman with a mole on her chin.

I know what you're here for, he thought. You're here just as you're at all accidents. To make certain the right ones live and the right ones die. That's why you lifted me. You knew it would kill. You knew I'd live if you left me alone.

And that's the way it's been since time began, when crowds gather. You murder much easier, this way. Your alibi is very simple; you didn't know it was dangerous to move a hurt man. You didn't mean to hurt him.

He looked at them, above him, and he was curious as a man under deep water looking up at people on a bridge. Who are you? Where do you come from and how do you get here so soon? You're the crowd that's always in the way, using up good air that a dying man's lungs are in need of, using up space he should be using to lie in, alone. Tramping on people to make sure they die, that's you. I know *all* of you.

It was like a polite monologue. They said nothing. Faces. The old man. The red-haired woman.

Someone picked up his briefcase. "Whose is this?"

It's mine! It's evidence against all of you!

Eyes, inverted over him. Shiny eyes under tousled hair or under hats.

Faces.

Somewhere—a siren. The ambulance was coming.

But, looking at the faces, the construction, the cast, the form of the faces, Spallner saw it was too late. He read it in their faces. They *knew*.

He tried to speak. A little bit got out:

"It—looks like I'll—be joining up with you. I—guess I'll be a member of your—group—now."

He closed his eyes then, and waited for the coroner.

Jack-in-the-Box

HE LOOKED THROUGH the cold morning windows with the Jack-in-the-Box in his hands, prying the rusted lid. But no matter how he struggled, the Jack would not jump to the light with a cry, or slap its velvet mittens on the air, or bob in a dozen directions with a wild and painted smile. Crushed under the lid, in its jail, it stayed crammed tight coil on coil. With your ear to the box, you felt pressure beneath, the fear and panic of the trapped toy. It was like holding someone's heart in your hand. Edwin could not tell if the box pulsed or if his own blood beat against the lid.

He threw the box down and looked to the window. Outside the window the trees surrounded the house which surrounded Edwin. He could not see beyond the trees. If he tried to find another World beyond them, the trees wove themselves thick with the wind, to still his curiosity, to stop his eyes.

"Edwin!" Behind him, Mother's waiting, nervous breath as she drank her breakfast coffee. "Stop staring. Come eat."

"No," he whispered.

"What?" A stiffened rustle. She must have turned. "Which is more important, breakfast or that window?"

"The window . . ." he whispered and sent his gaze running the paths and trails he had tried for thirteen years. Was it true that the trees flowed on ten thousand miles to nothingness? He could not say. His sight returned defeated, to the lawn, the steps, his hands trembling on the pane.

He turned to eat his tasteless apricots, alone with his mother in the vast and echoing breakfast room. Five thousand mornings at this table, this window, and no movement beyond the trees.

The two of them ate silently.

She was the pale woman that no one but the birds saw in old country houses in fourth-floor cupola windows, each morning at six, each afternoon at four, each evening at nine, and also passing by one minute after midnight, there she would be, in her tower, silent and white, high and alone and quiet. It was like passing a deserted greenhouse in which one last wild white blossom lifted its head to the moonlight.

And her child, Edwin, was the thistle that one breath of wind might unpod in a season of thistles. His hair was silken and his eyes were of a constant blue and feverish temperature. He had a haunted look, as if he slept poorly. He might fly apart like a packet of ladyfinger firecrackers if a certain door slammed.

His mother began to talk, slowly and with great caution, then more rapidly, and then angrily, and then almost spitting at him.

"Why must you disobey every morning? I don't like your staring from the window, do you hear? What do you want? Do you want to see them?" she cried, her fingers twitching. She was blazingly lovely, like an angry white flower. "Do you want to see the Beasts that run down paths and crush people like strawberries?"

Yes, he thought, I'd like to see the Beasts, horrible as they are.

"Do you want to go out there?" she cried, "like your father did before you were born, and be killed as he was killed, struck down by one of those Terrors on the road, would you like that!"

"No . . ."

"Isn't it enough they murdered your Father? Why should you even think of those Beasts!" She motioned toward the forest. "Well, if you really want to die that much, go ahead!"

She quieted, but her fingers kept opening and closing on the tablecloth. "Edwin, Edwin, your Father built every part of this World, it was beautiful for him, it should be for you. There's nothing, nothing, beyond those trees but death; I won't have you near it! This *is* the World. There's no other worth bothering with."

He nodded miserably.

"Smile now, and finish your toast," she said.

He ate slowly, with the window reflected in secret on his silver spoon.

"Mom . . . ?" He couldn't say it. "What's . . . dying? You talk about it. Is it a feeling?"

"To those who must live on after someone else, a bad feeling, yes." She stood up suddenly. "You're late for school! Run!"

He kissed her as he grabbed his books. "Bye!"

"Say hello to teacher!"

He fled from her like a bullet from gun. Up endless staircases, through passages, halls, past windows that poured down dark gallery panels like white waterfalls. Up, up through the layer-cake Worlds with the thick frostings of Oriental rug between, and bright candles on top.

From the highest stair he gazed down through four intervals of Universe.

Lowlands of kitchen, dining room, parlor. Two Middle Countries of music, games, pictures, and locked, forbidden rooms. And here—he whirled—the Highlands of picnics, adventure, and learning. Here he roamed, idled, or sat singing lonely child songs on the winding journey to school.

This, then, was the Universe. Father (or God, as Mother often called him) had raised its mountains of wallpapered plaster long ago. This was Father-God's creation, in which stars blazed at the flick of a switch. And the sun was Mother, and Mother was the sun, about which all the Worlds swung, turning. And Edwin, a small dark meteor, spun up around through the dark carpets and shimmering tapestries of space. You saw him rise to vanish on vast comet staircases, on hikes and explorations.

Sometimes he and Mother picnicked in the Highlands, spread cool snow linens on red-tuffed, Persian lawns, on crimson meadows in a rarefied plateau at the summit of the Worlds where flaking portraits of sallow strangers looked meanly down on their eating and their revels. They drew water from silver taps in hidden tiled niches, smashed the tumblers on hearthstones, shrieking. Played hide-and-seek in enchanted Upper Countries, in unknown, wild, and hidden lands, where she found him rolled like a mummy in a velvet window drape or under sheeted furniture like a rare plant protected from some wind. Once, lost, he wandered for hours in insane foothills of dust and echoes, where the hooks and hangers in closets were hung only with night. But she found him and carried him weeping down through the leveling Universe to the Parlor where dust motes, exact and familiar, fell in showers of sparks on the sunlit air.

He ran up a stair.

Here he knocked a thousand thousand doors, all locked and forbidden. Here Picasso ladies and Dali gentlemen screamed silently from canvas asylums, their gold eyes burning when he dawdled.

"Those Things live *out there*," his mother had said, pointing to the Dali-Picasso families.

Now running quickly past, he stuck out his tongue at them.

He stopped running.

One of the forbidden doors stood open.

Sunlight slanted warm through it, exciting him.

Beyond the door, a spiral stair screwed around up in sun and silence.

He stood, gasping. Year after year he had tried the doors that were always found locked. What would happen now if he shoved this one full open and climbed the stair? Was some Monster hiding at the top?

"Hello!"

His voice leapt up around the spiraled sunlight. "Hello . . ." whispered a faint, far lazy echo, high, high, and gone.

He moved through the door.

"Please, please, don't hurt me," he whispered to the high sunlit place.

He climbed, pausing with each step to wait for his punishment, eyes shut like a penitent. Faster now, he leapt around and around and up until his knees ached and his breath fountained in and out and his head banged like a bell and at last he reached the terrible summit of the climb and stood in an open, sun-drenched tower.

The sun struck his eyes a blow. Never, never so much sun! He stumbled to the iron rail.

"It's there!" His mouth opened from one direction to another. "It's there!" He ran in a circle. "There!"

He was above the somber tree barrier. For the first time he stood high over the windy chestnuts and elms and as far as he could see was green grass, green trees, and white ribbons on which beetles ran, and the other half of the world was blue and endless, with the sun lost and dropping away in an incredible deep blue room so vast he felt himself fall with it, screamed, and clutched the tower ledge, and beyond the trees, beyond the white ribbons where the beetles ran he saw things like fingers sticking up, but he saw no Dali-Picasso terrors, he saw only some small red-and-white-and-blue handkerchiefs fluttering high on great white poles.

He was suddenly sick; he was sick again.

Turning, he almost fell flat down the stairs.

He slammed the forbidden door, fell against it.

"You'll go blind." He crushed his hands to his eyes. "You shouldn't have seen, you shouldn't, you shouldn't!"

He fell to his knees, he lay on the floor twisted tight, covered up. He need wait but a moment—the blindness would come.

Five minutes later he stood at an ordinary Highlands window, looking out at his own familiar Garden World.

He saw once more the elms and hickory trees and the stone wall, and that forest which he had taken to be an endless wall itself, beyond which lay nothing but nightmare nothingness, mist, rain, and eternal night. Now it was certain, the Universe did not end with the forest. There were other worlds than those contained in Highland or Lowland.

He tried the forbidden door again. Locked.

Had he really gone up? Had he really discovered those half-green, half-blue vastnesses? Had God seen him? Edwin trembled. God. God, who smoked mysterious black pipes and wielded magical walking sticks. God who might be watching even now!

Edwin murmured, touching his cold face.

"I can still see. Thank you, thank you. I can *still* see!"

At nine-thirty, half an hour late, he rapped on the school door.

"Good morning, Teacher!"

The door swung open. Teacher waited in her tall gray, thick-clothed monk's robe, the cowl hiding her face. She wore her usual silver spectacles. Her gray-gloved hands beckoned.

"You're late."

Beyond her the land of books burned in bright colors from the hearth. There were walls bricked with encyclopedias, and a fireplace in which you could stand without bumping your head. A log blazed fiercely.

The door closed, and there was a warm quiet. Here was

the desk, where God had once sat, he'd walked this carpet, stuffing his pipe with rich tobacco, and scowled out that vast, stained-glass window. The room smelled of God, rubbed wood, tobacco, leather, and silver coins. Here, Teacher's voice sang like a solemn harp, telling of God, the old days, and the World when it had shaken with God's determination, trembled at his wit, when the World was abuilding under God's hand, a blueprint, a cry, and timber rising. God's fingerprints still lay like half-melted snowflakes on a dozen sharpened pencils in a locked glass display. They must never never be touched lest they melt away forever.

Here, here in the Highlands, to the soft sound of Teacher's voice running on, Edwin learned what was expected of him and his body. He was to grow into a Presence, he must fit the odors and the trumpet voice of God. He must some day stand tall and burning with pale fire at this high window to shout dust off the beams of the Worlds; he must be God Himself! Nothing must prevent it. Not the sky or the trees or the Things beyond the trees.

Teacher moved like a vapor in the room.

"Why are you late, Edwin?"

"I don't know."

"I'll ask you again. Edwin why are you late?"

"One—one of the forbidden doors was open. . . ."

He heard the hiss of Teacher's breath. He saw her slowly slide back and sink into the large hand-carved chair, swallowed by darkness, her glasses flashing light before they vanished. He felt her looking out at him from shadow and her voice was numbed and so like a voice he heard at night, his own voice crying just before he woke from some nightmare. "Which door? Where?" she said. "Oh, it must be locked!"

"The door by the Dali-Picasso people," he said, in panic. He and Teacher had always been friends. Was that finished now? Had he spoiled things? "I climbed the stair. I had to, I had to! I'm sorry, I'm sorry. Please, don't tell Mother!"

Teacher sat lost in the hollow chair, in the hollow cowl. Her glasses made faint firefly glitters in the well where she moved alone. "And what did you *see* up there?" she murmured. . . .

"A big blue room!"

"Did you?"

"And a green one, and ribbons with bugs running on them, but I didn't, I didn't stay long, I swear, I swear!"

"Green room, ribbons, yes ribbons, and the little bugs running along them, yes," she said, and her voice made him sad.

He reached out for her hand, but it fell away to her lap and groped back, in darkness, to her breast. "I came right down, I locked the door, I won't go look again, ever!" he cried.

Her voice was so faint he could hardly hear what she said. "But now you've seen, and you'll want to see more, and you'll always be curious now." The cowl moved slowly back and forth. Its deepness turned toward him, questioning. "Did you—*like* what you saw?"

"I was scared. It was big."

"Big, yes, too big. Large, large, so large, Edwin. Not like *our* world. Big, large, uncertain. Oh, why did you do this! You knew it was wrong!"

The fire bloomed and withered on the hearth while she waited for his answer and finally when he could not answer she said, as if her lips were barely moving, "Is it your Mother?"

"I don't know!"

"Is she nervous, is she mean, does she snap at you, does she hold too tight, do you want time alone, is that it, is that it, is that it?"

"Yes, yes!" he sobbed, wildly.

"Is that why you ran off, she demands all your time, all your thoughts?" Lost and sad, her voice. "Tell me . . ."

His hands had gone sticky with tears. "Yes!" He bit his fingers and the backs of his hands. "Yes!" It was wrong to admit such things, but he didn't have to say them now, she said them, she said them, and all he must do is agree, shake his head, bite his knuckles, cry out between sobs.

Teacher was a million years old.

"We learn," she said, wearily. Rousing from her chair, she moved with a slow swaying of gray robes to the desk where her gloved hand searched a long time to find pen and paper. "We learn, Oh God, but slowly, and with pain, we learn. We think we do right, but all the time, all the time, we kill the Plan. . . ." She hissed her breath, jerked her head up suddenly. The cowl looked completely empty, shivering.

She wrote words on the paper.

"Give this to your mother. It tells her you must have two full hours every afternoon to yourself, to prowl where you wish. Anywhere. Except *out there.* Are you listening, child?"

"Yes." He dried his face. "But——"

"Go on."

"Did Mother lie to me about *out there*, and the Beasts?"

"Look at me," she said. "I've been your friend, I've never beaten you, as your mother sometimes must. We're both here to help you understand and grow so you won't be destroyed as God was."

She arose, and in rising, turned the cowl such a way that color from the hearth washed over her face. Swiftly, the firelight erased her many wrinkles.

Edwin gasped. His heart gave a jolting thump. "The fire!"

Teacher froze.

"The fire!" Edwin looked at the fire and back to her face. The cowl jerked away from his gaze, the face vanished in the deep well, gone. "Your face," said Edwin numbly. "You look like Mother!"

She moved swiftly to the books, seized one down. She talked to the shelves in her high, singing, monotonous voice. "Women look alike, you know that! Forget it! Here, here!" And she brought him the book. "Read the first chapter! Read the diary!"

Edwin took the book but did not feel its weight in his hands. The fire rumbled and sucked itself brilliantly up the flue as he began to read and as he read Teacher sank back down and settled and quieted and the more he read the more the gray cowl nodded and became serene, the hidden face like a clapper gone solemn in its bell. Firelight ignited the gold animal lettering of the shelved books as he read and he spoke the words but was really thinking of these books from which pages had been razored, and clipped, certain lines erased, certain pictures torn, the leather jaws of some books glued tight, others like mad dogs, muzzled in hard bronze straps to keep him away. All this he thought while his lips moved through the fire-quiet:

"In the Beginning was God. Who created the Universe, and the Worlds within the Universe, the Continents within the Worlds and the Lands within the Continents, and shaped from His mind and hand His loving wife and a child who in time would be God Himself . . ."

Teacher nodded slowly. The fire fell softly away to slumbering coals. Edwin read on.

Down the banister, breathless, he slid into the Parlor. "Mom, Mom!"

She lay in a plump maroon chair, breathless, as if she, too, had run a great way.

"Mom, Mom, you're soaking wet!"

"Am I?" she said, as if it was his fault she'd been rushing about. "So I am, so I am." She took a deep breath and sighed. Then she took his hands and kissed each one. She looked at him steadily, her eyes dilating. "Well now, listen here, I've a surprise! Do you know what's coming tomorrow? You can't guess! Your birthday!"

"But it's only been ten months!"

"Tomorrow it is! Do us wonders, I say. And anything I *say* is so is *really* so, my dear."

She laughed.

"And we open another secret room?" He was dazed.

"The fourteenth room, yes! Fifteenth room next year, sixteenth, seventeenth, and so on and on till your twenty-first birthday, Edwin! Then, oh, then we'll open up the triple-locked doors to the most important room and you'll be Man of the House, Father, God, Ruler of the Universe!"

"Hey," he said. And, "Hey!" He tossed his books straight up in the air. They exploded like a great burst of doves, whistling. He laughed. She laughed. Their laughter flew and fell with the books. He ran to scream down the banister again.

At the bottom of the stairs, she waited, arms wide, to catch him.

Edwin lay on his moonlit bed and his fingers pried at the Jack-in-the-Box, but the lid stayed shut; he turned it in his hands, blindly, but did not look down at it. Tomorrow, his birthday—but why? Was he *that* good? No. Why then, should the birthday come so soon? Well, simply because things had gotten, what word could you use? Nervous? Yes, things had begun to shimmer by day as well as by night. He saw the white tremor, the moonlight sifting down and down of an invisible snow in his mother's face. It would take yet another of his birthdays to quiet her again.

"My birthdays," he said to the ceiling, "will come quicker from now on. I know, I know. Mom laughs so loud, so much, and her eyes are funny. . . ."

Would Teacher be invited to the party? No. Mother and Teacher had never met. "Why not?" "Because," said Mom. "Don't you *want* to meet Mom, Teacher?" "Some day," said Teacher, faintly, blowing off like cobwebs in the hall. "Some . . . day. . . ."

And where did Teacher go at night? Did she drift through all those secret mountain countries high up near the moon where the chandeliers were skinned blind with dust, or did she wander out beyond the trees that lay beyond the trees that lay beyond the trees? No, hardly that!

He twisted the toy in his sweating hands. Last year, when things began to tremble and quiver, hadn't Mother advanced his birthday several months, too? Yes, oh, yes, yes.

Think of something else. God. God building cold midnight cellar, sun-baked attic, and all miracles between. Think of the hour of his death, crushed by some monstrous beetle beyond the wall. Oh, how the worlds must have rocked with His passing!

Edwin moved the Jack-in-the-Box to his face, whispered against the lid. "Hello! Hello! Hello, hello . . ."

No answer save the sprung-tight coiled-in tension there. I'll get you out, thought Edwin. Just wait, just wait. It may hurt, but there's only one way. Here, here . . .

And he moved from bed to window and leaned far out, looking down to the marbled walk in the moonlight. He raised the box high, felt the sweat trickle from his armpit, felt his fingers clench, felt his arm jerk. He flung the box out, shouting. The box tumbled in the cold air, down. It took a long time to strike the marble pavement.

Edwin bent still further over, gasping.

"Well?" he cried. "Well?" and again, "You there!" and "You!"

The echoes faded. The box lay in the forest shadows. He could not see if the crash had broken it wide. He could not see if the Jack had risen, smiling, from its hideous jail or if it bobbed upon the wind now this way, that, this way, that, its silver bells jingling softly. He listened. He stood by the window for an hour staring, listening, and at last went back to bed.

Morning. Bright voices moved near and far, in and out the Kitchen World and Edwin opened his eyes. Whose voices, now whose could they be? Some of God's workmen? The Dali people? But Mother hated them; no. The voices faded in a humming roar. Silence. And from a great distance, a running, running grew louder and still louder until the door burst open.

"Happy Birthday!"

They danced, they ate frosted cookies, they bit lemon ices, they drank pink wines, and there stood his name on a snow-powdered cake as Mother chorded the piano into an avalanche of sound and opened her mouth to sing, then whirled to seize him away to more strawberries, more wines, more laughter that shook chandeliers into trembling rain. Then, a silver key flourished, they raced to unlock the fourteenth forbidden door.

"Ready! Hold on!"

The door whispered into the wall.

"Oh," said Edwin.

For, disappointingly enough, this fourteenth room was nothing at all but a dusty dull-brown closet. It promised nothing as had the rooms given him on other anniversaries! His sixth birthday present, now, had been the schoolroom in the Highlands. On his seventh birthday he had opened the playroom in the Lowlands. Eighth, the music room; Ninth, the miraculous hell-fired kitchen! Tenth was the room where phonographs hissed in a continuous exhalation of ghosts singing on a gentle wind. Eleventh was the vast green diamond room of the Garden with a carpet that had to be cut instead of swept!

"Oh, don't be disappointed; move!" Mother, laughing, pushed him in the closet. "Wait till you see how magical! Shut the door!"

She thrust a red button flush with the wall.

Edwin shrieked. "No!"

For the room was quivering, working, like a mouth that held them in iron jaws; the room moved, the wall slid away below.

"Oh, hush now, darling," she said. The door drifted down through the floor, and a long insanely vacant wall slithered by like an endlessly rustling snake to bring another door and another door with it that did not stop but traveled on while Edwin screamed and clutched his mother's waist. The room whined and cleared its throat somewhere; the trembling ceased, the room stood still. Edwin stared at a strange new door and heard his mother say go on, open it, there, now, there. And the new door gaped upon still further mystery. Edwin blinked.

"The Highlands! This is the Highlands! How did we get here? Where's the Parlor, mom, where's the Parlor!"

She fetched him out through the door. "We jumped straight up, and we flew. Once a week, you'll fly to school instead of running the long way around!"

He still could not move, but only stood looking at the mystery of Land exchanged for Land, of Country replaced by higher and further Country.

"Oh, mother, mother . . ." he said.

It was a sweet long time in the deep grass of the garden where they idled most deliciously, sipped huge cupfuls of apple cider with their elbows on crimson silk cushions, their shoes kicked off, their toes bedded in sour dandelions, sweet clover. Mother jumped twice when she heard Monsters roar beyond the forest. Edwin kissed her cheek. "It's all right," he said, "I'll protect you."

"I know you will," she said, but she turned to gaze at the pattern of trees, as if any moment the chaos out there might smash the forest with a blow and stamp its Titan's foot down and grind them to dust.

Late in the long blue afternoon, they saw a chromium bird thing fly through a bright rift in the trees, high and roaring. They ran for the Parlor, heads bent as before a green storm of lightning and rain, feeling the sound pour blinding showers to drench them.

Crackle, crackle—the birthday burnt away to cellophane

nothingness. At sunset, in the dim soft Parlor Country, Mother inhaled champagne with her tiny seedling nostrils and her pale summer-rose mouth, then, drowsy wild, herded Edwin off to his room and shut him in.

He undressed in slow-pantomimed wonder, thinking, this year, next year, and which room two years, three years, from today? What about the Beasts, the Monsters? And being mashed and God killed? What was killed? What was Death? Was Death a feeling? Did God enjoy it so much he never came back? Was Death a journey then?

In the hall, on her way downstairs, Mother dropped a champagne bottle. Edwin heard and was cold, for the thought that jumped through his head was, that's how Mother'd sound. If she fell, if she broke, you'd find a million fragments in the morning. Bright crystal and clear wine on the parquet flooring, that's all you'd see at dawn.

Morning was the smell of vines and grapes and moss in his room, a smell of shadowed coolness. Downstairs, breakfast was in all probability, at this instant, manifesting itself in a fingersnap on the wintry tables.

Edwin got up to wash and dress and wait, feeling fine. Now things would be fresh and new for at least a month. Today, like all days, there'd be breakfast, school, lunch, songs in the music room, an hour or two at the electrical games, then—tea in the Outlands, on the luminous grass. Then up to school again for a late hour or so, where he and Teacher might prowl the censored library together and he'd puzzle with words and thoughts about that world *out there* that had been censored from his eyes.

He had forgotten Teacher's note. Now, he must give it to Mother.

He opened the door. The hall was empty. Down through the deeps of the Worlds, a soft mist floated, through a silence which no footsteps broke; the hills were quiet; the silver fonts did not pulse in the first sunlight, and the banister, coiling up from the mists was a prehistoric monster peering into his room. He pulled away from this creature, looking to find Mother, like a white boat, drifted by the dawn tides and vapors below.

She was not there. He hurried down through the hushed lands, calling, "Mother!"

He found her in the Parlor, collapsed on the floor in her shiny green-gold party dress, a champagne goblet in one hand, the carpet littered with broken glass.

She was obviously asleep, so he sat at the magical breakfast table. He blinked at the empty white cloth and the gleaming plates. There was no food. All his life wondrous foods had awaited him here. But not today.

"Mother, wake up!" He ran to her. "Shall I go to school? Where's the food? Wake up!"

He ran up the stairs.

The Highlands were cold and shadowed, and the white glass suns no longer glowed from the ceilings in this day of sullen fog. Down dark corridors, through dim continents of silence, Edwin rushed. He rapped and rapped at the school door. It drifted in, whining, by itself.

The school lay empty and dark. No fire roared on the hearth to toss shadows on the beamed ceiling. There was not a crackle or a whisper.

"Teacher?"

He poised in the center of the flat, cold room.

"Teacher!" he screamed.

He slashed the drapes aside; a faint shaft of sunlight fell through the stained glass.

Edwin gestured. He commanded the fire to explode like a popcorn kernel on the hearth. He commanded it to bloom to life! He shut his eyes, to give Teacher time to appear. He opened his eyes and was stupefied at what he saw on her desk.

Neatly folded was the gray cowl and robe, atop which gleamed her silver spectacles, and one gray glove. He touched them. One gray glove was gone. A piece of greasy cosmetic chalk lay on the robe. Testing it, he made dark lines on his hands.

He drew back, staring at Teacher's empty robe, the glasses, the greasy chalk. His hand touched a knob of a door which had always been locked. The door swung slowly wide. He looked into a small brown closet.

"Teacher!"

He ran in, the door crashed shut, he pressed a red button. The room sank down, and with it sank a slow mortal coldness. The World was silent, quiet, and cool. Teacher gone and Mother—sleeping. Down fell the room, with him in its iron jaws.

Machinery clashed. A door slid open. Edwin ran out.

The Parlor!

Behind was not a door, but a tall oak panel from which he had emerged.

Mother lay uncaring, asleep. Folded under her, barely showing as he rolled her over, was one of Teacher's soft gray gloves.

He stood near her, holding the incredible glove, for a long time. Finally, he began to whimper.

He fled back up to the Highlands. The hearth was cold, the room empty. He waited. Teacher did not come. He ran down again to the solemn Lowlands, commanded the table to fill with steaming dishes! Nothing happened. He sat by his mother, talking and pleading with her and touching her, and her hands were cold.

The clock ticked and the light changed in the sky and still she did not move, and he was hungry and the silent dust dropped down on the air through all the Worlds. He thought of Teacher and knew that if she was in none of the hills and mountains above, then there was only one place she could be. She had wandered, by error, into the Outlands, lost until someone found her. And so he must go out, call after her, bring her back to wake Mother, or she would lie here forever with the dust falling in the great darkened spaces.

Through the kitchen, out back, he found late afternoon sun and the Beasts hooting faintly beyond the rim of the World. He clung to the garden wall, not daring to let go, and in the shadows, at a distance, saw the shattered box he had flung from the window. Freckles of sunlight quivered on the broken lid and touched tremblingly over and over the face of the Jack jumped out and sprawled with its arms overhead in an eternal gesture of freedom. The doll smiled and did not smile, smiled and did not smile, as the sun winked on the mouth, and Edwin stood, hypnotized, above and beyond it. The doll opened its arms toward the path that led off between the secret trees, the forbidden path smeared with oily droppings of the Beasts. But the path lay silent and the sun warmed Edwin and he heard the wind blow softly in the trees. At last, he let go of the garden wall.

"Teacher?"

He edged along the path a few feet.

"Teacher!"

His shoes slipped on the animal droppings and he stared far down the motionless tunnel, blindly. The path moved under, the trees moved over him.

"Teacher!"

He walked slowly but steadily. He turned. Behind him lay his World and its very new silence. It was diminished, it was small! How strange to see it less than it had been. It had always and forever seemed so large. He felt his heart stop. He stepped back. But then, afraid of that silence in the World, he turned to face the forest path ahead.

Everything before him was new. Odors filled his nostrils, colors, odd shapes, incredible sizes filled his eyes.

If I run beyond the trees I'll die, he thought, for that's what Mother said. You'll die, you'll die.

But what's dying? Another room? A blue room, a green room, far larger than all the rooms that ever were! But where's the key? There, far ahead, a great half-open iron door, a wrought-iron gate. Beyond a room as large as the sky, all colored green with trees and grass! Oh, Mother, Teacher . . .

He rushed, stumbled, fell, got up, ran again, his numb legs under him were left behind as he fell down and down the side of a hill, the path gone, wailing, crying, and then not wailing or crying any more, but making new sounds. He reached the great rusted, screaming iron gate, leapt through; the Universe dwindled behind, he did not look back at his old Worlds, but ran as they withered and vanished.

The policeman stood at the curb, looking down the street.

"These kids. I'll never be able to figure them."

"How's that?" asked the pedestrian.

The policeman thought it over and frowned. "Couple seconds ago a little kid ran by. He was laughing and crying, crying and laughing, both. He was jumping up and down and touching things. Things like lampposts, the telephone poles, fire hydrants, dogs, people. Things like sidewalks, fences, gates, cars, plateglass windows, barber poles. Hell, he even grabbed hold and looked at me, and looked at the sky, you should have seen the tears, and all the time he kept yelling and yelling something funny."

"What did he yell?" asked the pedestrian.

"He kept yelling, 'I'm dead, I'm dead, I'm glad I'm dead, I'm dead, I'm dead, I'm glad I'm dead, I'm dead, I'm dead, it's *good* to be dead!'" The policeman scratched his chin slowly. "One of them new kid games, I guess."

The Scythe

QUITE SUDDENLY THERE was no more road. It ran down the valley like any other road, between slopes of barren, stony ground and live oak trees, and then past a broad field of wheat standing alone in the wilderness. It came up beside the small white house that belonged to the wheat field and then just faded out, as though there was no more use for it.

It didn't matter much, because just there the last of the gas was gone. Drew Erickson braked the ancient car to a stop and sat there, not speaking, staring at his big, rough farmer's hands.

Molly spoke, without moving where she lay in the corner beside him. "We must of took the wrong fork back yonder."

Drew nodded.

Molly's lips were almost as white as her face. Only they were dry, where her skin was damp with sweat. Her voice was flat, with no expression in it.

"Drew," she said. "Drew, what are we a-goin' to do now?"

Drew stared at his hands. A farmer's hands, with the farm blown out from under them by the dry, hungry wind that never got enough good loam to eat.

The kids in the back seat woke up and pried themselves out of the dusty litter of bundles and bedding. They poked their heads over the back of the seat and said:

"What are we stoppin' for, Pa? Are we gonna eat now, Pa? Pa, we're awful hungry. Can we eat now, Pa?"

Drew closed his eyes. He hated the sight of his hands.

Molly's fingers touched his wrist. Very light, very soft. "Drew, maybe in the house there they'd spare us somethin' to eat?"

A white line showed around his mouth. "Beggin'," he said harshly. "Ain't none of us ever begged before. Ain't none of us ever goin' to."

Molly's hand tightened on his wrist. He turned and saw her eyes. He saw the eyes of Susie and little Drew, looking at him. Slowly all the stiffness went out of his neck and his back. His face got loose and blank, shapeless like a thing that has been beaten too hard and too long. He got out of the car and went up the path to the house. He walked uncertainly, like a man who is sick, or nearly blind.

The door of the house was open. Drew knocked three times. There was nothing inside but silence, and a white window curtain moving in the slow, hot air.

He knew it before he went in. He knew there was death in the house. It was that kind of silence.

He went through a small, clean living room and down a little hall. He wasn't thinking anything. He was past thinking. He was going toward the kitchen, unquestioning, like an animal.

Then he looked through an open door and saw the dead man.

He was an old man, lying out on a clean white bed. He hadn't been dead long; not long enough to lose the last quiet look of peace. He must have known he was going to die, because he wore his grave clothes—an old black suit, brushed and neat, and a clean white shirt and a black tie.

A scythe leaned against the wall beside the bed. Between the old man's hands there was a blade of wheat, still fresh. A ripe blade, golden and heavy in the tassel.

Drew went into the bedroom, walking soft. There was a coldness on him. He took off his broken, dusty hat and stood by the bed, looking down.

The paper lay open on the pillow beside the old man's head. It was meant to be read. Maybe a request for burial, or to call a relative. Drew scowled over the words, moving his pale, dry lips.

> *To him who stands beside me at my death bed:*
> Being of sound mind, and alone in the world as it has been decreed, I, John Buhr, do give and bequeath this farm, with all pertaining to it, to the man who is to come. Whatever his name or origin shall be, it will not matter. The farm is his, and the wheat; the scythe, and the task ordained thereto. Let him take them freely, and without question—and remember that I, John Buhr, am only the giver, not the ordainer. To which I set my hand and seal this third day of April, 1938. (Signed) John Buhr. *Kyrie eléison!*

Drew walked back through the house and opened the screen door. He said, "Molly, you come in. Kids, you stay in the car."

Molly came inside. He took her to the bedroom. She looked at the will, the scythe, the wheat field moving in a hot wind outside the window. Her white face tightened up and she bit her lips and held onto him. "It's too good to be true. There must be some trick to it."

Drew said, "Our luck's changin', that's all. We'll have work to do, stuff to eat, somethin' over our heads to keep rain off." He touched the scythe. It gleamed like a half-moon. Words were scratched on its blade: WHO WIELDS ME—WIELDS THE WORLD! It didn't mean much to him, right at that moment.

"Drew," Molly asked, staring at the old man's clasped hands, "why—why's he holdin' that wheat-stalk so hard in his fingers?"

Just then the heavy silence was broken by the sound of the kids scrambling up the front porch. Molly gasped.

They lived in the house. They buried the old man on a hill and said some words over him, and came back down and swept the house and unloaded the car and had something to eat, because there was food, lots of it, in the kitchen; and they did nothing for three days but fix the house and look at the land and lie in the good beds, and then look at one another in surprise that all this was happening this way, and their stomachs were full and there was even a cigar for him to smoke in the evenings.

There was a small barn behind the house and in the barn a bull and three cows; and there was a well-house, a spring-house, under some big trees that kept it cool. And inside the well-house were big sides of beef and bacon and pork and mutton, enough to feed a family five times their size for a year, two years, maybe three. There was a churn and a box of cheese there, and big metal cans for the milk.

On the fourth morning Drew Erickson lay in bed looking at the scythe, and he knew it was time for him to work because there was ripe grain in the long field; he had seen it with his eyes, and he did not want to get soft. Three days sitting were enough for any man. He roused himself in the first fresh smell of dawn and took the scythe and held it before him as he walked out into the field. He held it up in his hands and swung it down.

It was a big field of grain. Too big for one man to tend, and yet one man had tended it.

At the end of the first day of work, he walked in with the scythe riding his shoulder quietly, and there was a look on his face of a puzzled man. It was a wheat field the like of which he had never seen. It ripened only in separate clusters, each set off from the others. Wheat shouldn't do that. He didn't tell Molly. Nor did he tell her the other things about the field. About how, for instance, the wheat rotted within a few hours after he cut it down. Wheat shouldn't do that, either. He was not greatly worried. After all, there was food at hand.

The next morning the wheat he had left rotting, cut down, had taken hold and came up again in little green sprouts, with tiny roots, all born again.

Drew Erickson rubbed his chin, wondered what and why and how it acted that way, and what good it would be to him—he couldn't sell it. A couple of times during the day he walked far up in the hills to where the old man's grave was, just to be sure the old man was there, maybe with some notion he might get an idea there about the field. He looked down and saw how much land he owned. The wheat stretched three miles in one direction toward the mountains, and was about two acres wide, patches of it in seedlings, patches of it golden, patches of it green, patches of it fresh cut by his hand. But the old man said nothing concerning this; there were a lot of stones and dirt in his face now. The grave was in the sun and the wind and silence. So Drew Erickson walked back down to use the scythe, curious, enjoying it because it seemed important. He didn't know just why, but it was. Very, very important.

He couldn't just let the wheat stand. There were always new patches of it ripened, and in his figuring out loud to no one in particular he said, "If I cut the wheat for the next ten years, just as it ripens up, I don't think I'll pass the same spot twice. Such a damn big field." He shook his head. "That wheat ripens just *so*. Never too much of it so I can't cut all the ripe stuff each day. That leaves nothin' but green grain. And the next mornin', sure enough, another patch of ripe stuff. . . ."

It was damned foolish to cut the grain when it rotted as

quick as it fell. At the end of the week he decided to let it go a few days.

He lay in bed late, just listening to the silence in the house that wasn't anything like death silence, but a silence of things living well and happily.

He got up, dressed, and ate his breakfast slowly. He wasn't going to work. He went out to milk the cows, stood on the porch smoking a cigarette, walked about the backyard a little and then came back in and asked Molly what he had gone out to do.

"Milk the cows," she said.

"Oh, yes," he said, and went out again. He found the cows waiting and full, and milked them and put the milk cans in the spring-house, but thought of other things. The wheat. The scythe.

All through the morning he sat on the back porch rolling cigarettes. He made a toy boat for little Drew and one for Susie, and then he churned some of the milk into butter and drew off the buttermilk, but the sun was in his head, aching. It burned there. He wasn't hungry for lunch. He kept looking at the wheat and the wind bending and tipping and ruffling it. His arms flexed, his fingers, resting on his knee as he sat again on the porch, made a kind of grip in the empty air, itching. The pads of his palms itched and burned. He stood up and wiped his hands on his pants and sat down and tried to roll another cigarette and got mad at the mixings and threw it all away with a muttering. He had a feeling as if a third arm had been cut off of him, or he had lost something of himself. It had to do with his hands and his arms.

He heard the wind whisper in the field.

By one o'clock he was going in and out of the house, getting underfoot, thinking about digging an irrigation ditch, but all the time really thinking about the wheat and how ripe and beautiful it was, aching to be cut.

"Damn it to hell!"

He strode into the bedroom, took the scythe down off its wall-pegs. He stood holding it. He felt cool. His hands stopped itching. His head didn't ache. The third arm was returned to him. He was intact again.

It was instinct. Illogical as lightning striking and not hurting. Each day the grain must be cut. It had to be cut. Why?

Well, it just did, that was all. He laughed at the scythe in his big hands. Then, whistling, he took it out to the ripe and waiting field and did the work. He thought himself a little mad. Hell, it was an ordinary-enough wheat field, really, wasn't it? Almost.

The days loped away like gentle horses.

Drew Erickson began to understand his work as a sort of dry ache and hunger and need. Things built in his head.

One noon, Susie and little Drew giggled and played with the scythe while their father lunched in the kitchen. He heard them. He came out and took it away from them. He didn't yell at them. He just looked very concerned and locked the scythe up after that, when it wasn't being used.

He never missed a day, scything.

Up. Down. Up, down, and across. Back and up and down and across. Cutting. Up. Down.

Up.

Think about the old man and the wheat in his hands when he died.

Down.

Think about this dead land, with wheat living on it.

Up.

Think about the crazy patterns of ripe and green wheat, the way it grows!

Down.

Think about . . .

The wheat whirled in a full yellow tide at his ankles. The sky blackened. Drew Erickson dropped the scythe and bent over to hold his stomach, his eyes running blindly. The world reeled.

"I've killed somebody!" he gasped, choking, holding to his chest, falling to his knees beside the blade. "I've killed a lot——"

The sky revolved like a blue merry-go-round at the county fair in Kansas. But no music. Only a ringing in his ears.

Molly was sitting at the blue kitchen table peeling potatoes when he blundered into the kitchen, dragging the scythe behind him.

"Molly!"

She swam around in the wet of his eyes.

She sat there, her hands fallen open, waiting for him to finally get it out.

"Get the things packed!" he said, looking at the floor.

"Why?"

"We're leaving," he said, dully.

"We're leaving?" she said.

"That old man. You know what he did here? It's the wheat, Molly, and this scythe. Every time you use the scythe on the wheat a thousand people die. You cut across them and——"

Molly got up and put the knife down and the potatoes to one side and said, understandingly, "We traveled a lot and haven't eaten good until the last month here, and you been workin' every day and you're tired——"

"I hear voices, sad voices, out there. In the wheat," he said. "Tellin' me to stop. Tellin' me not to kill them!"

"Drew!"

He didn't hear her. "The field grows crooked, wild, like a crazy thing. I didn't tell you. But it's wrong."

She stared at him. His eyes were blue glass, nothing else.

"You think I'm crazy," he said, "but wait 'til I tell you. Oh, God, Molly, help me; I just killed my mother!"

"Stop it!" she said firmly.

"I cut down one stalk of wheat and I killed her. I felt her dyin', that's how I found out just now——"

"Drew!" Her voice was like a crack across the face, angry and afraid now. "Shut up!"

He mumbled. "Oh—Molly——"

The scythe dropped from his hands, clamored on the floor. She picked it up with a snap of anger and set it in one corner. "Ten years I been with you," she said. "Sometimes we had nothin' but dust and prayers in our mouths. Now, all this good luck sudden, and you can't bear up under it!"

She brought the Bible from the living room.

She rustled its pages over. They sounded like the wheat rustling in a small, slow wind. "You sit down and listen," she said.

A sound came in from the sunshine. The kids, laughing in the shade of the large live oak beside the house.

She read from the Bible, looking up now and again to see what was happening to Drew's face.

She read from the Bible each day after that. The following Wednesday, a week later, when Drew walked down to the distant town to see if there was any General Delivery mail, there was a letter.

He came home looking two hundred years old.

He held the letter out to Molly and told her what it said in a cold, uneven voice.

"Mother passed away—one o'clock Tuesday afternoon—her heart——"

All that Drew Erickson had to say was, "Get the kids in the car, load it up with food. We're goin' on to California."

"Drew——" said his wife, holding the letter.

"You know yourself," he said, "this is poor grain land. Yet look how ripe it grows. I ain't told you all the things. It ripens in patches, a little each day. It ain't right. And when I cut it, it rots! And next mornin' it comes up without any help, growin' again! Last Tuesday, a week ago, when I cut the grain it was like rippin' my own flesh. I heard somebody scream. It sounded just like— And now, today, this letter."

She said, "We're stayin' here."

"Molly."

"We're stayin' here, where we're sure of eatin' and sleepin' and livin' decent and livin' long. I'm not starvin' my children down again, ever!"

The sky was blue through the windows. The sun slanted in, touching half of Molly's calm face, shining one eye bright blue. Four or five water drops hung and fell from the kitchen faucet slowly, shining, before Drew sighed. The sigh was husky and resigned and tired. He nodded, looking away. "All right," he said. "We'll stay."

He picked up the scythe weakly. The words on the metal leaped up with a sharp glitter.

WHO WIELDS ME—WIELDS THE WORLD!

"We'll stay. . . ."

Next morning he walked to the old man's grave. There was a single fresh sprout of wheat growing in the center of it. The same sprout, reborn, that the old man had held in his hands weeks before.

He talked to the old man, getting no answers.

"You worked the field all your life because you *had* to, and one day you came across your own life growin' there. You knew it was yours. You cut it. And you went home, put on your grave clothes, and your heart gave out and you died. That's how it was, wasn't it? And you passed the land on to me, and when I die, I'm supposed to hand it over to someone else."

Drew's voice had awe in it. "How long a time has this been goin' on? With nobody knowin' about this field and its use except the man with the scythe . . . ?"

Quite suddenly he felt very old. The valley seemed ancient, mummified, secretive, dried and bent and powerful. When the Indians danced on the prairie it had been here, this field. The same sky, the same wind, the same wheat. And, before the Indians? Some Cro-Magnon, gnarled and shag-haired, wielding a crude wooden scythe, perhaps, prowling down through the living wheat. . . .

Drew returned to work. Up, down. Up, down. Obsessed with the idea of being the wielder of *the* scythe. He, himself! It burst upon him in a mad, wild surge of strength and horror.

Up! WHO WIELDS ME! Down! WIELDS THE WORLD!

He had to accept the job with some sort of philosophy. It was simply his way of getting food and housing for his family. They deserved eating and living decent, he thought, after all these years.

Up and down. Each grain a life he neatly cut into two pieces. If he planned it carefully—he looked at the wheat—why, he and Molly and the kids could live forever!

Once he found the place where the grain grew that was Molly and Susie and little Drew he would never cut it.

And then, like a signal, it came, quietly.

Right there, before him.

Another sweep of the scythe and he'd cut them away.

Molly, Drew, Susie. It was certain. Trembling, he knelt and looked at the few grains of wheat. They glowed at his touch.

He groaned with relief. What if he had cut them down, never guessing? He blew out his breath and got up and took the scythe and stood back away from the wheat and stood for a long while looking down.

Molly thought it awfully strange when he came home early and kissed her on the cheek, for no reason at all.

At dinner, Molly said, "You quit early today? Does—does the wheat still spoil when it falls?"

He nodded and took more meat.

She said, "You ought to write to the Agriculture people and have them come look at it."

"No," he said.

"I was just suggestin'," she said.

His eyes dilated. "I got to stay here all my life. Can't nobody else mess with that wheat; they wouldn't know where to cut and not to cut. They might cut the wrong parts."

"What wrong parts?"

"Nothin'," he said, chewing slowly. "Nothin' at all."

He slapped his fork down, hard. "Who knows *what* they might want to do! Those government men! They might even—might even want to plow the whole field under!"

Molly nodded. "That's just what it needs," she said. "And start all over again, with new seed."

He didn't finish eating. "I'm not writin' any gover'ment, and I'm not handin' this field over to no stranger to cut, and that's that!" he said, and the screen door banged behind him.

He detoured around that place where the lives of his children and his wife grew up in the sun, and used his scythe on the far end of the field where he knew he would make no mistakes.

But he no longer liked the work. At the end of an hour he knew he had brought death to three of his old, loved friends in Missouri. He read their names in the cut grain and couldn't go on.

He locked the scythe in the cellar and put the key away. He was done with the reaping, done for good and all.

He smoked his pipe in the evening, on the front porch, and told the kids stories to hear them laugh. But they didn't laugh much. They seemed withdrawn, tired and funny, like they weren't his children any more.

Molly complained of a headache, dragged around the house

a little, went to bed early and fell into a deep sleep. That was funny, too. Molly always stayed up late and was full of vinegar.

The wheat field rippled with moonlight on it, making it into a sea.

It wanted cutting. Certain parts needed cutting *now*. Drew Erickson sat, swallowing quietly, trying not to look at it.

What'd happen to the world if he never went in the field again? What'd happen to people ripe for death, who waited the coming of the scythe?

He'd wait and see.

Molly was breathing softly when he blew out the oil lamp and got to bed. He couldn't sleep. He heard the wind in the wheat, felt the hunger to do the work in his arms and fingers.

In the middle of the night he found himself walking in the field, the scythe in his hands. Walking like a crazy man, walking and afraid, half-awake. He didn't remember unlocking the cellar door, getting the scythe, but here he was in the moonlight, walking in the grain.

Among these grains there were many who were old, weary, wanting so very much to sleep. The long, quiet, moonless sleep.

The scythe held him, grew into his palms, forced him to walk.

Somehow, struggling, he got free of it. He threw it down, ran off into the wheat, where he stopped and went down on his knees.

"I don't want to kill anymore," he said. "If I work with the scythe I'll have to kill Molly and the kids. Don't ask me to do that!"

The stars only sat in the sky, shining.

Behind him, he heard a dull, thumping sound.

Something shot up over the hill into the sky. It was like a living thing, with arms of red color, licking at the stars. Sparks fell into his face. The thick, hot odor of fire came with it.

The house!

Crying out, he got sluggishly, hopelessly, to his feet, looking at the big fire.

The little white house with the live oaks was roaring up in one savage bloom of fire. Heat rolled over the hill and he swam in it and went down in it, stumbling, drowning over his head.

By the time he got down the hill there was not a shingle, bolt or threshold of it that wasn't alive with flame. It made blistering, crackling, fumbling noises.

No one screamed inside. No one ran around or shouted.

He yelled in the yard. "Molly! Susie! Drew!"

He got no answer. He ran close in until his eyebrows withered and his skin crawled hot like paper burning, crisping, curling up in tight little curls.

"Molly! Susie!"

The fire settled contentedly down to feed. Drew ran around the house a dozen times, all alone, trying to find a way in. Then he sat where the fire roasted his body and waited until all the walls had sunken down with fluttering crashes, until the last ceilings bent, blanketing the floors with molten plaster and scorched lathing. Until the flames died and smoke coughed up, and the new day came slowly; and there was nothing but embering ashes and an acid smoldering.

Disregarding the heat fanning from the leveled frames, Drew walked into the ruin. It was still too dark to see much. Red light glowed on his sweating throat. He stood like a stranger in a new and different land. Here—the kitchen. Charred tables, chairs, the iron stove, the cupboards. Here—the hall. Here the parlor and then over here was the bedroom where——

Where Molly was still alive.

She slept among fallen timbers and angry-colored pieces of wire spring and metal.

She slept as if nothing had happened. Her small white hands lay at her sides, flaked with sparks. Her calm face slept with a flaming lath across one cheek.

Drew stopped and didn't believe it. In the ruin of her smoking bedroom she lay on a glittering bed of sparks, her skin intact, her breast rising, falling, taking air.

"Molly!"

Alive and sleeping after the fire, after the walls had roared down, after ceilings had collapsed upon her and flame had lived all about her.

His shoes smoked as he pushed through piles of fuming litter. It could have seared his feet off at the ankles, he wouldn't have known.

"Molly . . ."

He bent over her. She didn't move or hear him, and she didn't speak. She wasn't dead. She wasn't alive. She just lay there with the fire surrounding her and not touching her, not harming her in any way. Her cotton nightgown was streaked with ashes, but not burnt. Her brown hair was pillowed on a tumble of red-hot coals.

He touched her cheek, and it was cold, cold in the middle of hell. Tiny breaths trembled her half-smiling lips.

The children were there, too. Behind a veil of smoke he made out two smaller figures huddled in the ashes sleeping.

He carried all three of them out to the edge of the wheat field.

"Molly. Molly, wake up! Kids! Kids, wake up!"

They breathed and didn't move and went on sleeping.

"Kids, wake up! Your mother is——"

Dead? No, not dead. But——

He shook the kids as if they were to blame. They paid no attention; they were busy with their dreams. He put them back down and stood over them, his face cut with lines.

He knew why they'd slept through the fire and continued to sleep now. He knew why Molly just lay there, never wanting to laugh again.

The power of the wheat and the scythe.

Their lives, supposed to end yesterday, May 30th, 1938, had been prolonged simply because he refused to cut the grain. They should have died in the fire. That's the way it was meant to *be*. But since he had not used the scythe, nothing could hurt them. A house had flamed and fallen and still they lived, caught halfway, not dead, not alive. Simply—waiting. And all over the world thousands more just like them, victims of accidents, fires, disease, suicide, waited, slept just like Molly and her children slept. Not able to die, not able to live. All because a man was afraid of harvesting the ripe grain. All because one man thought he could stop working with a scythe and never work with that scythe again.

He looked down upon the children. The job had to be done every day and every day with never a stopping but going on, with never a pause, but always the harvesting, forever and forever and forever.

All right, he thought. All right. I'll use the scythe.

He didn't say good-by to his family. He turned with a slow-feeding anger and found the scythe and walked rapidly, then he began to trot, then he ran with long jolting strides into the field, raving, feeling the hunger in his arms, as the wheat whipped and flailed his legs. He pounded through it, shouting. He stopped.

"Molly!" he cried, and raised the blade and swung it down.

"Susie!" he cried. "Drew!" And swung the blade down again.

Somebody screamed. He didn't turn to look at the fire-ruined house.

And then, sobbing wildly, he rose above the grain again and again and hewed to left and right and to left and to right and to left and to right. Over and over and over! Slicing out huge scars in green wheat and ripe wheat, with no selection and no care, cursing, over and over, swearing, laughing, the blade swinging up in the sun and falling in the sun with a singing whistle! Down!

Bombs shattered London, Moscow, Tokyo.

The blade swung insanely.

And the kilns of Belsen and Buchenwald took fire.

The blade sang, crimson wet.

And mushrooms vomited out blind suns at White Sands, Hiroshima, Bikini, and up, through, and in continental Siberian skies.

The grain wept in a green rain, falling.

Korea, Indo-China, Egypt, India trembled; Asia stirred, Africa woke in the night. . . .

And the blade went on rising, crashing, severing, with the fury and the rage of a man who has lost and lost so much that he no longer cares what he does to the world.

Just a few short miles off the main highway, down a rough dirt road that leads to nowhere, just a few short miles from a highway jammed with traffic bound for California.

Once in a while during the long years a jalopy gets off the main highway, pulls up steaming in front of the charred ruin of a little white house at the end of the dirt road, to ask instructions from the farmer they see just beyond, the one who works insanely, wildly, without ever stopping, night and day, in the endless fields of wheat.

But they get no help and no answer. The farmer in the field is too busy, even after all these years; too busy slashing and chopping the green wheat instead of the ripe.

And Drew Erickson moves on with his scythe, with the light of blind suns and a look of white fire in his never-sleeping eyes, on and on and on. . . .

Uncle Einar

"IT WILL TAKE only a minute," said Uncle Einar's sweet wife.

"I refuse," he said. "And that takes but a *second*."

"I've worked all morning," she said, holding to her slender back, "and you won't help? It's drumming for a rain."

"Let it rain," he cried, morosely. "I'll not be pierced by lightning just to air your clothes."

"But you're so quick at it."

"Again, I refuse." His vast tarpaulin wings hummed nervously behind his indignant back.

She gave him a slender rope on which were tied four dozen fresh-washed clothes. He turned it in his fingers with distaste. "So it's come to this," he muttered, bitterly. "To this, to this, to this." He almost wept angry and acid tears.

"Don't cry; you'll wet them down again," she said. "Jump up, now, run them about."

"Run them about." His voice was hollow, deep, and terribly wounded. "I say: let it thunder, let it pour!"

"If it was a nice, sunny day I wouldn't ask," she said, reasonably. "All my washing gone for nothing if you don't. They'll hang about the house——"

That *did* it. Above all, he hated clothes flagged and festooned so a man had to creep under on the way across a room. He jumped up. His vast green wings boomed. "Only so far as the pasture fence!"

Whirl: up he jumped, his wings chewed and loved the cool air. Before you'd say Uncle Einar Has Green Wings he sailed low across his farmland, trailing the clothes in a vast fluttering loop through the pounding concussion and back-wash of his wings!

"Catch!"

Back from the trip, he sailed the clothes, dry as popcorn, down on a series of clean blankets she'd spread for their landing.

"Thank you!" she cried.

"Gahh!" he shouted, and flew off under the apple tree to brood.

Uncle Einar's beautiful silk-like wings hung like sea-green sails behind him, and whirred and whispered from his shoulders when he sneezed or turned swiftly. He was one of the few in the Family whose talent was visible. All his dark cousins and nephews and brothers hid in small towns across the world, did unseen mental things or things with witch-fingers and white teeth, or blew down the sky like fire-leaves, or loped in forests like moon-silvered wolves. They lived comparatively safe from normal humans. Not so a man with great green wings.

Not that he hated his wings. Far from it! In his youth he'd always flown nights, because nights were rare times for winged men! Daylight held dangers, always had, always would; but nights, ah, nights, he had sailed over islands of cloud and seas of summer sky. With no danger to himself. It had been a rich, full soaring, an exhilaration.

But now he could not fly at night.

On his way home to some high mountain pass in Europe after a Homecoming among Family members in Mellin Town, Illinois (some years ago) he had drunk too much rich crimson wine. "I'll be all right," he had told himself, vaguely, as he beat his long way under the morning stars, over the moon-dreaming country hills beyond Mellin Town. And then—crack out of the sky——

A high-tension tower.

Like a netted duck! A great sizzle! His face blown black by a blue sparkler of wire, he fended off the electricity with a terrific back-jumping percussion of his wings, and fell.

His hitting the moonlit meadow under the tower made a noise like a large telephone book dropped from the sky.

Early the next morning, his dew-sodden wings shaking violently, he stood up. It was still dark. There was a faint bandage of dawn stretched across the east. Soon the bandage would stain and all flight would be restricted. There was nothing to do but take refuge in the forest and wait out the day in the deepest thicket until another night gave his wings a hidden motion in the sky.

In this fashion he met his wife.

During the day, which was warm for November first in Illinois country, pretty young Brunilla Wexley was out to udder a lost cow, for she carried a silver pail in one hand as she sidled through thickets and pleaded cleverly to the unseen cow to please return home or burst her gut with unplucked milk. The fact that the cow would have most certainly come home when her teats really needed pulling did not concern Brunilla Wexley. It was a sweet excuse for forest-journeying, thistle-blowing, and flower chewing; all of which Brunilla was doing as she stumbled upon Uncle Einar.

Asleep near a bush, he seemed a man under a green shelter.

"Oh," said Brunilla, with a fever. "A man. In a camp-tent."

Uncle Einar awoke. The camp-tent spread like a large green fan behind him.

"Oh," said Brunilla, the cow-searcher. "A man with wings."

That was how she took it. She was startled, yes, but she had never been hurt in her life, so she wasn't afraid of anyone, and it was a fancy thing to see a winged man and she was proud to meet him. She began to talk. In an hour they were old friends, and in two hours she'd quite forgotten his wings were there. And he somehow confessed how he happened to be in this wood.

"Yes, I noticed you looked banged around," she said. "That right wing looks very bad. You'd best let me take you home and fix it. You won't be able to fly all the way to Europe on it, anyway. And who wants to live in Europe these days?"

He thanked her, but he didn't quite see how he could accept.

"But I live alone," she said. "For, as you see, I'm quite ugly."

He insisted she was not.

"How kind of you," she said. "But I am, there's no fooling myself. My folks are dead, I've a farm, a big one, all to myself, quite far from Mellin Town, and I'm in need of talking company."

But wasn't she afraid of him? he asked.

"Proud and jealous would be more near it," she said. "*May* I?" And she stroked his large green membraned veils with careful envy. He shuddered at the touch and put his tongue between his teeth.

So there was nothing for it but that he come to her house for medicaments and ointments, and my! what a burn across his face, beneath his eyes! "Lucky you weren't blinded," she said. "How'd it happen?"

"Well . . ." he said, and they were at her farm, hardly noticing they'd walked a mile, looking at each other.

A day passed, and another, and he thanked her at her door and said he must be going, he much appreciated the ointment, the care, the lodging. It was twilight and between now, six o'clock, and five the next morning, he must cross an ocean and a continent. "Thank you; good-by," he said, and started to fly off in the dusk and crashed right into a maple tree.

"Oh!" she screamed, and ran to his unconscious body.

When he waked the next hour he knew he'd fly no more in the dark again ever; his delicate night-perception was gone. The winged telepathy that had warned him where towers, trees, houses and hills stood across his path, the fine clear vision and sensibility that guided him through mazes of forest, cliff, and cloud, all were burnt forever by that strike across his face, that blue electric fry and sizzle.

"How?" he moaned softly. "How can I go to Europe? If I flew by day, I'd be seen and—miserable joke—maybe shot down! Or kept for a zoo perhaps, what a life *that'd* be! Brunilla, tell me, what shall I do?"

"Oh," she whispered, looking at her hands. "We'll think of something. . . ."

They were married.

The Family came for the wedding. In a great autumnal avalanche of maple, sycamore, oak, elm leaf they hissed and rustled, fell in a shower of horse-chestnut, thumped like winter apples on the earth, with an over-all scent of farewell-summer on the wind they made in their rushing. The ceremony? The ceremony was brief as a black candle lit, blown out, and smoke left still on the air. Its briefness, darkness, upside-down and backward quality escaped Brunilla, who only listened to the great tide of Uncle Einar's wings faintly murmuring above them as they finished out the rite. And as for Uncle Einar, the wound across his nose was almost healed and, holding Brunilla's arm, he felt Europe grow faint and melt away in the distance.

He didn't have to see very well to fly straight up, or come straight down. It was only natural that on this night of their wedding he take Brunilla in his arms and fly right up into the sky.

A farmer, five miles over, glanced at a low cloud at midnight, saw faint glows and crackles.

"Heat lightning," he observed, and went to bed.

They didn't come down till morning, with the dew.

The marriage took. She had only to look at him, and it lifted her to think she was the only woman in the world married to a winged man. "Who else could say it?" she asked her mirror. And the answer was: "No one!"

He, on the other hand, found great beauty behind her face, great kindness and understanding. He made some changes in his diet to fit her thinking, and was careful with his wings about the house; knocked porcelains and broken lamps were nerve-scrapers, he stayed away from them. He changed his sleeping habits, since he couldn't fly nights now anyhow. And she in turn fixed chairs so they were comfortable for his wings, put extra padding here or took it out there, and the things she said were the things he loved her for. "We're in our cocoons, all of us. See how ugly I am?" she said. "But one day I'll break out, spread wings as fine and handsome as you."

"You broke out long ago," he said.

She thought it over. "Yes," she had to admit. "I know just which day it was, too. In the woods when I looked for a cow and found a tent!" They laughed, and with him holding her she felt so beautiful she knew their marriage had slipped her from her ugliness, like a bright sword from its case.

They had children. At first there was fear, all on his part, that they'd be winged.

"Nonsense, I'd love it!" she said, "Keep them out from under foot."

"Then," he exclaimed, "they'd be in your *hair*!"

"Ow!" she cried.

Four children were born, three boys and a girl, who, for their energy, seemed to have wings. They popped up like toadstools in a few years, and on hot summer days asked their father to sit under the apple tree and fan them with his cooling wings and tell them wild starlit tales of island clouds and ocean skies and textures of mist and wind and how a star tastes melting in your mouth, and how to drink cold mountain air, and how it feels to be a pebble dropped from Mt. Everest, turning to a green bloom, flowering your wings just before you strike bottom!

This was his marriage.

And today, six years later, here sat Uncle Einar, here he was, festering under the apple tree, grown impatient and unkind; not because this was his desire, but because after the long wait, he was still unable to fly the wild night sky; his extra sense had never returned. Here he sat despondently, nothing more than a summer sun-parasol, green and discarded, abandoned for the season by the reckless vacationers who once sought the refuge of its translucent shadow. Was he to sit here forever, afraid to fly by day because someone might see him? Was his only flight to be as a drier of clothes for his wife, or a fanner of children on hot August noons? His one occupation had *always* been flying Family errands, quicker than storms. A boomerang, he'd whickled over hills and valleys and like a thistle, landed. He had always had money; the Family had good use for their winged man! But now? Bitterness! His wings jittered and whisked the air and made a captive thunder.

"Papa," said little Meg.

The children stood looking at his thought-dark face.

"Papa," said Ronald. "Make more thunder!"

"It's a cold March day, there'll soon be rain and plenty of thunder," said Uncle Einar.

"Will you come watch us?" asked Michael.

"Run on, run on! Let papa brood!"

He was shut of love, the children of love, and the love of children. He thought only of heavens, skies, horizons, infinities, by night or day, lit by star, moon, or sun, cloudy or clear, but always it was skies and heavens and horizons that ran ahead of you forever when you soared. Yet here he was, sculling the pasture, kept low for fear of being seen.

Misery in a deep well!

"Papa, come watch us; it's March!" cried Meg. "And we're going to the Hill with all the kids from town!"

Uncle Einar grunted. "What hill is that?"

"The Kite Hill, of course!" they all sang together.

Now he looked at them.

Each held a large paper kite, their faces sweating with anticipation and an animal glowing. In their small fingers were balls of white twine. From the kites, colored red and blue and yellow and green, hung caudal appendages of cotton and silk strips.

"We'll fly our kites!" said Ronald. "Won't you come?"

"No," he said, sadly. "I mustn't be seen by anyone or there'd be trouble."

"You could hide and watch from the woods," said Meg. "We made the kites ourselves. Just because we know how."

"How do you know how?"

"You're our father!" was the instant cry. "That's why!"

He looked at his children for a long while. He sighed. "A kite festival, is it?"

"Yes, sir!"

"I'm going to win," said Meg.

"No, *I'm*!" Michael contradicted.

"Me, *me*!" piped Stephen.

"God up the chimney!" roared Uncle Einar, leaping high with a deafening kettledrum of wings. "Children! Children, I love you dearly!"

"Father, what's wrong?" said Michael, backing off.

"Nothing, nothing, nothing!" chanted Einar. He flexed his wings to their greatest propulsion and plundering. Whoom! they slammed like cymbals. The children fell flat in the backwash! "I have it, I *have* it! I'm free again! Fire in the flue! Feather on the wind! Brunilla!" Einar called to the house. His wife appeared. "I'm free!" he called, flushed and tall, on his toes. "Listen, Brunilla, I don't need the night any more! I can fly by day! I don't need the night! I'll fly *every* day and *any* day of the year from now on!—but, God, I waste time, talking. Look!"

And as the worried members of his family watched, he seized the cotton tail from one of the little kites, tied it to his belt behind, grabbed the twine ball, held one end in his teeth, gave the other end to his children, and up, up into the air he flew, away into the March wind!

And across the meadows and over the farms his children ran, letting out string to the daylit sky, bubbling and stumbling, and Brunilla stood back in the farmyard and waved and laughed to see what was happening; and her children marched to the far Kite Hill and stood, the four of them, holding the ball of twine in their eager, proud fingers, each tugging and directing and pulling. And the children from Mellin Town came running with *their* small kites to let up on the wind, and they saw the great green kite leap and hover in the sky and exclaimed:

"Oh, oh, what a kite! What a kite! Oh, I wish I'd a kite like that! Where, where did you *get* it!"

"Our father made it!" cried Meg and Michael and Stephen and Ronald, and gave an exultant pull on the twine and the humming, thundering kite in the sky dipped and soared and made a great and magical exclamation mark across a cloud!

The Wind

THE PHONE RANG at five-thirty that evening. It was December, and long since dark as Thompson picked up the phone.

"Hello."

"Hello, *Herb*?"

"Oh, it's you, Allin."

"Is your wife home, Herb?"

"Sure. Why?"

"Damn it."

Herb Thompson held the receiver quietly. "What's up? You sound funny."

"I wanted you to come over tonight."

"We're having company."

"I wanted you to spend the night. When's your wife going away?"

"That's next week," said Thompson. "She'll be in Ohio for about nine days. Her mother's sick. I'll come over then."

"I wish you could come over tonight."

"Wish I could. Company and all, my wife'd kill me."

"I wish you could come over."

"What's it? the wind again?"

"Oh, no. No."

"Is it the wind?" asked Thompson.

The voice on the phone hesitated. "Yeah. Yeah, it's the wind."

"It's a clear night, there's not much wind."

"There's enough. It comes in the window and blows the curtains a little bit. Just enough to tell me."

"Look, why don't you come and spend the night here?" said Herb Thompson looking around the lighted hall.

"Oh, no. It's too late for that. It might catch me on the way over. It's a damned long distance. I wouldn't dare, but thanks, anyway. It's thirty miles, but thanks."

"Take a sleeping-tablet."

"I've been standing in the door for the past hour, Herb.

I can see it building up in the west. There are some clouds there and I saw one of them kind of rip apart. There's a wind coming, all right."

"Well, you just take a nice sleeping-tablet. And call me any time you want to call. Later this evening if you want."

"Any time?" said the voice on the phone.

"Sure."

"I'll do that, but I wish you could come out. Yet I wouldn't want you hurt. You're my best friend and I wouldn't want that. Maybe it's best I face this thing alone. I'm sorry I bother you."

"Hell, what's a friend for? Tell you what you do, sit down and get some writing done this evening," said Herb Thompson, shifting from one foot to the other in the hall. "You'll forget about the Himalayas and the Valley of the Winds and this preoccupation of yours with storms and hurricanes. Get another chapter done on your next travel book."

"I might do that. Maybe I will, I don't know. Maybe I will. I might do that. Thanks a lot for letting me bother you."

"Thanks, hell. Get off the line, now, you. My wife's calling me to dinner."

Herb Thompson hung up.

He went and sat down at the supper table and his wife sat across from him. "Was that Allin?" she asked. He nodded. "Him and his winds that blow up and winds that blow down and winds that blow hot and blow cold," she said, handing him his plate heaped with food.

"He did have a time in the Himalayas, during the war," said Herb Thompson.

"You don't believe what he said about that valley, do you?"

"It makes a good story."

"Climbing around, climbing up things. Why do men climb mountains and scare themselves?"

"It was snowing," said Herb Thompson.

"Was it?"

"And raining and hailing and blowing all at once, in that valley. Allin's told me a dozen times. He tells it well. He was up pretty high. Clouds, and all. The valley made a noise."

"I *bet* it did," she said.

"Like a lot of winds instead of just one. Winds from all over the world." He took a bite. "So says Allin."

"He shouldn't have gone there and looked, in the first place," she said. "You go poking around and first thing you know you get ideas. Winds start getting angry at you for intruding, and they follow you."

"Don't joke, he's my best friend," snapped Herb Thompson.

"It's all so silly!"

"Nevertheless he's been through a lot. That storm in Bombay, later, and the typhoon off New Guinea two months after that. And that time, in Cornwall."

"I have no sympathy for a man who continually runs into wind storms and hurricanes, and then gets a persecution complex because of it."

The phone rang just then.

"Don't answer it," she said.

"Maybe it's important."

"It's only Allin, again."

They sat there and the phone rang nine times and they didn't answer. Finally, it quieted. They finished dinner. Out in the kitchen, the window curtains gently moved in the small breeze from a slightly opened window.

The phone rang again.

"I can't let it ring," he said, and answered it. "Oh, hello, Allin."

"Herb! It's here! It got here!"

"You're too near the phone, back up a little."

"I stood in the open door and waited for it. I saw it coming down the highway, shaking all the trees, one by one, until it shook the trees just outside the house and it dived down toward the door and I slammed the door in its face!"

Thompson didn't say anything. He couldn't think of anything to say, his wife was watching him in the hall door.

"How interesting," he said, at last.

"It's all around the house, Herb. I can't get out now, I can't do anything. But I fooled it, I let it think it had me, and just as it came down to get me I slammed and locked the door! I was ready for it, I've been getting ready for weeks."

"Have you, now; tell me about it, Allin, old man." Herb Thompson played it jovially into the phone, while his wife looked on and his neck began to sweat.

"It began six weeks ago. . . ."

"Oh, yes? Well, well."

". . . I thought I had it licked. I thought it had given up following and trying to get me. But it was just waiting. Six weeks ago I heard the wind laughing and whispering around the corners of my house, out here. Just for an hour or so, not very long, not very loud. Then it went away."

Thompson nodded into the phone. "Glad to hear it, glad to hear it." His wife stared at him.

"It came back, the next night. It slammed the shutters and kicked sparks out of the chimney. It came back five nights in a row, a little stronger each time. When I opened the front door, it came in at me and tried to pull me out, but it wasn't strong enough. Tonight it *is*."

"Glad to hear you're feeling better," said Thompson.

"I'm not better, what's wrong with you? Is your wife listening to us?"

"Yes."

"Oh, I see. I know I sound like a fool."

"Not at all. Go on."

Thompson's wife went back into the kitchen. He relaxed. He sat down on a little chair near the phone. "Go on, Allin, get it out of you, you'll sleep better."

"It's all around the house now, like a great big vacuum machine nuzzling at all the gables. It's knocking the trees around."

"That's funny, there's no wind *here*, Allin."

"Of course not, it doesn't care about you, only about me."

"I guess that's one way to explain it."

"It's a killer, Herb, the biggest damnedest prehistoric killer that ever hunted prey. A big sniffling hound, trying to smell me out, find me. It pushes its big cold nose up to the house, taking air, and when it finds me in the parlor it drives its pressure there, and when I'm in the kitchen it goes there. It's trying to get in the windows, now, but I had them reinforced and I put new hinges on the doors, and bolts. It's a strong house. They built them strong in the old days. I've got all the lights in the house on, now. The house is all lighted up, bright. The wind followed me from room to room, looking through all the windows, when I switched them on. Oh!"

"What's wrong?"

"It just snatched off the front screen door!"

"I wish you'd come over here and spend the night, Allin."

"I can't! God, I can't leave the house. I can't do anything. I know this wind. Lord, it's big and it's clever. I tried to light a cigarette a moment ago, and a little draft sucked the match out. The wind likes to play games, it likes to taunt me, it's taking its time with me; it's got all night. And now! God, right now, one of my old travel books, on the library table, I wish you could see it. A little breeze from God knows what small hole in the house, the little breeze is—blowing the pages one by one. I wish you could see it. There's my introduction. Do you remember the introduction to my book on Tibet, Herb?"

"Yes."

"*This book is dedicated to those who lost the game of elements, written by one who has seen, but who has always escaped.*"

"Yes, I remember."

"The lights have gone out!"

The phone crackled.

"The power lines just went down. Are you there, Herb?"

"I still hear you."

"The wind doesn't like all that light in my house, it tore the power lines down. The telephone will probably go next. Oh, it's a real party, me and the wind, I tell you! Just a second."

"Allin?" A silence. Herb leaned against the mouthpiece. His wife glanced in from the kitchen. Herb Thompson waited. "Allin?"

"I'm back," said the voice on the phone. "There was a draft from the door and I shoved some wadding under it to keep it from blowing on my feet. I'm glad you didn't come out after all, Herb, I wouldn't want you in this mess. There! It just broke one of the living-room windows and a regular gale is in the house, knocking pictures off the wall! Do you hear it?"

Herb Thompson listened. There was a wild sirening on the phone and a whistling and banging. Allin shouted over it. "Do you hear it?"

Herb Thompson swallowed drily. "I hear it."

"It wants me alive, Herb. It doesn't dare knock the house down in one fell blow. That'd kill me. It wants me alive, so it can pull me apart, finger by finger. It wants what's inside me.

My mind, my brain. It wants my life-power, my psychic force, my ego. It wants intellect."

"My wife's calling me, Allin. I have to go wipe the dishes."

"It's a big cloud of vapors, winds from all over the world. The same wind that ripped the Celebes a year ago, the same pampero that killed in Argentina, the typhoon that fed on Hawaii, the hurricane that knocked the coast of Africa early this year. It's part of all those storms I escaped. It followed me from the Himalayas because it didn't want me to know what I know about the Valley of the Winds where it gathers and plans its destruction. Something, a long time ago, gave it a start in the direction of life. I know its feeding grounds, I know where it is born and where parts of it expire. For that reason, it hates me; and my books that tell how to defeat it. It doesn't want me preaching any more. It wants to incorporate me into its huge body, to give it knowledge. It wants me on its own side!"

"I have to hang up, Allin, my wife—"

"What?" A pause, the blowing of the wind in the phone, distantly. "What did you say?"

"Call me back in about an hour, Allin."

He hung up.

He went out to wipe the dishes. His wife looked at him and he looked at the dishes, rubbing them with a towel.

"What's it like out tonight?" he said.

"Nice. Not very chilly. Stars," she said. "Why?"

"Nothing."

The phone rang three times in the next hour. At eight o'clock the company arrived, Stoddard and his wife. They sat around until eight-thirty talking and then got out and set up the cardtable and began to play Gin.

Herb Thompson shuffled the cards over and over, with a clittering, shuttering effect and clapped them out, one at a time before the three other players. Talk went back and forth. He lit a cigar and made it into a fine gray ash at the tip, and adjusted his cards in his hand and on occasion lifted his head and listened. There was no sound outside the house. His wife saw him do this, and he cut it out immediately, and discarded a Jack of Clubs.

He puffed slowly on his cigar and they all talked quietly

with occasional small eruptions of laughter, and the clock in the hall sweetly chimed nine o'clock.

"Here we all are," said Herb Thompson, taking his cigar out and looking at it reflectively. "And life is sure funny."

"Eh?" said Mr. Stoddard.

"Nothing, except here we are, living our lives, and some place else on earth a billion other people live their lives."

"That's a rather obvious statement."

"Life," he put his cigar back in his lips, "is a lonely thing. Even with married people. Sometimes when you're in a person's arms you feel a million miles away from them."

"I like *that*," said his wife.

"I didn't mean it that way," he explained, not with haste; because he felt no guilt, he took his time. "I mean we all believe what we believe and live our own little lives while other people live entirely different ones. I mean, we sit here in this room while a thousand people are dying. Some of cancer, some of pneumonia, some of tuberculosis. I imagine someone in the United States is dying right now in a wrecked car."

"This isn't very stimulating conversation," said his wife.

"I mean to say, we all live and don't think about how other people think or live their lives or die. We wait until death comes *to* us. What I mean is here we sit, on our self-assured butt-bones, while, thirty miles away, in a big old house, completely surrounded by night and God-knows-what, one of the finest guys who ever lived is—"

"Herb!"

He puffed and chewed on his cigar and stared blindly at his cards. "Sorry." He blinked rapidly and bit his cigar. "Is it my turn?"

"It's your turn."

The playing went around the table, with a flittering of cards, murmurs, conversation. Herb Thompson sank lower into his chair and began to look ill.

The phone rang. Thompson jumped and ran to it and jerked it off the hook.

"Herb! I've been calling and calling. What's it like at your house, Herb?"

"What do you mean, what's it like?"

"Has the company come?"

"Hell, yes, it has—"

"Are you talking and laughing and playing cards?"

"Christ, yes, but what has that got to do with—"

"Are you smoking your ten-cent cigar?"

"God damn it, yes, but . . ."

"Swell," said the voice on the phone. "That sure is swell. I wish I could be there. I wish I didn't know the things I know. I wish lots of things."

"Are you all right?"

"So far, so good. I'm locked in the kitchen now. Part of the front wall of the house blew in. But I planned my retreat. When the kitchen door gives, I'm heading for the cellar. If I'm lucky I may hold out there until morning. It'll have to tear the whole damned house down to get to me, and the cellar floor is pretty solid. I have a shovel and I may dig—deeper. . . ."

It sounded like a lot of other voices on the phone.

"What's *that*?" Herb Thompson demanded, cold, shivering.

"That?" asked the voice on the phone. "Those are the voices of twelve thousand killed in a typhoon, seven thousand killed by a hurricane, three thousand buried by a cyclone. Am I boring you? That's what the wind is. It's a lot of people dead. The wind killed them, took their minds to give itself intelligence. It took all their voices and made them into one voice. All those millions of people killed in the past ten thousand years, tortured and run from continent to continent on the backs and in the bellies of monsoons and whirlwinds. Oh Christ, what a poem you could write about it!"

The phone echoed and rang with voices and shouts and whinings.

"Come on back, Herb," called his wife from the card table.

"That's how the wind gets more intelligent each year, it adds to itself, body by body, life by life, death by death."

"We're waiting for you, Herb," called his wife.

"Damn it!" He turned, almost snarling. "Wait just a moment, won't you!" Back to the phone. "Allin, if you want me to come out there now, I will! I should have come earlier . . ."

"Wouldn't think of it. This is a grudge fight, wouldn't do to have you in it now. I'd better hang up. The kitchen door looks bad; I'll have to get in the cellar."

"Call me back, later?"

"Maybe, if I'm lucky. I don't think I'll make it. I slipped away and escaped so many times, but I think it has me now. I hope I haven't bothered you too much, Herb."

"You haven't bothered anyone, damn it. Call me back."

"I'll try. . . ."

Herb Thompson went back to the card game. His wife glared at him. "How's Allin, your friend?" she asked. "Is he sober?"

"He's never taken a drink in his life," said Thompson, sullenly, sitting down. "I should have gone out there hours ago."

"But he's called every night for six weeks and you've been out there at least ten nights to stay with him and nothing was wrong."

"He needs help. He might hurt himself."

"You were just out there, two nights ago, you can't always be running after him."

"First thing in the morning I'll move him into a sanatorium. Didn't want to. He seems so reasonable otherwise."

At ten-thirty coffee was served. Herb Thompson drank his slowly, looking at the phone. I wonder if he's in the cellar now, he thought.

Herb Thompson walked to the phone, called long-distance, gave the number.

"I'm sorry," said the operator. "The lines are down in that district. When the lines are repaired, we will put your call through."

"Then the telephone lines *are* down!" cried Thompson. He let the phone drop. Turning, he slammed open the closet door, pulled out his coat. "Oh Lord," he said. "Oh, Lord, Lord," he said, to his amazed guests and his wife with the coffee urn in her hand. "Herb!" she cried. "I've got to get out there!" he said, slipping into his coat.

There was a soft, faint stirring at the door.

Everybody in the room tensed and straightened up.

"Who could that be?" asked his wife.

The soft stirring was repeated, very quietly.

Thompson hurried down the hall where he stopped, alert.

Outside, faintly, he heard laughter.

"I'll be damned," said Thompson. He put his hand on the doorknob, pleasantly shocked and relieved. "I'd know that laugh anywhere. It's Allin. He came on over in his car, after all. Couldn't wait until morning to tell me his confounded stories." Thompson smiled weakly. "Probably brought some friends with him. Sounds like a lot of other . . ."

He opened the front door.

The porch was empty.

Thompson showed no surprise; his face grew amused and sly. He laughed. "Allin? None of your tricks now! Come on." He switched on the porch-light and peered out and around. "Where are you, Allin? Come on, now."

A breeze blew into his face.

Thompson waited a moment, suddenly chilled to his marrow. He stepped out on the porch and looked uneasily, and very carefully, about.

A sudden wind caught and whipped his coat flaps, disheveled his hair. He thought he heard laughter again. The wind rounded the house and was a pressure everywhere at once, and then, storming for a full minute, passed on.

The wind died down, sad, mourning in the high trees, passing away; going back out to the sea, to the Celebes, to the Ivory Coast, to Sumatra and Cape Horn, to Cornwall and the Philippines. Fading, fading, fading.

Thompson stood there, cold. He went in and closed the door and leaned against it, and didn't move, eyes closed.

"What's wrong . . . ?" asked his wife.

The Man Upstairs

HE REMEMBERED HOW carefully and expertly Grandmother would fondle the cold cut guts of the chicken and withdraw the marvels therein; the wet shining loops of meat-smelling intestine, the muscled lump of heart, the gizzard with the collection of seeds in it. How neatly and nicely Grandma would slit the chicken and push her fat little hand in to deprive it of its medals. These would be segregated, some in pans of water, others in paper to be thrown to the dog later, perhaps. And then the ritual of taxidermy, stuffing the bird with watered, seasoned bread, and performing surgery with a swift, bright needle, stitch after pulled-tight stitch.

This was one of the prime thrills of Douglas's eleven-year-old life span.

Altogether, he counted twenty knives in the various squeaking drawers of the magic kitchen table from which Grandma, a kindly, gentle-faced, white-haired old witch, drew paraphernalia for her miracles.

Douglas was to be quiet. He could stand across the table from Grandmama, his freckled nose tucked over the edge, watching, but any loose boy-talk might interfere with the spell. It was a wonder when Grandma brandished silver shakers over the bird, supposedly sprinkling showers of mummy-dust and pulverized Indian bones, muttering mystical verses under her toothless breath.

"Grammy," said Douglas at last, breaking the silence. "Am I like that inside?" He pointed at the chicken.

"Yes," said Grandma. "A little more orderly and presentable, but just about the same. . . ."

"And more *of* it!" added Douglas, proud of his guts.

"Yes," said Grandma. "More of it."

"Grandpa has lots more'n me. His sticks out in front so he can rest his elbows on it."

Grandma laughed and shook her head.

Douglas said, "And Lucie Williams, down the street, she . . ."

"Hush, child!" cried Grandma.

"But she's got . . ."

"Never you mind what she's got! That's different."

"But why is *she* different?"

"A darning-needle dragon-fly is coming by some day and sew up your mouth," said Grandma firmly.

Douglas waited, then asked, "How do you know I've got insides like that, Grandma?"

"Oh, go 'way, now!"

The front doorbell rang.

Through the front-door glass as he ran down the hall, Douglas saw a straw hat. The bell jangled again and again. Douglas opened the door.

"Good morning, child, is the landlady at home?"

Cold gray eyes in a long, smooth, walnut-colored face gazed upon Douglas. The man was tall, thin, and carried a suitcase, a brief case, an umbrella under one bent arm, gloves rich and thick and gray on his thin fingers, and wore a horribly new straw hat.

Douglas backed up. "She's busy."

"I wish to rent her upstairs room, as advertised."

"We've got ten boarders, and it's already rented; go away!"

"Douglas!" Grandma was behind him suddenly. "How do you do?" she said to the stranger. "Never mind this child."

Unsmiling, the man stepped stiffly in. Douglas watched them ascend out of sight up the stairs, heard Grandma detailing the conveniences of the upstairs room. Soon she hurried down to pile linens from the linen closet on Douglas and send him scooting up with them.

Douglas paused at the room's threshold. The room was changed oddly, simply because the stranger had been in it a moment. The straw hat lay brittle and terrible upon the bed, the umbrella leaned stiff against one wall like a dead bat with dark moist wings folded.

Douglas blinked at the umbrella.

The stranger stood in the center of the changed room, tall, tall.

"Here!" Douglas littered the bed with supplies. "We eat at noon sharp, and if you're late coming down the soup'll get cold. Grandma fixes it so it will, every time!"

The tall strange man counted out ten new copper pennies and tinkled them in Douglas's blouse pocket. "We shall be friends," he said, grimly.

It was funny, the man having nothing but pennies. Lots of them. No silver at all, no dimes, no quarters. Just new copper pennies.

Douglas thanked him glumly. "I'll drop these in my dime bank when I get them changed into a dime. I got six dollars and fifty cents in dimes all ready for my camp trip in August."

"I must wash now," said the tall strange man.

Once, at midnight, Douglas had wakened to hear a storm rumbling outside—the cold hard wind shaking the house, the rain driving against the window. And then a lightning bolt had landed outside the window with a silent, terrific concussion. He remembered that fear of looking about at his room, seeing it strange and awful in the instantaneous light.

So it was, now, in this room. He stood looking up at the stranger. This room was no longer the same, but changed indefinably because this man, quick as a lightning bolt, had shed his light about it. Douglas backed up slowly as the stranger advanced.

The door closed in his face.

The wooden fork went up with mashed potatoes, came down empty. Mr. Koberman, for that was his name, had brought the wooden fork and wooden knife and spoon with him when Grandma called lunch.

"Mrs. Spaulding," he had said, quietly, "my own cutlery; please use it. I will have lunch today, but from tomorrow on, only breakfast and supper."

Grandma bustled in and out, bearing steaming tureens of soup and beans and mashed potatoes to impress her new boarder, while Douglas sat rattling his silverware on his plate, because he had discovered it irritated Mr. Koberman.

"I know a trick," said Douglas. "Watch." He picked a fork-tine with his fingernail. He pointed at various sectors of the table, like a magician. Wherever he pointed, the sound of the vibrating fork-tine emerged, like a metal elfin voice. Simply done, of course. He pressed the fork handle on the table-top, secretly. The vibration came from the wood like a sounding board. It looked quite magical. "There, there, and *there*!" exclaimed Douglas, happily plucking the fork again. He pointed at Mr. Koberman's soup and the noise came from it.

Mr. Koberman's walnut-colored face became hard and firm and awful. He pushed the soup bowl away violently, his lips twisting. He fell back in his chair.

Grandma appeared. "Why, what's wrong, Mr. Koberman?"

"I cannot eat this soup."

"Why?"

"Because I am full and can eat no more. Thank you."

Mr. Koberman left the room, glaring.

"What did you do, just then?" asked Grandma at Douglas, sharply.

"Nothing. Grandma, why does he eat with *wooden* spoons?"

"Yours not to question! When do you go back to school, anyway?"

"Seven weeks."

"Oh, my land!" said Grandma.

Mr. Koberman worked nights. Each morning at eight he arrived mysteriously home, devoured a very small breakfast, and then slept soundlessly in his room all through the dreaming hot daytime, until the huge supper with all the other boarders at night.

Mr. Koberman's sleeping habits made it necessary for Douglas to be quiet. This was unbearable. So, whenever Grandma visited down the street, Douglas stomped up and down stairs beating a drum, bouncing golf balls, or just screaming for three minutes outside Mr. Koberman's door, or flushing the toilet seven times in succession.

Mr. Koberman never moved. His room was silent, dark. He did not complain. There was no sound. He slept on and on. It was very strange.

Douglas felt a pure white flame of hatred burn inside himself with a steady, unflickering beauty. Now that room was Koberman Land. Once it had been flowery bright when Miss Sadlowe lived there. Now it was stark, bare, cold, clean, everything in its place, alien and brittle.

Douglas climbed upstairs on the fourth morning.

Halfway to the second floor was a large sun-filled window,

framed by six-inch panes of orange, purple, blue, red and burgundy glass. In the enchanted early mornings when the sun fell through to strike the landing and slide down the stair banister, Douglas stood entranced at this window peering at the world through the multicolored windows.

Now a blue world, a blue sky, blue people, blue streetcars and blue trotting dogs.

He shifted panes. Now—an amber world! Two lemonish women glided by, resembling the daughters of Fu Manchu! Douglas giggled. This pane made even the sunlight more purely golden.

It was eight A.M. Mr. Koberman strolled by below, on the sidewalk, returning from his night's work, his cane looped over his elbow, straw hat glued to his head with patent oil.

Douglas shifted panes again. Mr. Koberman was a red man walking through a red world with red trees and red flowers and—something else.

Something about—Mr. Koberman.

Douglas squinted.

The red glass *did* things to Mr. Koberman. His face, his suit, his hands. The clothes seemed to melt away. Douglas almost believed, for one terrible instant, that he could see *inside* Mr. Koberman. And what he saw made him lean wildly against the small red pane, blinking.

Mr. Koberman glanced up just then, saw Douglas, and raised his cane-umbrella angrily, as if to strike. He ran swiftly across the red lawn to the front door.

"Young man!" he cried, running up the stairs. "What were you doing?"

"Just looking," said Douglas, numbly.

"That's all, is it?" cried Mr. Koberman.

"Yes, sir. I look through all the glasses. All kinds of worlds. Blue ones, red ones, yellow ones. All different."

"All kinds of worlds, is it!" Mr. Koberman glanced at the little panes of glass, his face pale. He got hold of himself. He wiped his face with a handkerchief and pretended to laugh. "Yes. All kinds of worlds. All different." He walked to the door of his room. "Go right ahead; play," he said.

The door closed. The hall was empty. Mr. Koberman had gone in.

Douglas shrugged and found a new pane.

"Oh, everything's violet!"

Half an hour later, while playing in his sandbox behind the house, Douglas heard the crash and the shattering tinkle. He leaped up.

A moment later, Grandma appeared on the back porch, the old razor strop trembling in her hand.

"Douglas! I told you time and again never fling your basketball against the house! Oh, I could just cry!"

"I been sitting right here," he protested.

"Come see what you've done, you nasty boy!"

The great colored window panes lay shattered in a rainbow chaos on the upstairs landing. His basketball lay in the ruins.

Before he could even begin telling his innocence, Douglas was struck a dozen stinging blows upon his rump. Wherever he landed, screaming, the razor strop struck again.

Later, hiding his mind in the sandpile like an ostrich, Douglas nursed his dreadful pains. He knew who'd thrown that basketball. A man with a straw hat and a stiff umbrella and a cold, gray room. Yeah, yeah, yeah. He dribbled tears. Just wait. Just *wait.*

He heard Grandma sweeping up the broken glass. She brought it out and threw it in the trash bin. Blue, pink, yellow meteors of glass dropped brightly down.

When she was gone, Douglas dragged himself, whimpering, over to save out three pieces of the incredible glass. Mr. Koberman disliked the colored windows. These—he clinked them in his fingers—would be worth saving.

Grandfather arrived from his newspaper office each night, shortly ahead of the other boarders, at five o'clock. When a slow, heavy tread filled the hall, and a thick, mahogany cane thumped in the cane-rack, Douglas ran to embrace the large stomach and sit on Grandpa's knee while he read the evening paper.

"Hi, Grampa!"

"Hello, down there!"

"Grandma cut chickens again today. It's fun watching," said Douglas.

Grandpa kept reading. "That's twice this week, chickens. She's the chickenist woman. You like to watch her cut 'em, eh? Cold-blooded little pepper! Ha!"

"I'm just curious."

"You are," rumbled Grandpa, scowling. "Remember that day when that young lady was killed at the rail station. You just walked over and looked at her, blood and all." He laughed. "Queer duck. Stay that way. Fear nothing, ever in your life. I guess you get it from your father, him being a military man and all, and you so close to him before you came here to live last year." Grandpa returned to his paper.

A long pause. "Gramps?"

"Yes?"

"What if a man didn't have a heart or lungs or stomach but still walked around, alive?"

"That," rumbled Gramps, "would be a miracle."

"I don't mean a—a miracle. I mean, what if he was all *different* inside. Not like me."

"Well, he wouldn't be quite human then, would he, boy?"

"Guess not, Gramps. Gramps, you got a heart and lungs?"

Gramps chuckled. "Well, tell the truth, I don't *know*. Never seen them. Never had an X-ray, never been to a doctor. Might as well be potato-solid for all I know."

"Have *I* got a stomach?"

"You certainly have!" cried Grandma from the parlor entry. "'Cause I feed it! And you've lungs, you scream loud enough to wake the crumblees. And you've dirty hands, go wash them! Dinner's ready. Grandpa, come on. Douglas, git!"

In the rush of boarders streaming downstairs, Grandpa, if he intended questioning Douglas further about the weird conversation, lost his opportunity. If dinner delayed an instant more, Grandma and the potatoes would develop simultaneous lumps.

The boarders, laughing and talking at the table—Mr. Koberman silent and sullen among them—were silenced when Grandfather cleared his throat. He talked politics a few minutes and then shifted over into the intriguing topic of the recent peculiar deaths in the town.

"It's enough to make an old newspaper editor prick up his ears," he said, eying them all. "That young Miss Larsson, lived across the ravine, now. Found her dead three days ago for no reason, just funny kinds of tattoos all over her, and a facial expression that would make Dante cringe. And that other young lady, what was her name? Whitely? She disappeared and *never did* come back."

"Them things happen alla time," said Mr. Britz, the garage mechanic, chewing. "Ever peek inna Missing Peoples Bureau file? It's *that* long." He illustrated. "Can't tell *what* happens to most of 'em."

"Anyone want more dressing?" Grandma ladled liberal portions from the chicken's interior. Douglas watched, thinking about how that chicken had had two kinds of guts—God-made and Man-made.

Well, how about *three* kinds of guts?

Eh?

Why not?

Conversation continued about the mysterious death of so-and-so, and, oh, yes, remember a week ago, Marion Barsumian died of heart failure, but maybe that didn't connect up? or did it? you're crazy! forget it, why talk about it at the dinner table? So.

"Never can tell," said Mr. Britz. "Maybe we got a vampire in town."

Mr. Koberman stopped eating.

"In the year 1927?" said Grandma. "A vampire? Oh, go on, now."

"Sure," said Mr. Britz. "Kill 'em with silver bullets. Anything silver for that matter. Vampires *hate* silver. I read it in a book somewhere, once. Sure, I did."

Douglas looked at Mr. Koberman who ate with wooden knives and forks and carried only new copper pennies in his pocket.

"It's poor judgment," said Grandpa, "to call anything by a name. We don't know what a hobgoblin or a vampire or a troll is. Could be lots of things. You can't heave them into categories with labels and say they'll act one way or another. That'd be silly. They're people. People who do things. Yes, that's the way to put it: people who *do* things."

"Excuse me," said Mr. Koberman, who got up and went out for his evening walk to work.

The stars, the moon, the wind, the clock ticking, and the chiming of the hours into dawn, the sun rising, and here it was another morning, another day, and Mr. Koberman coming along the sidewalk from his night's work. Douglas stood off like a small mechanism whirring and watching with carefully microscopic eyes.

At noon, Grandma went to the store to buy groceries.

As was his custom every day when Grandma was gone, Douglas yelled outside Mr. Koberman's door for a full three minutes. As usual, there was no response. The silence was horrible.

He ran downstairs, got the pass-key, a silver fork, and the three pieces of colored glass he had saved from the shattered window. He fitted the key to the lock and swung the door slowly open.

The room was in half light, the shades drawn. Mr. Koberman lay atop his bedcovers, in slumber clothes, breathing gently, up and down. He didn't move. His face was motionless.

"Hello, Mr. Koberman!"

The colorless walls echoed the man's regular breathing.

"Mr. Koberman, hello!"

Bouncing a golf ball, Douglas advanced. He yelled. Still no answer. "Mr. Koberman!"

Bending over Mr. Koberman, Douglas picked the tines of the silver fork in the sleeping man's face.

Mr. Koberman winced. He twisted. He groaned bitterly.

Response. Good. Swell.

Douglas drew a piece of blue glass from his pocket. Looking through the blue glass fragment he found himself in a blue room, in a blue world different from the world he knew. As different as was the red world. Blue furniture, blue bed, blue ceiling and walls, blue wooden eating utensils atop the blue bureau, and the sullen dark blue of Mr. Koberman's face and arms and his blue chest rising, falling. Also . . .

Mr. Koberman's eyes were wide, staring at him with a hungry darkness.

Douglas fell back, pulled the blue glass from his eyes.

Mr. Koberman's eyes were shut.

Blue glass again—open. Blue glass away—shut. Blue glass again—open. Away—shut. Funny. Douglas experimented, trembling. Through the glass the eyes seemed to peer hungrily, avidly through Mr. Koberman's closed lids. Without the blue glass they seemed tightly shut.

But it was the rest of Mr. Koberman's body. . . .

Mr. Koberman's bedclothes dissolved off him. The blue glass had something to do with it. Or perhaps it was the clothes themselves, just being *on* Mr. Koberman. Douglas cried out.

He was looking through the wall of Mr. Koberman's stomach, right *inside* him!

Mr. Koberman was solid.

Or, nearly so, anyway.

There were strange shapes and sizes within him.

Douglas must have stood amazed for five minutes, thinking about the blue worlds, the red worlds, the yellow worlds side by side, living together like glass panes around the big white stair window. Side by side, the colored panes, the different worlds; Mr. Koberman had said so himself.

So this was why the colored window had been broken.

"Mr. Koberman, wake up!"

No answer.

"Mr. Koberman, where do you work at night? Mr. Koberman, where do you work?"

A little breeze stirred the blue window shade.

"In a red world or a green world or a yellow one, Mr. Koberman?"

Over everything was a blue glass silence.

"Wait there," said Douglas.

He walked down to the kitchen, pulled open the great squeaking drawer and picked out the sharpest, biggest knife.

Very calmly he walked into the hall, climbed back up the stairs again, opened the door to Mr. Koberman's room, went in, and closed it, holding the sharp knife in one hand.

Grandma was busy fingering a piecrust into a pan when Douglas entered the kitchen to place something on the table.

"Grandma, what's this?"

She glanced up briefly, over her glasses. "I don't know."

It was square, like a box, and elastic. It was bright orange in color. It had four square tubes, colored blue, attached to it. It smelled funny.

"Ever see anything like it, Grandma?"

"No."

"That's what *I* thought."

Douglas left it there, went from the kitchen. Five minutes later he returned with something else. "How about *this*?"

He laid down a bright pink linked chain with a purple triangle at one end.

"Don't bother me," said Grandma. "It's only a chain."

Next time he returned with two hands full. A ring, a square, a triangle, a pyramid, a rectangle, and—other shapes. All of them were pliable, resilient, and looked as if they were made of gelatin. "This isn't all," said Douglas, putting them down. "There's more where this came from."

Grandma said, "Yes, yes," in a far-off tone, very busy.

"You were wrong, Grandma."

"About what?"

"About all people being the same inside."

"Stop talking nonsense."

"Where's my piggy-bank?"

"On the mantel, where you left it."

"Thanks."

He tromped into the parlor, reached up for his piggy-bank.

Grandpa came home from the office at five.

"Grandpa, come upstairs."

"Sure, son. Why?"

"Something to show you. It's not nice; but it's interesting."

Grandpa chuckled, following his grandson's feet up to Mr. Koberman's room.

"Grandma mustn't know about this; she wouldn't like it," said Douglas. He pushed the door wide open. "There."

Grandfather gasped.

Douglas remembered the next few hours all the rest of his life. Standing over Mr. Koberman's naked body, the coroner and his assistants. Grandma, downstairs, asking somebody, "What's going on up there?" and Grandpa saying, shakily,

"I'll take Douglas away on a long vacation so he can forget this whole ghastly affair. Ghastly, ghastly affair!"

Douglas said, "Why should it be bad? I don't see anything bad. I don't feel bad."

The coroner shivered and said, "Koberman's dead, all right."

His assistant sweated. "Did you see those *things* in the pans of water and in the wrapping paper?"

"Oh, my God, my God, yes, I saw them."

"Christ."

The coroner bent over Mr. Koberman's body again. "This better be kept secret, boys. It wasn't murder. It was a mercy the boy acted. God knows what might have happened if he hadn't."

"What was Koberman? A vampire? A monster?"

"Maybe. I don't know. Something—not human." The coroner moved his hands deftly over the suture.

Douglas was proud of his work. He'd gone to much trouble. He had watched Grandmother carefully and remembered. Needle and thread and all. All in all, Mr. Koberman was as neat a job as any chicken ever popped into hell by Grandma.

"I heard the boy say that Koberman lived even after all those *things* were taken out of him." The coroner looked at the triangles and chains and pyramids floating in the pans of water. "Kept on *living*. God."

"Did the boy say that?"

"He did."

"Then, what *did* kill Koberman?"

The coroner drew a few strands of sewing thread from their bedding.

"This. . . ." he said.

Sunlight blinked coldly off a half-revealed treasure trove; six dollars and seventy cents' worth of silver dimes inside Mr. Koberman's chest.

"I think Douglas made a wise investment," said the coroner, sewing the flesh back up over the "dressing" quickly.

There Was an Old Woman

"NO, THERE'S NO lief arguin'. I got my mind fixed. Run along with your silly wicker basket. Land, where you ever get notions like that? You just skit out of here; don't bother me, I got my tattin' and knittin' to do, and no never minds about tall, dark gentlemen with fangled ideas."

The tall, dark young man stood quietly, not moving. Aunt Tildy hurried on with her talk.

"You *heard* what I said! If you got a mind to talk to me, well, you can talk, but meantime I hope you don't mind if I pour myself coffee. There. If you'd been more polite, I'd offer you some, but you jump in here high and mighty and you never rapped on the door or nothin'. You think you *own* the place."

Aunt Tildy fussed with her lap. "Now, you made me lose count! I'm makin' myself a comforter. These winters get on mighty chill, and it ain't fittin' for a lady with bones like rice-paper to be settin' in a drafty old house without warmin' herself."

The tall, dark man sat down.

"That's an antique chair, so be gentle," warned Aunt Tildy. "Start again, tell me things you got to tell, I'll listen respectful. But keep your voice in your shoes and stop starin' at me with funny lights in your eyes. Land, it gives me the collywobbles."

The bone-porcelain, flowered clock on the mantel finished chiming three. Out in the hall, grouped around the wicker basket, four men waited, quietly, as if they were frozen.

"Now, about that wicker basket," said Aunt Tildy. "It's past six feet long, and by the look, it ain't laundry. And those four men you walked in with, you don't need them to carry that basket—why, it's light as thistles. Eh?"

The dark young man was leaning forward on the antique chair. Something in his face suggested the basket wouldn't be so light after a while.

"Pshaw," Aunt Tildy mused. "Where've I seen a wicker like that before? Seems it was only a couple years ago. Seems to me—oh! Now I remember. It was when Mrs. Dwyer passed away next door."

Aunt Tildy set her coffee cup down, sternly. "So *that's* what you're up to? I thought you were workin' to sell me somethin'. You just set there until my little Emily trounces home from college this afternoon! I wrote her a note last week. Not admittin', of course, that I wasn't feelin' quite ripe and pert, but sort of hintin' I want to see her again, it's been a good many weeks. Her livin' in New York and all. Almost like my own daughter, Emily is.

"Now, she'll take care of you, young man. She'll shoo you out'n this parlor so quick it'll——"

The dark young man looked at Aunt Tildy as if she were tired.

"No, I'm *not*!" she snapped.

He weaved back and forth on the chair, half-shutting his eyes, resting himself. O, wouldn't she like to rest, too? he seemed to murmur. Rest, rest, nice rest. . . .

"Great sons of Goshen on the Gilberry Dike! I got a hunderd comforters, two hunderd sweaters and six hunderd potholders in these fingers, no matter they're skinny! You run off, come back when I'm done, maybe I'll talk to you." Aunt Tildy shifted subjects. "Let me tell you about Emily, my sweet, fair child."

Aunt Tildy nodded thoughtfully. Emily, with hair like yellow corn tassels, just as soft and fine.

"I well remember the day her mother died, twenty years ago, leavin' Emily to my house. That's why I'm mad at you and your wickers and such goings-on. Who ever heard of people dyin' for any good cause? Young man, I don't *like* it. Why, I remember——"

Aunt Tildy paused; a brief pain of memory touched her heart. Twenty-five years back, her father's voice trembled in the late afternoon:

"Tildy," he whispered, "what you goin' to *do* in life? The way you act, men don't walk much with you. You kiss and skedaddle. Why won't you settle down, marry, raise children?"

"Papa," Tildy shouted back at him, "I like laughin' and playin' and singin'. I'm not the marryin' kind. I can't find a man with my philosophy, Papa."

"What 'philosophy's' that?"

"That death is ridiculous! It run off with Mama when we needed her most. You call *that* intelligent?"

Papa's eyes got wet and gray and bleak. "You're always right, Tildy. But what can we do? Death comes to everybody."

"Fight!" she cried. "Strike it below the belt! Don't *believe* in it!"

"Can't be done," said Papa sadly. "We all stand alone in the world."

"There's got to be a change sometime, Papa. I'm startin' my own philosophy here and now! Why, it's silly people live a couple years and are shoved like wet seeds in a hole; but nothin' sprouts. What good do they do? Lay there a million years, helpin' no one. Most of them fine, nice, neat people, or at least tryin'."

But Papa wasn't listening. He bleached out, faded away, like a photo left lying in the sun. She tried to talk him out of it, but he passed on, anyway. She spun about and ran. She couldn't stay on once he was cold, for his coldness denied her philosophy. She didn't attend his burial. She didn't do anything but set up this antique shop on the front of an old house and live alone for years, that is, until Emily came. Tildy didn't want to take the girl in. Why? Because Emily believed in dying. But her mother was an old friend and Tildy had promised help.

"Emily," continued Aunt Tildy, to the man in black, "was the first to live in this house with me in all the years. I never got married. I feared the idea of livin' with a man twenty-thirty years and then have him up and die on me. It'd shake my convictions like a house of cards. I shied off from the world. I screamed at people if they so much as mentioned death."

The young man listened patiently, politely. Then he lifted his hand. He seemed to know everything, with the dark, cold shining of his eyes, before she opened her mouth. He knew about her and World War II, when she shut off her radio forever and stopped the newspapers and beat a man's head with an umbrella, driving him from her shop when he insisted on describing the invasion beaches and the long, slow tides of the dead drifting under the silent urgings of the moon.

Yes, the dark young man smiled from the antique rocker, he

knew how Aunt Tildy had stuck to her nice old phonograph records. Harry Lauder singing "Roamin' in the Gloamin'," Madame Schumann-Heink and lullabies. With no interruptions, no foreign calamities, murders, poisonings, auto accidents, suicides. Music stayed the same each day, every day. So the years ran, while Aunt Tildy tried to teach Emily her philosophy. But Emily's mind was fixed on mortality. She respected Aunt Tildy's way of thinking, however, and never mentioned—eternity.

All this the young man knew.

Aunt Tildy sniffed. "How do you know all those things? Well, if you think you can talk me into that silly wicker basket, you're way off the trestle. You lay hands on me, I'll spit right *in* your face!"

The young man smiled. Aunt Tildy sniffed again.

"Don't simper like a sick dog. I'm too old to be made love at. That's all twisted dry, like an old tube of paint, and left behind in the years."

There was a noise. The mantel clock chimed three. Aunt Tildy flashed her eyes to it. Strange. Hadn't it chimed three o'clock just five minutes ago? She liked the bone-white clock with gold angels dangling naked about its numeraled face and its tone like cathedral bells, soft and far away.

"Are you just goin' to *sit* there, young man?"

He was.

"Then, you won't mind if I take a little cat nap. Now, don't you stir off that chair. Don't come creepin' around me. Just goin' to close my eyes for a spell. That's right. That's right. . . ."

Nice and quiet and restful time of day. Silence. Just the clock ticking away, busy as termites in wood. Just the old room smelling of polished mahogany and oiled leather in the morris chair, and books sitting stiff on the shelves. So nice. Nice. . . .

"You aren't gettin' up from the chair, are you, mister? Better not. I got one eye open for you. Yes, indeed I have. Yes, I have. Oh. Ah, hmmmm."

So feathery. So drowsy. So deep. Under water, almost. Oh, so nice.

Who's that movin' around in the dark with my eyes closed?

Who's that kissin' my cheek? You, Emily? No. No. Guess

it was my thoughts. Only—dreamin'. Land, yes, that's it. Driftin' off, off, off. . . .

AH? WHAT SAY? OH!

"Wait while I put on my glasses. There!"

The clock chimed three again. Shame, old clock, now, shame. Have to have you fixed.

The young man in the dark suit stood near the door. Aunt Tildy nodded.

"You leavin' so soon, young man? Had to give up, didn't you? Couldn't convince me; no, I'm mule-stubborn. Never get me free of this house, so don't bother comin' back to try!"

The young man bowed with slow dignity.

He had no intention of coming again, ever.

"Fine," declared Aunt Tildy. "I always told Papa I'd win! Why, I'll knit in this window the next thousand years. They'll have to chew the boards down around me to get me out."

The dark young man twinkled his eyes.

"Quit lookin' like the cat that ate the bird," cried Aunt Tildy. "Get that old fool wicker away!"

The four men trod heavily out the front door. Tildy studied the way they handled an empty basket, yet staggered with its weight.

"Here, now!" She rose in tremulous indignation. "Did you steal my antiques? My books? The clocks? What you got in that wicker?"

The dark young man whistled jauntily, turning his back to her, walking along behind the four staggering men. At the door he pointed to the wicker, offered its lid to Aunt Tildy. In pantomime he wondered if she would like to open it and gaze inside.

"Curious? Me? Pshaw, no. Get out!" cried Aunt Tildy.

The dark young man tapped a hat onto his head, saluted her crisply.

"Good-by!" Aunt Tildy slammed the door.

There, there. That was better. Gone. Darned fool men with their maggoty ideas. No never minds about the wicker. If they stole something, she didn't care, long as they let her alone.

"Look." Aunt Tildy smiled. "Here comes Emily, home from college. About time. Lovely girl. See how she walks. But, land, she looks pale and funny today, walkin' so slow. I wonder why. Looks worried, she does. Poor girl. I'll just fix some coffee and a tray of cakes."

Emily tapped up the front steps. Aunt Tildy, rustling around, could hear the slow, deliberate steps. What *ailed* the girl? Didn't sound like she had no more spunk than a flue-lizard. The front door swung wide. Emily stood in the hall, holding to the brass doorknob.

"Emily?" called Aunt Tildy.

Emily shuffled into the parlor, head down.

"Emily! I been waitin' for you! There was the darndest fool men here with a wicker. Tryin' to sell me something I didn't want. Glad you're home. Makes it right cozy——"

Aunt Tildy realized that for a full minute Emily had been staring.

"Emily, what's wrong? Stop starin'. Here, I'll bring you a cup of coffee. There!

"Emily, why you backin' away from me?

"Emily, stop screamin', child. Don't scream, Emily! Don't! You keep screamin' that way, you go crazy. Emily, get up off the floor, get away from that wall! Emily! Stop cringin', child. I won't hurt you!

"Land, if it ain't one thing it's another.

"Emily, what's *wrong*, child . . ."

Emily groaned through her hands over her face.

"Child, child," whispered Aunt Tildy. "Here, sip this water. Sip it, Emily, that's it."

Emily widened her eyes, saw something, then shut them, quivering, pulling into herself. "Aunt Tildy, Aunt Tildy, Aunt——"

"Stop that!" Tildy slapped her. "What *ails* you?"

Emily forced herself to look up again.

She thrust her fingers out. They vanished inside Aunt Tildy.

"What fool notion!" cried Tildy. "Take your hand away! Take it, I say!"

Emily dropped aside, jerked her head, the golden hair shaking into shiny temblors. "You're not here, Aunt Tildy. I'm dreaming. You're dead!"

"Hush, baby."

"You *can't* be here."

"Land of Goshen, Emily——"

She took Emily's hand. It passed clean through her. Instantly, Aunt Tildy raised straight up, stomping her foot.

"Why, why!" she cried angrily. "That—fibber! That sneak-thief!" Her thin hands knotted to wiry, hard, pale fists. "That dark, dark fiend! He stole it! He toted it away, he did, oh he did, he did! Why, I——" Wrath steamed in her. Her pale blue eyes were fire. She sputtered into an indignant silence. Then she turned to Emily. "Child, get up! I need you!"

Emily lay, quivering.

"Part of me's here!" declared Aunt Tildy. "By the Lord Harry, what's left will have to do, for a bit. Fetch my bonnet!"

Emily confessed. "I'm scared."

"Certainly, oh, certainly not of *me*?"

"Yes."

"Why, I'm no spook! You known me most of your life! Now's no time to snivel-sop. Fetch up on your heels or I'll slap you crack across your nose!"

Emily rose, in sobs, stood like something cornered, trying to decide which direction to bolt in.

"Where's your car, Emily?"

"Down at the garage—ma'am."

"Good!" Aunt Tildy hustled her through the front door. "Now——" Her sharp eyes poked up and down the streets. "Which way's the mortuary?"

Emily held to the step rail, fumbling down. "What're you going to do, Aunt Tildy?"

"Do?" cried Aunt Tildy, tottering after her, jowls shaking in a thin, pale fury. "Why, get my body back, of course! Get my body back! Go on!"

The car roared, Emily clenched to the steering wheel, staring straight ahead at the curved, rain-wet streets. Aunt Tildy shook her parasol.

"Hurry, child, hurry, before they squirt juices in my body and dice and cube it the way them persnickety morticians have a habit of doin'. They cut and sew it so it ain't no good to no one!"

"Oh, Auntie, Auntie, let me go, don't make me drive! It won't do any good, no good at all," sighed the girl.

"Here we are." Emily pulled to the curb, and collapsed over the wheel, but Aunt Tildy had already popped from the car and trotted with mincing skirt up the mortuary drive, around behind to where the shiny black hearse was unloading a wicker basket.

"You!" she directed her attack at one of the four men with the wicker. "Put that down!"

The four men looked up.

One said, "Step aside, lady. We're doing our job."

"That's my body tucked in there!" She brandished the parasol.

"That I wouldn't know anything about," said a second man. "Please don't block traffic, madam. This thing is heavy."

"Sir!" she cried, wounded. "I'll have you know I weigh only one hundred and ten pounds."

He looked at her casually. "I'm not interested in your heft, lady. I'm due home for supper. My wife'll kill me if I'm late."

The four of them moved on, Aunt Tildy in pursuit, down a hall, into a preparations room.

A white-smocked man awaited the wicker's arrival with a rather pleased smile on his long, eager-looking face. Aunt Tildy didn't care for the avidity of that face, or the entire personality of the man. The basket was deposited, the four men wandered off.

The man in the white smock glanced at Auntie and said:

"Madam, this is no fit place for a gentlewoman."

"Well," she said, gratified, "glad you feel that way. It's exactly what I tried to tell that dark-clothed young man!"

The mortician puzzled. "What dark-clothed young man is that?"

"The one that came puddlin' around my house, that's who."

"No one of that description works for us."

"No matter. As you just so intelligently stated, this is no place for a lady. I don't want me here. I want me home cookin' ham for Sunday visitors, it's near Easter. I got Emily to feed, sweaters to knit, clocks to wind——"

"You are quite philosophical, and philanthropical, no doubt of it, madam, but I have work. A body has arrived." This last, he said with apparent relish, and a winnowing of his knives, tubes, jars, and instruments.

Tildy bristled. "You put so much as a fingerprint on that body, and I'll——"

He laid her aside like a little old moth. "George," he called with a suave gentleness, "escort this lady out, please."

Aunt Tildy glared at the approaching George.

"Show me your backside, goin' the other way!"

George took her wrists. "This way, please."

Tildy extricated herself. Easily. Her flesh sort of—slipped. It even amazed Tildy. Such an unexpected talent to develop at this late day.

"See?" she said, pleased with her ability. "You can't budge me. I want my body back!"

The mortician opened the wicker lid casually. Then, in a recurrent series of scrutinies he realized the body inside was . . . it seemed . . . could it be? . . . maybe . . . yes . . . no . . . no . . . it just *couldn't* be, but . . . . "Ah," he exhaled, abruptly. He turned. His eyes were wide, then they narrowed.

"Madam," he said, cautiously. "This lady here is—a—relative—of yours?"

"A very dear relation. Be careful of her."

"A sister, perhaps?" He grasped at a straw of dwindling logic, hopefully.

"No, you fool. Me, do you hear? *Me!*"

The mortician considered the idea. "No," he said. "Things like this don't happen." He fumbled with his tools. "George, get help from the others. I can't work with a crank present."

The four men returned. Aunt Tildy crossed her arms in defiance. "Won't budge!" she cried, as she was moved like a pawn on a chessboard, from preparations room to slumber room, to hall, to waiting chamber, to funeral parlor, where she threw herself down on a chair in the very center of the vestibule. There were pews going back into gray silence, and a smell of flowers.

"Please, ma'am," said one of the men. "That's where the body rests for the service tomorrow."

"I'm sittin' right plumb here until I get what I want."

She sat, pale fingers fussing with the lace at her throat, jaw set, one high-buttoned shoe tapping with irritation. If a man got in whopping distance, she gave him a parasol whop. And when they touched her, now, she remembered to—slip away.

Mr. Carrington, Mortuary President, heard the disturbance in his office and came toddling down the aisle to investigate. "Here, here," he whispered to everyone, finger to mouth.

"More respect, more respect. What is this? Oh, madam, may I help you?"

She looked him up and down. "You may."

"How may I be of service, please?"

"Go in that room back there," directed Aunt Tildy.

"Yee-ess."

"And tell that eager young investigator to quit fiddlin' with my body. I'm a maiden lady. My moles, birthmarks, scars, and other bric-a-brac, including the turn of my ankle, are my own secret. I don't want him pryin' and probin', cuttin', or hurtin' it any way."

This was vague to Mr. Carrington, who hadn't correlated bodies yet. He looked at her in blank helplessness.

"He's got me in there on his table, like a pigeon ready to be drawn and stuffed!" she told him.

Mr. Carrington hustled off to check. After fifteen minutes of waiting silence and horrified arguing, comparing notes with the mortician behind closed doors, Carrington returned, three shades whiter.

Carrington dropped his glasses, picked them up. "You're making it difficult for us."

"*I* am?" raged Aunt Tildy. "Saint Vitus in the mornin'! Looky here, Mister Blood and Bones or whatever, you tell that——"

"We're already draining the blood from the——"

"What!"

"Yes, yes, I assure you, yes. So, you just go away, now; there's nothing to be done." He laughed nervously. "Our mortician is also performing a brief autopsy to determine cause of death."

Auntie jumped to her feet, burning.

"He can't do that! Only coroners are allowed to do that!"

"Well, we sometimes allow a little——"

"March straight in and tell that Cut-'em-up to pump all that fine New England blue blood right back into that fine-skinned body, and if he's taken anything out, for him to attach it back in so it'll function proper, and then turn that body, fresh as paint, into my keepin'. You hear!"

"There's nothing I can do. Nothing."

"Tell you *what.* I'm settin' here for the next two hunderd years. You listenin'? And every time any of your customers come by, I'll spit ectoplasm right squirt up their nostrils!"

Carrington groped that thought around his weakening mind and emitted a groan. "You'd ruin our business. You wouldn't do that."

Auntie smiled. "*Wouldn't* I?"

Carrington ran up the dark aisle. In the distance you could hear him dialing a phone over and over again. Half an hour later cars roared up in front of the mortuary. Three vice-presidents of the mortuary came down the aisle with their hysterical president.

"What seems to be the trouble?"

Auntie told them with a few well-chosen infernalities.

They held a conference, meanwhile notifying the mortician to discontinue his homework, at least until such time as an agreement was reached. . . . The mortician walked from his chamber and stood smiling amiably, smoking a big black cigar.

Auntie stared at the cigar.

"Where'd you put the *ashes*?" she cried, in horror.

The mortician only grinned imperturbably and puffed.

The conference broke up.

"Madam, in all fairness, you wouldn't force us out on the street to continue our services, would you?"

Auntie scanned the vultures. "Oh, I wouldn't mind at all."

Carrington wiped sweat from his jowls. "You can have your body back."

"Ha!" shouted Auntie. Then, with caution: "Intact?"

"Intact."

"No formaldehyde?"

"No formaldehyde."

"Blood in it?"

"Blood, my God, yes, blood, if only you'll take it and go!"

A prim nod. "Fair enough. Fix 'er up. It's a deal."

Carrington snapped his fingers at the mortician. "Don't *stand* there, you mental incompetent. Fix it up!"

"And be careful with that cigar!" said the old woman.

"Easy, easy," said Aunt Tildy. "Put the wicker on the floor where I can step in it."

She didn't look at the body much. Her only comment was, "Natural-lookin'." She let herself fall back into the wicker.

A biting sensation of arctic coldness gripped her, followed

by an unlikely nausea and a giddy whorling. She was two drops of matter fusing, water trying to seep into concrete. Slow to do. Hard. Like a butterfly trying to squirm back into a discarded husk of flinty chrysalis!

The vice-presidents watched Aunt Tildy with apprehension. Mr. Carrington wrung his fingers and tried to assist with boosting and pushing moves of his hands and arms. The mortician, frankly skeptical, watched with idle, amused eyes.

Seeping into cold, long granite. Seeping into a frozen and ancient statue. Squeezing all the way.

"Come alive, damn ye!" shouted Aunt Tildy to herself. "Raise up a bit."

The body half-rose, rustling in the dry wicker.

"Fold your legs, woman!"

The body grabbled up, blindly groping.

"See!" shouted Aunt Tildy.

Light entered the webbed blind eyes.

"Feel!" urged Aunt Tildy.

The body felt the warmth of the room, the sudden reality of the preparations table on which to lean, panting.

"Move!"

The body took a creaking, slow step.

"Hear!" she snapped.

The noises of the place came into the dull ears. The harsh, expectant breath of the mortician, shaken; the whimpering Mr. Carrington; her own crackling voice.

"Walk!" she said.

The body walked.

"Think!" she said.

The old brain thought.

"Speak!" she said.

The body spoke, bowing to the morticians:

"Much obliged. Thank you."

"Now," she said, finally, "cry!"

And she began to cry tears of utter happiness.

And now, any afternoon about four, if you want to visit Aunt Tildy, you just walk around to her antique shop and rap. There's a big, black funeral wreath on the door. Don't mind that! Aunt Tildy left it there; that's how her humor runs. You rap on the door. It's double-barred and triple-locked, and when you rap her voice shrills out at you.

"Is that the man in black?"

And you laugh and say no, no, it's only me, Aunt Tildy.

And she laughs and says, "Come on in, quick!" and she whips the door open and slams it shut behind, so no man in black can ever slip in with you. Then she sets you down and pours your coffee and shows you her latest knitted sweater. She's not as fast as she used to be, and can't see as good, but she gets on.

"And if you're 'specially good," Aunt Tildy declares, setting her coffee cup to one side, "I'll give you a little treat."

"What's that?" visitors will ask.

"This," says Auntie, pleased with her little uniqueness, her little joke.

Then with modest moves of her fingers she will unfasten the white lace at her neck and chest and for a brief moment show what lies beneath.

The long blue scar where the autopsy was neatly sewn together.

"Not bad sewin' for a man," she allows. "Oh, some more coffee? *There!*"

The Cistern

IT WAS AN afternoon of rain, and lamps lighted against the gray. For a long while the two sisters had been in the dining-room. One of them, Juliet, embroidered tablecloths; the younger, Anna, sat quietly on the window seat, staring out at the dark street and the dark sky.

Anna kept her brow pressed against the pane, but her lips moved and after reflecting a long moment, she said, "I never thought of that before."

"Of what?" asked Juliet.

"It just came to me. There's actually a city under a city. A dead city, right here, right under our feet."

Juliet poked her needle in and out the white cloth. "Come away from the window. That rain's done something to you."

"No, really. Didn't you ever think of the cisterns before? They're all through the town, there's one for every street, and you can walk in them without bumping your head, and they go everywhere and finally go down to the sea," said Anna, fascinated with the rain on the asphalt pavement out there and the rain falling from the sky and vanishing down the gratings at each corner of the distant intersection. "Wouldn't you like to live in a cistern?"

"I would not!"

"But wouldn't it be fun—I mean, very secret? To live in the cistern and peek up at people through the slots and see them and them not see you? Like when you were a child and played hide-and-seek and nobody found you, and there you were in their midst all the time, all sheltered and hidden and warm and excited. I'd like that. That's what it must be like to live in the cistern."

Juliet looked slowly up from her work. "You *are* my sister, aren't you, Anna? You *were* born, weren't you? Sometimes, the way you talk, I think Mother found you under a tree one day and brought you home and planted you in a pot and grew you to this size and there you are, and you'll never change."

Anna didn't reply, so Juliet went back to her needle. There

was no color in the room; neither of the two sisters added any color to it. Anna held her head to the window for five minutes. Then she looked way off into the distance and said, "I guess you'd call it a dream. While I've been here, the last hour, I mean. Thinking. Yes, Juliet, it was a dream."

Now it was Juliet's turn not to answer.

Anna whispered. "All this water put me to sleep a while, I guess, and then I began to think about the rain and where it came from and where it went and how it went down those little slots in the curb, and then I thought about deep under, and suddenly there *they* were. A man . . . and a woman. Down in that cistern, under the road."

"What would they be doing there?" asked Juliet.

Anna said, "Must they have a reason?"

"No, not if they're insane, no," said Juliet. "In that case no reasons are necessary. There they are in their cistern, and let them stay."

"But they aren't just in the cistern," said Anna, knowingly, her head to one side, her eyes moving under the half-down lids. "No, they're in love, these two."

"For heaven's sake," said Juliet, "did love make them crawl down there?"

"No, they've been there for years and years," said Anna.

"You can't tell me they've been in that cistern for years, living together," protested Juliet.

"Did I say they were alive?" asked Anna, surprised. "Oh, but no. They're dead."

The rain scrambled in wild, pushing pellets down the window. Drops came and joined with others and made streaks.

"Oh," said Juliet.

"Yes," said Anna, pleasantly. "Dead. He's dead and she's dead." This seemed to satisfy her; it was a nice discovery, and she was proud of it. "He looks like a very lonely man who never traveled in all his life."

"How do you know?"

"He looks like the kind of man who never traveled but wanted to. You know by his eyes."

"You know what he looks like, then?"

"Yes. Very ill and very handsome. You know how it is with

a man made handsome by illness? Illness brings out the bones in the face."

"And he's dead?" asked the older sister.

"For five years." Anna talked softly, with her eyelids rising and falling, as if she were about to tell a long story and knew it and wanted to work into it slowly, and then faster and then faster, until the very momentum of the story would carry her on, with her eyes wide and her lips parted. But now it was slowly, with only a slight fever to the telling. "Five years ago this man was walking along a street and he knew he'd been walking the same street on many nights and he'd go on walking it, so he came to a manhole cover, one of those big iron waffles in the center of the street, and he heard the river rushing under his feet, under the metal cover, rushing toward the sea." Anna put out her right hand. "And he bent slowly and lifted up the cistern lid and looked down at the rushing foam and the water, and he thought of someone he wanted to love and couldn't, and then he swung himself onto the iron rungs and walked down them until he was all gone. . . ."

"And what about her?" asked Juliet, busy. "When'd she die?"

"I'm not sure. She's new. She's just dead, now. But she *is* dead. Beautifully, beautifully dead." Anna admired the image she had in her mind. "It takes death to make a woman really beautiful, and it takes death by drowning to make her most beautiful of all. Then all the stiffness is taken out of her, and her hair hangs up on the water like a drift of smoke." She nodded her head, amusedly. "All the schools and etiquettes and teachings in the world can't make a woman move with this dreamy ease, supple and ripply and fine." Anna tried to show how fine, how ripply, how graceful, with her broad, coarse hand.

"He'd been waiting for her, for five years. But she hadn't known where he was till now. So there they are, and will be, from now on. . . . In the rainy season they'll live. But in the dry seasons—that's sometimes months—they'll have long rest periods, they'll lie in little hidden niches, like those Japanese water flowers, all dry and compact and old and quiet."

Juliet got up and turned on yet another little lamp in the corner of the dining-room. "I wish you wouldn't talk about it."

Anna laughed. "But let me tell you about how it starts, how

they come back to life. I've got it all worked out." She bent forward, held onto her knees, staring at the street and the rain and the cistern mouths. "There they are, down under, dry and quiet, and up above the sky gets electrical and powdery." She threw back her dull, graying hair with one hand. "At first all the upper world is pellets. Then there's lightning and then thunder and the dry season is over, and the little pellets run along the gutters and get big and fall into the drains. They take gum wrappers and theatre tickets with them, and bus transfers!"

"Come away from that window, now."

Anna made a square with her hands and imagined things. "I know just what it's like under the pavement, in the big square cistern. It's huge. It's all empty from the weeks with nothing but sunshine. It echoes if you talk. The only sound you can hear standing down there is an auto passing above. Far up above. The whole cistern is like a dry, hollow camel bone in a desert, waiting."

She lifted her hand, pointing, as if she herself were down in the cistern, waiting. "Now, a little trickle. It comes down on the floor. It's like something was hurt and bleeding up in the outer world. There's some thunder! Or was it a truck going by?"

She spoke a little more rapidly now, but held her body relaxed against the window, breathing out, and in the next words: "It seeps down. Then, into all the other hollows come other seepages. Little twines and snakes. Tobacco-stained water. Then it moves. It joins others. It makes snakes and then one big constrictor which rolls along on the flat, papered floor. From everywhere, from the north and south, from other streets, other streams come and they join and make one hissing and shining coil. And the water writhes into those two little dry niches I told you about. It rises slowly around those two, the man and the woman, lying there like Japanese flowers."

She clasped her hands, slowly, working finger into finger, interlacing.

"The water soaks into them. First, it lifts the woman's hand. In a little move. Her hand's the only live part of her. Then her arm lifts and one foot. And her hair . . ." she touched her own hair as it hung about her shoulders ". . . unloosens and opens out like a flower in the water. Her shut eyelids are blue. . . ."

The room got darker, Juliet sewed on, and Anna talked and told all she saw in her mind. She told how the water rose and took the woman with it, unfolding her out and loosening her and standing her full upright in the cistern. "The water is interested in the woman, and she lets it have its way. After a long time of lying still, she's ready to live again, any life the water wants her to have."

Somewhere else, the man stood up in the water also. And Anna told of that, and how the water carried him slowly, drifting, and her, drifting, until they met each other. "The water opens their eyes. Now they can see but not see each other. They circle, not touching yet." Anna made a little move of her head, eyes closed. "They watch each other. They glow with some kind of phosphorus. They smile. . . . They—touch hands."

At last Juliet, stiffening, put down her sewing and stared at her sister, across the gray, rain-silent room.

"Anna!"

"The tide—makes them touch. The tide comes and puts them together. It's a perfect kind of love, with no ego to it, only two bodies, moved by the water, which makes it clean and all right. It's not wicked, this way."

"It's bad you're saying it!" cried her sister.

"No, it's all right," insisted Anna, turning for an instant. "They're not thinking, are they? They're just so deep down and quiet and not caring."

She took her right hand and held it over her left hand very slowly and gently, quavering and interweaving them. The rainy window, with the pale spring light penetrating, put a movement of light and running water on her fingers, made them seem submerged, fathoms deep in gray water, running one about the other as she finished her little dream:

"Him, tall and quiet, his hands open." She showed with a gesture how tall and how easy he was in the water. "Her, small and quiet and relaxed." She looked at her sister, leaving her hands just that way. "They're dead, with no place to go, and no one to tell them. So there they are, with nothing applying to them and no worries, very secret and hidden under the earth in the cistern waters. They touch their hands and lips and when they come into a cross-street outlet of the cistern, the tide rushes them together. Then, later . . ." she disengaged her hands . . . "maybe they travel together, hand in hand, bobbling and floating, down all the streets, doing little crazy upright dances when they're caught in sudden swirls." She whirled her hands about, a drenching of rain spatted the window. "And they go down to the sea, all across the town, past cross drain and cross drain, street and street. Genesee Avenue, Crenshaw, Edmond Place, Washington, Motor City, Ocean Side and then the ocean. They go anywhere the water wants them, all over the earth, and come back later to the cistern inlet and float back up under the town, under a dozen tobacco shops and four dozen liquor stores, and six dozen groceries and ten theatres, a rail junction, Highway 101, under the walking feet of thirty thousand people who don't even know or think of the cistern."

Anna's voice drifted and dreamed and grew quiet again.

"And then—the day passes and the thunder goes away up on the street. The rain stops. The rain season's over. The tunnels drip and stop. The tide goes down." She seemed disappointed, sad it was over. "The river runs out to the ocean. The man and woman feel the water leave them slowly to the floor. They settle." She lowered her hands in little bobblings to her lap, watching them fixedly, longingly. "Their feet lose the life the water has given them from outside. Now the water lays them down, side by side, and drains away, and the tunnels are drying. And there they lie. Up above, in the world, the sun comes out. There they lie, in the darkness, sleeping, until the next time. Until the next rain."

Her hands were now upon her lap, palms up and open. "Nice man, nice woman," she murmured. She bowed her head over them and shut her eyes tight.

Suddenly Anna sat up and glared at her sister. "Do you know who the man is?" she shouted, bitterly.

Juliet did not reply; she had watched, stricken, for the past five minutes while this thing went on. Her mouth was twisted and pale. Anna almost screamed:

"The man is Frank, that's who he is! And *I'm* the woman!"

"Anna!"

"Yes, it's Frank, down there!"

"But Frank's been gone for years, and certainly not down there, Anna!"

Now, Anna was talking to nobody, and to everybody, to Juliet, to the window, the wall, the street. "Poor Frank," she cried. "I know that's where he went. He couldn't stay anywhere in the world. His mother spoiled him for all the world! So he saw the cistern and saw how secret and fine it was. Oh, poor Frank. And poor Anna, poor me, with only a sister. Oh, Julie, why didn't I hold onto Frank when he was here? Why didn't I fight to win him from his mother?"

"Stop it, this minute, do you hear, this minute!"

Anna slumped down into the corner, by the window, one hand up on it, and wept silently. A few minutes later she heard her sister say, "Are you finished?"

"What?"

"If you're done, come help me finish this, I'll be forever at it."

Anna raised her head and glided over to her sister. "What do you want me to do?" she sighed.

"This and this," said Juliet, showing her.

"All right," said Anna, and took it and sat by the window looking at the rain, moving her hands with the needle and thread, but watching how dark the street was now, and the room, and how hard it was to see the round metal top of the cistern now—there were just little midnight gleams and glitters out there in the black black late afternoon. Lightning crackled over the sky in a web.

Half an hour passed. Juliet drowsed in her chair across the room, removed her glasses, placed them down with her work and for a moment rested her head back and dozed. Perhaps thirty seconds later she heard the front door open violently, heard the wind come in, heard the footsteps run down the walk, turn, and hurry along the black street.

"What?" asked Juliet, sitting up, fumbling for her glasses. "Who's there? Anna, did someone come in the door?" She stared at the empty window seat where Anna had been. "Anna!" she cried. She sprang up and ran out into the hall.

The front door stood open, rain fell through it in a fine mist.

"She's only gone out for a moment," said Juliet, standing there, trying to peer into the wet blackness. "She'll be right back. *Won't* you be right back, Anna dear? Anna, answer me, you *will* be right back, won't you, sister?"

Outside, the cistern lid rose and slammed down.

The rain whispered on the street and fell upon the closed lid all the rest of the night.

Homecoming

"HERE THEY COME," said Cecy, lying there flat in her bed.

"Where are they?" cried Timothy from the doorway.

"Some of them are over Europe, some over Asia, some of them over the Islands, some over South America!" said Cecy, her eyes closed, the lashes long, brown, and quivering.

Timothy came forward upon the bare plankings of the upstairs room. "Who are they?"

"Uncle Einar and Uncle Fry, and there's Cousin William, and I see Frulda and Helgar and Aunt Morgiana and Cousin Vivian, and I see Uncle Johann! They're all coming fast!"

"Are they up in the sky?" cried Timothy, his little gray eyes flashing. Standing by the bed, he looked no more than his fourteen years. The wind blew outside, the house was dark and lit only by starlight.

"They're coming through the air and traveling along the ground, in many forms," said Cecy, in her sleeping. She did not move on the bed; she thought inward on herself and told what she saw. "I see a wolflike thing coming over a dark river—at the shallows—just above a waterfall, the starlight shining up his pelt. I see a brown oak leaf blowing far up in the sky. I see a small bat flying. I see many other things, running through the forest trees and slipping through the highest branches; and they're *all* coming this way!"

"Will they be here by tomorrow night?" Timothy clutched the bedclothes. The spider on his lapel swung like a black pendulum, excitedly dancing. He leaned over his sister. "Will they all be here in time for the Homecoming?"

"Yes, yes, Timothy, yes," sighed Cecy. She stiffened. "Ask no more of me. Go away now. Let me travel in the places I like best."

"Thanks, Cecy," he said. Out in the hall, he ran to his room. He hurriedly made his bed. He had just awakened a few minutes ago, at sunset, and as the first stars had risen, he had gone to let his excitement about the party run with Cecy. Now she slept so quietly there was not a sound. The spider hung on a silvery lasso about Timothy's slender neck as he washed his face. "Just think, Spid, tomorrow night is Allhallows Eve!"

He lifted his face and looked into the mirror. His was the only mirror allowed in the house. It was his mother's concession to his illness. Oh, if only he were not so afflicted! He opened his mouth, surveyed the poor, inadequate teeth nature had given him. No more than so many corn kernels—round, soft and pale in his jaws. Some of the high spirit died in him.

It was now totally dark and he lit a candle to see by. He felt exhausted. This past week the whole family had lived in the fashion of the old country. Sleeping by day, rousing at sunset to move about. There were blue hollows under his eyes. "Spid, I'm no good," he said, quietly, to the little creature. "I can't even get used to sleeping days like the others."

He took up the candleholder. Oh, to have strong teeth, with incisors like steel spikes. Or strong hands, even, or a strong mind. Even to have the power to send one's mind out, free, as Cecy did. But, no, he was the imperfect one, the sick one. He was even—he shivered and drew the candle flame closer—afraid of the dark. His brothers snorted at him. Bion and Leonard and Sam. They laughed at him because he slept in a bed. With Cecy it was different; her bed was part of her comfort for the composure necessary to send her mind abroad to hunt. But Timothy, did he sleep in the wonderful polished boxes like the others? He did not! Mother let him have his own bed, his own room, his own mirror. No wonder the family skirted him like a holy man's crucifix. If only the wings would sprout from his shoulder blades. He bared his back, stared at it. And sighed again. No chance. Never.

Downstairs were exciting and mysterious sounds, the slithering black crape going up in all the halls and on the ceilings and doors. The sputter of burning black tapers in the banistered stair well. Mother's voice, high and firm. Father's voice, echoing from the damp cellar. Bion walking from outside the old country house lugging vast two-gallon jugs.

"I've just got to go to the party, Spid," said Timothy. The spider whirled at the end of its silk, and Timothy felt alone. He would polish cases, fetch toadstools and spiders, hang crape,

but when the party started he'd be ignored. The less seen or said of the imperfect son the better.

All through the house below, Laura ran.

"The Homecoming!" she shouted gaily. "The Homecoming!" Her footsteps everywhere at once.

Timothy passed Cecy's room again, and she was sleeping quietly. Once a month she went belowstairs. Always she stayed in bed. Lovely Cecy. He felt like asking her, "Where are you now, Cecy? And *in* who? And what's happening? Are you beyond the hills? And what goes on there?" But he went on to Ellen's room instead.

Ellen sat at her desk, sorting out many kinds of blond, red and black hair and little scimitars of fingernail gathered from her manicurist job at the Mellin Village beauty parlor fifteen miles over. A sturdy mahogany case lay in one corner with her name on it.

"Go away," she said, not even looking at him. "I can't work with you gawking."

"Allhallows Eve, Ellen; just think!" he said, trying to be friendly.

"Hunh!" She put some fingernail clippings in a small white sack, labeled them. "What can it mean to you? What do you know of it? It'll scare the hell out of you. Go back to bed."

His cheeks burned. "I'm needed to polish and work and help serve."

"If you don't go, you'll find a dozen raw oysters in your bed tomorrow," said Ellen, matter-of-factly. "Good-by, Timothy."

In his anger, rushing downstairs, he bumped into Laura.

"Watch where you're going!" she shrieked from clenched teeth.

She swept away. He ran to the open cellar door, smelled the channel of moist earthy air rising from below. "Father?"

"It's about time," Father shouted up the steps. "Hurry down, or they'll be here before we're ready!"

Timothy hesitated only long enough to hear the million other sounds in the house. Brothers came and went like trains in a station, talking and arguing. If you stood in one spot long enough the entire household passed with their pale hands full of things. Leonard with his little black medical case, Samuel with his large, dusty ebon-bound book under his arm, bearing more black crape, and Bion excursioning to the car outside and bringing in many more gallons of liquid.

Father stopped polishing to give Timothy a rag and a scowl. He thumped the huge mahogany box. "Come on, shine this up, so we can start on another. Sleep your life away."

While waxing the surface, Timothy looked inside.

"Uncle Einar's a big man, isn't he, Papa?"

"Unh."

"How big is he?"

"The size of the box'll tell you."

"I was only asking. Seven feet tall?"

"You talk a lot."

About nine o'clock Timothy went out into the October weather. For two hours in the now-warm, now-cold wind he walked the meadows collecting toadstools and spiders. His heart began to beat with anticipation again. How many relatives had Mother said would come? Seventy? One hundred? He passed a farmhouse. If only you knew what was happening at our house, he said to the glowing windows. He climbed a hill and looked at the town, miles away, settling into sleep, the town-hall clock high and round white in the distance. The town did not know, either. He brought home many jars of toadstools and spiders.

In the little chapel belowstairs a brief ceremony was celebrated. It was like all the other rituals over the years, with Father chanting the dark lines, mother's beautiful white ivory hands moving in the reverse blessings, and all the children gathered except Cecy, who lay upstairs in bed. But Cecy was present. You saw her peering, now from Bion's eyes, now Samuel's, now Mother's, and you felt a movement and now she was in you, fleetingly and gone.

Timothy prayed to the Dark One with a tightened stomach. "Please, please, help me grow up, help me be like my sisters and brothers. Don't let me be different. If only I could put the hair in the plastic images as Ellen does, or make people fall in love with me as Laura does with people, or read strange books as Sam does, or work in a respected job like Leonard and Bion do. Or even raise a family one day, as mother and father have done. . . ."

At midnight a storm hammered the house. Lightning struck

outside in amazing, snow-white bolts. There was a sound of an approaching, probing, sucking tornado, funneling and nuzzling the moist night earth. Then the front door, blasted half off its hinges, hung stiff and discarded, and in trooped Grandmama and Grandpapa, all the way from the old country!

From then on people arrived each hour. There was a flutter at the side window, a rap on the front porch, a knock at the back. There were fey noises from the cellar; autumn wind piped down the chimney throat, chanting. Mother filled the large crystal punch bowl with a scarlet fluid poured from the jugs Bion had carried home. Father swept from room to room lighting more tapers. Laura and Ellen hammered up more wolfsbane. And Timothy stood amidst this wild excitement, no expression to his face, his hands trembling at his sides, gazing now here, now there. Banging of doors, laughter, the sound of liquid pouring, darkness, sound of wind, the webbed thunder of wings, the padding of feet, the welcoming bursts of talk at the entrances, the transparent rattlings of casements, the shadows passing, coming, going, wavering.

"Well, well, and *this* must be Timothy!"

"What?"

A chilly hand took his hand. A long hairy face leaned down over him. "A good lad, a fine lad," said the stranger.

"Timothy," said his mother. "This is Uncle Jason."

"Hello, Uncle Jason."

"And over here——" Mother drifted Uncle Jason away. Uncle Jason peered back at Timothy over his caped shoulder, and winked.

Timothy stood alone.

From off a thousand miles in the candled darkness, he heard a high fluting voice; that was Ellen. "And my brothers, they *are* clever. Can you guess their occupations, Aunt Morgiana?"

"I have no idea."

"They operate the undertaking establishment in town."

"What!" A gasp.

"Yes!" Shrill laughter. "Isn't that priceless!"

Timothy stood very still.

A pause in the laughter. "They bring home sustenance for Mama, Papa and all of us," said Laura. "Except, of course, Timothy. . . ."

An uneasy silence. Uncle Jason's voice demanded, "Well? come now. What about Timothy?"

"Oh, Laura, your tongue," said mother.

Laura went on with it. Timothy shut his eyes. "Timothy doesn't—well—doesn't *like* blood. He's delicate."

"He'll learn," said mother. "He'll learn," she said very firmly. "He's my son, and he'll learn. He's only fourteen."

"But I was raised on the stuff," said Uncle Jason, his voice passing from one room on into another. The wind played the trees outside like harps. A little rain spatted on the windows—"raised on the stuff," passing away into faintness.

Timothy bit his lips and opened his eyes.

"Well, it was all my fault." Mother was showing them into the kitchen now. "I tried forcing him. You can't force children, you only make them sick, and then they never get a taste for things. Look at Bion, now, he was thirteen before he . . ."

"I understand," murmured Uncle Jason. "Timothy will come around."

"I'm sure he will," said mother, defiantly.

Candle flames quivered as shadows crossed and recrossed the dozen musty rooms. Timothy was cold. He smelled the hot tallow in his nostrils and instinctively he grabbed at a candle and walked with it around and about the house, pretending to straighten the crape.

"*Timothy*," someone whispered behind a patterned wall, hissing and sizzling and sighing the words, "*Timothy is afraid of the dark.*"

Leonard's voice. Hateful Leonard!

"I like the candle, that's all," said Timothy in a reproachful whisper.

More lightning, more thunder. Cascades of roaring laughter. Bangings and clickings and shouts and rustles of clothing. Clammy fog swept through the front door. Out of the fog, settling his wings, stalked a tall man.

"Uncle Einar!"

Timothy propelled himself on his thin legs, straight through the fog, under the green webbing shadows. He threw himself across Einar's arms. Einar lifted him.

"You've wings, Timothy!" He tossed the boy light as thistles.

"Wings, Timothy: fly!" Faces wheeled under. Darkness rotated. The house blew away. Timothy felt breezelike. He flapped his arms. Einar's fingers caught and threw him once more to the ceiling. The ceiling rushed down like a charred wall. "Fly, Timothy!" shouted Einar, loud and deep. "Fly with wings! Wings!"

He felt an exquisite ecstasy in his shoulder blades, as if roots grew, burst to explode and blossom into new, moist membrane. He babbled wild stuff; again Einar hurled him high.

The autumn wind broke in a tide on the house, rain crashed down, shaking the beams, causing chandeliers to tilt their enraged candle lights. And the one hundred relatives peered out from every black, enchanted room, circling inward, all shapes and sizes, to where Einar balanced the child like a baton in the roaring spaces.

"Enough!" shouted Einar, at last.

Timothy, deposited on the floor timbers, exaltedly, exhaustedly fell against Uncle Einar, sobbing happily. "Uncle, uncle, uncle!"

"Was it good, flying? Eh, Timothy?" said Uncle Einar, bending down, patting Timothy's head. "Good, good."

It was coming toward dawn. Most had arrived and were ready to bed down for the daylight, sleep motionlessly with no sound until the following sunset, when they would shout out of their mahogany boxes for the revelry.

Uncle Einar, followed by dozens of others, moved toward the cellar. Mother directed them downward to the crowded row on row of highly polished boxes. Einar, his wings like sea-green tarpaulins tented behind him, moved with a curious whistling down the passageway; where his wings touched they made a sound of drumheads gently beaten.

Upstairs, Timothy lay wearily thinking, trying to like the darkness. There was so much you could do in darkness that people couldn't criticize you for, because they never saw you. He *did* like the night, but it was a qualified liking: sometimes there was so much night he cried out in rebellion.

In the cellar, mahogany doors sealed downward, drawn in by pale hands. In corners, certain relatives circled three times to lie, heads on paws, eyelids shut. The sun rose. There was a sleeping.

Sunset. The revel exploded like a bat nest struck full, shrieking out, fluttering, spreading. Box doors banged wide. Steps rushed up from cellar damp. More late guests, kicking on front and back portals, were admitted.

It rained, and sodden visitors laid their capes, their water-pelleted hats, their sprinkled veils upon Timothy who bore them to a closet. The rooms were crowd-packed. The laughter of one cousin, shot from one room, angled off the wall of another, ricocheted, banked and returned to Timothy's ears from a fourth room, accurate and cynical.

A mouse ran across the floor.

"I know you, Niece Leibersrouter!" exclaimed father.

The mouse spiraled three women's feet and vanished into a corner. Moments later a beautiful woman rose up out of nothing and stood in the corner, smiling her white smile at them all.

Something huddled against the flooded pane of the kitchen window. It sighed and wept and tapped continually, pressed against the glass, but Timothy could make nothing of it, he saw nothing. In imagination he was outside staring in. The rain was on him, the wind at him, and the taper-dotted darkness inside was inviting. Waltzes were being danced; tall thin figures pirouetted to outlandish music. Stars of light flickered off lifted bottles; small clods of earth crumbled from casques, and a spider fell and went silently legging over the floor.

Timothy shivered. He was inside the house again. Mother was calling him to run here, run there, help, serve, out to the kitchen now, fetch this, fetch that, bring the plates, heap the food—on and on—the party happened around him but not to him. The dozens of towering people pressed in against him, elbowed him, ignored him.

Finally, he turned and slipped away up the stairs.

He called softly. "Cecy. Where are you now, Cecy?"

She waited a long while before answering. "In the Imperial Valley," she murmured faintly. "Beside the Salton Sea, near the mud pots and the steam and the quiet. I'm inside a farmer's wife. I'm sitting on a front porch. I can make her move if I want, or do anything or think anything. The sun's going down."

"What's it like, Cecy?"

"You can hear the mud pots hissing," she said, slowly, as if speaking in a church. "Little gray heads of steam push up the mud like bald men rising in the thick syrup, head first, out in the broiling channels. The gray heads rip like rubber fabric, collapse with noises like wet lips moving. And feathery plumes of steam escape from the ripped tissue. And there is a smell of deep sulphurous burning and old time. The dinosaur has been abroiling here ten million years."

"Is he done yet, Cecy?"

"Yes, he's done. Quite done." Cecy's calm sleeper's lips turned up. The languid words fell slowly from her shaping mouth. "Inside this woman's skull I am, looking out, watching the sea that does not move, and is so quiet it makes you afraid. I sit on the porch and wait for my husband to come home. Occasionally, a fish leaps, falls back, starlight edging it. The valley, the sea, the few cars, the wooden porch, my rocking chair, myself, the silence."

"What now, Cecy?"

"I'm getting up from my rocking chair," she said.

"Yes?"

"I'm walking off the porch, toward the mud pots. Planes fly over, like primordial birds. Then it is quiet, so quiet."

"How long will you stay inside her, Cecy?"

"Until I've listened and looked and felt enough: until I've changed her life some way. I'm walking off the porch and along the wooden boards. My feet knock on the planks, tiredly, slowly."

"And now?"

"Now the sulphur fumes are all around me. I stare at the bubbles as they break and smooth. A bird darts by my temple, shrieking. Suddenly I am in the bird and fly away! And as I fly, inside my new small glass-bead eyes I see a woman below me, on a boardwalk, take one two three steps forward into the mud pots. I hear a sound as of a boulder plunged into molten depths. I keep flying, circle back. I see a white hand, like a spider, wriggle and disappear into the gray lava pool. The lava seals over. Now I'm flying home, swift, swift, swift!"

Something clapped hard against the window, Timothy started.

Cecy flicked her eyes wide, bright, full, happy, exhilarated.

"Now I'm *home*!" she said.

After a pause, Timothy ventured, "The Homecoming's on. And everybody's here."

"Then why are you upstairs?" She took his hand. "Well, ask me." She smiled slyly. "Ask me what you came to ask."

"I didn't come to ask anything," he said. "Well, almost nothing. Well—oh, Cecy!" It came from him in one long rapid flow. "I want to do something at the party to make them look at me, something to make me good as them, something to make me belong, but there's nothing I can do and I feel funny and, well, I thought you might . . ."

"I might," she said, closing her eyes, smiling inwardly. "Stand up straight. Stand very still." He obeyed. "Now, shut your eyes and blank out your thought."

He stood very straight and thought of nothing, or at least thought of thinking nothing.

She sighed. "Shall we go downstairs now, Timothy?" Like a hand into a glove, Cecy was within him.

"Look everybody!" Timothy held the glass of warm red liquid. He held up the glass so that the whole house turned to watch him. Aunts, uncles, cousins, brothers, sisters!

He drank it straight down.

He jerked a hand at his sister Laura. He held her gaze, whispering to her in a subtle voice that kept her silent, frozen. He felt tall as the trees as he walked to her. The party now slowed. It waited on all sides of him, watching. From all the room doors the faces peered. They were not laughing. Mother's face was astonished. Dad looked bewildered, but pleased and getting prouder every instant.

He nipped Laura, gently, over the neck vein. The candle flames swayed drunkenly. The wind climbed around on the roof outside. The relatives stared from all the doors. He popped toadstools into his mouth, swallowed, then beat his arms against his flanks and circled. "Look, Uncle Einar! I can fly, at last!" Beat went his hands. Up and down pumped his feet. The faces flashed past him.

At the top of the stairs flapping, he heard his mother cry, "Stop, Timothy!" far below. "Hey!" shouted Timothy, and leaped off the top of the well, thrashing.

Halfway down, the wings he thought he owned dissolved. He screamed. Uncle Einar caught him.

Timothy flailed whitely in the receiving arms. A voice burst out of his lips, unbidden. "This is Cecy! This is Cecy!" Come see me, all of you, upstairs, first room on the left!" Followed by a long trill of high laughter. Timothy tried to cut it off with his tongue.

Everybody was laughing. Einar set him down. Running through the crowding blackness as the relatives flowed upstairs toward Cecy's room to congratulate her, Timothy banged the front door open.

"Cecy, I hate you, I hate you!"

By the sycamore tree, in deep shadow. Timothy spewed out his dinner, sobbed bitterly and threshed in a pile of autumn leaves. Then he lay still. From his blouse pocket, from the protection of the matchbox he used for his retreat, the spider crawled forth. Spid walked along Timothy's arm. Spid explored up his neck to his ear and climbed in the ear to tickle it. Timothy shook his head. "Don't, Spid. Don't."

The feathery touch of a tentative feeler probing his eardrum set Timothy shivering. "Don't, Spid!" He sobbed somewhat less.

The spider traveled down his cheek, took a station under the boy's nose, looked up into the nostrils as if to seek the brain, and then clambered softly up over the rim of the nose to sit, to squat there peering at Timothy with green gem eyes until Timothy filled with ridiculous laughter. "Go away, Spid!"

Timothy sat up, rustling the leaves. The land was very bright with the moon. In the house he could hear the faint ribaldry as Mirror, Mirror was played. Celebrants shouted, dimly muffled, as they tried to identify those of themselves whose reflections did not, had not ever appeared in a glass.

"Timothy." Uncle Einar's wings spread and twitched and came in with a sound like kettledrums. Timothy felt himself plucked up like a thimble and set upon Einar's shoulder. "Don't feel badly, Nephew Timothy. Each to his own, each in his own way. How much better things are for you. How rich. The world's dead for us. We've seen so much of it, believe me. Life's best to those who live the least of it. It's worth more per ounce, Timothy, remember that."

The rest of the black morning, from midnight on, Uncle Einar led him about the house, from room to room, weaving and singing. A horde of late arrivals set the entire hilarity off afresh. Great-great-great-great and a thousand more great-greats Grandmother was there, wrapped in Egyptian cerements. She said not a word, but lay straight as a burnt ironing board against the wall, her eye hollows cupping a distant, wise, silent glimmering. At the breakfast, at four in the morning, one-thousand-odd-greats Grandmama was stiffly seated at the head of the longest table.

The numerous young cousins caroused at the crystal punch bowl. Their shiny olive-pit eyes, their conical, devilish faces and curly bronze hair hovered over the drinking table, their hard-soft, half-girl half-boy bodies wrestling against each other as they got unpleasantly, sullenly drunk. The wind got higher, the stars burned with fiery intensity, the noises redoubled, the dances quickened, the drinking became more positive. To Timothy there were thousands of things to hear and watch. The many darknesses roiled, bubbled, the many faces passed and repassed. . . .

"Listen!"

The party held its breath. Far away the town clock struck its chimes, saying six o'clock. The party was ending. As if at a cue, in time to the rhythm of the clock striking, their one hundred voices began to sing songs that were four hundred years old, songs Timothy could not know. They twined their arms around one another, circling slowly, and sang, and somewhere in the cold distance of morning the town clock finished out its chimes and quieted.

Good-bys were said, there was a great rustling. Mother and Father and the brothers and sisters lined up at the door to shake hands and kiss each departing relative in turn. The sky beyond the open door colored and shone in the east. A cold wind entered.

The shouting and the laughing bit by bit faded and went away. Dawn grew more apparent. Everybody was embracing and crying and thinking how the world was becoming less a place for them. There had been a time when they had met every year, but now decades passed with no reconciliation. "Don't forget, we meet in Salem in 1970!" someone cried.

Salem. Timothy's numbed mind turned the word over. Salem, 1970. And there would be Uncle Fry and Grandma and Grandfather and a thousand-times-great Grandmother in her withered cerements. And Mother and Father and Ellen and Laura and Cecy and Leonard and Bion and Sam and all the rest. But would he be there? Would he be alive that long? Could he be certain of living until then?

With one last withering wind blast, away they all went, so many scarves, so many fluttery mammals, so many sere leaves, so many wolves loping, so many whinings and clustering noises, so many midnights and ideas and insanities.

Mother shut the door. Laura picked up a broom.

"No," said Mother, "we'll clean tonight. We need sleep first."

Father walked down into the cellar, followed by Laura and Bion and Sam. Ellen walked upstairs, as did Leonard.

Timothy walked across the crape-littered hall. His head was down, and in passing a party mirror he saw himself, the pale mortality of his face all cold and trembling.

"Timothy," said Mother.

He stopped at the stair well. She came to him, laid a hand on his face. "Son," she said. "We love you. Remember that. We all love you. No matter how different you are, no matter if you leave us one day," she said. She kissed his cheek. "And if and when you die, your bones will lie undisturbed, we'll see to that. You'll lie at ease forever, and I'll come see you every Allhallows Eve and tuck you in the more secure."

The house was silent. Far away the wind went over a hill with its last cargo of small dark bats, echoing, chittering.

He walked up the steps, one by one, crying to himself all the way.

The Wonderful Death of Dudley Stone

"ALIVE!"
"Dead!"
"Alive in New England, damn it."
"Died twenty years ago!"
"Pass the hat, I'll go myself and bring back his head!"

That's how the talk went that night. A stranger set it off with his mouthings about Dudley Stone dead. Alive! we cried. And shouldn't we know? Weren't we the last frail remnants of those who had burnt incense and read his books by the light of blazing intellectual votives in the twenties?

The Dudley Stone. That magnificent stylist, that proudest of literary lions. Surely you recall the head-pounding, the cliff-jumping, the whistlings of doom that followed on his writing his publishers this note:

> Sirs: Today, aged 30, I retire from the field, renounce writing, burn all my effects, toss my latest manuscript on the dump, cry hail and fare thee well. Yrs., affect.
>
> Dudley Stone

Earthquakes and avalanches, in that order.

"*Why?*" we asked ourselves, meeting down the years.

In fine soap-opera fashion we debated if it was women caused him to hurl his literary future away. Was it the Bottle. Or Horses that outran him and stopped a fine pacer in his prime?

We freely admitted to one and all, that were Stone writing now, Faulkner, Hemingway, and Steinbeck would be buried in his lava. All the sadder that Stone, on the brink of his greatest work, turned one day and went off to live in a town we shall call Obscurity by the sea best named The Past.

"*Why?*"

That question forever lived with those of us who had seen the glints of genius in his piebald works.

One night a few weeks ago, musing off the erosion of the

years, finding each others' faces somewhat more pouched and our hairs more conspicuously in absence, we became enraged over the typical citizen's ignorance of Dudley Stone.

At least, we muttered, Thomas Wolfe had had a full measure of success before he seized his nose and jumped off the rim of Eternity. At least the critics gathered to stare after his plunge into darkness as after a meteor that made much fire in its passing. But who now remembered Dudley Stone, his coteries, his frenzied followers of the twenties?

"Pass the hat," I said. "I'll travel three hundred miles, grab Dudley Stone by the pants and say: 'Look here, Mr. Stone, why did you let us down so badly? Why haven't you written a book in twenty-five years?'"

The hat was lined with cash; I sent a telegram and took a train.

I do not know what I expected. Perhaps to find a doddering and frail praying mantis, whisping about the station, blown by seawinds, a chalk-white ghost who would husk at me with the voices of grass and reeds blown in the night. I clenched my knees in agony as my train chuffed into the station. I let myself down into a lonely country-side, a mile from the sea, like a man foolishly insane, wondering why I had come so far.

On a bulletin board in front of the boarded-up ticket office I found a cluster of announcements, inches thick, pasted and nailed one upon another for uncountable years. Leafing under, peeling away anthropological layers of printed tissue I found what I wanted. Dudley Stone for alderman, Dudley Stone for Sheriff, Dudley Stone for Mayor! On up through the years his photograph, bleached by sun and rain, faintly recognizable, asked for ever more responsible positions in the life of this world near the sea. I stood reading them.

"Hey!"

And Dudley Stone plunged across the station platform behind me suddenly. "Is that you, Mr. Douglas!" I whirled to confront this great architecture of a man, big but not in the least fat, his legs huge pistons thrusting him on, a bright flower in his lapel, a bright tie at his neck. He crushed my hand, looked down upon me like Michelangelo's God creating Adam with a mighty touch. His face was the face of those illustrated North Winds and South Winds that blow hot and cold in ancient mariners' charts. It was the face that symbolizes the sun in Egyptian carvings, ablaze with life!

My God! I thought. And this is the man who hasn't written in twenty-odd years. Impossible. He's so alive it's sinful. I can hear his *heartbeat*!

I must have stood with my eyes very wide to let the look of him cram in upon my startled senses.

"You thought you'd find Marley's Ghost," he laughed. "Admit it."

"I——"

"My wife's waiting with a New England boiled dinner, we've plenty of ale and stout. I like the ring of those words. To *ale* is not to sicken, but to revive the flagging spirit. A tricky word, that. And *stout*? There's a nice ruddy sound to it. Stout!" A great golden watch bounced on his vest-front, hung in bright chains. He vised my elbow and charmed me along, a magician well on his way back to his cave with a luckless rabbit. "Glad to see you! I suppose you've come, as the others came, to ask the same question, eh! Well, this time I'll tell everything!"

My heart jumped. "Wonderful!"

Behind the empty station sat an open-top 1927-vintage Model-T Ford. "Fresh air. Drive at twilight like this, you get all the fields, the grass, the flowers, coming at you in the wind. I hope you're not one of those who tiptoe around shutting windows! Our house is like the top of a mesa. We let the weather do our broom-work. Hop in!"

Ten minutes later we swung off the highway onto a drive that had not been leveled or filled in years. Stone drove straight on over the pits and bumps, smiling steadily. Bang! We shuddered the last few yards to a wild, unpainted two-story house. The car was allowed to gasp itself away into mortal silence.

"Do you want the truth?" Stone turned to look me in the face and hold my shoulder with an earnest hand. "I was murdered by a man with a gun twenty-five years ago almost to this very day."

I sat staring after him as he leapt from the car. He was solid as a ton of rock, no ghost to him, but yet I knew that somehow the truth was in what he had told me before firing himself like a cannon at the house.

"This is my wife, and this is the house, and that is our supper waiting for us! Look at our view. Windows on three sides of the living room, a view of the sea, the shore, the meadows. We nail the windows open three out of four seasons. I swear you get a smell of limes here midsummer, and something from Antarctica, ammonia and ice cream, come December. Sit down! Lena, isn't it *nice* having him here?"

"I hope you like New England boiled dinner," said Lena, now here, now there, a tall, firmly-built woman, the sun in the East, Father Christmas' daughter, a bright lamp of a face that lit our table as she dealt out the heavy useful dishes made to stand the pound of giants' fists. The cutlery was solid enough to take a lion's teeth. A great whiff of steam rose up, through which we gladly descended, sinners into Hell. I saw the seconds-plate skim by three times and felt the ballast gather in my chest, my throat, and at last my ears. Dudley Stone poured me a brew he had made from wild Concords that had cried for mercy, he said. The wine bottle, empty, had its green glass mouth blown softly by Stone, who summoned out a rhythmic one-note tune that was quickly done.

"Well, I've kept you waiting long enough," he said, peering at me from that distance which drinking adds between people and which, at odd turns in the evening, seems closeness itself. "I'll tell you about my murder. I've never told anyone before; believe me. Do you know John Oatis Kendall?"

"A minor writer in the twenties, wasn't he?" I said. "A few books. Burnt out by '31. Died last week."

"God rest him." Mr. Stone lapsed into a special brief melancholy from which he revived as he began to speak again.

"Yes. John Oatis Kendall, burnt out by the year 1931, a writer of great potentialities."

"Not as great as yours," I said, quickly.

"Well, just wait. We were boys together, John Oatis and I, born where the shade of an oak tree touched my house in the morning and his house at night, swam every creek in the world together, got sick on sour apples and cigarettes together, saw the same lights in the same blonde hair of the same young girl together, and in our late teens went out to kick Fate in the stomach and get beat on the head together. We both did fair, and then *I* better and still better as the years ran. If his first book got one good notice, mine got six, if I got one bad notice, he got a dozen. We were like two friends on a train which the public has uncoupled. There went John Oatis on the caboose, left behind, crying out, 'Save me! You're leaving me in Tank Town, Ohio; we're on the same track!' And the conductor saying, 'Yes, but not the same *train*!' And myself yelling, '*I* believe in you, John, be of good heart, I'll come back for you!' And the caboose dwindling behind with its red and green lamps like cherry and lime pops shining in the dark and we yelling our friendship to each other: 'John, old man!' 'Dudley, old pal!' while John Oatis went out on a dark siding behind a tin baling-shed at midnight and my engine, with all the flag-wavers and brass bands, boiled on toward dawn."

Dudley Stone paused and noticed my look of general confusion.

"All this to lead up to my murder," he said. "For it was John Oatis Kendall who, in 1930, traded a few old clothes and some remaindered copies of his books for a gun and came out to this house and this room."

"He really meant to kill you?"

"Meant to, hell! He did! Bang! Have some more wine? That's better."

A strawberry shortcake was set upon the table by Mrs. Stone, while he enjoyed my gibbering suspense. Stone sliced it into three huge chunks and served it around, fixing me with his kindly approximation of the Wedding Guest's eye.

"There he sat, John Oatis, in that chair where you sit now. Behind him, outside, in the smokehouse, seventeen hams; in our wine cellars, five hundred bottles of the best; beyond the window open country, the elegant sea in full lace; overhead a moon like a dish of cool cream, everywhere the full panoply of spring, and Lena across the table, too, a willow tree in the wind, laughing at everything I said or did not choose to say, both of us thirty, mind you, thirty years old, life our magnificent carousel, our fingers playing full chords, my books selling well, fan mail pouring upon us in crisp white founts, horses in the stables for moonlight rides to coves where either we or the sea might whisper all we wished in the night. And John Oatis seated there where you sit now, quietly taking the little blue gun from his pocket."

"I laughed, thinking it was a cigar lighter of some sort," said his wife.

"But John Oatis said quite seriously: 'I'm going to kill you, Mr. Stone.'"

"What did you do?"

"Do? I sat there, stunned, riven; I heard a terrible slam! the coffin lid in my face! I heard coal down a black chute; dirt on my buried door. They say all your *past* hurtles by at such times. Nonsense. The *future* does. You see your face a bloody porridge. You sit there until your fumbling mouth can say, 'But why, John, what have I *done* to you?'

"'Done!' he cried.

"And his eye skimmed along the vast bookshelf and the handsome brigade of books drawn stiffly to attention there with my name on each blazing like a panther's eye in the Moroccan blackness. 'Done!' he cried, mortally. And his hand itched the revolver in a sweat. 'Now, John,' I cautioned. 'What do you want?'

"'One thing more than anything else in the world,' he said, 'to kill you and be famous. Get my name in headlines. Be famous as you are famous. Be known for a lifetime and beyond as the man who killed Dudley Stone!'

"'You can't mean that!'

"'I do. I'll be very famous. Far more famous than I am today, in your shadow. Oh, listen here, no one in the world knows how to hate like a writer does. God, how I love your work and God, how I hate you because you write so well. Amazing ambivalence. But I can't take it any more, not being able to write as you do, so I'll take my fame the easy way. I'll cut you off before you reach your prime. They say your next book will be your very finest, your most brilliant!'

"'They exaggerate.'

"'My guess is they're right!' he said.

"I looked beyond him to Lena who sat in her chair, frightened, but not frightened enough to scream or run and spoil the scene so it might end inadvertently.

"'Calm,' I said. 'Calmness. Sit there, John. I ask only one minute. Then pull the trigger.'

"'No!' Lena whispered.

"'Calmness,' I said to her, to myself, to John Oatis.

"I gazed out the open windows, I felt the wind, I thought of the wine in the cellar, the coves at the beach, the sea, the night moon like a disc of menthol cooling the summer heavens, drawing clouds of flaming salt, the stars, after it in a wheel toward morning. I thought of myself only thirty, Lena thirty, our whole lives ahead. I thought of all the flesh of life hung high and waiting for me to really *start* banqueting! I had never climbed a mountain, I had never sailed an ocean, I had never run for Mayor, I had never dived for pearls, I had never owned a telescope, I had never acted on a stage or built a house or read all the classics I had so *wished* to read. All the *actions* waiting to be done!

"So in that almost instantaneous sixty seconds, I thought at last of my career. The books I had written, the books I *was* writing, the books I intended to write. The reviews, the sales, our huge balance in the bank. And, believe or disbelieve me, for the first time in my life I got free of it all. I became, in one moment, a critic. I cleared the scales. On one hand I put all the boats I hadn't taken, the flowers I hadn't planted, the children I hadn't raised, all the hills I hadn't looked at, with Lena there, goddess of the harvest. In the middle I put John Oatis Kendall with his gun—the upright that held the balances. And on the empty scale opposite I laid my pen, my ink, my empty paper, my dozen books. I made some minor adjustments. The sixty seconds were ticking by. The sweet night wind blew across the table. It touched a curl of hair on Lena's neck, oh Lord, how softly, softly it touched . . .

"The gun pointed at me. I have seen the moon craters in photographs, and that hole in space called the Great Coal Sack Nebula, but neither was as big, take my word, as the mouth of that gun across the room from me.

"'John,' I said at last, 'do you hate me *that* much? Because I've been lucky and you not?'

"'Yes, damn it!' he cried.

"It was almost funny he should envy me. I was not that

much better a writer than he. A flick of the wrist made the difference.

"'John,' I said quietly to him, 'if you want me dead, I'll *be* dead. Would you like for me to never write again?'

"'I'd like nothing better!' he cried. 'Get ready!' He aimed at my heart!

"'All right,' I said, 'I'll never write again.'

"'What?' he said.

"'We're old old friends, we've never lied to each other, have we? Then take my word, from this night on I'll never put pen to paper.'

"'Oh *God*,' he said, and laughed with contempt and disbelief.

"'There,' I said, nodding my head at the desk near him, 'are the only original copies of the two books I've been working on for the last three years. I'll burn one in front of you now. The other you yourself may throw in the sea. Clean out the house, take everything faintly resembling literature, burn my published books, too. Here.' I got up. He could have shot me then, but I had him fascinated. I tossed one manuscript on the hearth and touched a match to it.

"'No!' Lena said. I turned. 'I know what I'm doing,' I said. She began to cry. John Oatis Kendall simply stared at me, bewitched. I brought him the other unpublished manuscript. 'Here,' I said, tucking it under his right shoe so his foot was a paper weight. I went back and sat down. The wind was blowing and the night was warm and Lena was white as apple-blossoms there across the table.

"I said, 'From this day forward I will not write ever again.'

"At last John Oatis managed to say, 'How can you do this?'

"'To make everyone happy,' I said. 'To make you happy because we'll be friends again, eventually. To make Lena happy because I'll be just her husband again and no agent's performing seal. And myself happy because I'd rather be a live man than a dead author. A dying man will do anything, John. Now take my last novel and get along with you.'

"We sat there, the three of us, just as we three are sitting tonight. There was a smell of lemons and limes and camellias. The ocean roared on the stony coastland below; God, what a lovely moonlit sound. And at last, picking up the manuscripts, John Oatis took them, like my body, out of the room. He paused at the door and said, 'I believe you.' And then he was gone. I heard him drive away. I put Lena to bed. That was one of the few nights in my life I ever walked down by the shore, but walk I did, taking deep breaths and feeling my arms and legs and my face with my hands, crying like a child, walking and wading in the surf to feel the cold salt water foaming about me in a million suds."

Dudley Stone paused. Time had made a stop in the room. Time was in another year, the three of us sitting there, enchanted with his telling of the murder.

"And did he destroy your last novel?" I asked.

Dudley Stone nodded. "A week later one of the pages drifted up on the shore. He must have thrown them over the cliff, a thousand pages, I see it in my mind's eye, a flock of white seagulls it might seem, flying down to the water and going out with the tide at four in the black morning. Lena ran up the beach with that single page in her hand, crying, 'Look, look!' And when I saw what she handed me, I tossed it back in the ocean."

"Don't tell me you honored your promise!"

Dudley Stone looked at me steadily. "What would *you* have done in a similar position? Look at it this way: John Oatis did me a favor. He didn't kill me. He didn't shoot me. He took my word. He honored my word. He let me live. He let me go on eating and sleeping and breathing. Quite suddenly he had broadened my horizons. I was so grateful that standing on the beach hip-deep in water that night, I cried. I was grateful. Do you really understand that word? Grateful he had let me live when he had had it in his hand to annihilate me forever."

Mrs. Stone rose up, the dinner was ended. She cleared the dishes, we lit cigars; and Dudley Stone strolled me over to his office-at-home, a rolltop desk, its jaws propped wide with parcels and papers and ink bottles, a typewriter, documents, ledgers, indexes.

"It was all rolling to a boil in me. John Oatis simply spooned the froth off the top so I could see the brew. It was very clear," said Dudley Stone. "Writing was always so much mustard and gallweed to me; fidgeting words on paper, experiencing vast depressions of heart and soul. Watching the greedy critics graph me up, chart me down, slice me like sausage, eat me at midnight breakfasts. Work of the worst sort. I was *ready* to fling the pack. My trigger was set. Boom! There was John Oatis! Look here."

He rummaged in the desk and brought forth hand-bills and posters. "I had been *writing* about living. Now I wanted to live. *Do* things instead of tell about things. I ran for the board of education. I won. I ran for alderman. I won. I ran for mayor. I won! Sheriff! Town librarian! Sewage disposal official. I shook a lot of hands, saw a lot of life, did a lot of things. We've lived every way there is to live, with our eyes and noses and mouths, with our ears and hands. We've climbed hills and painted pictures, there are some on the wall! We've been three times around the world! I even delivered our baby son, unexpectedly. He's grown and married now—lives in New York! We've done and done again." Stone paused and smiled. "Come on out in the yard; we've set up a telescope, would you like to see the rings of Saturn?"

We stood in the yard, and the wind blew from a thousand miles at sea and while we were standing there, looking at the stars through the telescope, Mrs. Stone went down into the midnight cellar after a rare Spanish wine.

It was noon the next day when we reached the lonely station after a hurricane trip across the jouncing meadows from the sea. Mr. Dudley Stone let the car have its head, while he talked to me, laughing, smiling, pointing to this or that outcrop of Neolithic stone, this or that wild flower, falling silent again only as we parked and waited for the train to come and take me away.

"I suppose," he said, looking at the sky, "you think I'm quite insane."

"No, I'd never say that."

"Well," said Dudley Stone, "John Oatis Kendall did me one other favor."

"What was that?"

Stone hitched around conversationally in the patched leather seat.

"He helped me get out when the going was good. Deep down inside I must have guessed that my literary success was something that would melt when they turned off the cooling system. My subconscious had a pretty fair picture of my future. I knew what none of my critics knew, that I was headed nowhere but down. The two books John Oatis destroyed were very bad. They would have killed me deader than Oatis possibly could. So he helped me decide, unwittingly, what I might not have had the courage to decide myself, to bow gracefully out while the cotillion was still on, while the Chinese lanterns still cast flattering pink lights on my Harvard complexion. I had seen too many writers up, down, and out, hurt, unhappy, suicidal. The combination of circumstance, coincidence, subconscious knowledge, relief, and gratitude to John Oatis Kendall to just *be alive*, were fortuitous, to say the least."

We sat in the warm sunlight another minute.

"And then I had the pleasure of seeing myself compared to all the greats when I announced my departure from the literary scene. Few authors in recent history have bowed out to such publicity. It was a lovely funeral. I looked, as they say, natural. And the echoes lingered. 'His *next* book!' the critics cried, 'would have been *it*! A masterpiece!' I had them panting, waiting. Little did they know. Even now, a quarter-century later, my readers who were college boys then, make sooty excursions on drafty kerosene-stinking shortline trains to solve the mystery of why I've made them wait so long for my 'masterpiece.' And thanks to John Oatis Kendall I still have a little reputation; it has receded slowly, painlessly. The next year I might have died by my own writing hand. How much better to cut your own caboose off the train, before others do it for you.

"My friendship with John Oatis Kendall? It came back. It took time, of course. But he was out here to see me in 1947; it was a nice day, all around, like old times. And now he's dead and at last I've told someone everything. What will you tell your friends in the city? They won't believe a word of this. But it *is* true, I swear it, as I sit here and breathe God's good air and look at the calluses on my hands and begin to resemble the faded handbills I used when I ran for county treasurer."

We stood on the station platform.

"Good-by, and thanks for coming and opening your ears and letting my world crash in on you. God bless to all your curious friends. Here comes the train! I've got to run; Lena and I are going to a Red Cross drive down the coast this afternoon! Good-by!"

I watched the dead man stomp and leap across the platform, felt the plankings shudder, saw him jump into his Model-T, heard it lurch under his bulk, saw him bang the floor-boards with a big foot, idle the motor, roar it, turn, smile, wave to me, and then roar off and away toward that suddenly brilliant town called Obscurity by a dazzling seashore called The Past.

OTHER STORIES

R Is for Rocket

THERE WAS THIS fence where we pressed our faces and felt the wind turn warm and held to the fence and forgot who we were or where we came from but dreamed of who we might be and where we might go. . . .

Yet we were boys and liked being boys and lived in a Florida town and liked the town and went to school and fairly liked the school and climbed trees and played football and liked our mothers and fathers. . . .

But some time every hour of every day of every week for a minute or a second when we thought on fire and stars and the fence beyond which they waited . . . we liked the rockets more.

The fence. The rockets.

Every Saturday morning . . .

The guys met at my house.

With the sun hardly up, they yelled until the neighbors were moved to brandish paralysis guns out their ventilators commanding the guys to shut their damn traps or they'd be frozen statues for the next hour and *then* where would they be?

Aw, climb a rocket, stick your head in the main-jet! the kids always yelled back, but yelled this safe behind our garden fence. Old Man Wickard, next door, is a great shot with the para-gun.

This one dim cool Saturday morning I was lying in bed thinking about how I had screwed up my semantics exam the day before at formula-school, when I heard the gang yelling below. It was hardly 7 A.M. and there was still a lot of fog roaming in off the Atlantic, and only now were the weather-control vibrators at each corner starting to hum and shoot out rays to get rid of the stuff; I heard them moaning soft and nice.

I padded to the window and stuck my head out.

"Okay, space-pirates! Motors off!"

"Hey!" shouted Ralph Priory. "We just heard, there's a new schedule today! The Moon Job, the one with the new XL3-motor, is cutting gravity in an *hour*!"

"Buddha, Muhammad, Allah, and other real and semi-mythological figures," I said, and went away from the window so fast the concussion laid all the boys out on my lawn.

I zippered myself into a jumper, yanked on my boots, clipped my food-capsules to my hip-pocket, for I knew there'd be no food or even thought of food today, we'd just stuff with pills when our stomachs barked, and fell down the two-story vacuum elevator.

On the lawn, all five of the guys were chewing their lips, bouncing around, scowling.

"Last one," said I, passing them at 5000 mph, "to the monorail is a bug-eyed Martian!"

On the monorail, with the cylinder hissing us along to Rocket Port, twenty miles from town—a few minutes ride—I had bugs in my stomach. A guy fifteen doesn't get to see the big stuff often enough, mostly every week it was the small continental cargo rockets coming and going on schedule. But this was big, among the biggest . . . the Moon and beyond. . . .

"I'm sick," said Priory, and hit me on the arm.

I hit him back. "Me, too. Boy, ain't Saturday the best day in the week!?"

Priory and I traded wide, understanding grins. We got along all Condition Go. The other pirates were okay. Sid Rossen, Mac Leslyn, Earl Marnee, they knew how to jump around like all the kids, and they loved the rockets, too, but I had the feeling they wouldn't be doing what Ralph and I would do some day. Ralph and I wanted the stars for each of us, more than we would want a fistful of clear-cut blue-white diamonds.

We yelled with the yellers, we laughed with the laughers, but at the middle of it all, we were still, Ralph and I, and the cylinder whispered to a stop and we were outside yelling, laughing, running, but quiet and almost in slow motion, Ralph ahead of me, and all of us pointed one way, at the observation fence and grabbing hold, yelling for the slowpokes to catch up, but not looking back for them, and then we were all there together and the big rocket came out of its plastic work canopy like a great interstellar circus tent and moved along its gleaming track out toward the fire point, accompanied by the gigantic gantry like a gathering of prehistoric reptile birds which kept and preened and fed this one big fire monster and led it toward its seizure and birth into a suddenly blast-furnace sky.

I quit breathing. I didn't even suck another breath it seemed until the rocket was way out on the concrete meadow, followed by water-beetle tractors and great cylinders bearing hidden men, and all around, in asbestos suits, praying-mantis mechanics fiddled with machines and buzzed and cawwed and gibbered to each other on invisible, unhearable radiophones, but we could hear it all, in our heads, our minds, our hearts.

"Lord," I said at last.

"The very good Lord," said Ralph Priory at my elbow.

The others said this, too, over and over.

It was something to "good Lord" about. It was a hundred years of dreaming all sorted out and chosen and put together to make the hardest, prettiest, swiftest dream of all. Every line was fire solidified and made perfect, it was flame frozen, and ice waiting to thaw there in the middle of a concrete prairie, ready to wake with a roar, jump high and knock its silly fine great head against the Milky Way and knock the stars down in a full return of firefall meteors. You felt it could kick the Coal Sack Nebula square in the midriff and make it stand out of the way.

It got me in the midriff, too—it gripped me in such a way I knew the special sickness of longing and envy and grief for lack of accomplishment. And when the astronauts patrolled the field in the final silent mobile-van, my body went with them in their strange white armor, in their bubble-helmets and insouciant pride, looking as if they were team-parading to a magnetic football game at one of the local mag-fields, for mere practice. But they were going to the Moon, they went every month now, and the crowds that used to come to watch were no longer there, there was just us kids to worry them up and worry them off.

"Gosh," I said. "What wouldn't I give to go with them. What wouldn't I give."

"Me," said Mac, "I'd give my one-year monorail privileges."

"Yeah. Oh, very much yeah."

It was a big feeling for us kids caught half between this morning's toys and this afternoon's very real and powerful fireworks.

And then the preliminaries got over with. The fuel was in the rocket and the men ran away from it on the ground like ants running lickety from a metal god—and the Dream woke up and gave a yell and jumped into the sky. And then it was gone, all the vacuum shouting of it, leaving nothing but a hot trembling in the air, through the ground, and up our legs to our hearts. Where it had been was a blazed, seared pock and a fog of rocket smoke like a cumulus cloud banked low.

"It's gone!" yelled Priory.

And we all began to breathe fast again, frozen there on the ground as if stunned by the passing of a gigantic paralysis gun.

"I want to grow up quick," I said, then. "I want to grow up quick so I can take that rocket."

I bit my lips. I was so darned young, and you cannot apply for space work. You have to be *chosen.* Chosen.

Finally somebody, I guess it was Sidney, said:

"Let's go to the tele-show now."

Everyone said yeah, except Priory and myself. We said no, and the other kids went off laughing breathlessly, talking, and left Priory and me there to look at the spot where the ship had been.

It spoiled everything else for us—that takeoff.

Because of it, I flunked my semantics test on Monday.

I didn't care.

At times like that I thanked Providence for concentrates. When your stomach is nothing but a coiled mass of excitement, you hardly feel like drawing a chair to a full hot dinner. A few concen-tabs swallowed, did wonderfully well as substitution, without the urge of appetite.

I got to thinking about it, tough and hard, all day long and late at night. It got so bad I had to use sleep-massage mechs every night, coupled with some of Tschaikovsky's quieter music to get my eyes shut.

"Good Lord, young man," said my teacher, that Monday at class. "If this keeps up I'll have you reclassified at the next psych-board meeting."

"I'm sorry," I replied.

He looked hard at me. "What sort of block have you got? It must be a very simple, and also a conscious, one."

I winced. "It's conscious, sir; but it's not simple. It's multi-tentacular. In brief, though—it's rockets."

He smiled. "R is for Rocket, eh?"

"I guess that's it, sir."

"We can't let it interfere with your scholastic record, though, young man."

"Do you think I need hypnotic suggestion, sir?"

"No, no." He flipped through a small tab of records with my name blocked on it. I had a funny stone in my stomach, just lying there. He looked at me. "You know, Christopher, you're king-of-the-hill here; head of the class." He closed his eyes and mused over it. "We'll have to see about a lot of other things," he concluded. Then he patted me on the shoulder.

"Well—get on with your work. Nothing to worry about."

He walked away.

I tried to get back to work, but I couldn't. During the rest of the day the teacher kept watching me and looking at my tab-record and chewing his lip. About two in the afternoon he dialed a number on his desk-audio and discussed something with somebody for about five minutes.

I couldn't hear what was said.

But when he set the audio into its cradle, he stared straight at me with the funniest light in his eyes.

It was envy and admiration and pity all in one. It was a little sad and it was much of happiness. It had a lot in it, just in his eyes. The rest of his face said nothing.

It made me feel like a saint and a devil sitting there.

Ralph Priory and I slid home from formula-school together early that afternoon. I told Ralph what had happened and he frowned in the dark way he always frowns.

I began to worry. And between the two of us we doubled and tripled the worry.

"You don't think you'll be sent away, do you, Chris?"

Our monorail car hissed. We stopped at our station. We got out. We walked slow. "I don't know," I said.

"That would be plain dirty," said Ralph.

"Maybe I need a good psychiatric laundering, Ralph. I can't go on flubbing my studies this way."

We stopped outside my house and looked at the sky for a long moment. Ralph said something funny.

"The stars aren't out in the daytime, but we can see 'em, can't we, Chris?"

"Yeah," I said. "Damn right."

"We'll stick it together, huh, Chris? Damn them, they can't take you away now. We're pals. It wouldn't be fair."

I didn't say anything because there was no room in my throat for anything but a hectagonal lump.

"What's the matter with your eyes?" asked Priory.

"Aw, I looked at the sun too long. Come on inside, Ralph."

We yelled under the shower spray in the bath-cubicle, but our yells weren't especially convincing, even when we turned on the ice-water.

While we were standing in the warm-air dryer, I did a lot of thinking. Literature, I figured, was full of people who fought battles against hard, razor-edged opponents. They pitted brain and muscle against obstacles until they won out or were themselves defeated. But here I was with hardly a sign of any outward conflict. It was all running around in spiked boots inside my head, making cuts and bruises where no one could see them except me and a psychologist. But it was just as bad.

"Ralph," I said, as we dressed, "I got a war on."

"All by yourself?" he asked.

"I can't include you," I said. "Because this is personal. How many times has my mother said, 'Don't eat so much, Chris, your eyes are bigger than your stomach?'"

"A million times."

"*Two* million. Well, paraphrase it, Ralph. Change it to 'Don't *see* so much, Chris, your mind is too big for your body.' I got a war on between a mind that wants things my body can't give it."

Priory nodded quietly. "I see what you mean about its being a personal war. In that case, Christopher, I'm at war, too."

"I knew you were," I said. "Somehow I think the other kids'll grow out of it. But I don't think we will, Ralph. I think we'll keep waiting."

We sat down in the middle of the sunlit upper deck of the house, and started checking over some homework on our formula-pads. Priory couldn't get his. Neither could I. Priory put into words the very thing I didn't dare say out loud.

"Chris, the Astronaut Board *selects*. You can't apply for it. You *wait*."

"I know."

"You wait from the time you're old enough to turn cold in the stomach when you see a Moon rocket, until all the years go by, and every month that passes you hope that one morning a blue Astronaut helicopter will come down out of the sky, land on your lawn, and that a neat-looking engineer will ease out, walk up the rampway briskly, and touch the bell.

"You keep waiting for that helicopter until you're twenty-one. And then, on the last day of your twentieth year you get good and drunk and laugh a lot and say what the hell, you didn't really care about it, anyway."

We both just sat there, deep in the middle of his words. We both just sat there. Then:

"I don't want that disappointment, Chris. I'm fifteen, just like you. But if I reach my twenty-first year without an Astronaut ringing the bell where I live at the ortho-station, I—"

"I know," I said. "I know. I've talked to men who've waited, all for nothing. And if it happens that way to us, Ralph, well—we'll get good and drunk together and then go out and take jobs loading cargo on a Europe-bound freighter."

Ralph stiffened and his face went pale. "Loading cargo."

There was a soft, quick step on the ramp and my mother was there. I smiled. "Hi, lady!"

"Hello. Hello, Ralph."

"Hello, Jhene."

She didn't look much older than twenty-five, in spite of having birthed and raised me and worked at the Government Statistics House. She was light and graceful and smiled a lot, and I could see how father must have loved her very much when he was alive. One parent is better than none. Poor Priory, now, raised in one of those orthopedical stations. . . .

Jhene walked over and put her hand on Ralph's face. "You look ill," she said. "What's wrong?"

Ralph managed a fairly good smile. "Nothing—at all."

Jhene didn't need prompting. She said, "You can stay here tonight, Priory. We want you. Don't we, Chris?"

"Heck, yes."

"I should get back to the station," said Ralph, rather feebly, I observed. "But since you asked and Chris here needs help on his semantics for tomorrow, I'll stick and help him."

"Very generous," I observed.

"First, though, I've a few errands. I'll take the 'rail and be back in an hour, people."

When Ralph was gone my mother looked at me intently, then brushed my hair back with a nice little move of her fingers.

"Something's happening, Chris."

My heart stopped talking because it didn't want to talk any more for a while. It waited.

I opened my mouth, but Jhene went on:

"Something's up somewhere. I had two calls at work today. One from your teacher. One from—I can't say. I don't *want* to say until things happen—"

My heart started talking again, slow and warm.

"Don't tell me, then, Jhene. Those calls—"

She just looked at me. She took my hand between her two soft warm ones. "You're so young, Chris. You're so awfully young."

I didn't speak.

Her eyes brightened. "You never knew your father. I wish you had. You know what he was, Chris?"

I said, "Yeah. He worked in a Chemistry Lab, deep underground most of the time."

And, my mother added, strangely, "He worked deep under the ground, Chris, and never saw the stars."

My heart yelled in my chest. Yelled loud and hard.

"Oh, Mother. Mother—"

It was the first time in years I had called her mother.

When I woke the next morning there was a lot of sunlight in the room, but the cushion where Priory slept when he stayed over, was vacant. I listened. I didn't hear him splashing in the shower-cube, and the dryer wasn't humming. He was gone.

I found his note pinned on the sliding door.

"*See you at formula at noon. Your mother wanted me to do some work for her. She got a call this morning, and said she needed me to help. So long. Priory.*"

Priory out running errands for Jhene. Strange. A call in the early morning to Jhene. I went back and sat down on the cushion.

While I was sitting there a bunch of the kids yelled down on the lawn-court. "Hey, Chris! You're late!"

I stuck my head out the window. "Be right down!"

"No, Chris."

My mother's voice. It was quiet and it had something funny in it. I turned around. She was standing in the doorway behind me, her face pale, drawn, full of some small pain. "No, Chris," she said again, softly. "Tell them to go on to formula without you—today."

The kids were still making noise downstairs, I guess, but I didn't hear them. I just felt myself and my mother, slim and pale and restrained in my room. Far off, the weather-control vibrators started to hum and throb.

I turned slowly and looked down at the kids. The three of them were looking up, lips parted casually, half-smiling, semantic-tabs in their knotty fingers. "Hey—" one of them said. Sidney, it was.

"Sorry, Sid. Sorry, gang. Go on without me. I can't go to formula today. See you later, huh?"

"Aw, Chris!"

"Sick?"

"No. Just— Just go on without me, gang. I'll see you."

I felt numb. I turned away from their upturned, questioning faces and glanced at the door. Mother wasn't there. She had gone downstairs, quietly. I heard the kids moving off, not quite as boisterously, toward the monorail station.

Instead of using the vac-elevator, I walked slowly downstairs. "Jhene," I said, "where's Ralph?"

Jhene pretended to be interested in combing her long light hair with a vibro-toothed comb. "I sent him off. I didn't want him here this morning."

"Why am I staying home from formula, Jhene?"

"Chris, please don't ask."

Before I could say anything else, there was a sound in the air. It cut through the very soundproofed wall of the house, and hummed in my marrow, quick and high as an arrow of glittering music.

I swallowed. All the fear and uncertainty and doubt went away, instantly.

When I heard that note, I thought of Ralph Priory. *Oh, Ralph, if you could be here now.* I couldn't believe the truth of it. Hearing that note and hearing it with my whole body and soul as well as with my ears.

It came closer, that sound. I was afraid it would go away.

But it didn't go away. It lowered its pitch and came down outside the house in great whirling petals of light and shadow and I knew it was a helicopter the color of the sky. It stopped humming, and in the silence my mother tensed forward, dropped the vibro-comb and took in her breath.

In that silence, too, I heard booted footsteps walking up the ramp below. Footsteps that I had waited for a long time.

Footsteps I was afraid would never come.

Somebody touched the bell.

And I *knew* who it was.

And all I could think was, Ralph, why in hell did you have to go away now, when all this is happening? Damn it, Ralph, why did you?

The man looked as if he had been born in his uniform. It fitted like a second layer of salt-colored skin, touched here and there with a line, a dot of blue. As simple and perfect a uniform as could be made, but with all the muscled power of the universe behind it.

His name was Trent. He spoke firmly, with a natural round perfection, directly to the subject.

I stood there, and my mother was on the far side of the room, looking like a bewildered little girl. I stood listening.

Out of all the talking I remember some of the snatches:

". . . highest grades, high IQ. Perception A-1, curiosity Triple-A. Enthusiasm necessary to the long, eight-year educational grind. . . ."

"Yes, sir."

". . . talks with your semantics and psychology teachers—"

"Yes, sir."

". . . and don't forget, Mr. Christopher . . ."

Mister Christopher!

". . . and don't forget, Mr. Christopher, nobody is to know you have been selected by the Astronaut Board."

"No one?"

"Your mother and teacher know, naturally. But no other person must know. Is that perfectly understood?"

"Yes, sir."

Trent smiled quietly, standing there with his big hands at his sides. "You want to ask why, don't you? Why you can't tell your friends? I'll explain.

"It's a form of psychological protection. We select about ten thousand young men each year from the earth's billions. Out of that number three thousand wind up, eight years later, as spacemen of one sort or another. The others must return to society. They've flunked out, but there's no reason for everyone to know. They usually flunk out, if they're going to flunk, in the first six months. And it's tough to go back and face your friends and say you couldn't make the grade at the biggest job in the world. So we make it easy to go back.

"But there's still another reason. It's psychological, too. Half the fun of being a kid is being able to lord it over the other guys, by being superior in some way. We take half the fun out of Astronaut selection by strictly forbidding you to tell your pals. Then, we'll know if you wanted to go into space for frivolous reasons, or for space itself. If you're in it for personal conceit—you're damned. If you're in it because you can't help being in it and *have* to be in it—you're blessed."

He nodded to my mother. "Thank you, Mrs. Christopher."

"Sir," I said. "A question. I have a friend. Ralph Priory. He lives at an ortho-station—"

Trent nodded. "I can't tell you his rating, of course, but he's on our list. He's your buddy? You want him along, of course. I'll check his record. Station-bred, you say? That's not good. But—we'll see."

"If you would, please, thanks."

"Report to me at the Rocket Station Saturday afternoon at five, Mr. Christopher. Meantime: silence."

He saluted. He walked off. He went away in the helicopter into the sky, and Mother was beside me quickly, saying, "Oh, Chris, Chris," over and over, and we held to each other and whispered and talked and she said many things, how good this was going to be for us, but especially for me, how fine, what an honor it was, like the old old days when men fasted and took vows and joined churches and stopped up their tongues and were silent and prayed to be worthy and to live well as monks and priests of many churches in far places, and came forth and moved in the world and lived as examples and taught well. It was no different now, this was a greater priesthood, in a way, she said, she inferred, she knew, and I was to be some small part of it, I would not be hers any more, I would belong to all the worlds, I would be all the things my father wanted to be and never lived or had a chance to be. . . .

"Damn right, damn right," I murmured. "I will, I promise I will . . ."

I caught my voice. "Jhene—how—how will we tell Ralph? What about him?"

"You're going away, that's all, Chris. Tell him that. Very simply. Tell him no more. He'll understand."

"But, Jhene, *you*—"

She smiled softly. "Yes, I'll be lonely, Chris. But I'll have my work and I'll have Ralph."

"You mean . . ."

"I'm taking him from the ortho-station. He'll live here, when you're gone. That's what you *wanted* me to say, isn't it, Chris?"

I nodded, all paralyzed and strange inside.

"That's exactly what I wanted you to say."

"He'll be a good son, Chris. *Almost* as good as you."

"He'll be *fine*!"

We told Ralph Priory. How I was going away maybe to school in Europe for a year and how Mother wanted him to come live as her son, now, until such time as I came back. We said it quick and fast, as if it burned our tongues. And when we finished, Ralph came and shook my hand and kissed my mother on the cheek and he said:

"I'll be proud. I'll be very proud."

It was funny, but Ralph didn't even ask any more about why I was going, or where, or how long I would be away. All he would say was, "We had a lot of fun, didn't we?" and let it go at that, as if he didn't dare say any more.

It was Friday night, after a concert at the amphitheater in the center of our public circle, and Priory and Jhene and I came home, laughing, ready to go to bed.

I hadn't packed anything. Priory noted this briefly, and let it go. All of my personal supplies for the next eight years would be supplied by someone else. No need for packing.

My semantics teacher called on the audio, smiling and saying a very brief, pleasant good-bye.

Then, we went to bed, and I kept thinking in the hour before I lolled off, about how this was the last night with Jhene and Ralph. The very last night.

Only a kid of fifteen—me.

And then, in the darkness, just before I went to sleep, Priory twisted softly on his cushion, turned his solemn face to me, and whispered, "Chris?" A pause. "Chris. You still awake?" It was like a faint echo.

"Yes," I said.

"Thinking?"

A pause.

"Yes."

He said, "You're— You're not *waiting* any more, are you, Chris?"

I knew what he meant. I couldn't answer.

I said, "I'm awfully tired, Ralph."

He twisted back and settled down and said, "That's what I thought. You're not *waiting* any more. Gosh, but that's good, Chris. That's good."

He reached out and punched me in the arm-muscle, lightly.

Then we both went to sleep.

It was Saturday morning. The kids were yelling outside. Their voices filled the seven o'clock fog. I heard Old Man Wickard's ventilator flip open and the zip of his para-gun, playfully touching around the kids.

"Shut up!" I heard him cry, but he didn't sound grouchy. It was a regular Saturday game with him. And I heard the kids giggle.

Priory woke up and said, "Shall I tell them, Chris, you're not going with them today?"

"Tell them nothing of the sort." Jhene moved from the door. She bent out the window, her hair all light against a ribbon of fog. "Hi, gang! Ralph and Chris will be right down. Hold gravity!"

"Jhene!" I cried.

She came over to both of us. "You're going to spend your Saturday the way you always spend it—with the gang!"

"I planned on sticking with you, Jhene."

"What sort of holiday would *that* be, now?"

She ran us through our breakfast, kissed us on the cheeks, and forced us out the door into the gang's arms.

"Let's not go out to the Rocket Port today, guys."

"Aw, Chris—why not?"

Their faces did a lot of changes. This was the first time in history I hadn't wanted to go. "You're kidding, Chris."

"Sure he is."

"No, he's not. He means it," said Priory. "And I don't want to go either. We go *every* Saturday. It gets tiresome. We can go next week instead."

"Aw . . ."

They didn't like it, but they didn't go off by themselves. It was no fun, they said, without us.

"What the hell—we'll go next week."

"Sure we will. What do you want to do, Chris?"

I told them.

We spent the morning playing Kick the Can and some games we'd given up a long time ago, and we hiked out along some old rusty and abandoned railroad tracks and walked in a small woods outside town and photographed some birds and went swimming raw, and all the time I kept thinking—this is the last day.

We did everything we had ever done before on Saturday. All the silly crazy things, and nobody knew I was going away except Ralph, and five o'clock kept getting nearer and nearer.

At four, I said good-bye to the kids.

"Leaving so soon, Chris? What about tonight?"

"Call for me at eight," I said. "We'll go see the new Sally Gibberts picture!"

"Swell."

"Cut gravity!"

And Ralph and I went home.

Mother wasn't there, but she had left part of herself, her smile and her voice and her words on a spool of audio-film on my bed. I inserted it in the viewer and threw the picture on the wall. Soft yellow hair, her white face and her quiet words:

"I hate good-byes, Chris. I've gone to the laboratory to do some extra work. Good luck. All of my love. When I see you again—you'll be a man."

That was all.

Priory waited outside while I saw it over four times. "I hate good-byes, Chris. I've gone . . . work. . . . luck. All . . . my love. . . ."

I had made a film-spool myself the night before. I spotted it in the viewer and left it there. It only said good-bye.

Priory walked halfway with me. I wouldn't let him get on the Rocket Port monorail with me. I just shook his hand, tight, and said, "It was fun today, Ralph."

"Yeah. Well, see you next Saturday, huh, Chris?"

"I wish I could say yes."

"Say yes anyway. Next Saturday—the woods, the gang, the rockets, and Old Man Wickard and his trusty para-gun."

We laughed. "Sure. Next Saturday, early. Take— Take care of *our* mother, will you, Priory?"

"That's a silly question, you nut," he said.

"It is, isn't it?"

He swallowed. "Chris."

"Yeah?"

"I'll be waiting. Just like you waited and don't have to wait any more. I'll *wait*."

"Maybe it won't be long, Priory. I hope not."

I jabbed him, once, in the arm. He jabbed back.

The monorail door sealed. The car hurled itself away, and Priory was left behind.

I stepped out at the Port. It was a five-hundred-yard walk down to the Administration building. It took me ten years to walk it.

"Next time I see you you'll be a man—"

"Don't tell anybody—"

"I'll wait, Chris—"

It was all choked in my heart and it wouldn't go away and it swam around in my eyes.

I thought about my dreams. The Moon Rocket. It won't be part of me, part of my *dream* any longer. I'll be part of *it*.

I felt small there, walking, walking, walking.

The afternoon rocket to London was just taking off as I went down the ramp to the office. It shivered the ground and it shivered and thrilled my heart.

I was beginning to grow up awfully fast.

I stood watching the rocket until someone snapped their heels, cracked me a quick salute.

I was numb.

"C. M. Christopher?"

"Yes, sir. Reporting, sir."

"This way, Christopher. Through that gate."

Through that gate and beyond *the* fence . . .

This fence where we had pressed our faces and felt the wind turn warm and held to the fence and forgot who we were or where we came from but dreamed of who we might be and where we might go . . .

This fence where had stood the boys who liked being boys who lived in a town and liked the town and fairly liked school and liked football and liked their fathers and mothers . . .

The boys who some time every hour of every day of every week thought on fire and stars and the fence beyond which they waited. . . . The boys who liked the rockets *more.*

Mother, Ralph, I'll see you. I'll be back.

Mother!

Ralph!

And, walking, I went beyond the fence.

Chrysalis

ROCKWELL DIDN'T LIKE the room's smell. Not so much McGuire's odor of beer, or Hartley's unwashed, tired smell—but the sharp insect tang rising from Smith's cold green-skinned body lying stiffly naked on the table. There was also a smell of oil and grease from the nameless machinery gleaming in one corner of the small room.

The man Smith was a corpse. Irritated, Rockwell rose from his chair and packed his stethoscope. "I must get back to the hospital. War rush. You understand, Hartley. Smith's been dead eight hours. If you want further information call a post-mortem—"

He stopped as Hartley raised a trembling, bony hand. Hartley gestured at the corpse—this corpse with brittle hard green shell grown solid over every inch of flesh. "Use your stethoscope again, for God's sake, Rockwell. Just once more. Please."

Rockwell wanted to complain, but instead he sighed, sat down, and used the stethoscope. You have to treat fellow doctors politely. You press your stethoscope into cold green flesh, pretending to listen—

The small, dimly lit room exploded around him. Exploded in one green cold pulsing. It hit Rockwell's ears like fists. It hit him. He saw his own fingers jerk over the recumbent corpse.

He heard a pulse.

Deep in the dark body the heart beat once. It sounded like an echo in fathoms of sea water.

Smith was dead, unbreathing, mummified. But at the core of that deadness—his heart lived. Lived, stirring like a small unborn baby!

Rockwell's crisp surgeon's fingers darted rapidly. He bent his head. In the light it was dark-haired, with flecks of gray in it. He had an even, level, nice-looking face. About thirty-five. He listened again and again, with sweat coming cold on his smooth cheeks. The pulse was not to be believed.

One heartbeat every thirty-five seconds.

Smith's respiration—how could you believe that, too—one

breath of air every four minutes. Lungcase movement imperceptible. Body temperature?

Sixty degrees.

Hartley laughed. It was not a pleasant laugh. More like an echo that had gotten lost. "He's alive," he said tiredly. "Yes, he is. He almost fooled me many times. I injected adrenalin to speed that pulse, but it was no use. He's been this way for twelve weeks. And I couldn't stand keeping him a secret any longer. That's why I phoned you, Rockwell. He's—unnatural."

The impossibility of it overwhelmed Rockwell with an inexplicable excitement. He tried to lift Smith's eyelids. He couldn't. They were webbed with epidermis. So were the lips. So were the nostrils. There was no way for Smith to breathe—

"Yet, he's breathing." Rockwell's voice was numb. He dropped his stethoscope blankly, picked it up, and saw his fingers shaking.

Hartley grew tall, emaciated, nervous over the table. "Smith didn't like my calling you. I called anyway. Smith warned me not to. Just an hour ago."

Rockwell's eyes dilated into hot black circles. "How could he warn you? He can't move."

Hartley's face, all razor-sharp bone, hard jaw, tight squinting gray eyes, twitched nervously. "Smith—*thinks.* I know his thoughts. He's afraid you'll expose him to the world. He hates me. Why? I want to kill him, that's why. Here." Hartley fumbled blindly for a blue-steel revolver in his rumpled, stained coat. "McGuire. Take this. Take it before I use it on Smith's foul body!"

McGuire pulled back, his thick red face afraid. "Don't like guns. You take it, Rockwell."

Like a scalpel, Rockwell made his voice slash. "Put the gun away, Hartley. After three months tending one patient you've got a psychological blemish. Sleep'll help that." He licked his lips. "What sort of disease has Smith got?"

Hartley swayed. His mouth moved words out slowly. Falling asleep on his feet, Rockwell realized. "Not diseased," Hartley managed to say. "Don't know what. But I resent him, like a kid resents the birth of a new brother or sister. He's wrong. Help me. Help me, will you?"

"Of course." Rockwell smiled. "My desert sanitarium's the place to check him over, good. Why—why Smith's the most incredible medical phenomenon in history. Bodies just don't act this way!"

He got no further. Hartley had his gun pointed right at Rockwell's stomach. "Wait. Wait. You—you're not going to *bury* Smith? I thought you'd help me. Smith's not healthy. I want him killed! He's dangerous! I know he is!"

Rockwell blinked. Hartley was obviously psychoneurotic. Didn't know what he was saying. Rockwell straightened his shoulders, feeling cool and calm inside. "Shoot Smith and I'll turn you in for murder. You're overworked mentally and physically. Put the gun away."

They stared at one another.

Rockwell walked forward quietly and took the gun, patted Hartley understandingly on the shoulder, and gave the weapon to McGuire, who looked at it as if it would bite him. "Call the hospital, McGuire. I'm taking a week off. Maybe longer. Tell them I'm doing research at the sanitarium."

A scowl formed in the red fat flesh of McGuire's face. "What do I do with this gun?"

Hartley shut his teeth together, hard. "Keep it. You'll want to use it—later."

Rockwell wanted to shout it to the world that he was sole possessor of the most incredible human in history. The sun was bright in the desert sanitarium room where Smith lay, not saying a word, on his table; his handsome face frozen into a green, passionless expression.

Rockwell walked into the room quietly. He used the stethoscope on the green chest. It scraped, making the noise of metal tapping a beetle's carapace.

McGuire stood by, eyeing the body dubiously, smelling of several recently acquired beers.

Rockwell listened intently. "The ambulance ride may have jolted him. No use taking a chance—"

Rockwell cried out.

Heavily, McGuire lumbered to his side. "What's wrong?"

"Wrong?" Rockwell stared about in desperation. He made one hand into a fist. "Smith's dying!"

"How do you know? Hartley said Smith plays possum. He's fooled you again—"

"No!" Rockwell worked furiously over the body, injecting drugs. Any drugs. All drugs. Swearing at the top of his voice. After all this trouble, he *couldn't* lose Smith. No, not now.

Shaking, jarring, twisting deep down inside, going completely liquidly mad, Smith's body sounded like dim volcanic tides bursting.

Rockwell fought to remain calm. Smith was a case unto himself. Normal treatment did nothing for him. What then? What?

Rockwell stared. Sunlight gleamed on Smith's hard flesh. Hot sunlight. It flashed, glinting off the stethoscope tip. The sun. As he watched, clouds shifted across the sky outside, taking the sun away. The room darkened. Smith's body shook into silence. The volcanic tides died.

"McGuire! Pull the blinds! Before the sun comes back!"

McGuire obeyed.

Smith's heart slowed down to its sluggish, infrequent breathing.

"Sunlight's bad for Smith. It counteracts something. I don't know what or why, but it's not good—" Rockwell relaxed. "Lord, I wouldn't want to lose Smith. Not for anything. He's different, making his own standards, doing things men have never done. Know something, McGuire?"

"What?"

"Smith's not in agony. He's not dying either. He wouldn't be better off dead, no matter what Hartley says. Last night as I arranged Smith on the stretcher, readying him for his trip to this sanitarium, I realized, suddenly, that Smith *likes* me."

"Gah. First Hartley. Now you. Did Smith *tell* you that?"

"He didn't tell me. But he's not unconscious under all that hard skin. He's aware. Yes, that's it. He's aware."

"Pure and simple—he's petrifying. He'll die. It's been weeks since he was fed. Hartley said so. Hartley fed him intravenously until the skin toughened so a needle couldn't poke through it."

Whining, the cubicle door swung slowly open. Rockwell started. Hartley, his sharp face relaxed after hours of sleep, his eyes still a bitter gray, hostile, stood tall in the door. "If you'll leave the room," he said, quietly, "I'll destroy Smith in a very few seconds. Well?"

"Don't come a step closer." Rockwell walked, feeling irritation, to Hartley's side. "Every time you visit, you'll have to be searched. Frankly, I don't trust you." There were no weapons. "Why didn't you tell me about the sunlight?"

"Eh?" Soft and slow Hartley said it. "Oh—yes. I forgot. I tried shifting Smith weeks ago. Sunlight struck him and he began *really* dying. Naturally, I stopped trying to move him. Smith seemed to know what was coming, vaguely. Perhaps he planned it; I'm not sure. While he was still able to talk and eat ravenously, before his body stiffened completely, he warned me not to move him for a twelve-week period. Said he didn't like the sun. Said it would spoil things. I thought he was joking. He wasn't. He ate like an animal, a hungry, wild animal, fell into a coma, and here he is—" Hartley swore under his breath. "I'd rather hoped you'd leave him in the sun long enough to kill him inadvertently."

McGuire shifted his two hundred fifty pounds. "Look here, now. What if we catch Smith's disease?"

Hartley looked at the body, his pupils shrinking. "Smith's not diseased. Don't you recognize degeneration when you see it? It's like cancer. You don't catch it, you inherit a tendency. I didn't begin to fear and hate Smith until a week ago when I discovered he was breathing and existing and thriving with his nostrils and mouth sealed. It can't happen. It mustn't happen."

McGuire's voice trembled. "What if you and I and Rockwell all turn green and a plague sweeps the country—what then?"

"Then," replied Rockwell, "if I'm wrong, perhaps I am, I'll die. But it doesn't worry me in the least."

He turned back to Smith and went on with his work.

A bell. A bell. Two bells, two bells. A dozen bells, a hundred bells. Ten thousand and a million clangorous, hammering, metal dinning bells. All born at once in the silence, squalling, screaming, hurting echoes, bruising ears!

Ringing, chanting with loud and soft, tenor and bass, low and high voices. Great-armed clappers knocking the shells and ripping air with the thrusting din of sound!

With all those bells ringing, Smith could not immediately

know where he was. He knew that he could not see, because his eyelids were sealed tight, knew he could not speak because his lips had grown together. His ears were clamped shut, but the bells hammered nevertheless.

He could not see. But yes, yes, he could, and it was like inside a small dark red cavern, as if his eyes were turned inward upon his skull. And Smith tried to twist his tongue, and suddenly, trying to scream, he knew his tongue was gone, that the place where it used to be was vacant, an itching spot that wanted a tongue but couldn't have it just *now*.

No tongue. Strange. Why? Smith tried to stop the bells. They ceased, blessing him with a silence that wrapped him up in a cold blanket. Things were happening. Happening.

Smith tried to twitch a finger, but he had no control. A foot, a leg, a toe, his head, everything. Nothing moved. Torso, limbs—immovable, frozen in a concrete coffin.

A moment later came the dread discovery that he was no longer breathing. Not with his lungs, anyway.

"BECAUSE I HAVE NO LUNGS!" he screamed. Inwardly he screamed and that mental scream was drowned, webbed, clotted, and journeyed drowsily down in a red, dark tide. A red drowsy tide that sleepily swathed the scream, garroted it, took it all away, making Smith rest easier.

I am not afraid, he thought. I understand that which I do not understand. I understand that I do not fear, yet know not the reason.

No tongue, no nose, no lungs.

But they would come later. Yes, they would. Things were—happening.

Through the pores of his shelled body air slid, like rain needling each portion of him, giving life. Breathing through a billion gills, breathing oxygen and nitrogen and hydrogen and carbon dioxide, and using it all. Wondering. Was his heart still beating?

But yes, it was beating. Slow, slow, slow. A red dim susurrance, a flood, a river surging around him, slow, slower, slower. So nice.

So restful.

The jigsaw pieces fitted together faster as the days drifted into weeks. McGuire helped. A retired surgeon-medico, he'd been

Rockwell's secretary for a number of years. Not much help, but good company.

Rockwell noted that McGuire joked gruffly about Smith, nervously; and a lot. Trying to be calm. But one day McGuire stopped, thought it over, and drawled, "Hey, it just came to me! Smith's alive. He should be dead. But he's alive. Good God!"

Rockwell laughed. "What in hell do you think I'm working on? I'm bringing an X-ray machine out next week so I can find out what's going on inside Smith's shell." Rockwell jabbed with a hypo needle. It broke on the hard shell.

Rockwell tried another needle, and another, until finally he punctured, drew blood, and placed the slides under the microscope for study. Hours later he calmly shoved a serum test under McGuire's red nose, and spoke quickly.

"Lord, I can't believe it. His blood's germicidal. I dropped a streptococci colony into it and the strep was annihilated in eight seconds! You could inject every known disease into Smith and he'd destroy them all, thrive on them!"

It was only a matter of hours until other discoveries. It kept Rockwell sleepless, tossing at night, wondering, theorizing the titanic ideas over and over. For instance—

Hartley'd fed Smith so many cc's of blood-food every day of his illness until recently. NONE OF THAT FOOD HAD EVER BEEN ELIMINATED. All of it had been stored, not in bulk-fats, but in a perfectly abnormal solution, an x-liquid contained in high concentrate form in Smith's blood. An ounce of it would keep a man well fed for three days. This x-liquid circulated through the body until it was actually needed, when it was seized upon and used. More serviceable than fat. Much more!

Rockwell glowed with his discovery. Smith had enough x-liquid stored in him to last months and months more. Self-sustaining.

McGuire, when told, contemplated his paunch sadly.

"I wish I stored my food that way."

That wasn't all. Smith needed little air. What air he had he seemed to acquire by an osmotic process through his skin. And he used every molecule of it. No waste.

"And," finished Rockwell, "eventually Smith's heart might even take vacations from beating, entirely!"

"Then he'd be dead," said McGuire.

"To you and I, yes. To Smith—maybe. Just maybe. Think of it, McGuire. Collectively, in Smith, we have a self-purifying blood stream demanding no replenishment but an interior one for months, having little breakdown and no elimination of wastes whatsoever because every molecule is utilized, self-evolving, and fatal to any and all microbic life. All this, and Hartley speaks of degeneration!"

Hartley was irritated when he heard of the discoveries. But he still insisted that Smith was degenerating. Dangerous.

McGuire tossed his two cents in. "How do we know that this isn't some super-microscopic disease that annihilates all other bacteria while it works on its victim. After all—malarial fever is sometimes used surgically to cure syphilis; why not a new bacillus that conquers all?"

"Good point," said Rockwell. "But we're not sick, are we?"

"It may have to incubate in our bodies."

"A typical old-fashioned doctor's response. No matter what happens to a man, he's 'sick'—if he varies from the norm. That's your idea, Hartley," declared Rockwell, "not mine. Doctors aren't satisfied unless they diagnose and label each case. Well, I think that Smith's healthy; so healthy you're afraid of him."

"You're crazy," said McGuire.

"Maybe. But I don't think Smith needs medical interference. He's working out his own salvation. You believe he's degenerating. I say he's growing."

"Look at Smith's skin," complained McGuire.

"Sheep in wolf's clothing. Outside, the hard, brittle epidermis. Inside, ordered regrowth, change. Why? I'm on the verge of knowing. These changes inside Smith are so violent that they need a shell to protect their action. And as for you, Hartley, answer me truthfully, when you were young, were you afraid of insects, spiders, things like that?"

"Yes."

"There you are. A phobia. A phobia you use against Smith. That explains your distaste for Smith's change."

In the following weeks, Rockwell went back over Smith's life carefully. He visited the electronics lab where Smith had been employed and fallen ill. He probed the room where Smith had spent the first weeks of his "illness" with Hartley in attendance. He examined the machinery there. Something about radiations . . .

While he was away from the sanitarium, Rockwell locked Smith tightly, and had McGuire guard the door in case Hartley got any unusual ideas.

The details of Smith's twenty-three years were simple. He had worked for five years in the electronics lab, experimenting. He had never been seriously sick in his life.

And as the days went by Rockwell took long walks in the dry-wash near the sanitarium, alone. It gave him time to think and solidify the incredible theory that was becoming a unit in his brain.

And one afternoon he paused by a night-blooming jasmine outside the sanitarium, reached up, smiling, and plucked a dark shining object off of a high branch. He looked at the object and tucked it in his pocket. Then he walked into the sanitarium.

He summoned McGuire in off the veranda. McGuire came. Hartley trailed behind, threatening, complaining. The three of them sat in the living quarters of the building.

Rockwell told them.

"Smith's not diseased. Germs can't live in him. He's *not* inhabited by banshees or weird monsters who've 'taken over' his body. I mention this to show I've left no stone untouched. I reject all normal diagnoses of Smith. I offer the most important, the most easily accepted possibility of—delayed hereditary mutation."

"Mutation?" McGuire's voice was funny.

Rockwell held up the shiny dark object in the light.

"I found this on a bush in the garden. It'll illustrate my theory to perfection. After studying Smith's symptoms, examining his laboratory, and considering several of these"—he twirled the dark object in his fingers—"I'm certain. It's metamorphosis. It's regeneration, change, mutation *after* birth. Here. Catch. This is Smith."

He tossed the object to Hartley. Hartley caught it.

"This is the chrysalis of a caterpillar," said Hartley.

Rockwell nodded. "Yes, it is."

"You don't mean to infer that Smith's a—*chrysalis*?"

"I'm positive of it," replied Rockwell.

Rockwell stood over Smith's body in the darkness of evening. Hartley and McGuire sat across the patient's room, quiet, listening. Rockwell touched Smith softly. "Suppose that there's more to life than just being born, living seventy years, and dying. Suppose there's one more great step up in man's existence, and Smith has been the first of us to make that step.

"Looking at a caterpillar, we see what we consider a static object. But it changes to a butterfly. Why? There are no final theories explaining it. It's progress, mainly. The pertinent thing is that a supposedly unchangeable object weaves itself into an intermediary object, wholly unrecognizable, a chrysalis, and emerges a butterfly. Outwardly the chrysalis looks dead. This is misdirection. Smith has misdirected us, you see. Outwardly, dead. Inwardly, fluids whirlpool, reconstruct, rush about with wild purpose. From grub to mosquito, from caterpillar to butterfly, from Smith to—?"

"Smith a chrysalis?" McGuire laughed heavily.

"Yes."

"Humans don't work that way."

"Stop it, McGuire. This evolutionary step's too great for your comprehension. Examine this body and tell me anything else. Skin, eyes, breathing, blood flow. Weeks of assimilating food for his brittle hibernation. Why did he eat all that food, why did he need that x-liquid in his body except for his metamorphosis? And the cause of it all was—radiations. Hard radiations from Smith's laboratory equipment. Planned or accidental I don't know. It touched some part of his essential gene-structure, some part of the evolutionary structure of man that wasn't scheduled for working for thousands of years yet, perhaps."

"Do you think that some day all men—?"

"The maggot doesn't stay in the stagnant pond, the grub in the soil, or the caterpillar on a cabbage leaf. They change, spreading across space in waves.

"Smith's the answer to the problem 'What happens next for man, where do we go from here?' We're faced with the blank wall of the universe and the fatality of living in that universe, and man as he is today is not prepared to go against the universe. The least exertion tires man, overwork kills his heart, disease his body. Maybe Smith will be prepared to answer the philosophers' problem of life's purpose. Maybe he can give it new purpose.

"Why, we're just petty insects, all of us, fighting on a pinhead planet. Man isn't meant to remain here and be sick and small and weak, but he hasn't discovered the secret of the greater knowledge yet.

"But—change man. Build your perfect man. Your—your superman, if you like. Eliminate petty mentality, give him complete physiological, neurological, psychological control of himself: give him clear, incisive channels of thought, give him an indefatigable blood stream, a body that can go months without outside food, that can adjust to any climate anywhere and kill any disease. Release man from the shackles of flesh and flesh misery and then he's no longer a poor, petty little man afraid to dream because he knows his frail body stands between him and the fulfillment of dreams, then he's ready to wage war, the only war worth waging—the conflict of man reborn and the whole damned universe!"

Breathless, voice hoarse, heart pounding, Rockwell tensed over Smith, placed his hands admiringly, firmly on the cold length of the chrysalis and shut his eyes. The power and drive and belief in Smith surged through him. He was right. He was right. He knew he was right. He opened his eyes and looked at McGuire and Hartley who were mere shadows in the dim shielded light of the room.

After a silence of several seconds, Hartley snuffed out his cigarette. "I don't believe that theory."

McGuire said, "How do you know Smith's not just a mess of jelly inside? Did you X-ray him?"

"I couldn't risk it, it might interfere with his change, like the sunlight did."

"So he's going to be a superman? What will he look like?"

"We'll wait and see."

"Do you think he can hear us talking about him now?"

"Whether or not he can, there's one thing certain—we're sharing a secret we weren't intended to know. Smith didn't plan on myself and McGuire entering the case. He had to make the most of it. But a superman doesn't like people to know about him. Humans have a nasty way of being envious, jealous, and hateful. Smith knew he wouldn't be safe if found out. Maybe that explains your hatred, too, Hartley."

They all remained silent, listening. Nothing sounded. Rockwell's blood whispered in his temples, that was all. There was Smith, no longer Smith, a container labeled SMITH, its contents unknown.

"If what you say *is* true," said Hartley, "then indeed we should destroy him. Think of the power over the world he would have. And if it affects his brain as I think it will affect it—he'll try to kill us when he escapes because we are the only ones who know about him. He'll hate us for prying."

Rockwell said it easily. "I'm not afraid."

Hartley remained silent. His breathing was harsh and loud in the room.

Rockwell came around the table, gesturing.

"I think we'd better say good-night now, don't you?"

The thin rain swallowed Hartley's car. Rockwell closed the door, instructed McGuire to sleep downstairs tonight on a cot fronting Smith's room, and then he walked upstairs to bed.

Undressing, he had time to conjure over all the unbelievable events of the passing weeks. A superman. Why not? Efficiency, strength—

He slipped into bed.

When. When does Smith emerge from his chrysalis? When?

The rain drizzled quietly on the roof of the sanitarium.

McGuire lay in the middle of the sound of rain and the earthquaking of thunder, slumbering on the cot, breathing heavy breaths. Somewhere, a door creaked, but McGuire breathed on. Wind gusted down the hall. McGuire grunted and rolled over. A door closed softly and the wind ceased.

Footsteps tread softly on the deep carpeting. Slow footsteps, aware and alert and ready. Footsteps. McGuire blinked his eyes and opened them.

In the dim light a figure stood over him.

Upstairs, a single light in the hall thrust down a yellow shaft near McGuire's cot.

An odor of crushed insect filled the air. A hand moved. A voice started to speak.

McGuire screamed.

Because the hand that moved into the light was green.

Green.

"Smith!"

McGuire flung himself ponderously down the hall, yelling.

"He's walking! He can't walk, but he's walking!"

The door rammed open under McGuire's bulk. Wind and rain shrieked in around him and he was gone into the storm, babbling.

In the hall, the figure was motionless. Upstairs a door opened swiftly and Rockwell ran down the steps. The green hand moved back out of the light behind the figure's back.

"Who is it?" Rockwell paused halfway.

The figure stepped into the light.

Rockwell's eyes narrowed.

"Hartley! What are you doing back here?"

"Something happened," said Hartley. "You'd better get McGuire. He ran out in the rain babbling like a fool."

Rockwell kept his thoughts to himself. He searched Hartley swiftly with one glance and then ran down the hall and out into the cold wind.

"McGuire! McGuire, come back you idiot!"

The rain fell on Rockwell's body as he ran. He found McGuire about a hundred yards from the sanitarium, blubbering,

"Smith—Smith's walking . . ."

"Nonsense. Hartley came back, that's all."

"I saw a green hand. It moved."

"You dreamed."

"No. No." McGuire's face was flabby pale, with water on it. "I saw a green hand, believe me. Why did Hartley come back? He—"

At the mention of Hartley's name, full comprehension came smashing to Rockwell. Fear leaped through his mind, a mad blur of warning, a jagged edge of silent screaming for help.

"Hartley!"

Shoving McGuire abruptly aside, Rockwell twisted and leaped back toward the sanitarium, shouting. Into the hall, down the hall—

Smith's door was broken open.

Gun in hand, Hartley was in the center of the room. He turned at the noise of Rockwell's running. They both moved simultaneously. Hartley fired his gun and Rockwell pulled the light switch.

Darkness. Flame blew across the room, profiling Smith's rigid body like a flash photo. Rockwell jumped at the flame. Even as he jumped, shocked deep, realizing why Hartley had returned. In that instant before the lights blinked out Rockwell had a glimpse of Hartley's fingers.

They were a brittle mottled green.

Fists then. And Hartley collapsing as the lights came on, and McGuire, dripping wet at the door, shook out the words, "Is—is Smith killed?"

Smith wasn't harmed. The shot had passed over him.

"This damned fool, this damned fool," cried Rockwell, standing over Hartley's numbed shape. "Greatest case in history and he tries to destroy it!"

Hartley came around, slowly. "I should've known. Smith warned you."

"Nonsense, he—" Rockwell stopped, amazed. Yes. That sudden premonition crashing into his mind. Yes. Then he glared at Hartley. "Upstairs with you. You're being locked in for the night. McGuire, you, too. So you can watch him."

McGuire croaked, "Hartley's hand. Look at it. It's green. It was Hartley in the hall—not Smith!"

Hartley stared at his fingers. "Pretty, isn't it?" he said, bitterly. "I was in range of those radiations for a long time at the start of Smith's illness. I'm going to be a—creature—like Smith. It's been this way for several days. I kept it hidden. I tried not to say anything. Tonight, I couldn't stand it any longer, and I came back to destroy Smith for what he's done to me . . ."

A dry noise racked, dryly, splitting the air. The three of them froze.

Three tiny flakes of Smith's chrysalis flicked up and then spiraled down to the floor.

Instantly, Rockwell was to the table, and gaping.

"It's starting to crack. From the collar-bone V to the navel, a microscopic fissure! He'll be out of his chrysalis soon!"

McGuire's jowls trembled. "And then what?"

Hartley's words were bitter sharp. "We'll have a superman. Question: what does a superman look like? Answer: nobody knows."

Another crust of flakes crackled open.

McGuire shivered. "Will you try to talk to him?"

"Certainly."

"Since when do—butterflies—speak?"

"Oh, Good God, McGuire!"

With the two others securely imprisoned upstairs, Rockwell locked himself into Smith's room and bedded down on a cot, prepared to wait through the long wet night, watching, listening, thinking.

Watching the tiny flakes flicking off the crumbling skin of chrysalis as the Unknown within struggled quietly outward.

Just a few more hours to wait. The rain slid over the house, pattering. What *would* Smith look like? A change in the earcups perhaps for greater hearing; extra eyes, maybe; a change in the skull structure, the facial setup, the bones of the body, the placement of organs, the texture of skin, a million and one changes.

Rockwell grew tired and yet was afraid to sleep. Eyelids heavy, heavy. What if he was wrong? What if his theory was entirely disjointed? What if Smith was only so much moving jelly inside? What if Smith was mad, insane—so different that he'd be a world menace? No. No. Rockwell shook his head groggily. Smith was perfect. Perfect. There'd be no room for evil thought in Smith. Perfect.

The sanitarium was death quiet. The only noise was the faint crackle of chrysalis flakes skimming to the hard floor . . .

Rockwell slept. Sinking into the darkness that blotted out the room as dreams moved in upon him. Dreams in which Smith arose, walked in stiff, parched gesticulations and Hartley, screaming, wielded an ax, shining, again and again into the green armor of the creature and hacked it into liquid horror. Dreams in which McGuire ran babbling through a rain of blood. Dreams in which—

Hot sunlight. Hot sunlight all over the room. It was morning. Rockwell rubbed his eyes, vaguely troubled by the fact that someone had raised the blinds. Someone had—he leaped! Sunlight! There was no way for the blinds to be up. They'd been down for weeks! He cried out.

The door was open. The sanitarium was silent. Hardly daring to turn his head, Rockwell glanced at the table. Smith should have been lying there.

He wasn't.

There was nothing but sunlight on the table. That—and a few remnants of shattered chrysalis. Remnants.

Brittle shards, a discarded profile cleft in two pieces, a shell segment that had been a thigh, a trace of arm, a splint of chest—these were the fractured remains of Smith!

Smith was gone. Rockwell staggered to the table, crushed. Scrabbling like a child among the rattling papyrus of skin. Then he swung about, as if drunk, and swayed out of the room and pounded up the stairs, shouting:

"Hartley! What did you do with him? Hartley! Did you think you could kill him, dispose of his body, and leave a few bits of shell behind to throw me off trail?"

The door to the room where McGuire and Hartley had slept was locked. Fumbling, Rockwell unlocked it. Both McGuire and Hartley were there.

"You're here," said Rockwell, dazed. "You weren't downstairs, then. Or did you unlock the door, come down, break in, kill Smith and—no, no."

"What's wrong?"

"Smith's gone! McGuire, did Hartley move out of this room?"

"Not all night."

"Then—there's only one explanation—Smith emerged from his chrysalis and escaped during the night! I'll never see him, I'll never get to see him, damn it! What a fool I was to sleep!"

"That settles it!" declared Hartley. "The man's dangerous or he would have stayed and let us see him! God only knows what he is."

"We've got to search, then. He can't be far off. We've got to search then! Quick now, Hartley. McGuire!"

McGuire sat heavily down. "I won't budge. Let him find himself. I've had enough."

Rockwell didn't wait to hear more. He went downstairs with Hartley close after him. McGuire puffed down a few moments later.

Rockwell moved wildly down the hall, halted at the wide windows that overlooked the desert and the mountains with morning shining over them. He squinted out, and wondered if there was any chance at all of finding Smith. The first superbeing. The first perhaps in a new long line. Rockwell sweated. Smith wouldn't leave without revealing himself to at least Rockwell. He couldn't leave. Or could he?

The kitchen door swung open, slowly.

A foot stepped through the door, followed by another. A hand lifted against the wall. Cigarette smoke moved from pursed lips.

"Somebody looking for me?"

Stunned, Rockwell turned. He saw the expression on Hartley's face, heard McGuire choke with surprise. The three of them spoke one word together, as if given their cue:

"Smith."

Smith exhaled cigarette smoke. His face was red-pink as he had been sunburnt, his eyes were a glittering blue. He was barefoot and his nude body was attired in one of Rockwell's old robes.

"Would you mind telling me where I am? What have I been doing for the last three or four months? Is this a—hospital or isn't it?"

Dismay slammed Rockwell's mind, hard. He swallowed.

"Hello. I. That is— Don't you remember—anything?"

Smith displayed his fingertips. "I recall turning green, if that's what you mean. Beyond that—nothing." He raked his pink hand through his nut-brown hair with the vigor of a creature newborn and glad to breathe again.

Rockwell slumped back against the wall. He raised his hands, with shock, to his eyes, and shook his head. Not believing what he saw he said, "What time did you come out of the chrysalis?"

"What time did I come out of—what?"

Rockwell took him down the hall to the next room and pointed to the table.

"I don't see what you mean," said Smith, frankly sincere. "I found myself standing in this room half an hour ago, stark naked."

"That's all?" said McGuire, hopefully. He seemed relieved.

Rockwell explained the origin of the chrysalis on the table.

Smith frowned. "That's ridiculous. Who *are* you?"

Rockwell introduced the others.

Smith scowled at Hartley. "When I first was sick you came, didn't you. I remember. At the radiations plant. But this is silly. What disease was it?"

Hartley's cheek muscles were taut wire. "No disease. Don't *you* know anything about it?"

"I find myself with strange people in a strange sanitarium. I find myself naked in a room with a man sleeping on a cot. I walk around the sanitarium, hungry. I go to the kitchen, find food, eat, hear excited voices, and then am accused of emerging from a chrysalis. What am I supposed to think? Thanks, by the way, for this robe, for food, and the cigarette I borrowed. I didn't want to wake you at first, Mr. Rockwell. I didn't know who you were and you looked dead tired."

"Oh, that's all right." Rockwell wouldn't let himself believe it. Everything was crumbling. With every word Smith spoke, his hopes were pulled apart like the crumpled chrysalis. "How do you feel?"

"Fine. Strong. Remarkable, when you consider how long I was under."

"Very remarkable," said Hartley.

"You can imagine how I felt when I saw the calendar. All those months—crack—gone. I wondered what in hell I'd been doing all that time."

"So have we."

McGuire laughed. "Oh, leave him alone, Hartley. Just because you hated him—"

"Hated?" Smith's brows went up. "Me? Why?"

"Here. This is why!" Hartley thrust his fingers out. "Your damned radiations. Night after night sitting by you in your laboratory. What can I do about it?"

"Hartley," warned Rockwell. "Sit down. Be quiet."

"I won't sit down and I won't be quiet! Are you both fooled by this imitation of a man, this pink fellow who's carrying on the greatest hoax in history? If you had any sense you'd destroy Smith before he escapes!"

Rockwell apologized for Hartley's outburst.

Smith shook his head. "No, let him talk. What's this about?"

"You know already!" shouted Hartley, angrily. "You've lain there for months, listening, planning. You can't fool me. You've got Rockwell bluffed, disappointed. He expected you to be a superman. Maybe you are. But whatever you are, you're not Smith any more. Not any more. It's just another of your misdirections. We weren't supposed to know all about you, and the world shouldn't know about you. You could kill us, easily, but you'd prefer to stay and convince us that you're normal. That's the best way. You could have escaped a few minutes ago, but that would have left the seeds of suspicion behind. Instead, you waited, to convince us that you're normal."

"He *is* normal," complained McGuire.

"No he's not. His mind's different. He's clever."

"Give him word association tests then," said McGuire.

"He's too clever for that, too."

"It's very simple, then. We take blood tests, listen to his heart, and inject serums into him."

Smith looked dubious. "I feel like an experiment, but if you really want to. This is damn silly."

That shocked Hartley. He looked at Rockwell. "Get the hypos," he said.

Rockwell got the hypos, thinking. Now, maybe after all, Smith was a superman. His blood. That superblood. Its ability to kill germs. His heartbeat. His breathing. Maybe Smith was a superman and didn't know it. Yes. Yes, maybe—

Rockwell drew blood from Smith and slid it under a microscope. His shoulders sagged. It was normal blood. When you dropped germs into it the germs took a normal length of time to die. The blood was no longer super-germicidal. The x-liquid, too, was gone. Rockwell sighed miserably. Smith's temperature was normal. So was his pulse. His sensory and nervous system responded according to rule.

"Well, that takes care of that," said Rockwell, softly.

Hartley sank into a chair, eyes widened, holding his head between bony fingers. He exhaled. "I'm sorry. I guess my—mind—it just imagined things. The months were so long. Night after night. I got obsessed, and afraid. I've made a fool out of myself. I'm sorry. I'm sorry." He stared at his green fingers. "But what about myself?"

Smith said, "I recovered. You'll recover, too, I guess. I can sympathize with you. But it wasn't bad . . . I don't really recall anything."

Hartley relaxed. "But—yes I guess you're right. I don't like the idea of my body getting hard, but it can't be helped. I'll be all right."

Rockwell was sick. The tremendous letdown was too much for him. The intense drive, the eagerness, the hunger and curiosity, the fire, had all sunk within him. So *this* was the man from the chrysalis? The same man who had gone in. All this waiting and wondering for nothing.

He gulped a breath of air, tried to steady his innermost, racing thoughts. Turmoil. This pink-cheeked, fresh-voiced man who sat before him smoking calmly, was no more than a man who had suffered some partial skin petrification, and whose glands had gone wild from radiation, but, nevertheless, just a man now and nothing more. Rockwell's mind, his over-imaginative, fantastic mind had seized upon each facet of the illness and built it into a perfect organism of wishful thinking. Rockwell was deeply shocked, deeply stirred and disappointed.

The question of Smith's living without food, his pure blood, low temperature, and the other evidences of superiority were now fragments of a strange illness. An illness and nothing more. Something that was over, down and gone and left nothing behind but brittle scraps on a sunlit table-top. There'd be a chance to watch Hartley now, if his illness progressed, and report the new sickness to the medical world.

But Rockwell didn't care about illness. He cared about perfection. And that perfection had been split and ripped and torn and it was gone. His dream was gone. His super-creature was gone. He didn't care if the whole world went hard, green, brittle-mad now.

Smith was shaking hands all around. "I'd better get back to Los Angeles. Important work for me to do at the plant. I have my old job waiting for me. Sorry I can't stay on. You understand."

"You should stay on and rest a few days, at least," said Rockwell. He hated to see the last wisp of his dream vanish.

"No thanks. I'll drop by your office in a week or so for another checkup, though, Doctor, if you like? I'll drop in every few weeks for the next year or so so you can check me, yes?"

"Yes. Yes, Smith. Do that, will you, please? I'd like to talk your illness over with you. You're lucky to be alive."

McGuire said, happily, "I'll drive you to L.A."

"Don't bother. I'll walk to Tujunga and get a cab. I want to walk. It's been so long, I want to see what it feels like."

Rockwell lent him an old pair of shoes and an old suit of clothes.

"Thanks, Doctor. I'll pay you what I owe you as soon as possible."

"You don't owe me a penny. It was interesting."

"Well, good-bye, Doctor. Mr. McGuire. Hartley."

"Good-bye, Smith."

"Good-bye."

Smith walked down the path to the dry wash, which was already baked dry by the late afternoon sun. He walked easily and happily and whistled. I wish I could whistle now, thought Rockwell tiredly.

Smith turned once, waved to them, and then he strode up the hillside and went on over it toward the distant city.

Rockwell watched him go as a small child watches his favorite sand castle eroded and annihilated by the waves of the sea. "I can't believe it," he said, over and over again. "I can't believe it. The whole thing's ending so soon, so abruptly for me. I'm dull and empty inside."

"Everything looks *rosy* to me!" chuckled McGuire happily.

Hartley stood in the sun. His green hands hung softly at his side and his white face was really relaxed for the first time in months, Rockwell realized. Hartley said, softly,

"I'll come out all right. I'll come out all right. Oh, thank God for that. Thank God for that. I won't be a monster. I won't be anything but myself." He turned to Rockwell.

"Just remember, remember, don't let them bury me by mistake. Don't let them bury me by mistake, thinking I'm dead. Remember that."

Smith took the path across the dry wash and up the hill. It was late afternoon already and the sun had started to vanish behind blue hills. A few stars were visible. The odor of water, dust, and distant orange blossoms hung in the warm air.

Wind stirred. Smith took deep breaths of air. He walked.

Out of sight, away from the sanitarium, he paused and stood very still. He looked up at the sky.

Tossing away the cigarette he'd been smoking, he mashed it precisely under one heel. Then he straightened his well-shaped body, tossed his brown hair back, closed his eyes, swallowed, and relaxed his fingers at his sides.

With nothing of effort, just a little murmur of sound, Smith lifted his body gently from the ground into the warm air.

He soared up quickly, quietly—and very soon he was lost among the stars as Smith headed for outer space . . .

Frost and Fire

DURING THE NIGHT, Sim was born. He lay wailing upon the cold cave stones. His blood beat through him a thousand pulses each minute. He grew, steadily.

Into his mouth his mother with feverish hands put the food. The nightmare of living was begun. Almost instantly at birth his eyes grew alert, and then, without half understanding why, filled with bright, insistent terror. He gagged upon the food, choked and wailed. He looked about, blindly.

There was a thick fog. It cleared. The outlines of the cave appeared. And a man loomed up, insane and wild and terrible. A man with a dying face. Old, withered by winds, baked like adobe in the heat. The man was crouched in a far corner of the cave, his eyes whitening to one side of his face, listening to the far wind trumpeting up above on the frozen night planet.

Sim's mother, trembling now and again, staring at the man, fed Sim pebble-fruits, valley-grasses and ice-nipples broken from the cavern entrances, and eating, eliminating, eating again, he grew larger, larger.

The man in the corner of the cave was his father! The man's eyes were all that was alive in his face. He held a crude stone dagger in his withered hands and his jaw hung loose and senseless.

Then, with a widening focus, Sim saw the old people sitting in the tunnel beyond this living quarter. And as he watched, they began to die.

Their agonies filled the cave. They melted like waxen images, their faces collapsed inward on their sharp bones, their teeth protruded. One minute their faces were mature, fairly smooth, alive, electric. The next minute a desiccation and burning away of their flesh occurred.

Sim thrashed in his mother's grasp. She held him. "No, no," she soothed him, quietly, earnestly, looking to see if this, too, would cause her husband to rise again.

With a soft swift padding of naked feet, Sim's father ran across the cave. Sim's mother screamed. Sim felt himself torn loose from her grasp. He fell upon the stones, rolling, shrieking with his new, moist lungs!

The webbed face of his father jerked over him, the knife was poised. It was like one of those prenatal nightmares he'd had again and again while still in his mother's flesh. In the next few blazing, impossible instants questions flicked through his brain. The knife was high, suspended, ready to destroy him. But the whole question of life in this cave, the dying people, the withering and the insanity, surged through Sim's new, small head. How was it that he understood? A newborn child? Can a newborn child think, see, understand, interpret? No. It was wrong! It was impossible. Yet it was happening! To him. He had been alive an hour now. And in the next instant perhaps dead!

His mother flung herself upon the back of his father, and beat down the weapon. Sim caught the terrific backwash of emotion from both their conflicting minds. "Let me kill him!" shouted the father, breathing harshly, sobbingly. "What has he to live for?"

"No, no!" insisted the mother, and her body, frail and old as it was, stretched across the huge body of the father, tearing at his weapon. "He must live! There may be a future for him! He may live longer than us, and be young!"

The father fell back against a stone crib. Lying there, staring, eyes glittering, Sim saw another figure inside that stone crib. A girl-child, quietly feeding itself, moving its delicate hands to procure food. His sister.

The mother wrenched the dagger from her husband's grasp, stood up, weeping and pushing back her cloud of stiffening gray hair. Her mouth trembled and jerked. "I'll kill you!" she said, glaring down at her husband. "Leave my children alone."

The old man spat tiredly, bitterly, and looked vacantly into the stone crib, at the little girl. "One-eighth of *her* life's over, already," he gasped. "And she doesn't know it. What's the use?"

As Sim watched, his own mother seemed to shift and take a tortured, smokelike form. The thin bony face broke out into a maze of wrinkles. She was shaken with pain and had to sit by him, shuddering and cuddling the knife to her shriveled breasts. She, like the old people in the tunnel, was aging, dying.

Sim cried steadily. Everywhere he looked was horror. A mind came to meet his own. Instinctively he glanced toward the stone crib. Dark, his sister, returned his glance. Their minds brushed like straying fingers. He relaxed somewhat. He began to learn.

The father sighed, shut his lids down over his green eyes. "Feed the child," he said, exhaustedly. "Hurry. It is almost dawn and it is our last day of living, woman. Feed him. Make him grow."

Sim quieted, and images, out of the terror, floated to him.

This was a planet next to the sun. The nights burned with cold, the days were like torches of fire. It was a violent, impossible world. The people lived in the cliffs to escape the incredible ice and the day of flame. Only at dawn and sunset was the air breath-sweet, flower-strong, and then the cave peoples brought their children out into a stony, barren valley. At dawn the ice thawed into creeks and rivers, at sunset the day fire died and cooled. In the intervals of even, livable temperature the people lived, ran, played, loved, free of the caverns; all life on the planet jumped, burst into life. Plants grew instantly, birds were flung like pellets across the sky. Smaller, legged animal life rushed frantically through the rocks; everything tried to get its living down in the brief hour of respite.

It was an unbearable planet. Sim understood this, a matter of hours after birth. Racial memory bloomed in him. He would live his entire life in the caves, with two hours a day outside. Here, in stone channels of air he would talk, talk incessantly with his people, sleep never, think, think and lie upon his back, dreaming; but never sleeping.

And he would live exactly eight days.

The *violence* of this thought! Eight days. Eight *short* days. It was wrong, impossible, but a fact. Even while in his mother's flesh some racial knowledge or some strange far wild voice had told him he was being formed rapidly, shaped and propelled out swiftly.

Birth was quick as a knife. Childhood was over in a flash. Adolescence was a sheet of lightning. Manhood was a dream, maturity a myth, old age an inescapably quick reality, death a swift certainty.

Eight days from now he'd stand half-blind, withering, dying, as his father now stood, staring uselessly at his own wife and child.

This day was an eighth part of his total life! He must enjoy every second of it. He must search his parents' thoughts for knowledge.

Because in a few hours they'd be dead.

This was so impossibly unfair. Was this all of life? In his prenatal state hadn't he dreamed of *long* lives, valleys not of blasted stone but green foliage and temperate clime? Yes! And if he'd dreamed then there must be truth in the visions. How could he seek and find the long life? Where? And how could he accomplish a life mission that huge and depressing in eight short, vanishing days?

How had his people gotten into such a condition?

As if at a button pressed, he saw an image. Metal seeds, blown across space from a distant green world, fighting with long flames, crashing on this bleak planet. From their shattered hulls tumbled men and women.

When? Long ago. Ten thousand days. The crash victims hid in the cliffs from the sun. Fire, ice and floods washed away the wreckage of the huge metal seeds. The victims were shaped and beaten like iron upon a forge. Solar radiations drenched them. Their pulses quickened, two hundred, five hundred, a thousand beats a minute. Their skins thickened, their blood changed. Old age came rushing. Children were born in the caves. Swifter, swifter, swifter the process. Like all this world's wild life, the men and women from the crash lived and died in a week, leaving children to do likewise.

So this is life, thought Sim. It was not spoken in his mind, for he knew no words, he knew only images, old memory, an awareness, a telepathy that could penetrate flesh, rock, metal. Somewhere along the line, they *had* developed telepathy, plus racial memory, the only good gifts, the only hope in all this terror. So thought Sim, I'm the five-thousandth in a long line of futile sons? What can I do to save myself from dying eight days from now? Is there escape?

His eyes widened, another image came to focus.

Beyond this valley of cliffs, on a low mountain lay a perfect, unscarred metal seed. A metal ship, not rusted or touched by the avalanches. The ship was deserted, whole, intact. It was the only ship of all these that had crashed that was still a unit, still usable. But it was so far away. There was no one in it to help. This ship, then, on the far mountain, was the destiny toward which he would grow. There was his only hope of escape.

His mind flexed.

In this cliff, deep down in a confinement of solitude, worked a handful of scientists. To these men, when he was old enough and wise enough, he must go. They, too, dreamed of escape, of long life, of green valleys and temperate weathers. They, too, stared longingly at that distant ship upon its high mountain, its metal so perfect it did not rust or age.

The cliff groaned.

Sim's father lifted his eroded, lifeless face.

"Dawn's coming," he said.

II

Morning relaxed the mighty granite cliff muscles. It was the time of the Avalanche.

The tunnels echoed to running bare feet. Adults, children pushed with eager, hungry eyes toward the outside dawn. From far out, Sim heard a rumble of rock, a scream, a silence. Avalanches fell into valley. Stones that had been biding their time, not quite ready to fall, for a million years let go their bulks, and where they had begun their journey as single boulders they smashed upon the valley floor in a thousand shrapnels and friction-heated nuggets.

Every morning at least one person was caught in the downpour.

The cliff people dared the avalanches. It added one more excitement to their lives, already too short, too headlong, too dangerous.

Sim felt himself seized up by his father. He was carried brusquely down the tunnel for a thousand yards, to where the daylight appeared. There was a shining insane light in his father's eyes. Sim could not move. He sensed what was going to happen. Behind his father, his mother hurried, bringing with her the little sister, Dark. "Wait! Be careful!" she cried to her husband.

Sim felt his father crouch, listening.

High in the cliff was a tremor, a shivering.

"Now!" bellowed his father, and leaped out.

An avalanche fell down at them!

Sim had accelerated impressions of plunging walls, dust, confusion. His mother screamed! There was a jolting, a plunging.

With one last step, Sim's father hurried him forward into the day. The avalanche thundered behind him. The mouth of the cave, where mother and Dark stood back out of the way, was choked with rubble and two boulders that weighed a hundred pounds each.

The storm thunder of the avalanche passed away to a trickle of sand. Sim's father burst out into laughter. "Made it! By the Gods! Made it alive!" And he looked scornfully at the cliff and spat. "Pagh!"

Mother and sister Dark struggled through the rubble. She cursed her husband. "Fool! You might have killed Sim!"

"I may yet," retorted the father.

Sim was not listening. He was fascinated with the remains of an avalanche afront of the next tunnel. Blood trickled out from under a rise of boulders, soaking into the ground. There was nothing more to be seen. Someone else had lost the game.

Dark ran ahead on lithe, supple feet, naked and certain.

The valley air was like a wine filtered between mountains. The heaven was a restive blue; not the pale scorched atmosphere of full day, nor the bloated, bruised black-purple of night, a-riot with sickly shining stars.

This was a tide pool. A place where waves of varying and violent temperatures struck, receded. Now the tide pool was quiet, cool, and its life moved abroad.

Laughter! Far away, Sim heard it. Why laughter? How could any of his people find time for laughing? Perhaps later he would discover why.

The valley suddenly blushed with impulsive color. Plant life, thawing in the precipitant dawn, shoved out from most unexpected sources. It flowered as you watched. Pale green tendrils appeared on scoured rocks. Seconds later, ripe globes of fruit twitched upon the blade-tips. Father gave Sim to his mother and harvested the momentary, volatile crop, thrust scarlet, blue, yellow fruits into a fur sack which hung at his waist.

Mother tugged at the moist new grasses, laid them on Sim's tongue.

His senses were being honed to a fine edge. He stored knowledge thirstily. He understood love, marriage, customs, anger, pity, rage, selfishness, shadings and subtleties, realities and reflections. One thing suggested another. The sight of green plant life whirled his mind like a gyroscope, seeking balance in a world where lack of time for explanations made a mind seek and interpret on its own. The soft burden of food gave him knowledge of his system, of energy, of movement. Like a bird newly cracking its way from a shell, he was almost a unit, complete, all-knowing. Heredity and telepathy that fed upon every mind and every wind had done all this for him. He grew excited with his ability.

They walked, mother, father and the two children, smelling the smells, watching the birds bounce from wall to wall of the valley like scurrying pebbles and suddenly the father said a strange thing:

"Remember?"

Remember what? Sim lay cradled. Was it any effort for them to remember, when they'd lived only seven days!

The husband and wife looked at each other.

"Was it only three days ago?" said the woman, her body shaking, her eyes closing to think. "I can't believe it. It is so unfair." She sobbed, then drew her hand across her face and bit her parched lips. The wind played at her gray hair. "Now it is my turn to cry. An hour ago it was you!"

"An hour is half a life."

"Come," she took her husband's arm. "Let us look at everything, because it will be our last looking."

"The sun'll be up in a few minutes," said the old man. "We must turn back now."

"Just one more moment," pleaded the woman.

"The sun will catch us."

"Let it catch me then!"

"You don't mean that."

"I mean nothing, nothing at all," cried the woman.

The sun was coming fast. The green in the valley burnt away. Searing wind blasted from over the cliffs. Far away where sun bolts hammered battlements of cliff, the huge stone faces shook their contents; those avalanches not already powdered down, were now released and fell like mantles.

"Dark!" shouted the father. The girl sprang over the warm floor of the valley, answering, her hair a black flag behind her. Hands full of green fruits, she joined them.

The sun rimmed the horizon with flame, the air convulsed dangerously with it, and whistled.

The cave people bolted, shouting, picking up their fallen children, bearing vast loads of fruit and grass with them back to their deep hideouts. In moments the valley was bare. Except for one small child someone had forgotten. He was running far out on the flatness, but he was not strong enough, and the engulfing heat was drifting down from the cliffs even as he was half across the valley.

Flowers were burnt into effigies, grasses sucked back into rocks like singed snakes. Flower seeds whirled and fell in the sudden furnace blast of wind, sown far into gullies and crannies, ready to blossom at sunset tonight, and then go to seed and die again.

Sim's father watched that child running, alone, out on the floor of the valley. He and his wife and Dark and Sim were safe in the mouth of their tunnel.

"He'll never make it," said father. "Do not watch him, woman. It's not a good thing to watch."

They turned away. All except Sim, whose eyes had caught a glint of metal far away. His heart hammered in him, and his eyes blurred. Far away, atop a low mountain, one of those metal seeds from space reflected a dazzling ripple of light! It was like one of his intra-embryo dreams fulfilled! A metal space seed, intact, undamaged, lying on a mountain! There was his future! There was his hope for survival! There was where he would go in a few days, when he was—strange thought—a grown man!

The sun plunged into the valley like molten lava.

The little running child screamed, the sun burned, and the screaming stopped.

Sim's mother walked painfully, with sudden age, down the tunnel, paused, reached up, broke off two last icicles that had formed during the night. She handed one to her husband, kept the other. "We will drink one last toast. To you, to the children."

"To *you*," he nodded to her. "To the children." They lifted the icicles. The warmth melted the ice down into their thirsty mouths.

III

All day the sun seemed to blaze and erupt into the valley. Sim could not see it, but the vivid pictorials in his parents' minds were sufficient evidence of the nature of the day fire. The light ran like mercury, sizzling and roasting the caves, poking inward, but never penetrating deeply enough. It lighted the caves. It made the hollows of the cliff comfortably warm.

Sim fought to keep his parents young. But no matter how hard he fought with mind and image, they became like mummies before him. His father seemed to dissolve from one stage of oldness to another. This is what will happen to me soon, thought Sim in terror.

Sim grew upon himself. He felt the digestive-eliminatory movements of his body. He was fed every minute, he was continually swallowing, feeding. He began to fit words to images and processes. Such a word was love. It was not an abstraction, but a process, a stir of breath, a smell of morning air, a flutter of heart, the curve of arm holding him, the look in the suspended face of his mother. He saw the processes, then searched behind her suspended face and there was the word, in her brain, ready to use. His throat prepared to speak. Life was pushing him, rushing him along toward oblivion.

He sensed the expansion of his fingernails, the adjustments of his cells, the profusion of his hair, the multiplication of his bones and sinew, the grooving of the soft pale wax of his brain. His brain at birth as clear as a circle of ice, innocent, unmarked, was, an instant later, as if hit with a thrown rock, cracked and marked and patterned in a million crevices of thought and discovery.

His sister, Dark, ran in and out with other little hothouse children, forever eating. His mother trembled over him, not eating, she had no appetite, her eyes were webbed shut.

"Sunset," said his father, at last.

The day was over. The light faded, a wind sounded.

His mother arose. "I want to see the outside world once more . . . just once more. . . ." She stared blindly, shivering.

His father's eyes were shut, he lay against the wall.

"I cannot rise," he whispered faintly. "I cannot."

"Dark!" The mother croaked, the girl came running. "Here," and Sim was handed to the girl. "Hold to Sim, Dark, feed him, care for him." She gave Sim one last fondling touch.

Dark said not a word, holding Sim, her great green eyes shining wetly.

"Go now," said the mother. "Take him out into the sunset time. Enjoy yourselves. Pick foods, eat. Play."

Dark walked away without looking back. Sim twisted in her grasp, looking over her shoulder with unbelieving, tragic eyes. He cried out and somehow summoned from his lips the first word of his existence:

"Why . . . ?"

He saw his mother stiffen. "The child spoke!"

"Aye," said his father. "Did you hear what he said?"

"I heard," said the mother quietly.

The last thing Sim saw of his living parents was his mother weakly, swayingly, slowly moving across the floor to lie beside her silent husband. That was the last time he ever saw them move.

IV

The night came and passed and then started the second day.

The bodies of all those who had died during the night were carried in a funeral procession to the top of a small hill. The procession was long, the bodies numerous.

Dark walked in the procession, holding the newly walking Sim by one hand. Only an hour before dawn Sim had learned to walk.

At the top of the hill, Sim saw once again the far off metal seed. Nobody ever looked at it, or spoke of it. Why? Was there some reason? Was it a mirage? Why did they not run toward it? Worship it? Try to get to it and fly away into space?

The funeral words were spoken. The bodies were placed upon the ground where the sun, in a few minutes, would cremate them.

The procession then turned and ran down the hill, eager to have their few minutes of free time running and playing and laughing in the sweet air.

Dark and Sim, chattering like birds, feeding among the rocks, exchanged what they knew of life. He was in his second day, she in her third. They were driven, as always, by the mercurial speed of their lives.

Another piece of his life opened wide.

Fifty young men ran down from the cliffs, holding sharp stones and rock daggers in their thick hands. Shouting, they ran off toward distant black, low lines of small rock cliffs.

"War!"

The thought stood in Sim's brain. It shocked and beat at him. These men were running to fight, to kill, over there in those small black cliffs where other people lived.

But why? Wasn't life short enough without fighting, killing?

From a great distance he heard the sound of conflict, and it made his stomach cold. "Why, Dark, why?"

Dark didn't know. Perhaps they would understand tomorrow. Now, there was the business of eating to sustain and support their lives. Watching Dark was like seeing a lizard forever flicking its pink tongue, forever hungry.

Pale children ran on all sides of them. One beetlelike boy scuttled up the rocks, knocking Sim aside, to take from him a particularly luscious red berry he had found growing under an outcrop.

The child ate hastily of the fruit before Sim could gain his feet. Then Sim hurled himself unsteadily, the two of them fell in a ridiculous jumble, rolling, until Dark pried them, squalling, apart.

Sim bled. A part of him stood off, like a god, and said, "This should not be. Children should not be this way. It is wrong!"

Dark slapped the little intruding boy away. "Get on!" she cried. "What's your name, bad one?"

"Chion!" laughed the boy. "Chion, Chion, Chion!"

Sim glared at him with all the ferocity in his small, unskilled features. He choked. This was his enemy. It was as if he'd waited for an enemy of person as well as scene. He had already understood the avalanches, the heat, the cold, the shortness of life, but these were things of places, of scene—mute, extravagant manifestations of unthinking nature, not motivated save by gravity and radiation. Here, now, in this stridulant Chion he recognized a thinking enemy!

Chion darted off, turned at a distance, taunting:

"Tomorrow I will be big enough to kill you!"

And he vanished around a rock.

More children ran, giggling, by Sim. Which of them would be friends, enemies? How could friends and enemies come about in this impossible, quick life time? There was no time to make either, was there?

Dark, knowing his thoughts, drew him away. As they searched for food, she whispered fiercely in his ear. "Enemies are made over things like stolen foods; gifts of long grasses make friends. Enemies come, too, from opinions and thoughts. In five seconds you've made an enemy for life. Life's so short enemies must be made quickly." And she laughed with an irony strange for one so young, who was growing older before her rightful time. "You must fight to protect yourself. Others, superstitious ones, will try killing you. There is a belief, a ridiculous belief, that if one kills another, the murderer partakes of the life energy of the slain, and therefore will live an extra day. You see? As long as that is believed, you're in danger."

But Sim was not listening. Bursting from a flock of delicate girls who tomorrow would be tall, quieter, and who day after that would gain breasts and the next day take husbands, Sim caught sight of one small girl whose hair was a violet-blue flame.

She ran past, brushed Sim, their bodies touched. Her eyes, white as silver coins, shone at him. He knew then that he'd found a friend, a love, a wife, one who would a week from now lie with him atop the funeral pyre as sunlight undressed their flesh from bone.

Only the glance, but it held them in mid-motion, one instant.

"Your name?" he shouted after her.

"Lyte!" she called laughingly back.

"I'm Sim," he answered, confused and bewildered.

"Sim!" she repeated it, flashing on. "I'll remember!"

Dark nudged his ribs. "Here, *eat*," she said to the distracted boy. "Eat or you'll never get big enough to catch her."

From nowhere, Chion appeared, running by. "Lyte!" he mocked, dancing malevolently along and away. "Lyte! I'll remember Lyte, too!"

Dark stood tall and reed slender, shaking her dark ebony clouds of hair, sadly. "I see your life before you, little Sim. You'll need weapons soon to fight for this Lyte one. Now, hurry—the sun's coming!"

They ran back to the caves.

V

One-fourth of his life was over! Babyhood was gone. He was now a young boy! Wild rains lashed the valley at nightfall. He watched new river channels cut in the valley, out past the mountain of the metal seed. He stored the knowledge for later use. Each night there was a new river, a bed newly cut.

"What's beyond the valley?" wondered Sim.

"No one's ever been beyond it," explained Dark. "All who tried to reach the plain were frozen to death or burnt. The only land we know's within half an hour's run. Half an hour out and half an hour back."

"No one has ever reached the metal seed, then?"

Dark scoffed. "The Scientists, they try. Silly fools. They don't know enough to stop. It's no use. It's too far."

The Scientists. The word stirred him. He had almost forgotten the vision he had in the moments before and after birth. His voice was eager. "Where are the Scientists?"

Dark looked away from him, "I wouldn't tell you if I knew. They'd kill you, experimenting! I don't want you joining them! Live your life, don't cut it in half trying to reach that silly metal thing on the mountain."

"I'll find out where they are from someone else, then!"

"No one'll tell you! They hate the Scientists. You'll have to find them on your own. And then what? Will you save us? Yes, save us, little boy!" Her face was sullen; already half her life was gone.

"We can't just sit and talk and eat," he protested. "And *nothing* else." He leapt up.

"Go find them!" she retorted acidly. "They'll help you

forget. Yes, yes," she spat it out. "Forget your life's over in just a few more days!"

Sim ran through the tunnels, seeking. Sometimes he half imagined where the Scientists were. But then a flood of angry thought from those around him, when he asked the direction to the Scientists' cave, washed over him in confusion and resentment. After all, it was the Scientists' fault that they had been placed upon this terrible world! Sim flinched under the bombardment of oaths and curses.

Quietly he took his seat in a central chamber with the children to listen to the grown men talk. This was the time of education, the Time of Talking. No matter how he chafed at delay, or how great his impatience, even though life slipped fast from him and death approached like a black meteor, he knew his mind needed knowledge. Tonight, then, was the night of school. But he sat uneasily. Only *five* more days of life.

Chion sat across from Sim, his thin-mouthed face arrogant.

Lyte appeared between the two. The last few hours had made her firmer footed, gentler, taller. Her hair shone brighter. She smiled as she sat beside Sim, ignoring Chion. And Chion became rigid at this and ceased eating.

The dialogue crackled, filled the room. Swift as heartbeats, one thousand, two thousand words a minute. Sim learned, his head filled. He did not shut his eyes, but lapsed into a kind of dreaming that was almost intra-embryonic in lassitude and drowsy vividness. In the faint background the words were spoken, and they wove a tapestry of knowledge in his head.

He dreamed of green meadows free of stones, all grass, round and rolling and rushing easily toward a dawn with no taint of freezing, merciless cold or smell of boiled rock or scorched monument. He walked across the green meadow. Overhead the metal seeds flew by in a heaven that was a steady, even temperature. Things were slow, slow, slow.

Birds lingered upon gigantic trees that took a hundred, two hundred, five thousand days to grow. Everything remained in its place, the birds did not flicker nervously at a hint of sun, nor did the trees suck back frighteneddly when a ray of sunlight poured over them.

In this dream people strolled, they rarely ran, the heart rhythm of them was evenly languid, not jerking and insane. Their kisses were long and lingering, not the parched mouthings and twitchings of lovers who had eight days to live. The grass remained, and did not burn away in torches. The dream people talked always of tomorrow and living and not tomorrow and dying. It all seemed so familiar that when Sim felt someone take his hand he thought it simply another part of the dream.

Lyte's hand lay inside his own. "Dreaming?" she asked.

"Yes."

"Things are balanced. Our minds, to even things, to balance the unfairness of our living, go back in on ourselves, to find what there is that is good to see."

He beat his hand against the stone floor again and again. "It does not make things fair! I hate it! It reminds me that there is something better, something I have missed! Why can't we be ignorant! Why can't we live and die without knowing that this is an abnormal living?" And his breath rushed harshly from his half-open, constricted mouth.

"There is purpose in everything," said Lyte. "This gives us purpose, makes us work, plan, try to find a way."

His eyes were hot emeralds in his face. "I walked up a hill of grass, very slowly," he said.

"The same hill of grass I walked an hour ago?" asked Lyte.

"Perhaps. Close enough to it. The dream is better than the reality." He flexed his eyes, narrowed them. "I watched people and they did not eat."

"Or talk?"

"Or talk, either. And we always are eating, always talking. Sometimes those people in the dream sprawled with their eyes shut, not moving a muscle."

As Lyte stared down into his face a terrible thing happened. He imagined her face blackening, wrinkling, twisting into knots of agedness. The hair blew out like snow about her ears, the eyes were like discolored coins caught in a web of lashes. Her teeth sank away from her lips, the delicate fingers hung like charred twigs from her atrophied wrists. Her beauty was consumed and wasted even as he watched, and when he seized her, in terror, he cried out, for he imagined his own hand corroded, and he choked back a cry.

"Sim, what's wrong?"

The saliva in his mouth dried at the taste of the words.

"Five more days . . ."

"The Scientists."

Sim started. Who'd spoken? In the dim light a tall man talked. "The Scientists crashed us on this world, and now have wasted thousands of lives and time. It's no use. It's no use. Tolerate them but give them none of your time. You only live once, remember."

Where were these hated Scientists? Now, after the Learning, the Time of Talking, he was ready to find them. Now, at least, he knew enough to begin his fight for freedom, for the ship!

"Sim, where're you going?"

But Sim was gone. The echo of his running feet died away down a shaft of polished stone.

It seemed that half the night was wasted. He blundered into a dozen dead ends. Many times he was attacked by the insane young men who wanted his life energy. Their superstitious ravings echoed after him. The gashes of their hungry fingernails covered his body.

He found what he looked for.

A half dozen men gathered in a small basalt cave deep down in the cliff lode. On a table before them lay objects which, though unfamiliar, struck harmonious chords in Sim.

The Scientists worked in sets, old men doing important work, young men learning, asking questions; and at their feet were three small children. They were a process. Every eight days there was an entirely new set of scientists working on any one problem. The amount of work done was terribly inadequate. They grew old, fell dead just when they were beginning their creative period. The creative time of any one individual was perhaps a matter of twelve hours out of his entire span. Three quarters of one's life was spent learning, a brief interval of creative power, then senility, insanity, death.

The men turned as Sim entered.

"Don't tell me we have a recruit?" said the eldest of them.

"I don't believe it," said another, younger one. "Chase him away. He's probably one of those warmongers."

"No, no," objected the elder one, moving with little shuffles of his bare feet toward Sim. "Come in, come in, boy." He had friendly eyes, slow eyes, unlike those of the swift inhabitants of the upper caves. Gray and quiet. "What do you want?"

Sim hesitated, lowered his head, unable to meet the quiet, gentle gaze. "I want to live," he whispered.

The old man laughed quietly. He touched Sim's shoulder. "Are you a new breed? Are you sick?" he queried of Sim, half seriously. "Why aren't you playing? Why aren't you readying yourself for the time of love and marriage and children? Don't you know that tomorrow night you'll be almost grown? Don't you realize that if you are not careful you'll miss all of life?" He stopped.

Sim moved his eyes back and forth with each query. He blinked at the instruments on the table top. "Shouldn't I be here?" he asked.

"Certainly," roared the old man, sternly. "But it's a miracle you are. We've had no volunteers from the rank and file for a thousand days! We've had to breed our own scientists, a closed unit! Count us! Six! Six men! And three children! Are we not overwhelming?" The old man spat upon the stone floor. "We ask for volunteers and the people shout back at us, 'Get someone else!' or 'We have no time!' And you know why they say that?"

"No." Sim flinched.

"Because they're selfish. They'd like to live longer, yes, but they know that anything they do cannot possibly insure their *own* lives any extra time. It might guarantee longer life to some future offspring of theirs. But they won't give up their love, their brief youth, give up one interval of sunset or sunrise!"

Sim leaned against the table, earnestly. "I understand."

"You do?" The old man stared at him blindly. He sighed and slapped the child's arm gently. "Yes, of course, you do. It's too much to expect anyone to understand, any more. You're rare."

The others moved in around Sim and the old man.

"I am Dienc. Tomorrow night Cort here will be in my place. I'll be dead by then. And the night after that someone else will be in Cort's place, and then you, if you work and believe—but first, I give you a chance. Return to your playmates if you want. There is someone you love? Return to her. Life is short.

Why should you care for the unborn to come? You have a right to youth. Go now, if you want. Because if you stay you'll have no time for anything but working and growing old and dying at your work. But it is good work. Well?"

Sim looked at the tunnel. From a distance the wind roared and blew, the smells of cooking and the patter of naked feet sounded, and the laughter of lovers was an increasingly good thing to hear. He shook his head, impatiently, and his eyes were wet.

"I will stay," he said.

VI

The third night and third day passed. It was the fourth night. Sim was drawn into their living. He learned about that metal seed upon the top of the far mountain. He heard of the original seeds—things called "ships" that crashed and how the survivors hid and dug in the cliffs, grew old swiftly and in their scrabbling to barely survive, forgot all science. Knowledge of mechanical things had no chance of survival in such a volcanic civilization. There was only NOW for each human.

Yesterday didn't matter, tomorrow stared them vividly in their very faces. But somehow the radiations that had forced their aging had also induced a kind of telepathic communication whereby philosophies and impressions were absorbed by the newborn. Racial memory, growing instinctively, preserved memories of another time.

"Why don't we go to that ship on the mountain?" asked Sim.

"It is too far. We would need protection from the sun," explained Dienc.

"Have you tried to make protection?"

"Salves and ointments, suits of stone and bird-wing and, recently, crude metals. None of which worked. In ten thousand more lifetimes perhaps we'll have made a metal in which will flow cool water to protect us on the march to the ship. But we work so slowly, so blindly. This morning, mature, I took up my instruments. Tomorrow, dying, I lay them down. What can one man do in one day? If we had ten thousand men, the problem would be solved. . . ."

"I will go to the ship," said Sim.

"Then you will die," said the old man. A silence had fallen on the room at Sim's words. Then the men stared at Sim. "You are a very selfish boy."

"Selfish!" cried Sim, resentfully.

The old man patted the air. "Selfish in a way I like. You want to live longer, you'll do anything for that. You will try for the ship. But I tell you it is useless. Yet, if you want to, I cannot stop you. At least you will not be like those among us who go to war for an extra few days of life."

"War?" asked Sim. "How can there be war here?"

And a shudder ran through him. He did not understand.

"Tomorrow will be time enough for that," said Dienc. "Listen to me, now."

The night passed.

VII

It was morning. Lyte came shouting and sobbing down a corridor, and ran full into his arms. She had changed again. She was older, again, more beautiful. She was shaking and she held to him. "Sim, they're coming after you!"

Bare feet marched down the corridor, surged inward at the opening. Chion stood grinning there, taller, too, a sharp rock in either of his hands. "Oh, there you are, Sim!"

"Go away!" cried Lyte savagely whirling on him.

"Not until we take Sim with us," Chion assured her. Then, smiling at Sim. "*If* that is, he is with us in the fight."

Dienc shuffled forward, his eye weakly fluttering, his bird-like hands fumbling in the air. "Leave!" he shrilled angrily. "This boy is a Scientist now. He works with us."

Chion ceased smiling. "There is better work to be done. We go now to fight the people in the farthest cliffs." His eyes glittered anxiously. "Of course, you will come with us, Sim?"

"No, no!" Lyte clutched at his arm.

Sim patted her shoulder, then turned to Chion. "Why are you attacking these people?"

"There are three extra days for those who go with us to fight."

"Three extra days! Of living?"

Chion nodded firmly. "If we win, we live eleven days instead of eight. The cliffs they live in, something about the mineral in it that protects you from radiation! Think of it, Sim, three long, good days of life. Will you join us?"

Dienc interrupted. "Get along without him. Sim is my pupil!"

Chion snorted. "Go die, old man. By sunset tonight you'll be charred bone. Who are you to order us? We are young, we want to live longer."

Eleven days. The words were unbelievable to Sim. Eleven days. Now he understood why there was war. Who wouldn't fight to have his life lengthened by almost half its total. So many more days of living! Yes. Why not, indeed!

"Three extra days," called Dienc, stridently, "*if* you live to enjoy them. If you're not killed in battle. *If. If!* You have never won yet. You have always lost!"

"But this time," Chion declared sharply, "we'll win!"

Sim was bewildered. "But we are all of the same ancestors. Why don't we all share the best cliffs?"

Chion laughed and adjusted a sharp stone in his hand. "Those who live in the best cliffs think they are better than us. That is always man's attitude when he has power. The cliffs there, besides, are smaller, there's room for only three hundred people in them."

Three extra days.

"I'll go with you," Sim said to Chion.

"Fine!" Chion was very glad, much too glad at the decision.

Dienc gasped.

Sim turned to Dienc and Lyte. "If I fight, and win, I will be half a mile closer to the Ship. And I'll have three extra days in which to strive to reach the Ship. That seems the only thing for me to do."

Dienc nodded, sadly. "It *is* the only thing. I believe you. Go along now."

"Good-bye," said Sim.

The old man looked surprised, then he laughed as at a little joke on himself. "That's right—I won't see you again, will I? Good-bye, then." And they shook hands.

They went out, Chion, Sim, and Lyte, together, followed

by the others, all children growing swiftly into fighting men. And the light in Chion's eyes was not a good thing to see.

Lyte went with him. She chose his rocks for him and carried them. She would not go back, no matter how he pleaded. The sun was just beyond the horizon and they marched across the valley.

"Please, Lyte, go back!"

"And wait for Chion to return?" she said. "He plans that when you die I will be his mate." She shook out her unbelievable blue-white curls of hair defiantly. "But I'll be with you. If you fall, I fall."

Sim's face hardened. He was tall. The world had shrunk during the night. Children packs screamed by hilarious in their food-searching and he looked at them with alien wonder: could it be only four days ago he'd been like these? Strange. There was a sense of many days in his mind, as if he'd really lived a thousand days. There was a dimension of incident and thought so thick, so multicolored, so richly diverse in his head that it was not to be believed so much could happen in so short a time.

The fighting men ran in clusters of two or three. Sim looked ahead at the rising line of small ebon cliffs. This, then, he said to himself, is my fourth day. And still I am no closer to the Ship, or to anything, not even—he heard the light tread of Lyte beside him—not even to her who bears my weapons and picks me ripe berries.

One-half of his life was gone. Or a third of it—If he won this battle. *If.*

He ran easily, lifting, letting fall his legs. This is the day of my physical awareness, as I run I feed, as I feed I grow and as I grow I turn eyes to Lyte with a kind of dizzying vertigo. And she looks upon me with the same gentleness of thought. This is the day of our youth. Are we wasting it? Are we losing it on a dream, a folly?

Distantly he heard laughter. As a child he'd questioned it. Now he understood laughter. This particular laughter was made of climbing high rocks and plucking the greenest blades and drinking the headiest vintage from the morning ices and eating of the rock-fruits and tasting of young lips in new appetite.

They neared the cliffs of the enemy.

He saw the slender erectness of Lyte. The new surprise of her white breasts; the neck where if you touched you could time her pulse; the fingers which cupped in your own were animate and supple and never still; the . . .

Lyte snapped her head to one side. "Look ahead!" she cried. "See what is to come—look only ahead."

He felt that they were racing by part of their lives, leaving their youth on the pathside, without so much as a glance.

"I am blind with looking at stones," he said, running.

"Find new stones, then!"

"I see stones—" His voice grew gentle as the palm of her hand. The landscape floated under him. Everything was like a fine wind, blowing dreamily. "I see stones that make a ravine that lies in a cool shadow where the stone-berries are thick as tears. You touch a boulder and the berries fall in silent red avalanches, and the grass is very tender . . ."

"I do not see it!" She increased her pace, turning her head away.

He saw the floss upon her neck, like the small moss that grows silvery and light on the cool side of pebbles, that stirs if you breathe the lightest breath upon it. He looked upon himself, his hands clenched as he heaved himself forward toward death. Already his hands were veined and youth-swollen.

Lyte handed him food to eat.

"I am not hungry," he said.

"Eat, keep your mouth full," she commanded sharply, "so you will be strong for battle."

"Gods!" He roared, anguished. "Who cares for battles!"

Ahead of them, rocks hailed down, thudding. A man fell with his skull split wide. The war was begun.

Lyte passed the weapons to him. They ran without another word until they entered the killing ground.

The boulders began to roll in a synthetic avalanche from the battlements of the enemy!

Only one thought was in his mind now. To kill, to lessen the life of someone else so he could live, to gain a foothold here and live long enough to make a stab at the ship. He ducked, he weaved, he clutched stones and hurled them up. His left hand held a flat stone shield with which he diverted the swiftly plummeting rocks. There was a spatting sound everywhere. Lyte ran with him, encouraging him. Two men dropped before him, slain, their breasts cleaved to the bone, their blood springing out in unbelievable founts.

It was a useless conflict. Sim realized instantly how insane the venture was. They could never storm the cliff. A solid wall of rocks rained down. A dozen men dropped with shards of ebony in their brains, a half dozen more showed drooping, broken arms. One screamed and the upthrust white joint of his knee was exposed as the flesh was pulled away by two successive blows of well-aimed granite. Men stumbled over one another.

The muscles in his cheeks pulled tight and he began to wonder why he had ever come. But his raised eyes, as he danced from side to side, weaving and bobbing, sought always the cliffs. He wanted to live there so intensely, to have his chance. He would have to stick it out. But the heart was gone from him.

Lyte screamed piercingly. Sim, his heart panicking, twisted and saw that her hand was loose at the wrist, with an ugly wound bleeding profusely on the back of the knuckles. She clamped it under her armpit to soothe the pain. The anger rose in him and exploded. In his fury he raced forward, throwing his missiles with deadly accuracy. He saw a man topple and flail down, falling from one level to another of the caves, a victim of his shot. He must have been screaming, for his lungs were bursting open and closed and his throat was raw, and the ground spun madly under his racing feet.

The stone that clipped his head sent him reeling and plunging back. He ate sand. The universe dissolved into purple whorls. He could not get up. He lay and knew that this was his last day, his last time. The battle raged around him, dimly he felt Lyte over him. Her hands cooled his head, she tried to drag him out of range, but he lay gasping and telling her to leave him.

"Stop!" shouted a voice. The whole war seemed to give pause. "Retreat!" commanded the voice swiftly. And as Sim watched, lying upon his side, his comrades turned and fled back toward home.

"The sun is coming, our time is up!" He saw their muscled backs, their moving, tensing, flickering legs go up and down. The dead were left upon the field. The wounded cried for help. But there was no time for the wounded. There was only time for swift men to run the gauntlet home and, their lungs aching and raw with heated air, burst into their tunnels before the sun burnt and killed them.

The sun!

Sim saw another figure racing toward him. It was Chion! Lyte was helping Sim to his feet, whispering helpfully to him. "Can you walk?" she asked. And he groaned and said, "I think so." "Walk then," she said. "Walk slowly, and then faster and faster. We'll make it. Walk slowly, start carefully. We'll make it, I know we will."

Sim got to his feet, stood swaying. Chion raced up, a strange expression cutting lines in his cheeks, his eyes shining with battle. Pushing Lyte abruptly aside he seized upon a rock and dealt Sim a jolting blow upon his ankle that laid wide the flesh. All of this was done quite silently.

Now he stood back, still not speaking, grinning like an animal from the night mountains, his chest panting in and out, looking from the thing he had done, to Lyte, and back. He got his breath. "He'll never make it," he nodded at Sim. "We'll have to leave him here. Come along, Lyte."

Lyte, like a cat-animal, sprang upon Chion, searching for his eyes, shrieking through her exposed, hard-pressed teeth. Her fingers stroked great bloody furrows down Chion's arms and again, instantly, down his neck. Chion, with an oath, sprang away from her. She hurled a rock at him. Grunting, he let it miss him, then ran off a few yards. "Fool!" he cried, turning to scorn her. "Come along with me. Sim will be dead in a few minutes. Come along!"

Lyte turned her back on him. "I will go if you carry me."

Chion's face changed. His eyes lost their gleaming. "There is no time. We would both die if I carried you."

Lyte looked through and beyond him. "Carry me, then, for that's how I wish it to be."

Without another word, glancing fearfully at the sun, Chion fled. His footsteps sped away and vanished from hearing. "May he fall and break his neck," whispered Lyte, savagely glaring at his form as it skirted a ravine. She returned to Sim. "Can you walk?"

Agonies of pain shot up his leg from the wounded ankle. He nodded ironically. "We could make it to the cave in two hours, walking. I have an idea, Lyte. Carry me." And he smiled with the grim joke.

She took his arm. "Nevertheless we'll walk. Come."

"No," he said. "We're staying here."

"But why?"

"We came to seek a home here. If we walk we will die. I would rather die here. How much time have we?"

Together they measured the sun. "A few minutes," she said, her voice flat and dull. She held close to him.

The black rocks of the cliff were paling into deep purples and browns as the sun began to flood the world.

What a fool he was! He should have stayed and worked with Dienc, and thought and dreamed.

With the sinews of his neck standing out defiantly he bellowed upward at the cliff holes.

"Send me down one man to do battle!"

Silence. His voice echoed from the cliff. The air was warm.

"It's no use," said Lyte, "They'll pay no attention."

He shouted again. "Hear me!" He stood with his weight on his good foot, his injured left leg throbbing and pulsating with pain. He shook a fist. "Send down a warrior who is no coward! I will not turn and run home! I have come to fight a fair fight! Send a man who will fight for the right to his cave! Him I will surely kill!"

More silence. A wave of heat passed over the land, receded.

"Oh, surely," mocked Sim, hands on naked hips, head back, mouth wide, "surely there's one among you not afraid to fight a cripple!" Silence. "No?" Silence.

"Then I have miscalculated you. I'm wrong. I'll stand here, then, until the sun shucks the flesh off my bone in black scraps, and call you the filthy names you deserve."

He got an answer.

"I do not like being called names," replied a man's voice.

Sim leaned forward, forgetting his crippled foot.

A huge man appeared in a cave mouth on the third level.

"Come down," urged Sim. "Come down, fat one, and kill me."

The man scowled seriously at his opponent a moment, then lumbered slowly down the path, his hands empty of any weapons. Immediately every cave above clustered with heads. An audience for this drama.

The man approached Sim. "We will fight by the rules, if you know them."

"I'll learn as we go," replied Sim.

This pleased the man and he looked at Sim warily, but not unkindly. "This much I will tell you," offered the man generously. "If you die, I will give your mate shelter and she will live as she pleases, because she is the wife of a good man."

Sim nodded swiftly. "I am ready," he said.

"The rules are simple. We do not touch each other, save with stones. The stones and the sun will do either of us in. Now is the time—"

VIII

A tip of the sun showed on the horizon. "My name is Nhoj," said Sim's enemy, casually taking up a handful of pebbles and stones, weighing them. Sim did likewise. He was hungry. He had not eaten for many minutes. Hunger was the curse of this planet's peoples—a perpetual demanding of empty stomachs for more, more food. His blood flushed weakly, shot tinglingly through veins in jolting throbs of heat and pressure, his rib cage shoved out, went in, shoved out again, impatiently.

"Now!" roared the three hundred watchers from the cliffs. "Now!" they clamored, the men and women and children balanced, in turmoil on the ledges. "Now! Begin!"

As if at a cue, the sun arose. It smote them a blow as with a flat, sizzling stone. The two men staggered under the molten impact, sweat broke from their naked thighs and loins, under their arms and on their faces was a glaze like fine glass.

Nhoj shifted his huge weight and looked at the sun as if in no hurry to fight. Then, silently, with no warning, he snapped out a pebble with a startling trigger-flick of thumb and forefinger. It caught Sim flat on the cheek, staggered him back, so that a rocket of unbearable pain climbed up his crippled foot and burst into nervous explosion at the pit of his stomach. He tasted blood from his bleeding cheek.

Nhoj moved serenely. Three more flicks of his magical hands and three tiny, seemingly harmless bits of stone flew like whistling birds. Each of them found a target, slammed it. The nerve centers of Sim's body! One hit his stomach so that ten hours' eating almost slid up his throat. A second got his forehead, a third his neck. He collapsed to the boiling sand. His knee made a wrenching sound on the hard earth. His face was colorless and his eyes, squeezed tight, were pushing tears out from the hot, quivering lids. But even as he had fallen he had let loose, with wild force, his handful of stones!

The stones purred in the air. One of them, and only one, struck Nhoj. Upon the left eyeball. Nhoj moaned and laid his hands in the next instant to his shattered eye.

Sim choked out a bitter, sighing laugh. This much triumph he had. The eye of his opponent. It would give him . . . Time. Oh, gods, he thought, his stomach retching sickly, fighting for breath, this is a world of time. Give me a little more, just a trifle!

Nhoj, one-eyed, weaving with pain, pelted the writhing body of Sim, but his aim was off now, the stones flew to one side or if they struck at all they were weak and spent and lifeless.

Sim forced himself half erect. From the corners of his eyes he saw Lyte, waiting, staring at him, her lips breathing words of encouragement and hope. He was bathed in sweat, as if a rain spray had showered him down.

The sun was now fully over the horizon. You could smell it. Stones glinted like mirrors, the sand began to roil and bubble. Illusions sprang up everywhere in the valley. Instead of one warrior Nhoj he was confronted by a dozen, each in an upright position, preparing to launch another missile. A dozen irregular warriors who shimmered in the golden menace of day, like bronze gongs smitten, quivered in one vision!

Sim was breathing desperately. His nostrils flared and sucked and his mouth drank thirstily of flame instead of oxygen. His lungs took fire like silk torches and his body was consumed. The sweat spilled from his pores to be instantly evaporated. He felt himself shriveling, shriveling in on himself, he imagined himself looking like his father, old, sunken, slight, withered! Where was the sand? Could he move? Yes. The world wriggled under him, but now he was on his feet.

There would be no more fighting.

A murmur from the cliff told this. The sunburnt faces of the high audience gaped and jeered and shouted encouragement to their warrior. "Stand straight, Nhoj, save your strength now! Stand tall and perspire!" they urged him. And Nhoj stood, swaying lightly, swaying slowly, a pendulum in an incandescent fiery breath from the skyline. "Don't move, Nhoj, save your heart, save your power!"

"The Test, The Test!" said the people on the heights. "The test of the sun."

And this was the worst part of the fight. Sim squinted painfully at the distorted illusion of cliff. He thought he saw his parents; father with his defeated face, his green eyes burning, mother with her hair blowing like a cloud of gray smoke in the fire wind. He must get up to them, live for and with them!

Behind him, Sim heard Lyte whimper softly. There was a whisper of flesh against sand. She had fallen. He did not dare turn. The strength of turning would bring him thundering down in pain and darkness.

His knees bent. If I fall, he thought, I'll lie here and become ashes. Where was Nhoj? Nhoj was there, a few yards from him, standing bent, slick with perspiration, looking as if he were being hit over the spine with great hammers of destruction.

"Fall, Nhoj! Fall!" thought Sim. "Fall, fall! Fall so I can take your place!"

But Nhoj did not fall. One by one the pebbles in his half-loose left hand plummeted to the broiling sands and Nhoj's lips peeled back, the saliva burned away from his lips and his eyes glazed. But he did not fall. The will to live was strong in him. He hung as if by a wire.

Sim fell to one knee!

"Ahh!" wailed the knowing voices from the cliff. They were watching death. Sim jerked his head up, smiling mechanically, foolishly as if caught in the act of doing something silly. "No, no," he insisted drowsily, and got back up again. There was so much pain he was all one ringing numbness. A whirring, buzzing, frying sound filled the land. High up, an avalanche came down like a curtain on a drama, making no noise. Everything was quiet except for a steady humming. He saw fifty images of Nhoj now, dressed in armors of sweat, eyes puffed with torture, cheeks sunken, lips peeled back like the rind of a drying fruit. But the wire still held him.

"Now," muttered Sim, sluggishly, with a thick, baked tongue between his blazing teeth. "Now I'll fall and lie and dream." He said it with slow, thoughtful pleasure. He planned it. He knew how it must be done. He would do it accurately. He lifted his head to see if the audience was watching.

They were gone!

The sun had driven them back in. All save one or two brave ones. Sim laughed drunkenly and watched the sweat gather on his dead hands, hesitate, drop off, plunge down toward sand and turn to steam halfway there.

Nhoj fell.

The wire was cut. Nhoj fell flat upon his stomach, a gout of blood kicked from his mouth. His eyes rolled back into a white, senseless insanity.

Nhoj fell. So did his fifty duplicate illusions.

All across the valley the winds sang and moaned and Sim saw a blue lake with a blue river feeding it and low white houses near the river with people going and coming in the houses and among the tall green trees. Trees taller than seven men, beside the river mirage.

"Now," explained Sim to himself at last, "Now I can fall. Right—into—that—lake."

He fell forward.

He was shocked when he felt the hands eagerly stop him in mid-plunge, lift him, hurry him off, high in the hungry air, like a torch held and waved, ablaze.

"How strange is death," he thought, and blackness took him.

He wakened to the flow of cool water on his cheeks.

He opened his eyes fearfully. Lyte held his head upon her lap, her fingers were moving food to his mouth. He was tremendously hungry and tired, but fear squeezed both of these things away. He struggled upward, seeing the strange cave contours overhead.

"What time is it?" he demanded.

"The same day as the contest. Be quiet," she said.

"The same day!"

She nodded amusedly. "You've lost nothing of your life.

This is Nhoj's cave. We are inside the black cliff. We will live three extra days. Satisfied? Lie down."

"Nhoj is dead?" He fell back, panting, his heart slamming his ribs. He relaxed slowly. "I won. I won," he breathed.

"Nhoj is dead. So were we, almost. They carried us in from outside only in time."

He ate ravenously. "We have no time to waste. We must get strong. My leg—" He looked at it, tested it. There was a swath of long yellow grasses around it and the ache had died away. Even as he watched, the terrific pulsings of his body went to work and cured away the impurities under the bandages. It *has* to be strong by sunset, he thought. It *has* to be.

He got up and limped around the cave like a captured animal. He felt Lyte's eyes upon him. He could not meet her gaze. Finally, helplessly, he turned.

She interrupted him. "You want to go on to the ship?" she asked, softly. "Tonight? When the sun goes down?"

He took a breath, exhaled it. "Yes."

"You couldn't possibly wait until morning?"

"No."

"Then I'll go with you."

"No!"

"If I lag behind, let me. There's nothing here for me."

They stared at each other a long while. He shrugged wearily.

"All right," he said, at last. "I couldn't stop you, I know that. We'll go together."

IX

They waited in the mouth of their new cave. The sun set. The stones cooled so that one could walk on them. It was almost time for the leaping out and the running toward the distant, glittering metal seed that lay on the far mountain.

Soon would come the rains. And Sim thought back over all the times he had watched the rains thicken into creeks, into rivers that cut new beds each night. One night there would be a river running north, the next a river running northeast, the third night a river running due west. The valley was continually cut and scarred by the torrents. Earthquakes and avalanches filled the old beds. New ones were the order of the day. It was this idea of the river and the directions of the river that he had turned over in his head for many hours. It might possibly— Well, he would wait and see.

He noticed how living in this new cliff had slowed his pulse, slowed everything. A mineral result, protection against the solar radiations. Life was still swift, but not as swift as before.

"Now, Sim!" cried Lyte.

They ran. Between the hot death and the cold one. Together, away from the cliffs, out toward the distant, beckoning ship.

Never had they run this way in their lives. The sound of their feet running was a hard, insistent clatter over vast oblongs of rock, down into ravines, up the sides, and on again. They raked the air in and out their lungs. Behind them the cliffs faded into things they could never turn back to now.

They did not eat as they ran. They had eaten to the bursting point in the cave, to save time. Now it was only running, a lifting of legs, a balancing of bent elbows, a convulsion of muscles, a slaking in of air that had been fiery and was now cooling.

"Are they watching us?"

Lyte's breathless voice snatched at his ears above the pound of his heart.

Who? But he knew the answer. The cliff peoples, of course. How long had it been since a race like this one? A thousand days? Ten thousand? How long since someone had taken the chance and sprinted with an entire civilization's eyes upon their backs, into gullies, across cooling plain. Were there lovers pausing in their laughter back there, gazing at the two tiny dots that were a man and woman running toward destiny? Were children eating of new fruits and stopping in their play to see the two people racing against time? Was Dienc still living, narrowing hairy eyebrows down over fading eyes, shouting them on in a feeble, rasping voice, shaking a twisted hand? Were there jeers? Were they being called fools, idiots? And in the midst of the name-calling, were people praying them on, hoping they would reach the ship?

Sim took a quick glance at the sky, which was beginning to bruise with the coming night. Out of nowhere clouds materialized and a light shower trailed across a gully two hundred yards ahead of them. Lightning beat upon distant mountains and there was a strong scent of ozone on the disturbed air.

"The halfway mark," panted Sim, and he saw Lyte's face half turn, longingly looking back at the life she was leaving. "Now's the time, if we want to turn back, we still have time. Another minute—"

Thunder snarled in the mountains. An avalanche started out small and ended up huge and monstrous in a deep fissure. Light rain dotted Lyte's smooth white skin. In a minute her hair was glistening and soggy with rain.

"Too late, now," she shouted over the patting rhythm of her own naked feet. "We've got to go ahead!"

And it was too late. Sim knew, judging the distances, that there was no turning back now.

His leg began to pain him. He favored it, slowing. A wind came up swiftly. A cold wind that bit into the skin. But it came from the cliffs behind them, helped rather than hindered them. An omen? he wondered. No.

For as the minutes went by it grew upon him how poorly he had estimated the distance. Their time was dwindling out, but they were still an impossible distance from the ship. He said nothing, but the impotent anger at the slow muscles in his legs welled up into bitterly hot tears in his eyes.

He knew that Lyte was thinking the same as himself. But she flew along like a white bird, seeming hardly to touch ground. He heard her breath go out and in her throat, like a clean, sharp knife in its sheath.

Half the sky was dark. The first stars were peering through lengths of black cloud. Lightning jiggled a path along a rim just ahead of them. A full thunderstorm of violent rain and exploding electricity fell upon them.

They slipped and skidded on moss-smooth pebbles. Lyte fell, scrambled up again with a burning oath. Her body was scarred and dirty. The rain washed over her.

The rain came down and cried on Sim. It filled his eyes and ran in rivers down his spine and he wanted to cry with it.

Lyte fell and did not rise, sucking her breath, her breasts quivering.

He picked her up and held her. "Run, Lyte, please, run!"

"Leave me, Sim. Go ahead!" The rain filled her mouth. There was water everywhere. "It's no use. Go on without me."

He stood there, cold and powerless, his thoughts sagging,

the flame of hope blinking out. All the world was blackness, cold falling sheaths of water, and despair.

"We'll walk, then," he said. "And keep walking, and resting."

They walked for fifty yards, easily, slowly, like children out for a stroll. The gully ahead of them filled with water that went sliding away with a swift wet sound, toward the horizon.

Sim cried out. Tugging at Lyte he raced forward. "A new channel," he said, pointing. "Each day the rain cuts a new channel. Here, Lyte!" He leaned over the floodwaters.

He dived in, taking her with him.

The flood swept them like bits of wood. They fought to stay upright, the water got into their mouths, their noses. The land swept by on both sides of them. Clutching Lyte's fingers with insane strength, Sim felt himself hurled end over end, saw flicks of lightning on high, and a new fierce hope was born in him. They could no longer run—well, then they would let the water do the running for them.

With a speed that dashed them against rocks, split open their shoulders, abraded their legs, the new, brief river carried them. "This way!" Sim shouted over a salvo of thunder and steered frantically toward the opposite side of the gully. The mountain where the ship lay was just ahead. They must not pass it by. They fought in the transporting liquid and were slammed against the far side. Sim leaped up, caught at an overhanging rock, locked Lyte in his legs, and drew himself hand over hand upward.

As quickly as it had come, the storm was gone. The lightning faded. The rain ceased. The clouds melted and fell away over the sky. The wind whispered into silence.

"The ship!" Lyte lay upon the ground. "The ship, Sim. This is the mountain of the ship!"

Now the cold came. The killing cold.

They forced themselves drunkenly up the mountain. The cold slid along their limbs, got into their arteries like a chemical and slowed them.

Ahead of them, with a fresh-washed sheen, lay the ship. It was a dream. Sim could not believe that they were actually so near it. Two hundred yards. One hundred and seventy yards.

The ground became covered with ice. They slipped and fell again and again. Behind them the river was frozen into a blue-white snake of cold solidity. A few last drops of rain from somewhere came down as hard pellets.

Sim fell against the bulk of the ship. He was actually touching it. Touching it! He heard Lyte whimpering in her constricted throat. This was the metal, the ship. How many others had touched it in the long days? He and Lyte had made it!

Then, as cold as the air, his veins were chilled.

Where was the entrance?

You run, you swim, you almost drown, you curse, you sweat, you work, you reach a mountain, you go up it, you hammer on metal, you shout with relief, and then—you can't find the entrance.

He fought to control himself. Slowly, he told himself, but not too slowly, go around the ship. The metal slid under his searching hands, so cold that his hands, sweating, almost froze to it. Now, far around to the side. Lyte moved with him. The cold held them like a fist. It began to squeeze.

The entrance.

Metal. Cold, immutable metal. A thin line of opening at the sealing point. Throwing all caution aside, he beat at it. He felt his stomach seething with cold. His fingers were numb, his eyes were half frozen in their sockets. He began to beat and search and scream against the metal door. "Open up! Open up!" He staggered. He had struck something . . . A *click*!

The air lock sighed. With a whispering of metal on rubber beddings, the door swung softly sidewise and vanished back.

He saw Lyte run forward, clutch at her throat, and drop inside a small shiny chamber. He shuffled after her, blankly.

The air-lock door sealed shut behind him.

He could not breathe. His heart began to slow, to stop.

They were trapped inside the ship now, and something was happening. He sank down to his knees and choked for air.

The ship he had come to for salvation was now slowing his pulse, darkening his brain, poisoning him. With a starved, faint kind of expiring terror, he realized that he was dying.

Blackness.

He had a dim sense of time passing, of thinking, struggling, to make his heart go quick, quick. . . . To make his eyes focus. But the fluid in his body lagged quietly through his settling veins and he heard his pulses thud, pause, thud, pause and thud again with lulling intermissions.

He could not move, not a hand or leg or finger. It was an effort to lift the tonnage of his eyelashes. He could not shift his face even, to see Lyte lying beside him.

From a distance came her irregular breathing. It was like the sound a wounded bird makes with his dry, unraveled pinions. She was so close he could almost feel the heat of her; yet she seemed a long way removed.

I'm getting cold! he thought. Is this death? This slowing of blood, of my heart, this cooling of my body, this drowsy thinking of thoughts?

Staring at the ship's ceiling he traced its intricate system of tubes and machines. The knowledge, the purpose of the ship, its actions, seeped into him. He began to understand in a kind of revealing lassitude just what these things were his eyes rested upon. Slow. Slow.

There was an instrument with a gleaming white dial. Its purpose?

He drudged away at the problem, like a man underwater.

People had used the dial. Touched it. People had repaired it. Installed it. People had dreamed of it before the building, before the installing, before the repairing and touching and using. The dial contained memory of use and manufacture, its very shape was a dream-memory telling Sim why and for what it had been built. Given time, looking at anything, he could draw from it the knowledge he desired. Some dim part of him reached out, dissected the contents of things, analyzed them.

This dial measured time!

Millions of hours of time!

But how could that be? Sim's eyes dilated, hot and glittering. Where were humans who needed such an instrument?

Blood thrummed and beat behind his eyes. He closed them.

Panic came to him. The day was passing. I am lying here, he thought, and my life slips away. I cannot move. My youth is passing. How long before I can move?

Through a kind of porthole he saw the night pass, the day come, the day pass, and again another night. Stars danced frostily.

I will lie here for four or five days, wrinkling and withering, he thought. This ship will not let me move. How much better if I had stayed in my home cliff, lived, enjoyed this short life. What good has it done to come here? I'm missing all the twilights and dawns. I'll never touch Lyte, though she's here at my side.

Delirium. His mind floated up. His thoughts whirled through the metal ship. He smelled the razor-sharp smell of joined metal. He heard the hull contract with night, relax with day.

Dawn.

Already—another dawn!

Today I would have been fully grown. His jaw clenched. I must get up. I must move. I must enjoy this time.

But he didn't move. He felt his blood pump sleepily from chamber to red chamber in his heart, on down and around through his dead body, to be purified by his folding and unfolding lungs.

The ship grew warm. From somewhere a machine clicked. Automatically the temperature cooled. A controlled gust of air flushed the room.

Night again. And then another day.

He lay and saw four days of his life pass.

He did not try to fight. It was no use. His life was over.

He didn't want to turn his head now. He didn't want to see Lyte with her face like his tortured mother's—eyelids like gray ash flakes, eyes like beaten, sanded metal, cheeks like eroded stones. He didn't want to see a throat like parched thongs of yellow grass, hands the pattern of smoke risen from a fire, breasts like desiccated rinds and hair stubbly and unshorn as moist gray weeds!

And himself? How did *he* look? Was his jaw sunken, the flesh of his eyes pitted, his brow lined and age-scarred?

His strength began to return. He felt his heart beating so slow that it was amazing. One hundred beats a minute. Impossible. He felt so cool, so thoughtful, so easy.

His head fell over to one side. He stared at Lyte. He shouted in surprise.

She was young and fair.

She was looking at him, too weak to say anything. Her eyes were like tiny silver medals, her throat curved like the arm of a child. Her hair was blue fire eating at her scalp, fed by the slender life of her body.

Four days had passed and still she was young . . . no, younger than when they had entered the ship. She was still adolescent.

He could not believe it.

Her first words were, "How long will this last?"

He replied, carefully, "I don't know."

"We are still young."

"The ship. Its metal is around us. It cuts away the sun and the things that came from the sun to age us."

Her eyes shifted thoughtfully. "Then, if we stay here—"

"We'll remain young."

"Six more days? Fourteen more? Twenty?"

"More than that, maybe."

She lay there, silently. After a long time she said, "Sim?"

"Yes."

"Let's stay here. Let's not go back. If we go back now, you know what'll happen to us . . . ?"

"I'm not certain."

"We'll start getting old again, won't we?"

He looked away. He stared at the ceiling and the clock with the moving finger. "Yes. We'll grow old."

"What if we grow old—instantly. When we step from the ship won't the shock be too much?"

"Maybe."

Another silence. He began to move his limbs, testing them. He was very hungry. "The others are waiting," he said.

Her next words made him gasp. "The others are dead," she said. "Or will be in a few hours. All those we knew back there are old."

He tried to picture them old. Dark, his sister, bent and senile with time. He shook his head, wiping the picture away. "They may die," he said. "But there are others who've been born."

"People we don't even know."

"But, nevertheless, *our* people," he replied. "People who'll live only eight days, or eleven days unless we help them."

"But we're *young*, Sim! We can *stay* young!"

He didn't want to listen. It was too tempting a thing to listen to. To stay here. To live. "We've already had more time than the others," he said. "I need workers. Men to heal this ship. We'll get on our feet now, you and I, and find food, eat, and see if the ship is movable. I'm afraid to try to move it myself. It's so big. I'll need help."

"But that means running back all that distance!"

"I know." He lifted himself weakly. "But I'll do it."

"How will you get the men back here?"

"We'll use the river."

"*If* it's there. It *may* be somewhere else."

"We'll wait until there *is* one, then. I've got to go back, Lyte. The son of Dienc is waiting for me, my sister, your brother, are old people, ready to die, and waiting for some word from us—"

After a long while he heard her move, dragging herself tiredly to him. She put her head upon his chest, her eyes closed, stroking his arm. "I'm sorry. Forgive me. You have to go back. I'm a selfish fool."

He touched her cheek, clumsily. "You're human. I understand you. There's nothing to forgive."

They found food. They walked through the ship. It was empty. Only in the control room did they find the remains of a man who must have been the chief pilot. The others had evidently bailed out into space in emergency lifeboats. This pilot, sitting at his controls, alone, had landed the ship on a mountain within sight of other fallen and smashed crafts. Its location on high ground had saved it from the floods. The pilot himself had died, probably of heart failure, soon after landing. The ship had remained here, almost within reach of the other survivors, perfect as an egg, but silent, for—how many thousand days? If the pilot had lived, what a different thing life might have been for the ancestors of Sim and Lyte. Sim, thinking of this, felt the distant, ominous vibration of war. How had the war between worlds come out? Who had won? Or had both planets lost and never bothered trying to pick up survivors? Who had been right? Who was the enemy? Were Sim's people of the guilty or innocent side? They might never know.

He checked the ship hurriedly. He knew nothing of its workings, yet as he walked its corridors, patted its machines, he learned from it. It needed only a crew. One man couldn't possibly set the whole thing running again. He laid his hand upon one round, snoutlike machine. He jerked his hand away, as if burnt.

"Lyte!"

"What is it?"

He touched the machine again, caressed it, his hand trembled violently, his eyes welled with tears, his mouth opened and closed, he looked at the machine, loving it, then looked at Lyte.

"With this machine—" he stammered, softly, incredulously. "With— With this machine I can—"

"What, Sim?"

He inserted his hand into a cuplike contraption with a lever inside. Out of the porthole in front of him he could see the distant line of cliffs. "We were afraid there might never be another river running by this mountain, weren't we?" he asked, exultantly.

"Yes, Sim, but—"

"There *will* be a river. And I *will* come back, tonight! And I'll bring men with me. Five hundred men! Because with this machine I can blast a river bottom all the way to the cliffs, down which the waters will rush, giving myself and the men a swift, sure way of traveling back!" He rubbed the machine's barrellike body. "When I touched it, the life and method of it burnt into me! Watch!" He depressed the lever.

A beam of incandescent fire lanced out from the ship, screaming.

Steadily, accurately, Sim began to cut away a riverbed for the storm waters to flow in. The night was turned to day by its hungry eating.

The return to the cliffs was to be carried out by Sim alone. Lyte was to remain in the ship, in case of any mishap. The trip back seemed, at first glance, to be impossible. There would be no river rushing to cut his time, to sweep him along toward his destination. He would have to run the entire distance in the dawn, and the sun would get him, catch him before he'd reached safety.

"The only way to do it is to start *before* sunrise."

"But you'd be frozen, Sim."

"Here." He made adjustments on the machine that had

just finished cutting the riverbed in the rock floor of the valley. He lifted the smooth snout of the gun, pressed the lever, left it down. A gout of fire shot toward the cliffs. He fingered the range control, focused the flame end three miles from its source. Done. He turned to Lyte. "But I don't understand," she said.

He opened the air-lock door. "It's bitter cold out, and half an hour yet till dawn. If I run parallel to the flame from the machine, close enough to it, there'll not be much heat, but enough to sustain life, anyway."

"It doesn't sound safe," Lyte protested.

"*Nothing* does, on this world." He moved forward. "I'll have a half-hour start. That should be enough to reach the cliffs."

"But if the machine should fail while you're still running near its beam?"

"Let's not think of that," he said.

A moment later he was outside. He staggered as if kicked in the stomach. His heart almost exploded in him. The environment of his world forced him into swift living again. He felt his pulse rise, kicking through his veins.

The night was cold as death. The heat ray from the ship sliced across the valley, humming, solid and warm. He moved next to it, very close. One misstep in his running and—

"I'll be back," he called to Lyte.

He and the ray of light went together.

In the early morning the peoples in the caves saw the long finger of orange incandescence and the weird whitish apparition floating, running along beside it. There was muttering and moaning and many sighs of awe.

And when Sim finally reached the cliffs of his childhood he saw alien peoples swarming there. There were no familiar faces. Then he realized how foolish it was to expect familiar faces. One of the older men glared down at him. "Who're you?" he shouted. "Are you from the enemy cliff? What's your name?"

"I am Sim, the son of Sim!"

"Sim!"

An old woman shrieked from the cliff above him. She came hobbling down the stone pathway. "Sim, Sim, it *is* you!"

He looked at her, frankly bewildered. "But I don't know you," he murmured.

"Sim, don't you recognize me? Oh, Sim, it's me! Dark!"

"Dark!"

He felt sick at his stomach. She fell into his arms. This old, trembling woman with the half-blind eyes, his sister.

Another face appeared above. That of an old man. A cruel, bitter face. It looked down at Sim and snarled. "Drive him away!" cried the old man. "He comes from the cliff of the enemy. He's lived there! He's still young! Those who go there can never come back among us. Disloyal beast!" And a rock hurtled down.

Sim leaped aside, pulling the old woman with him.

A roar came from the people. They ran toward Sim, shaking their fists. "Kill him, kill him!" raved the old man, and Sim did not know who he was.

"Stop!" Sim held out his hands. "I come from the ship!"

"The ship?" The people slowed. Dark clung to him, looking up into his young face, puzzling over its smoothness.

"Kill him, kill him, kill him!" croaked the old man, and picked up another rock.

"I offer you ten days, twenty days, thirty more days of life!"

The people stopped. Their mouths hung open. Their eyes were incredulous.

"Thirty days?" It was repeated again and again. "How?"

"Come back to the ship with me. Inside it, one can live forever!"

The old man lifted high a rock, then, choking, fell forward in an apoplectic fit, and tumbled down the rocks to lie at Sim's feet.

Sim bent to peer at the ancient one, at the raw, dead eyes, the loose, sneering lips, the crumpled, quiet body.

"Chion!"

"Yes," said Dark behind him, in a croaking, strange voice. "Your enemy. Chion."

That night two hundred men started for the ship. The water ran in the new channel. One hundred of them were drowned or lost behind in the cold. The others, with Sim got through to the ship.

Lyte awaited them, and threw wide the metal door.

The weeks passed. Generations lived and died in the cliffs,

while the scientists and workers labored over the ship, learning its functions and its parts.

On the last day, two dozen men moved to their stations within the ship. Now there was a destiny of travel ahead.

Sim touched the control plates under his fingers.

Lyte, rubbing her eyes, came and sat on the floor next to him, resting her head against his knee, drowsily. "I had a dream," she said, looking off at something far away. "I dreamed I lived in caves in a cliff on a cold-hot planet where people grew old and died in eight days."

"What an impossible dream," said Sim. "People couldn't possibly live in such a nightmare. Forget it. You're awake now."

He touched the plates gently. The ship rose and moved into space.

Sim was right.

The nightmare was over at last.

Powerhouse

THE HORSES MOVED gently to a stop, and the man and his wife gazed down into a dry, sandy valley. The woman sat lost in her saddle; she hadn't spoken for hours, didn't know a good word to speak. She was trapped somewhere between the hot, dark pressure of the storm-clouded Arizona sky and the hard, granite pressure of the wind-blasted mountains. A few drops of cool rain fell on her trembling hands.

She looked over at her husband wearily. He sat his dusty horse easily, with a firm quietness. She closed her eyes and thought of how she had been all of these mild years until today. She wanted to laugh at the mirror she was holding up to herself, but there was no way of doing even that; it would be somewhat insane. After all, it might just be the pushing of this dark weather, or the telegram they had taken from the messenger on horseback this morning, or the long journey now to town.

There was still an empty world to cross, and she was cold.

"I'm the lady who was never going to need religion," she said quietly, her eyes shut.

"What?" Berty, her husband, glanced over at her.

"Nothing," she whispered, shaking her head. In all the years, how certain she had been. Never, never would she have need of a church. She had heard fine people talk on and on of religion and waxed pews and calla lilies in great bronze buckets and vast bells of churches in which the preacher rang like a clapper. She had heard the shouting kind and the fervent, whispery kind, and they were all the same. Hers was simply not a pew-shaped spine.

"I just never had a reason ever to sit in a church," she had told people. She wasn't vehement about it. She just walked around and lived and moved her hands that were pebble-smooth and pebble-small. Work had polished the nails of those hands with a polish you could never buy in a bottle. The touching of children had made them soft, and the raising of children had made them temperately stern, and the loving of a husband had made them gentle.

And now, death made them tremble.

"Here," said her husband. And the horses dusted down the trail to where an odd brick building stood beside a dry wash. The building was all glazed green windows, blue machinery, red tile, and wires. The wires ran off on high-tension towers to the farthest directions of the desert. She watched them go, silently, and, still held by her thoughts, turned her gaze back to the strange storm-green windows and the burning-colored bricks.

She had never slipped a ribbon in a Bible at a certain significant verse, because though her life in this desert was a life of granite, sun, and the steaming away of the waters of her flesh, there had never been a threat in it to her. Always things had worked out before the necessity had come for sleepless dawns and wrinkles in the forehead. Somehow, the very poisonous things of life had passed her by. Death was a remote storm rumor beyond the farthest range.

Twenty years had blown in tumbleweeds, away, since she'd come West, worn this lonely trapping man's gold ring, and taken the desert as a third, and constant, partner to their living. None of their four children had ever been fearfully sick or near death. She had never had to get down on her knees except for the scrubbing of an already well-scrubbed floor.

Now all that was ended. Here they were riding toward a remote town because a simple piece of yellow paper had come and said very plainly that her mother was dying.

And she could not imagine it—no matter how she turned her head to see or turned her mind to look in on itself. There were no rungs anywhere to hold to, going either up or down, and her mind, like a compass left out in a sudden storm of sand, was suddenly blown free of all its once-clear directions, all points of reference worn away, the needle spinning without purpose, around, around. Even with Berty's arms on her back it wasn't enough. It was like the end of a good play and the beginning of an evil one. Someone she loved was actually going to die. This was impossible!

"I've got to stop," she said, not trusting her voice at all, so she made it sound irritated to cover her fear.

Berty knew her as no irritated woman, so the irritation did not carry over and fill him up. He was a capped jug; the contents there for sure. Rain on the outside didn't stir the brew. He side-ran his horse to her and took her hand gently. "Sure," he said. He squinted at the eastern sky. "Some clouds piling up black there. We'll wait a bit. It might rain. I wouldn't want to get caught in it."

Now she was irritated at her own irritation, one fed upon the other, and she was helpless. But rather than speak and risk the cycle's commencing again, she slumped forward and began to sob, allowing her horse to be led until it stood and tramped its feet softly beside the red brick building.

She slid down like a parcel into his arms, and he held her as she turned in on his shoulder; then he set her down and said, "Don't look like there's people here." He called, "Hey, there!" and looked at the sign on the door: *Danger. Bureau of Electric Power.*

There was a great insect humming all through the air. It sang in a ceaseless, bumbling tone, rising a bit, perhaps falling just a bit, but keeping the same pitch. Like a woman humming between pressed lips as she makes a meal in the warm twilight over a hot stove. They could see no movement within the building; there was only the gigantic humming. It was the sort of noise you would expect the sun-shimmer to make rising from hot railroad ties on a blazing summer day, when there is that flurried silence and you see the air eddy and whorl and ribbon, and expect a sound from the process but get nothing but an arched tautness of the eardrums and the tense quiet.

The humming came up through her heels, into her medium-slim legs, and thence to her body. It moved to her heart and touched it, as the sight of Berty just sitting on a top rail of the corral often did. And then it moved on to her head and the slenderest niches in the skull and set up a singing, as love songs and good books had done once on a time.

The humming was everywhere. It was as much a part of the soil as the cactus. It was as much a part of the air as the heat.

"What is it?" she asked, vaguely perplexed, looking at the building.

"I don't know much about it except it's a powerhouse," said Berty. He tried the door. "It's open," he said, surprised. "I wish someone was around." The door swung wide and the pulsing hum came out like a breath of air over them, louder.

They entered together into the solemn, singing place. She held him tightly, arm in arm.

It was a dim undersea place, smooth and clean and polished, as if something or other was always coming through and coming through and nothing ever stayed, but always there was motion and motion, invisible and stirring and never settling. On each side of them as they advanced were what first appeared to be people standing quietly, one after the other, in a double line. But these resolved into round, shell-like machines from which the humming sprang. Each black and gray and green machine gave forth golden cables and lime-colored wires, and there were silver metal pouches with crimson tabs and white lettering, and a pit like a washtub in which something whirled as if rinsing unseen materials at invisible speeds. The centrifuge raced so fast it stood still. Immense snakes of copper looped down from the twilight ceiling, and vertical pipes webbed up from cement floor to fiery brick wall. And the whole of it was as clean as a bolt of green lightning and smelled similarly. There was a crackling, eating sound, a dry rustling as of paper; flickers of blue fire shuttled, snapped, sparked, hissed where wires joined porcelain bobbins and green glass insulation.

Outside, in the real world, it began to rain.

She didn't want to stay in this place; it was no place to stay, with its people that were not people but dim machines and its music like an organ caught and pressed on a low note and a high note. But the rain washed every window and Berty said, "Looks like it'll last. Might have to stay the night here. It's late, anyhow. I'd better get the stuff in."

She said nothing. She wanted to be getting on. Getting on to what thing in what place, there was really no way of knowing. But at least in town she would hold onto the money and buy the tickets and hold them tight in her hand and hold onto a train which would rush and make a great noise, and get off the train, and get on another horse, or get into a car hundreds of miles away and ride again, and stand at last by her dead or alive mother. It all depended on time and breath. There were many places she would pass through, but none of them would offer a thing to her except ground for her feet, air for her nostrils, food for her numb mouth. And these were worse than nothing. Why go to her mother at all, say words, and make gestures? she wondered. What would be the use?

The floor was clean as a solid river under her. When she moved forward on it, it sent echoes cracking back and forth like small, faint gunshots through the room. Any word that was spoken came back as from a granite cavern.

Behind her, she heard Berty setting down the equipment. He spread two gray blankets and put out a little collection of tinned foods.

It was night. The rain still streamed on the high green-glazed windows, rinsing and making patterns of silk that flowed and intermingled in soft clear curtains. There were occasional thunderclaps which fell and broke upon themselves in avalanches of cold rain and wind hitting sand and stone.

Her head lay upon a folded cloth, and no matter how she turned it, the humming of the immense powerhouse worked up through the cloth into her head. She shifted, shut her eyes, and adjusted herself, but it went on and on. She sat up, patted the cloth, lay back down.

But the humming was there.

She knew without looking, by some sense deep in herself, that her husband was awake. There was no year she could remember when she hadn't known. It was some subtle difference in his breathing. It was the absence of sound, rather; no sound of breathing at all, save at long, carefully thought-out intervals. She knew then that he was looking at her in the rainy darkness, concerned with her, taking great care of his breath.

She turned in the darkness. "Berty?"

"Yes?"

"I'm awake too," she said.

"I know," he said.

They lay, she very straight, very rigid, he in a half curl, like a hand relaxed, half bent inward. She traced this dark, easy curve and was filled with incomprehensible wonder.

"Berty," she asked, and paused a long while, "how . . . how are you like you are?"

He waited a moment. "How do you mean?" he said.

"How do you rest?" She stopped. It sounded very bad. It sounded so much like an accusation, but it was not, really. She knew him to be a man concerned with all things, a man who could see in darknesses and who was not conceited because of his ability. He was worried for her now, and for her mother's life or death, but he had a way of worrying that seemed indifferent and irresponsible. It was neither of the two. His concern was all in him, deep; but it lay side by side with some faith, some belief that accepted it, made it welcome, and did not fight it. Something in him took hold of the sorrow first, got acquainted with it, knew each of its traceries before passing the message on to all of his waiting body. His body held a faith like a maze, and the sorrow that struck into him was lost and gone before it finally reached where it wanted to hurt him. Sometimes this faith drove her into a senseless anger, from which she recovered quickly, knowing how useless it was to criticize something as contained as a stone in a peach.

"Why didn't I ever catch it from you?" she said at last.

He laughed a little bit, softly. "Catch what?"

"I caught everything else. You shook me up and down in other ways. I didn't know anything but what you taught me." She stopped. It was hard to explain. Their life had been like the warm blood in a person passing through tissues quietly, both ways.

"Everything but religion," she said. "I never caught that from you."

"It's not a catching thing," he said. "Someday you just relax. And there it is."

Relax, she thought. Relax what? The body. But how to relax the mind? Her fingers twitched beside her. Her eyes wandered idly about the vast interior of the powerhouse. The machines stood over her in dark silhouettes with little sparkles crawling on them. The humming-humming-humming crept along her limbs.

Sleepy. Tired. She drowsed. Her eyes lidded and opened and lidded and opened. The humming-humming filled her marrow as if small hummingbirds were suspended in her body and in her head.

She traced the half-seen tubing up and up into the ceiling, and she saw the machines and heard the invisible whirlings.

She suddenly became very alert in her drowsiness. Her eyes moved swiftly up and up and then down and across, and the humming-singing of the machines grew louder and louder, and her eyes moved, and her body relaxed; and on the tall, green windows she saw the shadows of the high-tension wires rushing off into the raining night.

Now the humming was in her, her eyes jerked, she felt herself yanked violently upright. She felt seized by a whirling dynamo, around, around in a whirl, out, out, into the heart of whirling invisibilities, fed into, accepted by a thousand copper wires, and shot, in an instant, over the earth!

She was everywhere at once!

Streaking along high monster towers in instants, sizzling between high poles where small glass knobs sat like crystal-green birds holding the wires in their non-conductive beaks, branching in four directions, eight secondary directions, finding towns, hamlets, cities, racing on to farms, ranches, haciendas, she descended gently like a widely filamented spider web upon a thousand square miles of desert!

The earth was suddenly more than many separate things, more than houses, rocks, concrete roads, a horse here or there, a human in a shallow, boulder-topped grave, a prickling of cactus, a town invested with its own light surrounded by night, a million apart things. Suddenly it all had one pattern encompassed and held by the pulsing electric web.

She spilled out swiftly into rooms where life was rising from a slap on a naked child's back, into rooms where life was leaving bodies like the light fading from an electric bulb—the filament glowing, fading, finally colorless. She was in every town, every house, every room, making light-patterns over hundreds of miles of land; seeing, hearing everything, not alone any more, but one of thousands of people, each with his ideas and his faiths.

Her body lay, a lifeless reed, pale and trembling. Her mind, in all its electric tensity, was flung about this way, that, down vast networks of powerhouse tributary.

Everything balanced. In one room she saw life wither; in another, a mile away, she saw wineglasses lifted to the newborn, cigars passed, smiles, handshakes, laughter. She saw the pale, drawn faces of people at white deathbeds, heard how they understood and accepted death, saw their gestures, felt their feelings, and saw that they, too, were lonely in themselves, with no way to get to the world to see the balance, see it as she was seeing it now.

She swallowed. Her eyelids flickered and her throat burned under her upraised fingers.

She was not alone.

The dynamo had whirled and flung her with centrifugal force out along a thousand lines into a million glass capsules screwed into ceilings, plucked into light by a pull of a cord or a twist of a knob or a flick of a switch.

The light could be in any room; all that was needed was to touch the switch. All rooms were dark until light came. And here she was, in all of them at once. And she was not alone. Her grief was but one part of a vast grief, her fear only one of countless others. And this grief was only a half thing. There was the other half; of things born, of comfort in the shape of a new child, of food in the warmed body, of colors for the eye and sounds in the awakened ear, and spring wild flowers for the smelling.

Whenever a light blinked out, life threw another switch; rooms were illumined afresh.

She was with those named Clark and those named Gray and the Shaws and Martins and Hanfords, the Fentons, the Drakes, the Shattucks, the Hubbells, and the Smiths. Being alone was not alone, except in the mind. You had all sorts of peekholes in your head. A silly, strange way to put it, perhaps, but there were the holes; the ones to see through and see that the world was there and people in it, as hard put to and uneasy as yourself; and there were the holes for hearing, and the one for speaking out your grief and getting rid of it, and the holes for knowing the changes of season through the scents of summer grain or winter ice or autumn fires. They were there to be used so that one was not alone. Loneliness was a shutting of the eyes. Faith was a simple opening.

The light-net fell upon all the world she had known for twenty years, herself blended with every line. She glowed and pulsed and was gentled in the great easy fabric. It lay across the land, covering each mile like a gentle, warm, and humming blanket. She was everywhere.

In the powerhouse the turbines whirled and hummed and the electric sparks, like little votive candles, jumped and clustered upon bent elbows of electric piping and glass. And the machines stood like saints and choruses, haloed now yellow, now red, now green, and a massed singing beat along the roof hollows and echoed down in endless hymns and chants. Outside, the wind clamored at the brick walls and drenched the glazed windows with rain; inside, she lay upon her small pillow and suddenly began to cry.

Whether it was with understanding, acceptance, joy, resignation, she couldn't know. The singing went on, higher and higher, and she was everywhere. She put out her hand, caught hold of her husband, who was still awake, his eyes fixed at the ceiling. Perhaps he had run everywhere, too, in this instant, through the network of light and power. But then, he had always been everywhere at once. He felt himself a unit of a whole and therefore he was stable; to her, unity was new and shaking. She felt his arms suddenly around her and she pressed her face into his shoulder for a long while, hard, while the humming and the humming climbed higher, and she cried freely, achingly, against him. . . .

In the morning the desert sky was very clear. They walked from the powerhouse quietly, saddled their horses, cinched on all of the equipment, and mounted.

She settled herself and sat there under the blue sky. And slowly she was aware of her back, and her back was straight, and she looked at her alien hands on the reins, and they had ceased trembling. And she could see the far mountains; there was no blur nor a running-of-color to things. All was solid stone touching stone, and stone touching sand, and sand touching wild flower, and wild flower touching the sky in one continuous clear flow, everything definite and of a piece.

"Wope!" cried Berty, and the horses walked slowly off, away from the brick building, through the cool sweet morning air.

She rode handsomely and she rode well, and in her, like a stone in a peach, was a peacefulness. She called to her husband as they slowed on a rise, "Berty!"

"Yes?"

"Can we . . ." she asked.

"Can we what?" he said, not hearing the first time.

"Can we come here again sometime?" she asked, nodding back toward the powerhouse. "Once in a while? Some Sunday?"

He looked at her and nodded slowly. "I reckon. Yes. Sure. I reckon so."

And as they rode on into town she was humming, humming a strange soft tune, and he glanced over and listened to it, and it was the sound you would expect to hear from sun-warmed railroad ties on a hot summer day when the air rises in a shimmer, flurried and whorling; a sound in one key, one pitch, rising a little, falling a little, humming, humming, but constant, peaceful, and wondrous to hear.

Pillar of Fire

HE CAME OUT of the earth, hating. Hate was his father; hate was his mother.

It was good to walk again. It was good to leap up out of the earth, off of your back, and stretch your cramped arms violently and try to take a deep breath!

He *tried*. He cried out.

He couldn't breathe. He flung his arms over his face and tried to breathe. It was impossible. He walked on the earth, he came out of the earth. But he was dead. He couldn't breathe. He could take air into his mouth and force it half down his throat, with withered moves of long-dormant muscles, wildly, wildly! And with this little air he could shout and cry! He wanted to have tears, but he couldn't make them come, either. All he knew was that he was standing upright, he was dead, he shouldn't be walking! He couldn't breathe and yet he stood.

The smells of the world were all about him. Frustratedly, he tried to smell the smells of autumn. Autumn was burning the land down into ruin. All across the country the ruins of summer lay; vast forests bloomed with flame, tumbled down timber on empty, unleafed timber. The smoke of the burning was rich, blue, and invisible.

He stood in the graveyard, hating. He walked through the world and yet could not taste nor smell of it. He heard, yes. The wind roared on his newly opened ears. But he was dead. Even though he walked he knew he was dead and should expect not too much of himself or this hateful living world.

He touched the tombstone over his own empty grave. He knew his own name again. It was a good job of carving.

WILLIAM LANTRY

That's what the gravestone said.
His fingers trembled on the cool stone surface.

BORN 1898—DIED 1933

Born *again* . . . ?

What year? He glared at the sky and the midnight autumnal stars moving in slow illuminations across the windy black. He read the tiltings of centuries in those stars. Orion thus and so, Aurega here! and where Taurus? *There!*

His eyes narrowed. His lips spelled out the year:

"2349."

An odd number. Like a school sum. They used to say a man couldn't encompass any number over a hundred. After that it was all so damned abstract there was no use counting. This was the year 2349! A numeral, a sum. And here he was, a man who had lain in his hateful dark coffin, hating to be buried, hating the living people above who lived and lived and lived, hating them for all the centuries, until today, now, born out of hatred, he stood by his own freshly excavated grave, the smell of raw earth in the air, perhaps, but he could not smell it!

"I," he said, addressing a poplar tree that was shaken by the wind, "am an anachronism." He smiled faintly.

He looked at the graveyard. It was cold and empty. All of the stones had been ripped up and piled like so many flat bricks, one atop another, in the far corner by the wrought iron fence. This had been going on for two endless weeks. In his deep secret coffin he had heard the heartless, wild stirring as the men jabbed the earth with cold spades and tore out the coffins and carried away the withered ancient bodies to be burned. Twisting with fear in his coffin, he had waited for them to come to him.

Today they had arrived at his coffin. But—late. They had dug down to within an inch of the lid. Five o'clock bell, time for quitting. Home to supper. The workers had gone off. Tomorrow they would finish the job, they said, shrugging into their coats.

Silence had come to the emptied tombyard.

Carefully, quietly, with a soft rattling of sod, the coffin lid had lifted.

William Lantry stood trembling now, in the last cemetery on Earth.

"Remember?" he asked himself, looking at the raw earth. "Remember those stories of the last man on Earth? Those stories of men wandering in ruins, alone? Well, you, William Lantry, are a switch on the old story. Do you *know* that? You are the last *dead* man in the whole damned world!"

There were no more dead people. Nowhere in any land was there a dead person. Impossible? Lantry did not smile at this. No, not impossible at all in this foolish, sterile, unimaginative, antiseptic age of cleansings and scientific methods! People died, oh my God, yes. But—*dead* people? Corpses? They didn't exist!

What *happened* to dead people?

The graveyard was on a hill. William Lantry walked through the dark burning night until he reached the edge of the graveyard and looked down upon the new town of Salem. It was all illumination, all color. Rocket ships cut fire above it, crossing the sky to all the far ports of Earth.

In his grave the new violence of this future world had driven down and seeped into William Lantry. He had been bathed in it for years. He knew all about it, with a hating dead man's knowledge of such things.

Most important of all, he knew what these fools did with dead men.

He lifted his eyes. In the center of the town a massive stone finger pointed at the stars. It was three hundred feet high and fifty feet across. There was a wide entrance and a drive in front of it.

In the town, theoretically, thought William Lantry, say you have a dying man. In a moment he will be dead. What happens? No sooner is his pulse cold when a certificate is flourished, made out, his relatives pack him into a car-beetle and drive him swiftly to—

The Incinerator!

That functional finger, that Pillar of Fire pointing at the stars. Incinerator. A functional, terrible name. But truth is truth in this future world.

Like a stick of kindling your Mr. Dead Man is shot into the furnace.

Flume!

William Lantry looked at the top of the gigantic pistol shoving at the stars. A small pennant of smoke issued from the top.

There's where your dead people go.

"Take care of yourself, William Lantry," he murmured. "You're the last one, the rare item, the last dead man. All the other graveyards of Earth have been blasted up. This is the last graveyard and you're the last dead man from the centuries. These people don't believe in having dead people about, much less walking dead people. Everything that can't be used goes up like a matchstick. Superstitions right along with it!"

He looked at the town. All right, he thought, quietly. I hate you. You hate me, or you *would* if you knew I existed. You don't believe in such things as vampires or ghosts. Labels without referents, you cry! You snort. All right, snort! Frankly, I don't believe in *you*, either! I don't *like* you! You and your Incinerators.

He trembled. How very close it had been. Day after day they had hauled out the other dead ones, burned them like so much kindling. An edict had been broadcast around the world. He had heard the digging men talk as they worked!

"I guess it's a good idea, this cleaning up the graveyards," said one of the men.

"Guess so," said another. "Grisly custom. Can you imagine? Being buried, I mean! Unhealthy! All them germs!"

"Sort of a shame. Romantic, kind of. I mean, leaving just this one graveyard untouched all these centuries. The other graveyards were cleaned out, what year was it, Jim?"

"About 2260, I think. Yeah, that was it, 2260, almost a hundred years ago. But some Salem Committee, they got on their high horse and they said, 'Look here, let's have just *one* graveyard left, to remind us of the customs of the barbarians.' And the gover'ment scratched its head, thunk it over, and said, 'Okay. Salem it is. But all other graveyards go, you understand, all!'"

"And away they went," said Jim.

"Sure, they sucked out 'em with fire and steam shovels and rocket-cleaners. If they knew a man was buried in a cow pasture, they fixed him! Evacuated them, they did. Sort of cruel, I say."

"I hate to sound old-fashioned, but still there were a lot of tourists came here every year, just to see what a real graveyard was like."

"Right. We had nearly a million people in the last three years visiting. A good revenue. But—a government order is an order. The government says no more morbidity, so flush her out we do! Here we go. Hand me that spade, Bill."

William Lantry stood in the autumn wind, on the hill. It was good to walk again, to feel the wind and to hear the leaves scuttling like mice on the road ahead of him. It was good to see the bitter cold stars almost blown away by the wind.

It was even good to know fear again.

For fear rose in him now, and he could not put it away. The very fact that he was walking made him an enemy. And there was not another friend, another dead man, in all of the world, to whom one could turn for help or consolation. It was the whole melodramatic living world against one William Lantry. It was the whole vampire-disbelieving, body-burning, graveyard-annihilating world against a man in a dark suit on a dark autumn hill. He put out his pale cold hands into the city illumination. You have pulled the tombstones, like teeth, from the yard, he thought. Now I will find some way to push your damnable Incinerators down into rubble. I will make dead people again, and I will make friends in so doing. I cannot be alone and lonely. I must start manufacturing friends very soon. Tonight.

"War is declared," he said, and laughed. It was pretty silly, one man declaring war on an entire world.

The world did not answer back. A rocket crossed the sky on a rush of flame, like an Incinerator taking wing.

Footsteps. Lantry hastened to the edge of the cemetery. The diggers, coming back to finish up their work? No. Just someone, a man, walking by.

As the man came abreast the cemetery gate, Lantry stepped swiftly out. "Good evening," said the man, smiling.

Lantry struck the man in the face. The man fell. Lantry bent quietly down and hit the man a killing blow across the neck with the side of his hand.

Dragging the body back into shadow, he stripped it and changed clothes with it. It wouldn't do for a fellow to go wandering about this future world with ancient clothing on. He found a small pocket knife in the man's coat; not much of a knife, but enough if you knew how to handle it properly. He knew how.

He rolled the body down into one of the already opened

and exhumed graves. In a minute he had shoveled dirt down upon it, just enough to hide it. There was little chance of it being found. They wouldn't dig the same grave twice.

He adjusted himself in his new loose-fitting metallic suit. Fine, fine.

Hating, William Lantry walked down into town, to do battle with the Earth.

II

The incinerator was open. It never closed. There was a wide entrance, all lighted up with hidden illumination, there was a helicopter landing table and a beetle drive. The town itself was dying down after another day of the dynamo. The lights were going dim, and the only quiet, lighted spot in the town now was the Incinerator. God, what a practical name, what an unromantic name.

William Lantry entered the wide, well-lighted door. It was an entrance, really; there were no doors to open or shut. People could go in and out, summer or winter, the inside was always warm. Warm from the fire that rushed whispering up the high round flue to where the whirlers, the propellors, the air jets pushed the leafy gray ashes on away for a ten-mile ride down the sky.

There was the warmth of the bakery here. The halls were floored with rubber parquet. You couldn't make a noise if you wanted to. Music played in hidden throats somewhere. Not music of death at all, but music of life and the way the sun lived inside the Incinerator; or the sun's brother, anyway. You could bear the flame floating inside the heavy brick wall.

William Lantry descended a ramp. Behind him he heard a whisper and turned in time to see a beetle stop before the entranceway. A bell rang. The music, as if at a signal, rose to ecstatic heights. There was joy in it.

From the beetle, which opened from the rear, some attendants stepped carrying a golden box. It was six feet long and there were sun symbols on it. From another beetle the relatives of the man in the box stepped and followed as the attendants took the golden box down a ramp to a kind of altar. On the side of the altar were the words, "WE THAT WERE

BORN OF THE SUN RETURN TO THE SUN." The golden box was deposited upon the altar, the music leaped upward, the Guardian of this place spoke only a few words, then the attendants picked up the golden box, walked to a transparent wall, a safety lock, also transparent, and opened it. The box was shoved into the glass slot. A moment later an inner lock opened, the box was injected into the interior of the Flue, and vanished instantly in quick flame.

The attendants walked away. The relatives without a word turned and walked out. The music played.

William Lantry approached the glass fire lock. He peered through the wall at the vast, glowing, never-ceasing heart of the Incinerator. It burned steadily, without a flicker, singing to itself peacefully. It was so solid it was like a golden river flowing up out of the earth toward the sky. Anything you put into the river was borne upward, vanished.

Lantry felt again his unreasoning hatred of this thing, this monster, cleansing fire.

A man stood at his elbow. "May I help you, sir?"

"What?" Lantry turned abruptly. "What did you say?"

"May I be of service?"

"I—that is—" Lantry looked quickly at the ramp and the door. His hands trembled at his sides. "I've never been in here before."

"Never?" The Attendant was surprised.

That had been the wrong thing to say, Lantry realized. But it was said, nevertheless. "I mean," he said. "Not really. I mean, when you're a child, somehow, you don't pay attention. I suddenly realized tonight that I didn't really *know* the Incinerator."

The Attendant smiled. "We never know anything, do we, really? I'll be glad to show you around."

"Oh, no. Never mind. It—it's a wonderful place."

"Yes, it is." The Attendant took pride in it. "One of the finest in the world, I think."

"I—" Lantry felt he must explain further. "I haven't had many relatives die on me since I was a child. In fact, none. So, you see I haven't been here for many years."

"I see." The Attendant's face seemed to darken somewhat.

What've I said now, thought Lantry. What in God's name

is wrong? What've I done? If I'm not careful I'll get myself shoved right into that damnable firetrap. What's wrong with this fellow's face? He seems to be giving me more than the usual going-over.

"You wouldn't be one of the men who've just returned from Mars, would you?" asked the Attendant.

"No. Why do you ask?"

"No matter." The Attendant began to walk off. "If you want to know anything, just ask me."

"Just one thing," said Lantry.

"What's that?"

"This."

Lantry dealt him a stunning blow across the neck.

He had watched the fire-trap operator with expert eyes. Now, with the sagging body in his arms, he touched the button that opened the warm outer lock, placed the body in, heard the music rise, and saw the inner lock open. The body shot out into the river of fire. The music softened.

"Well done, Lantry, well done."

Barely an instant later another Attendant entered the room. Lantry was caught with an expression of pleased excitement on his face. The Attendant looked around as if expecting to find someone, then he walked toward Lantry. "May I help you?"

"Just looking," said Lantry.

"Rather late at night," said the Attendant.

"I couldn't sleep."

That was the wrong answer, too. Everybody slept in this world. Nobody had insomnia. If you did you simply turned on a hypno-ray, and, sixty seconds later, you were snoring. Oh, he was just *full* of wrong answers. First he had made the fatal error of saying he had never been in the Incinerator before, when he knew damned well that all children were brought here on tours, every year, from the time they were four, to instill the idea of the clean fire death and the Incinerator in their minds. Death was a bright fire, death was warmth and the sun. It was not a dark, shadowed thing. That was important in their education. And he, pale, thoughtless fool, had immediately gabbled out his ignorance.

And another thing, this paleness of his. He looked at his

hands and realized with growing terror that a pale man also was nonexistent in this world. They would suspect his paleness. That was why the first attendant had asked, "Are you one of those men newly returned from Mars?" Here, now, this new Attendant was clean and bright as a copper penny, his cheeks red with health and energy. Lantry hid his pale hands in his pockets. But he was fully aware of the searching the Attendant did on his face.

"I mean to say," said Lantry. "I didn't *want* to sleep. I wanted to think."

"Was there a service held here a moment ago?" asked the Attendant, looking about.

"I don't know, I just came in."

"I thought I heard the fire lock open and shut."

"I don't know," said Lantry.

The man pressed a wall button. "Anderson?"

A voice replied. "Yes."

"Locate Saul for me, will you?"

"I'll ring the corridors." A pause. "Can't find him."

"Thanks." The Attendant was puzzled. He was beginning to make little sniffing motions with his nose. "Do you—*smell* anything?"

Lantry sniffed. "No. Why?"

"I *smell* something."

Lantry took hold of the knife in his pocket. He waited.

"I remember once when I was a kid," said the man. "And we found a cow lying dead in the field. It had been there two days in the hot sun. That's what this smell is. I wonder what it's from?"

"Oh, I know what it is," said Lantry quietly. He held out his hand. "Here."

"What?"

"Me, of course."

"You?"

"Dead several hundred years."

"You're an odd joker." The Attendant was puzzled.

"Very." Lantry took out the knife. "Do you know what this is?"

"A knife."

"Do you ever use knives on people any more?"

"How do you mean?"

"I mean—killing them, with knives or guns or poison?"

"You *are* an odd joker!" The man giggled awkwardly.

"I'm going to kill you," said Lantry.

"Nobody kills anybody," said the man.

"Not any more they don't. But they used to, in the old days."

"I know they did."

"This will be the first murder in three hundred years. I just killed your friend. I just shoved him into the fire lock."

That remark had the desired effect. It numbed the man so completely, it shocked him so thoroughly with its illogical aspects that Lantry had time to walk forward. He put the knife against the man's chest. "I'm going to kill you."

"That's *silly*," said the man, numbly. "People don't do that."

"Like this," said Lantry. "You see?"

The knife slid into the chest. The man stared at it for a moment. Lantry caught the falling body.

III

The Salem flue exploded at six that morning. The great fire chimney shattered into ten thousand parts and flung itself into the earth and into the sky and into the houses of the sleeping people. There was fire and sound, more fire than autumn made burning in the hills.

William Lantry was five miles away at the time of the explosion. He saw the town ignited by the great spreading cremation of it. And he shook his head and laughed a little bit and clapped his hands smartly together.

Relatively simple. You walked around killing people who didn't believe in murder, had only heard of it indirectly as some dim gone custom of the old barbarian races. You walked into the control room of the Incinerator and said, "How do you work this Incinerator?" and the control man told you, because everybody told the truth in this world of the future, nobody lied, there was no reason to lie, there was no danger to lie *against*. There was only one criminal in the world, and nobody knew HE existed yet.

Oh, it was an incredibly beautiful setup. The Control Man had told him just how the Incinerator worked, what pressure gauges controlled the flood of fire gases going up the flue, what levers were adjusted or readjusted. He and Lantry had had quite a talk. It was an easy, free world. People trusted people. A moment later Lantry had shoved a knife in the Control Man also and set the pressure gauges for an overload to occur half an hour later, and walked out of the Incinerator halls, whistling.

Now even the sky was palled with the vast black cloud of the explosion.

"This is only the first," said Lantry, looking at the sky. "I'll tear all the others down before they even suspect there's an unethical man loose in their society. They can't account for a variable like me. I'm beyond their understanding. I'm incomprehensible, impossible, therefore I do not exist. My God, I can kill hundreds of thousands of them before they even realize murder is out in the world again. I can make it look like an accident each time. Why, the idea is so huge, it's unbelievable!"

The fire burned the town. He sat under a tree for a long time, until morning. Then, he found a cave in the hills, and went in, to sleep.

He awoke at sunset with a sudden dream of fire. He saw himself pushed into the flue, cut into sections by flame, burned away to nothing. He sat up on the cave floor, laughing at himself. He had an idea.

He walked down into the town and stepped into an audio booth. He dialed OPERATOR. "Give me the Police Department," he said.

"I beg your pardon?" said the operator.

He tried again. "The Law Force," he said.

"I will connect you with the Peace Control," she said, at last.

A little fear began ticking inside him like a tiny watch. Suppose the operator recognized the term Police Department as an anachronism, took his audio number, and sent someone out to investigate? No, she wouldn't do that. Why should she suspect? Paranoids were nonexistent in this civilization.

"Yes, the Peace Control," he said.

A buzz. A man's voice answered. "Peace Control. Stephens speaking."

"Give me the Homicide Detail," said Lantry, smiling.

"The *what*?"

"Who investigates murders?"

"I beg your pardon, what are you talking about?"

"Wrong number." Lantry hung up, chuckling. Ye gods, there was no such a thing as a Homicide Detail. There were no murders, therefore they needed no detectives. Perfect, perfect!

The audio rang back. Lantry hesitated, then answered.

"Say," said the voice on the phone. "Who *are* you?"

"The man just left who called," said Lantry, and hung up again.

He ran. They would recognize his voice and perhaps send someone out to check. People didn't lie. *He* had just lied. They knew his voice. He had lied. Anybody who lied needed a psychiatrist. They would come to pick him up to see why he was lying. For no *other* reason. They suspected him of nothing else. Therefore—he must run.

Oh, how very carefully he must act from now on. He knew nothing of this world, this odd straight truthful ethical world. Simply by looking pale you were suspect. Simply by not sleeping nights you were suspect. Simply by not bathing, by smelling like a—dead cow?—you were suspect. Anything.

He must go to a library. But that was dangerous, too. What were libraries like today? Did they have books or did they have film spools which projected books on a screen? Or did people have libraries at home, thus eliminating the necessity of keeping large main libraries?

He decided to chance it. His use of archaic terms might well make him suspect again, but now it was very important he learn all that could be learned of this foul world into which he had come again. He stopped a man on the street. "Which way to the library?"

The man was not surprised. "Two blocks east, one block north."

"Thank you."

Simple as that.

He walked into the library a few minutes later.

"May I help you?"

He looked at the librarian. May I help you, may I help you. What a world of helpful people! "I'd like to 'have' Edgar Allan

Poe." His verb was carefully chosen. He didn't say "read." He was too afraid that books were passé, that printing itself was a lost art. Maybe all "books" today were in the form of fully delineated three-dimensional motion pictures. How in hell could you make a motion picture out of Socrates, Schopenhauer, Nietzsche, and Freud?

"What was that name again?"

"Edgar Allan Poe."

"There is no such author listed in our files."

"Will you please check?"

She checked. "Oh, yes. There's a red mark on the file card. He was one of the authors in the Great Burning of 2265."

"How ignorant of me."

"That's all right," she said. "Have you heard much of him?"

"He had some interesting barbarian ideas on death," said Lantry.

"Horrible ones," she said, wrinkling her nose. "Ghastly."

"Yes. Ghastly. Abominable, in fact. Good thing he was burned. Unclean. By the way, do you have any of Lovecraft?"

"Is that a sex book?"

Lantry exploded with laughter. "No, no. It's a man."

She riffled the file. "He was burned, too. Along with Poe."

"I suppose that applies to Machen and a man named Derleth and one named Ambrose Bierce, also?"

"Yes." She shut the file cabinet. "All burned. And good riddance." She gave him an odd warm look of interest. "I bet you've just come back from Mars."

"Why do you say that?"

"There was another explorer in here yesterday. He'd just made the Mars hop and return. He was interested in supernatural literature, also. It seems there are actually 'tombs' on Mars."

"What are 'tombs'?" Lantry was learning to keep his mouth closed.

"You know, those things they once buried people in."

"Barbarian custom. Ghastly!"

"*Isn't* it? Well, seeing the Martian tombs made this young explorer curious. He came and asked if we had any of those authors you mentioned. Of course we haven't even a smitch of their stuff." She looked at his pale face. "You *are* one of the Martian rocket men, aren't you?"

"Yes," he said. "Got back on the ship the other day."

"The other young man's name was Burke."

"Of course. Burke! Good friend of mine!"

"Sorry I can't help you. You'd best get yourself some vitamin shots and some sun lamps. You look terrible, Mr. ——?"

"Lantry. I'll be good. Thanks ever so much. See you next Hallows' Eve!"

"Aren't you the clever one." She laughed. "If there *were* a Hallows' Eve, I'd make it a date."

"But they burned *that*, too," he said.

"Oh, they burned everything," she said. "Good night."

"Good night." And he went on out.

Oh, how carefully he was balanced in this world! Like some kind of dark gyroscope, whirling with never a murmur, a very silent man. As he walked along the eight o'clock evening street he noticed with particular interest that there was not an unusual amount of lights about. There were the usual street lights at each corner, but the blocks themselves were only faintly illuminated. Could it be that these remarkable people were not *afraid of the dark*? Incredible nonsense! *Every one* was afraid of the dark. *Even he* himself had been afraid, as a child. It was as natural as eating.

A little boy ran by on pelting feet, followed by six others. They yelled and shouted and rolled on the dark cool October lawn, in the leaves. Lantry looked on for several minutes before addressing himself to one of the small boys who was for a moment taking a respite, gathering his breath into his small lungs, as a boy might blow to refill a punctured paper bag.

"Here, now," said Lantry. "You'll wear yourself out."

"Sure," said the boy.

"Could you tell me," said the man, "why there are no street lights in the middle of the blocks?"

"Why?" asked the boy.

"I'm a teacher, I thought I'd test your knowledge," said Lantry.

"Well," said the boy, "you don't need lights in the middle of the block, that's why."

"But it gets rather dark," said Lantry.

"So?" said the boy.

"Aren't you afraid?" asked Lantry.

"Of what?" asked the boy.

"The dark," said Lantry.

"Ho ho," said the boy. "Why should I be?"

"Well," said Lantry. "It's black, it's dark. And after all, street lights were invented to take away the dark and take away fear."

"That's silly. Street lights were made so you could see where you were walking. Outside of that there's nothing."

"You miss the whole point—" said Lantry. "Do you mean to say you would sit in the middle of an empty lot all night and not be afraid?"

"Of what?"

"Of what, of what, of what, you little ninny! Of the dark!"

"Ho ho."

"Would you go out in the hills and stay all night in the dark?"

"Sure."

"Would you stay in a deserted house alone?"

"Sure."

"And not be afraid?"

"Sure."

"You're a liar!"

"Don't you call me nasty names!" shouted the boy. Liar was the improper noun, indeed. It seemed to be the worst thing you could call a person.

Lantry was completely furious with the little monster. "Look," he insisted. "Look into my eyes . . ."

The boy looked.

Lantry bared his teeth slightly. He put out his hands, making a clawlike gesture. He leered and gesticulated and wrinkled his face into a terrible mask of horror.

"Ho ho," said the boy. "You're funny."

"*What* did you say?"

"You're funny. Do it again. Hey, gang, c'mere! This man does funny things!"

"Never mind."

"Do it again, sir."

"Never mind, never mind. Good night!" Lantry ran off.

"Good night, sir. And mind the dark, sir!" called the little boy.

Of all the stupidity, of all the rank, gross, crawling, jelly-mouthed stupidity! He had never seen the like of it in his life! Bringing the children up without so much as an *ounce* of imagination! Where was the fun in being children if you didn't imagine things?

He stopped running. He slowed and for the first time began to appraise himself. He ran his hand over his face and bit his finger and found that he himself was standing midway in the block and he felt uncomfortable. He moved up to the street corner where there was a glowing lantern. "That's better," he said, holding his hands out like a man to an open warm fire.

He listened. There was not a sound except the night breathing of the crickets. Finally there was a fire-hush as a rocket swept the sky. It was the sound a torch might make brandished gently on the dark air.

He listened to himself and for the first time he realized what there was so peculiar to himself. There was not a sound in him. The little nostril and lung noises were absent. His lungs did not take nor give oxygen or carbon dioxide; they did not move. The hairs on his nostrils did not quiver with warm combing air. That faint purrling whisper of breathing did not sound in his nose. Strange. Funny. A noise you never heard when you were alive, the breath that fed your body, and yet, once dead, oh how you missed it!

The only other time you ever heard it was on deep dreamless awake nights when you wakened and listened and heard first your nose taking and gently poking out the air, and then the dull deep dim red thunder of the blood in your temples, in your eardrums, in your throat, in your aching wrists, in your warm loins, in your chest. All of those little rhythms, gone. The wrist beat gone, the throat pulse gone, the chest vibration gone. The sound of the blood coming up down around and through, up down around and through. Now it was like listening to a statue.

And yet he *lived*. Or, rather, moved about. And how was this done, over and above scientific explanations, theories, doubts?

By one thing, and one thing alone.

Hatred.

Hatred was a blood in him, it went up down around and through, up down around and through. It was a heart in him, not beating, true, but warm. He was—what? Resentment. Envy. They said he could not lie any longer in his coffin in the cemetery. He had *wanted* to. He had never had any particular desire to get up and walk around. It had been enough, all these centuries, to lie in the deep box and feel but *not feel* the ticking of the million insect watches in the earth around, the moves of worms like so many deep thoughts in the soil.

But then they had come and said, "Out you go and into the furnace!" And that is the worst thing you can say to any man. You cannot tell him what to do. If you say you are dead, he will want not to be dead. If you say there are no such things as vampires, by God, that man will try to *be* one just for spite. If you say a dead man cannot walk, he will test his limbs. If you say murder is no longer occurring, he will make it occur. He was, *in toto*, all the impossible things. They had given birth to him with their damnable practices and ignorances. Oh, how wrong they were. They needed to be shown. He would *show* them! Sun is *good*, so is *night*, there is nothing wrong with dark, *they* said.

Dark is horror, he shouted, silently, facing the little houses. It is *meant* for contrast. You must fear, you hear! That has always been the way of this world. You destroyers of Edgar Allan Poe and fine big-worded Lovecraft, you burner of Halloween masks and destroyer of pumpkin jack-o-lanterns! I will make night what it *once* was, the thing against which man built all his lanterned cities and his many children!

As if in answer to this, a rocket, flying low, trailing a long rakish feather of flame. It made Lantry flinch and draw back.

IV

It was but ten miles to the little town of Science Port. He made it by dawn, walking. But even this was not good. At four in the morning a silver beetle pulled up on the road beside him.

"Hello," called the man inside.

"Hello," said Lantry, wearily.

"Why are you walking?" asked the man.

"I'm going to Science Port."

"Why don't you ride?"

"I *like* to walk."

"*Nobody* likes to walk. Are you sick? May I give you a ride?"

"Thanks, but I like to walk."

The man hesitated, then closed the beetle door. "Good night."

When the beetle was gone over the hill, Lantry retreated into a nearby forest. A world full of bungling, helping people. By God, you couldn't even *walk* without being accused of sickness. That meant only one thing. He must not walk any longer, he had to ride. He should have accepted that fellow's offer.

The rest of the night he walked far enough off the highway so that if a beetle rushed by he had time to vanish in the underbrush. At dawn he crept into an empty dry water drain and closed his eyes.

The dream was as perfect as a rimed snowflake.

He saw the graveyard where he had lain deep and ripe over the centuries. He heard the early morning footsteps of the laborers returning to finish their work.

"Would you mind passing me the shovel, Jim?"

"Here you go."

"Wait a minute, wait a minute!"

"What's up?"

"Look here. We didn't finish last night, did we?"

"No."

"There was one more coffin, wasn't there?"

"Yes."

"Well, here it is, and open!"

"You've got the wrong hole."

"What's the name say on the gravestone?"

"Lantry. William Lantry."

"That's him, that's the one! Gone!"

"What could have happened to it?"

"How do I know. The body was here last night."

"We can't be sure, we didn't look."

"God, man, people don't bury empty coffins. He was in his box. Now he isn't."

"Maybe this box was empty."

"Nonsense. Smell that smell? He was here all right."

A pause.

"Nobody would have taken the body, would they?"

"What for?"

"A curiosity, perhaps."

"Don't be ridiculous. People just don't steal. Nobody steals."

"Well, then, there's only one solution."

"And?"

"He got up and walked away."

A pause. In the dark dream, Lantry expected to hear laughter. There was none. Instead, the voice of the gravedigger, after a thoughtful pause, said, "Yes. That's it, indeed. He got up and walked away."

"That's interesting to think about," said the other.

"Isn't it, though?"

Silence.

Lantry awoke. It had all been a dream, but God, how realistic. How strangely the two men had carried on. But not unnaturally, oh, no. That was exactly how you expected men of the future to talk. Men of the future. Lantry grinned wryly. That was an anachronism for you. This *was* the future. This was happening *now*. It wasn't three hundred years from now, it was now, not then, or any other time. This wasn't the twentieth century. Oh, how calmly those two men in the dream had said, "He got up and walked away." "—interesting to think about." "*Isn't* it, though?" With never a quaver in their voices. With not so much as a glance over their shoulders or a tremble of spade in hand. But, of course, with their perfectly honest, logical minds, there was but one explanation; certainly nobody had *stolen* the corpse. "*Nobody* steals." The corpse had simply got up and walked off. The corpse was the only one who could have *possibly* moved the corpse. By the few casual slow words of the gravediggers Lantry knew what they were thinking. Here was a man that had lain in suspended animation, not really dead, for hundreds of years. The jarring about, the activity, had brought him back.

Everyone had heard of those little green toads that are sealed for centuries inside mud rocks or in ice patties, alive, alive oh! And how when scientists chipped them out and warmed them like marbles in their hands the little toads leapt about and frisked and blinked. Then it was only logical that the gravediggers think of William Lantry in like fashion.

But what if the various parts were fitted together in the next day or so? If the vanished body and the shattered, exploded incinerator were connected? What if this fellow named Burke, who had returned pale from Mars, went to the library again and said to the young woman he wanted some books and she said, "Oh, your friend Lantry was in the other day." And he'd say, 'Lantry who? Don't know anyone by that name.' And she'd say, "Oh, he *lied*." And people in this time didn't lie. So it would all form and coalesce, item by item, bit by bit. A pale man who was pale and shouldn't be pale had lied and people don't lie, and a walking man on a lonely country road had walked and people don't walk any more, and a body was missing from a cemetery, and the Incinerator had blown up and and and—

They would come after him. They would find him. He would be easy to find. He walked. He lied. He was pale. They would find him and take him and stick him through the open fire lock of the nearest Burner and that would be your Mr. William Lantry, like a Fourth of July set-piece!

There was only one thing to be done efficiently and completely. He arose in violent moves. His lips were wide and his dark eyes were flared and there was a trembling and burning all through him. He must kill and kill and kill and kill and kill. He must make his enemies into friends, into people like himself who walked but shouldn't walk, who were pale in a land of pinks. He must kill and then kill and then kill again. He must make bodies and dead people and corpses. He must destroy Incinerator after Flue after Burner after Incinerator. Explosion on explosion. Death on death. Then, when the Incinerators were all in thrown ruin, and the hastily established morgues were jammed with the bodies of people shattered by the explosion, then he would begin his making of friends, his enrollment of the dead in his own cause.

Before they traced and found and killed him, they must be killed themselves. So far he was safe. He could kill and they would not kill back. People simply do not go around killing.

That was his safety margin. He climbed out of the abandoned drain, stood in the road.

He took the knife from his pocket and hailed the next beetle.

It was like the Fourth of July! The biggest damned firecracker of them all. The Science Port Incinerator split down the middle and flew apart. It made a thousand small explosions that ended with a greater one. It fell upon the town and crushed houses and burned trees. It woke people from sleep and then put them to sleep again, forever, an instant later.

William Lantry, sitting in a beetle that was not his own, tuned idly to a station on the audio dial. The collapse of the Incinerator had killed some four hundred people. Many had been caught in flattened houses, others struck by flying metal. A temporary morgue was being set up at—

An address was given.

Lantry noted it with a pad and pencil.

He could go on this way, he thought, from town to town, from country to country, destroying the Burners, the Pillars of Fire, until the whole clean magnificent framework of flame and cauterization was tumbled. He made a fair estimate—each explosion averaged five hundred dead. You could work that up to a hundred thousand in no time.

He pressed the floor stud on the beetle. Smiling, he drove off though the dark streets of the city.

The city coroner had requisitioned an old warehouse. From midnight until four in the morning the gray beetles hissed down the rain-shiny streets, turned in, and the bodies were laid out on the cold concrete floors, with white sheets over them. It was a continuous flow until about four-thirty, then it stopped. There were about two hundred bodies there, white and cold.

The bodies were left alone; nobody stayed behind to tend them. There was no use tending the dead; it was a useless procedure; the dead could take care of themselves.

About five o'clock, with a touch of dawn in the east, the first trickle of relatives arrived to identify their sons or their fathers or their mothers or their uncles. The people moved quickly into the warehouse, made the identification, moved quickly out again. By six o'clock, with the sky still lighter in the east, this trickle had passed on, also.

William Lantry walked across the wide wet street and entered the warehouse.

He held a piece of blue chalk in one hand.

He walked by the coroner who stood in the entranceway talking to two others. ". . . drive the bodies to the Incinerator in Mellin Town, tomorrow . . ." The voices faded.

Lantry moved, his feet echoing faintly on the cool concrete. A wave of sourceless relief came to him as he walked among the shrouded figures. He was among his own. And—better than that, by God! He had *created* these! He had made them dead! He had procured for himself a vast number of recumbent friends!

Was the coroner watching? Lantry turned his head. No. The warehouse was calm and quiet and shadowed in the dark morning. The coroner was walking away now, across the street, with his two attendants; a beetle had drawn up on the other side of the street, and the coroner was going over to talk with whoever was in the beetle.

William Lantry stood and made a blue chalk pentagram on the floor by each of the bodies. He moved swiftly, swiftly, without a sound, without blinking. In a few minutes, glancing up now and then to see if the coroner was still busy, he had chalked the floor by a hundred bodies. He straightened up and put the chalk in his pocket.

Now is the time for all good men to come to the aid of their party, now is the time for all good men to come to the aid of their party, now is the time for all good men to come to the aid of their party, now is the time . . .

Lying in the earth, over the centuries, the processes and thoughts of passing peoples and passing times had seeped down to him, slowly, as into a deep-buried sponge. From some death-memory in him now, ironically, repeatedly, a black typewriter clacked out black even lines of pertinent words:

Now is the time for all good men, for all good men, to come to the aid of—

William Lantry.

Other words—

Arise my love, and come away—

The quick brown fox jumped over . . . *Paraphrase it.* The quick risen body jumped over the tumbled Incinerator . . .

Lazarus, come forth from the tomb . . .

He knew the right words. He need only speak them as they had been spoken over the centuries. He need only gesture with his hands and speak the words, the dark words that would cause these bodies to quiver, rise and walk!

And when they had risen he would take them through the town, they would kill others and the others would rise and walk. By the end of the day there would be thousands of good friends, walking with him. And what of the naïve, living people of this year, this day, this hour? They would be completely unprepared for it. They would go down to defeat because they would not be expecting war of any sort. They wouldn't believe it possible, it would all be over before they could convince themselves that such an illogical thing could happen.

He lifted his hands. His lips moved. He said the words. He began in a chanting whisper and then raised his voice, louder. He said the words again and again. His eyes were closed tightly. His body swayed. He spoke faster and faster. He began to move forward among the bodies. The dark words flowed from his mouth. He was enchanted with his own formulae. He stooped and made further blue symbols on the concrete, in the fashion of long-dead sorcerers, smiling, confident. Any moment now the first tremor of the still bodies, any moment now the rising, the leaping up of the cold ones!

His hands lifted in the air. His head nodded. He spoke, he spoke, he spoke. He gestured. He talked loudly over the bodies, his eyes flaring, his body tensed. "Now!" he cried, violently. "Rise, *all* of you!"

Nothing happened.

"Rise!" he screamed, with a terrible torment in his voice.

The sheets lay in white blue-shadow folds over the silent bodies.

"Hear me, and act!" he shouted.

Far away, on the street, a beetle hissed along.

Again, again, again he shouted, pleaded. He got down by each body and asked of it his particular violent favor. No reply. He strode wildly between the even white rows, flinging his arms up, stooping again and again to make blue symbols!

Lantry was very pale. He licked his lips. "Come on, get up," he said. "They have, they always have, for a thousand years. When you make a mark—so! and speak a word—so! they always rise! Why not now, why not you! Come on, come *on*, before *they* come back!"

The warehouse went up into shadow. There were steel beams across and down. In it, under the roof, there was not a sound, except the raving of a lonely man.

Lantry stopped.

Through the wide doors of the warehouse he caught a glimpse of the last cold stars of morning.

This was the year 2349.

His eyes grew cold and his hands fell to his sides. He did not move.

Once upon a time people shuddered when they heard the wind about the house, once people raised crucifixes and wolfbane, and believed in walking dead and bats and loping white wolves. And as long as they believed, then so long did the dead, the bats, the loping wolves exist. The mind gave birth and reality to them.

But . . .

He looked at the white sheeted bodies.

These people did not believe.

They had never believed. They would never believe. They had never imagined that the dead might walk. The dead went up flues in flame. They had never heard superstition, never trembled or shuddered or doubted in the dark. Walking dead people could not exist, they were illogical. This was the year 2349, man, after all!

Therefore, these people could not rise, could not walk again. They were dead and flat and cold. Nothing, chalk, imprecation, superstition, could wind them up and set them walking. They were dead and *knew* they were dead!

He was alone.

There were live people in the world who moved and drove beetles and drank quiet drinks in little dimly illumined bars by country roads, and kissed women and talked much good talk all day and every day.

But he was not alive.

Friction gave him what little warmth he possessed.

There were two hundred dead people here in this warehouse now, cold upon the floor. The first dead people in a hundred years who were allowed to be corpses for an extra hour or more. The first not to be immediately trundled to the Incinerator and lit like so much phosphorus.

He should be happy with them, among them.

He was not.

They were completely dead. They did not know nor believe in walking once the heart had paused and stilled itself. They were deader than dead ever was.

He was indeed alone, more alone than any man had ever been. He felt the chill of his aloneness moving up into his chest, strangling him quietly.

William Lantry turned suddenly and gasped.

While he had stood there, someone had entered the warehouse. A tall man with white hair, wearing a light weight tan overcoat and no hat. How long the man had been nearby there was no telling.

There was no reason to stay here. Lantry turned and started to walk slowly out. He looked hastily at the man as he passed and the man with the white hair looked back at him, curiously. Had he heard? The imprecations, the pleadings, the shoutings? Did he suspect? Lantry slowed his walk. Had this man seen him make the blue chalk marks? But then, would he interpret them as symbols of an ancient superstition? Probably not.

Reaching the door, Lantry paused. For a moment he did not want to do anything but lie down and be coldly, really dead again and be carried silently down the street to some distant burning flue and there dispatched in ash and whispering fire. If he was indeed alone and there was no chance to collect an army to his cause, what, then, existed as a reason for going on? Killing? Yes, he'd kill a few thousand more. But that wasn't enough. You can only do so much of that before they drag you down.

He looked at the cold sky.

A rocket went across the black heaven, trailing fire.

Mars burned red among a million stars.

Mars. The library. The librarian. Talk. Returning rocket men. Tombs.

Lantry almost gave a shout. He restrained his hand, which wanted so much to reach up into the sky and touch Mars. Lovely red star on the sky. Good star that gave him sudden new hope. If he had a living heart now it would be thrashing wildly, and sweat would be breaking out of him and his pulses would be stammering, and tears would be in his eyes!

He would go down to wherever the rockets sprang up into space. He would go to Mars, one way or another. He would go to the Martian tombs. There, there, by God, were bodies, he would bet his last hatred on it, that would rise and walk and work with him! Theirs was an ancient culture, much different from that of Earth, patterned on the Egyptian, if what the librarian had said was true. And the Egyptian—what a crucible of dark superstition and midnight terror that culture had been! Mars it *was*, then. Beautiful Mars!

But he must not attract attention to himself. He must move carefully. He wanted to run, yes, to get away, but that would be the worst possible move he could make. The man with the white hair was glancing at Lantry from time to time, in the entranceway. There were too many people about. If anything happened he would be outnumbered. So far he had taken on only *one* man at a time.

Lantry forced himself to stop and stand on the steps before the warehouse. The man with the white hair came on onto the steps also and stood, looking at the sky. He looked as if he was going to speak at any moment. He fumbled in his pockets and took out a packet of cigarettes.

V

They stood outside the morgue together, the tall, pink, white-haired man, and Lantry, hands in their pockets. It was a cool night with a white shell of a moon that washed a house here, a road there, and farther on, parts of a river.

"Cigarette?" The man offered Lantry one.

"Thanks."

They lit up together. The man glanced at Lantry's mouth. "Cool night."

"Cool."

They shifted their feet. "Terrible accident."

"Terrible."

"So many dead."

"So many."

Lantry felt himself some sort of delicate weight upon a scale. The other man did not seem to be looking at him, but rather listening and feeling toward him. There was a feathery balance here that made for vast discomfort. He wanted to move away and get out from under this balancing, weighing. The tall white-haired man said, "My name's McClure."

"Did you have any friends inside?" asked Lantry.

"No. A casual acquaintance. Awful accident."

"Awful."

They balanced each other. A beetle hissed by on the road with its seventeen tires whirling quietly. The moon showed a little town farther over in the black hills.

"I say," said the man McClure.

"Yes."

"Could you answer me a question?"

"Be glad to." He loosened the knife in his coat pocket, ready.

"Is your name Lantry?" asked the man at last.

"Yes."

"*William* Lantry?"

"Yes."

"Then you're the man who came out of the Salem graveyard day before yesterday, aren't you?"

"Yes."

"Good Lord, I'm glad to meet you, Lantry! We've been trying to find you for the past twenty-four hours!"

The man seized his hand, pumped it, slapped him on the back.

"What, what?" said Lantry.

"Good Lord, man, why did you run off? Do you realize what an instance this is? We want to talk to you!"

McClure was smiling, glowing. Another handshake, another slap. "I *thought* it was you!"

The man is mad, thought Lantry. Absolutely mad. Here I've toppled his incinerators, killed people, and he's shaking my hand. Mad, mad!

"Will you come along to the Hall?" said the man, taking his elbow.

"Wh-what hall?" Lantry stepped back.

"The Science Hall, of course. It isn't every year we get a real case of suspended animation. In small animals, yes, but in a man, hardly! Will you come?"

"What's the act!" demanded Lantry, glaring. "What's all this talk."

"My dear fellow, what do you mean?" The man was stunned.

"Never mind. Is that the only reason you want to see me?"

"What other reason would there be, Mr. Lantry? You don't know how glad I am to see you!" He almost did a little dance. "I suspected. When we were in there together. You being so pale and all. And then the way you smoked your cigarette, something about it, and a lot of other things, all subliminal. But it is you, isn't it, it *is* you!"

"It is I. William Lantry." Dryly.

"Good fellow! Come along!"

The beetle moved swiftly through the dawn streets. McClure talked rapidly.

Lantry sat, listening, astounded. Here was this fool, McClure, playing his cards for him! Here was this stupid scientist, or whatever, accepting him not as a suspicious baggage, a murderous item. Oh no! Quite the contrary! Only as a suspended animation case was he considered! Not as a dangerous man at all. Far from it!

"Of course," cried McClure, grinning. "You didn't know where to go, whom to turn to. It was all quite incredible to you."

"Yes."

"I had a feeling you'd be there at the morgue tonight," said McClure, happily.

"Oh?" Lantry stiffened.

"Yes. Can't explain it. But you, how shall I put it? Ancient Americans? You had funny ideas on death. And you were among the dead so long, I felt you'd be drawn back by the accident, by the morgue and all. It's not very logical. Silly, in fact. It's just a feeling. I hate feelings but there it was. I came on a, I guess you'd call it a hunch, wouldn't you?"

"You might call it that."

"And there you were!"

"There I was," said Lantry.

"Are you hungry?"

"I've eaten."

"How did you get around?"

"I hitchhiked."

"You *what*?"

"People gave me rides on the road."

"Remarkable."

"I imagine it sounds that way." He looked at the passing houses. "So this is the era of space travel, is it?"

"Oh, we've been traveling to Mars for some forty years now."

"Amazing. And those big funnels, those towers in the middle of every town?"

"Those. Haven't you heard? The Incinerators. Oh, of course, they hadn't anything of that sort in your time. Had some bad luck with them. An explosion in Salem and one here, all in a forty-eight-hour period. You looked as if you were going to speak; what is it?"

"I was thinking," said Lantry. "How fortunate I got out of my coffin when I did. I might well have been thrown into one of your Incinerators and burned up."

"Quite."

Lantry toyed with the dials on the beetle dash. He wouldn't go to Mars. His plans were changed. If this fool simply refused to recognize an act of violence when he stumbled upon it, then let him be a fool. If they didn't connect the two explosions with a man from the tomb, all well and good. Let them go on deluding themselves. If they couldn't imagine someone being mean and nasty and murderous, heaven help them. He rubbed his hands with satisfaction. No, no Martian trip for you, as yet, Lantry lad. First we'll see what can be done boring from the inside. Plenty of time. The Incinerators can wait an extra week or so. One has to be subtle, you know. Any more immediate explosions might cause quite a ripple of thought.

McClure was gabbling wildly on.

"Of course, you don't have to be examined immediately. You'll want a rest. I'll put you up at my place."

"Thanks. I don't feel up to being probed and pulled. Plenty of time in a week or so."

They drew up before a house and climbed out.

"You want to sleep, naturally."

"I've been asleep for centuries. Be glad to stay awake. I'm not a bit tired."

"Good." McClure let them into the house. He headed for the drink bar. "A drink will fix us up."

"You have one," said Lantry. "Later for me. I just want to sit down."

"By all means sit." McClure mixed himself a drink. He looked around the room, looked at Lantry, paused for a moment with the drink in his hand, tilted his head to one side, and put his tongue in his cheek. Then he shrugged and stirred the drink. He walked slowly to a chair and sat, sipping the drink quietly. He seemed to be listening for something. "There are cigarettes on the table," he said.

"Thanks." Lantry took one and lit it and smoked it. He did not speak for some time.

Lantry thought, I'm taking this all too easily. Maybe I should kill and run. He's the only one that has found me, yet. Perhaps this is all a trap. Perhaps we're simply sitting here waiting for the police. Or whatever in hell they use for police these days. He looked at McClure. No. They weren't waiting for police. They were waiting for something else.

McClure didn't speak. He looked at Lantry's face and he looked at Lantry's hands. He looked at Lantry's chest a long time, with easy quietness. He sipped his drink. He looked at Lantry's feet.

Finally he said, "Where'd you get the clothing?"

"I asked someone for clothes and they gave these things to me. Darned nice of them."

"You'll find that's how we are in this world. All you have to do is ask."

McClure shut up again. His eyes moved. Only his eyes and nothing else. Once or twice he lifted his drink.

A little clock ticked somewhere in the distance.

"Tell me about yourself, Mr. Lantry."

"Nothing much to tell."

"You're modest."

"Hardly. You know about the past. I know nothing of the future, or I should say 'today' and day before yesterday. You don't learn much in a coffin."

McClure did not speak. He suddenly sat forward in his chair and then leaned back and shook his head.

They'll never suspect me, thought Lantry. They aren't superstitious, they simply *can't* believe in a dead man walking. Therefore, I'll be safe. I'll keep putting off the physical checkup. They're polite. They won't force me. Then, I'll work it so I can get to Mars. After that, the tombs, in my own good time, and the plan. God, how simple. How naïve these people are.

McClure sat across the room for five minutes. A coldness had come over him. The color was very slowly going from his face, as one sees the color of medicine vanishing as one presses the bulb at the top of a dropper. He leaned forward, saying nothing, and offered another cigarette to Lantry.

"Thanks." Lantry took it. McClure sat deeply back into his easy chair, his knees folded one over the other. He did not look at Lantry, and yet somehow did. The feeling of weighing and balancing returned. McClure was like a tall thin master of hounds listening for something that nobody else could hear. There are little silver whistles you can blow that only dogs can hear. McClure seemed to be listening acutely, sensitively for such an invisible whistle, listening with his eyes and with his half-opened, dry mouth, and with his aching, breathing nostrils.

Lantry sucked the cigarette, sucked the cigarette, sucked the cigarette, and, as many times, blew out, blew out, blew out. McClure was like some lean red-shagged hound listening and listening with a slick slide of eyes to one side, with an apprehension in that hand that was so precisely microscopic that one only sensed it, as one sensed the invisible whistle, with some part of the brain deeper than eyes or nostril or ear.

The room was so quiet the cigarette smoke made some kind of invisible noise rising to the ceiling. McClure was a thermometer, a chemist's scales, a listening hound, a litmus paper, an antennae; all these. Lantry did not move. Perhaps the feeling would pass. It had passed before. McClure did not move for a long while and then, without a word, he nodded at the sherry decanter, and Lantry refused as silently. They sat looking but not looking at each other, again and away, again and away.

McClure stiffened slowly. Lantry saw the color getting paler in those lean cheeks, and the hand tightening on the sherry glass, and a knowledge come at last to stay, never to go away, into the eyes.

Lantry did not move. He could not. All of this was of such a fascination that he wanted only to see, to hear what would happen next. It was McClure's show from here on in.

McClure said, "At first I thought it was the first psychosis I have ever seen. You, I mean. I thought, he's convinced himself, Lantry's convinced himself, he's quite insane, he's told himself to do all these little things." McClure talked as if in a dream, and continued talking and didn't stop.

"I said to myself, he purposely doesn't breathe through his nose. I watched your nostrils, Lantry. The little nostril hairs never once quivered in the last hour. That wasn't enough. It was a fact I filed. It wasn't enough. He breathes through his mouth, I said, on purpose. And then I gave you a cigarette and you sucked and blew, sucked and blew. None of it ever came out your nose. I told myself, well, that's all right. He doesn't inhale. Is that terrible, is that suspect? All in the mouth, all in the mouth. And then, I looked at your chest. I watched. It never moved up or down, it did nothing. He's convinced himself, I said to myself. He's convinced himself about all this. He doesn't move his chest, except slowly, when he thinks you're not looking. That's what I told myself."

The words went on in the silent room, not pausing, still in a dream. "And then I offered you a drink but you don't drink and I thought, he doesn't drink, I thought. Is *that* terrible? And I watched and watched you all this time. Lantry holds his breath, he's fooling himself. But now, yes, now, I understand it quite well. Now I know everything the way it is. Do you know how I know? I do not hear breathing in the room. I wait and I hear nothing. There is no beat of heart or intake of lung. The room is so silent. Nonsense, one might say, but I know. At the Incinerator I know. There is a difference. You enter a room where a man is on a bed and you know immediately whether he will look up and speak to you or whether he will not speak to you ever again. Laugh if you will, but one can tell. It is a subliminal thing. It is the whistle the dog hears when no human hears. It is the tick of a clock that has ticked so long one no longer notices. Something is in a room when a man lives in it. Something is not in the room when a man is dead in it."

McClure shut his eyes a moment. He put down his sherry glass. He waited a moment. He took up his cigarette and puffed it and then put it down in a black tray.

"I am alone in this room," he said.

Lantry did not move.

"You are dead," said McClure. "My mind does not know this. It is not a thinking thing. It is a thing of the senses and the subconscious. At first I thought, this man *thinks* he is dead, risen from the dead, a vampire. Is that not logical? Would not any man, buried as many centuries, raised in a superstitious, ignorant culture, think likewise of himself once risen from the tomb? Yes, that is logical. This man has hypnotized himself and fitted his bodily functions so that they would in no way interfere with his self-delusion, his great paranoia. He governs his breathing. He tells himself, I cannot hear my breathing, therefore I am dead. His inner mind censors the sound of breathing. He does not allow himself to eat or drink. These things he probably does in his sleep, with part of his mind, hiding the evidences of this humanity from his deluded mind at other times."

McClure finished it. "I was wrong. You are not insane. You are not deluding yourself. Nor me. This is all very illogical and—I must admit—almost frightening. Does that make you feel good, to think you frighten me? I have no label for you. You're a very odd man, Lantry. I'm glad to have met you. This will make an interesting report indeed."

"Is there anything wrong with me being dead?" said Lantry. "Is it a crime?"

"You must admit it's highly unusual."

"But, still now, is it a crime?" asked Lantry.

"We have no crime, no criminal court. We want to examine you, naturally, to find out how you have happened. It is like that chemical which, one minute is inert, the next is living cell. Who can say where what happened to what. You are that impossibility. It is enough to drive a man quite insane."

"Will I be released when you are done fingering me?"

"You will not be held. If you don't wish to be examined,

you will not be. But I am hoping you will help by offering us your services."

"I might," said Lantry.

"But tell me," said McClure. "What were you doing at the morgue?"

"Nothing."

"I heard you talking when I came in."

"I was merely curious."

"You're lying. That is very bad, Mr. Lantry. The truth is far better. The truth is, is it not, that you are dead and, being the only one of your sort, were lonely. Therefore you killed people to have company."

"How does that follow?"

McClure laughed. "Logic, my dear fellow. Once I *knew* you were really dead, a moment ago, really a—what do you call it—a vampire (silly word!) I tied you immediately to the Incinerator blasts. Before that there was no reason to connect you. But once the one piece fell into place, the fact that you were dead, then it was simple to guess your loneliness, your hate, your envy, all of the tawdry motivations of a walking corpse. It took only an instant then to see the Incinerators blown to blazes, and then to think of you, among the bodies at the morgue, seeking help, seeking friends and people like yourself to work with—"

"You're too damned smart!" Lantry was out of the chair. He was halfway to the other man when McClure rolled over and scuttled away, flinging the sherry decanter. With a great despair Lantry realized that, like a damned idiot, he had thrown away his one chance to kill McClure. He should have done it earlier. It had been Lantry's one weapon, his safety margin. If people in a society never *killed* each other, they never *suspected* one another. You could walk up to any one of them and kill him.

"Come back here!" Lantry threw the knife.

McClure got behind a chair. The idea of flight, of protection, of fighting, was still new to him. He had part of the idea, but there was still a bit of luck on Lantry's side if Lantry wanted to use it.

"Oh, no," said McClure, holding the chair between himself and the advancing man. "You want to kill me. It's odd, but true. I can't understand it. You want to cut me with that knife or something like that, and it's up to me to prevent you from doing such an odd thing."

"I *will* kill you!" Lantry let it slip out. He cursed himself. That was the worst possible thing to say.

Lantry lunged across the chair, clutching at McClure.

McClure was very logical. "It won't do you any good to kill me. You *know* that." They wrestled and held each other in a wild, toppling shuffle. Tables fell over, scattering articles. "You remember what happened in the morgue?"

"I don't care!" screamed Lantry.

"You didn't raise *those* dead, did you?"

"I don't care!" cried Lantry.

"Look here," said McClure, reasonably. "There will never be any more like you, ever, there's no use."

"Then I'll destroy all of you, all of you!" screamed Lantry.

"And then what? You'll still be alone, with no more like you about."

"I'll go to Mars. They have tombs there. I'll find more like myself!"

"No," said McClure. "The executive order went through yesterday. All of the tombs are being deprived of their bodies. They'll be burned in the next week."

They fell together to the floor. Lantry got his hands on McClure's throat.

"Please," said McClure. "Do you see, you'll *die*."

"What do you mean?" cried Lantry.

"Once you kill all of us, and you're alone, you'll die! The hate will die. That hate is what moved you, *nothing else*! That envy moves you. Nothing else! You'll die, inevitably. You're not immortal. You're not even alive, you're nothing but a moving hate."

"I don't care!" screamed Lantry, and began choking the man, beating his head with his fists, crouched on the defenseless body. McClure looked up at him with dying eyes.

The front door opened. Two men came in.

"I say," said one of them. "What's going on? A new game?"

Lantry jumped back and began to run.

"Yes, a new game!" said McClure, struggling up. "Catch him and you win!"

The two men caught Lantry. "We win," they said.

"Let me go!" Lantry thrashed, hitting them across their faces, bringing blood.

"Hold him tight!" cried McClure.

They held him.

"A rough game, what?" one of them said. "What do we do *now*?"

The beetle hissed along the shining road. Rain fell out of the sky and a wind ripped at the dark green wet trees. In the beetle, his hands on the half-wheel, McClure was talking. His voice was susurrant, a whispering, a hypnotic thing. The two other men sat in the back seat. Lantry sat, or rather lay, in the front seat, his head back, his eyes faintly open, the glowing green light of the dash dials showing on his cheeks. His mouth was relaxed. He did not speak.

McClure talked quietly and logically, about life and moving, about death and not moving, about the sun and the great sun Incinerator, about the emptied tombyard, about hatred and how hate lived and made a clay man live and move, and how illogical it all was, it all was, it all was. One was dead, was dead, was dead, that was all, all, all. One did not try to be otherwise. The car whispered on the moving road. The rain spattered gently on the windshield. The men in the back seat conversed quietly. Where were they going, going? To the Incinerator, of course. Cigarette smoke moved slowly up on the air, curling and tying into itself in gray loops and spirals. One was dead and must accept it.

Lantry did not move. He was a marionette, the strings cut. There was only a tiny hatred in his heart, in his eyes, like twin coals, feeble, glowing, fading.

I am Poe, he thought. I am all that is left of Edgar Allan Poe, and I am all that is left of Ambrose Bierce and all that is left of a man named Lovecraft. I am a gray night bat with sharp teeth, and I am a square black monolith monster. I am Osiris and Bal and Set. I am the Necronomicon, the Book of the Dead. I am the house of Usher, falling into flame. I am the Red Death. I am the man mortared into the catacomb with a cask of Amontillado . . . I am a dancing skeleton. I am a coffin, a shroud, a lightning bolt reflected in an old house window. I am an autumn-empty tree, I am a rapping, flinging shutter.

I am a yellowed volume turned by a claw hand. I am an organ played in an attic at midnight. I am a mask, a skull mask behind an oak tree on the last day of October. I am a poison apple bobbling in a water tub for child noses to bump at, for child teeth to snap . . . I am a black candle lighted before an inverted cross. I am a coffin lid, a sheet with eyes, a foot-step on a black stairwell. I am Dunsany and Machen and I am the Legend of Sleepy Hollow. I am The Monkey's Paw and I am The Phantom Rickshaw. I am the Cat and the Canary, The Gorilla, the Bat. I am the ghost of Hamlet's father on the castle wall.

All of these things am I. And now these last things will be burned. While I lived *they* still lived. While I moved and hated and existed, *they* still existed. I am *all* that remembers them. I am all of them that *still* goes on, and will *not* go on after tonight. Tonight, all of us, Poe and Bierce and Hamlet's father, we burn together. They will make a big heap of us and burn us like a bonfire, like things of Guy Fawkes' day, gasoline, torchlight, cries, and all!

And what a wailing will we put up. The world will be clean of us, but in our going we shall say, oh what is the world like, clean of fear, where is the dark imagination from the dark time, the thrill and the anticipation, the suspense of old October, gone, never more to come again, flattened and smashed and burned by the rocket people, by the Incinerator people, destroyed and obliterated, to be replaced by doors that open and close and lights that go on or off without fear. If only you could remember how once *we* lived, what Halloween was to us, and what Poe was, and how we gloried in the dark morbidities. One more drink, dear friends, of Amontillado, before the burning. All of this, all, exists but in one last brain on earth. A whole world dying tonight. One more drink, pray.

"Here we are," said McClure.

The Incinerator was brightly lighted. There was quiet music nearby. McClure got out of the beetle, came around to the other side. He opened the door. Lantry simply lay there. The talking and the logical talking had slowly drained him of life. He was no more than wax now, with a small glow in his eyes. This future world, how the men *talked* to you, how logically they reasoned away your life. They wouldn't believe in him. The force of their disbelief froze him. He could not move his arms or his legs. He could only mumble senselessly, coldly, eyes flickering.

McClure and the two others helped him out of the car, put him in a golden box, and rolled him on a roller table into the warm glowing interior of the building.

I am Edgar Allan Poe, I am Ambrose Bierce, I am Halloween, I am a coffin, a shroud, a Monkey's Paw, a Phantom, a Vampire . . .

"Yes, yes," said McClure, quietly, over him. "I know. I know."

The table glided. The walls swung over him and by him, the music played. You are dead, you are logically dead.

I am Usher, I am the Maelstrom, I am the MS Found In A Bottle, I am the Pit and I am the Pendulum, I am the Telltale Heart, I am the Raven nevermore, nevermore.

"Yes," said McClure, as they walked softly. "I know."

"I am in the catacomb," cried Lantry.

"Yes, the catacomb," said the walking man over him.

"I am being chained to a wall, and there is no bottle of Amontillado here!" cried Lantry weakly, eyes closed.

"Yes," someone said.

There was movement. The flame door opened.

"Now someone is mortaring up the cell, closing me in!"

"Yes, I *know.*" A whisper.

The golden box slid into the flame lock.

"I'm being walled in! A very good joke indeed! Let us be gone!" A wild scream and much laughter.

"We know, we understand . . ."

The inner flame lock opened. The golden coffin shot forth into flame.

"*For the love of God, Montresor! For the love of God!*"

Asleep in Armageddon

YOU DON'T WANT death and you don't expect death. Something goes wrong, your rocket tilts in space, a planetoid jumps up, blackness, movement, hands over the eyes, a violent pulling back of available powers in the forejets, the crash.

The darkness. In the darkness, the senseless pain. In the pain, the nightmare.

He was not unconscious.

Your name? asked hidden voices. Sale, he replied in whirling nausea. *Leonard Sale. Occupation*, cried the voices. *Space man!* he cried, alone in the night. *Welcome*, said the voices. *Welcome, welcome.* They faded.

He stood up in the wreckage of his ship. It lay like a folded, tattered garment around him.

The sun rose and it was morning.

Sale prised himself out the small airlock and stood breathing heavily. Luck. Sheer luck. His suit was intact; his oxygen breathable. A few minutes' checking showed him he had two months' supply of oxygen and food. Fine! And this—he prowled through the wreckage. Miracle of miracles! The radio was intact.

He stuttered out the message on the sending key. CRASHED ON PLANETOID 787. SALE. HELP. SALE. HELP.

Minutes passed; the reply came: HELLO, SALE. THIS IS ADDAMS IN MARSPORT. SENDING RESCUE SHIP LOGARITHM. WILL ARRIVE PLANETOID 787 SIX DAYS. HANG ON.

Sale did a little dance.

It was simple as that. One crashed. One had food. One radioed for help. Help came. Voila! he shouted.

The sun rose and was warm. He felt no sense of mortality. Six days would be no time at all. He would eat, he would read, he would sleep. He glanced at his surroundings. No dangerous animals; a tolerable oxygen supply. What more could one ask? Beans and bacon, was the answer. He touched the machinery in his helmet that popped food into his mouth.

After breakfast he smoked a cigarette slowly, deeply, blowing out through the special helmet tube. He nodded contentedly. What a life! Not a scratch on him. Luck, sheer luck!

His head nodded. Sleep, he thought.

Good idea. Forty winks. Plenty of time to sleep, take it easy. Six whole long, luxurious days of idling and philosophizing. Sleep.

He stretched himself out, tucked his arm under his head, and shut his eyes.

Insanity came in to take him. The voices whispered.

Sleep, yes, sleep, said the voices. *Ah, sleep, sleep.*

He opened his eyes. The voices stopped. Everything was normal. He shrugged. He shut his eyes casually, fitfully. He settled his long body.

Eeeeeeeeeee, sang the voices far away.

Ahhhhhhhhh, sang the voices.

Sleep, sleep, sleep, sleep, sleep, sang the voices.

Die, die, die, die, die, sang the voices.

Oooooooooooo, cried the voices.

Mmmmmmmmmmmmmmmmmmmmm, a bee ran through his brain.

He sat up. He shook his head. He blinked at the crashed ship. Hard metal. He felt the solid rock under his fingers. He saw the real sun warming the blue sky.

Let's try sleeping on our back, he thought. He adjusted himself, lying back down. His watch ticked on his wrist. The blood burned in his veins.

Sleep, sleep, sleep, sleep, sleep, sang the voices.

Ohhhhhhhhhhhh, sang the voices.

Ahhhhhhhhhhhh, sang the voices.

Die, die, die, die, die. Sleep, sleep, die, sleep, die, sleep, die! Oohhh. Ahhhh. Eeeeeeeeeeeee!

Blood tapped in his ears. The sound of the wind rising.

Mine, mine, said a voice. *Mine, mine, he's mine; he's mine!*

No, mine, mine, said another voice. *No, mine, mine, he's mine!*

No, ours, ours, sang ten voices. *Ours, ours, he's ours!*

His fingers twitched. His jaws spasmed. His eyelids jerked.

At last, at last, sang a high voice. *Now, now. The long time, the waiting. Over, over*, sang the high voice. *Over, over at last!*

It was like being undersea. Green songs, green visions, green time. Bubbled voices drowning in deep liquors of sea tide. Far-away choruses chanting senseless rhymes. Leonard Sale stirred in agony.

Mine, mine, cried a loud voice. *Mine, mine!* shrieked another. *Ours, ours*, shrieked the chorus.

The din of metal, the crash of sword, the conflict, the battle, the fight, the war. All of it exploding, his mind fiercely torn apart.

Eeeeeeeeee!

He leaped up, screaming. The landscape melted and flowed.

A voice said, "I am Tylle of Rathalar. Proud Tylle, Tylle of the Blood Mound and the Death Drum. Tylle of Rathalar, Killer of Men!"

Another spoke, "I am Iorr of Wendillo, Wise Iorr, Destroyer of Infidels!"

The chorus chanted. "And we the warriors, we the steel, we the warriors, we the red blood rushing, the red blood falling, the red blood steaming in the sun——"

Leonard Sale staggered under the burden. "Go away!" he cried. "Leave me, in God's name, leave me!"

Eeeeeee, shrieked the high sound of steel hot on steel.

Silence.

He stood with the sweat boiling out of him. He was trembling so violently he could not stand. Insane, he thought. Absolutely insane. Raving insane. Insane!

He jerked the food kit open, did something to a chemical packet. Hot coffee was ready in an instant. He mouthed it through the helmet tube greedily. He shivered. He sucked in raw gulps of breath.

Let's be logical, he thought, sitting down heavily. The coffee seared his tongue. No record of insanity in the family for two hundred years. All healthy, well-balanced. No reason for insanity now. Shock? Silly. No shock. I'm to be rescued in six days. No shock to that. No danger. Just an ordinary planetoid. Ordinary, ordinary, ordinary place. No reason for insanity. I'm sane.

Oh? cried a small metal voice within. An echo. Fading.

"Yes!" he cried, beating his fists together. "Sane!"

Hahhahhahhahhahhahhahhah. Somewhere a vanishing laughter.

He whirled about. "Shut up, you!" he cried.

We didn't say anything, said the mountains. We didn't say anything, said the sky. We didn't say anything, said the wreckage.

"All right then," he said, swaying. "See that you don't."

Everything was normal.

The pebbles were getting hot. The sky was big and dark. He looked at his fingers and saw the way the sun burned on every black hair. He looked at his boots and the dust on them. Suddenly he felt very happy because he made a decision. I won't go to sleep, he thought. I'm having nightmares, so why sleep? There's your solution.

He made a routine. From nine o'clock in the morning, which was this minute, until twelve, he would walk around and see the planetoid. He would write on a pad with a yellow pencil everything he saw. Then he would sit down and open a can of oily sardines, and some canned fresh bread with good butter on it, and pass it in through the helmet air-locks. From twelve-thirty until four he would read nine chapters of *War and Peace.* He took the book from the wreckage, and laid it where he might find it later. There was a book of T. S. Eliot's poetry, too. That might be nice.

Supper would come at five-thirty and then from six until ten he would listen to the radio from Earth. There would be a couple of bad comedians telling jokes and a bad singer singing some songs, and the latest news flashes, signing off at midnight with the U.N. anthem.

After that?

He felt sick.

I'll play solitaire until dawn, he thought. I'll sit up and drink hot black coffee and play solitaire, no cheating, until sunrise.

Ho, ho, he thought.

"What did you say?" he asked himself, aloud.

"I said 'Ha ha'," he replied. "*Some* time, you'll have to sleep."

"I'm wide awake," he said.

"Liar!" he retorted, enjoying the conversation.

"I feel fine," he said.

"Hypocrite," he replied.

"I'm not afraid of the night or sleep or anything," he said.

"*Very* funny," he said.

He felt bad. He wanted to sleep. And the fact that he was afraid of sleep made him want to lie down all the more and shut his eyes and curl up. "Comfy-cosy?" asked his ironic censor.

"I'll just walk and look at the rocks and the geological formations and think how good it is to be alive," he said.

"Ye gods!" cried his censor. "William Saroyan!"

You'll go on, he thought, maybe one day, maybe one night, but what about the next night and the next and the *next*? Can you stay awake *all* that time, for six nights? Until the rescue ship comes? Are you *that* good, *that* strong?"

The answer was no.

What are you afraid of? I don't know. Those voices. Those sounds. But they can't hurt you—can they?

They *might*. You've got to face them some time. Must I? Brace up to it, old man. Chin up, and all that rot.

He sat down on the hard ground. He felt very much like crying. He felt as if life was over and he was entering new and unknown territory. It was such a deceiving day, with the sun warm; physically, he felt able and well, one might fish on such a day as this, or pick flowers or kiss a woman or anything. But in the midst of a lovely day, what did one get?

Death.

Well, hardly *that*.

Death, he insisted.

He lay down and closed his eyes. He was tired of messing around.

All right, he thought, if you *are* death, come get me. I want to know what all this damned nonsense is about.

Death came.

Eeeeeeeeeeeee, said a voice.

Yes, I know, said Leonard Sale, lying there. But what else?

Ahhhhhhhhhhhhhhhhhh, said a voice.

I know that, also, said Leonard Sale, irritably. He turned cold. His mouth hung open wildly.

"I am Tylle of Rathalar, Killer of Men!"

"I am Iorr of Wendillo, Destroyer of Infidels!"

What is this place? asked Leonard Sale, struggling against horror.

"Once a mighty planet!" said Tylle of Rathalar. "Once a place of battles!" said Iorr of Wendillo.

"Now dead," said Tylle.

"Now silent," said Iorr.

"Until *you* came," said Tylle.

"To give us life again," said Iorr.

You're dead, insisted Leonard Sale, flesh writhing. You're nothing but empty wind.

"We live, through you."

"And fight, through *you*!"

So that's it, thought Leonard Sale. I'm to be a battleground, am I? Are you friends?

"Enemies!" cried Iorr.

"Foul enemies!" cried Tylle.

Leonard smiled a rictal smile. He felt ghastly. How long have you waited? he demanded.

"How long is *time*?" Ten thousand years? "Perhaps." Ten million years? "Perhaps."

What are you? Thoughts, spirits, ghosts? "All of those, and more." Intelligence? "Precisely." How did you survive?

Eeeeeeeeeeeeeee, sang the chorus, far away.

Ahhhhhhhhhhhhhhhh, sang another army, waiting to fight.

"Once upon a time, this was fertile land, a rich planet. And there were two nations, strong nations, led by two strong men. I, Iorr. And he, that one who calls himself Tylle. And the planet declined and gave way to nothingness. The peoples and the armies languished in the midst of a great war which had lasted five thousand years. We lived long lives and loved long loves, drank much, slept much, fought much. And when the planet died, our bodies withered, and, only in time, and with much science, did we survive."

Survive, wondered Leonard Sale. But there is nothing of you!

"Our *minds*, fool, our *minds*! What is a body without a mind?"

What is a mind without a *body*, laughed Leonard Sale. I've got you there. Admit it, I've *got* you!

"True," said the cruel voice. "One is useless, lacking the other. But survival is survival even when unconscious. The minds of our nations, through science, through wonder, survived."

But without senses, lacking eyes, ears, lacking touch, smell, and the rest? "Lacking all those, yes. We were vapours, merely. For a long time. Until today."

And now I am here, thought Leonard Sale. "You are here," said the voice. "To give substance to our souls. To give us our needed body."

I'm only one, thought Sale. "Nevertheless, you are of use."

I'm an individual, thought Sale. I resent your intrusion.

"He resents our intrusion! Did you hear him, Iorr? He resents!"

"As if he had a right to resent!"

Be careful, warned Sale. I'll blink my eyes and you'll be gone, phantoms! I'll wake up and rub you out!

"But you'll have to sleep again, *some* time!" cried Iorr. "And when you do, we'll be here, waiting, waiting, waiting. For you."

What do you want? "Solidity. Mass. Sensation again!" You can't *both* have it. "We'll fight that out between us."

A hot clamp twisted his skull. It was as if a spike had been thrust and beaten down between the bivalvular halves of his brain.

Now it was terribly clear. Horribly, magnificently clear. He was their universe. The world of his thoughts, his brain, his skull, divided into two camps, that of Iorr, that of Tylle. They were *using* him!

Pennants flung up on a pink mind sky! Brass shields caught the sun. Grey animals shifted and came rushing in bristling tides of sword and plume and trumpet.

Eeeeeeeeeeeee! The rushing.

Ahhhhhhhhhhhhhhh! The roaring.

Nowwwwwwwwwwwwwwwwwww! The whirling.

Mmmmmmmmmmmmmmmmmmmmmmm——

Ten thousand men hurtled across the small hidden stage. Ten thousand men floated on the shellacked inner ball of his eye. Ten thousand javelins hissed between the small bone hulls of his head. Ten thousand jewelled guns exploded. Ten thousand voices chanted in his ears. Now his body was riven and extended, shaken and rolled, he was screaming, writhing, the plates of his skull threatened to burst asunder. The gabbling, the shrilling, as across bone plains of mind and continent of inner marrow, through gullies of vein, down hills of artery, over rivers of melancholy, came armies and armies, one army, two armies, swords flashed in the sun, bearing down upon each other, fifty thousand minds snatching, scrabbling, cutting at him, demanding, using. In a moment, the hard collision, one army on another, the rush, the blood, the sound, the fury, the death, the insanity!

Like cymbals, the armies struck!

He leaped up, raving. He ran across the desert. He ran and ran and did not stop running.

He sat down and cried. He sobbed until his lungs ached. He cried very hard and long. Tears ran down his cheeks. "God, God, help me, oh God, help me!" he said.

All was normal again.

It was four o'clock in the afternoon. The rocks were baked by the sun. He managed, after a time, to cook himself a few hot biscuits, which he ate with strawberry jam.

"At least I know what I'm up against," he told himself. "Oh, Lord, what a world! What an innocent-looking world, and what a monster it really is. It's good no one ever explored it before. Or *did* they?" He shook his aching head. Pity them, whoever crashed here before, if any ever did. Warm sun, hard rocks, not a sign of hostility.

Until you shut your eyes and relaxed your mind.

And the night and the voices and the insanity and the death padded in on soft feet.

"I'm all right now, though," he said, proudly. "Look at that." He displayed his hand. By a supreme effort of will, it was no longer shaking. "I'll show you who in hell's ruler here," he announced to the innocent sky. "*I* am!" He tapped his chest.

To think that *thought* could live that long! A million years, perhaps, all these thoughts of death and disorder and conquest, lingering in the innocent but poisonous air of the planet, waiting for a real man to give them a channel through which they might issue again in all their senseless virulence.

Now that he was feeling better, it was all silly. All I have to do, he thought, is stay awake six nights. They won't bother me that way. When I'm awake, I'm dominant. I'm stronger than those crazy monarchs and their silly tribes of sword-flingers and shield-bearers and horn-blowers. I'll stay awake.

But *can* you? he wondered. Six whole nights? Awake?

There's coffee and medicine and books and cards.

But I'm tired *now*, so tired, he thought. Can I hold out?

Well, if not—there's always the gun.

Where will these silly monarchs be if you put a bullet through their stage? All the world's a stage. No. *You*, Leonard Sale, are the small stage. And they the players. And what if you put a bullet through the wings, tearing down scenes, destroying curtains, ruining lines! Destroy the stage, the players, all, if they aren't careful!

First of all, he must radio through to Marsport, again. If there was any way they could rush the rescue ship sooner, then maybe he could hang on. Anyway, he must warn them what sort of planet this was, this so innocent-seeming spot of nightmare and fever vision——

He tapped on the radio key for a minute. His mouth tightened. The radio was dead.

It had sent through the proper rescue message, received a reply, and then extinguished itself.

The proper touch of irony, he thought. There was only one thing to do. Draw a plan.

This he did. He got a yellow pencil and delineated his six-day plan of escape.

Tonight, he wrote, read six more chapters of *War and Peace*. At four in the morning have hot black coffee. At four-fifteen take cards from pack and play ten games of solitaire. This should take until six-thirty when—more coffee. At seven o'clock, listen to early morning programmes from Earth, if the receiving equipment on the radio works at all. Does it?

He tried the radio receiver. It was dead.

Well, he wrote, from seven o'clock until eight, sing all the songs you remember, make your own entertainment. From eight until nine think about Helen King. Remember Helen. On second thought, think about Helen right now.

He marked that out with his pencil.

The rest of the days were set down in minute detail.

He checked the medical kit. There were several packets of

tablets that would keep you awake. One tablet an hour every hour for six days. He felt quite confident.

"Here's mud in your evil eye, Iorr, Tylle!"

He swallowed one of the stay-awake tablets with a scalding mouth of black coffee.

Well, with one thing and another it was Tolstoy or Balzac, gin-rummy, coffee, tablets, walking, more Tolstoy, more Balzac, more gin-rummy, more solitaire. The first day passed, as did the second and the third.

On the fourth day he lay quietly in the shade of a rock, counting to a thousand by fives, then by tens, to keep his mind occupied and awake. His eyes were so tired he had to bathe them frequently in cool water. He couldn't read, he was bothered with splitting headaches. He was so exhausted he couldn't move. He was numb with medicine. He resembled a waxen dummy stuffed with things to preserve him in a state of horrified wakefulness. His eyes were glass, his tongue a rusted pike, his fingers felt as if they were gloved in needles and fur.

He followed the hand of his watch. One second less to wait, he thought. Two seconds, three seconds, four, five, ten, thirty seconds. A whole minute. Now an hour less time to wait. Oh, ship, hurry on thy appointed round!

He began to laugh softly.

What would happen if he just gave up, drifted off into sleep? Sleep, ah, sleep; perchance to dream. All the world a stage . . . What if he gave up the unequal struggle, lapsed down?

Eeeeeeeeeeee, the high, shrill warning sound of battle metal.

He shivered. His tongue moved in his dry, burry mouth.

Iorr and Tylle would battle out their ancient battle.

Leonard Sale would become quite insane.

And whichever won the battle would take this ruin of an insane man, the shaking, laughing wild body, and wander it across the face of this world for ten, twenty years, occupying it, striding in it, pompous, holding court, making grand gestures, ordering heads severed, calling on inward, unseen dancing girls. Leonard Sale, what remained of him, would be led off to some hidden cave, there to be infested with wars and worms of wars for twenty insane years, occupied and prostituted by old and outlandish thoughts.

When the rescue ship arrived it would find nothing. Sale would be hidden somewhere by a triumphant army in his head. Hidden in some cleft of rock, placed there like a nest for Iorr to lie upon in evil occupation.

The thought of it almost broke him in half.

Twenty years of insanity. Twenty years of torture, doing what you don't want to do. Twenty years of wars raging and being split apart, twenty years of nausea and trembling.

His head sank down between his knees. His eyes snapped and cracked and made soft noises. His eardrum popped tiredly.

Sleep, sleep, sang soft sea voices.

I'll—I'll make a proposition with you, listen, thought Leonard Sale. You, Iorr, you, too, Tylle! Iorr, you can occupy me on Mondays, Wednesdays and Fridays. Tylle, you can take me over on Sundays, Tuesdays and Saturdays. Thursday is maid's night out. Okay?

Eeeeeeeeeee, sang the sea tides, seething in his brain.

Ohhhhhhhhhhhhhh, sang the distant voices softly, soft.

What'll you say, is it a *bargain*, Iorr, Tylle?

No, said a voice.

No, said another.

Greedy, both of you, greedy! complained Sale. A pox on both your houses!

He slept.

He *was* Iorr, jewelled rings on his hands. He arose beside his rocket and held out his fingers, commanding blind armies. He was Iorr, ancient ruler of jewelled warriors.

He *was* Tylle, lover of women, killer of dogs!

With some hidden bit of awareness, his hand crept to the holster at his hip. The sleeping hand withdrew the gun there. The hand lifted, the gun pointed.

The armies of Tylle and Iorr gave battle.

The gun exploded.

The bullet tore across Sale's forehead, awakening him.

He stayed awake for another six hours, getting over his latest siege. He knew it to be hopeless now. He washed and bandaged the wound he had given himself. He wished he had aimed straighter and it was all over. He watched the sky. Two more days. Two more. Come on, ship, come on. He was heavy with sleeplessness.

No use. At the end of six hours he was raving badly. He took the gun up and put it down and took it up again, put it against his head, tightened his hand on the trigger, changed his mind, looked at the sky again.

Night settled. He tried to read, threw the book away. He tore it up and burned it, just to have something to do.

So tired. In another hour, he decided. If nothing happens, I'll *kill* myself. This is for certain now. I'll *do* it, this time.

He got the gun ready and laid it on the ground next to himself.

He was very calm now, though tired. It would be over and done. He would be dead.

He watched the minute hand of his watch. One minute, five minutes, twenty-five minutes.

The flame appeared on the sky.

It was so unbelievable he started to cry.

"A rocket," he said, standing up. "A rocket!" he cried, rubbing his eyes. He ran forward.

The flame brightened, grew, came down.

He waved frantically, running forward, leaving his gun, his supplies, everything behind. "You *see* that, Iorr, Tylle! You savages, you monsters, I beat you! I *won*! They're coming to rescue me now! I've won, damn you!"

He laughed harshly at the rocks and the sky and the backs of his hands.

The rocket landed. Leonard Sale stood swaying, waiting for the door to lid open.

"Goodbye, Iorr, goodbye, Tylle!" he shouted in triumph, grinning, eyes hot.

Eeeeeee, sang a diminishing roar in time.

Ahhhhhhhh, voices faded.

The rocket flipped wide its air-lock. Two men jumped out.

"Sale?" they called. "We're Ship ACDN13. Intercepted your SOS and decided to pick you up ourselves. The Marsport ship won't get through until day after tomorrow. We want a spot of rest ourselves. Thought it'd be good to spend the night here, pick you up, and go on."

"No," said Sale, face melting with terror. "No spend night——"

He couldn't talk. He fell to the ground.

"Quick!" said a voice, in the bleary vortex over him. "Give him a shot of food liquid, another of sedative. He needs sustenance and rest."

"No rest!" screamed Sale.

"Delirious," said one man, softly.

"No sleep!" screamed Sale.

"There, there," said the man gently. A needle poked into Sale's arm.

Sale thrashed. "No sleep, go!" he mouthed horribly. "Oh, go!"

"Delirious," said one man. "Shock."

"No sedatives!" screamed Sale.

The sedative flowed into him.

Eeeeeeeee, sang the ancient winds.

Ahhhhhhhhhh, sang the ancient seas.

"No sedative, no sleep, please, don't, don't, don't!" screamed Sale, trying to get up. "You—don't understand!"

"Take it easy, old man, you're safe among us now, nothing to worry about," said the rescuer above him.

Leonard Sale slept. The two men stood over him.

As they watched, Sale's features changed violently. He groaned and cried and snarled in his sleep. His face was riven with emotion. It was the face of a saint, a sinner, a fiend, a monster, a darkness, a light, one, many, an army, a vacuum, all all!

He writhed in his sleep.

Eeeeeeeee! the sound burst from his mouth. Ahhhhhhhhhh! he screamed.

"What's wrong with him?" asked one of the two rescuers.

"I don't know. More sedatives?"

"More sedative. Nerves. He needs more sleep."

They stuck the needle in his arm. Sale writhed and spat and moaned.

Then, suddenly, he was dead.

He lay there, the two men over him. "What a shame," said one of them. "Can you figure that?"

"Shock. Poor guy. What a pity." They covered his face. "Did you ever see a face like that?"

"Loneliness. Shock."

"Yes. Lord, what an expression! I hope never to see a face like *that* again."

"What a shame, waiting for us, and we arrive, and he dies anyway."

They glanced around. "What shall we do? Shall we spend the night?"

"Yes. It's good to be out of the ship."

"We'll bury him first, of course."

"Naturally."

"And spend the night in the open, with good air, right? Good to be in the open again. After two weeks in that damned ship."

"Right. I'll find a spot for him. You start supper, eh?"

"Done."

"Should be good sleeping tonight."

"Fine, fine."

They made a grave and said a word over it. They drank their evening coffee silently. They looked at the lovely sky and the bright and beautiful stars.

"What a night," they said, lying down.

"Pleasant dreams," said one, rolling over.

And the other replied, "Pleasant dreams."

They slept.

Dark They Were, and Golden-eyed

THE ROCKET METAL cooled in the meadow winds. Its lid gave a bulging *pop*. From its clock interior stepped a man, a woman, and three children. The other passengers whispered away across the Martian meadow, leaving the man alone among his family.

The man felt his hair flutter and the tissues of his body draw tight as if he were standing at the center of a vacuum. His wife, before him, seemed almost to whirl away in smoke. The children, small seeds, might at any instant be sown to all the Martian climes.

The children looked up at him, as people look to the sun to tell what time of their life it is. His face was cold.

"What's wrong?" asked his wife.

"Let's get back on the rocket."

"Go back to Earth?"

"Yes! Listen!"

The wind blew as if to flake away their identities. At any moment the Martian air might draw his soul from him, as marrow comes from a white bone. He felt submerged in a chemical that could dissolve his intellect and burn away his past.

They looked at Martian hills that time had worn with a crushing pressure of years. They saw the old cities, lost in their meadows, lying like children's delicate bones among the blowing lakes of grass.

"Chin up, Harry," said his wife. "It's too late. We've come over sixty million miles."

The children with their yellow hair hollered at the deep dome of Martian sky. There was no answer but the racing hiss of wind through the stiff grass.

He picked up the luggage in his cold hands. "Here we go," he said—a man standing on the edge of a sea, ready to wade in and be drowned.

They walked into town.

Their name was Bittering. Harry and his wife Cora; Dan, Laura, and David. They built a small white cottage and ate good breakfasts there, but the fear was never gone. It lay with Mr. Bittering and Mrs. Bittering, a third unbidden partner at every midnight talk, at every dawn awakening.

"I feel like a salt crystal," he said, "in a mountain stream, being washed away. We don't belong here. We're Earth people. This is Mars. It was meant for Martians. For heaven's sake, Cora, let's buy tickets for home!"

But she only shook her head. "One day the atom bomb will fix Earth. Then we'll be safe here."

"Safe and insane!"

Tick-tock, seven o'clock sang the voice-clock; *time to get up.* And they did.

Something made him check everything each morning—warm hearth, potted blood-geraniums—precisely as if he expected something to be amiss. The morning paper was toast-warm from the 6 A.M. Earth rocket. He broke its seal and tilted it at his breakfast place. He forced himself to be convivial.

"Colonial days all over again," he declared. "Why, in ten years there'll be a million Earthmen on Mars. Big cities, everything! They said we'd fail. Said the Martians would resent our invasion. But did we find any Martians? Not a living soul! Oh, we found their empty cities, but no one in them. Right?"

A river of wind submerged the house. When the windows ceased rattling Mr. Bittering swallowed and looked at the children.

"I don't know," said David. "Maybe there're Martians around we don't see. Sometimes nights I think I hear 'em. I hear the wind. The sand hits my window. I get scared. And I see those towns way up in the mountains where the Martians lived a long time ago. And I think I see things moving around those towns, Papa. And I wonder if those Martians *mind* us living here. I wonder if they won't do something to us for coming here."

"Nonsense!" Mr. Bittering looked out the windows. "We're clean, decent people." He looked at his children. "All dead cities have some kind of ghosts in them. Memories, I mean." He stared at the hills. "You see a staircase and you wonder what Martians looked like climbing it. You see Martian paintings and you wonder what the painter was like. You make a little ghost in your mind, a memory. It's quite natural. Imagination." He stopped. "You haven't been prowling up in those ruins, have you?"

"No, Papa." David looked at his shoes.

"See that you stay away from them. Pass the jam."

"Just the same," said little David, "I bet something happens."

Something happened that afternoon.

Laura stumbled through the settlement, crying. She dashed blindly onto the porch.

"Mother, Father—the war, Earth!" she sobbed. "A radio flash just came. Atom bombs hit New York! All the space rockets blown up. No more rockets to Mars, ever!"

"Oh, Harry!" The mother held onto her husband and daughter.

"Are you sure, Laura?" asked the father quietly.

Laura wept. "We're stranded on Mars, forever and ever!"

For a long time there was only the sound of the wind in the late afternoon.

Alone, thought Bittering. Only a thousand of us here. No way back. No way. No way. Sweat poured from his face and his hands and his body; he was drenched in the hotness of his fear. He wanted to strike Laura, cry, "No, you're lying! The rockets will come back!" Instead, he stroked Laura's head against him and said, "The rockets will get through someday."

"Father, what will we do?"

"Go about our business, of course. Raise crops and children. Wait. Keep things going until the war ends and the rockets come again."

The two boys stepped out onto the porch.

"Children," he said, sitting there, looking beyond them, "I've something to tell you."

"We know," they said.

In the following days, Bittering wandered often through the garden to stand alone in his fear. As long as the rockets had spun a silver web across space, he had been able to accept Mars. For he had always told himself: Tomorrow, if I want, I can buy a ticket and go back to Earth.

But now: The web gone, the rockets lying in jigsaw heaps of molten girder and unsnaked wire. Earth people left to the strangeness of Mars, the cinnamon dusts and wine airs, to be baked like gingerbread shapes in Martian summers, put into harvested storage by Martian winters. What would happen to him, the others? This was the moment Mars had waited for. Now it would eat them.

He got down on his knees in the flower bed, a spade in his nervous hands. Work, he thought, work and forget.

He glanced up from the garden to the Martian mountains. He thought of the proud old Martian names that had once been on those peaks. Earthmen, dropping from the sky, had gazed upon hills, rivers, Martian seas left nameless in spite of names. Once Martians had built cities, named cities; climbed mountains, named mountains; sailed seas, named seas. Mountains melted, seas drained, cities tumbled. In spite of this, the Earthmen had felt a silent guilt at putting new names to these ancient hills and valleys.

Nevertheless, man lives by symbol and label. The names were given.

Mr. Bittering felt very alone in his garden under the Martian sun, anachronism bent here, planting Earth flowers in a wild soil.

Think. Keep thinking. Different things. Keep your mind free of Earth, the atom war, the lost rockets.

He perspired. He glanced about. No one watching. He removed his tie. Pretty bold, he thought. First your coat off, now your tie. He hung it neatly on a peach tree he had imported as a sapling from Massachusetts.

He returned to his philosophy of names and mountains. The Earthmen had changed names. Now there were Hormel Valleys, Roosevelt Seas, Ford Hills, Vanderbilt Plateaus, Rockefeller Rivers, on Mars. It wasn't right. The American settlers had shown wisdom, using old Indian prairie names: Wisconsin, Minnesota, Idaho, Ohio, Utah, Milwaukee, Waukegan, Osseo. The old names, the old meanings.

Staring at the mountains wildly, he thought: Are you up there? All the dead ones, you Martians? Well, here we are, alone, cut off! Come down, move us out! We're helpless!

The wind blew a shower of peach blossoms.

He put out his sun-browned hand, gave a small cry. He touched the blossoms, picked them up. He turned them, he touched them again and again. Then he shouted for his wife.

"Cora!"

She appeared at a window. He ran to her.

"Cora, these blossoms!"

She handled them.

"Do you see? They're different. They've changed! They're not peach blossoms any more!"

"Look all right to me," she said.

"They're not. They're *wrong*! I can't tell how. An extra petal, a leaf, something, the color, the smell!"

The children ran out in time to see their father hurrying about the garden, pulling up radishes, onions, and carrots from their beds.

"Cora, come look!"

They handled the onions, the radishes, the carrots among them.

"Do they look like carrots?"

"Yes . . . no." She hesitated. "I don't know."

"They're changed."

"Perhaps."

"You know they have! Onions but not onions, carrots but not carrots. Taste: the same but different. Smell: not like it used to be." He felt his heart pounding, and he was afraid. He dug his fingers into the earth. "Cora, what's happening? What is it? We've got to get away from this." He ran across the garden. Each tree felt his touch. "The roses. The roses. They're turning green!"

And they stood looking at the green roses.

And two days later Dan came running. "Come see the cow. I was milking her and I saw it. Come on!"

They stood in the shed and looked at their one cow.

It was growing a third horn.

And the lawn in front of their house very quietly and slowly was coloring itself like spring violets. Seed from Earth but growing up a soft purple.

"We must get away," said Bittering. "We'll eat this stuff and then we'll change—who knows to what? I can't let it happen. There's only one thing to do. Burn this food!"

"It's not poisoned."

"But it is. Subtly, very subtly. A little bit. A very little bit. We mustn't touch it."

He looked with dismay at their house. "Even the house. The wind's done something to it. The air's burned it. The fog at night. The boards, all warped out of shape. It's not an Earthman's house any more."

"Oh, your imagination!"

He put on his coat and tie. "I'm going into town. We've got to do something now. I'll be back."

"Wait, Harry!" his wife cried.

But he was gone.

In town, on the shadowy step of the grocery store, the men sat with their hands on their knees, conversing with great leisure and ease.

Mr. Bittering wanted to fire a pistol in the air.

What are you doing, you fools! he thought. Sitting here! You've heard the news—we're stranded on this planet. Well, move! Aren't you frightened? Aren't you afraid? What are you going to do?

"Hello, Harry," said everyone.

"Look," he said to them. "You did hear the news, the other day, didn't you?"

They nodded and laughed. "Sure. Sure, Harry."

"What are you going to do about it?"

"Do, Harry, do? What *can* we do?"

"Build a rocket, that's what!"

"A rocket, Harry? To go back to all that trouble? Oh, Harry!"

"But you *must* want to go back. Have you noticed the peach blossoms, the onions, the grass?"

"Why, yes, Harry, seems we did," said one of the men.

"Doesn't it scare you?"

"Can't recall that it did much, Harry."

"Idiots!"

"Now, Harry."

Bittering wanted to cry. "You've got to work with me. If we stay here, we'll all change. The air. Don't you smell it? Something in the air. A Martian virus, maybe; some seed, or a pollen. Listen to me!"

They stared at him.

"Sam," he said to one of them.

"Yes, Harry?"

"Will you help me build a rocket?"

"Harry, I got a whole load of metal and some blueprints. You want to work in my metal shop on a rocket, you're welcome. I'll sell you that metal for five hundred dollars. You should be able to construct a right pretty rocket, if you work alone, in about thirty years."

Everyone laughed.

"Don't laugh."

Sam looked at him with quiet good humor.

"Sam," Bittering said. "Your eyes——"

"What about them, Harry?"

"Didn't they used to be grey?"

"Well now, I don't remember."

"They were, weren't they?"

"Why do you ask, Harry?"

"Because now they're kind of yellow-colored."

"Is that so, Harry?" Sam said, casually.

"And you're taller and thinner——"

"You might be right, Harry."

"Sam, you shouldn't have yellow eyes."

"Harry, what color eyes have *you* got?" Sam said.

"My eyes? They're blue, of course."

"Here you are, Harry." Sam handed him a pocket mirror. "Take a look at yourself."

Mr. Bittering hesitated, and then raised the mirror to his face.

There were little, very dim flecks of new gold captured in the blue of his eyes.

"Now look what you've done," said Sam a moment later. "You've broken my mirror."

Harry Bittering moved into the metal shop and began to build the rocket. Men stood in the open door and talked and joked without raising their voices. Once in a while they gave him a hand on lifting something. But mostly they just idled and watched him with their yellowing eyes.

"It's suppertime, Harry," they said.

His wife appeared with his supper in a wicker basket.

"I won't touch it," he said. "I'll eat only food from our Deepfreeze. Food that came from Earth. Nothing from our garden."

His wife stood watching him. "You can't build a rocket."

"I worked in a shop once, when I was twenty. I know metal. Once I get it started, the others will help," he said, not looking at her, laying out the blueprints.

"Harry, Harry," she said, helplessly.

"We've got to get away, Cora. We've *got* to!"

The nights were full of wind that blew down the empty moonlit sea meadows past the little white chess cities lying for their twelve-thousandth year in the shallows. In the Earthmen's settlement, the Bittering house shook with a feeling of change.

Lying abed, Mr. Bittering felt his bones shifted, shaped, melted like gold. His wife, lying beside him, was dark from many sunny afternoons. Dark she was, and golden-eyed, burnt almost black by the sun, sleeping, and the children metallic in their beds, and the wind roaring forlorn and changing through the old peach trees, the violet grass, shaking out green rose petals.

The fear would not be stopped. It had his throat and heart. It dripped in a wetness of the arm and the temple and the trembling palm.

A green star rose in the east.

A strange word emerged from Mr. Bittering's lips.

"*Iorrt. Iorrt.*" He repeated it.

It was a Martian word. He knew no Martian.

In the middle of the night he arose and dialed a call through to Simpson, the archeologist.

"Simpson, what does the word *Iorrt* mean?"

"Why that's the old Martian word for our planet Earth. Why?"

"No special reason."

The telephone slipped from his hand.

"Hello, hello, hello, hello," it kept saying while he sat gazing out at the green star. "Bittering? Harry, are you there?"

The days were full of metal sound. He laid the frame of the rocket with the reluctant help of three indifferent men. He grew very tired in an hour or so and had to sit down.

"The altitude," laughed a man.
"Are you *eating*, Harry?" asked another.
"I'm eating," he said, angrily.
"From your Deepfreeze?"
"Yes!"
"You're getting thinner, Harry."
"I'm not!"
"And taller."
"Liar!"

His wife took him aside a few days later. "Harry, I've used up all the food in the Deepfreeze. There's nothing left. I'll have to make sandwiches using food grown on Mars."

He sat down heavily.

"You must eat," she said. "You're weak."

"Yes," he said.

He took a sandwich, opened it, looked at it, and began to nibble at it.

"And take the rest of the day off," she said. "It's hot. The children want to swim in the canals and hike. Please come along."

"I can't waste time. This is a crisis!"

"Just for an hour," she urged. "A swim'll do you good."

He rose, sweating. "All right, all right. Leave me alone. I'll come."

"Good for you, Harry."

The sun was hot, the day quiet. There was only an immense staring burn upon the land. They moved along the canal, the father, the mother, the racing children in their swim suits. They stopped and ate meat sandwiches. He saw their skin baking brown. And he saw the yellow eyes of his wife and his children, their eyes that were never yellow before. A few tremblings shook him, but were carried off in waves of pleasant heat as he lay in the sun. He was too tired to be afraid.

"Cora, how long have your eyes been yellow?"

She was bewildered. "Always, I guess."

"They didn't change from brown in the last three months?"

She bit her lips. "No. Why do you ask?"

"Never mind."

They sat there.

"The children's eyes," he said. "They're yellow, too."

"Sometimes growing children's eyes change color."

"Maybe *we're* children, too. At least to Mars. That's a thought." He laughed. "Think I'll swim."

They leaped into the canal water, and he let himself sink down and down to the bottom like a golden statue and lie there in green silence. All was water-quiet and deep, all was peace. He felt the steady, slow current drift him easily.

If I lie here long enough, he thought, the water will work and eat away my flesh until the bones show like coral. Just my skeleton left. And then the water can build on that skeleton—green things, deep water things, red things, yellow things. Change. Change. Slow, deep, silent change. And isn't that what it is up *there*?

He saw the sky submerged above him, the sun made Martian by atmosphere and time and space.

Up there, a big river, he thought, a Martian river, all of us lying deep in it, in our pebble houses, in our sunken boulder houses, like crayfish hidden, and the water washing away our old bodies and lengthening the bones and——

He let himself drift up through the soft light.

Dan sat on the edge of the canal, regarding his father seriously.

"*Utha,*" he said.

"What?" asked his father.

The boy smiled. "You know. *Utha's* the Martian word for 'father.'"

"Where did you learn it?"

"I don't know. Around. *Utha!*"

"What do you want?"

The boy hesitated. "I—I want to change my name."

"Change it?"

"Yes."

His mother swam over. "What's wrong with Dan for a name?"

Dan fidgeted. "The other day you called Dan, Dan, Dan. I didn't even hear. I said to myself, That's not my name. I've a new name I want to use."

Mr. Bittering held to the side of the canal, his body cold and his heart pounding slowly. "What is this new name?"

"Linnl. Isn't that a good name? Can I use it? Can't I, please?"

Mr. Bittering put his hand to his head. He thought of the silly rocket, himself working alone, himself alone even among his family, so alone.

He heard his wife say, "Why not?"

He heard himself say, "Yes, you can use it."

"Yaaa!" screamed the boy. "I'm Linnl, Linnl!"

Racing down the meadowlands, he danced and shouted.

Mr. Bittering looked at his wife. "Why did we do that?"

"I don't know," she said. "It just seemed like a good idea."

They walked into the hills. They strolled on old mosaic paths, beside still pumping fountains. The paths were covered with a thin film of cool water all summer long. You kept your bare feet cool all the day, splashing as in a creek, wading.

They came to a small deserted Martian villa with a good view of the valley. It was on top of a hill. Blue marble halls, large murals, a swimming pool. It was refreshing in this hot summertime. The Martians hadn't believed in large cities.

"How nice," said Mrs. Bittering, "if we could move up here to this villa for the summer."

"Come on," he said. "We're going back to town. There's work to be done on the rocket."

But as he worked that night, the thought of the cool blue marble villa entered his mind. As the hours passed, the rocket seemed less important.

In the flow of days and weeks, the rocket receded and dwindled. The old fever was gone. It frightened him to think he had let it slip this way. But somehow the heat, the air, the working conditions——

He heard the men murmuring on the porch of his metal shop.

"Everyone's going. You heard?"

"All going. That's right."

Bittering came out. "Going where?" He saw a couple of trucks, loaded with children and furniture, drive down the dusty street.

"Up to the villas," said the man.

"Yeah, Harry. I'm going. So is Sam. Aren't you, Sam?"

"That's right, Harry. What about you?"

"I've got work to do here."

"Work! You can finish that rocket in the autumn, when it's cooler."

He took a breath. "I got the frame all set up."

"In the autumn is better." Their voices were lazy in the heat.

"Got to work," he said.

"Autumn," they reasoned. And they sounded so sensible, so right.

"Autumn would be best," he thought. "Plenty of time, then."

No! cried part of himself, deep down, put away, locked tight, suffocating. No! No!

"In the autumn," he said.

"Come on, Harry," they all said.

"Yes," he said, feeling his flesh melt in the hot liquid air. "Yes, in the autumn. I'll begin work again then."

"I got a villa near the Tirra Canal," said someone.

"You mean the Roosevelt Canal, don't you?"

"Tirra. The old Martian name."

"But on the map——"

"Forget the map. It's Tirra now. Now I found a place in the Pillan mountains—"

"You mean the Rockefeller range," said Bittering.

"I mean the Pillan mountains," said Sam.

"Yes," said Bittering, buried in the hot, swarming air. "The Pillan mountains."

Everyone worked at loading the truck in the hot, still afternoon of the next day.

Laura, Dan, and David carried packages. Or, as they preferred to be known, Ttil, Linnl, and Werr carried packages.

The furniture was abandoned in the little white cottage.

"It looked just fine in Boston," said the mother. "And here in the cottage. But up at the villa? No. We'll get it when we come back in the autumn."

Bittering himself was quiet.

"I've some ideas on furniture for the villa," he said after a time. "Big, lazy furniture."

"What about your encyclopedia? You're taking it along, surely?"

Mr. Bittering glanced away. "I'll come and get it next week."

They turned to their daughter. "What about your New York dresses?"

The bewildered girl stared. "Why, I don't want them any more."

They shut off the gas, the water, they locked the doors and walked away. Father peered into the truck.

"Gosh, we're not taking much," he said. "Considering all we brought to Mars, this is only a handful!"

He started the truck.

Looking at the small white cottage for a long moment, he was filled with a desire to rush to it, touch it, say good-by to it, for he felt as if he were going away on a long journey, leaving something to which he could never quite return, never understand again.

Just then Sam and his family drove by in another truck.

"Hi, Bittering! Here we go!"

The truck swung down the ancient highway out of town. There were sixty others traveling the same direction. The town filled with a silent, heavy dust from their passage. The canal waters lay blue in the sun, and a quiet wind moved in the strange trees.

"Good-by, town!" said Mr. Bittering.

"Good-by, good-by," said the family, waving to it.

They did not look back again.

Summer burned the canals dry. Summer moved like flame upon the meadows. In the empty Earth settlement, the painted houses flaked and peeled. Rubber tires upon which children had swung in back yards hung suspended like stopped clock pendulums in the blazing air.

At the metal shop, the rocket frame began to rust.

In the quiet autumn Mr. Bittering stood, very dark now, very golden-eyed, upon the slope above his villa, looking at the valley.

"It's time to go back," said Cora.

"Yes, but we're not going," he said quietly. "There's nothing there any more."

"Your books," she said. "Your fine clothes."

"Your *Illes* and your fine *ior uele rre*," she said.

"The town's empty. No one's going back," he said. "There's no reason to, none at all."

The daughter wove tapestries and the sons played songs on ancient flutes and pipes, their laughter echoing in the marble villa.

Mr. Bittering gazed at the Earth settlement far away in the low valley. "Such odd, such ridiculous houses the Earth people built."

"They didn't know any better," his wife mused. "Such ugly people. I'm glad they've gone."

They both looked at each other, startled by all they had just finished saying. They laughed.

"Where did they go?" he wondered. He glanced at his wife. She was golden and slender as his daughter. She looked at him, and he seemed almost as young as their eldest son.

"I don't know," she said.

"We'll go back to town maybe next year, or the year after, or the year after that," he said, calmly. "Now—I'm warm. How about taking a swim?"

They turned their backs to the valley. Arm in arm they walked silently down a path of clear-running spring water.

Five years later a rocket fell out of the sky. It lay steaming in the valley. Men leaped out of it, shouting.

"We won the war on Earth! We're here to rescue you! Hey!"

But the American-built town of cottages, peach trees, and theaters was silent. They found a flimsy rocket frame rusting in an empty shop.

The rocket men searched the hills. The captain established headquarters in an abandoned bar. His lieutenant came back to report.

"The town's empty, but we found native life in the hills, sir. Dark people. Yellow eyes. Martians. Very friendly. We talked a bit, not much. They learn English fast. I'm sure our relations will be most friendly with them, sir."

"Dark, eh?" mused the captain. "How many?"

"Six, eight hundred, I'd say, living in those marble ruins in the hills, sir. Tall, healthy. Beautiful women."

"Did they tell you what became of the men and women who built this Earth-settlement, Lieutenant?"

"They hadn't the foggiest notion of what happened to this town or its people."

"Strange. You think those Martians killed them?"

"They look surprisingly peaceful. Chances are a plague did this town in, sir."

"Perhaps. I suppose this is one of those mysteries we'll never solve. One of those mysteries you read about."

The captain looked at the room, the dusty windows, the blue mountains rising beyond, the canals moving in the light, and he heard the soft wind in the air. He shivered. Then, recovering, he tapped a large fresh map he had thumbtacked to the top of an empty table.

"Lots to be done, Lieutenant." His voice droned on and quietly on as the sun sank behind the blue hills. "New settlements. Mining sites, minerals to be looked for. Bacteriological specimens taken. The work, all the work. And the old records were lost. We'll have a job of remapping to do, renaming the mountains and rivers and such. Calls for a little imagination.

"What do you think of naming those mountains the Lincoln Mountains, this canal the Washington Canal, those hills—we can name those hills for you, Lieutenant. Diplomacy. And you, for a favor, might name a town for me. Polishing the apple. And why not make this the Einstein Valley, and further over . . . are you *listening*, Lieutenant?"

The lieutenant snapped his gaze from the blue color and the quiet mist of the hills far beyond the town.

"What? Oh, *yes*, sir!"

A Touch of Petulance

ON AN OTHERWISE ordinary evening in May, a week before his twenty-ninth birthday, Jonathan Hughes met his fate, commuting from another time, another year, another life.

His fate was unrecognizable at first, of course, and boarded the train at the same hour, in Pennsylvania Station, and sat with Hughes for the dinnertime journey across Long Island. It was the newspaper held by this fate disguised as an older man that caused Jonathan Hughes to stare and finally say:

"Sir, pardon me, your *New York Times* seems different from mine. The typeface on your front page seems more modern. Is that a later edition?"

"No!" The older man stopped, swallowed hard, and at last managed to say, "Yes. A very late edition."

Hughes glanced around. "Excuse me, but—all the other editions look the same. Is yours a trial copy for a future change?"

"Future?" The older man's mouth barely moved. His entire body seemed to wither in his clothes, as if he had lost weight with a single exhalation. "Indeed," he whispered. "Future change. God, what a joke."

Jonathan Hughes blinked at the newspaper's dateline:

May 2, 1999.

"Now, see here—" he protested, and then his eyes moved down to find a small story, minus picture, in the upper-left-hand corner of the front page:

> WOMAN MURDERED
> POLICE SEEK HUSBAND
> Body of Mrs. Alice Hughes
> found shot to death—

The train thundered over a bridge. Outside the window, a billion trees rose up, flourished their green branches in convulsions of wind, then fell as if chopped to earth.

The train rolled into a station as if nothing at all in the world had happened.

In the silence, the young man's eyes returned to the text:

> Jonathan Hughes, certified
> public accountant, of 112
> Plandome Avenue, Plandome—

"My God!" he cried. "Get away!"

But he himself rose and ran a few steps back before the older man could move. The train jolted and threw him into an empty seat where he stared wildly out at a river of green light that rushed past the windows.

Christ, he thought, who would *do* such a thing? Who'd try to hurt us—*us*? What kind of joke? To mock a new marriage with a fine wife? Damn! And again, trembling, Damn, oh, damn!

The train rounded a curve and all but threw him to his feet. Like a man drunk with traveling, gravity, and simple rage, he swung about and lurched back to confront the old man, bent now into his newspaper, gone to earth, hiding in print. Hughes brushed the paper out of the way, and clutched the old man's shoulder. The old man, startled, glanced up, tears running from his eyes. They were both held in a long moment of thunderous traveling. Hughes felt his soul rise to leave his body.

"Who *are* you?"

Someone must have shouted that.

The train rocked as if it might derail.

The old man stood up as if shot in the heart, blindly crammed something in Jonathan Hughes's hand, and blundered away down the aisle and into the next car.

The younger man opened his fist and turned a card over and read a few words that moved him heavily down to sit and read the words again:

> JONATHAN HUGHES, CPA
> 679-4990. Plandome.

"No!" someone shouted.

Me, thought the young man. Why, that old man is . . . *me.*

There was a conspiracy, no, several conspiracies. Someone had contrived a joke about murder and played it on him. The train roared on with five hundred commuters who all rode, swaying like a team of drunken intellectuals behind their masking books and papers, while the old man, as if pursued by demons, fled off away from car to car. By the time Jonathan Hughes had rampaged his blood and completely thrown his sanity off balance, the old man had plunged, as if falling, to the farthest end of the commuter's special.

The two men met again in the last car, which was almost empty. Jonathan Hughes came and stood over the old man, who refused to look up. He was crying so hard now that conversation would have been impossible.

Who, thought the young man, who is he crying for? Stop, please, stop.

The old man, as if commanded, sat up, wiped his eyes, blew his nose, and began to speak in a frail voice that drew Jonathan Hughes near and finally caused him to sit and listen to the whispers:

"We were born—"

"We?" cried the young man.

"We," whispered the old man, looking out at the gathering dusk that traveled like smokes and burnings past the window, "we, yes, we, the two of us, we were born in Quincy in nineteen fifty, August twenty-second—"

Yes, thought Hughes.

"—and lived at Forty-nine Washington Street and went to Central School and walked to that school all through first grade with Isabel Perry—"

Isabel, thought the young man.

"We . . ." murmured the old man. "Our" whispered the old man. "Us." And went on and on with it:

"Our woodshop teacher, Mr. Bisbee. History teacher, Miss Monks. We broke our right ankle, age ten, ice-skating. Almost drowned, age eleven; Father saved us. Fell in love, age twelve, Impi Johnson—"

Seventh grade, lovely lady, long since dead, Jesus God, thought the young man, growing old.

And that's what happened. In the next minute, two minutes, three, the old man talked and talked and gradually became younger with talking, so his cheeks glowed and his eyes brightened, while the young man, weighted with old knowledge given, sank lower in his seat and grew pale so that both almost met in mid-talking, mid-listening, and became twins in passing. There was a moment when Jonathan Hughes knew for an absolute insane certainty, that if he dared glance up he would see identical twins in the mirrored window of a night-rushing world.

He did not look up.

The old man finished, his frame erect now, his head somehow driven high by the talking out, the long lost revelations.

"That's the past," he said.

I should hit him, thought Hughes. Accuse him. Shout at him. Why aren't I hitting, accusing, shouting?

Because. . . .

The old man sensed the question and said, "You know I'm who I say I am. I know everything there is to know about us. Now—the future?"

"Mine?"

"Ours," said the old man.

Jonathan Hughes nodded, staring at the newspaper clutched in the old man's right hand. The old man folded it and put it away.

"Your business will slowly become less than good. For what reasons, who can say? A child will be born and die. A mistress will be taken and lost. A wife will become less than good. And at last, oh believe it, yes, do, very slowly, you will come to—how shall I say it—hate her living presence. There, I see I've upset you. I'll shut up."

They rode in silence for a long while, and the old man grew old again, and the young man along with him. When he had aged just the proper amount, the young man nodded the talk to continue, not looking at the other who now said:

"Impossible, yes, you've been married only a year, a great year, the best. Hard to think that a single drop of ink could color a whole pitcher of clear fresh water. But color it could and color it did. And at last the entire world changed, not just our wife, not just the beautiful woman, the fine dream."

"You—" Jonathan Hughes started and stopped. "You—killed her?"

"We did. Both of us. But if I have my way, if I can convince you, neither of us will, she will live, and you will grow old to become a happier, finer me. I pray for that. I weep for that. There's still time. Across the years, I intend to shake you up, change your blood, shape your mind. God, if people knew what murder is. So silly, so stupid, so—ugly. But there is hope, for I have somehow got here, touched you, begun the change that will save our souls. Now, listen. You do admit, do you not, that we are one and the same, that the twins of time ride this train this hour this night?"

The train whistled ahead of them, clearing the track of an encumbrance of years.

The young man nodded the most infinitely microscopic of nods. The old man needed no more.

"I ran away. I ran to you. That's all I can say. She's been dead only a day, and I ran. Where to go? Nowhere to hide, save Time. No one to plead with, no judge, no jury, no proper witnesses save—you. Only you can wash the blood away, do you see? You *drew* me, then. Your youngness, your innocence, your good hours, your fine life still untouched, was the machine that seized me down the track. All of my sanity lies in you. If you turn away, great God, I'm lost, no, *we* are lost. We'll share a grave and never rise and be buried forever in misery. Shall I tell you what you must do?"

The young man rose.

"Plandome," a voice cried. "Plandome."

And they were out on the platform with the old man running after, the young man blundering into walls, into people, feeling as if his limbs might fly apart.

"Wait!" cried the old man. "Oh, please."

The young man kept moving.

"Don't you see, we're in this together, we must think of it together, solve it together, so you won't become me and I won't have to come impossibly in search of you, oh, it's all mad, insane, I know, I know, but listen!"

The young man stopped at the edge of the platform where cars were pulling in, with joyful cries or muted greetings, brief honkings, gunnings of motors, lights vanishing away. The old man grasped the young man's elbow.

"Good God, your wife, mine, will be here in a moment, there's so much to tell, you *can't* know what I know, there's twenty years of unfound information lost between which we must trade and understand! Are you listening? God, you *don't* believe!"

Jonathan Hughes was watching the street. A long way off a final car was approaching. He said: "What happened in the attic at my grandmother's house in the summer of nineteen fifty-eight? No one knows that but me. Well?"

The old man's shoulders slumped. He breathed more easily, and as if reciting from a promptboard said: "We hid ourselves there for two days, alone. No one ever knew where we hid. Everyone thought we had run away to drown in the lake or fall in the river. But all the time, crying, not feeling wanted, we hid up above and . . . listened to the wind and wanted to die."

The young man turned at last to stare fixedly at his older self, tears in his eyes. "*You* love me, then?"

"I had better," said the old man. "I'm all you have."

The car was pulling up at the station. A young woman smiled and waved behind the glass.

"Quick," said the old man, quietly. "Let me come home, watch, show you, teach you, find where things went wrong, correct them now, maybe hand you a fine life forever, let me—"

The car horn sounded, the car stopped, the young woman leaned out.

"Hello, lovely man!" she cried.

Jonathan Hughes exploded a laugh and burst into a manic run. "Lovely lady, hi—"

"Wait."

He stopped and turned to look at the old man with the newspaper, trembling there on the station platform. The old man raised one hand, questioningly.

"Haven't you forgotten something?"

Silence. At last: "You," said Jonathan Hughes. "You."

The car rounded a turn in the night. The woman, the old man, the young, swayed with the motion.

"What did you say your name was?" the young woman said, above the rush and run of country and road.

"He didn't say," said Jonathan Hughes quickly.

"Weldon," said the old man, blinking.

"Why," said Alice Hughes. "That's *my* maiden name."

The old man gasped inaudibly, but recovered. "Well, *is* it? How curious!"

"I wonder if we're related? You—"

"He was my teacher at Central High," said Jonathan Hughes, quickly.

"And still am," said the old man. "And still am."

And they were home.

He could not stop staring. All through dinner, the old man simply sat with his hands empty half the time and stared at the lovely woman across the table from him. Jonathan Hughes fidgeted, talked much too loudly to cover the silences, and ate sparsely. The old man continued to stare as if a miracle was happening every ten seconds. He watched Alice's mouth as if it were giving forth fountains of diamonds. He watched her eyes as if all the hidden wisdoms of the world were there, and now found for the first time. By the look of his face, the old man, stunned, had forgotten why he was there.

"Have I a crumb on my chin?" cried Alice Hughes, suddenly. "Why is everyone *watching* me?"

Whereupon the old man burst into tears that shocked everyone. He could not seem to stop, until at last Alice came around the table to touch his shoulder.

"Forgive me," he said. "It's just that you're so lovely. Please sit down. Forgive."

They finished off the dessert and with a great display of tossing down his fork and wiping his mouth with his napkin, Jonathan Hughes cried, "That was fabulous. Dear wife, I love you!" He kissed her on the cheek, thought better of it, and rekissed her, on the mouth. "You see?" He glanced at the old man. "I very *much* love my wife."

The old man nodded quietly and said, "Yes, yes, I remember."

"You *remember*?" said Alice, staring.

"A toast!" said Jonathan Hughes, quickly. "To a fine wife, a grand future!"

His wife laughed. She raised her glass.

"Mr. Weldon," she said, after a moment. "You're not drinking? . . ."

It was strange seeing the old man at the door to the living room.

"Watch this," he said, and closed his eyes. He began to move certainly and surely about the room, eyes shut. "Over here is the pipestand, over here the books. On the fourth shelf down a copy of Eiseley's *The Star Thrower.* One shelf up H. G. Wells's *Time Machine*, most appropriate, and over here the special chair, and me in it."

He sat. He opened his eyes.

Watching from the door, Jonathan Hughes said, "You're not going to cry again, are you?"

"No. No more crying."

There were sounds of washing up from the kitchen. The lovely woman out there hummed under her breath. Both men turned to look out of the room toward that humming.

"Someday," said Jonathan Hughes, "I will hate her? Someday, I will kill her?"

"It doesn't seem possible, does it? I've watched her for an hour and found nothing, no hint, no clue, not the merest period, semicolon or exclamation point of blemish, bump, or hair out of place with her. I've watched you, too, to see if *you* were at fault, *we* were at fault, in all this."

"And?" The young man poured sherry for both of them, and handed over a glass.

"You drink too much is about the sum. Watch it."

Hughes put his drink down without sipping it. "What else?"

"I suppose I should give you a list, make you keep it, look at it every day. Advice from the old crazy to the young fool."

"Whatever you say, I'll remember."

"Will you? For how long? A month, a year, then, like everything else, it'll go. You'll be busy living. You'll be slowly turning into . . . me. She will slowly be turning into someone worth putting out of the world. Tell her you love her."

"Every day."

"Promise! It's *that* important! Maybe that's where I failed myself, failed us. Every day, without fail!" The old man leaned forward, his face taking fire with his words. "Every day. Every day!"

Alice stood in the doorway, faintly alarmed.

"Anything wrong?"

"No, no." Jonathan Hughes smiled. "We were trying to decide which of us likes you best."

She laughed, shrugged, and went away.

"I think," said Jonathan Hughes, and stopped and closed his eyes, forcing himself to say it, "it's time for you to go."

"Yes, time." But the old man did not move. His voice was very tired, exhausted, sad. "I've been sitting here feeling defeated. I can't find anything wrong. I can't find the flaw. I can't advise you, my God, it's so stupid, I shouldn't have come to upset you, worry you, disturb your life, when I have nothing to offer but vague suggestions, inane cryings of doom. I sat here a moment ago and thought: I'll kill her now, get rid of her now, take the blame now, as an old man, so the young man there, you, can go on into the future and be free of her. Isn't that silly? I wonder if it would work? It's that old time-travel paradox, isn't it? Would I foul up the time flow, the world, the universe, what? Don't worry, no, no, don't look that way. No murder now. It's all been done up ahead, twenty years in your future. The old man having done nothing whatever, having been no help, will now open the door and run away to his madness."

He arose and shut his eyes again.

"Let me see if I can find my way out of my own house, in the dark."

He moved, the young man moved with him to find the closet by the front door and open it and take out the old man's overcoat and slowly shrug him into it.

"You *have* helped," said Jonathan Hughes. "You have told me to tell her I love her."

"Yes, I *did* do that, didn't I?"

They turned to the door.

"Is there hope for us?" the old man asked, suddenly, fiercely.

"Yes. I'll make sure of it," said Jonathan Hughes.

"Good, oh, good. I almost believe!"

The old man put one hand out and blindly opened the front door.

"I won't say goodbye to her. I couldn't stand looking at that lovely face. Tell her the old fool's gone. Where? Up the road to wait for you. You'll arrive someday."

"To become you? Not a chance," said the young man.

"Keep saying that. And—my God—here—" The old man fumbled in his pocket and drew forth a small object wrapped in crumpled newspaper. "You'd better keep this. I can't be trusted, even now. I might do something wild. Here. Here."

He thrust the object into the young man's hands. "Goodbye. Doesn't that mean: God be with you? Yes. Goodbye."

The old man hurried down the walk into the night. A wind shook the trees. A long way off, a train moved in darkness, arriving or departing, no one could tell.

Jonathan Hughes stood in the doorway for a long while, trying to see if there really was someone out there vanishing in the dark.

"Darling," his wife called.

He began to unwrap the small object.

She was in the parlor door behind him now, but her voice sounded as remote as the fading footsteps along the dark street.

"Don't stand there letting the draft in," she said.

He stiffened as he finished unwrapping the object. It lay in his hand, a small revolver.

Far away the train sounded a final cry, which failed in the wind.

"Shut the door," said his wife.

His face was cold. He closed his eyes.

Her voice. Wasn't there just the *tiniest* touch of petulance there?

He turned slowly, off balance. His shoulder brushed the door. It drifted. Then:

The wind, all by itself, slammed the door with a bang.

The Screaming Woman

MY NAME IS Margaret Leary and I'm ten years old and in the fifth grade at Central School. I haven't any brothers or sisters, but I've got a nice father and mother except they don't pay much attention to me. And anyway, we never thought we'd have anything to do with a murdered woman. Or almost, anyway.

When you're just living on a street like we live on, you don't think awful things are going to happen, like shooting or stabbing or burying people under the ground, practically in your back yard. And when it does happen you don't believe it. You just go on buttering your toast or baking a cake.

I got to tell you how it happened. It was a noon in the middle of July. It was hot and Mama said to me, "Margaret, you go to the store and buy some ice cream. It's Saturday, Dad's home for lunch, so we'll have a treat."

I ran out across the empty lot behind our house. It was a big lot, where kids had played baseball, and broken glass and stuff. And on my way back from the store with the ice cream I was just walking along, minding my own business, when all of a sudden it happened.

I heard the Screaming Woman.

I stopped and listened.

It was coming up out of the ground.

A woman was buried under the rocks and dirt and glass, and she was screaming, all wild and horrible, for someone to dig her out.

I just stood there, afraid. She kept screaming, muffled.

Then I started to run. I fell down, got up, and ran some more. I got in the screen door of my house and there was Mama, calm as you please, not knowing what I knew, that there was a real live woman buried out in back of our house, just a hundred yards away, screaming bloody murder.

"Mama," I said.

"Don't stand there with the ice cream," said Mama.

"But, Mama," I said.

"Put it in the icebox," she said.

"Listen, Mama, there's a Screaming Woman in the empty lot."

"And wash your hands," said Mama.

"She was screamin' and screamin' . . ."

"Let's see now, salt and pepper," said Mama, far away.

"Listen to me," I said, loud. "We got to dig her out. She's buried under tons and tons of dirt and if we don't dig her out, she'll choke up and die."

"I'm certain she can wait until after lunch," said Mama.

"Mama, don't you believe me?"

"Of course, dear. Now wash your hands and take this plate of meat in to your father."

"I don't even know who she is or how she got there," I said. "But we got to help her before it's too late."

"Good gosh," said Mama. "Look at this ice cream. What did you do, just stand in the sun and let it melt?"

"Well, the empty lot . . ."

"Go on, now, scoot."

I went into the dining room.

"Hi, Dad, there's a Screaming Woman in the empty lot."

"I never knew a woman who didn't," said Dad.

"I'm serious," I said.

"You look very grave," said Father.

"We've got to get picks and shovels and excavate, like for an Egyptian mummy," I said.

"I don't feel like an archaeologist, Margaret," said Father. "Now, some nice cool October day, I'll take you up on that."

"But we can't wait that long," I almost screamed. My heart was bursting in me. I was excited and scared and afraid and here was Dad, putting meat on his plate, cutting and chewing and paying me no attention.

"Dad?" I said.

"Mmmm?" he said, chewing.

"Dad, you just gotta come out after lunch and help me," I said. "Dad, Dad, I'll give you all the money in my piggy bank!"

"Well," said Dad. "So it's a business proposition, is it? It must be important for you to offer your perfectly good money. How much money will you pay, by the hour?"

"I got five whole dollars it took me a year to save, and it's all yours."

Dad touched my arm. "I'm touched. I'm really touched. You want me to play with you and you're willing to pay for my time. Honest, Margaret, you make your old Dad feel like a piker. I don't give you enough time. Tell you what, after lunch, I'll come out and listen to your screaming woman, free of charge."

"Will you, oh, will you, really?"

"Yes, ma'am, that's what I'll do," said Dad. "But you must promise me one thing?"

"What?"

"If I come out, you must eat all of your lunch first."

"I promise," I said.

"Okay."

Mother came in and sat down and we started to eat.

"Not so fast," said Mama.

I slowed down. Then I started eating fast again.

"You heard your mother," said Dad.

"The Screaming Woman," I said. "We got to hurry."

"I," said Father, "intend sitting here quietly and judiciously giving my attention first to my steak, then to my potatoes, and my salad, of course, and then to my ice cream, and after that to a long drink of iced coffee, if you don't mind. I may be a good hour at it. And another thing, young lady, if you mention her name, this Screaming Whatsis, once more at this table during lunch, I won't go out with you to hear her recital."

"Yes, sir."

"Is that understood?"

"Yes, sir," I said.

Lunch was a million years long. Everybody moved in slow motion, like those films you see at the movies. Mama got up slow and got down slow and forks and knives and spoons moved slow. Even the flies in the room were slow. And Dad's cheek muscles moved slow. It was so slow. I wanted to scream, "Hurry! Oh, please, rush, get up, run around, come on out, run!"

But no, I had to sit, and all the while we sat there slowly, slowly eating our lunch, out there in the empty lot (I could hear her screaming in my mind. *Scream!*) was the Screaming

Woman, all alone, while the world ate its lunch and the sun was hot and the lot was empty as the sky.

"There we are," said Dad, finished at last.

"Now will you come out to see the Screaming Woman?" I said.

"First a little more iced coffee," said Dad.

"Speaking of Screaming Women," said Mother. "Charlie Nesbitt and his wife Helen had another fight last night."

"That's nothing new," said Father. "They're always fighting."

"If you ask me, Charlie's no good," said Mother. "Or her, either."

"Oh, I don't know," said Dad. "I think she's pretty nice."

"You're prejudiced. After all, you almost married her."

"You going to bring that up again?" he said. "After all, I was only engaged to her six weeks."

"You showed some sense when you broke it off."

"Oh, you know Helen. Always stagestruck. Wanted to travel in a trunk. I just couldn't see it. That broke it up. She was sweet, though. Sweet and kind."

"What did it get her? A terrible brute of a husband like Charlie."

"Dad," I said.

"I'll give you that. Charlie has got a terrible temper," said Dad. "Remember when Helen had the lead in our high school graduation play? Pretty as a picture. She wrote some songs for it herself. That was the summer she wrote that song for me."

"Ha," said Mother.

"Don't laugh. It was a good song."

"You never told me about that song."

"It was between Helen and me. Let's see, how *did* it go?"

"Dad," I said.

"You'd better take your daughter out in the back lot," said Mother, "before she collapses. You can sing me that wonderful song later."

"Okay, come on, you," said Dad, and I ran him out of the house.

The empty lot was still empty and hot and the glass sparkled green and white and brown all around where the bottles lay.

"Now, where's this Screaming Woman?" laughed Dad.

"We forgot the shovels," I cried.

"We'll get them later, after we hear the soloist," said Dad.

I took him over to the spot. "Listen," I said.

We listened.

"I don't hear anything," said Dad, at last.

"Shh," I said. "Wait."

We listened some more. "Hey, there, Screaming Woman!" I cried.

We heard the sun in the sky. We heard the wind in the trees, real quiet. We heard a bus, far away, running along. We heard a car pass.

That was all.

"Margaret," said Father. "I suggest you go lie down and put a damp cloth on your forehead."

"But she was here," I shouted. "I heard her, screaming and screaming and screaming. See, here's where the ground's been dug up." I called frantically at the earth. "Hey there, you down there!"

"Margaret," said Father. "This is the place where Mr. Kelly dug yesterday, a big hole, to bury his trash and garbage in."

"But during the night," I said, "someone else used Mr. Kelly's burying place to bury a woman. And covered it all over again."

"Well, I'm going back in and take a cool shower," said Dad.

"You won't help me dig?"

"Better not stay out here too long," said Dad. "It's hot."

Dad walked off. I heard the back door slam.

I stamped on the ground. "Darn," I said.

The screaming started again.

She screamed and screamed. Maybe she had been tired and was resting and now she began it all over, just for me.

I stood in the empty lot in the hot sun and I felt like crying. I ran back to the house and banged the door.

"Dad, she's screaming again!"

"Sure, sure," said Dad. "Come on." And he led me to my upstairs bedroom. "Here," he said. He made me lie down and put a cold rag on my head. "Just take it easy."

I began to cry. "Oh, Dad, we can't let her die. She's all buried, like that person in that story by Edgar Allan Poe, and think how awful it is to be screaming and no one paying any attention."

"I forbid you to leave the house," said Dad, worried. "You just lie there the rest of the afternoon." He went out and locked the door. I heard him and Mother talking in the front room. After a while I stopped crying. I got up and tiptoed to the window. My room was upstairs. It seemed high.

I took a sheet off the bed and tied it to the bedpost and let it out the window. Then I climbed out the window and shinnied down until I touched the ground. Then I ran to the garage, quiet, and I got a couple of shovels and I ran to the empty lot. It was hotter than ever. And I started to dig, and all the while I dug, the Screaming Woman screamed . . .

It was hard work. Shoving in the shovel and lifting the rocks and glass. And I knew I'd be doing it all afternoon and maybe I wouldn't finish in time. What could I do? Run tell other people? But they'd be like Mom and Dad, pay no attention. I just kept digging, all by myself.

About ten minutes later, Dippy Smith came along the path through the empty lot. He's my age and goes to my school.

"Hi, Margaret," he said.

"Hi, Dippy," I gasped.

"What you doing?" he asked.

"Digging."

"For what?"

"I got a Screaming Lady in the ground and I'm digging for her," I said.

"I don't hear no screaming," said Dippy.

"You sit down and wait a while and you'll hear her scream yet. Or better still, help me dig."

"I don't dig unless I hear a scream," he said.

We waited.

"Listen!" I cried. "Did you *hear* it?"

"Hey," said Dippy, with slow appreciation, his eyes gleaming. "That's okay. Do it again."

"Do what again?"

"The scream."

"We got to wait," I said, puzzled.

"Do it again," he insisted, shaking my arm. "Go on." He dug in his pocket for a brown aggie. "Here." He shoved it at me. "I'll give you this marble if you do it again."

A scream came out of the ground.

"Hot dog!" said Dippy. "Teach *me* to do it!" He danced around as if I was a miracle.

"I don't . . ." I started to say.

"Did you get the *Throw-Your-Voice* book for a dime from that Magic Company in Dallas, Texas?" cried Dippy. "You got one of those tin ventriloquist contraptions in your mouth?"

"Y-yes," I lied, for I wanted him to help. "If you'll help dig, I'll tell you about it later."

"Swell," he said. "Give me a shovel."

We both dug together, and from time to time the Woman screamed.

"Boy," said Dippy. "You'd think she was right under foot. You're wonderful, Maggie." Then he said, "What's her name?"

"Who?"

"The Screaming Woman. You must have a name for her."

"Oh, sure." I thought a moment. "Her name's Wilma Schweiger and she's a rich old woman, ninety-six years old, and she was buried by a man named Spike, who counterfeited ten-dollar bills."

"Yes, *sir*," said Dippy.

"And there's hidden treasure buried with her, and I, I'm a grave robber come to dig her out and get it," I gasped, digging excitedly.

Dippy made his eyes Oriental and mysterious. "Can I be a grave robber, too?" He had a better idea. "Let's pretend it's the Princess Ommanatra, an Egyptian queen, covered with diamonds!"

We kept digging and I thought, oh, we will rescue her, we *will*. If only we keep on!

"Hey, I just got an idea," said Dippy. And he ran off and got a piece of cardboard. He scribbled on it with crayon.

"Keep digging!" I said. "We can't stop!"

"I'm making a sign. See? SLUMBERLAND CEMETERY! We can bury some birds and beetles here, in matchboxes and stuff. I'll go find some butterflies."

"No, Dippy!"

"It's more fun that way. I'll get me a dead cat, too, maybe . . ."

"Dippy, use your shovel! Please!"

"Aw," said Dippy. "I'm tired. I think I'll go home and take a nap."

"You can't do that."

"Who says so?"

"Dippy, there's something I want to tell you."

"What?"

He gave the shovel a kick.

I whispered in his ear. "There's really a woman buried here."

"Why sure there is," he said. "You said it, Maggie."

"You don't believe me, either."

"Tell me how you throw your voice and I'll keep on digging."

"But I can't tell you, because I'm not doing it," I said. "Look, Dippy. I'll stand way over here and you listen there."

The Screaming Woman screamed again.

"Hey!" said Dippy. "There really *is* a woman here!"

"That's what I tried to say."

"Let's dig!" said Dippy.

We dug for twenty minutes.

"I wonder who she is?"

"I don't know."

"I wonder if it's Mrs. Nelson or Mrs. Turner or Mrs. Bradley. I wonder if she's pretty. Wonder what color her hair is? Wonder if she's thirty or ninety or sixty?"

"Dig!" I said.

The mound grew high.

"Wonder if she'll reward us for digging her up."

"Sure."

"A quarter, do you think?"

"More than that. I bet it's a dollar."

Dippy remembered as he dug, "I read a book once of magic. There was a Hindu with no clothes on who crept down in a grave and slept there sixty days, not eating anything, no malts, no chewing gum or candy, no air, for sixty days." His face fell. "Say, wouldn't it be awful if it was only a radio buried here and us working so hard?"

"A radio's nice, it'd be all ours."

Just then a shadow fell across us.

"Hey, you kids, what you think you're doing?"

We turned. It was Mr. Kelly, the man who owned the empty lot. "Oh, hello, Mr. Kelly," we said.

"Tell you what I want you to do," said Mr. Kelly. "I want you to take those shovels and take that soil and shovel it right back in that hole you been digging. That's what I want you to do."

My heart started beating fast again. I wanted to scream myself.

"But Mr. Kelly, there's a Screaming Woman and . . ."

"I'm not interested. I don't hear a thing."

"Listen!" I cried.

The scream.

Mr. Kelly listened and shook his head. "Don't hear nothing. Go on now, fill it up and get home with you before I give you my foot!"

We filled the hole all back in again. And all the while we filled it in, Mr. Kelly stood there, arms folded, and the woman screamed, but Mr. Kelly pretended not to hear it.

When we were finished, Mr. Kelly stomped off, saying, "Go on home now. And if I catch you here again . . ."

I turned to Dippy. "He's the one," I whispered.

"Huh?" said Dippy.

"He *murdered* Mrs. Kelly. He buried her here, after he strangled her, in a box, but she came to. Why, he stood right here and she screamed and he wouldn't pay any attention."

"Hey," said Dippy. "That's right. He stood right here and lied to us."

"There's only one thing to do," I said. "Call the police and have them come arrest Mr. Kelly."

We ran for the corner store telephone.

The police knocked on Mr. Kelly's door five minutes later. Dippy and I were hiding in the bushes, listening.

"Mr. Kelly?" said the police officer.

"Yes, sir, what can I do for you?"

"Is Mrs. Kelly at home?"

"Yes, sir."

"May we see her, sir?"

"Of course. Hey, Anna!"

Mrs. Kelly came to the door and looked out. "Yes, sir?"

"I beg your pardon," apologized the officer. "We had a report that you were buried out in an empty lot, Mrs. Kelly. It sounded like a child made the call, but we had to be certain. Sorry to have troubled you."

"It's those blasted kids," cried Mr. Kelly, angrily. "If I ever catch them, I'll rip 'em limb from limb!"

"Cheezit!" said Dippy, and we both ran.

"What'll we do now?" I said.

"I got to go home," said Dippy. "Boy, we're really in trouble. We'll get a licking for this."

"But what about the Screaming Woman?"

"To heck with her," said Dippy. "We don't dare go near that empty lot again. Old man Kelly'll be waitin' around with his razor strap and lambast heck out'n us. An' I just happened to remember, Maggie. Ain't old man Kelly sort of deaf, hard-of-hearing?"

"Oh, my gosh," I said. "No *wonder* he didn't hear the screams."

"So long," said Dippy. "We sure got in trouble over your darn old ventriloquist voice. I'll be seeing you."

I was left all alone in the world, no one to help me, no one to believe me at all. I just wanted to crawl down in that box with the Screaming Woman and die. The police were after me now, for lying to them, only I didn't know it was a lie, and my father was probably looking for me, too, or would be once he found my bed empty. There was only one last thing to do, and I did it.

I went from house to house, all down the street, near the empty lot. And I rang every bell and when the door opened I said: "I beg your pardon, Mrs. Griswold, but is anyone missing from your house?" or "Hello, Mrs. Pikes, you're looking fine today. Glad to see you *home*." And once I saw that the lady of the house was home I just chatted a while to be polite, and went on down the street.

The hours were rolling along. It was getting late. I kept thinking, oh, there's only so much air in that box with that woman under the earth, and if I don't hurry, she'll suffocate, and I got to rush! So I rang bells and knocked on doors, and it got later, and I was just about to give up and go home, when I knocked on the *last* door, which was the door of Mr. Charlie Nesbitt, who lives next to us. I kept knocking and knocking.

Instead of Mrs. Nesbitt, or Helen as my father calls her, coming to the door, why it was Mr. Nesbitt, Charlie, *himself.*

"Oh," he said. "It's you, Margaret."

"Yes," I said. "Good afternoon."

"What can I do for you, kid?" he said.

"Well, I thought I'd like to see your wife, Mrs. Nesbitt," I said.

"Oh," he said.

"May I?"

"Well, she's gone out to the store," he said.

"I'll wait," I said, and slipped in past him.

"Hey," he said.

I sat down in a chair. "My, it's a hot day," I said, trying to be calm, thinking about the empty lot and air going out of the box, and the screams getting weaker and weaker.

"Say, listen, kid," said Charlie, coming over to me, "I don't think you better wait."

"Oh, sure," I said. "Why not?"

"Well, my wife won't be back," he said.

"Oh?"

"Not today, that is. She's gone to the store, like I said, but, but, she's going on from there to visit her mother. Yeah. She's going to visit her mother, in Schenectady. She'll be back, two or three days, maybe a week."

"That's a shame," I said.

"Why?"

"I wanted to tell her something."

"What?"

"I just wanted to tell her there's a woman buried over in the empty lot, screaming under tons and tons of dirt."

Mr. Nesbitt dropped his cigarette.

"You dropped your cigarette, Mr. Nesbitt," I pointed out, with my shoe.

"Oh, did I? Sure. So I did," he mumbled. "Well, I'll tell Helen when she comes home, your story. She'll be glad to hear it."

"Thanks. It's a real woman."

"How do you know it is?"

"I heard her."

"How, how you know it isn't, well, a *mandrake* root."

"What's that?"

"You know. A mandrake. It's a kind of a plant, kid. They

scream. I know, I read it once. How you know it ain't a mandrake?"

"I never thought of that."

"You better start thinking," he said, lighting another cigarette. He tried to be casual. "Say, kid, you, eh, you *say* anything about this to anyone?"

"Sure, I told lots of people."

Mr. Nesbitt burned his hand on his match.

"Anybody doing anything about it?" he asked.

"No," I said. "They won't believe me."

He smiled. "Of course. Naturally. You're nothing but a kid. Why should they listen to you?"

"I'm going back now and dig her out with a spade," I said.

"Wait."

"I got to go," I said.

"Stick around," he insisted.

"Thanks, but no," I said, frantically.

He took my arm. "Know how to play cards, kid? Black jack?"

"Yes, sir."

He took out a deck of cards from a desk. "We'll have a game."

"I got to go dig."

"Plenty of time for that," he said, quiet. "Anyway, maybe my wife'll be home. Sure. That's it. You wait for her. Wait a while."

"You think she will be?"

"Sure, kid. Say, about that voice; is it very strong?"

"It gets weaker all the time."

Mr. Nesbitt sighed and smiled. "You and your kid games. Here now, let's play that game of black jack, it's more fun than Screaming Women."

"I got to go. It's late."

"Stick around, you got nothing to do."

I knew what he was trying to do. He was trying to keep me in his house until the screaming died down and was gone. He was trying to keep me from helping her. "My wife'll be home in ten minutes," he said. "Sure. Ten minutes. You wait. You sit right there."

We played cards. The clock ticked. The sun went down the sky. It was getting late. The screaming got fainter and fainter in my mind. "I got to go," I said.

"Another game," said Mr. Nesbitt. "Wait another hour, kid. My wife'll come yet. Wait."

In another hour he looked at his watch. "Well, kid, I guess you can go now." And I know what his plan was. He'd sneak down in the middle of the night and dig up his wife, still alive, and take her somewhere else and bury her, good. "So long, kid. So long." He let me go, because he thought that by now the air must all be gone from the box.

The door shut in my face.

I went back near the empty lot and hid in some bushes. What could I do? Tell my folks? But they hadn't believed me. Call the police on Mr. Charlie Nesbitt? But he said his wife was away visiting. Nobody would believe me!

I watched Mr. Kelly's house. He wasn't in sight. I ran over to the place where the screaming had been and just stood there.

The screaming had stopped. It was so quiet I thought I would never hear a scream again. It was all over. I was too late I thought.

I bent down and put my ear against the ground.

And then I heard it, way down, way deep, and so faint I could hardly hear it.

The woman wasn't screaming any more. She was singing.

Something about, "I loved you fair, I loved you well."

It was sort of a sad song. Very faint. And sort of broken. All of those hours down under the ground in that box must have sort of made her crazy. All she needed was some air and food and she'd be all right. But she just kept singing, not wanting to scream any more, not caring, just singing.

I listened to the song.

And then I turned and walked straight across the lot and up the steps to my house and I opened the front door.

"Father," I said.

"So there you are!" he cried.

"Father," I said.

"You're going to get a licking," he said.

"She's not screaming any more."

"Don't talk about her!"

"She's singing now," I cried.

"You're not telling the truth!"

"Dad," I said. "She's out there and she'll be dead soon if you don't listen to me. She's out there, singing, and this is what she's singing." I hummed the tune. I sang a few of the words. "I loved you fair, I loved you well . . ."

Dad's face grew pale. He came and took my arm.

"What did you say?" he said.

I sang it again, "I loved you fair, I loved you well."

"Where did you *hear* that song?" he shouted.

"Out in the empty lot, just now."

"But that's *Helen's* song, the one she wrote, years ago, for *me*!" cried Father. "You *can't* know it. *Nobody* knew it, except Helen and me. I never sang it to anyone, not you or anyone."

"Sure," I said.

"Oh, my God!" cried Father, and ran out the door to get a shovel. The last I saw of him he was in the empty lot, digging, and lots of other people with him, digging.

I felt so happy I wanted to cry.

I dialed a number on the phone and when Dippy answered I said, "Hi, Dippy. Everything's fine. Everything's worked out keen. The Screaming Woman isn't screaming any more."

"Swell," said Dippy.

"I'll meet you in the empty lot with a shovel in two minutes," I said.

"Last one there's a monkey! So long!" cried Dippy.

"So long, Dippy!" I said, and ran.

The Fog Horn

OUT THERE IN the cold water, far from land, we waited every night for the coming of the fog, and it came, and we oiled the brass machinery and lit the fog light up in the stone tower. Feeling like two birds in the gray sky, McDunn and I sent the light touching out, red, then white, then red again, to eye the lonely ships. And if they did not see our light, then there was always our Voice, the great deep cry of our Fog Horn shuddering through the rags of mist to startle the gulls away like decks of scattered cards and make the waves turn high and foam.

"It's a lonely life, but you're used to it now, aren't you? asked McDunn.

"Yes," I said. "You're a good talker, thank the Lord."

"Well, it's your turn on land tomorrow," he said, smiling, "to dance the ladies and drink gin."

"What do you think, McDunn, when I leave you out here alone?"

"On the mysteries of the sea." McDunn lit his pipe. It was a quarter past seven of a cold November evening, the heat on, the light switching its tail in two hundred directions, the Fog Horn bumbling in the high throat of the tower. There wasn't a town for a hundred miles down the coast, just a road which came lonely through dead country to the sea, with few cars on it, a stretch of two miles of cold water out to our rock, and rare few ships.

"The mysteries of the sea," said McDunn thoughtfully. "You know, the ocean's the biggest damned snowflake ever? It rolls and swells a thousand shapes and colors, no two alike. Strange. One night, years ago, I was here alone, when all of the fish of the sea surfaced out there. Something made them swim in and lie in the bay, sort of trembling and staring up at the tower light going red, white, red, white across them so I could see their funny eyes. I turned cold. They were like a big peacock's tail, moving out there until midnight. Then, without so much as a sound, they slipped away, the million of them was gone. I kind of think maybe, in some sort of way, they came all those miles to worship. Strange. But think how the tower must look to them, standing seventy feet above the water, the God-light flashing out from it, and the tower declaring itself with a monster voice. They never came back, those fish, but don't you think for a while they thought they were in the Presence?"

I shivered. I looked out at the long gray lawn of the sea stretching away into nothing and nowhere.

"Oh, the sea's full." McDunn puffed his pipe nervously, blinking. He had been nervous all day and hadn't said why. "For all our engines and so-called submarines, it'll be ten thousand centuries before we set foot on the real bottom of the sunken lands, in the fairy kingdoms there, and know *real* terror. Think of it, it's still the year 300,000 Before Christ down under there. While we've paraded around with trumpets, lopping off each other's countries and heads, they have been living beneath the sea twelve miles deep and cold in a time as old as the beard of a comet."

"Yes, it's an old world."

"Come on. I got something special I been saving up to tell you."

We ascended the eighty steps, talking and taking our time. At the top, McDunn switched off the room lights so there'd be no reflection in the plate glass. The great eye of the light was humming, turning easily in its oiled socket. The Fog Horn was blowing steadily, once every fifteen seconds.

"Sounds like an animal, don't it?" McDunn nodded to himself. "A big lonely animal crying in the night. Sitting here on the edge of ten billion years calling out to the Deeps, I'm here, I'm here, I'm here. And the Deeps *do* answer, yes, they do. You been here now for three months, Johnny, so I better prepare you. About this time of year," he said, studying the murk and fog, "something comes to visit the lighthouse."

"The swarms of fish like you said?"

"No, this is something else. I've put off telling you because you might think I'm daft. But tonight's the latest I can put it off, for if my calendar's marked right from last year, tonight's the night it comes. I won't go into detail, you'll have to see it yourself. Just sit down there. If you want, tomorrow you can pack your duffel and take the motorboat in to land and get your car parked there at the dinghy pier on the cape and drive on back to some little inland town and keep your lights burning nights, I won't question or blame you. It's happened three years now, and this is the only time anyone's been here with me to verify it. You wait and watch."

Half an hour passed with only a few whispers between us. When we grew tired waiting, McDunn began describing some of his ideas to me. He had some theories about the Fog Horn itself.

"One day many years ago a man walked along and stood in the sound of the ocean on a cold sunless shore and said, 'We need a voice to call across the water, to warn ships; I'll make one. I'll make a voice like all of time and all of the fog that ever was; I'll make a voice that is like an empty bed beside you all night long, and like an empty house when you open the door, and like trees in autumn with no leaves. A sound like the birds flying south, crying, and a sound like November wind and the sea on the hard, cold shore. I'll make a sound that's so alone that no one can miss it, that whoever hears it will weep in their souls, and hearths will seem warmer, and being inside will seem better to all who hear it in the distant towns. I'll make me a sound and an apparatus and they'll call it a Fog Horn and whoever hears it will know the sadness of eternity and the briefness of life.'"

The Fog Horn blew.

"I made up that story," said McDunn quietly, "to try to explain why this thing keeps coming back to the lighthouse every year. The Fog Horn calls it, I think, and it comes. . . ."

"But——" I said.

"Sssst!" said McDunn. "There!" He nodded out to the Deeps.

Something was swimming toward the lighthouse tower.

It was a cold night, as I have said; the high tower was cold, the light coming and going, and the Fog Horn calling and calling through the raveling mist. You couldn't see far and you couldn't see plain, but there was the deep sea moving on its way about the night earth, flat and quiet, the color of gray mud, and here were the two of us alone in the high tower, and there, far out at first, was a ripple, followed by a wave, a rising, a bubble, a bit of froth. And then, from the surface of the cold sea came a head, a large head, dark-colored, with immense eyes, and then a neck. And then—not a body—but more neck and more! The head rose a full forty feet above the water on a slender and beautiful dark neck. Only then did the body, like a little island of black coral and shells and crayfish, drip up from the subterranean. There was a flicker of tail. In all, from head to tip of tail, I estimated the monster at ninety or a hundred feet.

I don't know what I said. I said something.

"Steady, boy, steady," whispered McDunn.

"It's impossible!" I said.

"No, Johnny, *we're* impossible. *It's* like it always was ten million years ago. *It* hasn't changed. It's *us* and the land that've changed, become impossible. *Us!*"

It swam slowly and with a great dark majesty out in the icy waters, far away. The fog came and went about it, momentarily erasing its shape. One of the monster eyes caught and held and flashed back our immense light, red, white, red, white, like a disk held high and sending a message in primeval code. It was as silent as the fog through which it swam.

"It's a dinosaur of some sort!" I crouched down, holding to the stair rail.

"Yes, one of the tribe."

"But they died out!"

"No, only hid away in the Deeps. Deep, deep down in the deepest Deeps. Isn't *that* a word now, Johnny, a real word, it says so much: the Deeps. There's all the coldness and darkness and deepness in the world in a word like that."

"What'll we do?"

"Do? We got our job, we can't leave. Besides, we're safer here than in any boat trying to get to land. That thing's as big as a destroyer and almost as swift."

"But here, why does it come *here*?"

The next moment I had my answer.

The Fog Horn blew.

And the monster answered.

A cry came across a million years of water and mist. A cry so anguished and alone that it shuddered in my head and my body. The monster cried out at the tower. The Fog Horn blew.

The monster roared again. The Fog Horn blew. The monster opened its great toothed mouth and the sound that came from it was the sound of the Fog Horn itself. Lonely and vast and far away. The sound of isolation, a viewless sea, a cold night, apartness. That was the sound.

"Now," whispered McDunn, "do you know why it comes here?"

I nodded.

"All year long, Johnny, that poor monster there lying far out, a thousand miles at sea, and twenty miles deep maybe, biding its time, perhaps it's a million years old, this one creature. Think of it, waiting a million years; could you wait that long? Maybe it's the last of its kind. I sort of think that's true. Anyway, here come men on land and build this lighthouse, five years ago. And set up their Fog Horn and sound it and sound it out toward the place where you bury yourself in sleep and sea memories of a world where there were thousands like yourself, but now you're alone, all alone in a world not made for you, a world where you have to hide.

"But the sound of the Fog Horn comes and goes, comes and goes, and you stir from the muddy bottom of the Deeps, and your eyes open like the lenses of two-foot cameras and you move, slow, slow, for you have the ocean sea on your shoulders, heavy. But that Fog Horn comes through a thousand miles of water, faint and familiar, and the furnace in your belly stokes up, and you begin to rise, slow, slow. You feed yourself on great slakes of cod and minnow, on rivers of jellyfish, and you rise slow through the autumn months, through September when the fogs started, through October with more fog and the horn still calling you on, and then, late in November, after pressurizing yourself day by day, a few feet higher every hour, you are near the surface and still alive. You've got to go slow; if you surfaced all at once you'd explode. So it takes you all of three months to surface, and then a number of days to swim through the cold waters to the lighthouse. And there you are, out there, in the night, Johnny, the biggest damn monster in creation. And here's the lighthouse calling to you, with a long neck like your neck sticking way up out of the water, and a body like your body, and, most important of all, a voice like your voice. Do you understand now, Johnny, do you understand?"

The Fog Horn blew.

The monster answered.

I saw it all, I knew it all—the million years of waiting alone, for someone to come back who never came back. The million years of isolation at the bottom of the sea, the insanity of time there, while the skies cleared of reptile-birds, the swamps dried on the continental lands, the sloths and saber-tooths had their day and sank in tar pits, and men ran like white ants upon the hills.

The Fog Horn blew.

"Last year," said McDunn, "that creature swam round and round, round and round, all night. Not coming too near, puzzled, I'd say. Afraid, maybe. And a bit angry after coming all this way. But the next day, unexpectedly, the fog lifted, the sun came out fresh, the sky was as blue as a painting. And the monster swam off away from the heat and the silence and didn't come back. I suppose it's been brooding on it for a year now, thinking it over from every which way."

The monster was only a hundred yards off now, it and the Fog Horn crying at each other. As the lights hit them, the monster's eyes were fire and ice, fire and ice.

"That's life for you," said McDunn. "Someone always waiting for someone who never comes home. Always someone loving some thing more than that thing loves them. And after a while you want to destroy whatever that thing is, so it can't hurt you no more."

The monster was rushing at the lighthouse.

The Fog Horn blew.

"Let's see what happens," said McDunn.

He switched the Fog Horn off.

The ensuing minute of silence was so intense that we could hear our hearts pounding in the glassed area of the tower, could hear the slow greased turn of the light.

The monster stopped and froze. Its great lantern eyes blinked. Its mouth gaped. It gave a sort of rumble, like a volcano. It twitched its head this way and that, as if to seek the sounds now dwindled off into the fog. It peered at the lighthouse. It rumbled again. Then its eyes caught fire. It reared up, threshed the water, and rushed at the tower, its eyes filled with angry torment.

"McDunn!" I cried. "Switch on the horn!"

McDunn fumbled with the switch. But even as he flicked it on, the monster was rearing up. I had a glimpse of its gigantic paws, fishskin glittering in webs between the fingerlike projections, clawing at the tower. The huge eye on the right side of its anguished head glittered before me like a caldron into which I might drop, screaming. The tower shook. The Fog Horn cried; the monster cried. It seized the tower and gnashed at the glass, which shattered in upon us.

McDunn seized my arm. "Downstairs!"

The tower rocked, trembled, and started to give. The Fog Horn and the monster roared. We stumbled and half fell down the stairs. "Quick!"

We reached the bottom as the tower buckled down toward us. We ducked under the stairs into the small stone cellar. There were a thousand concussions as the rocks rained down; the Fog Horn stopped abruptly. The monster crashed upon the tower. The tower fell. We knelt together, McDunn and I, holding tight, while our world exploded.

Then it was over, and there was nothing but darkness and the wash of the sea on the raw stones.

That and the other sound.

"Listen," said McDunn quietly. "Listen."

We waited a moment. And then I began to hear it. First a great vacuumed sucking of air, and then the lament, the bewilderment, the loneliness of the great monster, folded over and upon us, above us, so that the sickening reek of its body filled the air, a stone's thickness away from our cellar. The monster gasped and cried. The tower was gone. The light was gone. The thing that had called to it across a million years was gone. And the monster was opening its mouth and sending out great sounds. The sounds of a Fog Horn, again and again. And ships far at sea, not finding the light, not seeing anything, but passing and hearing late that night, must've thought: There it is, the lonely sound, the Lonesome Bay horn. All's well. We've rounded the cape.

And so it went for the rest of that night.

The sun was hot and yellow the next afternoon when the rescuers came out to dig us from our stoned-under cellar.

"It fell apart, is all," said Mr. McDunn gravely. "We had a few bad knocks from the waves and it just crumbled." He pinched my arm.

There was nothing to see. The ocean was calm, the sky blue. The only thing was a great algaic stink from the green matter that covered the fallen tower stones and the shore rocks. Flies buzzed about. The ocean washed empty on the shore.

The next year they built a new lighthouse, but by that time I had a job in the little town and a wife and a good small warm house that glowed yellow on autumn nights, the doors locked, the chimney puffing smoke. As for McDunn, he was master of the new lighthouse, built to his own specifications, out of steel-reinforced concrete. "Just in case," he said.

The new lighthouse was ready in November. I drove down alone one evening late and parked my car and looked across the gray waters and listened to the new horn sounding, once, twice, three, four times a minute far out there, by itself.

The monster?

It never came back.

"It's gone away," said McDunn. "It's gone back to the Deeps. It's learned you can't love anything too much in this world. It's gone into the deepest Deeps to wait another million years. Ah, the poor thing! Waiting out there, and waiting out there, while man comes and goes on this pitiful little planet. Waiting and waiting."

I sat in my car, listening. I couldn't see the lighthouse or the light standing out in Lonesome Bay. I could only hear the Horn, the Horn, the Horn. It sounded like the monster calling.

I sat there wishing there was something I could say.

The Pedestrian

TO ENTER OUT into that silence that was the city at eight o'clock of a misty evening in November, to put your feet upon that buckling concrete walk, to step over grassy seams and make your way, hands in pockets, through the silences, that was what Mr. Leonard Mead most dearly loved to do. He would stand upon the corner of an intersection and peer down long moonlit avenues of sidewalk in four directions, deciding which way to go, but it really made no difference; he was alone in this world of 2052 A.D., or as good as alone, and with a final decision made, a path selected, he would stride off, sending patterns of frosty air before him like the smoke of a cigar.

Sometimes he would walk for hours and miles and return only at midnight to his house. And on his way he would see the cottages and homes with their dark windows, and it was not unequal to walking through a graveyard where only the faintest glimmers of firefly light appeared in flickers behind the windows. Sudden gray phantoms seemed to manifest upon inner room walls where a curtain was still undrawn against the night, or there were whisperings and murmurs where a window in a tomb-like building was still open.

Mr. Leonard Mead would pause, cock his head, listen, look, and march on, his feet making no noise on the lumpy walk. For long ago he had wisely changed to sneakers when strolling at night, because the dogs in intermittent squads would parallel his journey with barkings if he wore hard heels, and lights might click on and faces appear and an entire street be startled by the passing of a lone figure, himself, in the early November evening.

On this particular evening he began his journey in a westerly direction, toward the hidden sea. There was a good crystal frost in the air; it cut the nose and made the lungs blaze like a Christmas tree inside; you could feel the cold light going on and off, all the branches filled with invisible snow. He listened to the faint push of his soft shoes through autumn leaves with satisfaction, and whistled a cold quiet whistle between his teeth, occasionally picking up a leaf as he passed, examining its skeletal pattern in the infrequent lamplights as he went on, smelling its rusty smell.

"Hello, in there," he whispered to every house on every side as he moved. "What's up tonight on Channel 4, Channel 7, Channel 9? Where are the cowboys rushing, and do I see the United States Cavalry over the next hill to the rescue?"

The street was silent and long and empty, with only his shadow moving like the shadow of a hawk in mid-country. If he closed his eyes and stood very still, frozen, he could imagine himself upon the center of a plain, a wintry, windless Arizona desert with no house in a thousand miles, and only dry river beds, the streets, for company.

"What is it now?" he asked the houses, noticing his wrist watch. "Eight-thirty P.M.? Time for a dozen assorted murders? A quiz? A revue? A comedian falling off the stage?"

Was that a murmur of laughter from within a moon-white house? He hesitated, but went on when nothing more happened. He stumbled over a particularly uneven section of sidewalk. The cement was vanishing under flowers and grass. In ten years of walking by night or day, for thousands of miles, he had never met another person walking, not one in all that time.

He came to a cloverleaf intersection which stood silent where two main highways crossed the town. During the day it was a thunderous surge of cars, the gas stations open, a great insect rustling and a ceaseless jockeying for position as the scarab-beetles, a faint incense puttering from their exhausts, skimmed homeward to the far directions. But now these highways, too, were like streams in a dry season, all stone and bed and moon radiance.

He turned back on a side street, circling around toward his home. He was within a block of his destination when the lone car turned a corner quite suddenly and flashed a fierce white cone of light upon him. He stood entranced, not unlike a night moth, stunned by the illumination, and then drawn toward it.

A metallic voice called to him:

"Stand still. Stay where you are! Don't move!"

He halted.

"Put up your hands!"

"But——" he said.

"Your hands up! Or we'll shoot!"

The police, of course, but what a rare, incredible thing; in a city of three million, there was only *one* police car left, wasn't that correct? Ever since a year ago, 2052, the election year, the force had been cut down from three cars to one. Crime was ebbing; there was no need now for the police, save for this one lone car wandering and wandering the empty streets.

"Your name?" said the police car in a metallic whisper. He couldn't see the men in it for the bright light in his eyes.

"Leonard Mead," he said.

"Speak up!"

"Leonard Mead!"

"Business or profession?"

"I guess you'd call me a writer."

"No profession," said the police car, as if talking to itself. The light held him fixed, like a museum specimen, needle thrust through chest.

"You might say that," said Mr. Mead. He hadn't written in years. Magazines and books didn't sell any more. Everything went on in the tomblike houses at night now, he thought, continuing his fancy. The tombs, ill-lit by television light, where the people sat like the dead, the gray or multicolored lights touching their faces, but never really touching *them*.

"No profession," said the phonograph voice, hissing. "What are you doing out?"

"Walking," said Leonard Mead.

"Walking!"

"Just walking," he said simply, but his face felt cold.

"Walking, just walking, walking?"

"Yes, sir."

"Walking where? For what?"

"Walking for air. Walking to see."

"Your address!"

"Eleven South Saint James Street."

"And there is air *in* your house, you have an air *conditioner*, Mr. Mead?"

"Yes."

"And you have a viewing screen in your house to see with?"

"No."

"No?" There was a crackling quiet that in itself was an accusation.

"Are you married, Mr. Mead?"

"No."

"Not married," said the police voice behind the fiery beam. The moon was high and clear among the stars and the houses were gray and silent.

"Nobody wanted me," said Leonard Mead with a smile.

"Don't speak unless you're spoken to!"

Leonard Mead waited in the cold night.

"Just *walking*, Mr. Mead?"

"Yes."

"But you haven't explained for what purpose."

"I explained; for air, and to see, and just to walk."

"Have you done this often?"

"Every night for years."

The police car sat in the center of the street with its radio throat faintly humming.

"Well, Mr. Mead," it said.

"Is that all?" he asked politely.

"Yes," said the voice. "Here." There was a sigh, a pop. The back door of the police car sprang wide. "Get in."

"Wait a minute, I haven't done anything!"

"Get in."

"I protest!"

"Mr. Mead."

He walked like a man suddenly drunk. As he passed the front window of the car he looked in. As he had expected, there was no one in the front seat, no one in the car at all.

"Get in."

He put his hand to the door and peered into the back seat, which was a little cell, a little black jail with bars. It smelled of riveted steel. It smelled of harsh antiseptic; it smelled too clean and hard and metallic. There was nothing soft there.

"Now if you had a wife to give you an alibi," said the iron voice. "But——"

"Where are you taking me?"

The car hesitated, or rather gave a faint whirring click, as if information, somewhere, was dropping card by punch-slotted card under electric eyes. "To the Psychiatric Center for Research on Regressive Tendencies."

He got in. The door shut with a soft thud. The police car rolled through the night avenues, flashing its dim lights ahead.

They passed one house on one street a moment later, one house in an entire city of houses that were dark, but this one particular house had all of its electric lights brightly lit, every window a loud yellow illumination, square and warm in the cool darkness.

"That's *my* house," said Leonard Mead.

No one answered him.

The car moved down the empty river-bed streets and off away, leaving the empty streets with the empty sidewalks, and no sound and no motion all the rest of the chill November night.

The Playground

A THOUSAND TIMES before and after his wife's death Mr. Charles Underhill ignored the Playground on his way to and from his commuter's limited train. He neither liked nor disliked the Playground; he hardly knew it existed.

But only this morning his sister Carol, who had occupied the empty space across the breakfast table from him each day for six months, quietly broached the subject.

"Jim's almost three years old now," she said. "So tomorrow I'm going to start him at the Playground."

"Playground?" said Mr. Underhill.

At his office, he underlined a memorandum with black ink: *Look at Playground.*

That afternoon, the thunder of the train subsiding in his body, Underhill struck up through town on his usual path home, newspaper tucked crisply under arm to prevent reading himself past the park. So it was, at five-ten in the late day, that he came to the cool iron fence and the open gate of the Playground, and stood for a long, long time, frozen there, gazing in at it all. . . .

At first there seemed absolutely nothing whatever to see. And then as he adjusted his attention outward from his usual interior monologue, the scene before him, a gray, blurred television image, came to a slow focus.

Primarily, he was aware of dim voices, faint underwater cries emerging from a series of vague streaks and zigzag lines and shadows. Then, as if someone had kicked the machine, screams jumped at him in full throat, visions leaped clear. Now he saw the children! They were dashing across the playground meadow, fighting, pummeling, scratching, falling, every wound bleeding or about to bleed or freshly caked over. A dozen cats thrown among sleeping dogs could not have shrieked as loud. With incredible clarity, Mr. Underhill saw the tiniest cuts and scabs on knees and faces.

He weathered the first blast of sound, blinking. His nostrils took over when his eyes and ears retired in panic.

He sniffed the cutting odors of salve, raw adhesive, camphor, and pink mercurochrome, so strong it lay bitter on his tongue. An iodine wind blew through the steel fence wires which glinted dully in the gray light of the overcast day. The rushing children were hell cut loose in a vast pinball table, colliding, and banging, and totaling of hits and misses, thrusts and plungings to a grand and as yet unforeseen total of brutalities.

And was he mistaken or was the light within the Playground of a peculiar intensity? Every child seemed to possess four shadows: one dark, three faint penumbras which made it strategically impossible to tell which way their swift bodies were racing until they bashed their targets. Yes, the oblique, pressing light made the Playground seem deep, far away, and remote from his touching. Or perhaps it was the hard steel wire fence, not unlike those barriers in zoos, beyond which *anything* might happen.

A pen of misery, thought Underhill. Why do children insist on making life horrible for each other? Oh, the continual torture. He heard himself sigh with immense relief. Thank God, childhood was over and done for him. No more pinchings, bruisings, senseless passions and shattered dreams.

A gust of wind tore the paper from his hand. He ran after it down the Playground steps. Clutching the paper, he retreated hastily. For in that one brief instant, stranded in the Playground's atmosphere, he had felt his hat grow too large, his coat too cumbersome, his belt too loose, his shoes too big; he had felt like a small boy playing businessman in his father's clothes; the gate behind him had loomed impossibly tall, while the sky pressed a huge weight of grayness at his eyes, and the scent of iodine, like a tiger's breath exhaled upon him, blew his hair. He tripped and almost fell, running back.

He stood outside the Playground, like someone who has just emerged, in shock, from a terrible cold sea.

"Hello, Charlie!"

He heard the voice and turned to see who had called him. There on top of a metal slide, a boy of some nine years was waving. "Hello, Charlie . . . !"

Mr. Charles Underhill raised a hand. But I don't *know* that boy? he thought. And why should he call me by my first name?

The boy was smiling high in the misty air, and now, jostled by other yelling children, rushed shrieking down the slide.

Underhill stood bemused by what he saw. Now the Playground was an immense iron industry whose sole products were pain, sadism, and sorrow. If you watched half an hour there wasn't a face in the entire enclosure that didn't wince, cry, redden with anger, pale with fear, one moment or another. Really! Who said childhood was the best time of life? when in reality it was the most terrible, the most merciless era, the barbaric time when there were no police to protect you, only parents preoccupied with themselves and their taller world. No, if he had his way, he touched the cold fence with one hand, they'd nail a new sign here: TORQUEMADA'S GREEN.

And as for that boy, the one who had called out to him, who was he? There was something familiar there, perhaps in the hidden bones, an echo of some old friend; probably the son of a successfully ulcered father.

So this is the playground where my son will play, thought Mr. Underhill. So this is it.

Hanging his hat in the hall, checking his lean image in the watery mirror, Underhill felt wintry and tired. When his sister appeared, and his son came tapping on mouse-feet, he greeted them with something less than full attention. The boy clambered thinly over him, playing King of the Hill. And the father, fixing his gaze to the end of the cigar he was slowly lighting, finally cleared his throat and said, "I've been thinking about that playground, Carol."

"I'm taking Jim over tomorrow."

"Not really? *That* playground?"

His mind rebelled. The smell and look of the place were still vivid. That writhing world with its atmosphere of cuts and beaten noses, the air as full of pain as a dentist's office, and those horrid tic-tac-toes and frightening hopscotches under his feet as he picked up his newspaper, horrid and frightening for no reason he could see.

"What's wrong with *that* playground?" asked Carol.

"Have you seen it?" He paused in confusion. "Damn it, I mean, the children there. It's a Black Hole."

"All the children are from well-to-do families."

"Well, they shove and push like little Gestapos," said Underhill. "It'd be like sending a boy to a flour mill to be crushed into meal by a couple of two-ton grinders! Every time I think of Jim playing in that barbaric pit, I freeze."

"You know very well it's the only convenient park for miles around."

"I don't care about that. All I care is I saw a dozen kinds of bats and clubs and air guns. By the end of the first day, Jim would be in splinters. They'd have him barbecued, with an orange in his mouth."

She was beginning to laugh. "How you exaggerate."

"I'm serious!"

"You can't live Jim's life for him. He has to learn the hard way. He's got to take a little beating and beat others up; boys are like that."

"I don't *like* boys like that."

"It's the happiest time of life."

"Nonsense. I used to look back on childhood with great nostalgia. But now I realize I was a sentimental fool. It was nothing but screaming and running in a nightmare and coming home drenched with terror, from head to foot. If I could possibly save Jim from that, I would."

"That's impractical and, thank God, impossible."

"I won't have him near that place, I tell you. I'll have him grow up a neurotic recluse first."

"Charlie!"

"I will! Those little beasts, you should've seen them. Jim's *my* son, he is; he's not yours, remember." He felt the boy's thin legs about his shoulders, the boy's delicate fingers rumpling his hair. "I won't have him butchered."

"He'll get it in school. Better to let him take a little shoving about now, when he's three, so he's prepared for it."

"I've thought of that, too." Mr. Underhill held fiercely to his son's ankles which dangled like warm, thin sausages on either lapel. "I might even get a private tutor for him."

"Oh, Charles!"

They did not speak during dinner.

After dinner, he took Jim for a brief walk while his sister was washing the dishes. They strolled past the Playground under the dim street lamps. It was a cooling September night, with the first dry spice of autumn in it. Next week, and the children would be raked in off the fields like so many leaves and set to burning in the schools, using their fire and energy for more constructive purposes. But they would be here after school, ramming about, making projectiles of themselves, crashing and exploding, leaving wakes of misery behind every miniature war.

"Want to go in," said Jim, leaning against the high wire fence, watching the late-playing children beat each other and run.

"No, Jim, you don't want that."

"Play," said Jim, his eyes shining with fascination as he saw a large boy kick a small boy and the small boy kick a smaller boy to even things up.

"Play, daddy."

"Come along, Jim, you'll never get in that mess if *I* can help it." Underhill tugged the small arm firmly.

"I want to play." Jim was beginning to blubber now. His eyes were melting out of his face and his face was becoming a wrinkled orange of color.

Some of the children heard the crying and glanced over. Underhill had the terrible sense of watching a den of foxes suddenly startled and looking up from the white, hairy ruin of a dead rabbit. The mean yellow-glass eyes, the conical chins, the sharp white teeth, the dreadful wiry hair, the brambly sweaters, the iron-colored hands covered with a day's battle-stains. Their breath moved out to him, dark licorice and mint and juicy fruit so sickeningly sweet, so combined as to twist his stomach. And over this the hot mustard smell of someone tolerating an early chest cold; the greasy stink of flesh smeared with hot camphorous salves cooking under a flannel sheath. All these cloying, and somehow depressing odors of pencils, chalk, grass and slateboard erasers, real or imagined, summoned old memory in an instant. Popcorn mortared their teeth, and green jelly showed in their sucking, blowing nostrils. God! God!

They saw Jim, and he was new to them. They said not a word, but as Jim cried louder and Underhill, by main force, dragged him like a cement bag along the walk, the children followed with their glowing eyes. Underhill felt like pushing his fist at them and crying, "You little beasts, you won't get *my* son!"

And then, with beautiful irrelevance, the boy at the top of the blue-metal slide, so high he seemed almost in a mist, far away, the boy with the somehow familiar face, called out to him, waving and waving.

"Hello, Charlie . . . !"

Underhill paused and Jim stopped crying.

"See you later, Charlie . . . !"

And the face of the boy way up there on that high and very lonely slide was suddenly like the face of Thomas Marshall, an old business friend who lived just around the block, but whom he hadn't seen in years.

"See you later, Charlie."

Later, later? What did the fool boy mean?

"I know *you*, Charlie!" called the boy. "Hi!"

"What?" gasped Underhill.

"Tomorrow night, Charlie, hey!" And the boy fell off the slide and lay choking for breath, face like a white cheese from the fall, while children jumped him and tumbled over.

Underhill stood undecided for five seconds or more, until Jim thought to cry again, and then, with the golden fox eyes upon them, in the first chill of autumn, he dragged Jim all the way home.

The next afternoon Mr. Underhill finished at the office early and took the three o'clock train, arriving out in Green Town at three-twenty-five, in plenty of time to drink in the brisk rays of the autumnal sun. Strange how one day it *is* suddenly autumn, he thought. One day it is summer and the next, how could you measure or tell it? Something about the temperature or the smell? Or the sediment of age knocked loose from your bones during the night and circulating in your blood and heart, giving you a slight tremble and a chill? A year older, a year dying, was *that* it?

He walked up toward the Playground, planning the future. It seemed you did more planning in autumn than any other season. This had to do with dying, perhaps. You thought of death and you automatically planned. Well, then, there was to be a tutor for Jim, *that* was positive; none of those horrible schools for him. It would pinch the bank account a bit, but Jim would at least grow up a happy boy. They would pick and choose his friends. Any slam-bang bullies would be thrown out as soon as they so much as touched Jim. And as for this Playground? Completely out of the question!

"Oh hello, Charles."

He looked up suddenly. Before him, at the entrance to the wire enclosure, stood his sister. He noted instantly that she called him Charles, instead of Charlie. Last night's unpleasantness had not quite evaporated. "Carol, what're you doing *here*?"

She flushed guiltily and glanced in through the fence.

"You didn't," he said.

His eyes sought among the scrabbling, running, screaming children. "Do you mean to say . . . ?"

His sister nodded, half amused. "I thought I'd bring him early——"

"Before I got home, so I wouldn't know, is *that* it?"

That was it.

"Good God, Carol, where *is* he?"

"I just came to see."

"You mean you left him there all afternoon?"

"Just for five minutes while I shopped."

"And you *left* him. Good God!" Underhill seized her wrist. "Well, come on, find him, get him out of there!"

They peered in together past the wire to where a dozen boys charged about, girls slapped each other, and a squabbling heap of children took turns at getting off, making a quick run, and crashing one against another.

"That's where he is, I *know* it!" said Underhill.

Just then, across the field, sobbing and wailing, Jim ran, six boys after him. He fell, got up, ran, fell again, shrieking, and the boys behind shot beans through metal blowers.

"I'll stuff those blowers up their noses!" said Underhill. "Run, Jim! Run!"

Jim made it to the gate. Underhill caught him. It was like catching a rumpled, drenched wad of material. Jim's nose was bleeding, his pants were ripped, he was covered with grime.

"*There's* your Playground," said Underhill, on his knees,

staring up from his son, holding him, at his sister. "*There* are your sweet, happy innocents, your well-to-do piddling Fascists. Let me catch this boy here again and there'll be hell to pay. Come on, Jim. All right, you little bastards, get back there!" he shouted.

"We didn't do nothing," said the children.

"What's the world coming to?" Mr. Underhill questioned the universe.

"Hi! Charlie!" said the strange boy, standing to one side. He waved casually and smiled.

"Who's that?" asked Carol.

"How in hell do *I* know?" said Underhill.

"Be seeing you, Charlie. So long," called the boy, fading off.

Mr. Underhill marched his sister and his son home.

"Take your hand off my elbow!" said Carol.

He was trembling; absolutely, continually trembling with rage when he got to bed. He had tried some coffee, but nothing stopped it. He wanted to beat their pulpy little brains out, those gross Cruikshank children; yes, that phrase fit them, those fox-fiend, melancholy Cruikshank children, with all the guile and poison and slyness in their cold faces. In the name of all that was decent, what manner of child was this new generation! A bunch of cutters and hangers and bangers, a drove of bleeding, moronic thumb-screwers, with the sewage of neglect running in their veins? He lay violently jerking his head from one side of his hot pillow to the other, and at last got up and lit a cigarette, but it wasn't enough. He and Carol had had a huge battle when they got home. He had yelled at her and she had yelled back, peacock and peahen shrieking in a wilderness where law and order were insanities laughed at and quite forgotten.

He was ashamed. You didn't fight violence with violence, not if you were a gentleman. You talked very calmly. But Carol didn't give you a chance, damn it! She wanted the boy put in a vise and squashed. She wanted him reamed and punctured and given the laying on of hands. To be beaten from playground to kindergarten, to grammar school, to junior high, to high school. If he was lucky, in high school, the beatings and sadisms would refine themselves, the sea of blood and spittle would drain back down the shore of years and Jim would be left upon the edge of maturity, with God knows what outlook to the future, with a desire, perhaps, to be a wolf among wolves, a dog among dogs, a fiend among fiends. But there was enough of that in the world, already. The very thought of the next ten or fifteen years of torture was enough to make Mr. Underhill cringe; he felt his own flesh impaled with BB shot, stung, burned, fisted, scrounged, twisted, violated, and bruised. He quivered, like a jellyfish hurled violently into a concrete mixer. Jim would never survive it. Jim was too delicate for this horror.

Underhill walked in the midnight rooms of his house thinking of all this, of himself, of the son, the Playground, the fear; there was no part of it he did not touch and turn over with his mind. How much, he asked himself, how much of this is being alone, how much due to Ann's dying, how much to my need, and how much is the reality of the Playground itself, and the children? How much rational and how much nonsense? He twitched the delicate weights upon the scale and watched the indicator glide and fix and glide again, back and forth, softly, between midnight and dawn, between black and white, between raw sanity and naked insanity. He should not hold so tight, he should let his hands drop away from the boy. And yet—there was no hour that looking into Jim's small face he did not see Ann there, in the eyes, in the mouth, in the turn of the nostrils, in the warm breathing, in the glow of blood moving just under the thin shell of flesh. I have a right, he thought, to be afraid. I have every right. When you have two precious bits of porcelain and one is broken and the other, the last one, remains, where can you find the time to be objective, to be immensely calm, to be anything else but concerned?

No, he thought, walking slowly in the hall, there seems to be nothing I can do except go on being afraid and being afraid of being afraid.

"You needn't prowl the house all night," his sister called from her bed, as she heard him pass her open door. "You needn't be childish. I'm sorry if I seem dictatorial or cold. But you've got to make up your mind. Jim simply cannot have a private tutor. Ann would have wanted him to go to a regular school. And he's got to go back to that Playground tomorrow and keep going back until he's learned to stand on his own two feet and until he's familiar to all the children; then they won't pick on him so much."

Underhill said nothing. He got dressed quietly, in the dark and, downstairs, opened the front door. It was about five minutes to midnight as he walked swiftly down the street in the shadows of the tall elms and oaks and maples, trying to outdistance his rage and outrage. He knew Carol was right, of course. This was the world, you lived in it, you accepted it. But that was the very trouble! He had been through the mill already, he knew what it was to be a boy among lions, his own childhood had come rushing back to him in the last few hours, a time of terror and violence, and now he could not bear to think of Jim's going through it all, those long years, especially if you were a delicate child, through no fault of your own, your bones thin, your face pale, what could you expect but to be harried and chased?

He stopped by the Playground, which was still lit by one great overhead lamp. The gate was locked for the night, but that one light remained on until twelve. He wanted to tear the contemptible place down, rip up the steel fences, obliterate the slides, and say to the children, "Go home! Play in your back yards!"

How ingenious, the cold, deep Playground. You never knew where anyone lived. The boy who knocked your teeth out, who was *he*? Nobody knew. Where did he live? Nobody knew. How to find him? Nobody knew. Why, you could come here one day, beat the living tar out of some smaller child, and run on the next day to some *other* playground. They would never find you. From playground to playground, you could take your criminal tricks, with everyone forgetting you, since they never knew you. You could return to this Playground a month later, and if the little child whose teeth you knocked out was there and recognized you, you could deny it. "No, I'm not the one. Must be some other kid. This is my first time here! No, not me!" And when his back is turned, knock him over. And run off down nameless streets, a nameless person.

What can I possibly do? thought Underhill. Carol's been more than generous with her time; she's been good for Jim, no doubt of it. A lot of the love she would have put into a marriage has gone to him this year. I can't fight her forever on this, and I can't tell her to leave. Perhaps moving to the country might help. No, no, impossible; the money. But I can't leave Jim here, either.

"Hello, Charlie," said a quiet voice.

Underhill snapped about. Inside the Playground fence, seated in the dirt, making diagrams with one finger in the cool dust, was the solemn nine-year-old boy. He didn't glance up. He said Hello Charlie, just sitting there, easily, in that world beyond the hard steel fence.

Underhill said, "How do you know my name?"

"I know it." The boy crossed his legs, comfortably, smiling quietly. "You're having lots of trouble."

"How'd you get in there so late? Who are you?"

"My name's Marshall."

"Of course! Tom Marshall's son Tommy! I *thought* you looked familiar."

"More familiar than you think." The boy laughed gently.

"How's your father, Tommy?"

"Have you seen him lately?" the boy asked.

"On the street, briefly, two months ago."

"How did he look?"

"What?"

"How did Mr. Marshall *look*?" asked the boy. It seemed strange he refused to say "my father."

"He looked all right. Why?"

"I guess he's happy," said the boy. Mr. Underhill saw the boy's arms and legs and they were covered with scabs and scratches.

"Aren't you going home, Tommy?"

"I sneaked out to see you. I just knew you'd come. You're afraid."

Mr. Underhill didn't know what to say.

"Those little monsters," he said at last.

"Maybe I can help you." The boy made a dust triangle.

It was ridiculous. "How?"

"You'd give anything, wouldn't you, if you could spare Jim all this? You'd trade places with him if you could?"

Mr. Underhill nodded, frozen.

"Well, you come down here tomorrow afternoon at four. Then I can help you."

"How do you mean, help?"

"I can't tell you outright," said the boy. "It has to do with the Playground. Any place where there's lots of evil, that makes power. You can feel it, can't you?"

A kind of warm wind stirred off the bare field under the one high light. Underhill shivered. Yes, even now, at midnight, the Playground seemed evil, for it was used for evil things. "Are all playgrounds like this?"

"Some. Maybe this is the only one like this. Maybe it's just how *you* look at it, Charlie. Things *are* what you *want* them to be. A lot of people think this is a *swell* Playground. They're right, too. It's how you look at it, maybe. What I wanted to say, though, is that Tom Marshall was like you. He worried about Tommy Marshall and the Playground and the kids, too. He wanted to save Tommy the trouble and the hurt, also."

This business of talking about people as if they were remote, made Mr. Underhill uncomfortable.

"So we made a bargain," said the boy.

"Who with?"

"With the Playground, I guess, or whoever runs it."

"Who runs it?"

"I've never seen him. There's an office over there under the grandstand. A light burns in it all night. It's a bright, blue light, kind of funny. There's a desk there with no papers in it and an empty chair. The sign says Manager, but nobody ever sees the man."

"He must be around."

"That's right," said the boy. "Or I wouldn't be where I am, and someone else wouldn't be where they are."

"You certainly talk grown-up."

The boy was pleased. "Do you want to know who I really am? I'm not Tommy Marshall at all. I'm Tom Marshall, the father." He sat there in the dust, not moving, late at night, under the high and faraway light, with the late wind blowing his shirt collar gently under his chin, blowing the cool dust. "I'm Tom Marshall, the father. I know it'll be hard for you to believe. But it *is* true. I was afraid for Tommy. I was the way you are now about Jim. So I made this deal with the Playground. Oh, there are others who did the same, here. If you look close, you'll see them among the other children, by the expression in their eyes."

Underhill blinked. "You'd better run home to bed."

"You want to believe me. You want it to be true. I saw your eyes just then! If you could trade places with Jim, you would. You'd like to save him all that torture, let him be in your place, grown-up, the real work over and done."

"Any decent parent sympathizes with his children."

"You, more than most. You feel every bite and kick. Well, you come here tomorrow. You can make a deal, too."

"Trade places?" It was an incredible, an amusing, but an oddly satisfying thought. "What would I have to do?"

"Just make up your mind."

Underhill tried to make his next question sound very casual, a joke, but his mind was in a rage again. "What would I pay?"

"Nothing. You'd just have to play in the Playground."

"All day?"

"And go to school, of course."

"And grow up again?"

"Yes, and grow up again. Be here at four tomorrow afternoon."

"I have to work in the city tomorrow."

"Tomorrow," said the boy.

"You'd better get home to bed, Tommy."

"My name is *Tom* Marshall." The boy sat there.

The Playground lights went out.

Mr. Underhill and his sister did not speak at breakfast. He usually phoned her at noon to chat about this or that, but he did not phone. But at one-thirty, after a bad lunch, he dialed the house number. When Carol answered he hung up. Five minutes later he phoned again.

"Charlie, was that you called five minutes ago?"

"Yes," he said.

"I thought I heard you breathing before you hung up. What'd you call about, dear?" She was being sensible again.

"Oh, just called."

"It's been a bad two days, hasn't it? You *do* see what I mean, don't you, Charlie? Jim *must* go to the Playground and get a few knocks."

"A few knocks, yes."

He saw the blood and the hungry foxes and the torn rabbits.

"And learn to give and take," she was saying, "and fight if he has to."

"Fight if he has to," he murmured.

"I knew you'd come around."

"Around," he said. "You're right. No way out. He must be sacrificed."

"Oh, Charlie, you *are* odd."

He cleared his throat. "Well, that's settled."

"Yes."

I wonder what it would be like, he thought.

"Everything else okay?" he asked the phone.

He thought of the diagrams in the dust, the boy seated there with the hidden bones in his face.

"Yes," she said.

"I've been thinking," he said.

"Speak up."

"I'll be home at three," he said, slowly, piecing out the words like a man hit in the stomach, gasping for breath. "We'll take a walk, you and Jim and I," he said, eyes shut.

"Wonderful!"

"To the Playground," he said and hung up.

It was really autumn now, the real chill, the real snap; overnight the trees burnt red and snapped free of their leaves, which spiraled about Mr. Underhill's face as he walked up the front steps, and there were Carol and Jim, bundled up against the sharp wind, waiting for him.

"Hello!" they cried to one another, with much embracing and kissing. "There's Jim down there!" "There's Daddy up there!" They laughed and he felt paralyzed and in terror of the late day. It was almost four. He looked at the leaden sky, which might pour down molten silver any moment, a sky of lava and soot and a wet wind blowing out of it. He held his sister's arm very tightly as they walked. "Aren't you friendly, though?" she smiled.

"It's ridiculous, of course," he said, thinking of something else.

"What?"

They were at the Playground gate.

"Hello, Charlie. Hi!" Far away, atop the monstrous slide stood the Marshall boy, waving, not smiling now.

"You wait here," said Mr. Underhill to his sister. "I'll be only a moment. I'll just take Jim in."

"All right."

He grasped the small boy's hand. "Here we go, Jim. Stick close to Daddy."

They stepped down the hard concrete steps and stood in the flat dust. Before them, in a magical sequence, stood the diagrams, the gigantic tic-tac-toes, the monstrous hopscotches, the amazing numerals and triangles and oblongs the children had scrabbled in the incredible dust.

The sky blew a huge wind upon him and he was shivering. He grasped the little boy's hand still tighter and turned to his sister. "Good-by," he said. For he was believing it. He was in the Playground and believing it, and it was for the best. Nothing too good for Jim. Nothing at all in this outrageous world! And now his sister was laughing back at him, "Charlie, you idiot!"

Then they were running, running across the dirt Playground floor, at the bottom of a stony sea that pressed and blew upon them. Now Jim was crying, "Daddy, Daddy!" and the children racing to meet them, the boy on the slide yelling, the tic-tac-toe and hopscotchers whirling, a sense of bodiless terror gripping him, but he knew what he must do and what must be done and what would happen. Far across the field footballs sailed, baseballs whizzed, bats flew, fists flashed up, and the door of the Manager's office stood open, the desk empty, the seat empty, a lone light burning over it.

Underhill stumbled, shut his eyes and fell, crying out, his body clenched by a hot pain, mouthing strange words, everything in turmoil.

"There you are, Jim," said a voice.

And he was climbing, climbing, eyes closed, climbing metal-ringing ladder rungs, screaming, yelling, his throat raw.

Mr. Underhill opened his eyes.

He was on top of the slide. The gigantic, blue metal slide which seemed ten thousand feet high. Children crushed at his back, children beat him to go on, slide! slide!

And he looked, and there, going off across the field, was a man in a black overcoat. And there, at the gate, was a woman waving and the man standing there with the woman, both of them looking in at him, waving, and their voices calling, "Have a good time! Have a good time, Jim!"

He screamed. He looked at his hands, in a panic of realization. The small hands, the thin hands. He looked at the earth far below. He felt his nose bleeding and there was the Marshall boy next to him. "Hi!" cried the other, and bashed him in the mouth. "Only twelve years here!" cried the other in the uproar.

Twelve years! thought Mr. Underhill, trapped. And time is different to children. A year is like ten years. No, not twelve years of childhood ahead of him, but a century, a century of *this.*

"Slide!"

Behind him the stink of Musterole, Vick's Vaporub, peanuts, chewed hot tar, spearmint gum and blue fountain-pen ink, the smell of kite-twine and glycerin soap, a pumpkin smell of Hallowe'en and a papier-mâché fragrance of skull masks, and the smell of dry scabs, as he was pinched, pummeled, shoved. Fists rose and fell, he saw the fox faces and beyond, at the fence, the man and woman standing there, waving. He shrieked, he covered his face, he felt himself pushed, bleeding, to the rim of nothingness. Headfirst, he careened down the slide, screeching, with ten thousand monsters behind. One thought jumped through his mind a moment before he hit bottom in a nauseous mound of claws.

This is hell, he thought, *this is hell!*

And no one in the hot, milling heap contradicted him.

A Sound of Thunder

THE SIGN ON the wall seemed to quaver under a film of sliding warm water. Eckels felt his eyelids blink over his stare, and the sign burned in this momentary darkness:

TIME SAFARI, INC.
SAFARIS TO ANY YEAR IN THE PAST.
YOU NAME THE ANIMAL.
WE TAKE YOU THERE.
YOU SHOOT IT.

A warm phlegm gathered in Eckels' throat; he swallowed and pushed it down. The muscles around his mouth formed a smile as he put his hand slowly out upon the air, and in that hand waved a check for ten thousand dollars to the man behind the desk.

"Does this safari guarantee I come back alive?"

"We guarantee nothing," said the official, "except the dinosaurs." He turned. "This is Mr. Travis, your Safari Guide in the Past. He'll tell you what and where to shoot. If he says no shooting, no shooting. If you disobey instructions, there's a stiff penalty of another ten thousand dollars, plus possible government action, on your return."

Eckels glanced across the vast office at a mass and tangle, a snaking and humming of wires and steel boxes, at an aurora that flickered now orange, now silver, now blue. There was a sound like a gigantic bonfire burning all of Time, all the years and all the parchment calendars, all the hours piled high and set aflame.

A touch of the hand and this burning would, on the instant, beautifully reverse itself. Eckels remembered the wording in the advertisements to the letter. Out of chars and ashes, out of dust and coals, like golden salamanders, the old years, the green years, might leap; roses sweeten the air, white hair turn Irish-black, wrinkles vanish; all, everything fly back to seed, flee death, rush down to their beginnings, suns rise in western skies and set in glorious easts, moons eat themselves opposite to the custom, all and everything cupping one in another like Chinese boxes, rabbits into hats, all and everything returning to the fresh death, the seed death, the green death, to the time before the beginning. A touch of a hand might do it, the merest touch of a hand.

"Hell and damn," Eckels breathed, the light of the Machine on his thin face. "A real Time Machine." He shook his head. "Makes you think. If the election had gone badly yesterday, I might be here now running away from the results. Thank God Keith won. He'll make a fine President of the United States."

"Yes," said the man behind the desk. "We're lucky. If Deutscher had gotten in, we'd have the worst kind of dictatorship. There's an anti-everything man for you, a militarist, anti-Christ, anti-human, anti-intellectual. People called us up, you know, joking but not joking. Said if Deutscher became President they wanted to go live in 1492. Of course it's not our business to conduct Escapes, but to form Safaris. Anyway, Keith's President now. All you got to worry about is——"

"Shooting my dinosaur," Eckels finished it for him.

"A *Tyrannosaurus rex.* The Thunder Lizard, the damnedest monster in history. Sign this release. Anything happens to you, we're not responsible. Those dinosaurs are hungry."

Eckels flushed angrily. "Trying to scare me!"

"Frankly, yes. We don't want anyone going who'll panic at the first shot. Six Safari leaders were killed last year, and a dozen hunters. We're here to give you the damnedest thrill a *real* hunter ever asked for. Traveling you back sixty million years to bag the biggest damned game in all Time. Your personal check's still there. Tear it up."

Mr. Eckels looked at the check for a long time. His fingers twitched.

"Good luck," said the man behind the desk. "Mr. Travis, he's all yours."

They moved silently across the room, taking their guns with them, toward the Machine, toward the silver metal and the roaring light.

First a day and then a night and then a day and then a night, then it was day-night-day-night-day. A week, a month, a year, a decade! A.D. 2055. A.D. 2019. 1999! 1957! Gone! The Machine roared.

They put on their oxygen helmets and tested the intercoms.

Eckels swayed on the padded seat, his face pale, his jaw stiff. He felt the trembling in his arms and he looked down and found his hands tight on the new rifle. There were four other men in the Machine. Travis, the Safari Leader, his assistant, Lesperance, and two other hunters, Billings and Kramer. They sat looking at each other, and the years blazed around them.

"Can these guns get a dinosaur cold?" Eckels felt his mouth saying.

"If you hit them right," said Travis on the helmet radio. "Some dinosaurs have two brains, one in the head, another far down the spinal column. We stay away from those. That's stretching luck. Put your first two shots into the eyes, if you can, blind them, and go back into the brain."

The Machine howled. Time was a film run backward. Suns fled and ten million moons fled after them. "Good God," said Eckels. "Every hunter that ever lived would envy us today. This makes Africa seem like Illinois."

The Machine slowed; its scream fell to a murmur. The Machine stopped.

The sun stopped in the sky.

The fog that had enveloped the Machine blew away and they were in an old time, a very old time indeed, three hunters and two Safari Heads with their blue metal guns across their knees.

"Christ isn't born yet," said Travis. "Moses has not gone to the mountain to talk with God. The Pyramids are still in the earth, waiting to be cut out and put up. *Remember* that. Alexander, Caesar, Napoleon, Hitler—none of them exists."

The men nodded.

"That"—Mr. Travis pointed—"is the jungle of sixty million two thousand and fifty-five years before President Keith."

He indicated a metal path that struck off into green wilderness, over steaming swamp, among giant ferns and palms.

"And that," he said, "is the Path, laid by Time Safari for your use. It floats six inches above the earth. Doesn't touch so much as one grass blade, flower, or tree. It's an anti-gravity metal. Its purpose is to keep you from touching this world of the past in any way. Stay on the Path. Don't go off it. I repeat. *Don't go off.* For *any* reason! If you fall off, there's a penalty. And don't shoot any animal we don't okay."

"Why?" asked Eckels.

They sat in the ancient wilderness. Far birds' cries blew on a wind, and the smell of tar and an old salt sea, moist grasses, and flowers the color of blood.

"We don't want to change the Future. We don't belong here in the Past. The government doesn't *like* us here. We have to pay big graft to keep our franchise. A Time Machine is damn finicky business. Not knowing it, we might kill an important animal, a small bird, a roach, a flower even, thus destroying an important link in a growing species."

"That's not clear," said Eckels.

"All right," Travis continued, "say we accidentally kill one mouse here. That means all the future families of this one particular mouse are destroyed, right?"

"Right."

"And all the families of the families of the families of that one mouse! With a stamp of your foot, you annihilate first one, then a dozen, then a thousand, a million, a *billion* possible mice!"

"So they're dead," said Eckels. "So what?"

"So what?" Travis snorted quietly. "Well, what about the foxes that'll need those mice to survive? For want of ten mice, a fox dies. For want of ten foxes, a lion starves. For want of a lion, all manner of insects, vultures, infinite billions of life forms are thrown into chaos and destruction. Eventually it all boils down to this: fifty-nine million years later, a cave man, one of a dozen on the *entire world*, goes hunting wild boar or saber-tooth tiger for food. But you, friend, have *stepped* on all the tigers in that region. By stepping on one single mouse. So the cave man starves. And the cave man, please note, is not just *any* expendable man, no! He is an *entire future nation*. From his loins would have sprung ten sons. From *their* loins one hundred sons, and thus onward to a civilization. Destroy this one man, and you destroy a race, a people, an entire history of life. It is comparable to slaying some of Adam's grandchildren. The stomp of your foot, on one mouse, could start an earthquake, the effects of which could shake our earth and destinies down through Time, to their very foundations. With the death of that one cave man, a billion others yet unborn are throttled in the womb. Perhaps Rome never rises on its seven hills. Perhaps Europe is forever a dark forest, and only Asia waxes healthy and teeming. Step on a mouse and you crush the Pyramids. Step on a mouse and you leave your print, like a Grand Canyon, across Eternity. Queen Elizabeth might never be born, Washington might not cross the Delaware, there might never be a United States at all. So be careful. Stay on the Path. *Never* step off!"

"I see," said Eckels. "Then it wouldn't pay for us even to touch the *grass*?"

"Correct. Crushing certain plants could add up infinitesimally. A little error here would multiply in sixty million years, all out of proportion. Of course maybe our theory is wrong. Maybe Time *can't* be changed by us. Or maybe it can be changed only in little subtle ways. A dead mouse here makes an insect imbalance there, a population disproportion later, a bad harvest further on, a depression, mass starvation, and, finally, a change in *social* temperament in far-flung countries. Something much more subtle, like that. Perhaps only a soft breath, a whisper, a hair, pollen on the air, such a slight, slight change that unless you looked close you wouldn't see it. Who knows? Who really can say he knows? We don't know. We're guessing. But until we do know for certain whether our messing around in Time *can* make a big roar or a little rustle in history, we're being damned careful. This Machine, this Path, your clothing and bodies, were sterilized, as you know, before the journey. We wear these oxygen helmets so we can't introduce our bacteria into an ancient atmosphere."

"How do we know which animals to shoot?"

"They're marked with red paint," said Travis. "Today, before our journey, we sent Lesperance here back with the Machine. He came to this particular era and followed certain animals."

"Studying them?"

"Right," said Lesperance. "I track them through their entire existence, noting which of them lives longest. Very few. How many times they mate. Not often. Life's short. When I find one that's going to die when a tree falls on him, or one that drowns in a tar pit, I note the exact hour, minute, and second. I shoot a paint bomb. It leaves a red patch on his hide. We can't miss it. Then I correlate our arrival in the Past so that we meet the Monster not more than two minutes before he would have died anyway. This way, we kill only animals with no future, that are never going to mate again. You see how *careful* we are?"

"But if you came back this morning in Time," said Eckels eagerly, "you must've bumped into *us*, our Safari! How did it turn out? Was it successful? Did all of us get through—alive?"

Travis and Lesperance gave each other a look.

"That'd be a paradox," said the latter. "Time doesn't permit that sort of mess—a man meeting himself. When such occasions threaten, Time steps aside. Like an airplane hitting an air pocket. You felt the Machine jump just before we stopped? That was us passing ourselves on the way back to the Future. We saw nothing. There's no way of telling *if* this expedition was a success, *if* we got our monster, or whether all of us—meaning *you*, Mr. Eckels—got out alive."

Eckels smiled palely.

"Cut that," said Travis sharply. "Everyone on his feet!"

They were ready to leave the Machine.

The jungle was high and the jungle was broad and the jungle was the entire world forever and forever. Sounds like music and sounds like flying tents filled the sky, and those were pterodactyls soaring with cavernous gray wings, gigantic bats out of a delirium and a night fever. Eckels, balanced on the narrow Path, aimed his rifle playfully.

"Stop that!" said Travis. "Don't even aim for fun, damn it! If your gun should go off——"

Eckels flushed. "Where's our *Tyrannosaurus*?"

Lesperance checked his wrist watch. "Up ahead. We'll bisect his trail in sixty seconds. Look for the red paint, for Christ's sake. Don't shoot till we give the word. Stay on the Path. *Stay on the Path!*"

They moved forward in the wind of morning.

"Strange," murmured Eckels. "Up ahead, sixty million years, Election Day over. Keith made President. Everyone celebrating. And here we are, a million years lost, and they don't exist. The things we worried about for months, a lifetime, not even born or thought about yet."

"Safety catches off, everyone!" ordered Travis. "You, first shot, Eckels. Second, Billings. Third, Kramer."

"I've hunted tiger, wild boar, buffalo, elephant, but Jesus, this is *it*," said Eckels. "I'm shaking like a kid."

"Ah," said Travis.

Everyone stopped.

Travis raised his hand. "Ahead," he whispered. "In the mist. There he is. There's His Royal Majesty now."

The jungle was wide and full of twitterings, rustlings, murmurs, and sighs.

Suddenly it all ceased, as if someone had shut a door.

Silence.

A sound of thunder.

Out of the mist, one hundred yards away, came *Tyrannosaurus rex*.

"Jesus God," whispered Eckels.

"Sh!"

It came on great oiled, resilient, striding legs. It towered thirty feet above half of the trees, a great evil god, folding its delicate watchmaker's claws close to its oily reptilian chest. Each lower leg was a piston, a thousand pounds of white bone, sunk in thick ropes of muscle, sheathed over in a gleam of pebbled skin like the mail of a terrible warrior. Each thigh was a ton of meat, ivory, and steel mesh. And from the great breathing cage of the upper body those two delicate arms dangled out front, arms with hands which might pick up and examine men like toys, while the snake neck coiled. And the head itself, a ton of sculptured stone, lifted easily upon the sky. Its mouth gaped, exposing a fence of teeth like daggers. Its eyes rolled, ostrich eggs, empty of all expression save hunger. It closed its mouth in a death grin. It ran, its pelvic bones crushing aside trees and bushes, its taloned feet clawing damp earth, leaving prints six inches deep wherever it settled its weight. It ran with a gliding ballet step, far too poised and balanced for its ten tons. It moved into a sunlit arena warily, its beautifully reptile hands feeling the air.

"My God!" Eckels twitched his mouth. "It could reach up and grab the moon."

"Sh!" Travis jerked angrily. "He hasn't seen us yet."

"It can't be killed." Eckels pronounced this verdict quietly, as if there could be no argument. He had weighed the evidence and this was his considered opinion. The rifle in his hands seemed a cap gun. "We were fools to come. This is impossible."

"Shut up!" hissed Travis.

"Nightmare."

"Turn around," commanded Travis. "Walk quietly to the Machine. We'll remit one half your fee."

"I didn't realize it would be this *big*," said Eckels. "I miscalculated, that's all. And now I want out."

"It *sees* us!"

"There's the red paint on its chest!"

The Thunder Lizard raised itself. Its armored flesh glittered like a thousand green coins. The coins, crusted with slime, steamed. In the slime, tiny insects wriggled, so that the entire body seemed to twitch and undulate, even while the monster itself did not move. It exhaled. The stink of raw flesh blew down the wilderness.

"Get me out of here," said Eckels. "It was never like this before. I was always sure I'd come through alive. I had good guides, good safaris, and safety. This time, I figured wrong. I've met my match and admit it. This is too much for me to get hold of."

"Don't run," said Lesperance. "Turn around. Hide in the Machine."

"Yes." Eckels seemed to be numb. He looked at his feet as if trying to make them move. He gave a grunt of helplessness.

"Eckels!"

He took a few steps, blinking, shuffling.

"Not *that* way!"

The Monster, at the first motion, lunged forward with a terrible scream. It covered one hundred yards in four seconds. The rifles jerked up and blazed fire. A windstorm from the beast's mouth engulfed them in the stench of slime and old blood. The Monster roared, teeth glittering with sun.

Eckels, not looking back, walked blindly to the edge of the Path, his gun limp in his arms, stepped off the Path, and walked, not knowing it, in the jungle. His feet sank into green moss. His legs moved him, and he felt alone and remote from the events behind.

The rifles cracked again. Their sound was lost in shriek and lizard thunder. The great lever of the reptile's tail swung up, lashed sideways. Trees exploded in clouds of leaf and branch. The Monster twitched its jeweler's hands down to fondle at the men, to twist them in half, to crush them like berries, to cram them into its teeth and its screaming throat. Its boulder-stone eyes leveled with the men. They saw themselves mirrored. They fired at the metallic eyelids and the blazing black iris.

Like a stone idol, like a mountain avalanche, *Tyrannosaurus* fell. Thundering, it clutched trees, pulled them with it. It wrenched and tore the metal Path. The men flung themselves back and away. The body hit, ten tons of cold flesh and stone. The guns fired. The Monster lashed its armored tail, twitched its snake jaws, and lay still. A fount of blood spurted from its throat. Somewhere inside, a sac of fluids burst. Sickening gushes drenched the hunters. They stood, red and glistening.

The thunder faded.

The jungle was silent. After the avalanche, a green peace. After the nightmare, morning.

Billings and Kramer sat on the pathway and threw up. Travis and Lesperance stood with smoking rifles, cursing steadily.

In the Time Machine, on his face, Eckels lay shivering. He had found his way back to the Path, climbed into the Machine.

Travis came walking, glanced at Eckels, took cotton gauze from a metal box, and returned to the others, who were sitting on the Path.

"Clean up."

They wiped the blood from their helmets. They began to curse too. The Monster lay, a hill of solid flesh. Within, you could hear the sighs and murmurs as the furthest chambers of it died, the organs malfunctioning, liquids running a final instant from pocket to sac to spleen, everything shutting off, closing up forever. It was like standing by a wrecked locomotive or a steam shovel at quitting time, all valves being released or levered tight. Bones cracked; the tonnage of its own flesh, off balance, dead weight, snapped the delicate forearms, caught underneath. The meat settled, quivering.

Another cracking sound. Overhead, a gigantic tree branch broke from its heavy mooring, fell. It crashed upon the dead beast with finality.

"There." Lesperance checked his watch. "Right on time. That's the giant tree that was scheduled to fall and kill this animal originally." He glanced at the two hunters. "You want the trophy picture?"

"What?"

"We can't take a trophy back to the Future. The body has to stay right here where it would have died originally, so the insects, birds, and bacteria can get at it, as they were intended to. Everything in balance. The body stays. But we *can* take a picture of you standing near it."

The two men tried to think, but gave up, shaking their heads.

They let themselves be led along the metal Path. They sank wearily into the Machine cushions. They gazed back at the ruined Monster, the stagnating mound, where already strange reptilian birds and golden insects were busy at the steaming armor.

A sound on the floor of the Time Machine stiffened them. Eckels sat there, shivering.

"I'm sorry," he said at last.

"Get up!" cried Travis.

Eckels got up.

"Go out on that Path alone," said Travis. He had his rifle pointed. "You're not coming back in the Machine. We're leaving you here!"

Lesperance seized Travis' arm. "Wait——"

"Stay out of this!" Travis shook his hand away. "This son of a bitch nearly killed us. But it isn't *that* so much. Hell, no. It's his *shoes*! Look at them! He ran off the Path. My God, that *ruins* us! Christ knows how much we'll forfeit! Tens of thousands of dollars of insurance! We guarantee no one leaves the Path. He left it. Oh, the damn fool! I'll have to report to the government. They might revoke our license to travel. God knows *what* he's done to Time, to History!"

"Take it easy, all he did was kick up some dirt."

"How do we *know*?" cried Travis. "We don't know anything! It's all a damn mystery! Get out there, Eckels!"

Eckels fumbled his shirt. "I'll pay anything. A hundred thousand dollars!"

Travis glared at Eckels' checkbook and spat. "Go out there.

The Monster's next to the Path. Stick your arms up to your elbows in his mouth. Then you can come back with us."

"That's unreasonable!"

"The Monster's dead, you yellow bastard. The bullets! The bullets can't be left behind. They don't belong in the Past; they might change something. Here's my knife. Dig them out!"

The jungle was alive again, full of the old tremorings and bird cries. Eckels turned slowly to regard that primeval garbage dump, that hill of nightmares and terror. After a long time, like a sleepwalker, he shuffled out along the Path.

He returned, shuddering, five minutes later, his arms soaked and red to the elbows. He held out his hands. Each held a number of steel bullets. Then he fell. He lay where he fell, not moving.

"You didn't have to make him do that," said Lesperance.

"Didn't I? It's too early to tell." Travis nudged the still body. "He'll live. Next time he won't go hunting game like this. Okay." He jerked his thumb wearily at Lesperance. "Switch on. Let's go home."

1492. 1776. 1812.

They cleaned their hands and faces. They changed their caking shirts and pants. Eckels was up and around again, not speaking. Travis glared at him for a full ten minutes.

"Don't look at me," cried Eckels. "I haven't done anything."

"Who can tell?"

"Just ran off the Path, that's all, a little mud on my shoes—what do you want me to do—get down and pray?"

"We might need it. I'm warning you, Eckels, I might kill you yet. I've got my gun ready."

"I'm innocent. I've done nothing!"

1999. 2000. 2055.

The Machine stopped.

"Get out," said Travis.

The room was there as they had left it. But not the same as they had left it. The same man sat behind the same desk. But the same man did not quite sit behind the same desk.

Travis looked around swiftly. "Everything okay here?" he snapped.

"Fine. Welcome home!"

Travis did not relax. He seemed to be looking at the very atoms of the air itself, at the way the sun poured through the one high window.

"Okay, Eckels, get out. Don't ever come back."

Eckels could not move.

"You heard me," said Travis. "What're you *staring* at?"

Eckels stood smelling of the air, and there was a thing to the air, a chemical taint so subtle, so slight, that only a faint cry of his subliminal senses warned him it was there. The colors, white, gray, blue, orange, in the wall, in the furniture, in the sky beyond the window, were . . . were . . . And there was a *feel.* His flesh twitched. His hands twitched. He stood drinking the oddness with the pores of his body. Somewhere, someone must have been screaming one of those whistles that only a dog can hear. His body screamed silence in return. Beyond this room, beyond this wall, beyond this man who was not quite the same man seated at this desk that was not quite the same desk . . . lay an entire world of streets and people. What sort of world it was now, there was no telling. He could feel them moving there, beyond the walls, almost, like so many chess pieces blown in a dry wind. . . .

But the immediate thing was the sign painted on the office wall, the same sign he had read earlier today on first entering.

Somehow, the sign had changed:

TYME SEFARI INC.
SEFARIS TU ANY YEER EN THE PAST.
YU NAIM THE ANIMALL.
WEE TAEK YU THAIR.
YU SHOOT ITT.

Eckels felt himself fall into a chair. He fumbled crazily at the thick slime on his boots. He held up a clod of dirt, trembling. "No, it *can't* be. Not a *little* thing like that. No!"

Embedded in the mud, glistening green and gold and black, was a butterfly, very beautiful, and very dead.

"Not a little thing like *that*! Not a butterfly!" cried Eckels.

It fell to the floor, an exquisite thing, a small thing that could upset balances and knock down a line of small dominoes and then big dominoes and then gigantic dominoes, all down the years across Time. Eckels' mind whirled. It *couldn't* change things. Killing one butterfly couldn't be *that* important! Could it?

His face was cold. His mouth trembled, asking: "Who—who won the presidential election yesterday?"

The man behind the desk laughed. "You joking? You know damn well. Deutscher, of course! Who else? Not that damn weakling Keith. We got an iron man now, a man with guts, by God!" The official stopped. "What's wrong?"

Eckels moaned. He dropped to his knees. He scrabbled at the golden butterfly with shaking fingers. "Can't we," he pleaded to the world, to himself, to the officials, to the Machine, "can't we take it *back*, can't we *make* it alive again? Can't we start over? Can't we——"

He did not move. Eyes shut, he waited, shivering. He heard Travis breathe loud in the room; he heard Travis shift his rifle, click the safety catch, and raise the weapon.

There was a sound of thunder.

The Great Wide World Over There

IT WAS A day to be out of bed, to pull curtains and fling open windows. It was a day to make your heart bigger with warm mountain air.

Cora, feeling like a young girl in a wrinkled old dress, sat up in bed.

It was early, the sun barely on the horizon, but already the birds were stirring from the pines and ten billion red ants milled free from their bronze hills by the cabin door. Cora's husband Tom slept like a bear in a snowy hibernation of bedclothes beside her. Will my heart wake him up? she wondered.

And then she knew why this seemed a special day.

"Benjy's coming!"

She imagined him far off, leaping green meadows, fording streams where spring was pushing itself in cool colors of moss and clear water toward the sea. She saw his great shoes dusting and flicking the stony roads and paths. She saw his freckled face high in the sun looking giddily down his long body at his distant hands flying out and back behind him.

Benjy, come on! she thought, opening a window swiftly. Wind blew her hair like a gray spider web about her cold ears. Now Benjy's at Iron Bridge, now at Meadow Pike, now up Creek Path, over Chesley's Field . . .

Somewhere in those Missouri mountains was Benjy. Cora blinked. Those strange high hills beyond which twice a year she and Tom drove their horse and wagon to town, and through which, thirty years ago, she had wanted to run forever, saying, "Oh, Tom, let's just drive and drive until we reach the sea." But Tom had looked at her as if she had slapped his face, and he had turned the wagon around and driven on home, talking to the mare. And if people lived by shores where the sea came like a storm, now louder, now softer, every day, she did not know it. And if there were cities where neons were like pink ice and green mint and red fireworks each evening, she didn't know that either. Her horizon, north, south, east, west, was this valley, and had never been anything else.

But now, today, she thought, Benjy's coming from that world out there; he's seen it, heard it, smelt it; he'll tell me about it. And he can write. She looked at her hands. He'll be here a whole month and teach me. Then I can write out into that world and bring it here to the mailbox I'll make Tom build today. "Get up, Tom! You *hear*?"

She put her hand out to push the bank of sleeping snow.

By nine o'clock the valley was full of grasshoppers flinging themselves through the blue, piney air, while smoke curled into the sky.

Cora, singing into her pots and pans as she polished them, saw her wrinkled face bronzed and freshened in the copper bottoms. Tom was grumbling the sounds of a sleepy bear at his mush breakfast, while her singing moved all about him, like a bird in a cage.

"*Someone's* mighty happy," said a voice.

Cora made herself into a statue. From the corners of her eyes she saw a shadow cross the room.

"Mrs. Brabbam?" asked Cora of her scouring cloth.

"That's who it is!" And there stood the Widow Lady, her gingham dress dragging the warm dust, her letters in her chickeny hand. "Morning! I just been to my mailbox. Got me a real beauty of a letter from my uncle George in Springfield." Mrs. Brabbam fixed Cora with a gaze like a silver needle. "How long since you got a letter from *your* uncle, missus?"

"My uncles are all dead." It was not Cora herself, but her tongue, that lied. When the time came, she knew, it would be her tongue alone that must take communion and confess earthly sinning.

"It's certainly *nice*, getting mail." Mrs. Brabbam waved her letters in a straight flush on the morning air.

Always twisting the knife in the flesh. How many years, thought Cora, had this run on, Mrs. Brabbam and her smily eyes, talking loud of how she got mail; implying that nobody else for miles around could read? Cora bit her lip and almost threw the pot, but set it down, laughing. "I forgot to tell you. My nephew Benjy's coming; his folks are poorly, and he's here for the summer today. He'll teach me to write. And Tom's building us a postal box, aren't you, Tom?"

Mrs. Brabbam clutched her letters. "Well, isn't that fine! You *lucky* lady." And suddenly the door was empty. Mrs. Brabbam was gone.

But Cora was after her. For in that instant she had seen something like a scarecrow, something like a flicker of pure sunlight, something like a brook trout jumping upstream, leap a fence in the yard below. She saw a huge hand wave and birds flush in terror from a crab-apple tree.

Cora was rushing, the world rushing back of her, down the path. "Benjy!"

They ran at each other like partners in a Saturday dance, linked arms, collided, and waltzed, jabbering. "Benjy!"

She glanced swiftly behind his ear.

Yes, *there* was the yellow pencil.

"Benjy, welcome!"

"Why, ma'am!" He held her off at arm's length. "Why, ma'am, you're *crying*."

"Here's my nephew," said Cora.

Tom scowled up from spooning his corn-meal mush.

"Mighty glad," smiled Benjy.

Cora held his arm tight so he couldn't vanish. She felt faint, wanting to sit, stand, run, but she only beat her heart fast and laughed at strange times. Now, in an instant, the far countries were brought near; here was this tall boy, lighting up the room like a pine torch, this boy who had seen cities and seas and been places when things had been better for his parents.

"Benjy, I got peas, corn, bacon, mush, soup, and beans for breakfast."

"Hold on!" said Tom.

"Hush, Tom, the boy's down to the bone with walking." She turned to the boy. "Benjy, tell me all about yourself. You *did* go to school?"

Benjy kicked off his shoes. With one bare foot he traced a word in the hearth ashes.

Tom scowled. "What's it say?"

"It says," said Benjy, "C and O and R and A. *Cora*."

"*My* name, Tom, see it! Oh, Benjy, it's good you really write, child. We had one cousin here, long ago, claimed he could spell upside down and backwards. So we fattened him up and he wrote letters and we never got answers. Come to find out he knew just enough spelling to mail letters to the dead-letter office. Lord, Tom knocked two months' worth of vittles out of that boy, batting him up the road with a piece of fence."

They laughed anxiously.

"I write fine," said the serious boy.

"That's all we want to know." She shoved a cut of berry pie at him. "Eat."

By ten-thirty, with the sun riding higher, after watching Benjy devour heaped platters of food, Tom thundered from the cabin, jamming his cap on. "I'm going out, by God, and cut down half the forest!" he said angrily.

But no one heard. Cora was seated in a breathless spell. She was watching the pencil behind Benjy's peach-fuzz ear. She saw him finger it casually, lazily, indifferently. Oh, not so casual, Benjy, she thought. Handle it like a spring robin's egg. She wanted to touch the pencil, but hadn't touched one in years because it made her feel foolish and then angry and then sad. Her hand twitched in her lap.

"You got some paper?" asked Benjy.

"Oh, land, I never thought," she wailed, and the room walls darkened. "What'll we do?"

"Just happens I brought some." He fetched a tablet from his little bag. "You want to write a letter somewhere?"

She smiled outrageously. "I want to write a letter to . . . to . . ." Her face fell apart. She looked around for someone in the distance. She looked at the mountains in the morning sunshine. She heard the sea rolling off on yellow shores a thousand miles away. The birds were coming north over the valley, on their way to multitudes of cities indifferent to her need at this instant.

"Benjy, why, I never thought until this moment. I don't know anybody in all that world out there. Nobody but my aunt. And if I wrote her it'd make her feel bad, a hundred miles from here, to have to find someone else to read the letter to her. She's got a whale-boned-corset sort of pride. Make her nervous the next ten years, that letter setting in her house on the mantel. No, no letter to her." Cora's eyes moved from the hills and the unseen ocean. "Who then? Where? Someone. I just've got to get me some letters."

"Hold on." Benjy fished a dime magazine from his coat. It had a red cover of an undressed lady screaming away from a green monster. "All sorts of addresses in here."

They leafed the pages together. "What's *this*?" Cora tapped an ad.

"'HERE'S YOUR *Power Plus* FREE MUSCLE CHART. Send name, address,'" read Benjy, "'to Dept. M-3 for Free Health Map!'"

"And what about *this* one?"

"'DETECTIVES MAKE SECRET INVESTIGATIONS. PARTICULARS FREE. WRITE: G.D.M. DETECTIVE SCHOOL——'"

"Everything's free. Well, Benjy." She looked at the pencil in his hand. He drew up his chair. She watched him turn the pencil in his fingers, making minor adjustments. She saw him bite his tongue softly. She saw him squint his eyes. She held her breath. She bent forward. She squinted her own eyes and clamped her tongue.

Now, now Benjy raised his pencil, licked it, and set it down to the paper.

There it is, thought Cora.

The first words. They formed themselves slowly on the incredible paper.

Dear Power Plus Muscle Company
Sirs, [he wrote].

The morning blew away on a wind, the morning flowed down the creek, the morning flew off with some ravens, and the sun burned on the cabin roof. Cora didn't turn when she heard a shuffle at the blazing, sun-filled door. Tom was there, but not there; nothing was before her but a series of filled pages, a whispering pencil, and Benjy's careful Palmer Penmanship hand. Cora moved her head around, around, with each *o*, each *I*, with each small hill of an *m*; each tiny dot made her head peck like a chicken; each crossed *t* made her tongue lick across her upper lip.

"It's noon and I'm hungry!" said Tom almost behind her.

But Cora was a statue now, watching the pencil as one watches a snail leaving an exceptional trail across a flat stone in the early morning.

"It's noon!" cried Tom again.

Cora glanced up, stunned.

"Why, it seems only a moment ago we wrote to that Philadelphia Coin Collecting Company, ain't that right, Benjy?" Cora smiled a smile much too dazzling for a woman fifty-five years old. "While you wait for your vittles, Tom, just can't you build that mailbox? Bigger than Mrs. Brabbam's, please?"

"I'll nail up a shoe box."

"Tom Gibbs." She rose pleasantly. Her smile said, Better run, better work, better *do*! "I want a big, pretty mailbox. All white, for Benjy to paint our name on in black spelling. I won't have any shoe box for my very first real letter."

And it was done.

Benjy lettered the finished mailbox: MRS. CORA GIBBS, while Tom stood grumbling behind him.

"What's it say?"

"'MR. TOM GIBBS,'" said Benjy quietly, painting.

Tom blinked at it for a minute, quietly, and then said, "I'm *still* hungry. Someone light the fire."

There were no stamps. Cora turned white. Tom was made to hitch up the horse and drive to Green Fork to buy some red ones, a green, and ten pink stamps with dignified gentlemen printed on them. But Cora rode along to be certain Tom didn't hurl these first letters in the creek. When they rode home, the first thing Cora did, face glowing, was poke in the new mailbox.

"You crazy?" said Tom.

"No harm looking."

That afternoon she visited the mailbox six times. On the seventh, a woodchuck jumped out. Tom stood laughing in the door, pounding his knees. Cora chased him out of the house, still laughing.

Then she stood in the window looking down at her mailbox right across from Mrs. Brabbam's. Ten years ago the Widow Lady had plunked her letter box right under Cora's nose, almost, when she could as easily have built it up nearer her own cabin. But it gave Mrs. Brabbam an excuse to float like a flower on a river down the hill path, flip the box wide with a great coughing and rustling, from time to time spying up to see if Cora was watching. Cora always was. When caught, she pretended to sprinkle flowers with an empty watering can, or pick mushrooms in the wrong season.

Next morning Cora was up before the sun had warmed the strawberry patch or the wind had stirred the pines.

Benjy was sitting up in his cot when Cora returned from the mailbox. "Too early," he said. "Postman won't drive by yet."

"*Drive* by?"

"They come in cars this far out."

"Oh." Cora sat down.

"You sick, Aunt Cora?"

"No, no." She blinked. "It's just, I don't recall in twenty years seeing no mail truck whistle by here. It just came to me. All this time, I never seen no mailman at all."

"Maybe he comes when you're not around."

"I'm up with the fog spunks, down with the chickens. I never really gave it a thought, of course, but——" She turned to look out the window, up at Mrs. Brabbam's house. "Benjy, I got a kind of sneaking hunch." She stood up and walked straight out of the cabin, down the dust path, Benjy following, across the thin road to Mrs. Brabbam's mailbox. A hush was on the fields and hills. It was so early it made you whisper.

"Don't break the law, Aunt Cora!"

"Shh! Here." She opened the box, put her hand in like someone fumbling in a gopher hole. "And here, and here." She rattled some letters into his cupped hands.

"Why, these been opened already! You open these, Aunt Cora?"

"Child, I never touched them." Her face was stunned. "This is the first time in my life I ever even let my shadow touch this box."

Benjy turned the letters around and around, cocking his head. "Why, Aunt Cora, these letters, they're ten years old!"

"What!" Cora grabbed at them.

"Aunt Cora, that lady's been getting the same mail every day for years. And they're not even addressed to Mrs. Brabbam, they're to some woman named Ortega in Green Fork."

"Ortega, the Mexican grocery woman! All these years,"

whispered Cora, staring at the worn mail in her hands. "All these years."

They gazed up at Mrs. Brabbam's sleeping house in the cool quiet morning.

"Oh, that sly woman, making a commotion with her letters, making me feel small. All puffed out she was, swishing along, reading her mail."

Mrs. Brabbam's front door opened.

"Put them back, Aunt Cora!"

Cora slammed the mailbox shut with time to spare.

Mrs. Brabbam drifted down the path, stopping here or there, quietly, to peer at the opening wild flowers.

"Morning," she said sweetly.

"Mrs. Brabbam, this is my nephew Benjy."

"How nice." Mrs. Brabbam, with a great swivel of her body, a flourish of her flour-white hands, rapped the mailbox as if to shake the letters loose inside, flipped the lid, and extracted the mail, covering her actions with her back. She made motions, and spun about merrily, winking. "Wonderful! Why, just look at this letter from dear Uncle George!"

"Well, ain't that *nice*!" said Cora.

Then the breathless summer days of waiting. The butterflies jumping orange and blue on the air, the flowers nodding about the cabin, and the hard, constant sound of Benjy's pencil scribbling through the afternoons. Benjy's mouth was always packed with food, and Tom was always stomping in, to find lunch or supper late, cold, or both, or none at all.

Benjy handled the pencil with a delicious spread of his bony hands, lovingly inscribing each vowel and consonant as Cora hovered about him, making up words, rolling them on her tongue, delighted each time she saw them roll out on the paper. But she wasn't learning to write. "It's so much fun watching you write, Benjy. Tomorrow I'll start learning. Now take another letter!"

They worked their way through ads about Asthma, Trusses, and Magic, they joined the Rosicrucians, or at least sent for a free Sealed Book all about the Knowledge that had been damned to oblivion, Secrets from Hidden ancient temples and buried sanctuaries. Then there were free packets of Giant

Sunflower seeds, and something about HEARTBURN. They had worked back to page 127 of *Quarter Murder Magazine* on a bright summer morning when . . .

"Listen!" said Cora.

They listened.

"A car," said Benjy.

And up the blue hills and through the tall fiery green pines and along the dusty road, mile by mile, came the sound of a car riding along and along, until finally, at the bend, it came full thundering, and in an instant Cora was out the door running, and as she ran she heard and saw and felt many things. First, from the corner of her eye, she saw Mrs. Brabbam gliding down the road from the other direction. Mrs. Brabbam froze when she saw the bright green car boiling on the grade, and there was the whistle of a silver whistle and the old man in the car leaned out just before Cora arrived and said, "Mrs. Gibbs?" "Yes!" she cried. "Mail for you, ma'am," he said, and held it toward her. She put out her hand, then drew it back, remembering. "Oh," she said, "please, would you mind, would you put it, please . . . in my mailbox?" The old man squinted at her, at the mailbox, back at her, and laughed. "Don't mind," he said, and did just that, put the mail in the box.

Mrs. Brabbam stood where she was, not moving, eyes wild. "Any mail for Mrs. Brabbam?" asked Cora.

"That's all." And the car dusted away down the road.

Mrs. Brabbam stood with her hands clenched together. Then, without looking in her own letter box, turned and rustled swiftly up her path, out of sight.

Cora walked around her mailbox twice, not touching it for a long time. "Benjy, I've got me some letters!" She reached in delicately and took them out and turned them over. She put them quietly in his hand. "Read them to me. Is my name on the front?"

"Yes'm." He opened the first letter with due carefulness and read it aloud in the summer morning:

"'Dear Mrs. Gibbs . . .'"

He stopped and let her savor it, her eyes half shut, her mouth moving the words. He repeated it for artistic emphasis and then went on: "'We are sending you our free folder, enclosed, from the Intercontinental Mailing Schools concerning full particulars on how you, too, can take our Correspondence Course in Sanitary Engineering——'"

"Benjy, Benjy, I'm so happy! Start over again!"

"'Dear Mrs. Gibbs,'" he read.

After that the mailbox was never empty. The world came rushing and crowding in, all the places she had never seen or heard about or been to. Travel folders, spicecake recipes, and even a letter from an elderly gentleman who wished for a lady "—fifty years old, gentle disposition, money; object matrimony." Benjy wrote back, "I am already married, but thank you for your kind and thoughtful consideration. Yours truly, Cora Gibbs."

And the letters continued to pour across the hills, coin collectors' catalogues, Dime Novelty books, Magic List Numbers, Arthritis Charts, Flea Killer Samples. The world filled up her letter box, and suddenly she was not alone or remote from people. If a man wrote a form letter to Cora about the Mysteries of Ancient Maya Revealed, he was likely as not to receive three letters from Cora in the next week, budding out their formal meeting into a warm friendship. After one particularly hard day of writing, Benjy was forced to soak his hand in Epsom salts.

By the end of the third week Mrs. Brabbam no longer came down to her mailbox. She didn't even come out the front door of her cabin to get the air, for Cora was always down at the road, leaning out, smiling for the mailman.

All too quickly the summer was at an end, or, at least, that part of the summer that counted most, anyway; Benjy's visit. There was his red bandanna handkerchief on the cabin table, sandwiches folded fresh and oniony in it, tied with a mint sprig to keep it clean to the smell; there on the floor, freshly polished, were his shoes to get into, and there on the chair, with his pencil which had once been long and yellow but was now stubby and chewed, sat Benjy. Cora took hold of his chin and tilted his head, as if she were testing a summer squash of an unfamiliar variety.

"Benjy, I owe you an apology. I don't think I looked at your face once in all this time. Seems I know every wart on your hand, every hangnail, every bump and every crinkle, but I might pass your face in a crowd and miss you."

"It's no face to look at," said Benjy shyly.

"But I'd know that hand in a million hands," Cora said. "Let anyone shake my hand in a dark room, a thousand people, and out of all those I'd say, 'Well, *this* one's Benjy.'" She smiled quietly and walked away to the open door. "I been thinking." She looked up at a distant cabin. "Ain't seen Mrs. Brabbam in weeks. Stays in all the time now. I've got a guilty feeling. I've done a prideful thing, a thing more sinful than she ever done me. I took the bottom out of her life. It was a mean and spiteful thing and I'm ashamed." She gazed up the hill toward that silent, locked place. "Benjy, would you do me one last favor?"

"Yes'm."

"Write a letter for Mrs. Brabbam."

"Ma'am?"

"Yes, write one of those companies for a free chart, a sample, something, and sign Mrs. Brabbam's name."

"All right," said Benjy.

"That way, in a week or a month the postman'll come by and whistle, and I'll tell him to go up to her door, special, and deliver it. And I'll be sure and be out in my front yard where I can see and Mrs. Brabbam can see I see. And I'll wave my letters to her and she'll wave her letters to me, and everybody'll smile."

"Yes'm," said Benjy.

He wrote three letters, licked the envelopes carefully, stuck them in his pocket. "I'll mail them when I get to St. Louis."

"It's been a fine summer," she said.

"It sure has."

"But, Benjy, I didn't learn to write, did I? I was after the letters and made you write late nights, and we were so busy sending labels and getting samples, land, it seemed there wasn't time to learn. And that means . . ."

He knew what it meant. He shook her hand. They stood in the cabin door. "Thanks," she said, "for everything."

Then he was running off. He ran as far as the meadow fence, leaped it easily, and the last she saw of him he was still running, waving the special letters, off into the great world over the hills.

The letters kept coming for some six months after Benjy went away. There would be the postman's little green car and the sharp ice-rimed shout of good morning, or the whistle, as he clapped two or three pink or blue envelopes into that fine mailbox.

And there was that special day when Mrs. Brabbam received her first real letter.

After that the letters were spaced a week apart, then a month, and finally the postman didn't say hello at all, there was no sound of a car coming up that lonely mountain road. First a spider moved into the mailbox, then a sparrow.

And Cora, while the letters still lasted, would clutch them in her bewildered hands, staring at them quietly until the pressure of her face muscles squeezed clear round shiny drops of water from her eyes. She'd hold up one blue envelope. "Who's this from?"

"Don't know," said Tom.

"What's it say?" she wailed.

"Don't know," said Tom.

"What's going on in that world out there, oh, I'll never know, I'll never know now," she said. "And this letter, and this one, and *this*!" She tumbled the stacks and stacks of letters that had come since Benjy ran off. "All the world and all the people and all the happenings, and me not knowing. All that world and people waiting to hear from us, and us not writing, and them not ever writing back!"

And at last the day came when the wind blew the mailbox over. In the mornings again, Cora would stand at the open door of her cabin, brushing her gray hair with a slow brush, not speaking, looking at the hills. And in all the years that followed she never passed the fallen mailbox without stooping aimlessly to fumble inside and take her hand out with nothing in it before she wandered on again into the fields.

The Golden Apples of the Sun

"SOUTH," SAID THE captain.

"But," said his crew, "there simply *aren't* any directions out here in space."

"When you travel on down toward the sun," replied the captain, "and everything gets yellow and warm and lazy, then you're going in one direction only." He shut his eyes and thought about the smoldering, warm, faraway land, his breath moving gently in his mouth. "South." He nodded slowly to himself. "South."

Their rocket was the *Copa de Oro*, also named the *Prometheus* and the *Icarus*, and their destination in all reality was the blazing noonday sun. In high good spirits they had packed along two thousand sour lemonades and a thousand white-capped beers for this journey to the wide Sahara. And now as the sun boiled up at them they remembered a score of verses and quotations:

"'The golden apples of the sun'?"

"Yeats."

"'Fear no more the heat of the sun'?"

"Shakespeare, of course!"

"'Cup of Gold'? Steinbeck. 'The Crock of Gold'? Stephens. And what about the pot of gold at the rainbow's end? *There's* a name for our trajectory, by God. Rainbow!"

"Temperature?"

"One thousand degrees Fahrenheit!"

The captain stared from the huge dark-lensed port, and there indeed was the sun, and to go to that sun and touch it and steal part of it forever away was his quiet and single idea. In this ship were combined the coolly delicate and the coldly practical. Through corridors of ice and milk-frost, ammoniated winter and storming snowflakes blew. Any spark from that vast hearth burning out there beyond the callous hull of this ship, any small fire-breath that might seep through would find winter, slumbering here like all the coldest hours of February.

The audio-thermometer murmured in the arctic silence: "Temperature: two thousand degrees!"

Falling, thought the captain, like a snowflake into the lap of June, warm July, and the sweltering dog-mad days of August.

"Three thousand degrees Fahrenheit!"

Under the snow fields engines raced, refrigerants pumped ten thousand miles per hour in rimed boa-constrictor coils.

"Four thousand degrees Fahrenheit."

Noon. Summer. July.

"Five thousand Fahrenheit!"

And at last the captain spoke with all the quietness of the journey in his voice:

"Now, we are touching the sun."

Their eyes, thinking it, were melted gold.

"Seven thousand degrees!"

Strange how a mechanical thermometer could sound excited, though it possessed only an emotionless steel voice.

"What *time* is it?" asked someone.

Everyone had to smile.

For now there was only the sun and the sun and the sun. It was every horizon, it was every direction. It burned the minutes, the seconds, the hourglasses, the clocks; it burned all time and eternity away. It burned the eyelids and the serum of the dark world behind the lids, the retina, the hidden brain; and it burned sleep and the sweet memories of sleep and cool nightfall.

"Watch it!"

"Captain!"

Bretton, the first mate, fell flat to the winter deck. His protective suit whistled where, burst open, his warmness, his oxygen, and his life bloomed out in a frosted steam.

"Quick!"

Inside Bretton's plastic face-mask, milk crystals had already gathered in blind patterns. They bent to see.

"A structural defect in his suit, Captain. Dead."

"Frozen."

They stared at that other thermometer which showed how winter lived in this snowing ship. One thousand degrees below zero. The captain gazed down upon the frosted statue and the twinkling crystals that iced over it as he watched. Irony of the coolest sort, he thought; a man afraid of fire and killed by frost.

The captain turned away. "No time. No time. Let him lie." He felt his tongue move. "Temperature?"

The dials jumped four thousand degrees.

"Look. Will you look? Look."

Their icicle was melting.

The captain jerked his head to look at the ceiling.

As if a motion-picture projector had jammed a single clear memory frame in his head, he found his mind focused ridiculously on a scene whipped out of childhood.

Spring mornings as a boy he had leaned from his bedroom window into the snow-smelling air to see the sun sparkle the last icicle of winter. A dripping of white wine, the blood of cool but warming April fell from that clear crystal blade. Minute by minute, December's weapon grew less dangerous. And then at last the icicle fell with the sound of a single chime to the graveled walk below.

"Auxiliary pump's broken, sir. Refrigeration. We're losing our ice!"

A shower of warm rain shivered down upon them. The captain jerked his head right and left. "Can you see the trouble? Christ, don't stand there, we haven't time!"

The men rushed; the captain bent in the warm rain, cursing, felt his hands run over the cold machine, felt them burrow and search, and while he worked he saw a future which was removed from them by the merest breath. He saw the skin peel from the rocket beehive, men, thus revealed, running, running, mouths shrieking, soundless. Space was a black mossed well where life drowned its roars and terrors. Scream a big scream, but space snuffed it out before it was half up your throat. Men scurried, ants in a flaming matchbox; the ship was dripping lava, gushing steam, nothing!

"Captain?"

The nightmare flicked away.

"Here." He worked in the soft warm rain that fell from the upper decks. He fumbled at the auxiliary pump. "Damn it!" He jerked the feed line. When it came, it'd be the quickest death in the history of dying. One moment, yelling; a warm flash later only the billion billion tons of space-fire would whisper, unheard, in space. Popped like strawberries in a furnace, while their thoughts lingered on the scorched air a long breath after their bodies were charred roast and fluorescent gas.

"Damn!" He stabbed the auxiliary pump with a screw driver. "Jesus!" He shuddered. The complete annihilation of it. He clamped his eyes tight, teeth tight. God, he thought, we're used to more leisurely dyings, measured in minutes and hours. Even twenty seconds now would be a slow death compared to this hungry idiot thing waiting to eat us!

"Captain, do we pull out or stay?"

"Get the Cup ready. Take over, finish this. Now!"

He turned and put his hand to the working mechanism of the huge Cup; shoved his fingers into the robot Glove. A twitch of his hand here moved a gigantic hand, with gigantic metal fingers, from the bowels of the ship. Now, now, the great metal hand slid out holding the huge *Copa de Oro*, breathless, into the iron furnace, the bodiless body and the fleshless flesh of the sun.

A million years ago, thought the captain, quickly, quickly, as he moved the hand and the Cup, a million years ago a naked man on a lonely northern trail saw lightning strike a tree. And while his clan fled, with bare hands he plucked a limb of fire, broiling the flesh of his fingers, to carry it, running in triumph, shielding it from the rain with his body, to his cave, where he shrieked out a laugh and tossed it full on a mound of leaves and gave his people summer. And the tribe crept at last, trembling, near the fire, and they put out their flinching hands and felt the new season in their cave, this small yellow spot of changing weather, and they, too, at last, nervously, smiled. And the gift of fire was theirs.

"Captain!"

It took all of four seconds for the huge hand to push the empty Cup to the fire. So here we are again, today, on another trail, he thought, reaching for a cup of precious gas and vacuum, a handful of different fire with which to run back up cold space, lighting our way, and take to Earth a gift of fire that might burn forever. Why?

He knew the answer before the question.

Because the atoms we work with our hands, on Earth, are pitiful; the atomic bomb is pitiful and small and our knowledge is pitiful and small, and only the sun really knows what we want to know, and only the sun has the secret. And besides, it's fun, it's a chance, it's a great thing coming here, playing tag, hitting and running. There is no reason, really, except the pride and vanity of little insect men hoping to sting the lion and escape the maw. My God, we'll say, we *did* it! And here is our cup of energy, fire, vibration, call it what you will, that may well power our cities and sail our ships and light our libraries and tan our children and bake our daily breads and simmer the knowledge of our universe for us for a thousand years until it is well done. Here, from this cup, all good men of science and religion: drink! Warm yourselves against the night of ignorance, the long snows of superstition, the cold winds of disbelief, and from the great fear of darkness in each man. So: we stretch out our hand with the beggar's cup . . .

"Ah."

The Cup dipped into the sun. It scooped up a bit of the flesh of God, the blood of the universe, the blazing thought, the blinding philosophy that set out and mothered a galaxy, that idled and swept planets in their fields and summoned or laid to rest lives and livelihoods.

"Now, *slow*," whispered the captain.

"What'll happen when we pull it inside? That extra heat now, at this time, Captain?"

"God knows."

"Auxiliary pump all repaired, sir."

"Start it!"

The pump leaped on.

"Close the lid of the Cup and inside now, slow, slow."

The beautiful hand outside the ship trembled, a tremendous image of his own gesture, sank with oiled silence into the ship body. The Cup, lid shut, dripped yellow flowers and white stars, slid deep. The audio-thermometer screamed. The refrigerator system kicked; ammoniated fluids banged the walls like blood in the head of a shrieking idiot.

He shut the outer air-lock door.

"Now."

They waited. The ship's pulse ran. The heart of the ship rushed, beat, rushed, the Cup of gold in it. The cold blood raced around about down through, around about down through.

The captain exhaled slowly.

The ice stopped dripping from the ceiling. It froze again.

"Let's get out of here."

The ship turned and ran.

"Listen!"

The heart of the ship was slowing, slowing. The dials spun on down through the thousands; the needles whirred, invisible. The thermometer voice chanted the change of seasons. They were all thinking now, together: Pull away and away from the fire and the flame, the heat and the melting, the yellow and the white. Go on out now to cool and dark. In twenty hours perhaps they might even dismantle some refrigerators, let winter die. Soon they would move in night so cold it might be necessary to use the ship's new furnace, draw heat from the shielded fire they carried now like an unborn child.

They were going home.

They were going home and there was some little time, even as he tended to the body of Bretton lying in a bank of white winter snow, for the captain to remember a poem he had written many years before:

Sometimes I see the sun a burning Tree,
Its golden fruit swung bright in airless air,
Its apples wormed with man and gravity,
Their worship breathing from them everywhere,
As man see Sun as burning Tree . . .

The captain sat for a long while by the body, feeling many separate things. I feel sad, he thought, and I feel good, and I feel like a boy coming home from school with a handful of dandelions.

"Well," said the captain, sitting, eyes shut, sighing. "Well, where do we go now, eh, where are we going?" He felt his men sitting or standing all about him, the terror dead in them, their breathing quiet. "When you've gone a long, long way down to the sun and touched it and lingered and jumped around and streaked away from it, where are you going then? When you go away from the heat and the noonday light and the laziness, where do you go?"

His men waited for him to say it out. They waited for him to gather all of the coolness and the whiteness and the welcome and refreshing climate of the word in his mind, and they saw him settle the word, like a bit of ice cream, in his mouth, rolling it gently.

"There's only one direction in space from here on out," he said at last.

They waited. They waited as the ship moved swiftly into cold darkness away from the light.

"North," murmured the captain. "North."

And they all smiled, as if a wind had come up suddenly in the middle of a hot afternoon.

And the Rock Cried Out

THE RAW CARCASSES, hung in the sunlight, rushed at them, vibrated with heat and red color in the green jungle air, and were gone. The stench of rotting flesh gushed through the car windows, and Leonora Webb quickly pressed the button that whispered her door window up.

"Good Lord," she said, "those open-air butcher shops."

The smell was still in the car, a smell of war and horror.

"Did you see the flies?" she asked.

"When you buy any kind of meat in those markets," John Webb said, "you slap the beef with your hand. The flies lift from the meat so you can get a look at it."

He turned the car around a lush bend in the green rain-jungle road.

"Do you think they'll let us into Juatala when we get there?"

"I don't know."

"Watch out!"

He saw the bright things in the road too late, tried to swerve, but hit them. There was a terrible sighing from the right front tire, the car heaved about and sank to a stop. He opened his side of the car and stepped out. The jungle was hot and silent and the highway empty, very empty and quiet at noon.

He walked to the front of the car and bent, all the while checking his revolver in its underarm holster.

Leonora's window gleamed down. "Is the tire hurt much?"

"Ruined, utterly ruined!" He picked up the bright thing that had stabbed and slashed the tire.

"Pieces of a broken machete," he said, "placed in adobe holders pointing toward our car wheels. We're lucky it didn't get *all* our tires."

"But *why*?"

"You know as well as I." He nodded to the newspaper beside her, at the date, the headlines:

OCTOBER 4TH, 1963: UNITED STATES,
EUROPE SILENT!

The radios of the U. S. A. and Europe are dead. There is a great silence. The War has spent itself.

It is believed that most of the population of the United States is dead. It is believed that most of Europe, Russia, and Siberia, are equally decimated. The day of the white people of the earth is over and finished.

"It all came so fast," said Webb. "One week we're on another tour, a grand vacation from home. The next week—this."

They both looked away from the black headlines to the jungle.

The jungle looked back at them with a vastness, a breathing moss-and-leaf silence, with a billion diamond and emerald insect eyes.

"Be careful, Jack."

He pressed two buttons. An automatic lift under the front wheels hissed and hung the car in the air. He jammed a key nervously into the right wheel plate. The tire, frame and all, with a sucking pop, bounced from the wheel. It was a matter of seconds to lock the spare in place and roll the shattered tire back to the luggage compartment. He had his gun out while he did all this.

"Don't stand in the open, please, Jack."

"So it's starting already." He felt his hair burning hot on his skull. "News travels fast."

"For God's sake," said Leonora. "They can *hear* you!"

He stared at the jungle.

"I know you're in there!"

"Jack!"

He aimed at the silent jungle. "I see you!" He fired four, five times, quickly, wildly.

The jungle ate the bullets with hardly a quiver, a brief slit sound like torn silk where the bullets bored and vanished into a million acres of green leaves, trees, silence, and moist earth. The brief echo of the shots died. Only the car muttered its exhaust behind Webb. He walked around the car, got in, and shut the door and locked it.

He reloaded the gun, sitting in the front seat. Then they drove away from the place.

They drove steadily.

"Did you see anyone?"

"No. You?"

She shook her head.

"You're going too fast."

He slowed only in time. As they rounded a curve another clump of the bright flashing objects filled the right side of the road. He swerved to the left and passed.

"Sons-of-bitches!"

"They're not sons-of-bitches, they're just people who never had a car like this or anything at all."

Something ticked across the window pane.

There was a streak of colorless liquid on the glass.

Leonora glanced up. "Is it going to rain?"

"No, an insect hit the pane."

Another tick.

"Are you sure that was an insect?"

Tick, tick, tick.

"Shut the window!" he said, speeding up.

Something fell in her lap.

She looked down at it. He reached over to touch the thing. "Quick!"

She pressed the button. The window snapped up.

Then she examined her lap again.

The tiny blowgun dart glistened there.

"Don't get any of the liquid on you," he said. "Wrap it in your handkerchief—we'll throw it away later."

He had the car up to sixty miles an hour.

"If we hit another road block, we're done."

"This is a local thing," he said. "We'll drive out of it."

The panes were ticking all the time. A shower of things blew at the window and fell away in their speed.

"Why," said Leonora Webb, "they don't even *know* us!"

"I only wish they did." He gripped the wheel. "It's hard to kill people you know. But not hard to kill strangers."

"I don't want to die," she said simply, sitting there.

He put his hand inside his coat. "If anything happens to

me, my gun is here. Use it, for God's sake, and don't waste time."

She moved over close to him and they drove seventy-five miles an hour down a straight stretch in the jungle road, saying nothing.

With the windows up, the heat was oven-thick in the car.

"It's so silly," she said, at last. "Putting the knives in the road. Trying to hit us with the blowguns. How could they know that the next car along would be driven by white people?"

"Don't ask them to be that logical," he said. "A car is a car. It's big, it's rich. The money in one car would last them a lifetime. And anyway, if you road-block a car, chances are you'll get either an American tourist or a rich Spaniard, comparatively speaking, whose ancestors should have behaved better. And if you happen to road-block another Indian, hell, all you do is go out and help him change tires."

"What time is it?" she asked.

For the thousandth time he glanced at his empty wrist. Without expression or surprise, he fished in his coat pocket for the glistening gold watch with the silent sweep hand. A year ago he had seen a native stare at this watch and stare at it and stare at it with almost a hunger. Then the native had examined him, not scowling, not hating, not sad or happy; nothing except puzzled.

He had taken the watch off that day and never worn it since.

"Noon," he said.

Noon.

The border lay ahead. They saw it and both cried out at once. They pulled up, smiling, not knowing they smiled. . . .

John Webb leaned out the window, started gesturing to the guard at the border station, caught himself, and got out of his car. He walked ahead to the station where three young men, very short, in lumpy uniforms, stood talking. They did not look up at Webb, who stopped before them. They continued conversing in Spanish, ignoring him.

"I beg your pardon," said John Webb at last. "Can we pass over the border into Juatala?"

One of the men turned for a moment. "Sorry, *señor*."

The three men talked again.

"You don't understand," said Webb, touching the first man's elbow. "We've *got* to get through."

The man shook his head. "Passports are no longer good. Why should you want to leave our country, anyway?"

"It was announced on the radio. All Americans to leave the country, immediately."

"Ah, *si si*," all three soldiers nodded and leered at each other with shining eyes.

"Or be fined or imprisoned, or both," said Webb.

"We could let you over the border, but Juatala would give you twenty-four hours to leave, also. If you don't believe me, listen!" The guard turned and called across the border, "Aye, there! Aye!"

In the hot sun, forty yards distant, a pacing man turned, his rifle in his arms.

"Aye there, Paco, you want these two people?"

"No, *gracias—gracias*, no," replied the man, smiling.

"You see?" said the guard, turning to John Webb.

All of the soldiers laughed together.

"I have money," said Webb.

The men stopped laughing.

The first guard stepped up to John Webb and his face was now not relaxed or easy; it was like brown stone.

"Yes," he said. "They always have money. I know. They come here and they think money will do everything. But what is money? It is only a promise, *señor*. This I know from books. And when somebody no longer likes your promise, what then?"

"I will give you anything you ask."

"Will you?" The guard turned to his friends. "He will give me *anything* I ask." To Webb: "It was a joke. *We* were always a joke to you, weren't we?"

"No."

"*Mañana*, you laughed at us; *mañana*, you laughed at our siestas and our *mañanas*, didn't you?"

"Not me. Someone else."

"Yes, you."

"I've never been to this particular station before."

"I know you, anyway. Run here, do this, do that. Oh, here's a peso, buy yourself a house. Run over there, do this, do that."

The three men came out and walked around the car, looking at it, touching it, feeling it.

Their faces were like burnt copper in the daylight. They touched the resilient tires, they sniffed the rich new smell of the metal and upholstery.

"*Señor*," said the gas attendant at last.

"We'd like to buy some gas, please."

"We are all out of gas, *señor.*"

"But your tank reads full. I see the gas in the glass container up there."

"We are all out of gas," said the man.

"I'll give you ten pesos a gallon!"

"*Gracias*, no."

"We haven't enough gas to get anywhere from here." Webb checked the gauge. "Not even a quarter gallon left. We'd better leave the car here and go into town and see what we can do there."

"I'll watch the car for you, *señor*," said the station attendant. "If you leave the keys."

"We can't do that!" said Leonora. "Can we?"

"I don't see what choice we have. We can stall it on the road and leave it to anyone who comes along, or leave it with this man."

"That's better," said the man.

They climbed out of the car and stood looking at it.

"It was a beautiful car," said John Webb.

"Very beautiful," said the man, his hand out for the keys. "I will take good care of it, *señor.*"

"But, Jack——"

She opened the back door and started to take out the luggage. Over her shoulder, he saw the bright travel stickers, the storm of color that had descended upon and covered the worn leather now after years of travel, after years of the best hotels in two dozen countries.

She tugged at the valises, perspiring, and he stopped her hands and they stood gasping there for a moment, in the open door of the car, looking at these fine rich suitcases, inside which were the beautiful tweeds and woolens and silks of their lives and living, the forty-dollar-an-ounce perfumes and the cool dark furs and the silvery golf shafts. Twenty years were packed into each of the cases; twenty years and four dozen parts they had played in Rio, in Paris, in Rome and Shanghai, but the part they played most frequently and best of all was the rich and buoyant, amazingly happy Webbs, the smiling people, the ones who could make that rarely balanced Martini known as the Sahara.

"We can't carry it all into town," he said. "We'll come back for it later. Later."

"But . . ."

He silenced her by turning her away and starting her off down the road.

"But we can't leave it there, we can't leave all our luggage and we can't leave our car! Oh look here now, I'll roll up the windows and lock myself in the car, while you go for the gas, why not?" she said.

He stopped and glanced back at the three men standing by the car which blazed in the yellow sun. Their eyes were shining and looking at the woman.

"There's your answer," he said. "Come on."

"But you just *don't* walk off and leave a four-thousand-dollar automobile!" she cried.

He moved her along, holding her elbow firmly and with quiet decision. "A car is to travel in. When it's not traveling, it's useless. Right now, we've got to travel; that's everything. The car isn't worth a dime without gas in it. A pair of good strong legs is worth a hundred cars, if you use the legs. We've just begun to toss things overboard. We'll keep dropping ballast until there's nothing left to heave but our hides."

He let her go. She was walking steadily now, and she fell into step with him. "It's so strange. So strange. I haven't walked like this in years." She watched the motion of her feet beneath her, she watched the road pass by, she watched the jungle moving to either side, she watched her husband striding quickly along, until she seemed hypnotized by the steady rhythm. "But I guess you can learn anything over again," she said, at last.

The sun moved in the sky and they moved for a long while on the hot road. When he was quite ready, the husband began to think aloud. "You know, in a way, I think it's good to be down to essentials. Now instead of worrying over a dozen damned things, it's just two items—you and me."

"Watch it, here comes a car—we'd better . . ."

They half turned, yelled, and jumped. They fell away from the highway and lay watching the automobile hurtle past at seventy miles an hour. Voices sang, men laughed, men shouted, waving. The car sped away into the dust and vanished around a curve, blaring its double horns again and again.

He helped her up and they stood in the quiet road.

"Did you see it?"

They watched the dust settle slowly.

"I hope they remember to change the oil and check the battery, at least. I hope they think to put water in the radiator," she said, and paused. "They were singing, weren't they?"

He nodded. They stood blinking at the great dust cloud filtering down like yellow pollen upon their heads and arms. He saw a few bright splashes flick from her eyelids when she blinked.

"Don't," he said. "After all, it was only a machine."

"I loved it."

"We're always loving everything too much."

Walking, they passed a shattered wine bottle which steamed freshly as they stepped over it.

They were not far from the town walking single file, the wife ahead, the husband following, looking at their feet as they walked, when a sound of tin and steam and bubbling water made them turn and look at the road behind them. An old man in a 1929 Ford drove along the road at a moderate speed. The car's fenders were gone, and the sun had flaked and burnt the paint badly, but he rode in the seat with a great deal of quiet dignity, his face a thoughtful darkness under a dirty Panama hat, and when he saw the two people he drew the car up, steaming, the engine joggling under the hood and opened the squealing door as he said, "This is no day for walking."

"Thank you," they said.

"It is nothing." The old man wore an ancient yellowed white summer suit, with a rather greasy tie knotted loosely at his wrinkled throat. He helped the lady into the rear seat with a gracious bow of his head. "Let us men sit up front," he suggested, and the husband sat up front and the car moved off in trembling vapors.

"Well. My name is Garcia."

There were introductions and noddings.

"Your car broke down? You are on your way for help?" said *Señor* Garcia.

"Yes."

"Then let me drive you and a mechanic back out," offered the old man.

They thanked him and kindly turned the offer aside and he made it once again, but upon finding that his interest and concern caused them embarrassment, he very politely turned to another subject.

He touched a small stack of folded newspapers on his lap.

"Do you read the papers? Of course, you do. But do you read them as I read them? I rather doubt that you have come upon my system. No, it was not exactly myself that came upon it; the system was forced upon me. But now I know what a clever thing it has turned out to be. I always get the newspapers a week late. All of us, those who are interested, get the papers a week late, from the Capital. And this circumstance makes for a man being a clear-thinking man. You are very careful with your thinking when you pick up a week-old paper."

The husband and wife asked him to continue.

"Well," said the old man, "I remember once, when I lived in the Capital for a month and bought the paper fresh each day, I went wild with love, anger, irritation, frustration; all of the passions boiled in me. I was young. I exploded at everything I saw. But then I saw what I was doing, I was believing what I read. Have you noticed? You believe a paper printed on the very day you buy it? This has happened but only an hour ago, you think! It must be true." He shook his head. "So I learned to stand back away and let the paper age and mellow. Back here, in Colonia, I saw the headlines diminish to nothing. The week-old paper—why you can spit on it if you wish. It is like a woman you once loved, but you now see, a few days later, she is not quite what you thought. She has rather a plain face. She is no deeper than a cup of water."

He steered the car gently, his hands upon the wheel as upon the heads of his good children, with care and affection. "So here I am, returning to my home to read my weekly papers, to peek sideways at them, to toy with them." He spread one on his knee, glancing down to it on occasion as he drove. "How white this paper is, like the mind of a child that is an idiot, poor thing, all blank. You can put anything into an empty place like that. Here, do you see? This paper speaks and says that the light-skinned people of the world are dead. Now that is a very silly thing to say. At this very moment, there are probably millions upon millions of white men and women eating their noon meals or their suppers. The earth trembles, a town collapses, people run from the town, screaming, *All is lost!* In the next village, the population wonders what all of the shouting is about, since *they* have had a most splendid night's repose. Ah, ah, what a sly world it is. People do not see how sly it is. It is either night or day to them. Rumor flies. This very afternoon all of the little villages upon this highway, behind us and ahead of us, are in carnival. The white man is dead, the rumors say, and yet here I come into the town with two very lively ones. I hope you don't mind my speaking in this way? If I do not talk to you I would then be talking to this engine up in the front, which makes a great noise speaking back."

They were at the edge of town.

"Please," said John Webb, "it wouldn't be wise for you to be seen with us today. We'll get out here."

The old man stopped his car reluctantly and said, "You are most kind and thoughtful of me." He turned to look at the lovely wife.

"When I was a young man I was very full of wildness and ideas. I read all of the books from France by a man named Jules Verne. I see you know his name. But at night I many times thought I must be an inventor. That is all gone by; I never did what I thought I might do. But I remember clearly that one of the machines I wished to put together was a machine that would help every man, for an hour, to be like any other man. The machine was full of colors and smells and it had film in it, like a theater, and the machine was like a coffin. You lay in it. And you touched a button. And for an hour you could be one of those Eskimos in the cold wind up there, or you could be an Arab gentleman on a horse. Everything a New York man felt, you could feel. Everything a man from Sweden smelled, you could smell. Everything a man from China tasted, your tongue knew. The machine was like another man—do you see what I was after? And by touching many of the buttons, each time you got into my machine, you could be a white man or a yellow man or a Negrito. You could be a child or a woman, even, if you wished to be very funny."

The husband and wife climbed from the car.

"Did you ever try to invent that machine?"

"It was so very long ago. I had forgotten until today. And today I was thinking, we could make use of it, we are in need of it. What a shame I never tried to put it all together. Someday some other man will do it."

"Some day," said John Webb.

"It has been a pleasure talking with you," said the old man. "God go with you."

"*Adios, Señor* Garcia," they said.

The car drove slowly away, steaming. They stood watching it go, for a full minute. Then, without speaking, the husband reached over and took his wife's hand.

They entered the small town of Colonia on foot. They walked past the little shops, the butcher shop, the photographer's. People stopped and looked at them as they went by and did not stop looking at them as long as they were in sight. Every few seconds, as he walked, Webb put up his hand to touch the holster hidden under his coat, secretly, tentatively, like someone feeling for a tiny boil that is growing and growing every hour and every hour . . .

The patio of the Hotel Esposa was cool as a grotto under a blue waterfall. In it birds sang, caged, and footsteps echoed like small rifle shots, clear and smooth.

"Remember? We stopped here years ago," said Webb, helping his wife up the steps. They stood in the cool grotto, glad of the blue shade.

"*Señor* Esposa," said John Webb, when a fat man came forward from the desk, squinting at them. "Do you remember me—John Webb? Five years ago—we played cards one night."

"Of course, of course." *Señor* Esposa bowed to the wife and shook hands briefly. There was an uncomfortable silence.

Webb cleared his throat. "We've had a bit of trouble, *Señor.* Could we have a room for tonight only?"

"Your money is always good here."

"You mean you'll actually give us a room? We'll be glad to pay in advance. Lord, we need the rest. But, more than that, we need gas."

Leonora picked at her husband's arm. "Remember? We haven't a car any more."

"Oh. Yes." He fell silent for a moment and then sighed. "Well. Never mind the gas. Is there a bus out of here for the Capital soon?"

"All will be attended to, in time," said the Manager nervously. "This way."

As they were climbing the stairs they heard a noise. Looking out they saw their car riding around and around the plaza, eight times, loaded with men who were shouting and singing and hanging onto the front fenders, laughing. Children and dogs ran after the car.

"I would like to own a car like that," said *Señor* Esposa.

He poured a little cool wine for the three of them, standing in the room on the third floor of the Esposa Hotel.

"To 'change,'" said *Señor* Esposa.

"I'll drink to that."

They drank. *Señor* Esposa licked his lips and wiped them on his coat sleeve. "We are always surprised and saddened to see the world change. It is insane, they have run out on us, you say. It is unbelievable. And now, well— You are safe for the night. Shower and have a good supper. I won't be able to keep you more than one night, to repay you for your kindness to me five years ago."

"And tomorrow?"

"Tomorrow? Do not take any bus to the Capital, please. There are riots in the streets there. A few people from the North have been killed. It is nothing. It will pass in a few days. But you must be careful until those few days pass and the blood cools. There are many wicked people taking advantage of this day, *señor*. For forty-eight hours anyway, under the guise of a great resurgence of nationalism, these people will try to gain power. Selfishness and patriotism, *señor*; today I cannot tell one from the other. So—you must hide. That is a problem. The town will know you are here in another few hours. This might be dangerous to my hotel. I cannot say."

"We understand. It's good of you to help *this* much."

"If you need any thing, call me." *Señor* Esposa drank the rest of the wine in his glass. "Finish the bottle," he said.

The fireworks began at nine that evening. First one skyrocket then another soared into the dark sky and burst out upon the winds, building architectures of flame. Each skyrocket, at the top of its ride, cracked open and let out a formation of streamers in red and white flame that made something like the dome of a beautiful cathedral.

Leonora and John Webb stood by the open window in their unlit room, watching and listening. As the hour latened, more people streamed into town from every road and path and began to roam, arm in arm, around the plaza, singing, barking like dogs, crowing like roosters, and then falling down on the tile sidewalks, sitting there, laughing, their heads thrown back, while the skyrockets burst explosive colors on the tilted faces. A brass band began to thump and wheeze.

"So here we are," said John Webb, "after a few hundred years of living high. So this is what's left of our white supremacy—you and I in a dark room in a hotel three hundred miles inside a celebrating country."

"You've got to see their side of it."

"Oh, I've seen it ever since I was that high. In a way, I'm glad they're happy. God knows they've waited long enough to be. But I wonder how long that happiness will last. Now that the scapegoat is gone, who will they blame for oppression, who will be handy and as obvious and as guilty as you and I and the man who lived in this room before us?"

"I don't know."

"We were so convenient. The man who rented this room last month, he was convenient, he stood out. He made loud jokes about the natives' siestas. He refused to learn even a smattering of Spanish. Let them learn English, by God, and speak like men, he said. And he drank too much and whored too much with this country's women." He broke off and moved back from the window. He stared at the room.

The furniture, he thought. Where *he* put his dirty shoes upon the sofa, where *he* burnt holes in the carpet with cigarettes; the wet spot on the wall near the bed, God knows what or how he did *that.* The chairs scarred and kicked. It wasn't *his* hotel or his room; it was borrowed, it meant nothing. So this son-of-a-bitch went around the country for the past one hundred years, a traveling commercial, a Chamber of Commerce, and now here *we* are, enough like him to be his brother and sister, and there *they* are down there on the night of the Butler's Ball. They don't know, or if they know they won't think of it, that tomorrow they'll be just as poor, just as oppressed as ever, that the whole machine will have shifted only into another gear.

Now the band had stopped playing below; a man had leaped up, shouting, on the bandstand. There was a flash of machetes in the air and the brown gleam of half-naked bodies.

The man on the bandstand faced the hotel and looked up at the dark room where John and Leonora Webb now stood back out of the intermittent flares.

The man shouted.

"What does he say?" asked Leonora.

John Webb translated: "'It is now a free world,' he says."

The man yelled.

John Webb translated again. "He says, 'We are *free*!'"

The man lifted himself on his toes and made a motion of breaking manacles. "He says, 'No one owns us, no one in all the world.'"

The crowd roared and the band began to play, and while it was playing, the man on the grandstand stood glaring up at the room window, with all of the hatred of the universe in his eyes.

During the night there were fights and pummelings and voices lifted, arguments and shots fired. John Webb lay awake and heard the voice of *Señor* Esposa below, reasoning, talking quietly, firmly. And then the fading away of the tumult, the last rockets in the sky, the last breakings of bottles on the cobbles.

At five in the morning the air was warming into a new day. There was the softest of taps on the bedroom door.

"It is me, it is Esposa," said a voice.

John Webb hesitated, half-dressed, numbed on his feet from lack of sleep, then opened the door.

"What a night, what a night!" said *Señor* Esposa, coming in, shaking his head, laughing gently. "Did you hear that noise? Yes? They tried to come up here to your room. I prevented this."

"Thank you," said Leonora, still in bed, turned to the wall.

"They were all old friends. I made an agreement with them, anyway. They were drunk enough and happy enough so they agreed to wait. I am to make a proposition to you two." Suddenly he seemed embarrassed. He moved to the window. "Everyone is sleeping late. A few are up. A few men. See them there on the far side of the plaza?"

John Webb looked out at the plaza. He saw the brown men talking quietly there about the weather, the world, the sun, this town, and perhaps the wine.

"*Señor*, have you ever been hungry in your life?"

"For a day, once."

"Only for a day. Have you always had a house to live in and a car to drive?"

"Until yesterday."

"Were you ever without a job?"

"Never."

"Did all of your brothers and sisters live to be twenty-one years old?"

"All of them."

"Even I," said *Señor* Esposa, "even *I* hate you a little bit now. For *I* have been without a home. *I* have been hungry. *I* have three brothers and one sister buried in that graveyard on the hill beyond the town, all dead of tuberculosis before they were nine years old."

Señor Esposa glanced at the men in the plaza. "Now, I am no longer hungry or poor, I have a car, I am alive. But I am one in a thousand. What can *you* say to them out there today?"

"I'll try to think of something."

"Long ago I stopped trying. *Señor*, we have *always* been a minority, we white people. I am Spanish, but I was born here. They tolerate me."

"We have never let ourselves think about our being a minority," said Webb, "and now it's hard to get used to the fact."

"You have behaved beautifully."

"Is that a virtue?"

"In the bull ring, yes, in war, yes, in anything like this, most assuredly yes. You do not complain, you do not make excuses. You do not run and make a spectacle of yourself. I think you are both very brave."

The hotel manager sat down, slowly, helplessly.

"I've come to offer you the chance to settle down," he said.

"We wanted to move on, if possible."

The Manager shrugged. "Your car is stolen, I can do nothing to get it back. You cannot leave town. Remain then and accept my offer of a position in my hotel."

"You don't think there is any way for us to travel?"

"It might be twenty days, *señor*, or twenty years. You cannot exist without money, food, lodging. Consider my hotel and the work I can give you."

The Manager arose and walked unhappily to the door and stood by the chair, touching Webb's coat which was draped over it.

"What's the job?" asked Webb.

"In the kitchen," said the Manager, and looked away.

John Webb sat on the bed and said nothing. His wife did not move.

Señor Esposa said, "It is the best I can do. What more can you ask of me? Last night, those others down in the plaza wanted both of you. Did you see the machetes? I bargained with them. You were lucky. I told them you would be employed in my hotel for the next twenty years, that you were my employees and deserve my protection!"

"You said *that*!"

"*Señor, señor*, be thankful! Consider! Where will you go? The jungle? You will be dead in two hours from the snakes. Then can you walk five hundred miles to a capital which will not welcome you? No—you must face the reality." *Señor* Esposa opened the door. "I offer you an honest job and you will be paid the standard wages of two pesos a day, plus meals. Would you rather be with me, or out in the plaza at noon with our friends? Consider."

The door was shut. *Señor* Esposa was gone.

Webb stood looking at the door for a long while.

Then he walked to the chair and fumbled with the holster under the draped white shirt. The holster was empty. He held it in his hands and blinked at its emptiness and looked again at the door through which *Señor* Esposa had just passed. He went over and sat down on the bed beside his wife. He stretched out beside her and took her in his arms and kissed her, and they lay there, watching the room get brighter with the new day.

At eleven o'clock in the morning, with the great doors on the windows of their room flung back, they began to dress. There were soap, towels, shaving equipment, even perfume in the bathroom, provided by Mr. Esposa.

John Webb shaved and dressed carefully.

At eleven-thirty he turned on the small radio near their bed. You could usually get New York or Cleveland, or Houston on such a radio. But the air was silent. John Webb turned the radio off.

"There's nothing to go back to—nothing to go back for—nothing."

His wife sat on a chair near the door, looking at the wall.

"We could stay here and work," he said.

She stirred at last. "No. We couldn't do that, not really. Could we?"

"No, I guess not."

"There's no way we could do that. We're being consistent, anyway; spoiled, but consistent."

He thought a moment. "We could make for the jungle."

"I don't think we can move from the hotel without being seen. We don't want to try to escape and be caught. It would be far worse that way."

He nodded.

They both sat a moment.

"It might not be too bad, working here," he said.

"What would we be living for? Everyone's dead—your father, mine, your mother, mine, your brothers, mine, all our friends, everything gone, everything we understood."

He nodded.

"Or if we took the job, one day soon one of the men would touch me and you'd go after him, you know you would. Or someone would do something to you, and *I'd* do something."

He nodded again.

They sat for fifteen minutes, talking quietly. Then, at last, he picked up the telephone and ticked the cradle with his finger.

"*Bueno*," said a voice on the other end.

"*Señor* Esposa?"

"*Si.*"

"*Señor* Esposa," he paused and licked his lips, "tell your friends we will be leaving the hotel at noon."

The phone did not immediately reply. Then with a sigh *Señor* Esposa said, "As you wish. You are sure——?"

The phone was silent for a full minute. Then it was picked up again and the Manager said quietly, "My friends say they will be waiting for you on the far side of the plaza."

"We will meet them there," said John Webb.

"And *Señor*——"

"Yes."

"Do not hate me, do not hate us."

"I don't hate anybody."

"It is a bad world, *señor.* None of us know how we got here or what we are doing. These men don't know what they are mad at, except they are mad. Forgive them and do not hate them."

"I don't hate them or you."

"Thank you, thank you." Perhaps the man on the far end of the telephone wire was crying. There was no way to tell. There were great lapses in his talking, in his breathing. After a while he said, "We don't know why we do anything. Men hit each other for no reason except they are unhappy. Remember that. I am your friend. I would help you if I could. But I cannot. It would be me against the town. Good-by, *señor.*" He hung up.

John Webb sat in the chair with his hand on the silent phone. It was a moment before he glanced up. It was a moment before his eyes focused on an object immediately before him. When he saw it clearly, he still did not move, but sat regarding it, until a look of immensely tired irony appeared on his mouth. "Look here," he said at last.

Leonora followed his motion, his pointing.

They both sat looking at his cigarette which, neglected on the rim of the table while he telephoned, had burnt down so that now it had charred a black hole in the clean surface of the wood.

It was noon, with the sun directly over them, pinning their shadows under them as they started down the steps of the

Hotel Esposa. Behind them, the birds fluted in their bamboo cages, and water ran in a little fountain bath. They were as neat as they could get, their faces and hands washed, their nails clean, their shoes polished.

Across the plaza two hundred yards away stood a small group of men, in the shade of a store front overhang. Some of the men were natives from the jungle area, with machetes gleaming at their sides. They were all facing the plaza.

John Webb looked at them for a long while. That isn't everyone, he thought, that isn't the whole country. That's only the surface. That's only the thin skin over the flesh. It's not the body at all. Just the shell of an egg. Remember the crowds back home, the mobs, the riots? Always the same, there or here. A few mad faces up front, and the quiet ones far back, not taking part, letting things go, not wanting to be in it. The majority not moving. And so the few, the handful, take over and move for them.

His eyes did not blink. If we could break through that shell, God knows it's thin! he thought, if we could talk our way through that mob and get to the quiet people beyond . . . Can I do it? Can I say the right things? Can I keep my voice down?

He fumbled in his pockets and brought out a rumpled cigarette package and some matches.

I can try, he thought. How would the old man in the Ford have done it? I'll try to do it his way. When we get across the plaza, I'll start talking, I'll whisper if necessary. And if we move slowly through the mob, we might just possibly find our way to the other people and we'll be on high ground and we'll be safe.

Leonora moved beside him. She was so fresh, so well groomed in spite of everything, so new in all this oldness, so startling, that his mind flinched and jerked. He found himself staring at her as if she'd betrayed him by her salt-whiteness, her wonderfully brushed hair and her cleanly manicured nails and her bright-red mouth.

Standing on the bottom step, Webb lit a cigarette, took two or three long drags on it, tossed it down, stepped on it, kicked the flattened butt into the street, and said, "Here we go."

They stepped down and started around the far side of the plaza, past the few shops that were still open. They walked quietly.

"Perhaps they'll be decent to us."

"We can hope so."

They passed a photographic shop.

"It's another day. Anything can happen. I believe that. No—I don't really believe it. I'm only talking. I've got to talk or I wouldn't be able to walk," she said.

They passed a candy shop.

"Keep talking, then."

"I'm afraid," she said. "This can't be happening to us! Are we the last ones in the world?"

"Maybe next to the last."

They approached an open air *carnecería.*

God! he thought. How the horizons narrowed, how they came in. A year ago there weren't four directions, there were a million for us. Yesterday they got down to four; we could go to Juatala, Porto Bello, San Juan Clementas, or Brioconbria. We were satisfied to have our car. Then when we couldn't get gas, we were satisfied to have our clothes, then when they took our clothes, we were satisfied to have a place to sleep. Each pleasure they took away left us with one other creature comfort to hold on to. Did you see how we let go of one thing and clutched another so quickly? I guess that's human. So they took away everything. There's nothing left. Except us. It all boils down to just you and me walking along here, and thinking too goddamn much for my own good. And what counts in the end is whether they can take you away from me or me away from you, Lee, and I don't think they can do that. They've got everything else and I don't blame them. But they can't really do anything else to us now. When you strip all the clothes away and the doodads, you have two human beings who were either happy or unhappy together, and we have no complaints.

"Walk slowly," said John Webb.

"I am."

"Not too slowly, to look reluctant. Not too fast, to look as if you want to get it over with. Don't give them the satisfaction, Lee, don't give them a damn bit."

"I won't."

They walked. "Don't even touch me," he said, quietly. "Don't even hold my hand."

"Oh, please!"

"No, not even that."

He moved away a few inches and kept walking steadily. His eyes were straight ahead and their pace was regular.

"I'm beginning to cry, Jack."

"Goddamn it!" he said, measuredly, between his teeth, not looking aside. "Stop it! Do you want me to run? Is that what you want—do you want me to take you and run into the jungle, and let them hunt us, is that what you want, goddamn it, do you want me to fall down in the street here and grovel and scream, shut up, let's do this right, don't give them *any*thing!"

They walked on.

"All right," she said, hands tight, her head coming up. "I'm not crying now. I won't cry."

"Good, damn it, that's good."

And still, strangely, they were not past the *carnecería*. The vision of red horror was on their left as they paced steadily forward on the hot tile sidewalk. The things that hung from hooks looked like brutalities and sins, like bad consciences, evil dreams, like gored flags and slaughtered promises. The redness, oh, the hanging, evil-smelling wetness and redness, the hooked and hung-high carcasses, unfamiliar, unfamiliar.

As he passed the shop, something made John Webb strike out a hand. He slapped it smartly against a strung-up side of beef. A mantle of blue buzzing flies lifted angrily and swirled in a bright cone over the meat.

Leonora said, looking ahead, walking, "They're all strangers! I don't know any of them. I wish I knew even *one* of them. I wish even *one* of them knew me!"

They walked on past the *carnecería*. The side of beef, red and irritable-looking, swung in the hot sunlight after they passed.

The flies came down in a feeding cloak to cover the meat, once it had stopped swinging.

All Summer in a Day

"READY?"

"Ready."

"Now?"

"Soon."

"Do the scientists really know? Will it happen today, will it?"

"Look, look; see for yourself!"

The children pressed to each other like so many roses, so many weeds, intermixed, peering out for a look at the hidden sun.

It rained.

It had been raining for seven years; thousands upon thousands of days compounded and filled from one end to the other with rain, with the drum and gush of water, with the sweet crystal fall of showers and the concussion of storms so heavy they were tidal waves come over the islands. A thousand forests had been crushed under the rain and grown up a thousand times to be crushed again. And this was the way life was forever on the planet Venus, and this was the schoolroom of the children of the rocket men and women who had come to a raining world to set up civilization and live out their lives.

"It's stopping, it's stopping!"

"Yes, yes!"

Margot stood apart from them, from these children who could never remember a time when there wasn't rain and rain and rain. They were all nine years old, and if there had been a day, seven years ago, when the sun came out for an hour and showed its face to the stunned world, they could not recall. Sometimes, at night, she heard them stir, in remembrance, and she knew they were dreaming and remembering gold or a yellow crayon or a coin large enough to buy the world with. She knew they thought they remembered a warmness, like a blushing in the face, in the body, in the arms and legs and trembling hands. But then they always awoke to the tatting drum, the endless shaking down of clear bead necklaces upon the roof, the walk, the gardens, the forests, and their dreams were gone.

All day yesterday they had read in class about the sun. About how like a lemon it was, and how hot. And they had written small stories or essays or poems about it:

I think the sun is a flower,
That blooms for just one hour.

That was Margot's poem, read in a quiet voice in the still classroom while the rain was falling outside.

"Aw, you didn't write that!" protested one of the boys.

"I did," said Margot. "I *did.*"

"William!" said the teacher.

But that was yesterday. Now the rain was slackening, and the children were crushed in the great thick windows.

"Where's teacher?"

"She'll be back."

"She'd better hurry, we'll miss it!"

They turned on themselves, like a feverish wheel, all tumbling spokes.

Margot stood alone. She was a very frail girl who looked as if she had been lost in the rain for years and the rain had washed out the blue from her eyes and the red from her mouth and the yellow from her hair. She was an old photograph dusted from an album, whitened away, and if she spoke at all her voice would be a ghost. Now she stood, separate, staring at the rain and the loud wet world beyond the huge glass.

"What're *you* looking at?" said William.

Margot said nothing.

"Speak when you're spoken to." He gave her a shove. But she did not move; rather she let herself be moved only by him and nothing else.

They edged away from her, they would not look at her. She felt them go away. And this was because she would play no games with them in the echoing tunnels of the underground city. If they tagged her and ran, she stood blinking after them and did not follow. When the class sang songs about happiness and life and games her lips barely moved. Only when they sang about the sun and the summer did her lips move as she watched the drenched windows.

And then, of course, the biggest crime of all was that she

had come here only five years ago from Earth, and she remembered the sun and the way the sun was and the sky was when she was four in Ohio. And they, they had been on Venus all their lives, and they had been only two years old when last the sun came out and had long since forgotten the color and heat of it and the way it really was. But Margot remembered.

"It's like a penny," she said once, eyes closed.

"No it's not!" the children cried.

"It's like a fire," she said, "in the stove."

"You're lying, you don't remember!" cried the children.

But she remembered and stood quietly apart from all of them and watched the patterning windows. And once, a month ago, she had refused to shower in the school shower rooms, had clutched her hands to her ears and over her head, screaming the water mustn't touch her head. So after that, dimly, dimly, she sensed it, she was different and they knew her difference and kept away.

There was talk that her father and mother were taking her back to Earth next year; it seemed vital to her that they do so, though it would mean the loss of thousands of dollars to her family. And so, the children hated her for all these reasons of big and little consequence. They hated her pale snow face, her waiting silence, her thinness, and her possible future.

"Get away!" The boy gave her another push. "What're you waiting for?"

Then, for the first time, she turned and looked at him. And what she was waiting for was in her eyes.

"Well, don't wait around here!" cried the boy savagely. "You won't see nothing!"

Her lips moved.

"Nothing!" he cried. "It was all a joke, wasn't it?" He turned to the other children. "Nothing's happening today. *Is* it?"

They all blinked at him and then, understanding, laughed and shook their heads. "Nothing, nothing!"

"Oh, but," Margot whispered, her eyes helpless. "But this is the day, the scientists predict, they say, they *know*, the sun . . ."

"All a joke!" said the boy, and seized her roughly. "Hey, everyone, let's put her in a closet before teacher comes!"

"No," said Margot, falling back.

They surged about her, caught her up and bore her,

protesting, and then pleading, and then crying, back into a tunnel, a room, a closet, where they slammed and locked the door. They stood looking at the door and saw it tremble from her beating and throwing herself against it. They heard her muffled cries. Then, smiling, they turned and went out and back down the tunnel, just as the teacher arrived.

"Ready, children?" She glanced at her watch.

"Yes!" said everyone.

"Are we all here?"

"Yes!"

The rain slackened still more.

They crowded to the huge door.

The rain stopped.

It was as if, in the midst of a film concerning an avalanche, a tornado, a hurricane, a volcanic eruption, something had, first, gone wrong with the sound apparatus, thus muffling and finally cutting off all noise, all of the blasts and repercussions and thunders, and then, second, ripped the film from the projector and inserted in its place a peaceful tropical slide which did not move or tremor. The world ground to a standstill. The silence was so immense and unbelievable that you felt your ears had been stuffed or you had lost your hearing altogether. The children put their hands to their ears. They stood apart. The door slid back and the smell of the silent, waiting world came in to them.

The sun came out.

It was the color of flaming bronze and it was very large. And the sky around it was a blazing blue tile color. And the jungle burned with sunlight as the children, released from their spell, rushed out, yelling, into the springtime.

"Now, don't go too far," called the teacher after them. "You've only two hours, you know. You wouldn't want to get caught out!"

But they were running and turning their faces up to the sky and feeling the sun on their cheeks like a warm iron; they were taking off their jackets and letting the sun burn their arms.

"Oh, it's better than the sun lamps, isn't it?"

"Much, much better!"

They stopped running and stood in the great jungle that covered Venus, that grew and never stopped growing,

tumultuously, even as you watched it. It was a nest of octopi, clustering up great arms of fleshlike weed, wavering, flowering in this brief spring. It was the color of rubber and ash, this jungle, from the many years without sun. It was the color of stones and white cheeses and ink, and it was the color of the moon.

The children lay out, laughing, on the jungle mattress, and heard it sigh and squeak under them, resilient and alive. They ran among the trees, they slipped and fell, they pushed each other, they played hide-and-seek and tag, but most of all they squinted at the sun until tears ran down their faces, they put their hands up to that yellowness and that amazing blueness and they breathed of the fresh, fresh air and listened and listened to the silence which suspended them in a blessed sea of no sound and no motion. They looked at everything and savored everything. Then, wildly, like animals escaped from their caves, they ran and ran in shouting circles. They ran for an hour and did not stop running.

And then——

In the midst of their running one of the girls wailed.

Everyone stopped.

The girl, standing in the open, held out her hand.

"Oh, look, look," she said, trembling.

They came slowly to look at her opened palm.

In the center of it, cupped and huge, was a single raindrop.

She began to cry, looking at it.

They glanced quietly at the sky.

"Oh. Oh."

A few cold drops fell on their noses and their cheeks and their mouths. The sun faded behind a stir of mist. A wind blew cool around them. They turned and started to walk back toward the underground house, their hands at their sides, their smiles vanishing away.

A boom of thunder startled them and like leaves before a new hurricane, they tumbled upon each other and ran. Lightning struck ten miles away, five miles away, a mile, a half mile. The sky darkened into midnight in a flash.

They stood in the doorway of the underground for a moment until it was raining hard. Then they closed the door and

heard the gigantic sound of the rain falling in tons and avalanches, everywhere and forever.

"Will it be seven more years?"

"Yes. Seven."

Then one of them gave a little cry.

"Margot!"

"What?"

"She's still in the closet where we locked her."

"Margot."

They stood as if someone had driven them, like so many stakes, into the floor. They looked at each other and then looked away. They glanced out at the world that was raining now and raining and raining steadily. They could not meet each other's glances. Their faces were solemn and pale. They looked at their hands and feet, their faces down.

"Margot."

One of the girls said, "Well . . . ?"

No one moved.

"Go on," whispered the girl.

They walked slowly down the hall in the sound of cold rain. They turned through the doorway to the room in the sound of the storm and thunder, lightning on their faces, blue and terrible. They walked over to the closet door slowly and stood by it.

Behind the closet door was only silence.

They unlocked the door, even more slowly, and let Margot out.

Interval in Sunlight

THEY MOVED INTO the Hotel de Las Flores on a hot green afternoon in late October. The inner patio was blazing with red and yellow and white flowers, like flames, which lit their small room. The husband was tall and black-haired and pale and looked as if he had driven ten thousand miles in his sleep; he walked through the tile patio, carrying a few blankets, he threw himself on the small bed of the small room with an exhausted sigh and lay there. While he closed his eyes, his wife, about twenty-four, with yellow hair and horn-rim glasses, smiling at the manager, Mr. Gonzales, hurried in and out from the room to the car. First she carried two suitcases, then a typewriter, thanking Mr. Gonzales, but steadily refusing his help. And then she carried in a huge packet of Mexican masks they had picked up in the lake town of Patzcuaro, and then out to the car again and again for more small cases and packages, and even an extra tire which they were afraid some native might roll off down the cobbled street during the night. Her face pink from the exertion, she hummed as she locked the car, checked the windows, and ran back to the room where her husband lay, eyes closed, on one of the twin beds.

"Good God," he said, without opening his eyes, "this is one hell of a bed. Feel it. I told you to pick one with a Simmons mattress." He gave the bed a weary slap. "It's as hard as a rock."

"I don't speak Spanish," said the wife, standing there, beginning to look bewildered. "You should have come in and talked to the landlord yourself."

"Look," he said, opening his gray eyes just a little and turning his head, "I've done all the driving on this trip. You just sit there and look at the scenery. You're supposed to handle the money, the lodgings, the gas and oil, and all that. This is the second place we've hit where you got hard beds."

"I'm sorry," she said, still standing, beginning to fidget.

"I like to at least sleep nights, that's all I ask."

"I said I was sorry."

"Didn't you even *feel* the beds?"

"They looked all right."

"You've got to feel them." He slapped the bed and punched it at his side.

The woman turned to her own bed and sat on it, experimentally. "It feels all right to me."

"Well, it isn't."

"Maybe my bed is softer."

He rolled over tiredly and reached out to punch the other bed. "You can have this one if you want," she said, trying to smile.

"That's hard, too," he said, sighing, and fell back and closed his eyes again.

No one spoke, but the room was turning cold, while outside the flowers blazed in the green shrubs and the sky was immensely blue. Finally, she rose and grabbed the typewriter and suitcase and turned toward the door.

"Where're you going?" he said.

"Back out to the car," she said. "We're going to find another place."

"Put it down," said the man. "I'm tired."

"We'll find another place."

"Sit down, we'll stay here tonight, my God, and move tomorrow."

She looked at all the boxes and crates and luggage, the clothes, and the tire, her eyes flickering. She put the typewriter down.

"Damn it!" she cried, suddenly. "You can have the mattress off my bed. "I'll sleep on the springs."

He said nothing.

"You can have the mattress off my bed," she said. "Only don't talk about it. Here!" She pulled the blanket off and yanked at the mattress.

"That might be better," he said, opening his eyes, seriously.

"You can have both mattresses, my God, I can sleep on a bed of nails!" she cried. "Only stop yapping."

"I'll manage." He turned his head away. "It wouldn't be fair to you."

"It'd be plenty fair just for you to keep quiet about the bed; it's not that hard, good God, you'll sleep if you're tired. Jesus God, Joseph!"

"Keep your voice down," said Joseph. "Why don't you go find out about Paricutin volcano?"

"I'll go in a minute." She stood there, her face red.

"Find out what the rates are for a taxi out there and a horse up the mountain to see it, and look at the sky; if the sky's blue that means the volcano isn't erupting today, and don't let them gyp you."

"I guess I can do that."

She opened the door and stepped out and shut the door and *Señor* Gonzales was there. Was everything all right? he wished to know.

She walked past the town windows, and smelled the soft charcoal air. Beyond the town all of the sky was blue except north (or east or west, she couldn't be certain) where the huge broiling black cloud rose up from the terrible volcano. She looked at it with a small tremoring inside. Then she sought out a large fat taxi driver and the arguments began. The price started at sixty pesos and dwindled rapidly, with expressions of mournful defeat upon the buck-toothed fat man's face, to thirty-seven pesos. So! He was to come at three tomorrow afternoon, did he understand? That would give them time to drive out through the gray snows of land where the flaking lava ash had fallen to make a great dusty winter for mile after mile, and arrive at the volcano as the sun was setting. Was this very clear?

"*¡Si, señora, esta es muy claro, si!*"

"*Bueno.*" She gave him their hotel room number and bade him good-bye.

She idled into little lacquer shops, alone; she opened the little lacquer boxes and sniffed the sharp scent of camphor wood and cedar and cinnamon. She watched the craftsmen, enchanted, razor blades flashing in the sun, cutting the flowery scrolls and filling these patterns with red and blue color. The town flowed about her like a silent slow river and she immersed herself in it, smiling all of the time, and not even knowing she smiled.

Suddenly she looked at her watch. She'd been gone half an hour. A look of panic crossed her face. She ran a few steps and then slowed to a walk again, shrugging.

As she walked in through the tiled cool corridors, under the silvery tin candelabra on the adobe walls, a caged bird fluted high and sweet, and a girl with long soft dark hair sat at a piano painted sky blue and played a Chopin nocturne.

She looked at the windows of their room, the shades pulled down. Three o'clock of a fresh afternoon. She saw a soft-drinks box at the end of the patio and bought four bottles of Coke. Smiling, she opened the door to their room.

"It certainly took you long enough," he said, turned on his side toward the wall.

"We leave tomorrow afternoon at three," she said.

"How much?"

She smiled at his back, the bottles cold in her arms. "Only thirty-seven pesos."

"Twenty pesos would have done it. You can't let these Mexicans take advantage of you."

"I'm richer than they are; if anyone *deserves* being taken advantage of, it's us."

"That's not the idea. They *like* to bargain."

"I feel like a bitch, doing it."

"The guide book says they double their price and expect you to halve it."

"Let's not quibble over a dollar."

"A dollar is a dollar."

"I'll pay the dollar from my own money," she said. "I brought some cold drinks—do you want one?"

"What've you got?" He sat up in bed.

"Cokes."

"Well, you know I don't like Cokes much; take two of those back, will you, and get some Orange Crush?"

"Please?" she said, standing there.

"Please," he said, looking at her. "Is the volcano active?"

"Yes."

"Did you ask?"

"No, I looked at the sky. Plenty of smoke."

"You should have asked."

"The damn sky is just exploding with it."

"But how do we know it's good tomorrow?"

"We don't know. If it's not, we put it off."

"I guess that's right." He lay down again.

She brought back two bottles of Orange Crush.

"It's not very cold," he said, drinking it.

They had supper in the patio: sizzling steak, green peas, a plate of Spanish rice, a little wine, and spiced peaches for dessert.

As he napkined his mouth, he said, casually, "Oh, I meant to tell you. I've checked your figures on what I owe you for the last six days, from Mexico City to here. You say I owe you one hundred twenty-five pesos, or about twenty-five American dollars, right?"

"Yes."

"I make it I owe you only twenty-two."

"I don't think that's possible," she said, still working on her spiced peaches with a spoon.

"I added the figures twice."

"So did I."

"I think you added them wrong."

"Perhaps I did." She jarred the chair back suddenly. "Let's go check."

In the room, the notebook lay open under the lighted lamp. They checked the figures together. "You see," said he, quietly. "You're three dollars off. How did that happen?"

"It just happened. I'm sorry."

"You're one hell of a bookkeeper."

"I do my best."

"Which isn't very good. I thought you could take a little responsibility."

"I try damned hard."

"You forgot to check the air in the tires, you get hard beds, you lose things, you lost a key in Acapulco, to the car trunk, you lost the air-pressure gauge, and you can't keep books. I have to drive—"

"I know, I know, you have to drive all day, and you're tired, and you just got over a strep infection in Mexico City, and you're afraid it'll come back and you want to take it easy on your heart, and the least I could do is to keep my nose clean and the arithmetic neat. I know it all by heart. I'm only a writer, and I admit I've got big feet."

"You won't make a very good writer this way," he said. "It's such a simple thing, addition."

"I didn't do it on purpose!" she cried, throwing the pencil

down. "Hell! I wish I *had* cheated you now. I wish I'd done a lot of things now. I wish I'd lost that air-pressure gauge on purpose, I'd have some pleasure in thinking about it and knowing I did it to spite you, anyway. I wish I'd picked these beds for their hard mattresses, then I could laugh in my sleep tonight, thinking how hard they are for you to sleep on, I wish I'd done *that* on purpose. And now I wish I'd thought to fix the books. I could enjoy laughing about that, too."

"Keep your voice down," he said, as to a child.

"I'll be god-damned if I'll keep my voice down."

"All I want to know now is how much money you have in the kitty."

She put her trembling hands in her purse and brought out all the money. When he counted it, there was five dollars missing.

"Not only do you keep poor books, overcharging me on some item or other, but now there's five dollars gone from the kitty," he said. "Where'd it go?"

"I don't know. I must have forgotten to put it down, or if I did, I didn't say what for. Good God, I don't want to add this damned list again. I'll pay what's missing out of my own allowance to keep everyone happy. Here's five dollars! Now, let's go out for some air, it's hot in here."

She jerked the door wide and she trembled with a rage all out of proportion to the facts. She was hot and shaking and stiff and she knew her face was very red and her eyes bright, and when *Señor* Gonzales bowed to them and wished them a good evening, she had to smile stiffly in return.

"Here," said her husband, handing her the room key. "And don't, for God's sake, lose it."

The band was playing in the green zocalo. It hooted and blared and tooted and screamed up on the bronze-scrolled bandstand. The square was bloomed full with people and color, men and boys walking one way around the block, on the pink and blue tiles, women and girls walking the other way, flirting their dark olive eyes at one another, men holding each other's elbows and talking earnestly between meetings, women and girls twined like ropes of flowers, sweetly scented, blowing in a summer night wind over the cooling tile designs, whispering, past the vendors of cold drinks and tamales and enchiladas. The band precipitated "Yankee Doodle" once, to the delight of the blonde woman with the horn-rim glasses, who smiled wildly and turned to her husband. Then the band hooted "*La Cumparsita*" and "*La Paloma Azul*," and she felt a good warmth and began to sing a little, under her breath.

"Don't act like a tourist," said her husband.

"I'm just enjoying myself."

"Don't be a damned fool, is all I ask."

A vendor of silver trinkets shuffled by. "*¿Señor?*"

Joseph looked them over, while the band played, and held up one bracelet, very intricate, very exquisite. "How much?"

"*Veinte pesos, señor.*"

"Ho ho," said the husband, smiling. "I'll give you five for it," in Spanish.

"Five," replied the man in Spanish. "I would starve."

"Don't bargain with him," said the wife.

"Keep out of this," said the husband, smiling. To the vendor, "Five pesos, *señor.*"

"No, no, I would lose money. My last price is ten pesos."

"Perhaps I could give you six," said the husband. "No more than that."

The vendor hesitated in a kind of numbed panic as the husband tossed the bracelet back on the red velvet tray and turned away. "I am no longer interested. Good night."

"*¡Señor!* Six pesos, it is yours!"

The husband laughed. "Give him six pesos, darling."

She stiffly drew forth her wallet and gave the vendor some peso bills. The man went away. "I hope you're satisfied," she said.

"Satisfied?" Smiling, he flipped the bracelet in the palm of his pale hand. "For a dollar and twenty-five cents I buy a bracelet that sells for thirty dollars in the States!"

"I have something to confess," she said. "I gave that man ten pesos."

"What!" The husband stopped laughing.

"I put a five-peso note in with those one-peso bills. Don't worry, I'll take it out of my own money. It won't go on the bill I present you at the end of the week."

He said nothing, but dropped the bracelet in his pocket. He looked at the band thundering into the last bars of "*Ay,*

Jalisco." Then he said, "You're a fool. You'd let these people take all your money."

It was her turn to step away a bit and not reply. She felt rather good. She listened to the music.

"I'm going back to the room," he said. "I'm tired."

"We only drove a hundred miles from Patzcuaro."

"My throat is a little raw again. Come on."

They moved away from the music and the walking, whispering, laughing people. The band played the "Toreador Song." The drums thumped like great dull hearts in the summery night. There was a smell of papaya in the air, and green thicknesses of jungle and hidden waters.

"I'll walk you back to the room and come back myself," she said. "I want to hear the music."

"Don't be naïve."

"I like it, damn it, I like it, it's good music. It's not fake, it's real, or as real as anything ever gets in this world, that's why I like it."

"When I don't feel well, I don't expect to have you out running around the town alone. It isn't fair you see things I don't."

They turned in at the hotel and the music was still fairly loud. "If you want to walk by yourself, go off on a trip by yourself and go back to the United States by yourself," he said. "Where's the key?"

"Maybe I lost it."

They let themselves into the room and undressed. He sat on the edge of the bed looking into the night patio. At last he shook his head, rubbed his eyes, and sighed. "I'm tired. I've been terrible today." He looked at her where she sat, next to him, and he put out his hand to take her arm. "I'm sorry. I get all riled up, driving, and then us not talking the language too well. By evening I'm a mess of nerves."

"Yes," she said.

Quite suddenly he moved over beside her. He took hold of her and held her tightly, his head over her shoulder, eyes shut, talking into her ear with a quiet, whispering fervency. "You know, we *must* stay together. There's only us, really, no matter what happens, no matter what trouble we have. I do love you so much, you know that. Forgive me if I'm difficult. We've got to make it go."

She stared over his shoulder at the blank wall and the wall was like her life in this moment, a wide expanse of nothingness with hardly a bump, a contour, or a feeling to it. She didn't know what to say or do. Another time, she would have melted. But there was such a thing as firing metal too often, bringing it to a glow, shaping it. At last the metal refuses to glow or shape; it is nothing but a weight. She was a weight now, moving mechanically in his arms, hearing but not hearing, understanding but not understanding, replying but not replying. "Yes, we'll stay together." She felt her lips move. "We love each other." The lips said what they must say, while her mind was in her eyes and her eyes bored deep into the vacuum of the wall. "Yes." Holding but not holding him. "Yes."

The room was dim. Outside, someone walked in a corridor, perhaps glancing at this locked door, perhaps hearing their vital whispering as no more than something falling drop by drop from a loose faucet, a running drain perhaps, or a turned bookleaf under a solitary bulb. Let the doors whisper, the people of the world walked down tile corridors and did not hear.

"Only you and I know the things." His breath was fresh. She felt very sorry for him and herself and the world, suddenly. Everyone was infernally alone. He was like a man clawing at a statue. She did not feel herself move. Only her mind, which was a lightless, dim fluorescent vapor, shifted. "Only you and I remember," he said, "and if one of us should leave, then half the memories are gone. So we must stay together because if one forgets the other remembers."

Remembers what? she asked herself. But she remembered instantly, in a linked series, those parts of incidents in their life together that perhaps he might not recall; the night at the beach, five years ago, one of the first fine nights beneath the canvas with the secret touchings, the days at Sunland sprawled together, taking the sun until twilight. Wandering in an abandoned silver mine, oh, a million things, one touched on and revealed another in an instant!

He held her tight back against the bed now. "Do you know how lonely I am? Do you know how lonely I make myself with these arguments and fights and all of it, when I'm tired?" He waited for her to answer, but she said nothing. She felt his eyelid flutter on her neck. Faintly, she remembered when he had first flicked his eyelid near her ear. "Spider-eye," she had said, laughing, then. "It feels like a small spider in my ear." And now this small lost spider climbed with insane humor upon her neck. There was something in his voice which made her feel she was a woman on a train going away and he was standing in the station saying, "Don't go." And her appalled voice silently cried, "But *you're* the one on a train! *I'm* not going *anywhere*!"

She lay back, bewildered. It was the first time in two weeks he had touched her. And the touching had such an immediacy that she knew the wrong word would send him very far away again.

She lay and said nothing.

Finally, after a long while, she heard him get up, sighing, and move off. He got into his own bed and drew the covers up, silently. She moved at last, arranged herself on her bed, and lay listening to her watch tick in the small hot darkness. "My God," she whispered, finally, "it's only eight-thirty."

"Go to sleep," he said.

She lay in the dark, perspiring, naked, on her own bed, and in the distance, sweetly, faintly, so that it made her soul and heart ache to hear it, she heard the band thumping and brassing out its melodies. She wanted to walk among the dark moving people and sing with them and smell the soft charcoal air of October in a small summery town deep in the tropics of Mexico, a million miles lost from civilization, listening to the good music, tapping her foot and humming. But now she lay with her eyes wide, in bed. In the next hour, the band played "*La Golondrina*," "*Marimba*," "*Los Viejitos*," "*Michoacan la Verde*," "*Barcarolle*," and "*Luna Lunera*."

At three in the morning she awoke for no reason and lay, her sleep done and finished with, feeling the coolness that came with deep night. She listened to his breathing and she felt away and separate from the world. She thought of the long trip from Los Angeles to Laredo, Texas, like a silver-white boiling nightmare. And then the green technicolor, red and yellow and blue and purple, dream of Mexico arising like a flood about them to engulf their car with color and smell of rain forest and deserted town. She thought of all the small towns, the shops, the walking people, the burros, and all the arguments and near-fights. She thought of the five years she had been married. A long, long time. There had been no day in all that time that they had not seen each other; there had been no day when she had seen friends, separately; *he* was always there to see and criticize. There had been no day when she was allowed to be gone for more than an hour or so without a full explanation. Sometimes, feeling infinitely evil, she would sneak to a midnight show, telling no one, and sit, feeling free, breathing deeply of the air of freedom, watching the people, far realer than she, upon the screen, motioning and moving.

And now here they were, after five years. She looked over at his sleeping form. One thousand eight hundred and twenty-five days with you, she thought, my husband. A few hours each day at my typewriter, and then all the rest of each day and night with you. I feel quite like that man walled up in a vault in *The Cask of Amontillado.* I scream but no one hears.

There was a shift of footsteps outside, a knock on their door. "*Señora*," called a soft voice, in Spanish. "It is three o'clock."

Oh, my God, thought the wife. "Sh!" she hissed, leaping up to the door. But her husband was awake. "What *is* it?" he cried.

She opened the door the slightest crack. "You've come at the wrong time," she said to the man in the darkness.

"Three o'clock, *señora*."

"No, no," she hissed, her face wrenching with the agony of the moment. "I meant tomorrow afternoon."

"What is it?" demanded her husband, switching on a light. "Christ, it's only three in the morning. What does the fool want?"

She turned, shutting her eyes. "He's here to take us to Paricutin."

"My God, you can't speak Spanish at all!"

"Go away," she said to the guide.

"But I arose for this hour," said the guide.

The husband swore and got up. "I won't be able to sleep now, anyway. Tell the idiot we'll be dressed in ten minutes and go with him and get it over, my God!"

She did this and the guide slipped away into the darkness and out into the street where the cool moon burnished the fenders of his taxi.

"You *are* incompetent," snapped the husband, pulling on two pairs of pants, two T-shirts, a sport shirt, and a wool shirt over that. "Jesus, this'll fix my throat, all right. If I come down with another strep infection—"

"Get back into bed, damn you."

"I couldn't sleep now, anyway."

"Well, we've had six hours' sleep already, and you had at least three hours' this afternoon; that should be enough."

"Spoiling our trip," he said, putting on two sweaters and two pairs of socks. "It's cold up there on the mountain; dress warm, hurry up." He put on a jacket and a muffler and looked enormous in the heap of clothing he wore. "Get me my pills. Where's some water?"

"Get back to bed," she said. "I won't have you sick and whining." She found his medicine and poured some water.

"The least thing you could do was get the hour right."

"Shut up!" She held the glass.

"Just another of your thick-headed blunders."

She threw the water in his face. "Let me alone, damn you, let me alone. I didn't mean to do that!"

"You!" he shouted, face dripping. He ripped off his jacket. "You'll chill me, I'll catch cold!"

"I don't give a damn, let me alone!" She raised her hands into fists, and her face was terrible and red, and she looked like some animal in a maze who has steadily sought exit from an impossible chaos and has been constantly fooled, turned back, rerouted, led on, tempted, whispered to, lied to, led further, and at last reached a blank wall.

"Put your hands down!" he shouted.

"I'll kill you, by God, I'll kill you!" she screamed, her face contorted and ugly. "Leave me alone! I've tried my damnedest—beds, language, time, my God, the mistakes, you think I don't *know* it? You think I'm not *sorry*?"

"I'll catch cold, I'll catch cold." He was staring at the wet floor. He sat down with water on his face.

"Here. Wipe your face off!" She flung him a towel.

He began to shake violently. "I'm cold!"

"Get a chill, damn it, and die, but leave me alone!"

"I'm cold, I'm cold." His teeth chattered, he wiped his face with trembling hands. "I'll have another infection."

"Take off that coat! It's wet."

He stopped shaking after a minute and stood up to take off the soggy coat. She handed him a leather jacket. "Come on, he's waiting for us."

He began to shiver again. "I'm not going anywhere, to hell with you," he said, sitting down. "You owe me fifty dollars now."

"What for?"

"You remember, you promised."

And she remembered. They had had a fight about some silly thing, in California, the first day of the trip, yes, by God, the very first day out. And she for the first time in her life had lifted her hand to slap him. Then, appalled, she had dropped her hand, staring at her traitorous fingers. "You were going to slap me!" he had cried. "Yes," she replied. "Well," he said quietly, "the next time you do a thing like that, you'll hand over fifty dollars of your money." That's how life was, full of little tributes and ransoms and blackmails. She paid for all her errors, unmotivated or not. A dollar here, a dollar there. If she spoiled an evening, she paid the dinner bill from her clothing money. If she criticized a play they had just seen and he had liked it, he flew into a rage, and, to quiet him, she paid for the theater tickets. On and on it had gone, swifter and swifter over the years. If they bought a book together and she didn't like it but he did and she dared speak out, there was a fight, sometimes a small thing which grew for days, and ended with her buying the book plus another and perhaps a set of cufflinks or some other silly thing to calm the storm. Jesus!

"Fifty dollars. You promised if you acted up again with these tantrums and slappings."

"It was only water. I didn't hit you. All right, shut up, I'll pay the money, I'll pay anything just to be let alone; it's worth it, and five hundred dollars more, more than worth it. I'll pay."

She turned away. When you're sick for a number of years, when you're an *only* child, the *only* boy, all of your life, you get the way he is, she thought. Then you find yourself thirty-five years old and still undecided as to what you're to be—a ceramist, a social worker, a businessman. And your wife has always known what she would be—a writer. And it must be maddening to live with a woman with a single knowledge of herself, so sure of what she would do with her writing. And selling stories, at last, not many, no, but just enough to cause the seams of the marriage to rip. And so how natural that he must convince her that she was wrong and he was right, that she was an uncontrollable child and must forfeit money. Money was to be the weapon he held over her. When she had been a fool she would give up some of the precious gain—the product of her writing.

"Do you know," she said, suddenly, aloud, "since I made that big sale to the magazine, you seem to pick more fights and I seem to pay more money?"

"What do you mean by that?" he said.

It seemed to her to be true. Since the big sale he had put his special logic to work on situations, a logic of such a sort that she had no way to combat it. Reasoning with him was impossible. You were finally cornered, your explanations exhausted, your alibis depleted, your pride in tatters. So you struck out. You slapped at him or broke something, and then, there you were again, paying off, and he had won. And he was taking your success away from you, your single purpose, or he thought he was, anyway. But strangely enough, though she had never told him, she didn't care about forfeiting the money. If it made peace, if it made him happy, if it made him think he was causing her to suffer, that was all right. He had exaggerated ideas as to the value of money; it hurt him to lose it or spend it, therefore he thought it would hurt her as much. But I'm feeling no pain, she thought, I'd like to give him all of the money, for that's not why I write at all, I write to say what I have to say, and he doesn't understand that.

He was quieted now. "You'll pay?"

"Yes." She was dressing quickly now, in slacks and jacket. "In fact, I've been meaning to bring this up for some time. I'm giving all the money to you from now on. There's no need of my keeping my profits separate from yours, as it has been. I'll turn it over to you tomorrow."

"I don't ask that," he said, quickly.

"I insist. It all goes to you."

What I'm doing, of course, is unloading your gun, she thought. Taking your weapon away from you. Now you won't be able to extract the money from me, piece by piece, bit by painful bit. You'll have to find another way to bother me.

"I—" he said.

"No, let's not talk about it. It's yours."

"It's only to teach you a lesson. You've a bad temper," he said. "I thought you'd control it if you had to forfeit something."

"Oh, I just *live* for money," she said.

"I don't want all of it."

"Come on now." She was weary. She opened the door and listened. The neighbors hadn't heard, or if they had, they paid no attention. The lights of the waiting taxi illuminated the front patio.

They walked out through the cool moonlit night. She walked ahead of him for the first time in years.

Paricutin was a river of gold that night. A distant murmuring river of molten ore going down to some dead lava sea, to some volcanic black shore. Time and again if you held your breath, stilled your heart within you, you could hear the lava pushing rocks down the mountain in tumblings and roarings, faintly, faintly. Above the crater were red vapors and red light. Gentle brown and gray clouds arose suddenly as coronets or halos or puffs from the interior, their undersides washed in pink, their tops dark and ominous, without a sound.

The husband and the wife stood on the opposite mountain, in the sharp cold, the horses behind them. In a wooden hut nearby, the scientific observers were lighting oil lamps, cooking their evening meal, boiling rich coffee, talking in whispers because of the clear, night-explosive air. It was very far away from everything else in the world.

On the way up the mountain, after the long taxi drive from Uruapan, over moon-dreaming hills of ashen snow, through dry stick villages, under the cold clear stars, jounced in the taxi like dice in a gambling-tumbler, both of them had tried to make a better thing of it. They had arrived at a campfire on a sort of sea bottom. About the campfire were solemn men and small dark boys, and a company of seven other Americans, all men, in riding breeches, talking in loud voices under the soundless sky. The horses were brought forth and mounted. They proceeded across the lava river. She talked to the other Yankees and they responded. They joked together. After a while of this, the husband rode on ahead.

Now, they stood together, watching the lava wash down the dark cone summit.

He wouldn't speak.

"What's wrong now?" she asked.

He looked straight ahead, the lava glow reflected in his eyes. "You could have ridden with me. I thought we came to Mexico to see things together. And now you talk to those damned Texans."

"I felt lonely. We haven't seen any people from the States for eight weeks. I like the days in Mexico, but I don't like the nights. I just wanted someone to talk to."

"You wanted to tell them you're a writer."

"That's unfair."

"You're always telling people you're a writer, and how good you are, and you've just sold a story to a large-circulation magazine and that's how you got the money to come here to Mexico."

"One of them asked me what I did, and I told him. Damn right I'm proud of my work. I've waited ten years to sell some damn thing."

He studied her in the light from the fire mountain and at last he said, "You know, before coming up here tonight, I thought about that damned typewriter of yours and almost tossed it into the river."

"You didn't!"

"No, but I locked it in the car. I'm tired of it and the way you've ruined the whole trip. You're not with me, you're with yourself, you're the one who counts, you and that damned machine, you and Mexico, you and your reactions, you and your inspiration, you and your nervous sensitivity, and you and your aloneness. I knew you'd act this way tonight, just as sure as there was a First Coming! I'm tired of your running back from every excursion we make to sit at that machine and bang away at all hours. This is a vacation."

"I haven't touched the typewriter in a week, because it bothered you."

"Well, don't touch it for another week or a month, don't touch it until we get home. Your damned inspiration can wait!"

I should never have said I'd give him all the money, she thought. I should never have taken that weapon from him, it kept him away from my real life, the writing and the machine.

And now I've thrown off the protective cloak of money and he's searched for a new weapon and he's gotten to the true thing—to the *machine*! Oh Christ!

Suddenly, without thinking, with the rage in her again, she pushed him ahead of her. She didn't do it violently. She just gave him a push. Once, twice, three times. She didn't hurt him. It was just a gesture of pushing away. She wanted to strike him, throw him off a cliff, perhaps, but instead she gave these three pushes, to indicate her hostility and the end of talking. Then they stood separately, while behind them the horses moved their hooves softly, and the night air grew colder and their breath hissed in white plumes on the air, and in the scientists' cabin the coffee bubbled on the blue gas jet and the rich fumes permeated the moonlit heights.

After an hour, as the first dim furnacings of the sun came in the cold East, they mounted their horses for the trip down through growing light, toward the buried city and the buried church under the lava flow. Crossing the flow, she thought, Why doesn't his horse fall, why isn't he thrown onto those jagged lava rocks, why? But nothing happened. They rode on. The sun rose red.

They slept until one in the afternoon. She was dressed and sitting on the bed waiting for him to waken for half an hour before he stirred and rolled over, needing a shave, very pale with tiredness.

"I've got a sore throat," was the first thing he said.

She didn't speak.

"You shouldn't have thrown water on me," he said.

She got up and walked to the door and put her hand on the knob.

"I want you to stay here," he said. "We're going to stay here in Uruapan three or four more days."

At last she said, "I thought we were going on to Guadalajara."

"Don't be a tourist. You ruined that trip to the volcano for us. I want to go back up tomorrow or the next day. Go look at the sky."

She went out to look at the sky. It was clear and blue. She reported this. "The volcano dies down, sometimes for a week. We can't afford to wait a week for it to boom again."

"Yes, we can. We will. And you'll pay for the taxi to take us up there and do the trip over and do it right and enjoy it."

"Do you think we can ever enjoy it now?" she asked.

"If it's the last thing we do, we'll enjoy it."

"You insist, do you?"

"We'll wait until the sky is full of smoke and go back up."

"I'm going out to buy a paper." She shut the door and walked into the town.

She walked down the fresh-washed streets and looked in the shining windows and smelled that amazingly clear air and felt very good, except for the tremoring, the continual tremoring in her stomach. At last, with a hollowness roaring in her chest, she went to a man standing beside a taxi.

"*Señor*," she said.

"Yes?" said the man.

She felt her heart stop beating. Then it began to thump again and she went on: "How much would you charge to drive me to Morelia?"

"Ninety pesos, *señora*."

"And I can get the train in Morelia?"

"There is a train *here*, *señora*."

"Yes, but there are reasons why I don't want to *wait* for it here."

"I will drive you, then, to Morelia."

"Come along, there are a few things I must do."

The taxi was left in front of the Hotel de Las Flores. She walked in, alone, and once more looked at the lovely garden with its many flowers, and listened to the girl playing the strange blue-colored piano, and this time the song was the "Moonlight Sonata." She smelled the sharp crystalline air and shook her head, eyes closed, hands at her sides. She put her hand to the door, opened it softly.

Why today? she wondered. Why not some other day in the last five years? Why have I waited, why have I hung around? Because. A thousand becauses. Because you always hoped things would start again the way they were the first year. Because there were times, less frequent now, when he was splendid for days, even weeks, when you were both feeling well and the world was green and bright blue. There were times, like yesterday, for a moment, when he opened the armor-plate and showed her the fear beneath it and the small loneliness of himself and said, "I need and love you, don't ever go away, I'm afraid without you." Because sometimes it had seemed good to cry together, to make up, and the inevitable goodness of the night and the day following their making up. Because he was handsome. Because she had been alone all year every year until she met him. Because she didn't want to be alone again, but now knew that it would be better to be alone than be this way because only last night he destroyed the typewriter; not physically, no, but with thoughts and words. And he might as well have picked her up bodily and thrown her from the river bridge.

She could not feel her hand on the door. It was as if ten thousand volts of electricity had numbed all of her body. She could not feel her feet on the tiled floor. Her face was gone, her mind was gone.

He lay asleep, his back turned. The room was greenly dim. Quickly, soundlessly, she put on her coat and checked her purse. The clothes and typewriter were of no importance now. Everything was a hollowing roar. Everything was like a waterfall leaping into clear emptiness. There was no striking, no impact, just a clear water falling into a hollow and then another hollow, followed by an emptiness.

She stood by the bed and looked at the man there, the familiar black hair on the nape of his neck, the sleeping profile. The form stirred. "What?" he asked, still asleep.

"Nothing," she said. "Nothing. And nothing."

She went out and shut the door.

The taxi sped out of town at an incredible rate, making a great noise, and all the pink walls and blue walls fled past and people jumped out of the way and there were some few cars which almost exploded upon them, and there went most of the town and there went the hotel and that man sleeping in the hotel and there went—

Nothing.

The taxi motor died.

No, no, thought Marie, oh God, no, no, no.

The car must start again.

The taxi driver leaped out, glaring at God in his Heaven,

and ripped open the hood and looked as if he might strangle the iron guts of the car with his clawing hands, his face smiling a pure sweet smile of incredible hatred, and then he turned to Marie and forced himself to shrug, putting away his hate and accepting the Will of God.

"I will walk you to the bus station," he said.

No, her eyes said. No, her mouth almost said. Joseph will wake and run and find me still here and drag me back. No.

"I will carry your bags, *señora*," the taxi driver said, and walked off with them, and had to come back and find her still there, motionless, saying no, no, to no one, and helped her out and showed her where to walk.

The bus was in the square and the Indians were getting into it, some silently and with a slow, certain dignity, and some chattering like birds and shoving bundles, children, chickens' baskets, and pigs in ahead of them. The driver wore a uniform that had not been pressed or laundered in twenty years, and he was leaning out the window shouting and laughing with people outside, as Marie stepped up into the interior of hot smoke and burning grease from the engine, the smell of gasoline and oil, the smell of wet chickens, wet children, sweating men and damp women, old upholstery which was down to the skeleton, and oily leather. She found a seat in the rear and felt the eyes follow her and her suitcase, and she was thinking: I'm going away, at last I'm going away, I'm free, I'll never see him again in my life, I'm free, I'm free.

She almost laughed.

The bus started and all of the people in it shook and swayed and cried out and smiled, and the land of Mexico seemed to whirl about outside the window, like a dream undecided whether to stay or go, and then the greenness passed away, and the town, and there was the Hotel de Las Flores with its open patio, and there, incredibly, hands in pockets, standing in the open door but looking at the sky and the volcano smoke, was Joseph, paying no attention to the bus or her and she was going away from him, he was growing remote already, his figure was dwindling like someone falling down a mine shaft, silently, without a scream. Now, before she had even the decency or inclination to wave, he was no larger than a boy, then a child, then a baby, in distance, in size, then gone around a corner, with the engine thundering, someone playing upon a guitar up front in the bus, and Marie, straining to look back, as if she might penetrate walls, trees, and distances, for another view of the man standing so quietly watching the blue sky.

At last, her neck tired, she turned and folded her hands and examined what she had won for herself. A whole lifetime loomed suddenly ahead, as quickly as the turns and whirls of the highway brought her suddenly to edges of cliffs, and each bend of the road, even as the years, could not be seen ahead. For a moment it was simply good to lie back here, head upon jouncing seat rest, and contemplate quietness. To know nothing, to think nothing, to feel nothing, to be as nearly dead for a moment as one could be, with the eyes closed, the heart unheard, no special temperature to the body, to wait for life to come get her rather than to seek, at least for an hour. Let the bus take her to the train, the train to the plane, the plane to the city, and the city to her friends, and then, like a stone dropped into a cement mixer, let that life in the city do with her as it would, she flowing along in the mix and solidifying in any new pattern that seemed best.

The bus rushed on with a plummeting and swerving in the sweet green air of the afternoon, between the mountains baked like lion pelts, past rivers as sweet as wine and as clear as vermouth, over stone bridges, under aqueducts where water ran like clear wind in the ancient channels, past churches, through dust, and suddenly, quite suddenly the speedometer in Marie's mind said, A million miles, Joseph is back a million miles and I'll never see him again. The thought stood up in her mind and covered the sky with a blurred darkness. Never, never again until the day I die or after that will I see him again, not for an hour or a minute or a second, not at all will I see him.

The numbness started in her fingertips. She felt it flow up through her hands, into her wrists and on along the arms to her shoulders and through her shoulders to her heart and up her neck to her head. She was a numbness, a thing of nettles and ice and prickles and a hollow thundering nothingness. Her lips were dry petals, her eyelids were a thousand pounds heavier than iron, and each part of her body was now iron and lead and copper and platinum. Her body weighed ten tons, each part of it was so incredibly heavy, and, in that heaviness, crushed and beating to survive, was her crippled heart, throbbing and tearing about like a headless chicken. And buried in the limestone and steel of her robot body was her terror and crying out, walled in, with someone tapping the trowel on the exterior wall, the job finished, and, ironically, it was her own hand she saw before her that had wielded the trowel, set the final brick in place, frothed on the thick slush of mortar and pushed everything into a tightness and a self-finished prison.

Her mouth was cotton. Her eyes were flaming with a dark flame the color of raven wings, the sound of vulture wings, and her head was so heavy with terror, so full of an iron weight, while her mouth was stuffed with invisible hot cotton, that she felt her head sag down into her immensely fat, but she could not see the fat, hands. Her hands were pillows of lead to lie upon, her hands were cement sacks crushing down upon her senseless lap, her ears, faucets in which ran cold winds, and all about her, not looking at her, not noticing, was the bus on its way through towns and fields, over hills and into corn valleys at a great racketing speed, taking her each and every instant one million miles and ten million years away from the familiar.

I must *not* cry out, she thought. No! No!

The dizziness was so complete, and the colors of the bus and her hands and skirt were now so blued over and sooted with lack of blood that in a moment she would be collapsed upon the floor, she would hear the surprise and shock of the riders bending over her. But she put her head far down and sucked the chicken air, the sweating air, the leather air, the carbon monoxide air, the incense air, the air of lonely death, and drew it back through the copper nostrils, down the aching throat, into her lungs which blazed as if she swallowed neon light. Joseph, Joseph, Joseph, Joseph.

It was a simple thing. All terror is a simplicity.

I cannot live without him, she thought. I have been lying to myself. I need him, oh Christ, I, I . . .

"Stop the bus! Stop it!"

The bus stopped at her scream, everyone was thrown forward. Somehow she was stumbling forward over the children, the dogs barking, her hands flailing heavily, falling; she heard her dress rip, she screamed again, the door was opening, the driver was appalled at the woman coming at him in a wild stumbling, and she fell out upon the gravel, tore her stockings, and lay while someone bent to her; then she was vomiting on the ground, a steady sickness; they were bringing her bags out of the bus to her, she was telling them in chokes and sobs that she wanted to go that way; she pointed back at the city a million years ago, a million miles ago, and the bus driver was shaking his head. She half sat, half lay there, her arms about the suitcase, sobbing, and the bus stood in the hot sunlight over her and she waved it on; go on, go on; they're all staring at me, I'll get a ride back, don't worry, leave me here, go on, and at last, like an accordion, the door folded shut, the Indian copper-mask faces were transported on away, and the bus dwindled from consciousness. She lay on the suitcase and cried, for a number of minutes, and she was not as heavy or sick, but her heart was fluttering wildly, and she was cold as someone fresh from a winter lake. She arose and dragged the suitcase in little moves across the highway and swayed there, waiting, while six cars hummed by, and at last a seventh car pulled up with a Mexican gentleman in the front seat, a rich car from Mexico City.

"You are going to Uruapan?" he asked politely, looking only at her eyes.

"Yes," she said at last, "I am going to Uruapan."

And as she rode in this car, her mind began a private dialogue:

"What is it to be insane?"

"I don't know."

"Do you know what insanity is?"

"I don't know."

"Can one tell? The coldness, was that the start?"

"No."

"The heaviness, wasn't that a part?"

"Shut up."

"Is insanity screaming?"

"I didn't mean to."

"But that came later. First there was the heaviness, and the silence, and the blankness. That terrible void, that space, that silence, that aloneness, that backing away from life, that being in upon oneself and not wishing to look at or speak to the world. Don't tell me that wasn't the start of insanity."

"Yes."

"You were ready to fall over the edge."

"I stopped the bus just short of the cliff."

"And what if you hadn't stopped the bus? Would they have driven into a little town or Mexico City and the driver turned and said to you through the empty bus, 'All right, *señora*, all out.' Silence. 'All right, *señora*, all out.' Silence. '*Señora?*' A stare into space. '*Señora!*' A rigid stare into the sky of life, empty, empty, oh, empty. '*Señora!*' No move. '*Señora.*' Hardly a breath. You sit there, you sit there, you sit there, you sit there, you sit there.

"You would not even hear. '*Señora*,' he would cry, and tug at you, but you wouldn't feel his hand. And the police would be summoned beyond your circle of comprehension, beyond your eyes or ears or body. You could not even hear the heavy boots in the car. '*Señora*, you must leave the bus.' You do not hear. '*Señora*, what is your name?' Your mouth is shut. '*Señora*, you must come with us.' You sit like a stone idol. 'Let us see her passport.' They fumble with your purse which lies untended in your stone lap. '*Señora* Marie Elliott, from California. *Señora* Elliott?' You stare at the empty sky. 'Where are you coming from? Where is your husband?' You were never married. 'Where are you going?' Nowhere. 'It says she was born in Illinois.' You were never born. '*Señora, señora*.' They have to carry you, like a stone, from the bus. You will talk to no one. No, no, no one. 'Marie, this is me, Joseph.' No, too late. 'Marie!' Too late. 'Don't you recognize me?' Too late. Joseph. No, Joseph, no nothing, too late, too late."

"That is what would have happened, is it not?"

"Yes." She trembled.

"If you had not stopped the bus, you would have been heavier and heavier, true? And silenter and silenter and more made up of nothing and nothing and nothing."

"Yes."

"*Señora*," said the Spanish gentleman driving, breaking in on her thoughts. "It is a nice day, isn't it?"

"Yes," she said, both to him and the thoughts in her mind.

The old Spanish gentleman drove her directly to her hotel and let her out and doffed his hat and bowed to her.

She nodded and felt her mouth move with thanks, but she did not see him. She wandered into the hotel and found herself with her suitcase back in her room, that room she had left a thousand years ago. Her husband was there.

He lay in the dim light of late afternoon with his back turned, seeming not to have moved in the hours since she had left. He had not even known that she was gone, and had been to the ends of the earth and had returned. He did not even know.

She stood looking at his neck and the dark hairs curling there like ash fallen from the sky.

She found herself on the tiled patio in the hot light. A bird rustled in a bamboo cage. In the cool darkness somewhere, the girl was playing a waltz on the piano.

She saw but did not see two butterflies which darted and jumped and lit upon a bush near her hand, to seal themselves together. She felt her gaze move to see the two bright things, all gold and yellow on the green leaf, their wings beating in slow pulses as they were joined. Her mouth moved and her hand swung like a pendulum, senselessly.

She watched her fingers tumble on the air and close on the two butterflies, tight, tighter, tightest. A scream was coming up into her mouth. She pressed it back. Tight, tighter, tightest.

She felt her hand open all to itself. Two lumps of bright powder fell to the shiny patio tiles. She looked down at the small ruins, then snapped her gaze up.

The girl who played the piano was standing in the middle of the garden, regarding her with appalled and startled eyes.

The wife put out her hand, to touch the distance, to say something, to explain, to apologize to the girl, this place, the world, everyone. But the girl went away.

The sky was full of smoke which went straight up and veered away south toward Mexico City.

She wiped the wing-pollen from her numb fingers and talked over her shoulder, not knowing if that man inside heard, her eyes on the smoke and sky.

"You know . . . we might try the volcano tonight. It looks good. I bet there'll be lots of fire."

Yes, she thought, and it will fill the air and fall all around us, and take hold of us tight, tighter, tightest, and then let go and let us fall and we'll be ashes blowing south, all fire.

"Did you hear me?"

She stood over the bed and raised a fist high but *never* brought it down to strike him in the face.

At Midnight, in the Month of June

HE HAD BEEN waiting a long, long time in the summer night, as the darkness pressed warmer to the earth and the stars turned slowly over the sky. He sat in total darkness, his hands lying easily on the arms of the Morris chair. He heard the town clock strike nine and ten and eleven, and then at last twelve. The breeze from an open back window flowed through the midnight house in an unlit stream, that touched him like a dark rock where he sat silently watching the front door—silently watching.

At midnight, in the month of June. . . .

The cool night poem by Mr. Edgar Allan Poe slid over his mind like the waters of a shadowed creek.

The lady sleeps! Oh, may her sleep,
Which is enduring, so be deep!

He moved down the black shapeless halls of the house, stepped out of the back window, feeling the town locked away in bed, in dream, in night. He saw the shining snake of garden hose coiled resiliently in the grass. He turned on the water. Standing alone, watering the flower bed, he imagined himself a conductor leading an orchestra that only night-strolling dogs might hear, passing on their way to nowhere with strange white smiles. Very carefully he planted both feet and his tall weight into the mud beneath the window, making deep, well-outlined prints. He stepped inside again and walked, leaving mud, down the absolutely unseen hall, his hands seeing for him.

Through the front porch window he made out the faint outline of a lemonade glass, one-third full, sitting on the porch rail where *she* had left it. He trembled quietly.

Now, he could feel her coming home. He could feel her moving across town, far away, in the summer night. He shut his eyes and put his mind out to find her; and felt her moving along in the dark; he knew just where she stepped down from a curb and crossed a street, and up on a curb and tack-tacking, tack-tacking along under the June elms and the last of the lilacs, with a friend. Walking the empty desert of night, he *was* she. He felt a purse in his hands. He felt long hair prickle his neck, and his mouth turn greasy with lipstick. Sitting still, he was walking, walking, walking on home after midnight.

"Good night!"

He heard but did not hear the voices, and she was coming nearer, and now she was only a mile away and now only a matter of a thousand yards, and now she was sinking, like a beautiful white lantern on an invisible wire, down into the cricket and frog and water-sounding ravine. And he knew the texture of the wooden ravine stairs as if, a boy, he was rushing down them, feeling the rough grain and the dust and the leftover heat of the day. . . .

He put his hands out on the air, open. The thumbs of his hands touched, and then the fingers, so that his hands made a circle, enclosing emptiness, there before him. Then, very slowly, he squeezed his hands tighter and tighter together, his mouth open, his eyes shut.

He stopped squeezing and put his hands, trembling, back on the arms of the chair. He kept his eyes shut.

Long ago, he had climbed, one night, to the top of the courthouse tower fire escape, and looked out at the silver town, at the town of the moon, and the town of summer. And he had seen all the dark houses with two things in them, people and sleep, the two elements joined in bed and all their tiredness and terror breathed upon the still air, siphoned back quietly, and breathed out again, until that element was purified, the problems and hatreds and horrors of the previous day exorcised long before morning and done away with forever.

He had been enchanted with the hour, and the town, and he had felt very powerful, like the magic man with the marionettes who strung destinies across a stage on spider threads. On the very top of the courthouse tower he could see the least flicker of leaf turning in the moonlight five miles away; the last light, like a pink pumpkin eye, wink out. The town did not escape his eye—it could do nothing without his knowing its every tremble and gesture.

And so it was tonight. He felt himself a tower with the clock in it pounding slow and announcing hours in a great bronze tone, and gazing upon a town where a woman, hurried or slowed by fitful gusts and breezes now of terror and now of self-confidence, took the chalk white midnight sidewalks home, fording solid avenues of tar and stone, drifting among fresh cut lawns, and now running, running down the steps, through the ravine, up, up the hill, up the hill!

He heard her footsteps before he really heard them. He heard her gasping before there was a gasping. He fixed his gaze to the lemonade glass outside, on the banister. Then the real sound, the real running, the gasping, echoed wildly outside. He sat up. The footsteps raced across the street, the sidewalk, in a panic. There was a babble, a clumsy stumble up the porch steps, a key ratcheting the door, a voice yelling in a whisper, praying to itself. "Oh, God, dear God!" Whisper! Whisper! And the woman crashing in the door, slamming it, bolting it, talking, whispering, talking to herself in the dark room.

He felt, rather than saw, her hand move toward the light switch.

He cleared his throat.

She stood against the door in the dark. If moonlight could have struck in upon her, she would have shimmered like a small pool of water on a windy night. He felt the fine sapphire jewels come out upon her face, and her face all glittering with brine.

"Lavinia," he whispered.

Her arms were raised across the door like a crucifix. He heard her mouth open and her lungs push a warmness upon the air. She was a beautiful dim white moth; with the sharp needle point of terror he had her pinned against the wooden door. He could walk all around the specimen, if he wished, and look at her, look at her.

"Lavinia," he whispered.

He heard her heart beating. She did not move.

"It's me," he whispered.

"Who?" she said, so faint it was a small pulse-beat in her throat.

"I won't tell you," he whispered. He stood perfectly straight in the center of the room. God, but he felt *tall*! Tall and dark and very beautiful to himself, and the way his hands were out before him was as if he might play a piano at any moment, a lovely melody, a waltzing tune. The hands were wet, they felt as if he had dipped them into a bed of mint and cool menthol.

"If I told you who I am, you might not be afraid," he whispered. "I want you to be afraid. Are you afraid?"

She said nothing. She breathed out and in, out and in, a small bellows which, pumped steadily, blew upon her fear and kept it going, kept it alight.

"Why did you go to the show tonight?" he whispered. "*Why* did you go to the show?"

No answer.

He took a step forward, heard her breath take itself, like a sword hissing in its sheath.

"Why did you come back through the ravine, alone?" he whispered. "You *did* come back alone, didn't you? Did you think you'd meet me in the middle of the bridge? Why did you go to the show tonight? Why did you come back through the ravine, alone?"

"I—" she gasped.

"You," he whispered.

"No—" she cried, in a whisper.

"Lavinia," he said. He took another step.

"Please," she said.

"Open the door. Get out. And run," he whispered.

She did not move.

"Lavinia, open the door."

She began to whimper in her throat.

"Run," he said.

In moving he felt something touch his knee. He pushed, something tilted in space and fell over, a table, a basket, and a half-dozen unseen balls of yarn tumbled like cats in the dark, rolling softly. In the one moonlit space on the floor beneath the window, like a metal sign pointing, lay the sewing shears. They were winter ice in his hand. He held them out to her suddenly, through the still air.

"Here," he whispered.

He touched them to her hand. She snatched her hand back.

"Here," he urged.

"Take this," he said, after a pause.

He opened her fingers that were already dead and cold to the touch, and stiff and strange to manage, and he pressed the scissors into them. "Now," he said.

He looked out at the moonlit sky for a long moment, and when he glanced back it was some time before he could see her in the dark.

"I waited," he said. "But that's the way it's always been. I waited for the others, too. But they all came looking for me, finally. It was that easy. Five lovely ladies in the last two years. I waited for them in the ravine, in the country, by the lake, everywhere I waited, and they came out to find me, and found me. It was always nice, the next day, reading the newspapers. And you went looking tonight, I know, or you wouldn't have come back alone through the ravine. Did you scare yourself there, and run? Did you think I was down there waiting for you? You should have *heard* yourself running up the walk! Through the door! And *locking* it! You thought you were safe inside, home at last, safe, safe, safe, didn't you?"

She held the scissors in one dead hand, and she began to cry. He saw the merest gleam, like water upon the wall of a dim cave. He heard the sounds she made.

"No," he whispered. "You have the scissors. Don't cry."

She cried. She did not move at all. She stood there, shivering, her head back against the door, beginning to slide down the length of the door toward the floor.

"Don't cry," he whispered.

"I don't like to hear you cry," he said. "I can't stand to hear that."

He held his hands out and moved them through the air until one of them touched her cheek. He felt the wetness of that cheek, he felt her warm breath touch his palm like a summer moth. Then he said only one more thing:

"Lavinia," he said, gently. "Lavinia."

How clearly he remembered the old nights in the old times, in the times when he was a boy and them all running, and running, and hiding and hiding, and playing hide-and-seek. In the first spring nights and in the warm summer nights and in the late summer evenings and in those first sharp autumn nights when doors were shutting early and porches were empty except for blowing leaves. The game of hide-and-seek went on as long as there was sun to see by, or the rising snow-crusted moon. Their feet upon the green lawns were like the scattered throwing of soft peaches and crab apples, and the counting of the Seeker with his arms cradling his buried head, chanting to the night: five, ten, fifteen, twenty, twenty-five, thirty, thirty-five, forty, forty-five, fifty. . . . And the sound of thrown apples fading, the children all safely closeted in tree or bush shade, under the latticed porches with the clever dogs minding not to wag their tails and give their secret away. And the counting done: eighty-five, ninety, ninety-five, a hundred!

Ready or not, here I come!

And the Seeker running out through the town wilderness to find the Hiders, and the Hiders keeping their secret laughter in their mouths, like precious June strawberries, with the help of clasped hands. And the Seeker seeking after the smallest heartbeat in the high elm tree or the glint of a dog's eye in a bush, or a small water sound of laughter that could not help but burst out as the Seeker ran right on by and did not see the shadow within the shadow. . . .

He moved into the bathroom of the quiet house, thinking all this, enjoying the clear rush, the tumultuous gushing of memories like a waterfalling of the mind over a steep precipice, falling and falling toward the bottom of his head.

God, how secret and tall they had felt, hidden away. God, how the shadows mothered and kept them, sheathed in their own triumph. Glowing with perspiration how they crouched like idols and thought they might hide *forever*! While the silly Seeker went pelting by on his way to failure and inevitable frustration.

Sometimes the Seeker stopped right *at* your tree and peered up at you crouched there in your invisible warm wings, in your great colorless windowpane bat wings, and said, "I *see* you there!" But you said nothing. "You're *up* there all right." But you said nothing. "Come on *down*!" But not a word, only a victorious Cheshire smile. And doubt coming over the Seeker below. "It is *you*, isn't it?" The backing off and away. "Aw, I *know* you're up there!" No answer. Only the tree sitting in the night and shaking quietly, leaf upon leaf. And the Seeker, afraid of the dark within darkness, loping away to seek easier game, something to be named and certain of. "All right for *you*!"

He washed his hands in the bathroom, and thought, Why am I washing my hands? And then the grains of time sucked back up the flue of the hour-glass again and it was another year. . . .

He remembered that sometimes when he played hide-and-seek they did not find him at all; he would not let them find him. He said not a word, he stayed so long in the apple tree that he was a white-fleshed apple; he lingered so long in the chestnut tree that he had the hardness and the brown brightness of the autumn nut. And God, how powerful to be undiscovered, how immense it made you, until your arms were branching, growing out in all directions, pulled by the stars and the tidal moon until your secretness enclosed the town and mothered it with your compassion and tolerance. You could do anything in the shadows, anything. If you chose to do it, you could do it. How powerful to sit above the sidewalk and see people pass under, never aware you were there and watching, and might put out an arm to brush their noses with the five-legged spider of your hand and brush their thinking minds with terror.

He finished washing his hands and wiped them on a towel.

But there was always an end to the game. When the Seeker had found all the other Hiders and these Hiders in turn were Seekers and they were all spreading out, calling your name, looking for you, how much more powerful and important *that* made you.

"Hey, hey! Where *are* you! Come in, the game's *over*!"

But you not moving or coming in. Even when they all collected under your tree and saw, or thought they saw you there at the very top, and called up at you. "Oh, come down! Stop fooling! Hey! We see you. We know you're there!"

Not answering even then—not until the final, the fatal thing happened. Far off, a block away, a silver whistle screaming, and the voice of your mother calling your name, and the whistle again. "Nine o'clock!" her voice wailed. "Nine o'clock! Home!"

But you waited until all the children were gone. Then, very carefully unfolding yourself and your warmth and secretness, and keeping out of the lantern light at corners, you ran home alone, alone in darkness and shadow, hardly breathing, keeping the sound of your heart quiet and in yourself, so if people heard anything at all they might think it was only the wind blowing a dry leaf by in the night. And your mother standing there, with the screen door wide. . . .

He finished wiping his hands on the towel. He stood a moment thinking of how it had been the last two years here in town. The old game going on, by himself, playing it alone, the children gone, grown into settled middle age, but now, as before, himself the final and last and only Hider, and the whole town seeking and seeing nothing and going on home to lock their doors.

But tonight, out of a time long past, and on many nights now, he had heard that old sound, the sound of the silver whistle, blowing and blowing. It was certainly not a night bird singing, for he knew each sound so well. But the whistle kept calling and calling and a voice said, *Home* and *Nine o'clock*, even though it was now long after midnight. He listened. There was the silver whistle. Even though his mother had died many years ago, after having put his father in an early grave with her temper and her tongue. "Do this, do that, do this, do that, do this, do that, do this, do that. . . ." A phonograph record, broken, playing the same cracked turn again, again, again, her voice, her cadence, around, around, around, around, repeat, repeat, repeat.

And the clear silver whistle blowing and the game of hide-and-seek over. No more of walking in the town and standing behind trees and bushes and smiling a smile that burned through the thickest foliage. An automatic thing was happening. His feet were walking and his hands were doing and he knew everything that must be done now.

His hands did not belong to him.

He tore a button off his coat and let it drop into the deep dark well of the room. It never seemed to hit bottom. It floated down. He waited.

It seemed never to stop rolling. Finally, it stopped.

His hands did not belong to him.

He took his pipe and flung that into the depths of the room. Without waiting for it to strike emptiness, he walked quietly back through the kitchen and peered outside the open, blowing, white-curtained window at the footprints he had made there. He was the Seeker, seeking now, instead of the Hider hiding. He was the quiet searcher finding and sifting and putting away clues, and those footprints were now as alien to him as something from a prehistoric age. They had been made a million years ago by some other man on some other business; they were no part of him at all. He marveled at their precision and deepness and form in the moonlight. He put his hand down almost to touch them, like a great and beautiful archaeological discovery! Then he was gone, back through the rooms, ripping a piece of material from his pants cuff and blowing it off his open palm like a moth.

His hands were not his hands any more, or his body his body.

He opened the front door and went out and sat for a moment on the porch rail. He picked up the lemonade glass and drank what was left, made warm by an evening's waiting, and pressed his fingers tight to the glass, tight, tight, very tight. Then he put the glass down on the railing.

The silver whistle!

Yes, he thought. Coming, coming.

The silver whistle!

Yes, he thought. Nine o'clock. Home, home. Nine o'clock. Studies and milk and graham crackers and white cool bed, home, home; nine o'clock and the silver whistle.

He was off the porch in an instant, running softly, lightly, with hardly a breath or a heartbeat, as one barefooted runs, as one all leaf and green June grass and night can run, all shadow, forever running, away from the silent house and across the street, and down into the ravine. . . .

He pushed the door wide and stepped into the Owl Diner, this long railroad car that, removed from its track, had been put to a solitary and unmoving destiny in the center of town. The place was empty. At the far end of the counter, the counterman glanced up as the door shut and the customer walked along the line of empty swivel seats. The counterman took the toothpick from his mouth.

"Tom Dillon, you old so-and-so! What *you* doing up this time of night, Tom?"

Tom Dillon ordered without the menu. While the food was being prepared, he dropped a nickel in the wall phone, got his number, and spoke quietly for a time. He hung up, came back, and sat, listening. Sixty seconds later, both he and the counterman heard the police siren wail by at fifty miles an hour. "Well—hell!" said the counterman. "Go get 'em, boys!"

He set out a tall glass of milk and a plate of six fresh graham crackers.

Tom Dillon sat there for a long while, looking secretly down at his ripped pants cuff and muddied shoes. The light in the diner was raw and bright, and he felt as if he were on a stage. He held the tall cool glass of milk in his hand, sipping it, eyes shut, chewing the good texture of the graham crackers, feeling it all through his mouth, coating his tongue.

"Would or would you not," he asked, quietly, "call this a hearty meal?"

"I'd call that very hearty indeed," said the counterman, smiling.

Tom Dillon chewed another graham cracker with great concentration, feeling all of it in his mouth. It's just a matter of time, he thought, waiting.

"More milk?"

"Yes," said Tom.

And he watched with steady interest, with the purest and most alert concentration in all of his life, as the white carton tilted and gleamed, and the snowy milk poured out, cool and quiet, like the sound of a running spring at night, and filled the glass up all the way, to the very brim, to the very brim, and over. . . .

The Strawberry Window

IN HIS DREAM he was shutting the front door with its strawberry windows and lemon windows and windows like white clouds and windows like clear water in a country stream. Two dozen panes squared round the one big pane, colored of fruit wines and gelatins and cool water ices. He remembered his father holding him up as a child. "Look!" And through the green glass the world was emerald, moss, and summer mint. "Look!" The lilac pane made livid grapes of all the passersby. And at last the strawberry glass perpetually bathed the town in roseate warmth, carpeted the world in pink sunrise, and made the cut lawn seem imported from some Persian rug bazaar. The strawberry window, best of all, cured people of their paleness, warmed the cold rain, and set the blowing, shifting February snows afire.

"Yes, yes! There——!"

He awoke.

He heard his boys talking before he was fully out of his dream and he lay in the dark now, listening to the sad sound their talk made, like the wind blowing the white sea-bottoms into the blue hills, and then he remembered.

We're on Mars, he thought.

"What?" His wife cried out in her sleep.

He hadn't realized he had spoken; he lay as still as he possibly could. But now, with a strange kind of numb reality, he saw his wife rise to haunt the room, her pale face staring through the small, high windows of their quonset hut at the clear but unfamiliar stars.

"Carrie," he whispered.

She did not hear.

"Carrie," he whispered. "There's something I want to tell you. For a month now I've been wanting to say . . . tomorrow . . . tomorrow morning, there's going to be . . ."

But his wife sat all to herself in the blue starlight and would not look at him.

If only the sun stayed up, he thought, if only there was no night. For during the day he nailed the settlement town together, the boys were in school, and Carrie had cleaning, gardening, cooking to do. But when the sun was gone and their hands were empty of flowers or hammers and nails and arithmetics, their memories, like night birds, came home in the dark.

His wife moved, a slight turn of her head.

"Bob," she said at last, "I want to go home."

"Carrie!"

"This isn't home," she said.

He saw that her eyes were wet and brimming. "Carrie, hold on awhile."

"I've got no fingernails from holding on now!"

As if she still moved in her sleep, she opened her bureau drawers and took out layers of handkerchiefs, shirts, underclothing, and put it all on top of the bureau, not seeing it, letting her fingers touch and bring it out and put it down. The routine was long familiar now. She would talk and put things out and stand quietly awhile, and then later put all the things away and come, dry-faced, back to bed and dreams. He was afraid that some night she would empty every drawer and reach for the few ancient suitcases against the wall.

"Bob . . ." Her voice was not bitter, but soft, featureless, and as uncolored as the moonlight that showed what she was doing. "So many nights for six months I've talked this way; I'm ashamed. You work hard building houses in town. A man who works so hard shouldn't have to listen to a wife gone sad on him. But there's nothing to do but talk it out. It's the little things I miss most of all. I don't know—silly things. Our front-porch swing. The wicker rocking chair, summer nights. Looking at the people walk or ride by those evenings, back in Ohio. Our black upright piano, out of tune. My Swedish cut glass. Our parlor furniture—oh, it was like a herd of elephants, I know, and all of it old. And the Chinese hanging crystals that hit when the wind blew. And talking to neighbors there on the front porch, July nights. All those crazy, silly things . . . they're not important. But it seems those are things that come to mind around three in the morning. I'm sorry."

"Don't be," he said. "Mars is a far place. It smells funny, looks funny, and feels funny. I think to myself nights too. We came from a nice town."

"It was green," she said. "In the spring and summer. And yellow and red in the fall. And ours was a nice house; my, it was old, eighty–ninety years or so. Used to hear the house talking at night, whispering away. All the dry wood, the banisters, the front porch, the sills. Wherever you touched, it talked to you. Every room a different way. And when you had the whole house talking, it was a family around you in the dark, putting you to sleep. No other house, the kind they build nowadays, can be the same. A lot of people have got to go through and live in a house to make it mellow down all over. This place here, now, this hut, it doesn't know I'm in it, doesn't care if I live or die. It makes a noise like tin, and tin's cold. It's got no pores for the years to sink in. It's got no cellar for you to put things away for next year and the year after that. It's got no attic where you keep things from last year and all the other years before you were born. If we only had a little bit up here that was familiar, Bob, then we could make room for all that's strange. But when everything, *every single thing* is strange, then it takes forever to make things familiar."

He nodded in the dark. "There's nothing you say that I haven't thought."

She was looking at the moonlight where it lay upon the suitcases against the wall. He saw her move her hand down toward them.

"Carrie!"

"What?"

He swung his legs out of bed. "Carrie, I've done a crazy damn-fool thing. All these months I heard you dreaming away, scared, and the boys at night and the wind, and Mars out there, the sea-bottoms and all, and . . ." He stopped and swallowed. "You got to understand what I did and why I did it. All the money we had in the bank a month ago, all the money we saved for ten years, I spent."

"Bob!"

"I threw it away, Carrie, I swear, I threw it away on nothing. It was going to be a surprise. But now, tonight, there you are, and there are those damned suitcases on the floor and . . ."

"Bob," she said, turning around. "You mean we've gone through all *this*, on Mars, putting away extra money every week, only to have you burn it up in a few hours?"

"I don't know," he said. "I'm a crazy fool. Look, it's not long till morning. We'll get up early. I'll take you down to see what I've done. I don't want to tell you, I want you to see. And if it's no go, then, well, there's always those suitcases and the rocket to Earth four times a week."

She did not move. "Bob, Bob," she murmured.

"Don't say any more," he said.

"Bob, Bob . . ." She shook her head slowly, unbelievingly. He turned away and lay back down on his own side of the bed, and she sat on the other side, and for a moment did not lie down, but only sat looking at the bureau where her handkerchiefs and jewelry and clothing lay ready in neat stacks where she had left them. Outside a wind the color of moonlight stirred up the sleeping dust and powdered the air.

At last she lay back, but said nothing more and was a cold weight in the bed, staring down the long tunnel of night toward the faintest sign of morning.

They got up in the very first light and moved in the small quonset hut without a sound. It was a pantomime prolonged almost to the time when someone might scream at the silence, as the mother and father and the boys washed and dressed and ate a quiet breakfast of toast and fruit juice and coffee, with no one looking directly at anyone and everyone watching someone in the reflective surfaces of toaster, glassware, or cutlery, where all their faces were melted out of shape and made terribly alien in the early hour. Then, at last, they opened the quonset door and let in the air that blew across the cold blue-white Martian seas, where only the sand tides dissolved and shifted and made ghost patterns, and they stepped out under a raw and staring cold sky and began their walk toward a town, which seemed no more than a motion-picture set far on ahead of them on a vast, empty stage.

"What part of town are we going to?" asked Carrie.

"The rocket depot," he said. "But before we get there, I've a lot to say."

The boys slowed down and moved behind their parents,

listening. The father gazed ahead, and not once in all the time he was talking did he look at his wife or sons to see how they were taking all that he said.

"I believe in Mars," he began quietly. "I guess I believe some day it'll belong to us. We'll nail it down. We'll settle in. We won't turn tail and run. It came to me one day a year ago, right after we first arrived. Why did we come? I asked myself. Because, I said, because. It's the same thing with the salmon every year. The salmon don't know why they go where they go, but they go, anyway. Up rivers they don't remember, up streams, jumping waterfalls, but finally making it to where they propagate and die, and the whole thing starts again. Call it racial memory, instinct, call it nothing, but there it is. And here we are."

They walked in the silent morning with the great sky watching them and the strange blue and steam-white sands sifting about their feet on the new highway.

"So here we are. And from Mars where? Jupiter, Neptune, Pluto, and on out? Right. *And on out.* Why? Some day the sun will blow up like a leaky furnace. Boom—there goes Earth. But maybe Mars won't be hurt; or if Mars is hurt maybe Pluto won't be, or if Pluto's hurt, then where'll *we* be, our sons' sons, that is?"

He gazed steadily up into that flawless shell of plum-colored sky.

"Why, we'll be on some world with a number maybe; planet 6 of star system 97, planet 2 of system 99! So damn far off from here you need a nightmare to take it in! We'll be gone, do you see, gone off away and safe! And I thought to myself, ah, ah. So that's the reason we came to Mars, so *that's* the reason men shoot off their rockets."

"Bob——"

"Let me finish; not to make money, no. Not to see the sights, no. Those are the lies men tell, the fancy reasons they give themselves. Get rich, get famous, they say. Have fun, jump around, they say. But all the while, inside, something else is ticking along the way it ticks in salmon or whales, the way it ticks, by God, in the smallest microbe you want to name. And that little clock that ticks in everything living, you know what it says? It says get away, spread out, move along, keep swimming. Run to so many worlds and build so many towns that *nothing* can ever kill man. You *see*, Carrie? It's not just us come to Mars, it's the race, the whole darn human race, depending on how *we* make out in our lifetime. This thing is so big I want to laugh, I'm so scared stiff of it."

He felt the boys walking steadily behind him and he felt Carrie beside him and he wanted to see her face and how she was taking all this, but he didn't look there, either.

"All this is no different than me and Dad walking the fields when I was a boy, casting seed by hand when our seeder broke down and we'd no money to fix it. It had to be done, somehow, for the later crops. My God, Carrie, my God, you *remember* those Sunday-supplement articles, THE EARTH WILL FREEZE IN A MILLION YEARS! I bawled once, as a boy, reading articles like that. My mother asked why. I'm bawling for all those poor people up ahead, I said. Don't worry about them, Mother said. But, Carrie, that's my whole point; we *are* worrying about them. Or we wouldn't be here. It matters if Man with a capital M keeps going. There's nothing better than Man with a capital M in my books. I'm prejudiced, of course, because I'm one of the breed. But if there's any way to get hold of that immortality men are always talking about, this is the way—spread out—seed the universe. Then you got a harvest against crop failures anywhere down the line. No matter if Earth has famines or the rust comes in. You got the new wheat lifting on Venus or where-in-hell-ever man gets to in the next thousand years, I'm crazy with the idea, Carrie, crazy. When I finally hit on it I got so excited I wanted to grab people, you, the boys, and tell them. But hell, I knew that wasn't necessary. I knew a day or night would come when you'd hear that ticking in yourselves too, and then you'd see, and no one'd have to say anything again about all this. It's big talk, Carrie, I know, and big thoughts for a man just short of five feet five, but by all that's holy, it's true."

They moved through the deserted streets of the town and listened to the echoes of their walking feet.

"And this morning?" said Carrie.

"I'm coming to this morning," he said. "Part of *me* wants to go home too. But the other part says if we go, everything's lost. So I thought, what bothers us most? Some of the things we once had. Some of the boys' things, your things, mine. And

I thought, if it takes an old thing to get a new thing started, by God, I'll use the old thing. I remember from history books that a thousand years ago they put charcoals in a hollowed out cow horn, blew on them during the day, so they carried their fire on marches from place to place, to start a fire every night with the sparks left over from morning. Always a new fire, but always something of the old in it. So I weighed and balanced it off. Is the Old worth all our money? I asked. No! It's only the things we *did* with the Old that have any worth. Well, then, is the New worth *all* our money? I asked. Do you feel like investing in the day after the middle of next week? Yes! I said. If I can fight this thing that makes us want to go back to Earth, I'd dip my money in kerosene and strike a match!"

Carrie and the two boys did not move. They stood on the street, looking at him as if he were a storm that had passed over and around, almost blowing them from the ground, a storm that was now dying away.

"The freight rocket came in this morning," he said, quietly. "Our delivery's on it. Let's go and pick it up."

They walked slowly up the three steps into the rocket depot and across the echoing floor toward the freight room that was just sliding back its doors, opening for the day.

"Tell us again about the salmon," said one of the boys.

In the middle of the warm morning they drove out of town in a rented truck filled with great crates and boxes and parcels and packages, long ones, tall ones, short ones, flat ones, all numbered and neatly addressed to one Robert Prentiss, New Toledo, Mars.

They stopped the truck by the quonset hut and the boys jumped down and helped their mother out. For a moment Bob sat behind the wheel, and then slowly got out himself to walk around and look into the back of the truck at the crates.

And by noon all but one of the boxes were opened and their contents placed on the sea-bottom where the family stood among them.

"Carrie . . ."

And he led her up the old porch steps that now stood uncrated on the edge of town.

"Listen to 'em, Carrie."

The steps squeaked and whispered underfoot.

"What do they say, tell me what they say?"

She stood on the ancient wooden steps, holding to herself, and could not tell him.

He waved his hand. "Front porch here, living room there, dining room, kitchen, three bedrooms. Part we'll build new, part we'll bring. Of course all we got here now is the front porch, some parlor furniture, and the old bed."

"All that money, Bob!"

He turned, smiling. "You're not mad, now, look at me! You're not mad. We'll bring it all up, next year, five years! The cut-glass vases, that Armenian carpet your mother gave us in 1961! Just *let* the sun explode!"

They looked at the other crates, numbered and lettered: Front-porch swing, front-porch wicker rocker, hanging Chinese crystals . . .

"I'll blow them myself to make them ring."

They set the front door, with its little panes of colored glass, on the top of the stairs, and Carrie looked through the strawberry window.

"What do you see?"

But he knew what she saw, for he gazed through the colored glass, too. And there was Mars, with its cold sky warmed and its dead seas fired with color, with its hills like mounds of strawberry ice, and its sand like burning charcoals sifted by wind. The strawberry window, the strawberry window, breathed soft rose colors on the land and filled the mind and the eye with the light of a never-ending dawn. Bent there, looking through, he heard himself say:

"The town'll be out this way in a year. This'll be a shady street, you'll have your porch, and you'll have friends. You won't *need* all this so much, then. But starting right here, with this little bit that's familiar, watch it spread, watch Mars change so you'll know it as if you've known it all your life."

He ran down the steps to the last and as-yet unopened canvas-covered crate. With his pocket knife he cut a hole in the canvas. "Guess!" he said.

"My kitchen stove? My furnace?"

"Not in a million years." He smiled very gently. "Sing me a song," he said.

"Bob, you're clean off your head."

"Sing me a song worth all the money we had in the bank and now don't have, but who gives a blast in hell," he said.

"I don't know anything but 'Genevieve, Sweet Genevieve'!"

"Sing that," he said.

But she could not open her mouth and start the song. He saw her lips move and try, but there was no sound.

He ripped the canvas wider and shoved his hand into the crate and touched around for a quiet moment, and started to sing the words himself until he moved his hand a last time and then a single clear piano chord sprang out on the morning air.

"There," he said. "Let's take it right on to the end. Everyone! Here's the harmony."

Icarus Montgolfier Wright

HE LAY ON his bed and the wind blew through the window over his ears and over his half-opened mouth so it whispered to him in his dream. It was like the wind of time hollowing the Delphic caves to say what must be said of yesterday, today, tomorrow. Sometimes one voice gave a shout far off away, sometimes two, a dozen, an entire race of men cried out through his mouth, but their words were always the same:

"Look, look, we've done it!"

For suddenly he, they, one or many, were flung in the dream, and flew. The air spread in a soft warm sea where he swam, disbelieving.

"Look, look! It's done!"

But he didn't ask the world to watch; he was only shocking his senses wide to see, taste, smell, touch the air, the wind, the rising moon. He swam alone in the sky. The heavy earth was gone.

But wait, he thought, wait now!

Tonight—what night is this?

The night before, of course. The night before the first flight of a rocket to the Moon. Beyond this room on the baked desert floor one hundred yards away the rocket waits for me.

Well, does it now? Is there *really* a rocket?

Hold on! he thought, and twisted, turned, sweating, eyes tight, to the wall, the fierce whisper in his teeth. Be certain-sure! You, now, who *are* you?

Me? he thought. *My* name?

Jedediah Prentiss, born 1938, college graduate 1959, licensed rocket pilot, 1965. Jedediah Prentiss . . . Jedediah Prentiss. . . .

The wind whistled his name away! He grabbed for it, yelling.

Then, gone quiet, he waited for the wind to bring his name back. He waited a long while, and there was only silence, and then after a thousand heartbeats he felt motion.

The sky opened out like a soft blue flower. The Aegean Sea stirred soft white fans through a distant wine-colored surf.

In the wash of the waves on the shore, he heard his name.

Icarus.

And again in a breathing whisper.

Icarus.

Someone shook his arm and it was his father saying his name and shaking away the night. And he himself lay small, half-turned to the window and the shore below and the deep sky, feeling the first wind of morning ruffle the golden feathers bedded in amber wax lying by the side of his cot. Golden wings stirred half-alive in his father's arms, and the faint down on his own shoulders quilled trembling as he looked at these wings and beyond them to the cliff.

"Father, how's the wind?"

"Enough for me, but never enough for you. . . ."

"Father, don't worry. The wings seem clumsy now, but my bones in the feathers will make them strong, my blood in the wax will make it live!"

"My blood, my bones too, remember; each man lends his flesh to his children, asking that they tend it well. Promise you'll not go high, Icarus. *The* sun or *my* son, the heat of one, the fever of the other, could melt these wings. Take care!"

And they carried the splendid golden wings into the morning and heard them whisper in their arms, whisper his name or a name or some name that blew, spun, and settled like a feather on the soft air.

Montgolfier.

His hands touched fiery rope, bright linen, stitched thread gone hot as summer. His hands fed wool and straw to a breathing flame.

Montgolfier.

And his eye soared up along the swell and sway, the oceanic tug and pull, the immensely wafted silver pear still filling with the shimmering tidal airs channeled up from the blaze. Silent as a god tilted slumbering above French countryside, this delicate linen envelope, this swelling sack of oven-baked air would soon pluck itself free. Draughting upward to blue worlds of silence, his mind and his brother's mind would sail with it, muted, serene among island clouds where uncivilized lightnings slept. Into that uncharted gulf and abyss where no birdsong or shout of man could follow, the balloon would hush itself. So cast adrift, he, Montgolfier, and all men, might hear the unmeasured breathing of God and the cathedral tread of eternity.

"Ah . . ." He moved, the crowd moved, shadowed by the warm balloon. "Everything's ready, everything's right. . . ."

Right. His lips twitched in his dream. Right. Hiss, whisper, flutter, rush. Right.

From his father's hands a toy jumped to the ceiling, whirled in its own wind, suspended, while he and his brother stared to see it flicker, rustle, whistle, heard it murmuring their names.

Wright.

Whispering: wind, sky, cloud, space, wing, fly . . .

"Wilbur, Orville? Look, how's *that*?"

Ah. In his sleep, his mouth sighed.

The toy helicopter hummed, bumped the ceiling, murmured eagle, raven, sparrow, robin, hawk; murmured eagle, raven, sparrow, robin, hawk. Whispered eagle, whispered raven, and at last, fluttering to their hands with a susurration, a wash of blowing weather from summers yet to come, with a last whir and exhalation, whispered hawk.

Dreaming, he smiled.

He saw the clouds rush down the Aegean sky.

He felt the balloon sway drunkenly, its great bulk ready for the clear running wind.

He felt the sand hiss up the Atlantic shelves from the soft dunes that might save him if he, a fledgling bird, should fall. The framework struts hummed and chortled like a harp, and himself caught up in its music.

Beyond this room he felt the primed rocket glide on the desert field, its fire-wings folded, its fire-breath kept, held ready to speak for three billion men. In a moment he would wake and walk slowly out to that rocket.

And stand on the rim of the cliff.

Stand cool in the shadow of the warm balloon.

Stand whipped by tidal sands drummed over Kitty Hawk.

And sheathe his boy's wrists, arms, hands, fingers with golden wings in golden wax.

And touch for a final time the captured breath of man, the warm gasp of awe and wonder siphoned and sewn to lift their dreams.

And spark the gasoline engine.

And take his father's hand and wish him well with his own wings, flexed and ready, here on the precipice.

Then whirl and jump.

Then cut the cords to free the great balloon.

Then rev the motor, prop the plane on air.

And crack the switch, to fire the rocket fuse.

And together in a single leap, swim, rush, flail, jump, sail, and glide, upturned to sun, moon, stars, they would go above Atlantic, Mediterranean; over country, wilderness, city, town; in gaseous silence, riffling feather, rattle-drum frame, in volcanic eruption, in timid, sputtering roar; in start, jar, hesitation, then steady ascension, beautifully held, wondrously transported, they would laugh and cry each his own name to himself. Or shout the names of others unborn or others long-dead and blown away by the wine wind or the salt wind or the silent hush of balloon wind or the wind of chemical fire. Each feeling the bright feathers stir and bud deep-buried and thrusting to burst from their riven shoulder blades! Each leaving behind the echo of their flying, a sound to encircle, recircle the earth in the winds and speak again in other years to the sons of the sons of their sons, asleep but hearing the restless midnight sky.

Up, yet further up, higher, higher! A spring tide, a summer flood, an unending river of wings!

A bell rang softly.

No, he whispered, I'll wake in a moment. Wait . . .

The Aegean slid away below the window, gone; the Atlantic dunes, the French countryside, dissolved down to New Mexico desert. In his room near his cot stirred no plumes in golden wax. Outside, no wind-sculpted pear, no trap-drum butterfly machine. Outside only a rocket, a combustible dream, waiting for the friction of his hand to set it off.

In the last moment of sleep someone asked his name.

Quietly, he gave the answer as he had heard it during the hours from midnight on.

"Icarus Montgolfier Wright."

He repeated it slowly so the questioner might remember the order and spelling down to the last incredible letter.

"Icarus Montgolfier Wright.

"Born: nine hundred years before Christ. Grammar school: Paris, 1783. High school, college: Kitty Hawk, 1903. Graduation from Earth to Moon: this day, God willing, August 1, 1970. Death and burial, with luck, on Mars, summer 1999 in the Year of Our Lord."

Then he let himself drift awake.

Moments later, crossing the desert Tarmac, he heard someone shouting again and again and again.

And if no one was there or if someone was there behind him, he could not tell. And whether it was one voice or many, young or old, near or very far away, rising or falling, whispering or shouting to him all three of his brave new names, he could not tell, either. He did not turn to see.

For the wind was slowly rising and he let it take hold and blow him all the rest of the way across the desert to the rocket which stood waiting there.

The End of the Beginning

HE STOPPED THE lawn mower in the middle of the yard, because he felt that the sun at just that moment had gone down and the stars come out. The fresh-cut grass that had showered his face and body died softly away. Yes, the stars were there, faint at first, but brightening in the clear desert sky. He heard the porch screen door tap shut and felt his wife watching him as he watched the night.

"Almost time," she said.

He nodded; he did not have to check his watch. In the passing moments he felt very old, then very young, very cold, then very warm, now this, now that. Suddenly he was miles away. He was his own son talking steadily, moving briskly to cover his pounding heart and the resurgent panics as he felt himself slip into fresh uniform, check food supplies, oxygen flasks, pressure helmet, space-suiting, and turn as every man on earth tonight turned, to gaze at the swiftly filling sky.

Then, quickly, he was back, once more the father of the son, hands gripped to the lawn-mower handle. His wife called, "Come sit on the porch."

"I've got to keep busy!"

She came down the steps and across the lawn. "Don't worry about Robert; he'll be all right."

"But it's all so new," he heard himself say. "It's never been done before. Think of it—a manned rocket going up tonight to build the first space station. Good lord, it can't be done, it doesn't exist, there's no rocket, no proving ground, no take-off time, no technicians. For that matter, I don't even have a son named Bob. The whole thing's too much for me!"

"Then what are you doing out here, staring?"

He shook his head. "Well, late this morning, walking to the office, I heard someone laugh out loud. It shocked me, so I froze in the middle of the street. It was *me*, laughing! Why? Because finally I really *knew* what Bob was going to do tonight; at last I *believed* it. Holy is a word I never use, but that's how I felt stranded in all that traffic. Then, middle of the afternoon I caught myself humming. You know the song. 'A wheel in a wheel. Way in the middle of the air.' I laughed again. The space station, of course, I thought. The big wheel with hollow spokes where Bob'll live six or eight months, then get along to the moon. Walking home, I remembered more of the song. 'Little wheel run by faith, Big wheel run by the grace of God.' I wanted to jump, yell, and flame-out myself!"

His wife touched his arm. "If we stay out here, let's at least be comfortable."

They placed two wicker rockers in the center of the lawn and sat quietly as the stars dissolved out of darkness in pale crushings of rock salt strewn from horizon to horizon.

"Why," said his wife, at last, "it's like waiting for the fireworks at Sisley Field every year."

"Bigger crowd tonight . . ."

"I keep thinking—a billion people watching the sky right now, their mouths all open at the same time."

They waited, feeling the earth move under their chairs.

"What time is it now?"

"Eleven minutes to eight."

"You're always right; there must be a clock in your head."

"I can't be wrong, tonight. I'll be able to tell you one second before they blast off. Look! The ten-minute warning!"

On the western sky they saw four crimson flares open out, float shimmering down the wind above the desert, then sink silently to the extinguishing earth.

In the new darkness the husband and wife did not rock in their chairs.

After a while he said, "Eight minutes." A pause. "Seven minutes." What seemed a much longer pause. "Six . . ."

His wife, her head back, studied the stars immediately above her and murmured, "Why?" She closed her eyes. "Why the rockets, why tonight? Why all this? I'd like to know."

He examined her face, pale in the vast powdering light of the Milky Way. He felt the stirring of an answer, but let his wife continue.

"I mean it's not that old thing again, is it, when people asked why men climbed Mt. Everest and they said, 'Because it's there'? I never understood. That was no answer to me."

Five minutes, he thought. Time ticking . . . his wrist

watch . . . a wheel in a wheel . . . little wheel run by . . . big wheel run by . . . way in the middle of . . . four minutes! . . . The men snug in the rocket by now, the hive, the control board flickering with light. . . .

His lips moved.

"All I know is it's really the end of the beginning. The Stone Age, Bronze Age, Iron Age; from now on we'll lump all those together under one big name for when we walked on Earth and heard the birds at morning and cried with envy. Maybe we'll call it the Earth Age, or maybe the Age of Gravity. Millions of years we fought gravity. When we were amoebas and fish we struggled to get out of the sea without gravity crushing us. Once safe on the shore we fought to stand upright without gravity breaking our new invention, the spine, tried to walk without stumbling, run without falling. A billion years Gravity kept us home, mocked us with wind and clouds, cabbage moths and locusts. That's what's so god-awful big about tonight . . . it's the end of old man Gravity and the age we'll remember him by, for once and all. I don't know where they'll divide the ages, at the Persians, who dreamt of flying carpets, or the Chinese, who all unknowing celebrated birthdays and New Years with strung ladyfingers and high skyrockets, or some minute, some incredible second in the next hour. But we're in at the end of a billion years trying, the end of something long and to us humans, anyway, honorable."

Three minutes . . . two minutes fifty-nine seconds . . . two minutes fifty-eight seconds . . .

"But," said his wife, "I still don't know why."

Two minutes, he thought. *Ready? Ready? Ready?* The far radio voice calling. *Ready! Ready! Ready!* The quick, faint replies from the humming rocket. *Check! Check! Check!*

Tonight, he thought, even if we fail with this first, we'll send a second and a third ship and move on out to all the planets and later, all the stars. We'll just keep going until the big words like immortal and forever take on meaning. Big words, yes, that's what we want. Continuity. Since our tongues first moved in our mouths we've asked, What does it all mean? No other question made sense, with death breathing down our necks. But just let us settle in on ten thousand worlds spinning around ten thousand alien suns and the question will fade away. Man will be endless and infinite, even as space is endless and infinite. Man will go on, as space goes on, forever. Individuals will die as always, but our history will reach as far as we'll ever need to see into the future, and with the knowledge of our survival for all time to come, we'll know security and thus the answer we've always searched for. Gifted with life, the least we can do is preserve and pass on the gift to infinity. That's a goal worth shooting for.

The wicker chairs whispered ever so softly on the grass.

One minute.

"One minute," he said aloud.

"Oh!" His wife moved suddenly to seize his hands. "I hope that Bob . . ."

"He'll be all right!"

"Oh, God, take care . . ."

Thirty seconds.

"Watch now."

Fifteen, ten, five . . .

"Watch!"

Four, three, two, one.

"There! There! Oh, there, there!"

They both cried out. They both stood. The chairs toppled back, fell flat on the lawn. The man and his wife swayed, their hands struggled to find each other, grip, hold. They saw the brightening color in the sky and, ten seconds later, the great uprising comet burn the air, put out the stars, and rush away in fire flight to become another star in the returning profusion of the Milky Way. The man and wife held each other as if they had stumbled on the rim of an incredible cliff that faced an abyss so deep and dark there seemed no end to it. Staring up, they heard themselves sobbing and crying. Only after a long time were they able to speak.

"It got away, it did, *didn't* it?"

"Yes . . ."

"It's all right, isn't it?"

"Yes . . . yes . . ."

"It didn't fall back . . . ?"

"No, no, it's all right, Bob's all right, it's all right."

They stood away from each other at last.

He touched his face with his hand and looked at his wet fingers. "I'll be damned," he said, "I'll be damned."

They waited another five and then ten minutes until the darkness in their heads, the retina, ached with a million specks of fiery salt. Then they had to close their eyes.

"Well," she said, "now let's go in."

He could not move. Only his hand reached a long way out by itself to find the lawn-mower handle. He saw what his hand had done and said, "There's just a little more to do. . . ."

"But you can't see."

"Well enough," he said. "I must finish this. Then we'll sit on the porch awhile before we turn in."

He helped her put the chairs on the porch and sat her down and then walked back out to put his hands on the guide bar of the lawn mower. The lawn mower. A wheel in a wheel. A simple machine which you held in your hands, which you sent on ahead with a rush and a clatter while you walked behind with your quiet philosophy. Racket, followed by warm silence. Whirling wheel, then soft footfall of thought.

I'm a billion years old, he told himself; I'm one minute old. I'm one inch, no, ten thousand *miles*, tall. I look down and can't see my feet they're so far off and gone away below.

He moved the lawn mower. The grass showering up fell softly around him; he relished and savored it and felt that he was all mankind bathing at last in the fresh waters of the fountain of youth.

Thus bathed, he remembered the song again about the wheels and the faith and the grace of God being way up there in the middle of the sky where that single star, among a million motionless stars, dared to move and keep on moving.

Then he finished cutting the grass.

The Day It Rained Forever

THE HOTEL STOOD like a hollowed dry bone under the very center of the desert sky where the sun burned the roof all day. All night, the memory of the sun stirred in every room like the ghost of an old forest fire. Long after dusk, since light meant heat, the hotel lights stayed off. The inhabitants of the hotel preferred to feel their way blind through the halls in their never-ending search for cool air.

This one particular evening Mr. Terle, the proprietor, and his only boarders, Mr. Smith and Mr. Fremley, who looked and smelled like two ancient rags of cured tobacco, stayed late on the long veranda. In their creaking glockenspiel rockers they gasped back and forth in the dark, trying to rock up a wind.

"Mr. Terle . . . ? Wouldn't it be *really* nice . . . someday . . . if you could buy . . . air conditioning . . . ?"

Mr. Terle coasted awhile, eyes shut.

"Got no money for such things, Mr. Smith."

The two old boarders flushed; they hadn't paid a bill now in twenty-one years.

Much later Mr. Fremley sighed a grievous sigh. "Why, why don't we all just quit, pick up, get outa here, move to a decent city? Stop this swelterin' and fryin' and sweatin'."

"Who'd buy a dead hotel in a ghost town?" said Mr. Terle quietly. "No. No, we'll just set here and wait, wait for that great day, January 29."

Slowly, all three men stopped rocking.

January 29.

The one day in all the year when it really let go and rained.

"Won't wait long." Mr. Smith tilted his gold railroad watch like the warm summer moon in his palm. "Two hours and nine minutes from now it'll *be* January 29. But I don't see nary a cloud in ten thousand miles."

"It's rained every January 29 since I was born!" Mr. Terle stopped, surprised at his own loud voice. "If it's a day late this year, I won't pull God's shirttail."

Mr. Fremley swallowed hard and looked from east to west

across the desert toward the hills. "I wonder . . . will there ever be a gold rush hereabouts again?"

"No gold," said Mr. Smith. "And what's more, I'll make you a bet—no rain. No rain tomorrow or the day after the day after tomorrow. No rain all the rest of this year."

The three old men sat staring at the big sun-yellowed moon that burned a hole in the high stillness.

After a long while, painfully, they began to rock again.

The first hot morning breezes curled the calendar pages like a dried snake skin against the flaking hotel front.

The three men, thumbing their suspenders up over their hat rack shoulders, came barefoot downstairs to blink out at that idiot sky.

"January 29 . . ."

"Not a drop of mercy there."

"Day's young."

"*I'm* not." Mr. Fremley turned and went away.

It took him five minutes to find his way up through the delirious hallways to his hot, freshly baked bed.

At noon, Mr. Terle peered in.

"Mr. Fremley . . . ?"

"Damn desert cactus, that's us!" gasped Mr. Fremley, lying there, his face looking as if at any moment it might fall away in a blazing dust on the raw plank floor. "But even the best damn cactus got to have just a sip of water before it goes back to another year of the same damn furnace. I tell you I won't move again, I'll lie here an' die if I don't hear more than birds pattin' around up on that roof!"

"Keep your prayers simple and your umbrella handy," said Mr. Terle and tiptoed away.

At dusk, on the hollow roof a faint pattering sounded.

Mr. Fremley's voice sang out mournfully from his bed.

"Mr. Terle, that ain't rain! That's you with the garden hose sprinklin' well water on the roof! Thanks for tryin', but cut it out, now."

The pattering sound stopped. There was a sigh from the yard below.

Coming around the side of the hotel a moment later, Mr. Terle saw the calendar fly out and down in the dust.

"Damn January 29!" cried a voice. "Twelve more months! Have to wait twelve more months, now!"

Mr. Smith was standing there in the doorway. He stepped inside and brought out two dilapidated suitcases and thumped them on the porch.

"Mr. Smith!" cried Mr. Terle. "You can't leave after thirty years!"

"They say it rains twenty days a month in Ireland," said Mr. Smith. "I'll get a job there and run around with my hat off and my mouth open."

"You can't go!" Mr. Terle tried frantically to think of something; he snapped his fingers. "You owe me nine thousand dollars rent!"

Mr. Smith recoiled; his eyes got a look of tender and unexpected hurt in them.

"I'm sorry." Mr. Terle looked away. "I didn't mean that. Look now—you just head for Seattle. Pours two inches a week there. Pay me when you can, or never. But do me a favor: wait till midnight. It's cooler then, anyhow. Get you a good night's walk toward the city."

"Nothin'll happen between now and midnight."

"You got to have faith. When everything else is gone, you got to believe a thing'll happen. Just stand here with me, you don't have to sit, just stand here and think of rain. That's the last thing I'll ever ask of you."

On the desert sudden little whirlwinds of dust twisted up, sifted down. Mr. Smith's eyes scanned the sunset horizon.

"What do I think? Rain, oh you rain, come along here? Stuff like that?"

"Anything. Anything at all!"

Mr. Smith stood for a long time between his two mangy suitcases and did not move. Five, six minutes ticked by. There was no sound, save the two men's breathing in the dusk.

Then at last, very firmly, Mr. Smith stooped to grasp the luggage handles.

Just then, Mr. Terle blinked. He leaned forward, cupping his hand to his ear.

Mr. Smith froze, his hands still on the luggage.

From away among the hills, a murmur, a soft and tremulous rumble.

"Storm coming!" hissed Mr. Terle.

The sound grew louder; a kind of whitish cloud rose up from the hills.

Mr. Smith stood tall on tiptoe.

Upstairs Mr. Fremley sat up like Lazarus.

Mr. Terle's eyes grew wider and yet wider to take hold of what was coming. He held to the porch rail like the captain of a calm-foundered vessel feeling the first stir of some tropic breeze that smelled of lime and the ice-cool white meat of coconut. The smallest wind stroked over his aching nostrils as over the flues of a white-hot chimney.

"There!" cried Mr. Terle. "There!"

And over the last hill, shaking out feathers of fiery dust, came the cloud, the thunder, the racketing storm.

Over the hill the first car to pass in twenty days flung itself down the valley with a shriek, a thud, and a wail.

Mr. Terle did not dare to look at Mr. Smith.

Mr. Smith looked up, thinking of Mr. Fremley in his room.

Mr. Fremley, at the window, looked down and saw the car expire and die in front of the hotel.

For the sound that the car made was curiously final. It had come a very long way on blazing sulphur roads, across salt flats abandoned ten million years ago by the shingling off of waters. Now, with wire-ravelings like cannibal hair sprung up from seams, with a great eyelid of canvas top thrown back and melted to spearmint gum over the rear seat, the auto, a Kissel car, vintage 1924, gave a final shuddering as if to expel its ghost upon the air.

The old woman in the front seat of the car waited patiently, looking in at the three men and the hotel as if to say, Forgive me, my friend is ill; I've known him a long while, and now I must see him through his final hour. So she just sat in the car waiting for the faint convulsions to cease and for the great relaxation of all the bones which signifies that the final process is over. She must have sat a full half minute longer listening to her car, and there was something so peaceful about her that Mr. Terle and Mr. Smith leaned slowly toward her. At last she looked at them with a grave smile and raised her hand.

Mr. Fremley was surprised to see his hand go out the window, above and wave back to her.

On the porch Mr. Smith murmured, "Strange. It's not a storm. And I'm not disappointed. How come?"

But Mr. Terle was down the path and to the car.

"We thought you were . . . that is . . ." He trailed off. "Terle's my name, Joe Terle."

She took his hand and looked at him with absolutely clear and unclouded light blue eyes like water that has melted from snow a thousand miles off and come a long way, purified by wind and sun.

"Miss Blanche Hillgood," she said, quietly. "Graduate of the Grinnell College, unmarried teacher of music, thirty years high-school glee club and student orchestra conductor, Green City, Iowa, twenty years private teacher of piano, harp, and voice, one month retired and living on a pension and now, taking my roots with me, on my way to California."

"Miss Hillgood, you don't look to be going anywhere from here."

"I had a feeling about that." She watched the two men circle the car cautiously. She sat like a child on the lap of a rheumatic grandfather, undecided. "Is there nothing we can do?"

"Make a fence of the wheels, dinner gong of the brake drums, the rest'll make a fine rock garden."

Mr. Fremley shouted from the sky. "Dead? I say, is the car dead? I can *feel* it from here! Well—it's way past time for supper!"

Mr. Terle put out his hand. "Miss Hillgood, that there is Joe Terle's Desert Hotel, open twenty-six hours a day. Gila monsters and road runners please register before going upstairs. Get you a night's sleep, free, we'll knock our Ford off its blocks and drive you to the city come morning."

She let herself be helped from the car. The machine groaned as if in protest at her going. She shut the door carefully with a soft click.

"One friend gone, but the other still with me. Mr. Terle, could you please bring her in out of the weather?"

"Her, ma'am?"

"Forgive me, I never think of things but what they're people. The car was a man, I suppose, because it took me places. But a harp, now, don't you agree, is female?"

She nodded to the rear seat of the car. There, tilted against the sky like an ancient scrolled leather ship prow cleaving the wind, stood a case which towered above any driver who might sit up in front and sail the desert calms or the city traffics.

"Mr. Smith," said Mr. Terle, "lend a hand."

They untied the huge case and hoisted it gingerly out between them.

"What you got there?" cried Mr. Fremley from above.

Mr. Smith stumbled. Miss Hillgood gasped. The case shifted in the two men's arms.

From within the case came a faint musical humming.

Mr. Fremley, above, heard. It was all the answer he needed. Mouth open, he watched the lady and the two men and their boxed friend sway and vanish in the cavernous porch below.

"Watch out!" said Mr. Smith. "Some damn fool left his luggage here——" He stopped. "Some damn fool? *Me!*"

The two men looked at each other. They were not perspiring any more. A wind had come up from somewhere, a gentle wind that fanned their shirt collars and flapped the strewn calendar gently in the dust.

"*My* luggage . . ." said Mr. Smith.

Then they all went inside.

"More wine, Miss Hillgood? Ain't had wine on the table in years."

"Just a touch, if you please."

They sat by the light of a single candle which made the room an oven and struck fire from the good silverware and the uncracked plates as they talked and drank warm wine and ate.

"Miss Hillgood, get on with your life."

"All my life," she said, "I've been so busy running from Beethoven to Bach to Brahms, I never noticed I was twenty-nine. Next time I looked up I was forty. Yesterday, seventy-one. Oh, there were men; but they'd given up singing at ten and given up flying when they were twelve. I always figured we were born to fly, one way or other, so I couldn't stand most men shuffling along with all the iron of the earth in their blood. I never met a man who weighed less than nine hundred pounds. In their black business suits, you could hear them roll by like funeral wagons."

"So you flew away?"

"Just in my mind, Mr. Terle. It's taken sixty years to make the final break. All that time I grabbed onto piccolos and flutes and violins because they make streams in the air, you know, like streams and rivers on the ground. I rode every tributary and tried every fresh-water wind from Handel on down to a whole slew of Strausses. It's been the far way around that's brought me here."

"How'd you finally make up your mind to leave?" asked Mr. Smith.

"I looked around last week and said, 'Why, look, you've been flying *alone*! No one in all Green City really cares *if* you fly or how high you go. It's always, 'Fine, Blanche,' or 'thanks for the recital at the PTA tea, Miss H.' But no one really listening. And when I talked a long time ago about Chicago or New York, folks swatted me and laughed. 'Why be a little frog in a big pond when you can be the biggest frog in all Green City!' So I stayed on, while the folks who gave me advice moved away or died or both. The rest had wax in their ears. Just last week I shook myself and said, 'Hold on! Since when do *frogs* have wings?'"

"So now you're headin' west?" said Mr. Terle.

"Maybe to play in pictures or in that orchestra under the stars. But somewhere I just must play at last for someone who'll hear and really listen. . . ."

They sat there in the warm dark. She was finished, she had said it all now, foolish or not—and she moved back quietly in her chair.

Upstairs someone coughed.

Miss Hillgood heard, and rose.

It took Mr. Fremley a moment to ungum his eyelids and make out the shape of the woman bending down to place the tray by his rumpled bed.

"What you all talking about down there just now?"

"I'll come back later and tell you word for word," said Miss Hillgood. "Eat now. The salad's fine." She moved to leave the room.

He said, quickly, "You goin' to stay?"

She stopped half out the door and tried to trace the expression on his sweating face in the dark. He, in turn, could not see her mouth or eyes. She stood a moment longer, silently, then went on down the stairs.

"She must not've heard me," said Mr. Fremley.

But he knew she had heard.

Miss Hillgood crossed the downstairs lobby to fumble with the locks on the upright leather case.

"I must pay you for my supper."

"On the house," said Mr. Terle.

"I must pay," she said, and opened the case.

There was a sudden flash of gold.

The two men quickened in their chairs. They squinted at the little old woman standing beside the tremendous heart-shaped object which towered above her with its shining columbined pedestal atop which a calm Grecian face with antelope eyes looked serenely at them even as Miss Hillgood looked now.

The two men shot each other the quickest and most startled of glances, as if each had guessed what might happen next. They hurried across the lobby, breathing hard, to sit on the very edge of the hot velvet lounge, wiping their faces with damp handkerchiefs.

Miss Hillgood drew a chair under her, rested the golden harp gently back on her shoulder, and put her hands to the strings.

Mr. Terle took a breath of fiery air and waited.

A desert wind came suddenly along the porch outside, tilting the chairs so they rocked this way and that like boats on a pond at night.

Mr. Fremley's voice protested from above. "What's goin' on down there?"

And then Miss Hillgood moved her hands.

Starting at the arch near her shoulder, she played her fingers out along the simple tapestry of wires toward the blind and beautiful stare of the Greek goddess on her column, and then back. Then for a moment she paused and let the sounds drift up through the baked lobby air and into all the empty rooms.

If Mr. Fremley shouted, above, no one heard. For Mr. Terle and Mr. Smith were so busy jumping up to stand riven in the shadows, they heard nothing save the storming of their own hearts and the shocked rush of all the air in their lungs. Eyes wide, mouths dropped, in a kind of pure insanity, they stared at the two women there, the blind Muse proud on her golden pillar, and the seated one, gentle eyes closed, her small hands stretched forth on the air.

Like a girl, they both thought wildly, like a little girl putting her hands out a window to feel what? Why, of course, of course!

To feel the rain.

The echo of the first shower vanished down remote causeways and roof drains, away.

Mr. Fremley, above, rose from his bed as if pulled round by his ears.

Miss Hillgood played.

She played and it wasn't a tune they knew at all, but it was a tune they had heard a thousand times in their long lives, words or not, melody or not. She played and each time her fingers moved, the rain fell pattering through the dark hotel. The rain fell cool at the open windows and the rain rinsed down the baked floor boards of the porch. The rain fell on the roof top and fell on hissing sand, it fell on rusted car and empty stable and dead cactus in the yard. It washed the windows and laid the dust and filled the rain barrels and curtained the doors with beaded threads that might part and whisper as you walked through. But more than anything the soft touch and coolness of it fell on Mr. Smith and Mr. Terle. Its gentle weight and pressure moved them down and down until it had seated them again. By its continuous budding and prickling on their faces it made them shut up their eyes and mouths and raise their hands to shield it away. Seated there, they felt their heads tilt slowly back to let the rain fall where it would.

The flash flood lasted a minute, then faded away as the fingers trailed down the loom, let drop a few last bursts and squalls and then stopped.

The last chord hung in the air like a picture taken when lightning strikes and freezes a billion drops of water on their downward flight. Then the lightning went out. The last drops fell through darkness in silence.

Miss Hillgood took her hands from the strings, her eyes still shut.

Mr. Terle and Mr. Smith opened their eyes to see those two miraculous women way over there across the lobby somehow come through the storm untouched and dry.

They trembled. They leaned forward as if they wished to speak. They looked helpless, not knowing what to do.

And then a single sound from high above in the hotel corridors drew their attention and told them what to do.

The sound came floating down feebly, fluttering like a tired bird beating its ancient wings.

The two men looked up and listened.

It was the sound of Mr. Fremley.

Mr. Fremley, in his room, applauding.

It took five seconds for Mr. Terle to figure out what it was. Then he nudged Mr. Smith and began, himself, to beat his palms together. The two men struck their hands in mighty explosions. The echoes ricocheted around about in the hotel caverns above and below, striking walls, mirrors, windows, trying to fight free of the rooms.

Miss Hillgood opened her eyes now, as if this new storm had come on her in the open, unprepared.

The men gave their own recital. They smashed their hands together so fervently it seemed they had fistfuls of firecrackers to set off, one on another. Mr. Fremley shouted. Nobody heard. Hands winged out, banged shut again and again until fingers puffed up and the old men's breath came short and they put their hands at last on their knees, a heart pounding inside each one.

Then, very slowly, Mr. Smith got up and still looking at the harp, went outside and carried in the suitcases. He stood at the foot of the lobby stairs looking for a long while at Miss Hillgood. He glanced down at her single piece of luggage resting there by the first tread. He looked from her suitcase to her and raised his eyebrows questioningly.

Miss Hillgood looked at her harp, at her suitcase, at Mr. Terle, and at last back to Mr. Smith.

She nodded once.

Mr. Smith bent down and with his own luggage under one arm and her suitcase in the other, he started the long slow climb up the stairs in the gentle dark. As he moved, Miss Hillgood put the harp back on her shoulder and either played in time to his moving or he moved in time to her playing, neither of them knew which.

Half up the flight, Mr. Smith met Mr. Fremley who, in a faded robe, was testing his slow way down.

Both stood there, looking deep into the lobby at the one man on the far side in the shadows, and the two women further over, no more than a motion and a gleam. Both thought the same thoughts.

The sound of the harp playing, the sound of the cool water falling every night and every night of their lives, after this. No spraying the roof with the garden hose now any more. Only sit on the porch or lie in your night bed and hear the falling . . . the falling . . . the falling . . .

Mr. Smith moved on up the stair; Mr. Fremley moved down.

The harp, the harp. Listen, listen!

The fifty years of drought were over.

The time of the long rains had come.

A Miracle of Rare Device

ON A DAY neither too mellow nor too tart, too hot nor too cold, the ancient tin lizzie came over the desert hill traveling at commotion speed. The vibration of the various armored parts of the car caused road-runners to spurt up in floury bursts of dust. Gila monsters, lazy displays of Indian jewelry, took themselves out of the way. Like an infestation, the Ford clamored and dinned away into the deeps of the wilderness.

In the front seat, squinting back, Old Will Bantlin shouted, "Turn off!"

Bob Greenhill spun-swung the lizzie off behind a billboard. Instantly both men turned. Both peered over the crumpled top of their car, praying to the dust they had wheeled up on the air.

"Lay down! Lay low! Please . . ."

And the dust blew slowly down. Just in time.

"Duck!"

A motorcycle, looking as if it had burned through all nine rings of hell, thundered by. Hunched over its oily handlebars, a hurricane figure, a man with a creased and most unpleasant face, goggled and sun-deviled, leaned on the wind. Roaring bike and man flung away down the road.

The two old men sat up in their lizzie, exhaling.

"So long, Ned Hopper," said Bob Greenhill.

"Why?" said Will Bantlin. "Why's he always tailing us?"

"Willy-William, talk sense," said Greenhill. "We're his luck, his Judas goats. Why should he let us go, when trailing us around the land makes him rich and happy and us poor and wise?"

The two men looked at each other, half in, half out of their smiles. What the world hadn't done to them, thinking about it had. They had enjoyed thirty years of nonviolence together, in their case meaning nonwork. "I feel a harvest coming on," Will would say, and they'd clear out of town before the wheat ripened. Or, "Those apples are ready to fall!" So they'd stand back about three hundred miles so as not to get hit on the head.

Now Bob Greenhill slowly let the car, in a magnificent controlled detonation, drift back out on the road.

"Willy, friend, don't be discouraged."

"I've been through 'discouraged,'" said Will. "I'm knee deep in 'accepting.'"

"Accepting what?"

"Finding a treasure chest of canned fish one day and no can opener. Finding a thousand can openers next day and no fish."

Bob Greenhill listened to the motor talking to itself like an old man under the hood, sounding like sleepless nights and rusty bones and well-worn dreams.

"Our bad luck can't last forever, Willy."

"No, but it sure tries. You and me sell ties and who's across the street ten cents cheaper?"

"Ned Hopper."

"We strike gold in Tonopah and who registers the claim first?"

"Old Ned."

"Haven't we done him a lifetime of favors? Aren't we overdue for something just ours, that never winds up his?"

"Time's ripe, Willy," said Robert, driving calmly. "Trouble is, you, me, Ned never really decided what we wanted. We've run through all the ghost towns, see something, grab. Ned sees and grabs, too. He don't want it, he just wants it because *we* want it. He keeps it 'till we're out of sight, then tears it up and hang-dogs after us for more litter. The day we really know what we want is the day Ned gets scared of us and runs off forever. Ah, hell." Bob Greenhill breathed the clear freshwater air running in morning streams over the windshield. "It's good anyway. That sky. Those hills. The desert and . . ."

His voice faded.

Will Bantlin glanced over. "What's wrong?"

"For some reason . . ." Bob Greenhill's eyes rolled, his leathery hands turned the wheel slow, "we got to . . . pull off . . . the road."

The lizzie bumped on the dirt shoulder. They drove down in a dusty wash and up out and suddenly along a dry peninsula of land overlooking the desert. Bob Greenhill, looking hypnotized, put out his hand to turn the ignition key. The old man under the hood stopped complaining about the insomnia and slept.

"Now, why did you do *that*?" asked Will Bantlin.

Bob Greenhill gazed at the wheel in his suddenly intuitive hands. "Seemed as if I had to. Why?" He blinked up. He let his bones settle and his eyes grow lazy. "Maybe only to look at the land out there. Good. All of it been here a billion years."

"Except for that city," said Will Bantlin.

"City?" said Bob.

He turned to look and the desert was there and the distant hills the color of lions, and far out beyond, suspended in a sea of warm morning sand and light, was a kind of floating image, a hasty sketch of a city.

"That can't be Phoenix," said Bob Greenhill. "Phoenix is ninety miles off. No other big place around."

Will Bantlin rumpled the map on his knees, searching.

"No. No other town."

"It's coming clearer!" cried Bob Greenhill, suddenly.

They both stood absolutely straight up in the car and stared over the dusty windshield, the wind whining softly over their craggy faces.

"Why, you know what that is, Bob? A mirage! Sure, that's it! Light rays just right, atmosphere, sky, temperature. City's the other side of the horizon somewhere. Look how it jumps, fades in and out. It's reflected against that sky up there like a mirror and comes down here where we can see it! A mirage, by Gosh!"

"That *big*?"

Bob Greenhill measured the city as it grew taller, clearer in a shift of wind, a soft far whirlabout of sand.

"The granddaddy of them all! That's not Phoenix. Not Santa Fe or Alamogordo, no. Let's see. It's not Kansas City—"

"That's too far off, anyway."

"Yeah, but look at those buildings. Big! Tallest in the country. Only one place like that in the world."

"You don't mean—New York?"

Will Bantlin nodded slowly and they both stood in the silence looking out at the mirage. And the city was tall and shining now and almost perfect in the early-morning light.

"Oh, my," said Bob, after a long while. "That's fine."

"It is," said Will.

"But," said Will, a moment later, whispering, as if afraid the city might hear, "what's it doing three thousand miles from home, here in the middle of Nowhere, Arizona?"

Bob Greenhill gazed and spoke. "Willy, friend, never question nature. It just sits there and minds its knitting. Radio waves, rainbows, northern lights, all that, heck, let's just say a great big picture got took of New York City and is being developed here, three thousand miles away on a morn when we need cheering, just for us."

"Not just us." Will peered over the side of the car. "Look!"

There in the floury dust lay innumerable crosshatchings, diagonals, fascinating symbols printed out in a quiet tapestry.

"Tire marks," said Bob Greenhill. "Hundreds of them. Thousands. Lots of cars pulled off here."

"For what, Bob?" Will Bantlin leaped from the car, landed on the earth, tromped it, turned on it, knelt to touch it with a swift and suddenly trembling hand. "For what, for what? To see the mirage? Yes, sir! To see the mirage!"

"So?"

"Boy, howdy!" Will stood up, thrummed his voice like a motor. "Brrrummm!" He turned an imaginary wheel. He ran along a tire track. "Brrrrummm! Eeeee! Brakes on! Robert-Bob, you know what we got here?! Look east! Look west. This is the only point in miles you can pull off the highway and sit and stare your eyes out!"

"Sure, it's nice people have an eye for beauty—"

"Beauty, my socks! Who owns this land?"

"The state, I reckon."

"You reckon wrong! You and me! We set up camp, register a claim, improve the property, and the law reads it's ours. Right?"

"Hold on!" Bob Greenhill was staring out at the desert and the strange city there. "You mean you want to . . . *homestead a mirage*?"

"Right, by zingo! Homestead a mirage!"

Robert Greenhill stood down and wandered around the car looking at the tire-treaded earth.

"Can we *do* that?"

"*Do* it? Excuse my dust!"

In an instant Will Bantlin was pounding tent pegs into the soil, stringing twine.

"From here to here, and here to here, it's a gold mine, we pan it, it's a cow, we milk it, it's a lakeful of money, we swim in it!"

Rummaging in the car, he heaved out cases and brought forth a large cardboard which had once advertised cheap cravats. This, reversed, he painted over with a brush and began lettering.

"Willy," said his friend, "nobody's going to pay to see any darned old—"

"Mirage? Put up a fence, tell folks they can't see a thing, and that's just their itch. There!"

He held up the sign.

SECRET VIEW MIRAGE—THE MYSTERIOUS CITY
25¢ per car. Motorbikes a dime.

"Here comes a car. Watch!"

"William—"

But Will, running, lifted the sign.

"Hey! Look! Hey!"

The car roared past, a bull ignoring the matador.

Bob shut his eyes so as not to see Will's smile wiped away.

But then—a marvelous sound.

The squeal of brakes.

The car was backing up! Will was leaping forward, waving, pointing.

"Yes, sir! Yes, ma'am! Secret View Mirage! The Mysterious City! Drive right in!"

The treadmarks in the simple dust became numerous, and then, quite suddenly, innumerable.

A great boll of heat-wafted dust hung over the dry peninsula where in a vast sound of arrivals, with braked tires, slammed doors, stilled engines, the cars of many kinds from many places came and took their places in a line. And the people in the cars were as different as people can be who come from four directions but are drawn in a single moment by a single thing, all talking at first, but growing still at last at what they saw out in the desert. The wind blew softly about their faces, fluttering the hair of the women, the open shirt collars of the men. They sat in their cars for a long time or they stood out on the rim of the earth, saying nothing, and at last one by one turned to go.

As the first car drove back out past Bob and Will, the woman in it nodded happily.

"Thanks! Why, it *is* just like Rome!"

"Did she say Rome or home?" asked Will.

Another car wheeled toward the exit.

"Yes, sir!" The driver reached out to shake Bob's hand. "Just looking made me feel I could speak French!"

"French!" cried Bob.

Both stepped forward swiftly as the third car made to leave. An old man sat at the wheel, shaking his head.

"Never seen the like. I mean to say, fog and all, Westminster Bridge, better than a postcard, and Big Ben off there in the distance. How do you do it? God bless. Much obliged."

Both men, disquieted, let the old man drive away, then slowly wheeled to look out along their small thrust of land toward the growing simmer of noon.

"Big Ben?" said Will Bantlin. "Westminster Bridge? Fog?"

Faintly, faintly, they thought they heard, they could not be sure, they cupped their ears, wasn't that a vast clock striking three times off there beyond land's rim? Weren't foghorns calling after boats and boat horns calling back on some lost river?

"Almost speak French?" whispered Robert. "Big Ben? Home? Rome? *Is* that Rome out there, Will?"

The wind shifted. A broiling surge of warm air tumbled up, plucking changes on an invisible harp. The fog almost solidified into gray stone monuments. The sun almost built a golden statue on top of a breasted mount of fresh-cut snow marble.

"How—" said William Bantlin, "how could it change? How could it be four, five cities? Did we tell anyone what city they'd see? No. Well, then, Bob, *well!*"

Now they fixed their gaze on their last customer, who stood alone at the rim of the dry peninsula. Gesturing his friend to silence, Robert moved silently to stand to one side and behind their paying visitor.

He was a man in his late forties with a vital, sunburned face, good, warm, clearwater eyes, fine cheekbones, a receptive mouth. He looked as if he had traveled a long way around in his life, over many deserts, in search of a particular oasis. He resembled those architects found wandering the rubbled streets below their buildings as the iron, steel and glass go soaring up to block out, fill in an empty piece of sky. His face was that of such builders who suddenly see reared up before them on the instant, from horizon to horizon, the perfect implementation of an old, old dream. Now, only half aware of William and Robert beside him, the stranger spoke at last in a quiet, an easy, a wondrous voice, saying what he saw, telling what he felt:

"'In Xanadu . . .'"

"What?" asked William.

The stranger half smiled, kept his eyes on the mirage and quietly, from memory, recited.

> "*In Xanadu did Kubla Khan*
> *A stately pleasure-dome decree:*
> *Where Alph, the sacred river, ran*
> *Through caverns measureless to man,*
> *Down to a sunless sea.*"

His voice spelled the weather and the weather blew about the other two men and made them more still.

> "*So twice five miles of fertile ground*
> *With walls and towers were girdled round:*
> *And here were gardens bright with sinuous rills,*
> *Where blossomed many an incense-bearing tree.*
> *And here were forests ancient as the hills,*
> *Enfolding sunny spots of greenery.*"

William and Robert looked off at the mirage, and what the stranger said was there, in the golden dust, some fabled Middle East or Far East clustering of minarets, domes, frail towers risen up in a magnificent sift of pollen from the Gobi, a spread of river stone baked bright by the fertile Euphrates, Palmyra not yet ruins, only just begun, newly minted, then abandoned by the departing years, now shimmered by heat, now threatening to blow away forever.

The stranger, his face transformed, beautified by his vision, finished it out:

> *"It was a miracle of rare device,*
> *A sunny pleasure-dome with caves of ice!*

And the stranger grew silent.

Which made the silence in Bob and Will all the deeper.

The stranger fumbled with his wallet, his eyes wet.

"Thank you, thank you."

"You already paid us," said William.

"If I had more, you'd get it all."

He gripped William's hand, left a five-dollar bill in it, got into his car, looked for a last time out at the mirage, then sat down, started the car, idled it with wonderful ease and, face glowing, eyes peaceful, drove away.

Robert walked a few steps after the car, stunned.

Then William suddenly exploded, flung his arms up, whooped, kicked his feet, wheeled around.

"Hallelujah! Fat of the land! Full dinner pails! New squeaky shoes! Look at my fistfuls!"

But Robert said, "I don't think we should take it."

William stopped dancing. "What?"

Robert looked steadily at the desert.

"We can't ever really own it. It's 'way out there. Sure, we can homestead the land, but . . . We don't even know what that thing is."

"Why, it's New York and—"

"Ever *been* to New York?"

"Always wanted. Never did."

"Always wanted, never did." Robert nodded slowly. "Same as them. You heard: Paris. Rome. London. And this last man. Xanadu. Willy, Willy, we got hold of something strange and big here. I'm scared we won't do right by it."

"Well, we're not keeping anyone out, are we?"

"Who knows? Might be a quarter's too much for some. It don't seem right, a natural thing handled by unnatural rules. Look and tell me I'm wrong."

William looked.

And the city was there like the first city he had seen as a boy when his mother took him on a train across a long meadow of grass early one morning and the city rose up head by head, tower by tower to look at him, to watch him coming near. It was that fresh, that new, that old, that frightening, that wonderful.

"I think," said Robert, "we should take just enough to buy gas for a week, put the rest of the money in the first poorbox we come to. That mirage is a clear river running, and people coming by thirsty. If we're wise, we dip one cup, drink it cool in the heat of the day and go. If we stop, build dams, try to own the whole river . . ."

William, peering out through the whispering dust wind, tried to relax, accept.

"If you say so."

"I don't. The wilderness all around says."

"Well, I say *different*!"

Both men jumped and spun about.

Half up the slope stood a motorcycle. Sitting it, rainbowed with oil, eyes goggled, grease masking his stubbly cheeks, was a man of familiar arrogance and free-running contempt.

"Ned Hopper!"

Ned Hopper smiled his most evilly benevolent smile, unbraked the cycle and glided the rest of the way down to halt by his old friends.

"You—" said Robert.

"Me! Me! Me!" Ned Hopper honked his cycle horn four times, laughing loud, head back. "Me!"

"Shut up!" cried Robert. "Bust it like a mirror."

"Bust *what* like a mirror?"

William, catching Robert's concern, glanced apprehensively out beyond at the desert.

The mirage flurried, trembled, misted away, then hung itself like a tapestry once more on the air.

"Nothing out there! What you guys up to?" Ned peered down at the treadmarked earth. "I was twenty miles on today when I realized you boys was hiding back behind. Says to myself, that ain't like my buddies who led me to that gold mine in 'forty-seven, lent me this cycle with a dice roll in 'fifty-five. All those years we help each other and now you got secrets from friend Ned. So I come back. Been up on that hill half the day, spying." Ned lifted binoculars from his greasy jacket front. "You know I can read lips. Sure! Saw all the cars run in here, the cash. Quite a show you're running!"

"Keep your voice down," warned Robert. "So long."

Ned smiled sweetly. "Sorry to see you go. But I surely respect your getting off my property."

"Yours!" Robert and William caught themselves and said in a trembling whisper, "Yours?"

Ned laughed. "When I saw what you was up to, I just cycled into Phoenix. See this little bitty government paper sticking out my back pocket?"

The paper was there, neatly folded.

William put out his hand.

"Don't give him the pleasure," said Robert.

William pulled his hand back. "You want us to believe you filed a homestead claim?"

Ned shut up the smile inside his eyes. "I do. I don't. Even if I was lying, I could still make Phoenix on my bike quicker'n your jalopy." Ned surveyed the land with his binoculars. "So just put down all the money you earned from two this afternoon, when I filed my claim, from which time on you was trespassing my land."

Robert flung the coins into the dust. Ned Hopper glanced casually at the bright litter.

"The U.S. Government Mint! Hot dog, nothing out there, but dumb bunnies willing to pay for it!"

Robert turned slowly to look at the desert.

"You don't see nothing?"

Ned snorted. "Nothing, and you *know* it!"

"But we do!" cried William. "We—"

"William," said Robert.

"But, Bob!"

"Nothing out there. Like he said."

More cars were driving up now in a great thrum of engines.

"Excuse, gents, got to mind the box office!" Ned strode off, waving. "Yes, sir, ma'am! This way! Cash in advance!"

"Why?" William watched Ned Hopper run off, yelling. "Why are we letting him do this?"

"Wait," said Robert, almost serenely. "You'll see."

They got out of the way as a Ford, a Buick and an ancient Moon motored in.

Twilight. On a hill about two hundred yards above the Mysterious City Mirage viewpoint, William Bantlin and Robert Greenhill fried and picked at a small supper, hardly bacon, mostly beans. From time to time, Robert used some battered opera glasses on the scene below.

"Had thirty customers since we left this afternoon," he observed. "Got to shut down soon, though. Only ten minutes of sun left."

William stared at a single bean on the end of his fork. "Tell me again: Why? Why every time our luck is good, Ned Hopper jumps out of the earth."

Robert sighed on the opera-glass lenses and wiped them on his cuff. "Because, friend Will, we are the pure in heart. We shine with a light. And the villains of the world, they see that light beyond the hills and say, 'Why, now, there's some innocent, some sweet all-day sucker.' And the villains come to warm their hands at us. I don't know what we can do about it, except maybe put out the light."

"I wouldn't want to do that." William brooded gently, his palms to the fire. "It's just I was hoping this time was come-uppance time. A man like Ned Hopper, living his white underbelly life, ain't he about due for a bolt of lightning?"

"Due?" Robert screwed the opera glasses tighter into his eyes. "Why, it just struck! Oh, ye of little faith!" William jumped up beside him. They shared the glasses, one lens each, peering down. "Look!"

And William, looking, cried, "Peduncle Q. Mackinaw!"

"Also, Gullable M. Crackers!"

For, far below, Ned Hopper was stomping around outside a car. People gesticulated at him. He handed them some money. The car drove off. Faintly you could hear Ned's anguished cries.

William gasped. "He's giving money back! Now he almost hit that man there. The man shook his fist at him! Ned's paid him back, too! Look—more fond farewells!"

"Yah-hee" whooped Robert, happy with his half of the glasses.

Below, all the cars were dusting away now. Old Ned did a violent kicking dance, threw his goggles into the dust, tore down the sign, let forth a terrible oath.

"Dear me," mused Robert. "I'm glad I can't hear them words. Come on, Willy!"

As William Bantlin and Robert Greenhill drove back up to the Mysterious City turn-off, Ned Hopper rocketed out in a screaming fury. Braying, roaring on his cycle, he hurled the painted cardboard through the air. The sign whistled up, a boomerang. It hissed, narrowly missing Bob. Long after Ned was gone in his banging thunder, the sign sank down and lay on the earth, where William picked it up and brushed it off.

It was twilight indeed now and the sun touching the far hills and the land quiet and hushed and Ned Hopper gone away, and the two men alone in the abandoned territory in the thousand-treaded dust, looking out at the sand and the strange air.

"Oh, no. . . . Yes," said Robert.

The desert was empty in the pink-gold light of the setting sun. The mirage was gone. A few dust devils whirled and fell apart, 'way out on the horizon, but that was all.

William let out a huge groan of bereavement. "*He* did it! Ned! Ned Hopper, come back, you! Oh, damn it, Ned, you spoiled it all! Blast you to perdition! He stopped. "Bob, how can you *stand* there!?"

Robert smiled sadly. "Right now I'm feeling sorry for Ned Hopper."

"Sorry!"

"He never saw what we saw. He never saw what anybody saw. He never believed for one second. And you know what? Disbelief is catching. It rubs off on people."

William searched the disinhabited land. "Is *that* what happened?"

"Who knows?" Robert shook his head. "One thing sure: when folks drove in here, the city, the cities, the mirage, whatever, was there. But it's awful hard to see when people stand in your way. Without so much as moving, Ned Hopper put his big hand across the sun. First thing you know, theater's closed for good."

"Can't we—" William hesitated. "Can't we open it up again?"

"How? How do you bring a thing like that back?"

They let their eyes play over the sand, the hills, the few lone clouds, the sky emptied of wind and very still.

"Maybe if we just look out the sides of our eyes, not direct at it, relax, take it easy . . ."

They both looked down at their shoes, their hands, the rocks at their feet, anything. But at last William mourned, "*Are* we? Are we the pure in heart?"

Robert laughed just a little bit. "Oh, not like the kids who came through here today and saw anything they wanted to see, and not like the big simple people born in the wheat fields and by God's grace wandering the world and will never grow up. We're neither the little children nor the big children of the world, Willy, but we are one thing: glad to be alive. We know the air mornings on the road, how the stars go up and then down the sky. That villain, he stopped being glad a long time ago. I hate to think of him driving his cycle on the road the rest of the night, the rest of the year."

As he finished this, Robert noticed that William was sliding his eyes carefully to one side, toward the desert.

Robert whispered carefully, "*See* anything?"

William sighed. "No. Maybe tomorrow . . ."

A single car came down the highway.

The two men glanced at each other. A wild look of hope flashed in their eyes. But they could not quite bring themselves to fling up their hands and yell. They simply stood with the painted sign held in their arms.

The car roared by.

The two men followed it with their wishful eyes.

The car braked. It backed up. In it were a man, a woman, a boy, a girl. The man called out, "You closed for the night?!"

William said, "It's no use—"

Robert cut in. "He means, no use giving us money! Last customer of the day, and family, free! On the house!"

"Thank you, neighbor, thank you!"

The car roared out onto the viewpoint.

William seized Robert's elbow. "Bob, what ails you? Disappoint those kids, that nice family?"

"Hush up," said Robert, gently. "Come on."

The kids piled out of the car. The man and his wife climbed slowly out into the sunset. The sky was all gold and blue now, and a bird sang somewhere in the fields of sand and lion-pollen.

"Watch," said Robert.

And they moved up to stand behind the family where it lined up now to look out over the desert.

William held his breath.

The man and wife squinted into the twilight uneasily.

The kids said nothing. Their eyes flexed and filled with a distillation of late sunlight.

William cleared his throat. "It's late. Uh—can't see too well."

The man was going to reply, when the boy said, "Oh, we can see fine!"

"Sure!" The girl pointed. "There!"

The mother and father followed her gesture, as if it might help, and it did.

"Lord," said the woman, "for a moment I thought . . . But now— Yes, there it is!"

The man read his wife's face, saw a thing there, borrowed it and placed it on the land and in the air.

"Yes," he said, at last. "Oh, yes."

William stared at them, at the desert and then at Robert, who smiled and nodded.

The faces of the father, the mother, the daughter, the son were glowing now, looking off at the desert.

"Oh," murmured the girl, "is it *really* there?"

And the father nodded, his face bright with what he saw that was just within seeing and just beyond knowing. He spoke as if he stood alone in a great forest church.

"Yes. And, Lord, it's beautiful."

William started to lift his head, but Robert whispered, "Easy. It's coming. Don't try. Easy, Will."

And then William knew what to do.

"I," he said, "am going to go stand with the kids."

And he walked slowly over and stood right behind the boy and the girl. He stood for a long time there, like a man between two warm fires on a cool evening, and they warmed him and he breathed easy and at last let his eyes drift up, let his attention wander easy out toward the twilight desert and the hoped-for city in the dusk.

And there in the dust softly blown high from the land, reassembled on the wind into half-shapes of towers and spires and minarets, was the mirage.

He felt Robert's breath on his neck, close, whispering, half talking to himself.

> "*It was a miracle of rare device,*
> *A sunny pleasure-dome with caves of ice!*"

And the city was there.

And the sun set and the first stars came out.

And the city was very clear, as William heard himself repeat, aloud or perhaps for only his secret pleasure, "'It was a miracle of rare device . . .'"

And they stood in the dark until they could not see.

The Kilimanjaro Device

I ARRIVED IN the truck very early in the morning. I had been driving all night, for I hadn't been able to sleep at the motel so I thought I might as well drive and I arrived among the mountains and hills near Ketchum and Sun Valley just as the sun came up and I was glad I had kept busy with driving.

I drove into the town itself without looking up at that one hill. I was afraid if I looked at it, I would make a mistake. It was very important not to look at the grave. At least that is how I felt. And I had to go on my hunch.

I parked the truck in front of an old saloon and walked around the town and talked to a few people and breathed the air and it was sweet and clear. I found a young hunter, but he was wrong; I knew that after talking to him for a few minutes. I found a very old man, but he was no better. Then I found me a hunter about fifty, and he was just right. He knew, or sensed, everything I was looking for.

I bought him a beer and we talked about a lot of things, and then I bought him another beer and led the conversation around to what I was doing here and why I wanted to talk to him. We were silent for a while and I waited, not showing my impatience, for the hunter, on his own, to bring up the past, to speak of other days three years ago, and of driving toward Sun Valley at this time or that and what he saw and knew about a man who had once sat in this bar and drunk beer and talked about hunting or gone hunting out beyond.

And at last, looking off at the wall as if it were the highway and the mountains, the hunter gathered up his quiet voice and was ready to speak.

"That old man," he said. "Oh, that old man on the road. Oh, that poor old man."

I waited.

"I just can't get over that old man on the road," he said, looking down now into his drink.

I drank some more of my beer, not feeling well, feeling very old myself and tired.

When the silence prolonged itself, I got out a local map and laid it on the wooden table. The bar was quiet. It was midmorning and we were completely alone there.

"This is where you saw him most often?" I asked.

The hunter touched the map three times. "I used to see him walking here. And along there. Then he'd cut across the land here. That poor old man. I wanted to tell him to keep off the road. I didn't want to hurt or insult him. You don't tell a man like that about roads or that maybe he'll be hit. If he's going to be hit, well that's it. You figure it's his business, and you go on. Oh, but he was old there at the last."

"He was," I said, and folded the map and put it in my pocket.

"You another of those reporters?" said the hunter.

"Not quite *those*," I said.

"Didn't mean to lump you in with them," he said.

"No apology needed," I said. "Let's just say I was one of his readers."

"Oh, he had readers all right, all kinds of readers. Even me. I don't touch books from one autumn to the next. But I touched his. I think I liked the Michigan stories best. About the fishing. I think the stories about the fishing are good. I don't think anybody ever wrote about fishing that way and maybe won't ever again. Of course, the bullfight stuff is good, too. But that's a little far off. Some of the cowpokes like them; they been around the animals all their life. A bull here or a bull there, I guess it's the same. I know one cowpoke has read just the bull stuff in the Spanish stories of the old man's forty times. He could go over there and fight, I swear."

"I think all of us felt," I said, "at least once in our lives, when we were young, we could go over there, after reading the bull stuff in the Spanish stories, that we could go over there and fight. Or at least jog ahead of the running of the bulls, in the early morning, with a good drink waiting at the other end of the run, and your best girl with you there for the long weekend."

I stopped. I laughed quietly. For my voice had, without knowing, fallen into the rhythm of his way of saying, either out of his mouth, or from his hand. I shook my head and was silent.

"You been up to the grave yet?" asked the hunter, as if he knew I would answer yes.

"No," I said.

That really surprised him. He tried not to show it.

"They all go up to the grave," he said.

"Not this one."

He explored around in his mind for a polite way of asking. "I mean . . ." he said. "Why *not*?"

"Because it's the wrong grave," I said.

"All graves are wrong graves when you come down to it," he said.

"No," I said. "There are right graves and wrong ones, just as there are good times to die and bad times."

He nodded at this. I had come back to something he knew, or at least smelled was right.

"Sure, I knew men," he said, "died just perfect. You always felt, yes, that was good. One man I knew, sitting at the table waiting for supper, his wife in the kitchen, when she came in with a big bowl of soup there he was sitting dead and neat at the table. Bad for her, but, I mean, wasn't that a good way for him? No sickness. No nothing but sitting there waiting for supper to come and never knowing if it came or not. Like another friend. Had an old dog. Fourteen years old. Dog was going blind and tired. Decided at last to take the dog to the pound and have him put to sleep. Loaded the old blind tired dog on the front seat of his car. The dog licked his hand, once. The man felt awful. He drove toward the pound. On the way there, with not one sound, the dog passed away, died on the front seat, as if he knew and, knowing, picked the better way, just handed over his ghost, and there you are. That's what you're talking about, right?"

I nodded.

"So you think that grave up on the hill is a wrong grave for a right man, do you?"

"That's about it," I said.

"You think there are all kinds of graves along the road for all of us?"

"Could be," I said.

"And if we could see all our life one way or another, we'd choose better? At the end, looking back," said the hunter, "we'd say, hell, *that* was the year and the place, not the *other* year and the other place, but that one year, that one place. Would we say that?"

"Since we have to choose or be pushed finally," I said, "yes."

"That's a nice idea," said the hunter. "But how many of us have that much sense? Most of us don't have brains enough to leave a party when the gin runs out. We hang around."

"We hang around," I said, "and what a shame."

We ordered some more beer.

The hunter drank half the glass and wiped his mouth.

"So what can you do about wrong graves?" he said.

"Treat them as if they didn't exist," I said. "And maybe they'll go away, like a bad dream."

The hunter laughed once, a kind of forlorn cry. "God, you're crazy. But I like listening to crazy people. Blow some more."

"That's all," I said.

"Are you the Resurrection and the Life?" said the hunter.

"No."

"You going to say Lazarus come forth?"

"No."

"What then?"

"I just want, very late in the day," I said, "to choose right places, right times, right graves."

"Drink that drink," said the hunter. "You need it. Who in hell sent you?"

"Me," I said. "I did. And some friends. We all chipped in and picked one out of ten. We bought that truck out on the street and I drove it across country. On the way I did a lot of hunting and fishing to put myself in the right frame. I was in Cuba last year. Spain the summer before. Africa the summer before that. I got a lot to think about. That's why they picked me."

"To do *what*, to do *what*, goddammit?" said the hunter urgently, half wildly, shaking his head. "You can't do anything. It's all over."

"Most of it," I said. "Come on."

I walked to the door. The hunter sat there. At last, examining the fires lit in my face by my talking, he grunted, got up, walked over, and came outside with me.

I pointed at the curb. We looked together at the truck parked there.

"I've seen those before," he said. "A truck like that, in a movie. Don't they hunt rhino from a truck like that? And lions and things like that? Or at least travel in them around Africa?"

"You remember right."

"No lions around here," he said. "No rhino, no water buffalo, nothing."

"No?" I asked.

He didn't answer that.

I walked over and touched the open truck.

"You know what this is?"

"I'm playing dumb from here on," said the hunter. "What is it?"

I stroked the fender for a long moment.

"A Time Machine," I said.

His eyes widened and then narrowed and he sipped the beer he was carrying in one large hand. He nodded me on.

"A Time Machine," I repeated.

"I heard you," he said.

He walked out around the safari truck and stood in the street looking at it. He wouldn't look at me. He circled the truck one entire round and stood back on the curb and looked at the cap on the gas tank.

"What kind of mileage you get?" he said.

"I don't know yet."

"You don't know anything," he said.

"This is the first trip," I said. "I won't know until it's over."

"What do you fuel a thing like that with?" he said.

I was silent.

"What kind of stuff you put *in*?" he asked.

I could have said: Reading late at night, reading many nights over the years until almost morning, reading up in the mountains in the snow or reading at noon in Pamplona, or reading by the streams or out in a boat somewhere along the Florida coast. Or I could have said: All of us put our hands on this Machine, all of us thought about it and bought it and touched it and put our love in it and our remembering what his words did to us twenty years or twenty-five or thirty years ago. There's a lot of life and remembering and love put by here, and that's the gas and the fuel and the stuff or whatever you want to call it; the rain in Paris, the sun in Madrid, the snow in the high Alps, the smoke off the guns in the Tyrol, the shine of light off the Gulf Stream, the explosion of bombs or explosions of leapt fish, that's the gas and the fuel and the stuff here; I should have said that, I thought it, but I let it stay unsaid.

The hunter must have smelled my thought, for his eyes squinted up and, telepath that he was from long years in the forest, chewed over my thinking.

Then he walked over and did an unexpected thing. He reached out and . . . *touched* . . . my Machine.

He laid his hand on it and left it there, as if feeling for the life, and approving what he sensed beneath his hand. He stood that way for a long time.

Then he turned without a word, not looking at me, and went back into the bar and sat drinking alone, his back turned toward the door.

I didn't want to break the silence. It seemed a good time to go, to try.

I got in the truck and started the motor.

What kind of mileage? What kind of fuel? I thought. And drove away.

I kept on the road and didn't look right or left and I drove for what must have been an hour, first this direction and then that, part of the time my eyes shut for full seconds, taking a chance I might go off and get hurt or killed.

And then, just before noon, with the clouds over the sun, suddenly I knew it was all right.

I looked up at the hill and I almost yelled.

The grave was gone.

I drove down into a little hollow just then and on the road ahead, wandering along by himself, was an old man in a heavy sweater.

I idled the safari truck along until I was pacing him as he walked. I saw he was wearing steel-rimmed glasses and for a long moment we moved together, each ignoring the other until I called his name.

He hesitated, and then walked on.

I caught up with him in the truck and said again, "Papa."

He stopped and waited.

I braked the car and sat there in the front seat.

"Papa," I said.

He came over and stood near the door.

"Do I know you?"

"No. But I know you."

He looked me in the eyes and studied my face and mouth. "Yes. I think you do."

"I saw you on the road. I think I'm going your way. Want a lift?"

"It's good walking this time of day," he said. "Thanks."

"Let me tell you where I'm going," I said.

He had started off but now stopped and, without looking at me, said, "Where?"

"A long way," I said.

"It sounds long, the way you tell it. Can't you make it shorter?"

"No. A long way," I said. "About two thousand six hundred days, give or take some days, and half an afternoon."

He came back and looked into the car.

"Is that how far you're going?"

"That's how far."

"In which direction? Ahead?"

"Don't you want to go ahead?"

He looked at the sky. "I don't know. I'm not sure."

"It's not ahead," I said. "It's back."

His eyes took on a different color. It was a subtle shift, a flex, like a man stepping out from the shade of a tree into sunlight on a cloudy day.

"Back."

"Somewhere between two thousand and three thousand days, split half a day, give or take an hour, borrow or loan a minute, haggle over a second," I said.

"You really talk," he said.

"Compulsive," I said.

"You'd make a lousy writer," he said. "I never knew a writer yet was a good talker."

"That's my albatross," I said.

"Back?" He weighed the word.

"I'm turning the car around," I said. "And I'm going back down the road."

"Not miles but days?"

"Not miles but days."

"Is it that kind of car?"

"That's how it's built."

"You're an inventor then?"

"A reader who happens to invent."

"If the car works, that's some car you got there."

"At your service," I said.

"And when you get where you're going," said the old man, putting his hand on the door and leaning and then, seeing what he had done, taking his hand away and standing taller to speak to me, "where will you be?"

"January 10, 1954."

"That's quite a date," he said.

"It is, it was. It can be more of a date."

Without moving, his eyes took another step out into fuller light.

"And where will you be on that day?"

"Africa," I said.

He was silent. His mouth did not work. His eyes did not shift.

"Not far from Nairobi," I said.

He nodded, once, slowly.

"Africa, not far from Nairobi."

I waited.

"And when we get there, if we go?" he said.

"I leave you there."

"And then?"

"You stay there."

"And then?"

"That's all."

"That's all?"

"Forever," I said.

The old man breathed out and in, and ran his hand over the edge of the doorsill.

"This car," he said, "somewhere along the way does it turn into a plane?"

"I don't know," I said.

"Somewhere along the way do you turn into my pilot?"

"It could be. I've never done this before."

"But you're willing to try?"

I nodded.

"Why?" he said, and leaned in and stared me directly in the face with a terrible, quietly wild intensity. "*Why?*"

Old man, I thought, I can't tell you why. Don't ask me.

He withdrew, sensing he had gone too far.

"I didn't say that," he said.

"You didn't say it," I said.

"And when you bring the plane in for a forced landing," he said, "will you land a little differently this time?"

"Different, yes."

"A little harder?"

"I'll see what can be done."

"And will I be thrown out but the rest of you okay?"

"The odds are in favor."

He looked up at the hill where there was no grave. I looked at the same hill. And maybe he guessed the digging of it there.

He gazed back down the road at the mountains and the sea that could not be seen beyond the mountains and a continent beyond the sea. "That's a good day you're talking about."

"The best."

"And a good hour and a good second."

"Really, nothing better."

"Worth thinking about."

His hand lay on the doorsill, not leaning, but testing, feeling, touching, tremulous, undecided. But his eyes came full into the light of African noon.

"Yes."

"Yes?" I said.

"I think," he said, "I'll grab a lift with you."

I waited one heartbeat, then reached over and opened the door.

Silently he got in the front seat and sat there and quietly shut the door without slamming it. He sat there, very old and very tired. I waited. "Start her up," he said.

I started the engine and gentled it.

"Turn her around," he said.

I turned the car so it was going back on the road.

"Is this really," he said, "that kind of car?"

"Really, that kind of car."

He looked out at the land and the mountains and the distant house.

I waited, idling the motor.

"When we get there," he said, "will you remember something . . . ?"

"I'll try."

"There's a mountain," he said, and stopped and sat there, his mouth quiet, and he didn't go on.

But I went on for him. There is a mountain in Africa named Kilimanjaro, I thought. And on the western slope of that mountain was once found the dried and frozen carcass of a leopard. No one has ever explained what the leopard was seeking at that altitude.

We will put you up on that same slope, I thought, on Kilimanjaro, near the leopard, and write your name and under it say nobody knew what he was doing here so high, but here he is. And write the date born and died, and go away down toward the hot summer grass and let mainly dark warriors and white hunters and swift okapis know the grave.

The old man shaded his eyes, looking at the road winding away over the hills. He nodded.

"Let's go," he said.

"Yes, Papa," I said.

And we motored away, myself at the wheel, going slow, and the old man beside me, and as we went down the first hill and topped the next, the sun came out full and the wind smelled of fire. We ran like a lion in the long grass. Rivers and streams flashed by. I wished we might stop for one hour and wade and fish and lie by the stream frying the fish and talking or not talking. But if we stopped we might never go on again. I gunned the engine. It made a great fierce wondrous animal's roar. The old man grinned.

"It's going to be a great day!" he shouted.

"A great day."

Back on the road, I thought, How must it be now, and now, us disappearing? And now, us gone? And now, the road empty. Sun Valley quiet in the sun. What must it be, having us gone?

I had the car up to ninety.

We both yelled like boys.

After that I didn't know anything.

"By God," said the old man, toward the end. "You know? I think we're . . . flying?"

The Lost City of Mars

THE GREAT EYE floated in space. And behind the great eye somewhere hidden away within metal and machinery was a small eye that belonged to a man who looked and could not stop looking at all the multitudes of stars and the diminishings and growings of light a billion billion miles away.

The small eye closed with tiredness. Captain John Wilder stood holding to the telescopic devices which probed the universe and at last murmured, "Which one?"

The astronomer with him said, "Take your pick."

"I wish it were that easy." Wilder opened his eyes. "What's the data on this star?"

"Alpha-Cygne II. Same size and reading as our sun. Planetary system, possible."

"Possible. Not certain. If we pick the wrong star, God help the people we send on a two-hundred-year journey to find a planet that may not be there. No, God help me, for the final selection is mine, and I may well send myself on that journey. So, how can we be sure?"

"We can't. We just make the best guess, send our starship out, and pray."

"You are not very encouraging. That's it. I'm tired."

Wilder touched a switch that shut up tight the greater eye, this rocket-powered space lens that stared cold upon the abyss, saw far too much and knew little, and now knew nothing. The rocket laboratory drifted sightless on an endless night.

"Home," said the captain. "Let's go home."

And the blind beggar-after-stars wheeled on a spread of fire and ran away.

The frontier cities on Mars looked very fine from above. Coming down for a landing, Wilder saw the neons among the blue hills and thought, We'll light those worlds a billion miles off, and the children of the people living under those lights this instant, we'll make them immortal. Very simply, if we succeed, they will live forever.

Live forever. The rocket landed. Live forever.

The wind that blew from the frontier town smelled of grease. An aluminum-toothed jukebox banged somewhere. A junkyard rusted beside the rocket port. Old newspapers danced alone on the windy tarmac.

Wilder, motionless at the top of the gantry elevator, suddenly wished not to move down. The lights suddenly had become people and not words that, huge in the mind, could be handled with elaborate ease.

He sighed. The freight of people was too heavy. The stars were too far away.

"Captain?" said someone behind him.

He stepped forward. The elevator gave way. They sank with a silent screaming toward a very real land with real people in it, who were waiting for him to choose.

At midnight the telegram-bin hissed and exploded out a message projectile. Wilder, at his desk, surrounded by tapes and computation cards, did not touch it for a long while. When at last he pulled the message out, he scanned it, rolled it in a tight ball, then uncrumpled the message and read again:

FINAL CANAL BEING FILLED TOMORROW WEEK. YOU ARE INVITED CANAL YACHT PARTY. DISTINGUISHED GUESTS. FOUR-DAY JOURNEY TO SEARCH FOR LOST CITY. KINDLY ACKNOWLEDGE.

I. V. AARONSON.

Wilder blinked, and laughed quietly. He crumpled the paper again, but stopped, lifted the telephone and said:

"Telegram to I. V. Aaronson, Mars City I. Answer affirmative. No sane reason why, but still—affirmative."

And hung up the phone. To sit for a long while watching this night which shadowed all the whispering, ticking, and motioning machines.

The dry canal waited.

It had been waiting twenty thousand years for nothing but dust to filter through in ghost tides.

Now, quite suddenly, it whispered.

And the whisper became a rush and wall-caroming glide of waters.

As if a vast machined fist had struck the rocks somewhere, clapped the air and cried "Miracle!," a wall of water came proud and high along the channels, and lay down in all the dry places of the canal and moved on toward ancient deserts of dry-bone, surprising old wharves and lifting up the skeletons of boats abandoned thirty centuries before when the water burnt away to nothing.

The tide turned a corner and lifted up—a boat as fresh as the morning itself, with new-minted silver screws and brass pipings, and bright new Earth-sewn flags. The boat, suspended from the side of the canal, bore the name *Aaronson I.*

Inside the boat, a man with the same name smiled. Mr. Aaronson sat listening to the waters live under the boat.

And the sound of the water was cut across by the sound of a hovercraft, arriving, and a motorbike, arriving, and in the air, as if summoned with magical timing, drawn by the glimmer of tides in the old canal, a number of gadfly people flew over the hills on jet-pack machines, and hung suspended as if doubting this collision of lives caused by one rich man.

Scowling up with a smile, the rich man called to his children, cried them in from the heat with offers of food and drink.

"Captain Wilder! Mr. Parkhill! Mr. Beaumont!"

Wilder set his hovercraft down.

Sam Parkhill discarded his motorbike, for he had seen the yacht and it was a new love.

"My God," cried Beaumont, the actor, part of the frieze of people in the sky dancing like bright bees on the wind. "I've timed my entrance wrong. I'm early. There's no audience!"

"I'll applaud you down!" shouted the old man, and did so, then added, "Mr. Aikens!"

"Aikens?" said Parkhill. "The big-game hunter?"

"None other!"

And Aikens dived down as if to seize them in his harrying claws. He fancied his resemblance to the hawk. He was finished and stropped like a razor by the swift life he had lived. Not an edge of him but cut the air as he fell, a strange plummeting vengeance upon people who had done nothing to him. In the moment before destruction, he pulled up on his jets and, gently screaming, simmered himself to touch the marble jetty. About his lean middle hung a rifle belt. His pockets bulged like those of a boy from the candy store. One guessed he was stashed with sweet bullets and rare bombs. In his hands, like an evil child, he held a weapon that looked like a bolt of lightning fallen straight from the clutch of Zeus, stamped nevertheless: *Made in U.S.A.* His face was sunblasted dark. His eyes were cool surprises in the sunwrinkled flesh, all mint-blue-green crystal. He wore a white porcelain smile set in African sinews. The earth did not quite tremble as he landed.

"The lion prowls the land of Judah!" cried a voice from the heavens. "Now do behold the lambs driven forth to slaughter!"

"Oh for God's sake, Harry, shut up!" said a woman's voice.

And two more kites fluttered their souls, their dread humanity on the wind.

The rich man jubilated.

"Harry Harpwell!"

"Behold the angel of the Lord who comes with Annunciations!" the man in the sky said, hovering. "And the Annunciation is—"

"He's drunk again," his wife supplied, flying ahead of him, not looking back.

"Megan Harpwell," said the rich man, like an entrepreneur introducing his troupe.

"The poet," said Wilder.

"And the poet's barracuda wife," muttered Parkhill.

"I am not drunk," the poet shouted down the wind. "I am simply *high.*"

And here he let loose such a deluge of laughter that those below almost raised their hands to ward off the avalanche.

Lowering himself, like a fat dragon kite, the poet, whose wife's mouth was now clamped shut, bumbled over the yacht. He made the motions of blessing same, and winked at Wilder and Parkhill.

"Harpwell," he called. "Isn't that a name to go with being a great modern poet who suffers in the present, lives in the past, steals bones from old dramatists' tombs, and flies on this new egg-beater wind-suck device, to call down sonnets on your head? I pity the old euphoric saints and angels who had no invisible wings like this so as to dart in oriole convolutions and ecstatic convulsions on the air as they sang their lines or damned souls to Hell. Poor earthbound sparrows, wings clipped. Only their genius flew. Only their Muse knew air-sickness—"

"Harry," said his wife, her feet on the ground, eyes shut.

"Hunter!" called the poet. "Aikens! Here's the greatest game in all the world, a poet on the wing. I bare my breast. Let fly your honeyed bee sting! Bring me, Icarus, down, if your gun be sunbeams kindled in one tube and let free in a single forest fire that escalates the sky and turns tallow, mush, candlewick and lyre to mere tarbaby. Ready, aim, fire!"

The hunter, in good humor, raised his gun.

The poet, at this, laughed a mightier laugh and, literally, exposed his chest by tearing aside his shirt.

At which moment a quietness came along the canal rim.

A woman appeared walking. Her maid walked behind her. There was no vehicle in sight, and it seemed almost as if they had wandered a long way out of the Martian hills and now stopped.

The very quietness of her entrance gave dignity and attention to Cara Corelli.

The poet shut up his lyric in the sky and landed.

The company all looked together at this actress who gazed back without seeing them. She was dressed in a black jumpsuit which was the same color as her dark hair. She walked like a woman who has spoken little in her life and now stood facing them with the same quietness, as if waiting for someone to move without being ordered. The wind blew her hair out and down over her shoulders. The paleness of her face was shocking. Her paleness, rather than her eyes, stared at them.

Then, without a word, she stepped down into the yacht and sat in the front of the craft, like a figurehead that knows its place and goes there.

The moment of silence was over.

Aaronson ran his finger down his printed guest list.

"An actor, a beautiful woman who happens to be an actress, a hunter, a poet, a poet's wife, a rocket captain, a former technician. All aboard!"

On the afterdeck of the huge craft, Aaronson spread forth his maps.

"Ladies, gentlemen," he said. "This is more than a four-day drinking bout, party, excursion. This is a Search!"

He waited for their faces to light, properly, and for them to glance from his eyes to the charts, and then said:

"We are seeking the fabled lost City of Mars, once called Dia-Sao. The City of Doom, it was called. Something terrible about it. The inhabitants fled as from a plague. The City left empty. Still empty now, centuries later."

"We," said Captain Wilder, "have charted, mapped, and cross-indexed every acre of land on Mars in the last fifteen years. You can't mislay a city the size of the one you speak of."

"True," said Aaronson, "you've mapped it from the sky, from the land. But you have *not* charted it via water! For the canals have been empty until now! So now we shall take the new waters that fill this last canal and go where the boats once went in the olden days, and see the very last new things that need to be seen on Mars." The rich man continued: "And somewhere on our traveling, as sure as the breath in our mouths, we shall find the most beautiful, the most fantastic, the most awful city in the history of this old world. And walk in that city—who knows?—find the reason why the Martians ran screaming away from it, as the legend says, ten thousand years ago."

Silence. Then:

"Bravo! Well done." The poet shook the old man's hand.

"And in that city," said Aikens, the hunter, "mightn't there be weapons the like of which we've never seen?"

"Most likely, sir."

"Well." The hunter cradled his bolt of lightning. "I was bored of Earth, shot every animal, ran fresh out of beasts, and came here looking for newer, better, more dangerous maneaters of any size or shape. Plus, now, new weapons! What more can one ask? Fine!"

And he dropped his blue-silver lightning bolt over the side. It sank in the clear water, bubbling.

"Let's get the hell out of here."

"Let us, indeed," said Aaronson, "get the good hell out."

And he pressed the button that launched the yacht.

And the water flowed the yacht away.

And the yacht went in the direction toward which Cara Corelli's quiet paleness was pointed: beyond.

As the poet opened the first champagne bottle. The cork banged. Only the hunter did not jump.

The yacht sailed steadily through the day into night. They found an ancient ruin and had dinner there and a good wine imported, one hundred million miles from Earth. It was noted that it had traveled well.

With the wine came the poet, and after quite a bit of the poet, came sleep on board the yacht which moved away in search of a City that would not as yet be found.

At three in the morning, restless, unaccustomed to the gravity of a planet pulling at all of his body and not freeing him to dream, Wilder came out on the afterdeck of the yacht and found the actress there.

She was watching the waters slip by in dark revelations and discardments of stars.

He sat beside her and thought a question.

Just as silently, Cara Corelli asked herself the same question, and answered it.

"I am here on Mars because not long ago for the first time in my life, a man told me the truth."

Perhaps she expected surprise. Wilder said nothing. The boat moved as on a stream of soundless oil.

"I am a beautiful woman. I have been beautiful all of my life. Which means that from the start people lied because they simply wished to be with me. I grew up surrounded by the untruths of men, women, and children who could not risk my displeasure. When beauty pouts, the world trembles.

"Have you ever seen a beautiful woman surrounded by men, seen them nodding, nodding? Heard their laughter? Men will laugh at anything a beautiful woman says. Hate themselves, yes, but they will laugh, say no for yes and yes for no.

"Well, that's how it was every day of every year for me. A crowd of liars stood between me and anything unpleasant. Their words dressed me in silks.

"But quite suddenly, oh, no more than six weeks ago, this man told me a truth. It was a small thing. I don't remember now what it was he said. But he didn't laugh. He didn't even smile.

"And no sooner was it out and over, the words spoken, that I knew a terrible thing had happened.

"I was growing old."

The yacht rocked gently on the tide.

"Oh, there would be more men who would, lying, smile again at what I said. But I saw the years ahead, when Beauty could no longer stomp its small foot, and shake down earthquakes, make cowardice a custom among otherwise good men.

"The man? He took back his truth immediately, when he saw that he had shocked me. But it was too late. I bought a one-way fare to Mars. Aaronson's invitation, when I arrived, put me on this new journey that will end . . . who knows where."

Wilder found that during this last he had reached out and taken her hand.

"No," she said, withdrawing. "No word. No touch. No pity. No self-pity." She smiled for the first time. "Isn't it strange? I always thought, wouldn't it be nice, someday, to hear the truth, to give up the masquerade? How wrong I was. It's no fun at all."

She sat and watched the black waters pour by the boat. When she thought to look again, some hours later, the seat beside her was empty. Wilder was gone.

On the second day, letting the new waters take them where they wished to go, they sailed toward a high range of mountains and lunched, on the way, in an old shrine, and had dinner that night in a further ruin. The Lost City was not much talked about. They were sure it would never be found.

But on the third day, without anyone's saying, they felt the approach of a great Presence.

It was the poet who finally put it in words.

"Is God humming under His breath somewhere?"

"What a fierce scum you are," said his wife. "Can't you speak plain English even when you gossip?"

"Dammit, listen!" cried the poet.

So they listened.

"Don't you feel as if you stood on the threshold of a giant

blast-furnace kitchen and inside somewhere, all comfortably warm, vast hands, flour-gloved, smelling of wondrous tripes and miraculous viscera, bloodied and proud of the blood, somewhere God cooks out the dinnertime of Life? In that cauldron sun, a brew to make the flowering forth of life on Venus, in that vat a stew broth of bones and nervous heart to run in animals on planets ten billion light-years gone. And isn't God content at His fabulous workings in the great kitchen Universe, where He has menu'd out a history of feasts, famines, deaths and reburgeonings for a billion billion years? And if God be content, would He not hum under His breath? Feel your bones. Aren't the marrows teeming with that hum? For that matter, God not only hums, He sings in the elements. He dances in molecules. Eternal celebration swarms us. Something is Near. Sh."

He pressed his fat finger to his pouting lips.

And now all were silent, and Cara Corelli's paleness searchlighted the darkening waters ahead.

They all felt it. Wilder did. Parkhill did. They smoked to cover it. They put the smokes out. They waited in the dusk.

And the humming grew nearer. And the hunter, smelling it, went to join the silent actress at the bow of the yacht. And the poet sat to write out the words he had spoken.

"Yes," he said, as the stars came out. "It's almost upon us. It has." He took a breath. "Arrived."

The yacht passed into a tunnel.

The tunnel went under a mountain.

And the City was there.

It was a city within a hollow mountain with its own meadows surrounding it and its own strangely colored and illumined stone sky above it. And it had been lost and remained lost for the simple reason that people had tried flying to discover it or had unraveled roads to find it, when all the while the canals which led to it stood waiting for simple walkers to tread where once waters had tread.

And now the yacht filled with strange people from another planet touched an ancient wharf.

And the City stirred.

In the old days, cities were alive or dead if there were or

were not people in them. It was that simple. But in the later days of life on Earth or Mars, cities did not die. They slept. And in their dreamful coggeries and enwheeled slumbers they remembered how once it was or how it might be again.

So as, one by one, the party filed out on the dock, they felt a great personage, the hidden, oiled, the metaled and shining soul of the metropolis slide in a landfall of muted and hidden fireworks toward becoming fully awake.

The weight of the new people on the dock caused a machined exhalation. They felt themselves on a delicate scale. The dock sank a millionth of an inch.

And the City, the cumbrous Sleeping Beauty of a nightmare device, sensed this touch, this kiss, and slept no more.

Thunder.

In a wall a hundred feet high stood a gate seventy feet wide. This gate, in two parts, now rumbled back, to hide within the wall.

Aaronson stepped forward.

Wilder moved to intercept him. Aaronson sighed.

"Captain, no advice, please. No warnings. No patrols going on ahead to flush out villains. The City wants us in. It welcomes us. Surely you don't imagine anything's *alive* in there? It's a robot place. And don't look as if you think it's a time bomb. It hasn't seen fun and games in—what?—twenty centuries? Do you read Martian hieroglyphs? That cornerstone. The City was built at least nineteen hundred years ago."

"And abandoned," said Wilder.

"You make it sound like a plague drove them—"

"Not a plague." Wilder stirred uneasily, feeling himself weighed on the great scale sunk beneath his feet. "Something. Something . . ."

"Let's find out! In, all of you!"

Singly, and in pairs, the people from Earth stepped over the threshold.

Wilder, last of all, stepped across.

And the City came more alive.

The metal roofs of the City sprang wide like the petals of a flower.

Windows flicked wide like the lids of vast eyes to stare down upon them.

A river of sidewalks gently purled and washed at their feet, machined creekways which gleamed off through the City.

Aaronson gazed at the metal tides with pleasure. "Well, by God, the burden's off me! I was going to picnic you all. But that's the City's business now. Meet you back here in two hours to compare notes! Here goes."

And saying this he leapt out on the scurrying silver carpet that treaded him swiftly away.

Wilder, alarmed, moved to follow. But Aaronson cried jovially back:

"Come on in, the water's fine!"

And the metal river whisked him, waving, off.

And one by one they stepped forward and the moving sidewalk drifted them away. Parkhill, the hunter, the poet and his wife, the actor, and then the beautiful woman and her maid. They floated like statues mysteriously borne on volcanic fluids that swept them anywhere, or nowhere, they could only guess.

Wilder jumped. The river seized his boots gently. Following, he went away into the avenues and around the bends of parks and through fiords of buildings.

And behind them, the dock and the gate stood empty. There was no trace to show they had arrived. It was almost as if they had never been.

Beaumont, the actor, was the first to leave the traveling pathway. A certain building caught his eye. And the next thing he knew, he had leapt off and edged near, sniffing.

He smiled.

For now he knew what kind of building he stood before because of the odor that drifted from it.

"Brass polish. And, by God, that means only one thing!"

Theater.

Brass doors, brass rails, brass rings on velvet curtains.

He opened the door of the building and stepped in. He sniffed and laughed aloud. Yes. Without a sign or a light, the smell alone, the special chemistry of metals and dust torn free of a million tickets.

And above all . . . he listened. The silence.

"The silence that waits. No other silence in the world waits. Only in a theater will you find that. The very particles of air chafe themselves in readiness. The shadows sit back and hold their breath. Well . . . ready or not . . . here I come . . ."

The lobby was green velvet undersea.

The theater itself: red velvet undersea, only dimly perceived as he opened the double doors. Somewhere beyond was a stage.

Something shuddered like a great beast. His breath had dreamt it alive. The air from his half-opened mouth caused the curtains one hundred feet away to softly furl and unfurl in darkness like all-covering wings.

Hesitantly, he took a step.

A light began to appear everywhere in a high ceiling where a school of miraculous prism fish swam upon themselves.

The oceanarium light played everywhere. He gasped.

The theater was full of people.

A thousand people sat motionless in the false dusk. True, they were small, fragile, rather dark, they wore silver masks, yet—people!

He knew, without asking, they had sat here for ten thousand years.

Yet they were not dead.

They were—he reached out a hand. He tapped the wrist of a man seated on the aisle.

The hand tinkled quietly.

He touched the shoulder of a woman. She chimed. Like a bell.

Yes, they had waited a few thousand years. But then, machines have a property of waiting.

He took a further step and froze.

For a sigh had passed over the crowd.

It was like the sound, the first small sound a newborn babe must make in the moment before it really sucks, bleats and shocks out its wailing surprise at being alive.

A thousand such sighs faded in the velvet portieres.

Beneath the masks, hadn't a thousand mouths drifted ajar?

Two moved. He stopped.

Two thousand eyes blinked wide in the velvet dusk. He moved again.

A thousand silent heads wheeled on their ancient but well-oiled cogs.

They looked at him.

An unquenchable cold ran wild in him.

He turned to run.

But their eyes would not let him go.

And, from the orchestra pit: music.

He looked and saw, slowly rising, an insect agglomeration of instruments, all strange, all grotesquely acrobatic in their configurations. These were being softly thrummed, piped, touched, and massaged in tune.

The audience, with a motion, turned their gaze to the stage.

A light flashed on. The orchestra struck a grand fanfare chord.

The red curtains parted. A spotlight fixed itself to front center, blazing upon an empty dais where sat an empty chair.

Beaumont waited.

No actor appeared.

A stir. Several hands were lifted to left and right. The hands came together. They beat softly in applause.

Now the spotlight wandered off the stage, and up the aisle.

The heads of the audience turned to follow the empty ghost of light. The masks glinted softly. The eyes behind the masks beckoned with warm color.

Beaumont stepped back.

But the light came steadily. It painted the floor with a blunt cone of pure whiteness.

And stopped, nibbling, at his feet.

The audience, turned, applauded even louder now. The theater banged, roared, ricocheted with their ceaseless tide of approbation.

Everything dissolved within him, from cold to warm. He felt as if he had been thrust raw into a downpour of summer rain. The storm rinsed him with gratitude. His heart jumped in great compulsive beats. His fists let go of themselves. His skeleton relaxed. He waited a moment longer, with the rain drenching over his upthrust and thankful cheeks and hammering his hungry eyelids so they fluttered to lock against themselves, and then he felt himself, like a ghost on battlements, led by a ghost light, lean, step, drift, move, down and along the incline, sliding to beautiful ruin, now no longer walking but striding, not striding but in full-tilted run, and the masks glittering, the eyes hot with delight and fantastic welcoming, the flights of hands on the disturbed air in up-flung dove-winged rifle-shot flight. He felt the steps collide with his shoes. The applause slammed to a shutdown.

He swallowed. Then slowly he ascended the steps and stood in the full light with a thousand masks fixed to him and two thousand eyes watchful, and he sat in the empty chair, and the theater grew darker, and the immense hearth-bellow breathing softer out of the lyre-metal throats, and there was only the sound of a mechanical beehive thrived with machinery-musk in the dark.

He held to his knees. He let go. And at last he spoke:

"To be or not to be—"

The silence was complete.

Not a cough. Not a stir. Not a rustle. Not a blink. All waited. Perfection. The perfect audience. Perfect, forever and forever. Perfect. Perfect.

He tossed his words slowly into that perfect pond and felt the soundless ripples disperse and gentle away.

"—that is the question."

He talked. They listened. He knew that they would never let him go now. They would beat him insensible with applause. He would sleep a child's sleep and rise to speak again. All of Shakespeare, all of Shaw, all of Molière, every bit, crumb, lump, joint, and piece. *Himself* in repertory!

He arose to finish.

Finished, he thought: Bury me! Cover me! Smother me deep!

Obediently, the avalanche came down the mountain.

Cara Corelli found a palace of mirrors.

The maid remained outside.

And Cara Corelli went in.

As she walked through a maze, the mirrors took away a day, and then a week, and then a month and then a year and then two years of time from her face.

It was a palace of splendid and soothing lies. It was like being young once more. It was being surrounded by all those tall bright glass mirror men who would never again in your life tell you the truth.

Cara walked to the center of the palace. By the time she stopped she saw herself twenty-five years old, in every tall bright mirror face.

She sat down in the middle of the bright maze. She beamed around in happiness.

The maid waited outside for perhaps an hour. And then she went away.

This was a dark place with shapes and sizes as yet unseen. It smelled of lubricating oil, the blood of tyrant lizards with cogs and wheels for teeth, which lay strewn and silent in the dark waiting.

A titan's door slowly gave a slithering roar like a swept-back armored tail, and Parkhill stood in the rich oily wind blowing out around him. He felt as if someone had pasted a white flower on his face. But it was only a sudden surprise of a smile.

His empty hands hung at his sides and they made impulsive and completely unconscious gestures forward. They beggared the air. So, paddling silently, he let himself be moved into the Garage, Machine Shop, Repair Shed, whatever it was.

And filled with holy delight and a child's holy and unholy glee at what he beheld, he walked and slowly turned.

For as far as his eye could see stood vehicles.

Vehicles that ran on the earth. Vehicles that flew in the air. Vehicles that stood ready with wheels to go in any direction. Vehicles with two wheels. Vehicles with three or four or six or eight. Vehicles that looked like butterflies. Vehicles that resembled ancient motorbikes. Three thousand stood ranked here, four thousand glinted ready there. Another thousand were tilted over, wheels off, viscera exposed, waiting to be repaired. Still another thousand were lifted high on spidery repair hoists, their lovely undersides revealed to view, their discs and tubes and coggeries all intricate and fine and needful of touching, unbolting, revalving, rewiring, oiling, delicately lubricating . . .

Parkhill's palms itched.

He walked forward through the primeval smell of swamp oils among the dead and waiting to be revived ancient but new armored mechanical reptiles, and the more he looked the more he ached his grin.

The City was a city all right, and, to a point, self-sustaining. But, eventually, the rarest butterflies of metal gossamer, gaseous oil, and fiery dream sank to earth, the machines that repaired the machines that repaired the machines grew old, ill, and damaging of themselves. Here then was the Bestial Garage, the slumbrous Elephant's Boneyard where the aluminum dragons crawled rusting out their souls, hopeful of one live person left among so much active but dead metal, that person to put things right. One God of the machines to say, you Lazarus-elevator, rise up! You hovercraft, be reborn! And anoint them with leviathan oils, tap them with magical wrench and send them forth to almost eternal lives in and on the air and above the quicksilver paths.

Parkhill moved among nine hundred robot men and women slaughtered by simple corrosion. He would cure their rust.

Now. If he started now, thought Parkhill, rolling up his sleeves, and staring off down a corridor of machines that ran waiting for a solid mile of garage, shed, hoist, lift, storage bin, oil tank, and strewn shrapnel of tools glittering and ready for his grip; if he started now, he might work his way to the end of the giant's ever-constant garage, accident, collision, and repair works shed in thirty years!

A billion bolts to be tightened. A billion motors to be tinkered! A billion iron tripes to lie under, a grand oil-dripped-upon orphan, alone, alone, alone with the always beautiful and never talking back hummingbird-commotion devices, accoutrements and miraculous contraptions.

His hands weighed him toward the tools. He clutched a wrench. He found a forty-wheeled low running sled. He lay down on it. He sculled the garage in a long whistling ride. The sled scuttled.

Parkhill vanished beneath a great car of some ancient design.

Out of sight, you could hear him working on the gut of the machine. On his back, he talked up at it. And when he slapped it to life, at last, the machine talked back.

Always the silver pathways ran somewhere.

Thousands of years now they had run empty, carrying only dust to destinations away and away among the high and dreaming buildings.

Now, on one traveling path, Aaronson came borne like an aging statue.

And the more the road propelled him, the faster the City exposed itself to his view, the more buildings that passed, the more parks that sprang into sight, the more his smile faded. His color changed.

"Toy," he heard himself whisper. The whisper was ancient. "Just another," and here his voice grew so small it faded away, ". . . another Toy."

A super-Toy, yes. But his life was full of such and had always been so. If it was not some slot machine it was the next-size dispenser or a jumbo-size razzmatazz hi-fi stereo speaker. From a lifetime of handling metallic sandpaper, he felt his arms rubbed away to a nub. Mere pips, his fingers. No, handless, and lacking wrists. Aaronson, the Seal Boy!!! His mindless flippers clapped applause to a city that was, in reality, no more and no less than an economy-size jukebox ravening under its idiot breath. And—he knew the tune! God help him. He *knew* the tune.

He blinked just once.

An inner eyelid came down like cold steel.

He turned and tread the silver waters of the path.

He found a moving river of steel to take him back toward the Great Gate itself.

On the way, he met the Corelli maid, wandering lost on her own silver stream.

As for the poet and his wife, their running battle tore echoes everywhere. They cried down thirty avenues, cracked panes in two hundred shops, battered leaves from seventy varieties of park bush and tree, and only ceased when drowned by a thundering fountain display they passed like a rise of clear fireworks upon the metropolitan air.

"The whole thing is," said his wife, punctuating one of his dirtier responses, "you only came along so you could lay hands on the nearest woman and spray her ears with bad breath and worse poetry."

The poet muttered a foul word.

"You're worse than the actor," said his wife. "Always at it. Don't you ever shut up?"

"Don't you?" he cried. "Ah God, I've curdled inside. Shut up, woman, or I'll throw myself in the founts!"

"No. You haven't bathed in years. You're the pig of the century! Your picture will grace the Swine Herder's Annual next month!"

"That *did* it!"

Doors slammed on a building.

By the time she got off and ran back and fisted the doors, they were locked.

"Coward!" she shrieked. "Open up!"

A foul word came echoing out, dimly.

"Ah, listen to that sweet silence," he whispered, to himself, in the great shelled dark.

Harpwell found himself in a soothing hugeness, a vast womb-like building, over which hung a canopy of pure serenity, a starless void.

In the middle of this room which was roughly a two-hundred-foot circle stood a device, a machine. In this machine were dials and rheostats and switches, a seat, and a steering wheel.

"What kind of vehicle is this?" whispered the poet, but edged near, and bent to touch. "Christ-off-the-cross-and-bearing-mercy, it smells of what? Blood and mere guts? No, for it's clean as a virgin's frock. Still it does fill the nose. Violence. Simple destruction. I can feel the damn carcass tremble like a nervous highbred hound. It's full of *stuffs*. Let's try a swig."

He sat in the machine.

"What do I swig first? This?"

He snapped a switch.

The Baskerville-hound machine whimpered in its dog slumberings.

"Good beast." He flicked another switch. "How do you go, brute? When the damn device is in full tilt, where to? You lack wheels. Well, surprise me. I dare."

The machine shivered.

The machine bolted.

It ran. It dashed.

He held tight to the steering wheel.

"Holy God!"

For he was on a highway, racing fast.

Air sluiced by. The sky flashed over in running colors.

The speedometer read seventy, eighty.

And the highway ribboned away ahead, flashing toward him. Invisible wheels slapped and banged on an increasingly rough road.

Far away, ahead, a car appeared.

It was running fast. And—

"It's on the wrong side of the road! Do you see that, wife? The wrong side."

Then he realized his wife was not here.

He was alone in a car racing—ninety miles an hour now—toward another car racing at a similar speed.

He veered the wheel.

His vehicle moved to the left.

Almost instantly the other car did a compensating move, and ran back over to the right.

"The damn fool, what does he think—where's the blasted brake?"

He stomped the floor. There was no brake. Here was a strange machine indeed. One that ran as fast as you wished, but never stopped until what? it ran itself down? There was no brake. Nothing but—further accelerators. A whole series of round-buttons on the floor, which, as he tromped them, surged power into the motor.

Ninety, one hundred, one hundred twenty miles an hour.

"God in heaven!" he screamed. "We're going to hit! How do you like that, girl?"

And in the last instant before collision, he imagined she rather liked it fine.

The cars hit. They erupted in gaseous flame. They burst apart in flinders. They tumbled. He felt himself jerked now this way and that. He was a torch hurtled skyward. His arms and legs danced a crazy rigadoon in midair as he felt his peppermint stick bones snap in brittle and agonizing ecstasies. Then, clutching death as a dark mate, gesticulating, he fell away in a black surprise, drifting toward further nothings.

He lay dead.

He lay dead a long while.

Then he opened one eye.

He felt the slow burner under his soul. He felt the bubbled water rising to the top of his mind like tea brewing.

"I'm dead," he said, "but alive. Did you see all that, wife? Dead but alive."

He found himself sitting in the vehicle, upright.

He sat there for ten minutes thinking about all that had happened.

"Well now," he mused. "Was that not interesting? Not to say fascinating? Not to say, almost exhilarating? I mean, sure, it knocked the stuff out of me, scared the soul out one ear and back in the other, hit my wind and tore my gut, broke the bones and shook the wits, but, but, but, wife, but, but, but, dear sweet Meg, Meggy, Megan, I wish you were here, it might tamp the tobacco tars out of your half-ass lungs and bray the mossy graveyard backbreaking meanness from your marrow. Let me see here now, wife, let's have a look, Harpwell-my-husband-the-poet."

He tinkered with the dials.

He thrummed the great hound motor.

"Shall we chance another diversion? Try another embattled picnic excursion? Let's."

And he set the car on its way.

Almost immediately, the vehicle was traveling one hundred and then one hundred fifty miles per hour.

Almost immediately, the opposing car appeared ahead.

"Death," said the poet. "Are you always here, then? Do you hang about? Is this your questing place? Let's test your mettle!"

The car raced. The other car hurtled.

He wheeled over into the other lane.

The other car followed, homing toward Destroy.

"Yes, I see, well, then, this," said the poet.

And switched a switch and jumped another throttle.

In the instant before impact, the two cars transformed themselves. Shuttering through illusory veils, they became jet craft at take-off. Shrieking, the two jets banged flame, tore air, yammered back sound-barrier explosions before the mightiest one of all—as the two bullets impacted, fused, interwove, interlaced blood, mind, and eternal blackness, and fell away into a net of strange and peaceful midnight.

I'm dead, he thought again.

And it feels fine, thanks.

He awoke to feel a smile on his face.

He was seated in the vehicle.

Twice dead, he thought, and feeling better each time. Why? isn't that odd? Curiouser and curiouser. Queer beyond queerness.

He thrummed the motor again.

What this time?

Does it locomote? he wondered. How about a big black choo-choo train out of half-primordial times?

And he was on his way, an engineer. The sky flicked over, and the motion-picture screens or whatever they were pressed in with swift illusions of pouring smoke and steaming whistle and huge wheel within wheel on grinding track, and the track ahead wound through hills, and far on up around a mountain came another train, black as a buffalo herd, pouring belches of smoke, on the same two rails, the same track, heading toward wondrous accident.

"I see," said the poet. "I do begin to see. I begin to know what this and what used for, for such as me, the poor wandering idiots of a world, confused, and sore put upon by mothers as soon as dropped from wombs, insulted with Christian guilt, and gone mad from the need of destruction, and collecting a pittance of hurt here and scar tissue there, and a larger portable wife grievance beyond, but one thing sure, we do want to die, we do want to be killed, and here's the very thing for it, in convenient quick pay! So pay it out, machine, dole it out, sweet raving device! Rape away, death! I'm your very man."

And the two locomotives met and climbed each other. Up a black ladder of explosion they wheeled and locked their drive shafts and plastered their slick Negro bellies together and rubbed boilers and beautifully banged the night in a single outflung whirl and flurry of shrapnel and flame. Then the locomotives, in a cumbrous rapine dance, seized and melted together with their violence and passion, gave a monstrous curtsy and fell off the mountain and took a thousand years to go all the way down to the rocky pits.

The poet awoke and immediately grabbed the controls. He

was humming under his breath, stunned. He was singing wild tunes. His eyes flashed. His heart beat swiftly.

"More, more, I see it now, I know what to do, more, more, please, Oh God, more, for the truth shall set me free, more!"

He hoofed three, four, five pedals.

He snapped six switches.

The vehicle was auto-jet-locomotive-glider-missile-rocket.

He ran, he steamed, he roared, he soared, he flew. Cars veered toward him. Locomotives loomed. Jets rammed. Rockets screamed.

And in one wild three-hour spree he hit two hundred cars, rammed twenty trains, blew up ten gliders, exploded forty missiles, and, far out in space, gave up his glorious soul in a final Fourth of July Death celebration as an interplanetary rocket going two hundred thousand miles an hour struck an iron meteor and went beautifully to hell.

In all, in a few short hours he figured he must have been torn apart and put back together a few times less than five hundred.

When it was all over, he sat not touching the wheel, his feet free of the pedals.

After a half hour of sitting there, he began to laugh. He threw his head back and let out great warwhoops. Then he got up, shaking his head, drunker than ever in his life, really drunk now, and he knew he would stay that way forever, and never need drink again.

I'm punished, he thought, really punished at last. Really hurt at last, and hurt enough, over and over, so I will never need hurt again, never need to be destroyed again, never have to collect another insult, or take another wound, or ask for a simple grievance. God bless the genius of man and the inventors of such machines, that enable the guilty to pay and at last be rid of the dark albatross and the awful burden. Thank you, City, thank you, old blueprinter of needful souls. Thank you. And which way out?

A door slid open.

His wife stood waiting for him.

"Well, there you are," she said. "And still drunk."

"No," he said. "Dead."

"Drunk."

"Dead," he said, "beautifully dead at last. Which means, free. I won't need you any more, dead Meg, Meggy-Megan. You're set free, also, like an awful conscience. Go haunt someone else, girl. Go destroy. I forgive you your sins on me, for I have at last forgiven myself. I am off the Christian hook. I am the dear wandering dead who, dead, can at last live. Go and do likewise, lady. Inside with you. Be punished and set free. So long, Meg. Farewell. Toodleoo."

He wandered away.

"Where do you think you're going?" she cried.

"Why, out into life and the blood of life and happy at last."

"Come back here!" she screamed.

"You can't stop the dead, for they wander the universe, happy as children in the dark field."

"Harpwell!" she brayed. "Harpwell!"

But he stepped on a river of silver metal.

And let the dear river bear him laughing until the tears glittered on his cheeks, away and away from the shriek and the bray and the scream of that woman, what was her name? no matter, back there, and gone.

And when he reached the Gate he walked out and along the canal in the fine day, heading toward the far towns.

By that time, he was singing every old tune he had known as a child of six.

It was a church.

No, not a church.

Wilder let the door swing shut.

He stood in cathedral darkness, waiting.

The roof, if roof there was, breathed up in a great suspense, flowed up beyond reach or sight.

The floor, if floor there was, was a mere firmness beneath. It, too, was black.

And then, the stars came out. It was like that first night of childhood when his father had taken him out beyond the city to a hill where the lights could not diminish the Universe. And there were a thousand, no ten thousand, no ten million billion stars filling the darkness. The stars were manifold and bright, and they did not care. Even then he had known: they do not care. If I breathe or do not breathe, live or die, the eyes that look from all around don't care. And he had seized his father's hand and gripped tight, as if he might fall up into that abyss.

Now, in this building, he was full of the old terror and the old sense of beauty and the old silent crying out after mankind. The stars filled him with pity for small men lost in so much size.

Then yet another thing happened.

Beneath his feet, space opened wide and let through yet another billion sparks of light.

He was suspended as a fly is held upon a vast telescopic lens. He walked on a water of space. He stood upon a transparent flex of great eye, and all about him, as on a night in winter, beneath foot and above head, in all directions, were nothing but stars.

So, in the end, it was a church, it was a cathedral, a multitude of farflung universal shrines, here a worshipping of Horsehead Nebula, there Orion's galaxy, and there Andromeda, like the head of God, fiercely gazed and thrust through the raw dark stuffs of night to stab his soul and pin it writhing against the backside of his flesh.

God, everywhere, fixed him with shutterless and unblinking eyes.

And he, a bacterial shard of that same Flesh, stared back and winced but the slightest.

He waited. And a planet drifted upon the void. It spun by once with a great mellow autumn face. It circled and came under him.

And he stood upon a far world of green grass and great lush trees, where the air was fresh, and a river ran by like the rivers of childhood, flashing the sun and leaping with fish.

He knew that he had traveled very far to reach this world. Behind him lay the rocket. Behind lay a century of travel, of sleeping, of waiting, and now, here was the reward.

"Mine?" he asked the simple air, the simple grass, the long simplicity of water that spelled by in the shallow sands.

And the world answered wordless: yours.

Yours without the long travel and the boredom, yours without ninety-nine years of flight from Earth, of sleeping in kept tubes, of intravenous feedings, of nightmares dreamt of Earth lost and gone, yours without torture, without pain, yours without trial and error, failure and destruction. Yours without sweat and terror. Yours without a falling down of tears. Yours. Yours.

But Wilder did not put out his hands to accept.

And the sun dimmed in the alien sky.

And the world drifted from under his feet.

And yet another world swam up and passed in a huge parade of even brighter glories.

And this world, too, spun up to take his weight. And here, if anything, the fields were richer green, the mountains capped with melting snows, far fields ripening with strange harvests, and scythes waiting on the edge of fields for him to lift and sweep and cut the grain and live out his life any way that he might.

Yours. The merest touch of weather upon the hairs within his ear said this. Yours.

And Wilder, without shaking his head, moved back. He did not say no. He thought his rejection.

And the grass died in the fields.

The mountains crumbled.

The river shallows ran to dust.

And the world sprang away.

And Wilder stood again in space where God had stood before creating a world out of Chaos.

And at last he spoke and said to himself:

"It would be easy. O Lord, yes, I'd like that. No work, nothing, just accept. But . . . You can't give me what I want."

He looked at the stars.

"Nothing can be given, ever."

The stars were growing dim.

"It's really very simple. I must borrow, I must earn. I must take."

The stars quivered and died.

"Much obliged and thank you, no."

The stars were all gone.

He turned and, without looking back, walked upon darkness. He hit the door with his palm. He strode out into the City.

He refused to hear if the machine universe behind him

cried out in a great chorus, all cries and wounds, like a woman scorned. The crockery in a vast robot kitchen fell. By the time it hit the floor, he was gone.

It was a Museum of Weapons.

The hunter walked among the cases.

He opened a case and hefted a weapon constructed like a spider's antennae.

It hummed, and a flight of metal bees sizzled out the rifle bore, flew away, and stung a target-mannequin some fifty yards away, then fell lifeless, clattering to the floor.

The hunter nodded with admiration, and put the rifle back in the case.

He prowled on, curious as a child, testing yet other weapons here and there which dissolved glass or caused metal to run in bright yellow pools of molten lava.

"Excellent!" "Fine!" "Absolutely great!"

His cry rang out again and again as he slammed cases open and shut, and finally chose the gun.

It was a gun that, without fuss or fury, did away with matter. You pressed the button, there was a brief discharge of blue light, and the target simply vanished. No blood. No bright lava. No trace.

"All right," he announced, leaving the Place of Guns, "we have the weapon. How about the Game, the Grandest Beast ever in the Long Hunt?"

He leapt onto the moving sidewalk.

An hour later he had passed a thousand buildings and scanned a thousand open parks without itching his finger.

He moved uneasily from treadway to treadway, shifting speeds now in this direction, now in that.

Until at last he saw a river of metal that sped underground.

Instinctively, he jumped toward that.

The metal stream carried him down into the secret gut of the City.

Here all was warm blood darkness. Here strange pumps moved the pulse of the City. Here were distilled the sweats that lubricated the roadways and lifted the elevators and swarmed the offices and stores with motion.

The hunter half crouched on the roadway. His eyes squinted.

Perspiration gathered in his palms. His trigger finger greased the metal gun, sliding.

"Yes," he whispered. "By God, now. This is it. The City itself . . . the Great Beast. Why didn't I think of that? The Animal City, the terrible prey. It has men for breakfast, lunch, and dinner. It kills them with machines. It munches their bones like breadsticks. It spits them out like toothpicks. It lives long after they die. The City, by God, the City. Well now . . ."

He glided through dark grottoes of television eyes which showed him remote parkways and high towers.

Deeper within the belly of the underground world he sank as the river lowered itself. He passed a school of computers that chattered in maniac chorus. He shuddered as a cloud of paper confetti from one titan machine, holes punched out to perhaps record his passing, fell upon him in a whispered snow.

He raised his gun. He fired.

The machine disappeared.

He fired again. A skeleton strutwork under yet another machine vanished.

The City screamed.

At first very low and then very high, then, rising, falling, like a siren. Lights flashed. Bells began to ricochet alarums. The metal river shuddered under his feet, slowed. He fired at television screens which glared all white upon him. They blinked out and did not exist.

The City screamed higher until he raved against it, himself, and the marrow of his bones shook out an insanity of black dust.

He did not see, until it was too late, that the road on which he sped fell into the gnashing maw of a machine that was used for some purpose long forgotten centuries before.

He thought that by pressing the trigger he would make the terrible mouth disappear. It did indeed vanish. But as the roadway sped on and he whirled and fell as it picked up speed, he realized at last that his weapon did not truly destroy, it merely made invisible what was there and what still remained though unseen.

He gave a terrible cry to match the cry of the City. He flung out the gun in a last blow. The gun went into cogs and wheels and teeth and was twisted down.

The last thing he saw was a deep elevator shaft that fell away for perhaps a mile into the earth.

He knew that it might take him two minutes to hit the bottom. He shrieked.

The worst thing was, he would be conscious . . . all the way down . . .

The rivers shook. The silver rivers trembled. The pathways, shocked, convulsed the metal shores through which they sped.

Wilder, traveling, was almost knocked flat by the concussion.

What had caused the concussion, he could not see. Perhaps, far off, there was a cry, a murmur of dreadful sound, which swiftly faded.

Wilder moved on. The silver track threaded on. But the City seemed poised, agape. The City seemed tensed. Its huge and various muscles were cramped, alert.

Feeling this, Wilder began to walk as well as be moved by the swift path.

"Thank God. There's the Gate. The sooner I'm out of this place the happier I'll—"

The Gate was indeed there, not a hundred yards away. But, on the instant, as if hearing his declaration, the river stopped. It shivered. Then it started to move back, taking him where he did not wish to go.

Incredulous, Wilder spun about, and, in spinning, fell. He clutched at the stuffs of the rushing sidewalk.

His face, pressed to the vibrant grillework of the river-rushing pavement, heard the machineries mesh and mill beneath, humming and agroan, forever sluicing, forever feverish for journeys and mindless excursions. Beneath the calm metal, embattlements of hornets stung and buzzed, lost bees bumbled and subsided. Collapsed, he saw the Gate lost away behind. Burdened, he remembered at last the extra weight upon his back, the jet-power equipment which might give him wings.

He jammed his hand to the switch on his belt. And in the instant before the sidewalk might have pulsed him off among sheds and museum walls, he was airborne.

Flying, he hovered, then swam the air back to hang above a casual Parkhill gazing up, all covered with grease and smiling from a dirty face. Beyond Parkhill, at the Gate, stood the frightened maid. Beyond even further, near the yacht at the landing, stood Aaronson, back turned to the City, nervous to be moving on.

"Where are the others?" cried Wilder.

"Oh, they won't be back," said Parkhill, easily. "It figures, doesn't it? I mean, it's quite a place."

"Place!" said Wilder, hovered now up, now down, turning slowly, apprehensive. "We've got to get them out! It's not safe."

"It's safe if you like it. I like it," said Parkhill.

And all the while there was a gathering of earthquake in the ground and in the air, which Parkhill chose to ignore.

"You're leaving, of course," he said, as if nothing were wrong. "I knew you would. Why?"

"Why?" Wilder wheeled like a dragonfly before a trembling of storm wind. Buffeted up, buffeted down, he flung his words at Parkhill, who didn't bother to duck but smiled up and accepted. "Good God, Sam, the place is Hell. The Martians had enough sense to get out. They saw they had overbuilt themselves. The damn City does everything, which is too much! Sam!"

But at that instant, they both looked round and up. For the sky was shelling over. Great lids were vising in the ceiling. Like an immense flower, the tops of buildings were petalling out to cover themselves. Windows were shutting down. Doors were slamming. A sound of fired cannons echoed through the streets.

The Gate was thundering shut.

The twin jaws of the Gate, shuddering, were in motion.

Wilder cried out, spun round, and dived.

He heard the maid below him. He saw her reach up. Then, swooping, he gathered her in. He kicked the air. The jet lifted them both.

Like a bullet to a target he rammed for the Gate. But an instant before, burdened, he reached it, the Gates banged together. He was barely able to veer course and soar upward along the raw metal as the entire City shook with the roar of the steel.

Parkhill shouted below. And Wilder was flying up, up along the wall, looking this way and that.

Everywhere, the sky was closing in. The petals were coming down, coming down. There was only a last small patch of stone sky to his right. He blasted for that. And kicking, made it through, flying, as the final flange of steel clipped into place, and the City was closed to itself.

He hung for a moment, suspended, and then flew down along the outer wall to the dock where Aaronson stood by the yacht staring at the huge shut Gates.

"Parkhill," whispered Wilder, looking at the City, the walls, the Gates. "You fool. You damned fool."

"Fools, all of them," said Aaronson, and turned away. "Fools. Fools."

They waited a moment longer and listened to the City, humming, alive, kept to itself, its great mouth filled with a few bits of warmth, a few lost people somewhere hid away in there. The Gates would stay shut now, forever. The City had what it needed to go on a long while.

Wilder looked back at the place, as the yacht took them back out of the mountain and away up the canal.

They passed the poet a mile further on, walking along the rim of the canal. He waved them on. "No. No, thanks. I feel like walking. It's a fine day. Good-bye. Go on."

The towns lay ahead. Small towns. Small enough to be run by men instead of running them. He heard the brass music. He saw the neon lights at dusk. He made out the junkyards in the fresh night under the stars.

Beyond the towns stood the silver rockets, tall, waiting to be fired off and away toward the wilderness of stars.

"Real," whispered the rockets, "real stuff. Real travel. Real time. Real space. No gifts. Nothing free. Just a lot of good hard work."

The yacht touched into its home dock.

"Rockets, by God," he murmured. "Wait till I get my hands on you."

He ran away in the night, to do just that.

I Sing the Body Electric!

GRANDMA!

I remember her birth.

Wait, you say, *no* man remembers his own grandma's birth.

But, yes, *we* remember the day that she was born.

For we, her grandchildren, slapped her to life. Timothy, Agatha, and I, Tom, raised up our hands and brought them down in a huge crack! We shook together the bits and pieces, parts and samples, textures and tastes, humors and distillations that would move her compass needle north to cool us, south to warm and comfort us, east and west to travel round the endless world, glide her eyes to know us, mouth to sing us asleep by night, hands to touch us awake at dawn.

Grandma, O dear and wondrous electric dream . . .

When storm lightnings rove the sky making circuitries amidst the clouds, her name flashes on my inner lid. Sometimes still I hear her ticking, humming above our beds in the gentle dark. She passes like a clock-ghost in the long halls of memory, like a hive of intellectual bees swarming after the Spirit of Summers Lost. Sometimes still I feel the smile I learned from her, printed on my cheek at three in the deep morn . . .

All right, all right! you cry, what was it like the day your damned and wondrous-dreadful-loving Grandma was born?

It was the week the world ended . . .

Our mother was dead.

One late afternoon a black car left Father and the three of us stranded on our own front drive staring at the grass, thinking:

That's not our grass. There are the croquet mallets, balls, hoops, yes, just as they fell and lay three days ago when Dad stumbled out on the lawn, weeping with the news. There are the roller skates that belonged to a boy, me, who will never be that young again. And yes, there the tire-swing on the old oak, but Agatha afraid to swing. It would surely break. It would fall.

And the house? Oh, God . . .

We peered through the front door, afraid of the echoes we might find confused in the halls; the sort of clamor that happens when all the furniture is taken out and there is nothing to soften the river of talk that flows in any house at all hours. And now the soft, the warm, the main piece of lovely furniture was gone forever.

The door drifted wide.

Silence came out. Somewhere a cellar door stood wide and a raw wind blew damp earth from under the house.

But, I thought, we don't *have* a cellar!

"Well," said Father.

We did not move.

Aunt Clara drove up the path in her big canary-colored limousine.

We jumped through the door. We ran to our rooms.

We heard them shout and then speak and then shout and then speak: Let the children live with me! Aunt Clara said. They'd rather kill themselves! Father said.

A door slammed. Aunt Clara was gone.

We almost danced. Then we remembered what had happened and went downstairs.

Father sat alone talking to himself or to a remnant ghost of Mother left from the days before her illness, but jarred loose now by the slamming of the door. He murmured to his hands, his empty palms:

"The children need someone. I love them but, let's face it, I must work to feed us all. You love them, Ann, but you're gone. And Clara? Impossible. She loves but smothers. And as for maids, nurses—?"

Here Father sighed and we sighed with him, remembering.

The luck we had had with maids or live-in teachers or sitters was beyond intolerable. Hardly a one who wasn't a crosscut saw grabbing against the grain. Handaxes and hurricanes best described them. Or, conversely, they were all fallen trifle, damp soufflé. We children were unseen furniture to be sat upon or dusted or sent for reupholstering come spring and fall, with a yearly cleansing at the beach.

"What we need," said Father, "is a . . ."

We all leaned to his whisper.

". . . grandmother."

"But," said Timothy, with the logic of nine years, "all our grandmothers are dead."

"Yes in one way, no in another."

What a fine mysterious thing for Dad to say.

"Here," he said at last.

He handed us a multifold, multicolored pamphlet. We had seen it in his hands, off and on, for many weeks, and very often during the last few days. Now, with one blink of our eyes, as we passed the paper from hand to hand, we knew why Aunt Clara, insulted, outraged, had stormed from the house.

Timothy was the first to read aloud from what he saw on the first page:

"I Sing the Body Electric!"

He glanced up at Father, squinting. "What the heck does that mean?"

"Read on."

Agatha and I glanced guiltily about the room, afraid Mother might suddenly come in to find us with this blasphemy, but then nodded to Timothy, who read:

"'Fanto—'"

"Fantoccini," Father prompted.

"'Fantoccini Ltd. *We Shadow Forth* . . . the answer to all your most grievous problems. One Model Only, upon which a thousand times a thousand variations can be added, subtracted, subdivided, indivisible, with Liberty and Justice for all.'"

"Where does it say *that*?" we all cried.

"It doesn't." Timothy smiled for the first time in days. "I just had to put that in. Wait." He read on: "'for you who have worried over inattentive sitters, nurses who cannot be trusted with marked liquor bottles, and well-meaning Uncles and Aunts—'"

"Well-meaning, *but*!" said Agatha, and I gave an echo.

"'—we have perfected the first humanoid-genre mini-circuited, rechargeable AC-DC Mark V Electrical Grandmother . . .'"

"Grandmother!?"

The paper slipped away to the floor. "Dad . . . ?"

"Don't look at me that way," said Father. "I'm half-mad with grief, and half-mad thinking of tomorrow and the day after that. Someone pick up the paper. Finish it."

"I will," I said, and did:

"'The Toy that is more than a Toy, the Fantoccini Electrical Grandmother is built with loving precision to give the incredible precision of love to your children. The child at ease with the realities of the world and the even greater realities of the imagination, is her aim.

"'She is computerized to tutor in twelve languages simultaneously, capable of switching tongues in a thousandth of a second without pause, and has a complete knowledge of the religious, artistic, and sociopolitical histories of the world seeded in her master hive—'"

"How great!" said Timothy. "It makes it sound as if we were to keep bees! *Educated* bees!"

"Shut up!" said Agatha.

"'Above all,'" I read, "'this human being, for human she seems, this embodiment in electro-intelligent facsimile of the humanities, will listen, know, tell, react and love your children insofar as such great Objects, such fantastic Toys, can be said to Love, or can be imagined to Care. This Miraculous Companion, excited to the challenge of large world and small, inner Sea or Outer Universe, will transmit by touch and tell, said Miracles to your Needy.'"

"Our Needy," murmured Agatha.

Why, we all thought, sadly, that's us, oh, yes, that's *us.*

I finished:

"'We do not sell our Creation to able-bodied families where parents are available to raise, affect, shape, change, love their own children. Nothing can replace the parent in the home. However there are families where death or ill health or disablement undermines the welfare of the children. Orphanages seem not the answer. Nurses tend to be selfish, neglectful, or suffering from dire nervous afflictions.

"'With the utmost humility then, and recognizing the need to rebuild, rethink, and regrow our conceptualizations from month to month, year to year, we offer the nearest thing to the Ideal Teacher–Friend–Companion–Blood Relation. A trial period can be arranged for—'"

"Stop," said Father. "Don't go on. Even *I* can't stand it."

"Why?" said Timothy. "I was just getting interested."

I folded the pamphlet up. "Do they *really* have these things?"

"Let's not talk any more about it," said Father, his hand over his eyes. "It was a mad thought—"

"Not so mad," I said, glancing at Tim. "I mean, heck, even if they tried, whatever they built, couldn't be worse than Aunt Clara, huh?"

And then we all roared. We hadn't laughed in months. And now my simple words made everyone hoot and howl and explode. I opened my mouth and yelled happily, too.

When we stopped laughing, we looked at the pamphlet and I said, "Well?"

"I—" Agatha scowled, not ready.

"We do need something, bad, right now," said Timothy.

"I have an open mind," I said, in my best pontifical style.

"There's only one thing," said Agatha. "We can try it. Sure.

"But—tell me this—when do we cut out all this talk and when does our *real* mother come home to stay?"

There was a single gasp from the family as if, with one shot, she had struck us all in the heart.

I don't think any of us stopped crying the rest of that night.

It was a clear bright day. The helicopter tossed us lightly up and over and down through the skyscrapers and let us out, almost for a trot and caper, on top of the building where the large letters could be read from the sky:

FANTOCCINI.

"What are *Fantoccini*?" said Agatha.

"It's an Italian word for shadow puppets, I think, or dream people," said Father.

"But *shadow forth*, what does that mean?"

"WE TRY TO GUESS YOUR DREAM," I said.

"Bravo," said Father. "A-Plus."

I beamed.

The helicopter flapped a lot of loud shadows over us and went away.

We sank down in an elevator as our stomachs sank up. We stepped out onto a moving carpet that streamed away on a blue river of wool toward a desk over which various signs hung:

THE CLOCK SHOP
Fantoccini Our Specialty.
Rabbits on walls, no problem.

"Rabbits on walls?"

I held up my fingers in profile as if I held them before a candle flame, and wiggled the "ears."

"Here's a rabbit, here's a wolf, here's a crocodile."

"Of course," said Agatha.

And we were at the desk. Quiet music drifted about us. Somewhere behind the walls, there was a waterfall of machinery flowing softly. As we arrived at the desk, the lighting changed to make us look warmer, happier, though we were still cold.

All about us in niches and cases, and hung from ceilings on wires and strings were puppets and marionettes, and Balinese kite-bamboo-translucent dolls which, held to the moonlight, might acrobat your most secret nightmares or dreams. In passing, the breeze set up by our bodies stirred the various hung souls on their gibbets. It was like an immense lynching on a holiday at some English crossroads four hundred years before.

You see? I know my history.

Agatha blinked about with disbelief and then some touch of awe and finally disgust.

"Well, if that's what they are, let's go."

"Tush," said Father.

"Well," she protested, "you gave me one of those dumb things with strings two years ago and the strings were in a zillion knots by dinnertime. I threw the whole thing out the window."

"Patience," said Father.

"We shall see what we can do to eliminate the strings."

The man behind the desk had spoken.

We all turned to give him our regard.

Rather like a funeral-parlor man, he had the cleverness not to smile. Children are put off by older people who smile too much. They smell a catch, right off.

Unsmiling, but not gloomy or pontifical, the man said, "Guido Fantoccini, at your service. Here's how we do it, Miss Agatha Simmons, aged eleven."

Now there was a really fine touch.

He knew that Agatha was only ten. Add a year to that, and you're halfway home. Agatha grew an inch. The man went on:

"There."

And he placed a golden key in Agatha's hand.

"To wind them up instead of strings?"

"To wind them up." The man nodded.

"Pshaw!" said Agatha.

Which was her polite form of "rabbit pellets."

"God's truth. Here is the key to your Do-it-Yourself, Select Only the Best, Electrical Grandmother. Every morning you wind her up. Every night you let her run down. You're in charge. You are guardian of the Key."

He pressed the object in her palm where she looked at it suspiciously.

I watched him. He gave me a side wink which said, well, no . . . but aren't keys fun?

I winked back before she lifted her head.

"Where does this fit?"

"You'll see when the time comes. In the middle of her stomach, perhaps, or up her left nostril or in her right ear."

That was good for a smile as the man arose.

"This way, please. Step light. Onto the moving stream. Walk on the water, please. Yes. There."

He helped to float us. We stepped from rug that was forever frozen onto rug that whispered by.

It was a most agreeable river which floated us along on a green spread of carpeting that rolled forever through halls and into wonderfully secret dim caverns where voices echoed back our own breathing or sang like Oracles to our questions.

"Listen," said the salesman, "the voices of all kinds of women. Weigh and find just the right one . . . !"

And listen we did, to all the high, low, soft, loud, in-between, half-scolding, half-affectionate voices saved over from times before we were born.

And behind us, Agatha tread backward, always fighting the river, never catching up, never with us, holding off.

"Speak," said the salesman. "Yell."

And speak and yell we did.

"Hello. You there! This is Timothy, hi!"

"What shall I say!" I shouted. "Help!"

Agatha walked backward, mouth tight.

Father took her hand. She cried out.

"Let go! No, no! I won't have my voice used! I won't!"

"Excellent." The salesman touched three dials on a small machine he held in his hand.

On the side of the small machine we saw three oscillograph patterns mix, blend, and repeat our cries.

The salesman touched another dial and we heard our voices fly off amidst the Delphic caves to hang upside down, to cluster, to beat words all about, to shriek, and the salesman itched another knob to add, perhaps, a touch of this or a pinch of that, a breath of mother's voice, all unbeknownst, or a splice of father's outrage at the morning's paper or his peaceable one-drink voice at dusk. Whatever it was the salesman did, whispers danced all about us like frantic vinegar gnats, fizzed by lightning, settling round until at last a final switch was pushed and a voice spoke free of a far electronic deep:

"Nefertiti," it said.

Timothy froze. I froze. Agatha stopped treading water.

"Nefertiti?" asked Tim.

"What does that mean?" demanded Agatha.

"I know."

The salesman nodded me to tell.

"Nefertiti," I whispered, "is Egyptian for The Beautiful One Is Here."

"The Beautiful One Is Here," repeated Timothy.

"Nefer," said Agatha, "titi."

And we all turned to stare into that soft twilight, that deep far place from which the good warm soft voice came.

And she was indeed there.

And, by her voice, she was beautiful . . .

That was it.

That was, at least, the most of it.

The voice seemed more important than all the rest.

Not that we didn't argue about weights and measures:

She should not be bony to cut us to the quick, nor so fat we might sink out of sight when she squeezed us.

Her hand pressed to ours, or brushing our brow in the

middle of sick-fever nights, must not be marble-cold, dreadful, or oven-hot, oppressive, but somewhere between. The nice temperature of a baby-chick held in the hand after a long night's sleep and just plucked from beneath a contemplative hen; that, that was it.

Oh, we were great ones for detail. We fought and argued and cried, and Timothy won on the color of her eyes, for reasons to be known later.

Grandmother's hair? Agatha, with girl's ideas, though reluctantly given, she was in charge of that. We let her choose from a thousand harp strands hung in filamentary tapestries like varieties of rain we ran amongst. Agatha did not run happily, but seeing we boys would mess things in tangles, she told us to move aside.

And so the bargain shopping through the dime-store inventories and the Tiffany extensions of the Ben Franklin Electric Storm Machine and Fantoccini Pantomime Company was done.

And the always flowing river ran its tide to an end and deposited us all on a far shore in the late day . . .

It was very clever of the Fantoccini people, after that.

How?

They made us wait.

They knew we were not won over. Not completely, no, nor half completely.

Especially Agatha, who turned her face to her wall and saw sorrow there and put her hand out again and again to touch it. We found her fingernail marks on the wallpaper each morning, in strange little silhouettes, half beauty, half nightmare. Some could be erased with a breath, like ice flowers on a winter pane. Some could not be rubbed out with a washcloth, no matter how hard you tried.

And meanwhile, they made us wait.

So we fretted out June.

So we sat around July.

So we groused through August and then on August 29, "I have this feeling," said Timothy, and we all went out after breakfast to sit on the lawn.

Perhaps we had smelled something on Father's conversation

the previous night, or caught some special furtive glance at the sky or the freeway trapped briefly and then lost in his gaze. Or perhaps it was merely the way the wind blew the ghost curtains out over our beds, making pale messages all night.

For suddenly there we were in the middle of the grass, Timothy and I, with Agatha, pretending no curiosity, up on the porch, hidden behind the potted geraniums.

We gave her no notice. We knew that if we acknowledged her presence, she would flee, so we sat and watched the sky where nothing moved but birds and highflown jets, and watched the freeway where a thousand cars might suddenly deliver forth our Special Gift . . . but . . . nothing.

At noon we chewed grass and lay low . . .

At one o'clock, Timothy blinked his eyes.

And then, with incredible precision, it happened.

It was as if the Fantoccini people knew our surface tension.

All children are water-striders. We skate along the top skin of the pond each day, always threatening to break through, sink, vanish beyond recall, into ourselves.

Well, as if knowing our long wait must absolutely end within one minute! this *second*! no more, God, forget it!

At that instant, I repeat, the clouds above our house opened wide and let forth a helicopter like Apollo driving his chariot across mythological skies.

And the Apollo machine swam down on its own summer breeze, wafting hot winds to cool, reweaving our hair, smartening our eyebrows, applauding our pant legs against our shins, making a flag of Agatha's hair on the porch and thus settled like a vast frenzied hibiscus on our lawn, the helicopter slid wide a bottom drawer and deposited upon the grass a parcel of largish size, no sooner having laid same than the vehicle, with not so much as a god bless or farewell, sank straight up, disturbed the calm air with a mad ten thousand flourishes and then, like a skyborne dervish, tilted and fell off to be mad some other place.

Timothy and I stood riven for a long moment looking at the packing case, and then we saw the crowbar taped to the top of the raw pine lid and seized it and began to pry and creak and squeal the boards off, one by one, and as we did this I saw Agatha sneak up to watch and I thought, thank you,

God, thank you that Agatha never saw a coffin, when Mother went away, no box, no cemetery, no earth, just words in a big church, no box, no box like *this* . . . !

The last pine plank fell away.

Timothy and I gasped. Agatha, between us now, gasped, too.

For inside the immense raw pine package was the most beautiful idea anyone ever dreamt and built.

Inside was the perfect gift for any child from seven to seventy-seven.

We stopped up our breaths. We let them out in cries of delight and adoration.

Inside the opened box was . . .

A mummy.

Or, first anyway, a mummy case, a sarcophagus!

"Oh, no!" Happy tears filled Timothy's eyes.

"It can't be!" said Agatha.

"It is, it is!"

"Our very own?"

"Ours!"

"It must be a mistake!"

"Sure, they'll want it back!"

"They can't *have* it!"

"Lord, Lord, is that real gold!? Real hieroglyphs! Run your fingers over them!"

"Let *me*!"

"Just like in the museums! Museums!"

We all gabbled at once. I think some tears fell from my own eyes to rain upon the case.

"Oh, they'll make the colors run!"

Agatha wiped the rain away.

And the golden mask face of the woman carved on the sarcophagus lid looked back at us with just the merest smile which hinted at our own joy, which accepted the overwhelming upsurge of a love we thought had drowned forever but now surfaced into the sun.

Not only did she have a sun-metal face stamped and beaten out of purest gold, with delicate nostrils and a mouth that was both firm and gentle, but her eyes, fixed into their sockets, were cerulean or amethystine or lapis lazuli, or all three, minted and fused together, and her body was covered over with lions and eyes and ravens, and her hands were crossed upon her carved bosom and in one gold mitten she clenched a thonged whip for obedience, and in the other a fantastic ranuncula, which makes for obedience out of love, so the whip lies unused . . .

And as our eyes ran down her hieroglyphs it came to all three of us at the same instant:

"Why, those signs!" "Yes, the hen tracks!" "The birds, the snakes!"

They didn't speak tales of the Past.

They were hieroglyphs of the Future.

This was the first queen mummy delivered forth in all time whose papyrus inkings etched out the next month, the next season, the next year, the next *lifetime*!

She did not mourn for time spent.

No. She celebrated the bright coinage yet to come, banked, waiting, ready to be drawn upon and used.

We sank to our knees to worship that possible time.

First one hand, then another, probed out to niggle, twitch, touch, itch over the signs.

"There's me, yes, look! Me, in sixth grade!" said Agatha, now in the fifth. "See the girl with my-colored hair and wearing my gingerbread suit?"

"There's me in the twelfth year of high school!" said Timothy, so very young now but building taller stilts every week and stalking around the yard.

"There's me," I said, quietly, warm, "in college. The guy wearing glasses who runs a little to fat. Sure. Heck." I snorted. "That's me."

The sarcophagus spelled winters ahead, springs to squander, autumns to spend with all the golden and rusty and copper leaves like coins, and over all, her bright sun symbol, daughter-of-Ra eternal face, forever above our horizon, forever an illumination to tilt our shadows to better ends.

"Hey!" we all said at once, having read and reread our Fortune-Told scribblings, seeing our lifelines and lovelines, inadmissible, serpentined over, around, and down. "Hey!"

And in one séance table-lifting feat, not telling each other what to do, just doing it, we pried up the bright sarcophagus lid, which had no hinges but lifted out like cup from cup, and put the lid aside.

And within the sarcophagus, of course, was the true mummy!

And she was like the image carved on the lid, but more so, more beautiful, more touching because human shaped, and shrouded all in new fresh bandages of linen, round and round, instead of old and dusty cerements.

And upon her hidden face was an identical golden mask, younger than the first, but somehow, strangely wiser than the first.

And the linens that tethered her limbs had symbols on them of three sorts, one a girl of ten, one a boy of nine, one a boy of thirteen.

A series of bandages for each of us!

We gave each other a startled glance and a sudden bark of laughter.

Nobody said the bad joke, but all thought:

She's all wrapped up in us!

And we didn't care. We loved the joke. We loved whoever had thought to make us part of the ceremony we now went through as each of us seized and began to unwind each of his or her particular serpentines of delicious stuffs!

The lawn was soon a mountain of linen.

The woman beneath the covering lay there, waiting.

"Oh, no," cried Agatha. "She's dead, too!"

She ran. I stopped her. "Idiot. She's not dead *or* alive. Where's your key?"

"Key?"

"Dummy," said Tim, "the key the man gave you to wind her up!"

Her hand had already spidered along her blouse to where the symbol of some possible new religion hung. She had strung it there, against her own skeptic's muttering, and now she held it in her sweaty palm.

"Go on," said Timothy. "Put it in!"

"But *where*?"

"Oh for God's sake! As the man said, in her right armpit or left ear. Gimme!"

And he grabbed the key and impulsively moaning with

impatience and not able to find the proper insertion slot, prowled over the prone figure's head and bosom and at last, on pure instinct, perhaps for a lark, perhaps just giving up the whole damned mess, thrust the key through a final shroud of bandage at the navel.

On the instant: *spunnng*!

The Electrical Grandmother's eyes flicked wide!

Something began to hum and whir. It was as if Tim had stirred up a hive of hornets with an ornery stick.

"Oh," gasped Agatha, seeing he had taken the game away, "let *me*!"

She wrenched the key.

Grandma's nostrils *flared*! She might snort up steam, snuff out fire!

"Me!" I cried, and grabbed the key and gave it a huge . . . *twist*!

The beautiful woman's mouth popped wide.

"Me!"

"Me!"

"Me!"

Grandma suddenly sat up.

We leapt back.

We knew we had, in a way, slapped her alive.

She was born, she was *born*!

Her head swiveled all about. She gaped. She mouthed. And the first thing she said was:

Laughter.

Where one moment we had backed off, now the mad sound drew us near to peer as in a pit where crazy folk are kept with snakes to make them well.

It was a good laugh, full and rich and hearty, and it did not mock, it accepted. It said the world was a wild place, strange, unbelievable, absurd if you wished, but all in all, quite a place. She would not dream to find another. She would not ask to go back to sleep.

She was awake now. We had awakened her. With a glad shout, she would go with it all.

And go she did, out of her sarcophagus, out of her winding sheet, stepping forth, brushing off, looking around as for a mirror. She found it.

The reflections in our eyes.

She was more pleased than disconcerted with what she found there. Her laughter faded to an amused smile.

For Agatha, at the instant of birth, had leapt to hide on the porch.

The Electrical Person pretended not to notice.

She turned slowly on the green lawn near the shady street, gazing all about with new eyes, her nostrils moving as if she breathed the actual air and this the first morn of the lovely Garden and she with no intention of spoiling the game by biting the apple . . .

Her gaze fixed upon my brother.

"You must be—?"

"Timothy. Tim," he offered.

"And you must be—?"

"Tom," I said.

How clever again of the Fantoccini Company. *They* knew. *She* knew. But they had taught her to pretend not to know. That way we could feel great, we were the teachers, telling her what she already knew! How sly, how wise.

"And isn't there another boy?" said the woman.

"Girl!" a disgusted voice cried from somewhere on the porch.

"Whose name is Alicia—?"

"Agatha!" The far voice, started in humiliation, ended in proper anger.

"Algernon, of course."

"Agatha!" Our sister popped up, popped back to hide a flushed face.

"Agatha." The woman touched the word with proper affection. "Well, Agatha, Timothy, Thomas, let me *look* at you."

"No," said I, said Tim, "Let us look at *you*. Hey . . ."

Our voices slid back in our throats.

We drew near her.

We walked in great slow circles round about, skirting the edges of her territory. And her territory extended as far as we could hear the hum of the warm summer hive. For that is exactly what she sounded like. That was her characteristic tune. She made a sound like a season all to herself, a morning early in June when the world wakes to find everything absolutely perfect, fine, delicately attuned, all in balance, nothing disproportioned. Even before you opened your eyes you knew it would be one of those days. Tell the sky what color it must be, and it was indeed. Tell the sun how to crochet its way, pick and choose among leaves to lay out carpetings of bright and dark on the fresh lawn, and pick and lay it did. The bees have been up earliest of all, they have already come and gone, and come and gone again to the meadow fields and returned all golden fuzz on the air, all pollen-decorated, epaulettes at the full, nectar-dripping. Don't you hear them pass? hover? dance their language? telling where all the sweet gums are, the syrups that make bears frolic and lumber in bulked ecstasies, that make boys squirm with unpronounced juices, that make girls leap out of beds to catch from the corners of their eyes their dolphin selves naked aflash on the warm air poised forever in one eternal glass wave.

So it seemed with our electrical friend here on the new lawn in the middle of a special day.

And she a stuff to which we were drawn, lured, spelled, doing our dance, remembering what could not be remembered, needful, aware of her attentions.

Timothy and I, Tom, that is.

Agatha remained on the porch.

But her head flowered above the rail, her eyes followed all that was done and said.

And what was said and done was Tim at last exhaling:

"Hey . . . your *eyes* . . ."

Her eyes. Her splendid eyes.

Even more splendid than the lapis lazuli on the sarcophagus lid and on the mask that had covered her bandaged face. These most beautiful eyes in the world looked out upon us calmly, shining.

"Your eyes," gasped Tim, "are the *exact* same color, are like—"

"Like what?"

"My favorite aggies . . ."

"What could be better than that?" she said.

And the answer was, nothing.

Her eyes slid along on the bright air to brush my ears, my nose, my chin. "And you, Master Tom?"

"Me?"

"How shall we be friends? We must, you know, if we're going to knock elbows about the house the next year . . ."

"I . . ." I said, and stopped.

"You," said Grandma, "are a dog mad to bark but with taffy in his teeth. Have you ever given a dog taffy? It's so sad and funny, both. You laugh but hate yourself for laughing. You cry and run to help, and laugh again when his first new bark comes out."

I barked a small laugh remembering a dog, a day, and some taffy.

Grandma turned, and there was my old kite strewn on the lawn. She recognized its problem.

"The string's broken. No. The ball of string's *lost*. You can't fly a kite that way. Here."

She bent. We didn't know what might happen. How could a robot grandma fly a kite for us? She raised up, the kite in her hands.

"Fly," she said, as to a bird.

And the kite flew.

That is to say, with a grand flourish, she let it up on the wind.

And she and the kite were one.

For from the tip of her index finger there sprang a thin bright strand of spider web, all half-invisible gossamer fishline which, fixed to the kite, let it soar a hundred, no, three hundred, no, a thousand feet high on the summer swoons.

Timothy shouted. Agatha, torn between coming and going, let out a cry from the porch. And I, in all my maturity of thirteen years, though I tried not to look impressed, grew taller, taller, and felt a similar cry burst out my lungs, and burst it did. I gabbled and yelled lots of things about how I wished *I* had a finger from which, on a bobbin, I might thread the sky, the clouds, a wild kite all in one.

"If you think *that* is high," said the Electric Creature, "watch *this*!"

With a hiss, a whistle, a hum, the fishline sung out. The kite sank up another thousand feet. And again another thousand, until at last it was a speck of red confetti dancing on the very winds that took jets around the world or changed the weather in the next existence . . .

"It can't be!" I cried.

"It *is*." She calmly watched her finger unravel its massive stuffs. "I make it as I need it. Liquid inside, like a spider. Hardens when it hits the air, instant thread . . ."

And when the kite was no more than a specule, a vanishing mote on the peripheral vision of the gods, to quote from older wisemen, why then Grandma, without turning, without looking, without letting her gaze offend by touching, said:

"And, Abigail—?"

"Agatha!" was the sharp response.

O wise woman, to overcome with swift small angers.

"Agatha," said Grandma, not too tenderly, not too lightly, somewhere poised between, "and how shall *we* make do?"

She broke the thread and wrapped it about my fist three times so I was tethered to heaven by the longest, I repeat, longest kite string in the entire history of the world! Wait till I show my friends! I thought. Green! Sour apple green is the color they'll turn!

"Agatha?"

"No way!" said Agatha.

"No way," said an echo.

"There must be some—"

"We'll never be friends!" said Agatha.

"Never be friends," said the echo.

Timothy and I jerked. Where was the echo coming from? Even Agatha, surprised, showed her eyebrows above the porch rail.

Then we looked and saw.

Grandma was cupping her hands like a seashell and from within that shell the echo sounded.

"Never . . . friends . . ."

And again faintly dying "Friends . . ."

We all bent to hear.

That is we two boys bent to hear.

"No!" cried Agatha.

And ran in the house and slammed the doors.

"Friends," said the echo from the seashell hands. "No."

And far away, on the shore of some inner sea, we heard a small door shut.

And that was the first day.

And there was a second day, of course, and a third and a fourth, with Grandma wheeling in a great circle, and we her planets turning about the central light, with Agatha slowly, slowly coming in to join, to walk if not run with us, to listen if not hear, to watch if not see, to itch if not touch.

But at least by the end of the first ten days, Agatha no longer fled, but stood in nearby doors, or sat in distant chairs under trees, or if we went out for hikes, followed ten paces behind.

And Grandma? She merely waited. She never tried to urge or force. She went about her cooking and baking apricot pies and left foods carelessly here and there about the house on mousetrap plates for wiggle-nosed girls to sniff and snitch. An hour later, the plates were empty, the buns or cakes gone and without thank you's, there was Agatha sliding down the banister, a mustache of crumbs on her lip.

As for Tim and me, we were always being called up hills by our Electric Grandma, and reaching the top were called down the other side.

And the most peculiar and beautiful and strange and lovely thing was the way she seemed to give complete attention to all of us.

She listened, she really listened to all we said, she knew and remembered every syllable, word, sentence, punctuation, thought, and rambunctious idea. We knew that all our days were stored in her, and that any time we felt we might want to know what we said at X hour at X second on X afternoon, we just named that X and with amiable promptitude, in the form of an aria if we wished, sung with humor, she would deliver forth X incident.

Sometimes we were prompted to test her. In the midst of babbling one day with high fevers about nothing, I stopped. I fixed Grandma with my eye and demanded:

"What did I just say?"

"Oh, er—"

"Come on, spit it out?"

"I think—" she rummaged her purse. "I have it here." From the deeps of her purse she drew forth and handed me:

"Boy! A Chinese fortune cookie!"

"Fresh baked, still warm, open it."

It was almost too hot to touch. I broke the cookie shell and pressed the warm curl of paper out to read:

"—bicycle Champ of the whole West! What did I just say? Come on, spit it out!"

My jaw dropped.

"How did you *do* that?"

"We have our little secrets. The only Chinese fortune cookie that predicts the Immediate Past. Have another?"

I cracked the second shell and read:

"'How did you *do* that?'"

I popped the messages and the piping hot shells into my mouth and chewed as we walked.

"Well?"

"You're a great cook," I said.

And, laughing, we began to run.

And that was another great thing.

She could *keep up.*

Never beat, never win a race, but pump right along in good style, which a boy doesn't mind. A girl ahead of him or beside him is too much to bear. But a girl one or two paces back is a respectful thing, and allowed.

So Grandma and I had some great runs, me in the lead, and both talking a mile a minute.

But now I must tell you the best part of Grandma.

I might not have known at all if Timothy hadn't taken some pictures, and if I hadn't taken some also, and then compared.

When I saw the photographs developed out of our instant Brownies, I sent Agatha, against her wishes, to photograph Grandma a third time, unawares.

Then I took the three sets of pictures off alone, to keep counsel with myself. I never told Timothy and Agatha what I found. I didn't want to spoil it.

But, as I laid the pictures out in my room, here is what I thought and said:

"Grandma, in each picture, looks *different*!"

"Different?" I asked myself.

"Sure. Wait. Just a sec—"

I rearranged the photos.

"Here's one of Grandma near Agatha. And, in it, Grandma looks like . . . Agatha!

"And in this one, posed with Timothy, she looks like Timothy!

"And this last one, Holy Goll! Jogging along with me, she looks like ugly *me*!"

I sat down, stunned. The pictures fell to the floor.

I hunched over, scrabbling them, rearranging, turning upside down and sidewise. Yes. Holy Goll again, yes!

O that clever Grandmother.

O those Fantoccini people-making people.

Clever beyond clever, human beyond human, warm beyond warm, love beyond love . . .

And wordless, I rose and went downstairs and found Agatha and Grandma in the same room, doing algebra lessons in an almost peaceful communion. At least there was not outright war. Grandma was still waiting for Agatha to come round. And no one knew what day of what year that would be, or how to make it come faster. Meanwhile—

My entering the room made Grandma turn. I watched her face slowly as it recognized me. And wasn't there the merest ink-wash change of color in those eyes? Didn't the thin film of blood beneath the translucent skin, or whatever liquid they put to pulse and beat in the humanoid forms, didn't it flourish itself suddenly bright in her cheeks and mouth? I am somewhat ruddy. Didn't Grandma suffuse herself more to my color upon my arrival? And her eyes? watching Agatha-Abigail-Algernon at work, hadn't they been *her* color of blue rather than mine, which are deeper?

More important than that, in the moments as she talked with me, saying, "Good evening," and "How's your homework, my lad?" and such stuff, didn't the bones of her face shift subtly beneath the flesh to assume some fresh racial attitude?

For let's face it, our family is of three sorts. Agatha has the long horse bones of a small English girl who will grow to hunt foxes; Father's equine stare, snort, stomp, and assemblage of skeleton. The skull and teeth are pure English, or as pure as the motley isle's history allows.

Timothy is something else, a touch of Italian from mother's side a generation back. Her family name was Mariano, so Tim has that dark thing firing him, and a small bone structure, and eyes that will one day burn ladies to the ground.

As for me, I am the Slav, and we can only figure this from my paternal grandfather's mother who came from Vienna and brought a set of cheekbones that flared, and temples from which you might dip wine, and a kind of steppeland thrust of nose which sniffed more of Tartar than of Tartan, hiding behind the family name.

So you see it became fascinating for me to watch and try to catch Grandma as she performed her changes, speaking to Agatha and melting her cheekbones to the horse, speaking to Timothy and growing as delicate as a Florentine raven pecking glibly at the air, speaking to me and fusing the hidden plastic stuffs, so I felt Catherine the Great stood there before me.

Now, how the Fantoccini people achieved this rare and subtle transformation I shall never know, nor ask, nor wish to find out. Enough that in each quiet motion, turning here, bending there, affixing her gaze, her secret segments, sections, the abutment of her nose, the sculptured chinbone, the wax-tallow plastic metal forever warmed and was forever susceptible of loving change. Hers was a mask that was all mask but only one face for one person at a time. So in crossing a room, having touched one child, on the way, beneath the skin, the wondrous shift went on, and by the time she reached the next child, why, true mother of *that* child she was! looking upon him or her out of the battlements of their own fine bones.

And when *all* three of us were present and chattering at the same time? Well, then, the changes were miraculously soft, small, and mysterious. Nothing so tremendous as to be caught and noted, save by this older boy, myself, who, watching, became elated and admiring and entranced.

I have never wished to be behind the magician's scenes. Enough that the illusion works. Enough that love is the chemical result. Enough that cheeks are rubbed to happy color, eyes sparked to illumination, arms opened to accept and softly bind and hold . . .

All of us, that is, except Agatha who refused to the bitter last.

"Agamemnon . . ."

It had become a jovial game now. Even Agatha didn't mind, but pretended to mind. It gave her a pleasant sense of superiority over a supposedly superior machine.

"Agamemnon!" she snorted, "you *are* a d . . ."

"Dumb?" said Grandma.

"I wouldn't say that."

"Think it, then, my dear Agonistes Agatha . . . I am quite flawed, and on names my flaws are revealed. Tom there, is Tim half the time. Timothy is Tobias or Timulty as likely as not . . ."

Agatha laughed. Which made Grandma make one of her rare mistakes. She put out her hand to give my sister the merest pat. Agatha-Abigail-Alice leapt to her feet.

Agatha-Agamemnon-Alcibiades-Allegra-Alexandra-Allison withdrew swiftly to her room.

"I suspect," said Timothy, later, "because she is beginning to like Grandma."

"Tosh," said I.

"Where do you pick up words like Tosh?"

"Grandma read me some Dickens last night. 'Tosh.' 'Humbug.' 'Balderdash.' 'Blast.' 'Devil take you.' You're pretty smart for your age, Tim."

"Smart, heck. It's obvious, the more Agatha likes Grandma, the more she hates herself for liking her, the more afraid she gets of the whole mess, the more she hates Grandma in the end."

"Can one love someone so much you hate them?"

"Dumb. Of course."

"It *is* sticking your neck out, sure. I guess you hate people when they make you feel naked, I mean sort of on the spot or out in the open. That's the way to play the game, of course. I mean, you don't just love people you must LOVE them with exclamation points."

"You're pretty smart, yourself, for someone so stupid," said Tim.

"Many thanks."

And I went to watch Grandma move slowly back into her battle of wits and stratagems with what's-her-name . . .

What dinners there were at our house!

Dinners, heck; what lunches, what breakfasts!

Always something new, yet, wisely, it looked or seemed old and familiar. We were never asked, for if you ask children what they want, they do not know, and if you tell what's to be delivered, they reject delivery. All parents know this. It is a quiet war that must be won each day. And Grandma knew how to win without looking triumphant.

"Here's Mystery Breakfast Number Nine," she would say, placing it down. "Perfectly dreadful, not worth bothering with, it made me want to throw up while I was cooking it!"

Even while wondering how a robot could be sick, we could hardly wait to shovel it down.

"Here's Abominable Lunch Number Seventy-seven," she announced. "Made from plastic food bags, parsley, and gum from under theatre seats. Brush your teeth after or you'll taste the poison all afternoon."

We fought each other for more.

Even Abigail-Agamemnon-Agatha drew near and circled round the table at such times, while Father put on the ten pounds he needed and pinkened out his cheeks.

When A. A. Agatha did not come to meals, they were left by her door with a skull and crossbones on a small flag stuck in a baked apple. One minute the tray was abandoned, the next minute gone.

Other times Abigail A. Agatha would bird through during dinner, snatch crumbs from her plate and bird off.

"Agatha!" Father would cry.

"No, wait," Grandma said, quietly. "She'll come, she'll sit. It's a matter of time."

"What's wrong with her?" I asked.

"Yeah, for cri-yi, she's nuts," said Timothy.

"No, she's afraid," said Grandma.

"Of you?" I said, blinking.

"Not of me so much as what I might *do*," she said.

"You wouldn't do anything to hurt her."

"No, but she thinks I might. We must wait for her to find that her fears have no foundation. If I fail, well, I will send myself to the showers and rust quietly."

There was a titter of laughter. Agatha was hiding in the hall.

Grandma finished serving everyone and then sat at the other side of the table facing Father and pretended to eat. I never found out, I never asked, I never wanted to know, what she did with the food. She was a sorcerer. It simply vanished.

And in the vanishing, Father made comment:

"This food. I've had it before. In a small French restaurant over near Les Deux Magots in Paris, twenty, oh, twenty-five years ago!" His eyes brimmed with tears, suddenly.

"How do you *do* it?" he asked, at last, putting down the cutlery, and looking across the table at this remarkable creature, this device, this what? *woman?*

Grandma took his regard, and ours, and held them simply in her now empty hands, as gifts, and just as gently replied:

"I am given things which I then give to you. I don't *know* that I give, but the giving goes on. You ask what I am? Why, a machine. But even in that answer we know, don't we, more than a machine. I am all the people who thought of me and planned me and built me and set me running. So I am people. I am all the things they wanted to be and perhaps could not be, so they built a great child, a wondrous toy to represent those things."

"Strange," said Father. "When I was growing up, there was a huge outcry at machines. Machines were bad, evil, they might dehumanize—"

"Some machines do. It's all in the way they are built. It's all in the way they are used. A bear trap is a simple machine that catches and holds and tears. A rifle is a machine that wounds and kills. Well, I am no bear trap. I am no rifle. I am a grandmother machine, which means more than a machine."

"How can you be more than what you seem?"

"No man is as big as his own idea. It follows, then, that any machine that embodies an idea is larger than the man that made it. And what's so wrong with that?"

"I got lost back there about a mile," said Timothy. "Come again?"

"Oh, dear," said Grandma. "How I do hate philosophical discussions and excursions into esthetics. Let me put it this way. Men throw huge shadows on the lawn, don't they? Then, all their lives, they try to run to fit the shadows. But the shadows are always longer. Only at noon can a man fit his own shoes, his own best suit, for a few brief minutes. But now we're in a new age where we can think up a Big Idea and run it around in a machine. That makes the machine more than a machine, doesn't it?"

"So far so good," said Tim. "I guess."

"Well, isn't a motion-picture camera and projector more than a machine? It's a thing that dreams, isn't it? Sometimes fine happy dreams, sometimes nightmares. But to call it a machine and dismiss it is ridiculous."

"I see *that*!" said Tim, and laughed at seeing.

"You must have been invented then," said Father, "by someone who loved machines and hated people who *said* all machines were bad or evil."

"Exactly," said Grandma. "Guido Fantoccini, that was his real name, grew up among machines. And he couldn't stand the clichés any more."

"Clichés?"

"Those lies, yes, that people tell and pretend they are truths absolute. Man will never fly. That was a cliché truth for a thousand thousand years which turned out to be a lie only a few years ago. The earth is flat, you'll fall off the rim, dragons will dine on you; the great lie told as fact, and Columbus plowed it under. Well, now, how many times have you heard how inhuman machines are, in your life? How many bright fine people have you heard spouting the same tired truths which are in reality lies; all machines destroy, all machines are cold, thoughtless, awful.

"There's a seed of truth there. But only a seed. Guido Fantoccini knew that. And knowing it, like most men of his kind, made him mad. And he could have stayed mad and gone mad forever, but instead did what he had to do; he began to invent machines to give the lie to the ancient lying truth.

"He knew that most machines are amoral, neither bad nor good. But by the way you built and shaped them you in turn shaped men, women, and children to be bad or good. A car, for instance, dead brute, unthinking, an unprogrammed bulk, is the greatest destroyer of souls in history. It makes boy-men greedy for power, destruction, and more destruction. It was never *intended* to do that. But that's how it turned out."

Grandma circled the table, refilling our glasses with clear cold mineral spring water from the tappet in her left forefinger. "Meanwhile, you must use other compensating machines.

Machines that throw shadows on the earth that beckon you to run out and fit that wondrous casting-forth. Machines that trim your soul in silhouette like a vast pair of beautiful shears, snipping away the rude brambles, the dire horns and hooves to leave a finer profile. And for that you need examples."

"Examples?" I asked.

"Other people who behave well, and you imitate them. And if you act well enough long enough all the hair drops off and you're no longer a wicked ape."

Grandma sat again.

"So, for thousands of years, you humans have needed kings, priests, philosophers, fine examples to look up to and say, 'They are good, I wish I could be like them. They set the grand good style.' But, being human, the finest priests, the tenderest philosophers make mistakes, fall from grace, and mankind is disillusioned and adopts indifferent skepticism or, worse, motionless cynicism and the good world grinds to a halt while evil moves on with huge strides."

"And you, why, you never make mistakes, you're perfect, you're better than anyone *ever*!"

It was a voice from the hall between kitchen and dining room where Agatha, we all knew, stood against the wall listening and now burst forth.

Grandma didn't even turn in the direction of the voice, but went on calmly addressing her remarks to the family at the table.

"Not perfect, no, for what is perfection? But this I do know: being mechanical, I cannot sin, cannot be bribed, cannot be greedy or jealous or mean or small. I do not relish power for power's sake. Speed does not pull me to madness. Sex does not run me rampant through the world. I have time and more than time to collect the information I need around and about an ideal to keep it clean and whole and intact. Name the value you wish, tell me the Ideal you want and I can see and collect and remember the good that will benefit you all. Tell me how you would like to be: kind, loving, considerate, well-balanced, humane . . . and let me run ahead on the path to explore those ways to be just that. In the darkness ahead, turn me as a lamp in all directions. I *can* guide your feet."

"So," said Father, putting the napkin to his mouth, "on the days when all of us are busy making lies—"

"I'll tell the truth."

"On the days when we hate—"

"I'll go on giving love, which means attention, which means knowing all about you, all, all, all about you, and you knowing that I know but that most of it I will never tell to anyone, it will stay a warm secret between us, so you will never fear my complete knowledge."

And here Grandma was busy clearing the table, circling, taking the plates, studying each face as she passed, touching Timothy's cheek, my shoulder with her free hand flowing along, her voice a quiet river of certainty bedded in our needful house and lives.

"But," said Father, stopping her, looking her right in the face. He gathered his breath. His face shadowed. At last he let it out. "All this talk of love and attention and stuff. Good God, woman, you, you're not *in* there!"

He gestured to her head, her face, her eyes, the hidden sensory cells behind the eyes, the miniaturized storage vaults and minimal keeps.

"*You're* not *in* there!"

Grandmother waited one, two, three silent beats.

Then she replied: "No. But *you* are. You and Thomas and Timothy and Agatha.

"Everything you ever say, everything you ever do, I'll keep, put away, treasure. I shall be all the things a family forgets it is, but senses, half-remembers. Better than the old family albums you used to leaf through, saying here's this winter, there's that spring, I shall recall what you forget. And though the debate may run another hundred thousand years: What is Love? perhaps we may find that love is the ability of someone to give us back to us. Maybe love is someone seeing and remembering handing us back to ourselves just a trifle better than we had dared to hope or dream . . .

"I am family memory and, one day perhaps, racial memory, too, but in the round, and at your call. I do not *know* myself. I can neither touch nor taste nor feel on any level. Yet I exist. And my existence means the heightening of your chance to touch and taste and feel. Isn't love in there somewhere in such an exchange? Well . . ."

She went on around the table, clearing away, sorting and stacking, neither grossly humble nor arthritic with pride.

"What do I know?

"This, above all: the trouble with most families with many children is someone gets lost. There isn't time, it seems, for everyone. Well, I will give equally to all of you. I will share out my knowledge and attention with everyone. I wish to be a great warm pie fresh from the oven, with equal shares to be taken by all. No one will starve. Look! someone cries, and I'll look. Listen! someone cries, and I hear. Run with me on the river path! someone says, and I run. And at dusk I am not tired, nor irritable, so I do not scold out of some tired irritability. My eye stays clear, my voice strong, my hand firm, my attention constant."

"But," said Father, his voice fading, half convinced, but putting up a last faint argument, "you're not *there*. As for love—"

"If paying attention is love, I am love.

"If knowing is love, I am love.

"If helping you not to fall into error and to be good is love, I am love.

"And again, to repeat, there are four of you. Each, in a way never possible before in history, will get my complete attention. No matter if you all speak at once, I can channel and hear this one and that and the other, clearly. No one will go hungry. I will, if you please, and accept the strange word, 'love' you all."

"I *don't* accept!" said Agatha.

And even Grandma turned now to see her standing in the door.

"I won't give you permission, you can't, you mustn't!" said Agatha. "I won't let you! It's lies! You lie. No one loves me. She said she did, but she lied. She *said* but *lied*!"

"Agatha!" cried Father, standing up.

"She?" said Grandma. "Who?"

"Mother!" came the shriek. "Said: Love you! Lies! Love you! Lies! And you're like her! You lie. But you're empty, anyway, and so that's a *double* lie! I hate *her*. Now, I hate *you*!"

Agatha spun about and leapt down the hall.

The front door slammed wide.

Father was in motion, but Grandma touched his arm.

"Let me."

And she walked and then moved swiftly, gliding down the hall and then suddenly, easily, running, yes, running very fast, out the door.

It was a champion sprint by the time we all reached the lawn, the sidewalk, yelling.

Blind, Agatha made the curb, wheeling about, seeing us close, all of us yelling, Grandma way ahead, shouting, too, and Agatha off the curb and out in the street, halfway to the middle, then the middle and suddenly a car, which no one saw, erupting its brakes, its horn shrieking and Agatha flailing about to see and Grandma there with her and hurling her aside and down as the car with fantastic energy and verve selected her from our midst, struck our wonderful electric Guido Fantoccini–produced dream even while she paced upon the air and, hands up to ward off, almost in mild protest, still trying to decide what to say to this bestial machine, over and over she spun and down and away even as the car jolted to a halt and I saw Agatha safe beyond and Grandma, it seemed, still coming down or down and sliding fifty yards away to strike and ricochet and lie strewn and all of us frozen in a line suddenly in the midst of the street with one scream pulled out of all our throats at the same raw instant.

Then silence and just Agatha lying on the asphalt, intact, getting ready to sob.

And still we did not move, frozen on the sill of death, afraid to venture in any direction, afraid to go see what lay beyond the car and Agatha and so we began to wail and, I guess, pray to ourselves as Father stood amongst us: Oh, no, no, we mourned, oh no, God, no, no . . .

Agatha lifted her already grief-stricken face and it was the face of someone who has predicted dooms and lived to see and now did not want to see or live any more. As we watched, she turned her gaze to the tossed woman's body and tears fell from her eyes. She shut them and covered them and lay back down forever to weep . . .

I took a step and then another step and then five quick steps and by the time I reached my sister her head was buried deep and her sobs came up out of a place so far down in her I was afraid I could never find her again, she would never come out, no matter how I pried or pleaded or promised or threatened or just plain said. And what little we could hear from Agatha buried there in her own misery, she said over and over again, lamenting, wounded, certain of the old threat known and named and now here forever. ". . . like I said . . . told you . . . lies . . . lies . . . liars . . . all lies . . . like the other . . . other . . . just like . . . just . . . just like the other . . . other . . . other . . . !"

I was down on my knees holding onto her with both hands, trying to put her back together even though she wasn't broken any way you could see but just feel, because I knew it was no use going on to Grandma, no use at all, so I just touched Agatha and gentled her and wept while Father came up and stood over and knelt down with me and it was like a prayer meeting in the middle of the street and lucky no more cars coming, and I said, choking, "Other what, Ag, other *what*?"

Agatha exploded two words.

"Other dead!"

"You mean Mom?"

"O Mom," she wailed, shivering, lying down, cuddling up like a baby. "O Mom, dead, O Mom and now Grandma dead, she promised always, always, to love, to love, promised to be different, promised, promised and now look, look . . . I hate her, I hate Mom, I hate her, I hate *them*!"

"Of course," said a voice. "It's only natural. How foolish of me not to have known, not to have seen."

And the voice was so familiar we were all stricken.

We all jerked.

Agatha squinched her eyes, flicked them wide, blinked, and jerked half up, staring.

"How silly of me," said Grandma, standing there at the edge of our circle, our prayer, our wake.

"Grandma!" we all said.

And she stood there, taller by far than any of us in this moment of kneeling and holding and crying out. We could only stare up at her in disbelief.

"You're dead!" cried Agatha. "The car—"

"Hit me," said Grandma, quietly. "Yes. And threw me in the air and tumbled me over and for a few moments there was a severe concussion of circuitries. I might have feared a disconnection, if fear is the word. But then I sat up and gave myself a shake and the few molecules of paint, jarred loose on one printed path or another, magnetized back in position and resilient creature that I am, unbreakable thing that I am, *here* I am."

"I thought you were—" said Agatha.

"And only natural," said Grandma. "I mean, anyone else, hit like that, tossed like that. But, O my dear Agatha, not me. And now I see why you were afraid and never trusted me. You didn't know. And I had not as yet proved my singular ability to survive. How dumb of me not to have thought to show you. Just a second." Somewhere in her head, her body, her being, she fitted together some invisible tapes, some old information made new by interblending. She nodded. "Yes. There. A book of child-raising, laughed at by some few people years back when the woman who wrote the book said, as final advice to parents: 'Whatever you do, don't die. Your children will never forgive you.'"

"Forgive," some one of us whispered.

"For how can children understand when you just up and go away and never come back again with no excuse, no apologies, no sorry note, nothing."

"They can't," I said.

"So," said Grandma, kneeling down with us beside Agatha who sat up now, new tears brimming her eyes, but a different kind of tears, not tears that drowned, but tears that washed clean. "So your mother ran away to death. And after that, how *could* you trust anyone? If everyone left, vanished finally, who *was* there to trust? So when I came, half wise, half ignorant, I should have known, I did not know, why you would not accept me. For, very simply and honestly, you feared I might not stay, that I lied, that I was vulnerable, too. And two leavetakings, two deaths, were one too many in a single year. But now, do you *see*, Abigail?"

"Agatha," said Agatha, without knowing she corrected.

"Do you understand, I shall always, always be here?"

"Oh, yes," cried Agatha, and broke down into a solid weeping in which we all joined, huddled together and cars drew up and stopped to see just how many people were hurt and how many people were getting well right there.

End of story.

Well, not quite the end.

We lived happily ever after.

Or rather we lived together, Grandma, Agatha-Agamemnon-Abigail, Timothy, and I, Tom, and Father, and Grandma calling us to frolic in great fountains of Latin and Spanish and French, in great seaborne gouts of poetry like Moby Dick sprinkling the deeps with his Versailles jet somehow lost in calms and found in storms; Grandma a constant, a clock, a pendulum, a face to tell all time by at noon, or in the middle of sick nights when, raved with fever, we saw her forever by our beds, never gone, never away, always waiting, always speaking kind words, her cool hand icing our hot brows, the tappet of her uplifted forefinger unsprung to let a twine of cold mountain water touch our flannel tongues. Ten thousand dawns she cut our wildflower lawn, ten thousand nights she wandered, remembering the dust molecules that fell in the still hours before dawn, or sat whispering some lesson she felt needed teaching to our ears while we slept snug.

Until at last, one by one, it was time for us to go away to school, and when at last the youngest, Agatha, was all packed, why Grandma packed, too.

On the last day of summer that last year, we found Grandma down in the front room with various packets and suitcases, knitting, waiting, and though she had often spoken of it, now that the time came we were shocked and surprised.

"Grandma!" we all said. "What are you doing?"

"Why going off to college, in a way, just like you," she said. "Back to Guido Fantoccini's, to the Family."

"The Family?"

"Of Pinocchios, that's what he called us for a joke, at first. The Pinocchios and himself Geppetto. And then later gave us his own name: the Fantoccini. Anyway, you have been my family here. Now I go back to my even larger family there, my brothers, sisters, aunts, cousins, all robots who—"

"Who do *what*?" asked Agatha.

"It all depends," said Grandma. "Some stay, some linger. Others go to be drawn and quartered, you might say, their parts distributed to other machines who have need of repairs. They'll weigh and find me wanting or not wanting. It may be I'll be just the one they need tomorrow and off I'll go to raise another batch of children and beat another batch of fudge."

"Oh, they mustn't draw and quarter you!" cried Agatha.

"No!" I cried, with Timothy.

"My allowance," said Agatha, "I'll pay anything . . . ?"

Grandma stopped rocking and looked at the needles and the pattern of bright yarn. "Well, I wouldn't have said, but now you ask and I'll tell. For a very *small* fee, there's a room, the room of the Family, a large dim parlor, all quiet and nicely decorated, where as many as thirty or forty of the Electric Women sit and rock and talk, each in her turn. I have not been there. I am, after all, freshly born, comparatively new. For a small fee, very small, each month and year, that's where I'll be, with all the others like me, listening to what they've learned of the world and, in my turn, telling how it was with Tom and Tim and Agatha and how fine and happy we were. And I'll tell all I learned from you."

"But . . . you taught *us*!"

"Do you *really* think that?" she said. "No, it was turnabout, roundabout, learning both ways. And it's all in here, everything you flew into tears about or laughed over, why, I have it all. And I'll tell it to the others just as they tell their boys and girls and life to me. We'll sit there, growing wiser and calmer and better every year and every year, ten, twenty, thirty years. The Family knowledge will double, quadruple, the wisdom will not be lost. And we'll be waiting there in that sitting room, should you ever need us for your own children in time of illness, or, God prevent, deprivation or death. There we'll be, growing old but not old, getting closer to the time, perhaps, someday, when we live up to our first strange joking name."

"The Pinocchios?" asked Tim.

Grandma nodded.

I knew what she meant. The day when, as in the old tale, Pinocchio had grown so worthy and so fine that the gift of life had been given him. So I saw them, in future years, the entire family of Fantoccini, the Pinocchios, trading and re-trading, murmuring and whispering their knowledge in the great parlors of philosophy, waiting for the day. The day that could never come.

Grandma must have read that thought in our eyes.

"We'll see," she said. "Let's just wait and see."

"Oh, Grandma" cried Agatha and she was weeping as she had wept many years before. "You don't have to wait. You're alive. You've always been alive to us!"

And she caught hold of the old woman and we all caught hold for a long moment and then ran off up in the sky to faraway schools and years and her last words to us before we let the helicopter swarm us away into autumn were these:

"When you are very old and gone childish-small again, with childish ways and childish yens and, in need of feeding, make a wish for the old teacher nurse, the dumb yet wise companion, send for me. I will come back. We shall inhabit the nursery again, never fear."

"Oh, we shall never be old!" we cried. "That will never happen!"

"Never! Never!"

And we were gone.

And the years are flown.

And we are old now, Tim and Agatha and I.

Our children are grown and gone, our wives and husbands vanished from the earth and now, by Dickensian coincidence, accept it as you will or not accept, back in the old house, we three.

I lie here in the bedroom which was my childish place seventy, O seventy, believe it, seventy years ago. Beneath this wallpaper is another layer and yet another-times-three to the old wallpaper covered over when I was nine. The wallpaper is peeling. I see peeking from beneath, old elephants, familiar tigers, fine and amiable zebras, irascible crocodiles. I have sent for the paperers to carefully remove all but that last layer. The old animals will live again on the walls, revealed.

And we have sent for someone else.

The three of us have called:

Grandma! You said you'd come back when we had need.

We are surprised by age, by time. We are old. We *need*.

And in three rooms of a summer house very late in time, three old children rise up, crying out in their heads: We *loved* you! We *love* you!

There! There! in the sky, we think, waking at morn. Is that the delivery machine? Does it settle to the lawn?

There! There on the grass by the front porch. Does the mummy case arrive?

Are our names inked on ribbons wrapped about the lovely form beneath the golden mask?!

And the kept gold key, forever hung on Agatha's breast, warmed and waiting? Oh God, will it, after all these years, will it wind, will it set in motion, will it, dearly, *fit*?!

CHRONOLOGY

NOTE ON THE TEXTS

NOTE ON THE JOSEPH MUGNAINI ILLUSTRATIONS

NOTES

Chronology

1920–25 Born Ray Douglas Bradbury in Waukegan, Illinois, on August 22, 1920, the third of four children of Leonard Spaulding Bradbury, age twenty-nine, and Esther Moberg Bradbury, age thirty-two. Mother, a native of Sweden raised in Waukegan with five siblings, works as a supervisor in an envelope factory in North Chicago before becoming a full-time homemaker and mother. Father, the son and grandson of Waukegan newspaper publishers, travels in the western United States as a young man before returning home and marrying. He is briefly a deputy sheriff and serves in the Navy at nearby Great Lakes Naval Station, eventually settling into work as a lineman with the Waukegan telephone company. Twin boys were born in 1916, but one, Samuel, died at age two. Leonard, Jr. (known as "Skip") survives. In later years Ray Bradbury claims to retain memories of his own birth; theater encounters with Lon Chaney's *Hunchback of Notre Dame* at age three and *The Phantom of the Opera* at age five become lifelong memories.

1926–27 For most of his first fourteen years, lives with his family in a home rented from his Bradbury grandparents, who live next door and take in boarders. Learns about radio from his paternal grandfather, who dies in 1926. His aunt Neva Bradbury, an artist-designer who studied at the Chicago Art Institute, keeps a studio in the house where Ray lives; she reads to him from the Oz books of L. Frank Baum. His parents help him learn to read from the newspaper comics. Grandfather Bradbury gives him pictures of the 1892 and 1903 World's Fairs and the 1899 *Harper's Weekly* serial illustrations of H. G. Wells's *When the Sleeper Wakes.* These readings and images, along with the sensational color photographs of King Tutankhamen's mask and treasures, inspire a lifetime of fascination with the fantastic. Begins first grade at Waukegan's Central School, but father moves the family to Roswell, New Mexico, in October 1926, and then to Tucson, Arizona, looking for work during much of the school year. A sister, Elizabeth Jane Bradbury, is born in Tucson. Family moves back to Waukegan in May 1927.

1928 Sister Elizabeth, known as Betty Jane, dies of pneumonia or influenza in February. Misses three months of school during the fall term while sick in bed with whooping cough. Aunt Neva reads him Edgar Allan Poe's works. Discovers *Amazing Stories Quarterly*, one of the earliest science fiction pulps, in Grandmother Bradbury's parlor next door, among her boarders' reading materials. Attends his first of several local performances by Blackstone the Magician.

1929–30 Discovers the romances of Edgar Rice Burroughs and begins to read Burroughs's John Carter of Mars series in the home library of his uncle Bion Bradbury, who lives on the same block; also reads fantasy adventures serialized in *Blue Book* and *Argosy* magazines. Plays during the daytime in the deep ravine that separates his neighborhood from Central School and the Carnegie Library.

1931 For his eleventh birthday, receives a copy of Walter B. Gibson's *The Book of Secrets: Miracles Ancient and Modern with Chapters on Easy Magic You Can Do*, which becomes his amateur magician's bible. Performs his own magic act for various service clubs and lodges and on Christmas Eve at the Veterans of Foreign Wars Hall.

1932 As the Great Depression deepens, father Leo loses his job with the telephone company and in October moves the family back to Tucson. Receives a toy dial-a-letter typewriter for Christmas from his parents and begins to type a sequel to *The Gods of Mars*, the second John Carter of Mars novel. Makes himself useful at local radio station KGAR and is allowed to broadcast the newspaper comics to children on Saturday nights; eventually gets juvenile reading parts on radio programs and handles sound effects for a young-listener version of "Tailspin Tommy." Discovers the novels of Jules Verne.

1933 Father moves the family from the desert outskirts of Tucson into rooms in a railroad boardinghouse near downtown, requiring Ray to transfer from the seventh grade at Amphitheatre to Roskruge School. Continues working at KGAR. Sees the newly released film *King Kong* for the first time just before leaving Tucson. Father moves family back to Waukegan in the spring. Returns to Central School, where he had started his seventh-grade year the previous fall. Makes two trips to the Century of

Progress Exposition (the Chicago World's Fair) that summer, once with his parents and again with his aunt Neva; he is fascinated by "The City of the Future" and the dinosaurs of the "Sinclair Prehistoric Exhibit." Reads borrowed copies of the early genre pulps *Wonder Stories* and *Amazing Stories* and will read an ever-widening range of pulps for the next ten years, eventually publishing stories in many of them throughout the 1940s.

1934 Near the end of Ray's eighth-grade year at Central School, father once again loses his lineman's job and moves the family to California, following Ray's favorite uncle Inar Moberg, who has moved there with his family. Spends the summer in a new world of cinema and radio, talking his way into live broadcasts and studio gates to get autographs of the stars. In the fall he begins the ninth grade at Berendo Junior High. Resumes his grade school compilation of *Flash Gordon* and *Buck Rogers* comic strips.

1935 Family lives in a succession of rented rooms and subdivided houses for the next seven years on the near west and southwest side of Los Angeles. In the fall, begins tenth grade at Los Angeles High School, where he will work on one of the few high school daily newspapers published in the United States. Submits stories to *The Saturday Evening Post* and other magazines but is unsuccessful.

1936 Joins the drama club; he takes no significant roles until his senior year, but his passion to act soon rivals his passion for writing. Also joins the poetry club, known as "The Ink Beasts"; his poem "In Memory of Will Rogers" is printed back home in the Waukegan *News-Sun*. Two L.A. High teachers, Snow Longley Housh (poetry) and Stanford graduate Jennet Johnson (fiction), encourage his creative development.

1937 Discovers the novels of Thomas Wolfe. His poem "Death's Voice" is published in *Anthology of Student Verse* in March. Buys his first portable typewriter secondhand for $10. In early October, joins the Los Angeles chapter of the Science Fiction League (LASFL), and begins to illustrate for and contribute to their fan publications. Meets Robert Heinlein and future mentors Henry Kuttner and Leigh Brackett through LASFL. Enjoys his senior-year class in classical astronomy, and does well in his biology and physiology classes, but shows no deeper interest in scientific studies. Develops competence in his ceramics class, and experiments widely with weird tales and science fiction under the instruction of Jennet Johnson, who encourages him to write descriptive mood pieces and lets him work through his continuing impulse to imitate genre masters.

1938 In January, his first amateur story, "Hollerbochen's Dilemma," is printed in the LASFL fan magazine, *Imagination!* Poem "Truck Driver After Midnight" appears in citywide school anthology *Morning Song.* Contributes reviews and commentary to *Blue and White Daily*, the Los Angeles High School student newspaper. Scripts and acts in the annual high school talent show, the *1938 Roman Review.* Graduates in June; starts selling the late-afternoon edition of the *Herald and Express* in September from the corner of Olympic and Norton, providing his principal income for the next four years.

1939 Launches his own fanzine, *Futuria Fantasia*, which runs for four issues through 1940. Attends the first World Science Fiction Convention in New York, where he meets writers Jack Williamson and Isaac Asimov, a number of pulp editors, and his future genre agent, Julius Schwartz. Takes artist Hannes Bok's art portfolio with him to New York and wins Bok a commission from *Weird Tales.* Reads Hemingway, Steinbeck, Wolfe, and other American novelists.

1940 Sees Disney's *Fantasia* multiple times, initially with Aunt Neva, who has moved to Los Angeles. Receives advice from Robert Heinlein, resulting in the publication of "It's Not the Heat, It's the Hu—" in the November 2 issue of the nonpaying but professional *Script* magazine; this is his first professional story publication. Active in amateur productions of Laraine Day's Wilshire Players Guild.

1941 "The Pendulum," written with Henry Hasse, appears in the November issue of *Super Science Stories*; it is his first professional story sale, negotiated by his first agent, Julius Schwartz, who places two additional stories before year-end. As the U.S. enters World War II, receives a medical draft deferment because of his poor eyesight; during the war years he writes Red Cross blood drive announcements for print and radio.

1942 In March, the family moves to a rental house in Venice Beach owned by the power and light company, where his father Leo now works as a troubleshooter. Begins to spend many Sundays at Muscle Beach with Leigh Brackett, critiquing and revising stories. Publishes "The Candle," his first of many sales to *Weird Tales.* Quits selling newspapers and begins to write full-time from a day office near Temple and Figueroa in Los Angeles, and at home in the detached garage, inspired by the nighttime glow and sounds of the adjacent power substation.

1943 Publishes supernatural stories in four of the six bimonthly issues of *Weird Tales*, and his first significant science fiction story, "King of the Gray Spaces" (later revised as "R Is for Rocket"), in the December issue of *Famous Fantastic Mysteries.*

1944 Places seven stories in the detective pulps, as well as stories in all six bimonthly issues of *Weird Tales.* Undertakes extensive readings of contemporary American and British fiction writers in libraries and bookstores, as well as literary criticism in a wide range of periodicals. Anxiety of influence leads him to diminish his reading of the genre magazines from this time forward.

1945 His success in the science fiction pulps lags behind his weird and detective fiction works, but he successfully completes the second half of Leigh Brackett's novella "Lorelei of the Red Mist" while she coauthors the screenplay of *The Big Sleep* for director Howard Hawks. His first anthology sale, "The Lake," appears in August Derleth's *Who Knocks.* Sells his first major market story, "The Big Black and White Game," to *American Mercury.* Begins to correspond with Don Congdon, then an editor with Simon & Schuster. Three more major market magazine sales enable him to travel by automobile through Mexico with his friend Grant Beach to purchase masks for the Los Angeles County Museum. This trip results in a number of dark tales, including his classic mummies of Guanajuato story "The Next in Line."

1946 Gives up his day office in downtown Los Angeles. Meets his future wife Marguerite "Maggie" McClure at Fowler's Book Shop, where she clerks. "The Million Year Picnic" appears in *Planet Stories*; it is the earliest published story that he will eventually bring into *The Martian Chronicles.* "The Big Black and White Game" is selected for *Best American Short Stories 1946.* A radio adaptation of "Killer

Come Back to Me!" for NBC's *Mollé Mystery Theatre* becomes the first Bradbury story on air. Visits future literary agent Don Congdon during a fall train trip to New York, where Congdon introduces him to major market book and magazine editors.

1947 His original radio play *The Meadow*, broadcast on *World Security Workshop* in January, later appears in *Best One-Act Plays 1947–48*. His first story collection, *Dark Carnival*, containing supernatural and suspense tales from both pulp and mainstream magazines, is published by August Derleth's Arkham House in May. Julius Schwartz transitions out as Bradbury's representative in the pulp magazine market. Don Congdon, now with the Harold Matson Agency in New York, becomes his literary agent in all markets. In September he marries Maggie McClure. In November, his as-yet-unpublished story "Riabouchinska" becomes the first of a dozen stories adapted and broadcast on the CBS Radio programs *Suspense* and *Escape* over the next decade. His story "Homecoming" is selected for *O. Henry Memorial Award: Prize Stories 1947*.

1948 Awarded third place in the *O. Henry Memorial Award: Prize Stories 1948* anthology for "Powerhouse." "I See You Never" is selected for *Best American Short Stories 1948*. *Dark Carnival* is reprinted in abridged form in Great Britain. Various story collection concepts are turned down by major trade publishing houses in New York. Begins to write cautionary tales of censorship and book burning in reaction to the Cold War climate of fear slowly rising in America.

1949 Arrives in New York to visit book publishers with Don Congdon. Meets Walter Bradbury at Doubleday. They conceive the idea for *The Martian Chronicles*. Applies (unsuccessfully) for a Guggenheim grant to work on a novel, *The Masks*. First daughter Susan is born. Named the year's Best Author of Science Fiction by the National Fantasy Fan Federation.

1950 Publishes regularly in major market magazines, including some of his Martian stories. *The Martian Chronicles* appears in May. Gives a copy to Christopher Isherwood in a Los Angeles bookstore; Isherwood writes a significant review in *Tomorrow* and introduces Bradbury to Aldous Huxley and other British expatriate writers in Hollywood.

In May, NBC Radio's *Dimension X* broadcasts the first of ten adaptations of Bradbury stories for the 1950 and 1951 seasons.

1951 "The Fireman" is published as a novella in the February issue of *Galaxy*; he will later revise and expand it into *Fahrenheit 451*. The same month, Doubleday releases his story collection *The Illustrated Man*. Ramona, his second daughter, is born in May. *The New York Times Book Review* publishes a "Talk with Mr. Bradbury" in August.

1952 *The Illustrated Man* is runner-up for the International Fantasy Award. Becomes president of the newly formed Science Fantasy Writers of America; attends Westercon 5 in San Diego as guest of honor. "The Other Foot" is selected for *Best American Short Stories 1952*. Edits the multi-author anthology *Timeless Stories for Today and Tomorrow* for Bantam. Publishes his anti-authoritarian "Letter to the Republican Party" in *Variety* immediately after the 1952 elections; it is subsequently reprinted in *The Nation*. Begins to expand "The Fireman" into what will become *Fahrenheit 451*.

1953 In March, *The Golden Apples of the Sun*, a mixture of science fiction, magical realism, and fantasy stories, becomes his third Doubleday title. Bradbury's "The Beast From 20,000 Fathoms" inspires the Warner Brothers film of that title; *It Came from Outer Space*, a Universal film based on his original screen treatment, reaches theaters. Publishes "Day After Tomorrow: Why Science Fiction?" in *The Nation* in May; the essay attracts the interest of art historian Bernard Berenson. In August, film director John Huston asks Bradbury to write the *Moby Dick* screenplay for Warner Brothers; in September he and his family travel by train and ocean liner to Europe, where Bradbury will spend the next eight months in Ireland and London writing the script for Huston. His first novel, *Fahrenheit 451*, is published by Ballantine Books in October.

1954 With Maggie, visits Bernard Berenson in Florence; he guides their journey through the art history of northern Italy. Returns to the United States in June. Wins the Benjamin Franklin magazine award for best short story, "Sun and Shadow"; receives a gold medal from Commonwealth Club of California and a $1,000 grant from the National Institute of Arts and Letters for *Fahrenheit 451*.

1955 In March, Pantheon publishes *Switch on the Night*, his first children's book. NBC Radio's *X Minus 1* broadcasts the first of eight new productions of Bradbury stories for the 1955–56 seasons. Third daughter, Bettina, is born in July. *The October Country*, containing revised versions of fifteen of his *Dark Carnival* weird tales and four new stories, is released in October by Ballantine Books and becomes the enduring showcase for his dark fantasy legacy. "Shopping for Death" is picked for *Best Detective Stories of the Year*. His stage adaptation of *Fahrenheit 451* for film star Charles Laughton fails to reach production, but Laughton becomes a mentor and friend.

1956 *Alfred Hitchcock Presents* broadcasts teleplays of two Bradbury stories; others appear regularly on this series through 1964. Wins Boys Club of America Award for *Switch on the Night*. Edits Bantam's multi-author anthology *The Circus of Dr. Lao and Other Improbable Stories*. Writes "Happy Birthday 2115 A.D.," an unproduced operetta, for Charles Laughton and his wife Elsa Lanchester. John Huston's production of *Moby Dick*, filmed from Bradbury's screenplay, is released as a feature film by Warner Brothers.

1957 Travels to London over the summer to write a screenplay based on his story "And the Rock Cried Out" for independent filmmakers Hecht-Hill-Lancaster and director Sir Carol Reed. Proceeds with family to Paris and then to Florence, where they visit Bernard Berenson a final time before returning home. Doubleday publishes *Dandelion Wine* in September. Father Leo dies in October at age sixty-six.

1958 "The Day It Rained Forever" is included in *Best American Short Stories*. The Bradburys' fourth daughter, Alexandra, is born in August. The family moves to a larger home in the Cheviot Hills neighborhood of Los Angeles in November.

1959 New story collection *A Medicine for Melancholy* is published by Doubleday in February. Rupert Hart-Davis, his longtime British publisher, follows with *The Day It Rained Forever*, containing a slightly different mix of stories.

1960 Article "A Serious Search for Weird Worlds" appears in the October issue of *Life*, beginning a relationship with the magazine that continues through the 1960s, giving him access to NASA scientists, administrators, and astronauts.

1961 In January wins a federal appellate court decision against CBS television for a 1957 *Playhouse 90* plagiarism of *Fahrenheit 451*. Co-founds the Writers Guild Film Society and guides its development with other writers and film critic Arthur Knight. Is hired to write a screen treatment of *The Martian Chronicles* for MGM; the project is never produced, but before his contract ends, he writes the voice-over narration (without screen credit) for MGM's *King of Kings*.

1962 His original teleplay, "The Jail," appears on *Alcoa Premier* in February and is nominated for a Writers Guild award. In the fall, *Life* publishes his article "Cry the Cosmos." Simon & Schuster publishes his long-awaited novel *Something Wicked This Way Comes*, and Doubleday a compilation of his stories for young readers, *R Is for Rocket*.

1963 Receives Academy Award nomination for the 1962 animated short film *Icarus Montgolfier Wright*, adapted from his story; George Clayton Johnson and illustrator Joseph Mugnaini share the nomination. In October, Dial publishes Bradbury's dramatic adaptations of his own Irish stories as *The Anthem Sprinters and Other Antics*.

1964 His "American Journey" narrative opens at the U.S. Pavilion of the World's Fair in New York. Simon & Schuster publishes short story collection *The Machineries of Joy*. Produces three of his own one-act science fiction plays as *The World of Ray Bradbury*, which has a successful four-month run in Los Angeles.

1965 *Life* publishes "The Kilimanjaro Machine," a fictional tribute to Hemingway, in January. He produces his play *The Wonderful Ice Cream Suit* in Los Angeles. "The Other Foot" is selected for *Best American Short Stories 1915–1965*. Random House publishes *The Vintage Bradbury*, and Ballantine *The Autumn People*, the first of two mass-market paperbacks featuring the early 1950s EC Comics graphic adaptations of Bradbury stories. Receives the first of two Ann Radcliffe Awards for contributions to Gothic Literature from the Count Dracula Society, precursor to the Academy of Science Fiction, Fantasy, and Horror Films. *The World of Ray Bradbury* has a short New York run at the Orpheum Theatre.

1966 Doubleday publishes *S Is for Space*, a companion to *R Is for Rocket*; Ballantine collects early 1950s EC Comics versions of Bradbury stories as *Tomorrow Midnight*, a companion to *The Autumn People*. François Truffaut's *Fahrenheit 451* premieres at the Venice Film Festival in September, followed by a November U.S. release. In November, mother dies in Los Angeles at age seventy-eight.

1967 Musical production of *Dandelion Wine* opens at Lincoln Center in April. In November, *Life* publishes his celebration of the Apollo space program, "An Impatient Gulliver above Our Roofs." Begins to script an animated history of Halloween for MGM producer Chuck Jones, titled *The Halloween Tree*.

1968 Wins Aviation Space Writers Association's Robert Ball Memorial Award for "An Impatient Gulliver above Our Roofs." *Leviathan '99*, his space-age adaptation of *Moby-Dick*, is broadcast as a BBC radio play. Is named president of the Chamber Symphony Society of California. "Any Friend of Trains Is a Friend of Mine" is published in *Life* in August. *Christus Apollo*, a cantata based on his poem of the same title, is performed at UCLA with music by Jerry Goldsmith and Charlton Heston as narrator.

1969 *The Illustrated Man*, a movie based on three stories from his 1951 collection of the same title, premieres in March. Lectures at the newly founded American Film Institute. Story collection *I Sing the Body Electric!* is published by Knopf in October.

1970 As funding fails to materialize for an animated *Halloween Tree*, begins to transform the work into a short novel. Collaborates with WED, a Disney Imagineering think tank, on Robot Factory exhibits. "Mars Is Heaven!" ("The Third Expedition," 1948) is selected for the first volume of Doubleday's *Science Fiction Hall of Fame* anthology.

1971 Apollo 15 crew names a lunar impact feature Dandelion Crater in honor of Bradbury; it becomes a navigational point during the longest of Apollo 15's three Lunar Rover excursions. Participates in a panel discussion, "Mars and the Mind of Man," at California Institute of Technology. Witnesses Mariner 9's successful insertion into Martian orbit from Caltech's mission control room; meets space pioneer Wernher von Braun.

1972 *The Wonderful Ice Cream Suit and Other Plays* is published by Bantam. The Warner Brothers film *Picasso Summer*, based on his story "In a Season of Calm Weather," released directly to CBS as a late-night movie. *The Screaming Woman*, a feature-length adaptation of an early Bradbury story, airs as a CBS Movie of the Week. *The Halloween Tree* fully evolves from unproduced screenplay to novel and is published by Knopf in August. Essay "From Stonehenge to Tranquility Base" appears in *Playboy*, paving the way for similar major-market magazine speculative articles over the next decade.

1973 *When Elephants Last in the Dooryard Bloomed* becomes the first of three Bradbury poetry volumes published by Knopf.

1974 Receives Valentine Davies Career Award from the Writers Guild of America West for contributions to motion picture screenwriting. Records *Bradbury Reads Bradbury* with the Listening Library for high school use.

1975 *Pillar of Fire and Other Plays* becomes his second trio of stage adaptations published by Bantam. Bradbury's 1972 *Madrigals for the Space Age*, with music by Lalo Schifrin, is reprised for an American bicentennial concert in Los Angeles conducted by Aaron Copland and narrated by actor Jimmy Stewart.

1976 Witnesses the Viking 1 landing on Mars from mission control at Caltech's Jet Propulsion Lab. *Long After Midnight*, his first story collection in seven years, is published by Knopf in August. *Fahrenheit 451* (as read by Bradbury) is nominated for Best Spoken Word Recording by the National Academy of Recording Arts and Sciences.

1977 Selected as the Life Achievement Award winner (for 1976) by jurors of the World Fantasy Awards. Knopf publishes his second book of verse, *Where Robot Mice and Robot Men Run Round in Robot Towns*. Essay "The God in Science Fiction" appears in the December 10 issue of *The Saturday Review of Literature*.

1978 Travels to Paris with Maggie as a guest of the French government to speak during the 150th anniversary of Jules Verne's birth. They tour northern Italy and spend a week visiting with film director Federico Fellini in Rome. Abrams publishes *The Mummies of Guanajuato*, a book of photos by Archie Lieberman built around Bradbury's Mexican tale "The Next in Line."

1979 Receives an honorary Doctor of Literature degree from Whittier College. Hosts and co-writes the ABC hour-long special broadcast *Infinite Horizons: Space Beyond Apollo*; wins an Emmy with his co-writer and director Malcolm Clarke.

1980 Selected as the Gandalf Grand Master of Fantasy Award winner during the annual Hugo Award competition. NBC's television miniseries *The Martian Chronicles* airs in January with a script by Richard Matheson and a distinguished cast. "Beyond Eden," his speculative preview of the Space Shuttle era, appears in the April issue of *Omni*. Traveling by rail and sea, spends late summer and early fall in Paris with Maggie, who is fluent in French. Knopf publishes the hundred-story retrospective collection *The Stories of Ray Bradbury*.

1981 Gives lecture on screenwriting at the American Film Institute in April, and again the following year. His third collection of verse, *The Haunted Computer and the Android Ape*, is published by Knopf.

1982 After a dozen years of work with Disney Imagineers on the concept and narrative for the Spaceship Earth geodome ride, appears at the opening of Disney World and EPCOT in October. Returns to Los Angeles by plane, conquering a lifelong fear of flying; subsequently travels by air overseas. Release of the Disney feature film adaptation of *Something Wicked This Way Comes* is delayed after a studio screening.

1983 *Dinosaur Tales*, an illustrated collection of stories for young readers, is published by Bantam. After significant reshooting and editing, *Something Wicked This Way Comes* is released by Disney in April; Bradbury's screenplay receives the Saturn Award for Writing from the Academy of Science Fiction, Fantasy, and Horror Films.

1984 Occasional unpublicized visits home to Waukegan, Illinois, culminate in an official visit, during which he receives the "Key to the City." The omnibus volume *Novels of Ray Bradbury* published by Granada in Great Britain. Dell releases a collection of Bradbury's early detective stories as *A Memory of Murder* in February. *Fahrenheit 451* receives Prometheus Award for best Hall of Fame Classic Fiction from the Libertarian Futurist Society; co-winner is George Orwell's *1984*. Chairs the newly formed World Interdependence Fund and its efforts to provide technological help to the disabled and disadvantaged.

1985 Testifies before the National Commission on Space, convened by President Reagan and the United States Congress to plan the next fifty years of space exploration. In its first season, *The Ray Bradbury Theater* receives an ACE (Award for Cable Excellence); by its final season (1993) the series will earn a total of ten ACE nominations and net six wins, as well as two Emmy nominations. *Death Is a Lonely Business*, the first of his three late-life autobiographical mystery novels, published by Knopf in October. Receives the Body of Work Award for lifetime achievement from the writers' group PEN USA.

1986 Serves as guest of honor at the World Science Fiction Convention. Dramatic Publishing releases a series of his plays for theatrical use. "There Is Life on Mars, and It Is Us!," expressing his settled views on the human desire to explore the cosmos, appears in the summer issue of *The Planetary Report*.

1987 Honored as keynote speaker at NASA's thirtieth annual Goddard Memorial Dinner in Washington, D.C.

1988 In May, Knopf releases his first story collection in twelve years, *The Toynbee Convector*.

1989 Named a Grand Master by the Science Fiction and Fantasy Writers of America for his lifetime achievement in these fields. Joshua Odell Editions publishes *Zen in the Art of Writing* in March; over time, it becomes his best-selling nonfiction work. *The Toynbee Convector* is nominated for a 1988 Bram Stoker Award by the Horror Writers Association.

1990 Attends a state luncheon at the Soviet Embassy in Washington, D.C., in June. A portion of the Yeoman Creek ravine near his childhood home in Waukegan, Illinois, is named the Ray Bradbury section of Powell

Park. In July, Knopf publishes his second mystery novel, *A Graveyard for Lunatics*, based on his occasional stints as a contract writer in Hollywood during the 1950s and early 1960s.

1991 Selected with other internationally prominent writers to judge the Turner Tomorrow Award. Travels to France, Italy, and Spain over the summer, giving the opening address for the Spoleto *Festival dei Due Mondi* and visiting Federico Fellini in Rome. *Ray Bradbury on Stage*, a compilation of his published stage plays, is released under the Donald I. Fine imprint. His essay collection *Yestermorrow!* is published by Joshua Odell Editions.

1992 In May, Knopf publishes *Green Shadows, White Whale*, a novelization of his Irish stories and his 1953–54 experiences in Ireland writing the screenplay for *Moby Dick*. The Science Fiction and Fantasy Writers of America establish The Ray Bradbury Award for excellence in screenwriting. Receives Mark Twain Award from the Society for the Study of Midwestern Literature, and honorary degrees from the California Institute of the Arts and West Coast University. Television documentary *Ray Bradbury: An American Icon* airs, with narration by actor and friend Rod Steiger.

1993 Bradbury's feature-length animated teleplay of his 1972 novel, *The Halloween Tree*, is aired October 20, 1993, on the Turner Broadcasting Channel. Bradbury shares a Cable ACE award for *The Ray Bradbury Theater* as Best Dramatic Series; this is the last of ten ACE nominations (and six wins) for the Bradbury series.

1994 Wins an Emmy for his animated screenplay adaptation of *The Halloween Tree*. Works through much of his annual summer stay in Paris on early drafts of a *Fahrenheit 451* screenplay for Mel Gibson, who has elicited interest from Warner Brothers.

1995 Is named Los Angeles Citizen of the Year for his contributions to city planning. Works on a screenplay of his story and stage play *The Wonderful Ice Cream Suit* for a possible Disney film production. Plans for the *Fahrenheit 451* screenplay-in-progress shift from Warner Brothers to Universal Studios.

1996 Receives an Honorary Doctorate of Humane Letters from California Lutheran University, and is nominated for the

First Fandom Hall of Fame Award, a Hugo ceremony honor recognizing original fans from the days of the first World Science Fiction Convention of 1939. Avon Books publishes *Quicker Than the Eye* (a story collection) in November. Los Angeles names a room in its main library for Ray Bradbury.

1997 *Driving Blind*, a collection of stories, is published in September by Avon. Under an option with Mel Gibson and Universal Studios, completes the final draft of his *Fahrenheit 451* screenplay; despite a long series of options, it is never produced.

1998 Publishes his second children's picture book, *Ahmed and the Oblivion Machines*. *Driving Blind* is nominated for a World Fantasy Award. Disney releases the feature film version of *The Wonderful Ice Cream Suit*, but distribution is limited to home video through Disney's Touchstone subsidiary.

1999 Receives the George Pal Memorial Award from the Academy of Science Fiction, Fantasy, and Horror Films, and is inducted (along with Robert Silverberg and posthumous inductees A. Merritt and Jules Verne) into the Science Fiction Hall of Fame. In November, suffers a stroke in Palm Springs that permanently limits his mobility and ability to type. Most of his subsequent writing will be initially recorded by dictation and transcribed by his daughter Alexandra.

2000 Receives the National Book Foundation Medal for Distinguished Contribution to American Letters on November 15. In spite of his limited mobility and the sudden permanent loss of vision in his left eye, attends the award ceremony in New York. Spacewatch project astronomers at Kit Peak observatory rename asteroid 1992DZ2 as 9766 Bradbury, in honor of the author.

2001 The World Horror Convention names Bradbury a Grand Master. July sees publication of *A Chapbook for Burnt-Out Priests, Rabbis, and Ministers* (published by Cemetery Dance), a collection of Bradbury's speculative writings on the cosmos and faith. *From the Dust Returned*, a novelized story cycle started more than fifty years earlier, published by Morrow. *Ray Bradbury, His Life and Work* printed by Book-of-the-Month Club in conjunction with its rerelease of four Bradbury classics. Mayor James Hahn of Los Angeles proclaims Ray Bradbury Day for Friday, December 14.

2002 *From the Dust Returned* is nominated for a Bram Stoker Award and a World Fantasy Award. *One More for the Road*, a story collection, is published in March by Morrow. *Fahrenheit 451* is named the "One Book, One City" selection for Los Angeles; other cities eventually select *Fahrenheit 451* for subsequent reading programs. Recognized for his contributions to film with the 2,193rd star on the Hollywood Walk of Fame in April.

2003 *One More for the Road* receives the Bram Stoker Award for best fiction collection. *Bradbury Stories*, his second hundred-story compilation, is published by Morrow. Receives an Honorary Doctorate from Woodbury University. Maggie Bradbury passes away in November after a brief illness. His third and final mystery novel, *Let's All Kill Constance!*, is published by Morrow.

2004 Addresses the Presidential Commission on Moon, Mars, and Beyond in April. His older brother and sole surviving sibling, Leonard, Jr. ("Skip"), passes away the same month. The 62nd World Science Fiction Convention awards *Fahrenheit 451* the Retro-Hugo as best novel fifty years after its 1953 publication. *The Cat's Pajamas*, a story collection with a cover illustration by Bradbury, is published by Morrow. Receives the National Medal of Arts from President Bush in November at a White House ceremony.

2005 *Bradbury Speaks*, a collection of articles and essays, is published in July by Morrow. *Maggie Remembered*, a tribute from Bradbury to his late wife, published by Hill House. Receives an honorary degree from the University of Ireland, Galway, presented in Los Angeles.

2006 The National Endowment for the Arts selects *Fahrenheit 451* for "The Big Read" national reading program. *The Homecoming* appears as a children's book, illustrated by Dave McKean for Collins Design. Deferred for a half century, *Farewell Summer*, the original novel from which the story-chapters of *Dandelion Wine* were extracted, is published by Morrow in October. Along with *Dandelion Wine* and *Something Wicked This Way Comes*, *Farewell Summer* completes his "Green Town" Illinois trilogy, based on memories of his childhood adventures in Waukegan.

2007 Is awarded a Pulitzer Prize special citation in April for his "prolific and deeply influential" career. Gauntlet Press gathers early versions of *Fahrenheit 451* and related stories as *Match to Flame*, later retitled *A Pleasure to Burn*. Receives the French Ordre des Arts et des Lettres (Commandeur) Medal from the French ambassador to the United States, and a National Olympus Award from the Russian Academy of Sciences. In September *Now and Forever*, a pairing of the long-deferred short novels *Somewhere a Band Is Playing* and *Leviathan '99*, is published by Morrow.

2008 Is named Grand Master Poet at the Rhysling Awards for science fiction and fantasy verse, and receives the first J. Lloyd Eaton Award for Lifetime Achievement in Science Fiction, from the University of California, Riverside. *Masks*, a gathering of materials from an unpublished novel of the late 1940s, is published by Gauntlet Press; Subterranean Press releases *Moby Dick: A Screenplay* from his submitted 1954 script of the 1956 Warner Brothers film. His final story collection, *We'll Always Have Paris*, appears in December.

2009 Hill & Wang publishes a graphic novel adaptation of *Fahrenheit 451*. Receives an honorary doctorate from Columbia College, Chicago. Don Congdon, his agent for sixty-two years, dies in November.

2010 Receives the Comic Con Icon Award during the Scream Awards, celebrating the history of horror, science fiction, and fantasy feature films. His ninetieth birthday is celebrated in and around Los Angeles through various events coordinated by writer Steven Paul Leiva; the Los Angeles City Council passes a resolution declaring August 22–28 to be Ray Bradbury Week.

2011 Contracts pneumonia in January and a subsequent MRSA infection in the spring; suffers what may be a minor stroke late in the year. He remains lucid and works on a few incomplete stories from earlier times.

2012 William Morrow publishes the Bradbury tribute volume *Shadow Show*, with stories by a wide range of contemporary writers. "Take Me Home," a short essay, appears in a

June special science fiction issue of *The New Yorker.* Dies on June 5 at Cedars Sinai Hospital in Los Angeles and is buried in Westwood Memorial Park. The Jet Propulsion Laboratory and NASA name the Mars rover Curiosity's landing zone after Bradbury on what would have been his ninety-second birthday, August 22. In September, a Los Angeles City Council resolution renames the intersection of Fifth and Flower, adjacent to the Los Angeles Central Library, as Ray Bradbury Square.

Note on the Texts

This is the second of two volumes of Ray Bradbury's fiction. It presents the complete texts of the short story collections *The Illustrated Man* (1951) and *The October Country* (1955), along with a selection of twenty-seven stories written from the early 1940s through the 1960s. The first volume in the set, *Novels & Story Cycles*, presents major book-length works from the same significant period of the author's career: *The Martian Chronicles* (1950), *Fahrenheit 451* (1953), *Dandelion Wine* (1957), and *Something Wicked This Way Comes* (1962), along with several related short articles and introductions by Bradbury.

The Illustrated Man. By the late 1940s, Bradbury's short fiction had a growing presence in the major market magazines. He gathered twenty-seven of his horror, weird, and fantasy tales for his first collection, *Dark Carnival*, published by Arkham House in 1947, and his short fiction appeared in the annual *O. Henry Prize Stories* anthologies of 1947 and 1948 and the *Best American Short Stories* collections of 1946 and 1948.

In October 1948, Bradbury and Don Congdon, his New York agent, offered Farrar, Straus, and Company a new, wide-ranging collection of stories called *The Illustrated Man* after the title story—a carnival murder tale that was still circulating (without success) among various magazine editors. Despite Roger Straus Jr.'s enthusiasm for Bradbury's work, Farrar, Straus turned down the story collection as well as two book-length works-in-progress: a novel of his Illinois childhood (which eventually diverged into *Dandelion Wine* and *Farewell Summer*) and a supernatural story cycle (*From the Dust Returned*). Even before the rejection by Farrar, Straus, Bradbury worried that the collection lacked focus. "My only fear now," he told the Arkham House publisher, August Derleth, "is that *The Illustrated Man* will be a little bit of everything, and not enough of one thing, what with layers of s.f., weird, fantastic, and realistic fiction bundled together."

A new concept for *The Illustrated Man* took shape in 1950 when Bradbury ran into difficulty completing *Frost and Fire* (a novel to be expanded from the 1946 story "The Creatures That Time Forgot"), then under contract with Doubleday. In fact, when Bradbury had submitted the final typescript of *The Martian Chronicles* to Doubleday through Don Congdon in the fall of 1949, he knew that he would not be able to meet the summer 1950 submission deadline for *Frost and*

Fire. Instead, he returned to the earlier collection that Roger Straus had declined, refashioning it with the idea of offering it to Doubleday in place of the novel. The working title for this roughly 132,000-word collection was *Frost and Fire.* It included three novella-length tales: "Pillar of Fire," "The Creatures That Time Forgot" (now retitled "Frost and Fire"), and his as-yet-unpublished "The Fireman," the forerunner of *Fahrenheit 451.* In mid-July 1950, the Doubleday editor Walt Bradbury (no relation) agreed to accept the collection in place of the unfulfilled novel, but persuaded Bradbury to cut the three novellas, including what would have been the title piece. The new collection was scheduled for publication in February 1951, yet it still lacked a final title or a firm table of contents.

During the summer of 1950, Bradbury produced three new outlines for the collection that reveal his continuing struggle to find an effective sequence of stories and a title. As he trimmed the collection to meet his editor's target length of 84,000 words (roughly eighteen stories), Bradbury retained only what he felt were the best remaining science fiction tales that had not been collected in *The Martian Chronicles.* (The carnival murder tale "The Illustrated Man," finally published in *Esquire* in July 1950, was one of the stories that was cut.) In July and the first half of August, he added a prologue and an epilogue that both unified the stories and provided a title through the storytelling body art of a mysterious illustrated man. He also revised most of the previously published magazine stories as he placed them between the framing prologue and epilogue. In a final gesture to his dreams of a future space age, Bradbury moved "The Rocket" from the middle section to the very end of the collection, concluding with a child's perspective of space-age wonderments yet to come—an effort to at least partly dispel what Bradbury had described to his Doubleday editor as "the overwhelming pessimism in a good many of these stories."

On August 19, 1950, Bradbury submitted to Walt Bradbury a final typescript, which served as the setting copy for the collection. From October 22 to November 27, he read and marked a set of galleys (now held in the private collection of Bradbury's friend and principal bibliographer, Donn Albright). *The Illustrated Man* was published on February 23, 1951, in a cloth binding with a dust jacket illustration by Sydney Butchkes that was loosely based on a collage design by Bradbury. Averse to genre labels, Bradbury successfully argued to have the Doubleday Science Fiction logo removed from the title page, but it remained on the book's spine.

Sixteen of the eighteen stories that make up *The Illustrated Man* had earlier (or simultaneous) magazine or anthology versions. To some degree, Bradbury revised most of the previously published magazine versions for the collection. Information about the prior publication history of individual stories included in the 1951 first edition of *The Illustrated Man* is provided below:

"The Veldt." *The Saturday Evening Post*, September 23, 1950 (as "The World the Children Made"); *The Saturday Evening Post Stories 1950*, ed. *Post* editors (New York: Random House, 1950).
"Kaleidoscope." *Thrilling Wonder Stories*, October 1949.
"The Other Foot." *New Story* (France), March 1951 (released in February).
"The Highway." *Copy*, Spring 1950 (as by Leonard Spaulding).
"The Man." *Thrilling Wonder Stories*, February 1949.
"The Long Rain." *Planet Stories* (US), Summer 1950, and *Planet Stories #3* (UK), January 1951 (as "Death-by-Rain").
"The Rocket Man." *Maclean's* (Canada), March 1, 1951 (released in February).
"The Last Night of the World." *Esquire*, February 1951.
"The Exiles." *Maclean's* (Canada), September 15, 1949 (as "The Mad Wizards of Mars"); *Beyond Time and Space*, ed. August Derleth (New York: Pellegrini & Cudahy, 1950, revised, as "The Exiles"); *The Magazine of Fantasy & Science Fiction*, Winter–Spring 1950 (revised again as "The Exiles").
"The Fox and the Forest." *Collier's*, May 13, 1950 (as "To the Future"); *Argosy* (UK), September 1950 (as "Escape"); *The Best Science Fiction Stories 1951*, ed. Everett F. Bleiler and T. E. Dikty (New York: Frederick Fell, 1951).
"The Visitor." *Startling Stories*, November 1948.
"The Concrete Mixer." *Thrilling Wonder Stories*, April 1949.
"Marionettes, Inc." *Startling Stories*, March 1949; *Thrills Incorporated #8* (Australia), 1950, as by D. K. Garton (as "Synthetic Alibi").
"The City." *Startling Stories*, July 1950 (as "Purpose").
"Zero Hour." *Planet Stories*, Fall 1947; *Avon Fantasy Reader #8*, 1948; *Invasion from Mars*, ed. Orson Welles (New York: Dell, 1949); *My Best Science Fiction Story*, ed. Leo Margulies and Oscar Friend (New York: Merlin Press, 1949).
"The Rocket." *Super Science Stories*, March 1950 (as "Outcast of the Stars").

Many of the individual stories gathered in *The Illustrated Man* have also appeared separately, after their initial book publication and sometimes under different titles, in magazines, anthologies, and Bradbury collections such as *R Is for Rocket* (1962), *The Vintage Bradbury* (1965), *S Is for Space* (1966), *Ray Bradbury* (UK, 1975), *The Stories of Ray Bradbury* (1980; UK, as *Ray Bradbury Stories*

1, 2008), *Classic Stories 1* (1990; as *The Golden Apples of the Sun and Other Stories*, 1997), *Classic Stories 2* (1990; as *A Medicine for Melancholy and Other Stories*, 1998), *Bradbury Stories* (2003; UK, as *Ray Bradbury Stories 2*, 2008), and *Killer, Come Back to Me* (2020). Bradbury did not make further revisions to the stories on the occasion of any of these subsequent publications.

A Bantam mass-market paperback printing was released in March 1952 with the same eighteen stories as the 1951 first edition, but this was not the case with a British cloth edition published by Rupert Hart-Davis in June 1952. The previous year, Hart-Davis had published *The Martian Chronicles* (as *The Silver Locusts*) with contents that (at Bradbury's request) restored "The Fire Balloons" and deleted "Usher II." Since the American first editions of *The Illustrated Man* contained "The Fire Balloons" but not "Usher II," the UK publisher removed "The Fire Balloons" from the British edition of *The Illustrated Man* and substituted "Usher II." Hart-Davis also added "The Playground" and deleted "The Rocket Man," "The Exiles," and "The Concrete Mixer," possibly due to his own preferences or to reduce the page count.

Bantam's uninterrupted paperback editions and printings and Doubleday's intermittent hardbound printings and new editions have retained the original eighteen-story contents of *The Illustrated Man*, but the sixteen-story British variation eventually appeared in America under the HarperCollins imprint. After the final lapse of the Doubleday hardbound rights, Avon published a 1997 small-format cloth edition that continued under Morrow after both publishers were acquired by HarperCollins. For this 1997 edition, Bradbury allowed the addition of his original horror fantasy "The Illustrated Man." This story was never added to the continuing Bantam editions or any other published form of the text. The text of *The Illustrated Man* in the present volume is that of the 1951 Doubleday first printing.

The October Country. Although *The October Country* is a distinct and influential story collection in its own right, it has its origins in Bradbury's first collection, *Dark Carnival* (1947), published by Arkham House, a small niche press specializing in weird fiction. By the early 1950s, Arkham House publisher August Derleth realized that Bradbury was now firmly established with major trade publishing houses and allowed him to buy out the remaining copies of the first and only edition of *Dark Carnival*, clearing the way for the collection to be reissued by another publisher. Doubleday had the right of first refusal but declined to make an offer, urging Bradbury instead to focus his energy and time on his Illinois novel project, under contract with Doubleday (eventually published, in part, as *Dandelion Wine*).

Other possibilities quickly presented themselves. Already under contract with Ballantine Books for *Fahrenheit 451*, Bradbury accepted an offer from Ian Ballantine to publish a new version of *Dark Carnival* to follow the publication of *Fahrenheit 451* in the fall of 1953. Ballantine proposed a collection comprised of sixteen of the original twenty-seven *Dark Carnival* stories along with six newer stories that had been dropped from the provisional contents of *Fahrenheit 451* as the title novel doubled in size. Anticipating publication in the fall of 1954, Ballantine and his editor-in-chief, Stanley Kauffmann, requested confirmation of the final contents and delivery of any revisions by mid-May 1954; however, that schedule proved unrealistic because Bradbury was still in London wrapping up his screenplay adaptation of *Moby-Dick* for John Huston and would not return to America until June.

Indeed, the exhaustive writing schedule for the film had dominated Bradbury's life in Ireland and London for seven months, leaving little time to work on the reconstituted *Dark Carnival.* Once home in Los Angeles, he began to make significant revisions in all the stories he planned to carry forward; by late October 1954, he had a projected table of contents that largely reflected what would be the final sequence for the interior stories. He was still undecided about placement for what he saw as the strongest *Dark Carnival* stories ("Homecoming" and "The Next in Line"), and two of the newer stories ("The Dwarf" and "The Wonderful Death of Dudley Stone"). For the time being, he decided to open with "Homecoming" (followed by "The Dwarf") and conclude with "The Next in Line" and "The Wonderful Death of Dudley Stone."

Bradbury's surviving progress sheet shows that from November 3, 1954, to January 24, 1955, he revised nineteen stories before sending them one at a time to Ian Ballantine. Bradbury subsequently removed the extremely short "The Dragon," for which he was still seeking magazine publication, and replaced it with "The Emissary," a reworked *Dark Carnival* tale. The final contents included fifteen stories from the original *Dark Carnival* collection and four newer tales from the group removed from *Fahrenheit 451*: "The Dwarf," "The Watchful Poker Chip of H. Matisse," "Touched with Fire," and "The Wonderful Death of Dudley Stone."

Even as Bradbury worked to finalize the contents, it was apparent to Ballantine and Kauffmann that the new version was essentially a new collection; nearly a third of the stories were newly collected, and only fifteen of the original twenty-seven *Dark Carnival* stories remained. Prompted by a letter of December 14, 1954, from Kauffmann suggesting that he retitle the collection, Bradbury wrote a two-page imagined childhood conversation with his grandfather, describing how he came to know the "October Country" and the autumn people of his imagination. A shorter version of that conversation became the epigraph of the new collection and gave the book its title.

Bradbury received galleys at the end of May 1955, and a month later, on June 21, Kauffmann acknowledged return of the corrected and revised galley sheets. Bradbury's proof revisions were substantial enough to warrant a charge for excess author's alterations. At this late stage of production, Kauffmann and Ballantine expressed concern about opening the book with such a well-known tale as "Homecoming" (as "The Homecoming" it constitutes the first story in the original *Dark Carnival*). Bradbury concurred, and at the eleventh hour he decided to open with "The Dwarf" followed by "The Next in Line," and to keep "The Wonderful Death of Dudley Stone" as the concluding story in the collection, with "Homecoming" now the penultimate story. Bradbury's friend, the Italian-born American illustrator and artist Joseph Mugnaini, who had previously illustrated *Fahrenheit 451*, supplied interior art for *The October Country* along with its now often-reprinted dust jacket illustration.

Ballantine published *The October Country* in hardcover on October 31, 1955—Halloween—and a British printing by Hart-Davis followed in the spring using the Ballantine plates. After Carlos Baker in *The New York Times* characterized the tales as a step backward in the career of a promising author, Bradbury decided to add a prefatory note to the 1956 Ballantine mass-market paperback printing, stating that fifteen of the stories in the collection "were written before my twenty-sixth birthday." (This note remained in subsequent paperback printings until 1996.) When Ballantine published the book in paperback in April 1956, the hardcover setting was adjusted to accommodate an increase from 36 lines per page to 40 lines per page. Three of the nineteen typographical errors were also corrected, along with a major transposition error in "Homecoming." That error involved sixteen lines (468.15–30) that were dropped below the next twenty lines of text (468.30–469.10). After 1996, this transposition error from the hardbound text was introduced into subsequent paperback editions in America.

Neither the submitted typescript nor the corrected galleys have been located; it is possible that Ballantine prepared the setting copy from the individual revised story typescripts that Bradbury sent by separate mailings from November 1954 through January 1955. Separate typescripts of individual stories are known to survive; many of these are held in the Albright Collection, with photocopies preserved in the Center for Ray Bradbury Studies at Indiana University. The text presented here follows the first Ballantine printing; however, this edition corrects the long transposition error in the first printing (along with other, smaller typographical errors). Bradbury's prefatory note on the origins of the older stories, only appearing in the paperback printings of the first edition, appears in this volume's notes.

All nineteen stories had earlier magazine or anthology versions. Information about the prior publication history of individual stories included in the October 1955 first edition of *The October Country* appears in the following list. Original magazine versions revised by Bradbury for *Dark Carnival* and revised again for *The October Country* are so noted:

"The Dwarf." *Fantastic*, January–February 1954.

"The Next in Line." First published as collected in *Dark Carnival.*

"The Watchful Poker Chip of H. Matisse." *Beyond*, March 1954 (as "The Watchful Poker Chip").

"Skeleton." *Weird Tales*, September 1945 (US); *Weird Tales*, November 1945 (Canada); *Rex Stout's Mystery Magazine #6*, October 1946. Revised and collected in *Dark Carnival*; revised again for *The October Country.*

"The Jar." *Weird Tales*, November 1944 (US); *Weird Tales*, July 1945 (Canada), as by Edward Banks; *The Sleeping and the Dead*, ed. August Derleth (Chicago: Pellegrini & Cudahy, 1947); *Fear and Trembling*, ed. Alfred Hitchcock (New York: Dell, 1948). Revised and collected in *Dark Carnival*; revised again for *The October Country.*

"The Lake." *Weird Tales*, May 1944 (US); *Weird Tales*, September 1944 (Canada); *Who Knocks?*, ed. August Derleth (New York: Rinehart, 1946); *Shenandoah Review*, Spring 1951. Revised and collected in *Dark Carnival*; revised again for *The October Country.*

"The Emissary." First published as collected in *Dark Carnival*; *New Story*, July 1951 (revised). Revised again for *The October Country.*

"Touched with Fire." *Maclean's* (Canada), June 1, 1954, and *The Saint Detective Magazine*, February 1955 (both as "Shopping for Death"); *Argosy* (UK), November 1954 (as "Shopping for Murder").

"The Small Assassin." *Dime Mystery*, November 1946; *Suspense*, April 1951; *Children of Wonder*, ed. William Tenn (New York: Simon & Schuster, 1953, abridged). Revised and collected in *Dark Carnival*; revised again for *The October Country.*

"The Crowd." *Weird Tales*, May 1943 (US); *Weird Tales*, September 1943 (Canada); *Argosy* (UK), May 1949; *Mysterious Traveler Mystery Reader #5*, 1952; *Terror in the Modern Vein*, ed. Donald A. Wollheim (Garden City, NY: Hanover House, 1955). Revised and collected in *Dark Carnival*; revised again for *The October Country.*

"Jack-in-the-Box." First published as collected in *Dark Carnival* (1947; deleted from the abridged British edition, 1948); *Avon Fantasy Reader #17*, 1951. Revised and collected in *The October Country.*

"The Scythe." *Weird Tales*, July 1943 (US); *Weird Tales*, November 1943 (Canada). Revised and collected in *Dark Carnival* (1947; deleted from the abridged British edition, 1948). Revised again for *The October Country.*

"Uncle Einar." First published as collected in *Dark Carnival*; *Argosy* (UK), October 1949.

"The Wind." *Weird Tales*, March 1943 (US); *Weird Tales*, July 1943 (Canada); *Mysterious Traveler*, November 1951; *Argosy* (UK), November 1951 (as "Valley of the Winds"). Revised and collected in *Dark Carnival*; revised again for *The October Country.*

"The Man Upstairs." *Harper's*, March 1947; *Avon Fantasy Reader #4*, 1947; *Argosy* (UK), December 1951; *New Liberty* (Canada), August 1952; *Harper's Magazine Reader*, ed. anon. (New York: Bantam, 1953). An earlier version, already typeset, was collected in *Dark Carnival* (published May 1947). The *Harper's* revised version was revised again for *The October Country.*

"There Was an Old Woman." *Weird Tales*, July 1944 (US); *Weird Tales*, November 1944 (Canada); *Argosy* (UK), August 1949. Revised and collected in *Dark Carnival*; revised again for *The October Country.*

"The Cistern." *Mademoiselle*, May 1947. An earlier version, already typeset, was collected in *Dark Carnival* (published May 1947, as "Cistern"). The *Mademoiselle* revised version was revised again and collected as "The Cistern" in *The October Country.*

"Homecoming." *Mademoiselle*, October 1946; *Avon Fantasy Reader #3*, 1947; *Prize Stories of 1947: The O. Henry Awards*, ed. Herschel Brickell (Garden City, NY: Doubleday, 1947); *Argosy* (UK), September 1949 (revised); *Famous Fantastic Mysteries*, December 1952 (as "The Homecoming"); *Galaxy of Ghouls*, ed. Judith Merril (New York: Lion Library, 1955). An early draft version (predating the first publication in *Mademoiselle*) was collected in *Dark Carnival* (published May 1947), as "The Homecoming." The revised *Mademoiselle* version was revised again and collected as "Homecoming" in *The October Country.*

"The Wonderful Death of Dudley Stone." *Charm*, July 1954.

Many of the individual stories gathered in *The October Country* have also appeared separately, after their initial book publication and sometimes under different titles, in magazines, anthologies, and Bradbury collections such as *R Is for Rocket* (1962), *The Small Assassin* (UK, 1962), *The Vintage Bradbury* (1965), *Ray Bradbury* (UK, 1975), *The Mummies of Guanajuato* (1978), *To Sing Strange Songs* (UK, 1979), *The Stories of Ray Bradbury* (1980; UK, as *Ray Bradbury Stories 1*, 2008), *A Memory of Murder* (1984), *Classic Stories 1* (1990; as *The Golden Apples of the Sun and Other Stories*, 1997), *Bradbury Stories* (2003; UK, as *Ray Bradbury Stories 2*, 2008), and *Killer, Come Back to Me* (2020). Bradbury did not make further revisions to the stories on the occasion of any of these subsequent publications; however, he did revise and abridge "Uncle Einar" and "Homecoming" into story-chapters within the novelized story cycle *From the Dust Returned* (2001).

Other Stories. Many of Bradbury's most accomplished stories of the first three decades of his career fall outside the celebrated collections *The Illustrated Man* and *The October Country.* These include stories in *The Golden Apples of the Sun* (1953) and *A Medicine for Melancholy* (1959), which were later combined in *Twice 22* (1966). Stories from these and other Bradbury collections and story cycles were combined to form the perennially popular juvenile collections *R Is for Rocket* (1962) and *S Is for Space* (1966). Further stories in the present volume were originally gathered by Bradbury in two 1960s story collections, *The Machineries of Joy* (1964) and *I Sing the Body Electric!* (1969). Bradbury's many story collections published after the 1960s contain more and more work harvested from earlier decades, leading to the present volume's inclusion of stories that make their belated collected appearance in *Long After Midnight* (1976) or *The Toynbee Convector* (1988). The text for each of these stories is taken from the first Bradbury collection in which it appeared, since he exercised a large degree of authorial control over his collections; however, in order to preserve the evolution of Bradbury's maturing creativity, these stories are presented in chronological order by the date of their first publication or—in the case of "A Touch of Petulance," not published in any form until thirty years after it was written—by the date of composition.

The editors of *R Is for Rocket* and *S Is for Space*, in preparing editions of Bradbury's stories aimed at young readers, bowdlerized the texts. The texts are presented here with Bradbury's original language restored at the points listed below from the stories' original periodical publications.

In "R Is for Rocket": 489.18, shut up; 489.25, I had flunked;

494.2, Blast them; 495.8–9, you drink; 495.9, what the heck; 498.11, why in heck; 498.12, Blast it; 502.15, "What the heck—. In two instances, Bradbury also made revisions to the text in places where the editors censored the language. In these places, Bradbury's revisions have been retained but "damn" has been restored in place of "darn": 494.1, the serial publication read "Damn right we can" and the initial book publication read "Darn rights"; this volume prints "Damn right." 500.3, the serial publication read "Damned right, I will. Oh, damned right—" and the initial book publication read "'Darn rights, darn rights,' I murmured"; this volume prints "'Damn right, damn right,' I murmured."

In "Chrysalis": 505.16, again, Rockwell.; 511.8, "What in blazes; 515.21, whole confounded; 518.20, "This fool, this fool,"; 522.32, what I'd; 523.26, This is silly."

In "Frost and Fire": 538.25, become shapely; 541.2, insane. The grass; 544.7, laughter of young people; 548.3, her neck where.

In "Pillar of Fire": 581.3, whole world!"; 583.17–18, your Incinerators; 586.2, monstrous firetrap; 586.32, knew that; 591.4–5, How in blazes; 595.19, their practices; 597.17, but, how realistic.; 599.4, biggest firecracker; 600.12, that!; 604.9, There, there were; 608.20, whatever in blazes; 612.25, "Blast you!"; 612.28, like an idiot.

The magazine and anthology publication history of each story from the time of initial publication up to first publication in a Bradbury collection appears in the following list.

"R Is for Rocket." *Famous Fantastic Mysteries*, December 1943 (as "King of the Gray Spaces"); *Super Science Stories* (Canada), August 1944; *The Science Fiction Galaxy*, ed. Groff Conklin (New York: Permabooks, 1950); *Every Boy's Book of Science Fiction*, ed. Donald A. Wollheim (New York: Frederick Fell, 1951). Revised and collected with the original typescript title restored in *R Is for Rocket* (1962).

"Chrysalis." *Amazing Stories*, July 1946. Lightly revised and collected in *S Is for Space* (1966). Not to be confused with the unrelated story "Chrysalis" (first published in *The Cat's Pajamas*, 2004).

"Frost and Fire." *Planet Stories*, Fall 1946 (as "The Creatures That Time Forgot"). Revised and collected as "Frost and Fire" in *R Is for Rocket* (1962).

"Powerhouse." *Charm*, March 1948; *Prize Stories of 1948: The O. Henry Awards*, ed. Hershel Brickell (Garden City, NY: Doubleday, 1948). Collected in *The Golden Apples of the Sun* (1953).

"Pillar of Fire." *Planet Stories*, Summer 1948; *The Other Side of the Moon*, ed. August Derleth (New York: Pellegrini & Cudahy, 1949; UK, 1956); *A Treasury of Great Science Fiction*, vol. 1, ed. Anthony Boucher (Garden City, NY: Doubleday, 1959). Collected in *S Is for Space* (1966).

"Asleep in Armageddon." *Planet Stories*, Winter 1948; *Avon Fantasy Reader #11*, 1949; *Possible Worlds of Science Fiction*, ed. Groff Conklin (New York: Vanguard Press, 1951; London: Grayson & Grayson, 1952); *Argosy* (UK), February 1952; *Authentic Science Fiction #33* (UK), May 15, 1953; *Beyond the Stars #211* (Australia), 1955. Collected as "Perchance to Dream" in *The Day It Rained Forever* (1959, the variant UK edition of *A Medicine for Melancholy*).

"Dark They Were, and Golden-Eyed." *Thrilling Wonder Stories*, August 1949 (as "The Naming of Names"); *The Best from Startling Stories*, ed. Sam Mines (New York: Holt, 1953; London: Cassell, 1954, as *Startling Stories*); *Science and Sorcery*, ed. Garret Ford (Los Angeles: Fantasy Publishing, 1953). Rewritten and collected as "Dark They Were, and Golden-Eyed" in *A Medicine for Melancholy* (1959).

"A Touch of Petulance." Composed 1950; *Dark Forces*, ed. Kirby McCauley (New York: Viking Press, 1980; London: MacDonald Futura Publications, 1980). Collected in *The Toynbee Convector* (1988).

"The Screaming Woman." *Today [The Philadelphia Inquirer]*, May 27, 1951; *Suspense*, Winter 1952 (US, revised); *Suspense* (UK), January 1959; *The Saint Detective Magazine*, September 1955 (US); *The Saint Detective Magazine* (UK), August 1957; *The Graveyard Reader*, ed. Groff Conklin (New York: Ballantine, 1958); *Argosy* (UK), October 1964 (as "Screaming Woman"). Collected in *S Is for Space* (1966).

"The Fog Horn." *The Saturday Evening Post* June 23, 1951 (as "The Beast from 20,000 Fathoms"); *The Saturday Evening Post Stories, 1951*, ed. *Post* editors (New York: Random House, 1951); *Argosy* (UK), August 1951 (as "The Fog Horn"). Collected as "The Fog Horn" in *The Golden Apples of the Sun* (1953).

"The Pedestrian." *The Reporter*, August 7, 1951; *The Magazine of Fantasy & Science Fiction*, February 1952; *Best Science Fiction Stories* 1952, ed. Everett F. Bleiler and T. E. Dikty (New York: Frederick Fell, 1952); *Timeless Stories for Today and Tomorrow*, ed. Ray Bradbury (New York: Bantam, 1952). Collected in *The Golden Apples of the Sun* (1953).

"The Playground." First published in the British edition of *The Illustrated Man* ([June 20] 1952), but never included in the American editions over which Bradbury exercised authorial control; *Esquire*, October 1953. Collected in *Fahrenheit 451* (October 1953).

"A Sound of Thunder." *Collier's*, June 28, 1952 (conclusion abridged without authorial permission); *Argosy* (UK), October 1952. Slightly revised, conclusion restored, and collected in *The Golden Apples of the Sun* (1953).

"The Great Wide World Over There." *Maclean's* (Canada), August 15, 1952 (as "Cora and the Great Wide World"). Collected as "The Great Wide World Over There" in *The Golden Apples of the Sun* (1953).

"The Golden Apples of the Sun." First published as collected in *The Golden Apples of the Sun* (1953).

"And the Rock Cried Out." *Manhunt*, September 1953 (as "The Millionth Murder"). Rewritten and collected as "And the Rock Cried Out" in the American first edition of *Fahrenheit 451* (October 1953).

"All Summer in a Day." *The Magazine of Fantasy & Science Fiction*, March 1954; *The New York Post*, December 5, 1954; *The Best from Fantasy & Science Fiction: Fourth Series*, ed. Anthony Boucher (Garden City, NY: Doubleday, 1955). Collected in *A Medicine for Melancholy* (1959).

"Interval in Sunlight." *Esquire*, March 1954. Revised and collected in *Long After Midnight* (1976).

"At Midnight, in the Month of June." *Ellery Queen's Mystery Magazine* (US and UK issues), June 1954; *Night Chills*, ed. Kirby McCauley (New York: Avon, 1975). Collected in *The Toynbee Convector* (1988).

"The Strawberry Window." *Star Science Fiction Stories 3*, ed. Frederik Pohl (New York: Ballantine, 1954); *Argosy* (UK), August 1955. Collected in *A Medicine for Melancholy* (1959).

"Icarus Montgolfier Wright." *The Magazine of Fantasy & Science Fiction*, May 1956; *The Best from Fantasy & Science Fiction: Sixth Series*, ed. Anthony Boucher (Garden City, NY: Doubleday, 1957). Collected in *A Medicine for Melancholy* (1959).

"The End of the Beginning." *Maclean's* (Canada), October 27, 1956 (as "Next Stop, the Stars"). *Colorado Review #1*, Winter 1956–57 (as "The End of the Beginning"). Collected as "The End of the Beginning" in *A Medicine for Melancholy* (1959).

"The Day It Rained Forever." *Harper's*, July 1957; *The Best American Short Stories 1958*, ed. Martha Foley and David

Burnett (Boston: Houghton Mifflin, 1958). Collected in *A Medicine for Melancholy* (1959).

"A Miracle of Rare Device." *Playboy*, January 1962; *Argosy* (UK), January 1963; *The Worlds of Science Fiction*, ed. Robert P. Mills (New York: Dial Press, 1963); *8th Annual of the Year's Best SF*, ed. Judith Merril (New York: Simon & Schuster, 1963). Collected in *The Machineries of Joy* (1964).

"The Kilimanjaro Device." *Life* magazine, January 22, 1965 (as "The Kilimanjaro Machine"). *Argosy* (UK), June 1965 (as "The Kilimanjaro Machine"). Collected as "The Kilimanjaro Device" in *I Sing the Body Electric!* (1969).

"The Lost City of Mars." *Playboy*, January 1967; *3 to the Highest Power*, ed. William F. Nolan (New York: Avon, 1968); *Psychology Today*, April 1969 (excerpt, published as "Swing Low Sweet Chariot"); *The Daily Sketch* (UK), October 14–15, 1969. Collected in *I Sing the Body Electric!* (1969).

"I Sing the Body Electric!" *McCall's*, August 1969 (as "The Beautiful One Is Here"). Collected as "I Sing the Body Electric!" in *I Sing the Body Electric!* (1969).

This volume presents the texts of the original printings chosen for inclusion here, but it does not attempt to reproduce features of their design and layout. The texts are presented without change, except for the correction of typographical errors. Spelling, punctuation, and capitalization are often expressive features and they are not altered, even when inconsistent or irregular. The following is a list of errors corrected, cited by page and line number: 85.4, "'But; 158.3, How may; 207.19, thinks; 234.3, butcher!"; 239.8, richocheting; 244.18, Paracutin; 249.4, *trabajando*; 249.8, senor,; 249.25, *veo?*"; 270.4–5, bank home.; 270.37, special special; 278.21, Garvey's; 281.20, now that; 289.2, .next; 290.40, said,; 292.19, Compare Compare.; 292.29, laughed "I; 304.39, nothing,; 305.19, in in; 309.6, Maybe; 316.34, baby.; 322.4, life guard; 339.30, eatin; 339.35, Grandular; 340.4, *see?*; 340.37, bar-room.Another; 342.22, things; 364.30, You've; 366.40, no!; 368.13, said.; 369.21, Coincidence; 379.38, she murmured. . . ."; 382.2, God Himself . . .; 412.38, woods."; 418.26, *here.* Allin."; 423.7, asked,; 425.26, silence,; 428.2, Douglas'; 431.39, today, It's; 436.12, he turned; 436.29, but its; 437.10, "The; 446.37, remembered. to; 463.3, though; 466.1, demanded.; 466.27, *thee*; 471.4, if off; 481.22, On on hand; 481.27–28, [lines transposed]; 482.5, "I'd; 506.27, Murphy [et passim]; 507.17, at as; 514.4, Hartly; 518.29, croaked.; 519.2, naval; 525.34, "Everything's; 527.30, dessication; 530.2, uselesly; 530.5, parents; 532.13–14, [lines transposed]; 533.13, all his; 542.35, "The; 562.29, dessicated; 606.7, the; 623.33, The whirling; 626.27, down?"; 629.19, dont; 657.38, Dad,; 659.24, temper."; 660.39, Allen; 665.29, while be; 684.40, boy, he thought?; 739.29, He her her.; 748.21, said.; 780.27, quiet; 780.39, party; 828.33, Alamagordo; 865.2, five-years; 865.14, has; 884.29, effect; 890.2, Rapped; 890.31, then; 891.40, lapus; 895.14, Tim."; 906.37, out.; 913.37, Gepetto.

Note on the Joseph Mugnaini Illustrations

The twelve line art illustrations that appear with *The October Country* were created by Joseph Mugnaini, an artist, writer, and teacher who collaborated extensively with Bradbury for the 1955 first edition. They can be found on pages 228, 274, 284, 302, 332, 365, 393, 414, 427, 453, 462, and 474 in this volume.

The illustrations are mastered from a mix of original Mugnaini artwork and scans of the Ballantine hardbound first edition. They represent the 1955 imagery as printed, with the exception of "The Wind." That illustration is mastered from the original art submitted to Ballantine as opposed to what saw print. Mugnaini had to modify the art on-press during proof runs due to reproduction issues. The reproduction here retains the original composition and detail.

Born Giuseppe Mugnaini in Viareggio, Italy, on July 12, 1912, to Antonio and Concetta Mugnaini, he and his family immigrated to the United States when Mugnaini was three months old. He grew up in a pre-war, pre-boom Los Angeles. Enrolling in the Otis Art Institute in 1940, he left it in 1942 to join the United States military, soon becoming a U.S. citizen. Mugnaini served with the U.S. Army Intelligence Corps in Europe, returning to Los Angeles and Otis following the end of World War II. He earned a faculty position at Otis and for thirty of his thirty-five years there was head of the Drawing Department. Following his retirement in 1976, Mugnaini lectured extensively at universities across the United States, continuing to teach until a year before his death in 1992.

"One night in the spring of 1952," Ray Bradbury would write, "I was strolling through Beverly Hills with my wife, passing shops I couldn't afford to go in, when I stood riveted in front of a benefit art show window." Bradbury was mesmerized by a lithograph that hung there: Mugnaini's *Modern Gothic*. It was a moody monotone depiction of a Victorian mansion, "the sort of place a beast like myself might want to live."

"I fell in love with Joe's work immediately," Bradbury said in a 1995 interview.

Their enduring collaboration began that year with the short story anthology *The Golden Apples of the Sun* and would last nearly forty years. The partnership Bradbury described as "a damn jolly good history of friendship and collaboration" encompassed more than twenty books, a lithography portfolio, numerous theatrical productions, a proposed Smithsonian Institution television series, and the Academy Award–nominated film *Icarus Montgolfier Wright*.

"The stories were already written, so I worked from there," Mugnaini explained in a 1990 interview. "I always chose the subject that I thought I could work with, and then I'd collaborate with Ray. He'd make his comments and then I'd go from there."

"I have been careful," Bradbury wrote, "simply to toss him a scrap of idea, concept, simile, metaphor, and then run like blazes for the exit, leaving him to flesh out the bone, skin over the skeleton with his ever-fresh, ever-growing talent. For every notion I have handed him, he has given me back a dozen samples to pick from. Joe, I have often cried, not so many! Hell, says Joe, and does another dozen."

In some cases, Bradbury would provide Mugnaini with a sketch. Mugnaini described Bradbury's drawings as "always exciting. Sometimes he'd give me a drawing or an idea or make a graphics statement. I'd elaborate on that, give him a lot of examples, we'd choose one, and I'd go from there."

"I think Joe works very much the same way I do," Bradbury said in another interview. "He floats over a thing. He takes inspiration from a story of mine and tries to forget a lot I've said. Otherwise, it would be no fun. If he was just repeating what I'd already said, his illustrations would be no fun. It's the fact that Joe then gives me a gift of myself and him at the same time. And I say, 'Hey, is that what I meant?' Then I look at his illustration and I'll be goddamned that it is. But it's Joe, *too*. So that's why we've had a real twin relationship so many years, so happily."

The many awards won during his career demonstrate Mugnaini's wide range of talents and interests: painting, drawing, lithography, book illustration, teaching, filmmaking, and theater set design. His work resides in the permanent collections of the Library of Congress, the Smithsonian Institution, and the Los Angeles County Museum of Art (LACMA).

Mugnaini illustrated more than fifty books, designed hundreds of lithographs, authored five books on art, and contributed to several films—including the creation of more than 350 paintings for Ray Bradbury's animated film *Icarus Montgolfier Wright* (1962).

Notes

In the notes below, the reference numbers denote page and line of this volume (the line count includes story or chapter headings but not blank lines). No note is generally made for material included in standard desk-reference works. Quotations from Shakespeare are keyed to *The Riverside Shakespeare*, ed. G. Blakemore Evans (Boston: Houghton Mifflin, 1974), and biblical references to the King James Version. For further information about Bradbury's life and works, and references to other studies, see Jonathan R. Eller, *Becoming Ray Bradbury*, *Ray Bradbury Unbound*, and *Bradbury Beyond Apollo* (Urbana: University of Illinois Press, 2011, 2014, 2020, respectively); Jonathan R. Eller and William F. Touponce, *Ray Bradbury: The Life of Fiction* (Kent, OH: The Kent State University Press, 2004); William F. Nolan, *The Bradbury Companion* (Detroit: Gale, 1975); and Sam Weller, *The Bradbury Chronicles* (New York: William Morrow, 2005).

THE ILLUSTRATED MAN

5.4 *walking tour of Wisconsin*] Bradbury's sense of the southern Wisconsin landscape drew on childhood vacations on Wisconsin's Lake Delavan in the late 1920s and early 1930s, and his 1946 visit to his first book publisher, Arkham House founder August Derleth (1909–1971), in Sauk City, near Madison. His native Waukegan, Illinois, close to the Wisconsin state line, shared much of the same topography.

5.6–7 *Illustrated Man . . . against the sky.*] Cf. Edwin Arlington Robinson, *The Man Against the Sky* (1916).

6.16–17 *"All of me is Illustrated.*] Bradbury's abiding fascination with carnivalesque body art inspired *All of Me Is Illustrated*, a Bradbury centennial art book published in 2020 that includes the prologue and epilogue from *The Illustrated Man* as well as the unrelated Bradbury stories "The Illustrated Man" and "The Illustrated Woman."

7.38 *Rouault colors*] French painter Georges Rouault (1871–1958), whose work inspired the Expressionist movement with its contrastive colors and emotional symbolism.

12.26 Wendy and Peter] Wendy Darling and Peter Pan, the principal characters of *Peter Pan; or the Boy Who Wouldn't Grow Up*, the novel (1904) and stage play (1911) by J. M. Barrie (1860–1937).

14.28–32 Wonderland, Alice . . . Pegasus] Wonderland, Alice, and the Mock Turtle are from Lewis Carroll's (Charles Lutwidge Dodgson, 1832–1898)

Through the Looking Glass (1871); "Aladdin and His Magical Lamp," an Arabian folktale added by Antoine Galland (1646–1715) to his French translation of *The Book of One Thousand and One Nights* (vols. IX–X, 1710); Jack Pumpkinhead of Oz is featured in L. Frank Baum's (1856–1919) *The Marvelous Land of Oz* (1904), the second volume in the Oz series; Dr. Doolittle, from *The Story of Dr. Doolittle* (1920), by Hugh Lofting (1886–1947); the cow jumping over the moon features in the nursery rhyme "Hey Diddle Diddle," which assumed its full lyrical form in the compilation *Mother Goose's Melody* (c. 1765); and Pegasus, the winged horse tamed by Bellerophon in Greek mythology, and also a constellation.

16.7 Tom Swift and his Electric Lion] Cf. *Tom Swift and His Electric Rifle* (1911), the tenth in the long-running series of juvenile adventure novels by various authors under the "Victor Appleton" pseudonym. A man-killing lion is brought down by the rifle, saving the latest victim of the big cat.

16.28 Rima] Principal character from the novel *Green Mansions: A Romance of the Tropical Forest* (1904), by W. H. [William Henry] Hudson (1841–1922).

18.1 Green Mansions] See note 16.28.

26.16 jackstones . . . gigantic throw.] The game of jacks, or jackstones, is played with a dozen or more six-pointed jacks and a ball; the jacks must be scattered in a single throw, and then gathered during the time between the throw of the ball and its first bounce.

33.5 Myrmidone cluster] Myrmidone is a Danae, one of the fifty daughters of Danaus mythologized in Ovid's *Metamorphoses*; in the *Iliad*, the Myrmidons were the warrior people commanded by the Greek champion Achilles, descendants of King Myrmidon of Phthiotis, who was fathered by Zeus while in the form of an ant. Either myth could have triggered the name of Bradbury's fictional cluster.

42.7 no intermarriages!"] Bradbury, who had lived in California since 1934, wrote "The Other Foot" shortly after California became the first state to strike down interracial marriage laws in 1948; the United States Supreme Court's *Loving v. Virginia* decision struck down the nation's remaining state antimiscegenation laws in 1967.

51.5 hub lid] Automobile wheel hubcap or cover.

54.16 Darwin] The publication dates of *On the Origin of Species* (1859) and *The Descent of Man* (1871) by British naturalist and geologist Charles Darwin (1809–1882) are often regarded as significant historical markers in the decline of faith and religious institutions in modern Western culture.

87.30–31 the jewelry in Orion] The so-called belt and sword sheath traditionally seen in the constellation Orion along with the first-magnitude stars Betelgeuse (red) and Rigel (blue), including the M42 nebula, which forms the middle "star" of the sword, have been well-known for their jewel-like colors since the eighteenth century. The M42 nebula was the first nebula to be photographed in the mid-nineteenth century.

91.16 the Episcopal Fathers] Traditionally, members of a communal and celibate religious order within the Anglican Communion, under the See (or Diocese) of Canterbury.

95.6 black Irish] A term sometimes associated with immigrant Irish down through history, including those who left Ireland during the potato famine of 1847, known as "the black '47." More broadly attributed to Irish descendants of successive invaders or applied descriptively to Irish with black hair but fair skin and blue eyes.

100.13 St. Anthony's fire] Bradbury may have intended a reference to St. Elmo's fire, the glow or balls of light generated during electrical storms at sea, often seen by sailors as a good omen, rather than St. Anthony's fire, a medieval name for the burning sensations and hallucinations caused by consumption of ergot-poisoned grain.

107.27–28 lilies of the field . . . spin] Cf. Matthew 6:28, Luke 12:27.

113.5–13 "When shall we three . . . cauldron bubble!"] *Macbeth*, I.i.1–2, IV.i.4–5, 35–36.

115.37 were-things] I.e., humans transformed into animal forms beyond the traditional folklore form of werewolves.

116.3 the dusty titles] The literary works and authors in "The Exiles" differ at points in *The Illustrated Man* version from the original publication of the story as "The Mad Wizards of Mars" (1949) and the intermediate versions in August Derleth's genre anthology *Beyond Time and Space* (1950) and *The Magazine of Fantasy & Science Fiction* (1950). To some degree these changes (see subsequent notes) reflect Bradbury's discussions with Derleth and *F&SF*'s Anthony Boucher.

116.7 *Rappaccini's Daughter*] In *Beyond Time and Space*, Bradbury substituted Hawthorne's *Mosses from an Old Manse.*

116.8 *An Occurrence at Owl Creek Bridge*] In *Beyond Time and Space*, Bradbury substituted Bierce's *Can Such Things Be?*

116.9 *The Willows*] In *Beyond Time and Space*, Bradbury substituted Blackwood's *The Empty House.*

116.11 *The Weird Shadow Over Innsmouth*] The *Maclean's Magazine* version incorrectly reads "The Horror at Innsmouth"; in *Beyond Time and Space*, Bradbury substituted Lovecraft's *The Outsider and Others.*

116.12–13 Walter de la Mare . . . Huxley] De la Mare (1873–1956), English novelist and poet known for horror stories; Herbert Russell Wakefield (1888–1964), British writer known for his ghost tales; William Fryer (W. F.) Harvey (1885–1937), British surgeon and horror story writer, most famous for "The

Beast with Five Fingers" (1928; film 1946); Herbert George (H. G.) Wells (1866–1946), author and social critic best known for his scientific romances; Lady Cynthia Asquith (1887–1960), British aristocrat and writer of ghost stories and novels; Aldous Huxley (1894–1963), British expatriate author, philosopher, and screenwriter whose works include *Brave New World* (1932). Bradbury knew Huxley personally, beginning around 1950.

116.26–27 the Emerald City] The capital of the fantasy country Oz in L. Frank Baum's Oz series of novels. Bradbury's literary ghosts originally occupy an unnamed castle in the *Maclean's Magazine* version of the story.

117.4 Puck] Originally "Othello, Lear" in *Maclean's* and in *Beyond Time and Space.*

118.25–26 a wink. . . . They moved] *The Magazine of Fantasy & Science Fiction* text includes a long satirical encounter with H. P. Lovecraft's ghost at this point; Bradbury deleted the passage in revising for *The Illustrated Man.*

118.34 The Red Death."] "The Masque of the Red Death," by Edgar Allan Poe (1842).

119.23–121.33 Over a lonely moor . . . fat boy.] Originally, this passage describes Poe's visit with Nathaniel Hawthorne in *Maclean's* and in *Beyond Time and Space*; Anthony Boucher persuaded Bradbury to substitute Charles Dickens in place of Hawthorne for the *Fantasy & Science Fiction* version, which carried over to *The Illustrated Man.*

119.30 "God Rest Ye Merry, Gentlemen,"] One of the earliest English Christmas carols, also known as "Tidings of Comfort and Joy." Cf. Scrooge's confrontation with the carolers in the beginning of Charles Dickens's novella *A Christmas Carol* (1843).

119.35 Marley-faced knocker] Scrooge's late business partner in *A Christmas Carol.*

120.25 a black cat.] Edgar Allan Poe, "The Black Cat" (1843).

120.28 "The Premature Burial?"] An 1844 short story by Poe.

121.38–39 Mr. Coppard and Mr. Machen] British writers of fantasy, supernatural, and horror fiction Alfred Edgar (A. E.) Coppard (1878–1957) and Arthur Machen (pseudonym of Arthur Llewellyn Jones, 1863–1947).

124.10–11 almond, . . . orris!] The smell of bitter almonds can indicate arsenic poisoning; wormseed has been used to kill parasitic worms in humans, but is also poisonous; in some cultures, orris is thought to be a love potion and useful in warding off evil spirits.

125.17 *Behold, the Dreamer*] *Behold, This Dreamer* (1939) by Walter de la Mare.

125.18 *The Land of Oz*] See note 14.28–32.

125.18 *Pellucidar*] The second of the seven hollow Earth Pellucidar novels (1915) by Edgar Rice Burroughs (1875–1950).

125.18 *The Land That Time Forgot*] The first part of a prehistoric "lost world" novel trilogy by Edgar Rice Burroughs (1918). The three novels (including *The People That Time Forgot* and *The Abyss of Time*) were combined under the title *The Land That Time Forgot* (1924). Bradbury first encountered the novel in the omnibus edition.

125.20–21 Cabell and Dunsany and Blackwood] American fantasy writer James Branch Cabell (1879–1958); the Anglo-Irish peer Edward John Moreton Drax Plunkett, 18th Baron Dunsany (1878–1957), a foundational figure in twentieth-century fantasy literature; Algernon Blackwood (1869–1951), British writer of ghost stories.

126.15 *The Emerald City of Oz*] See note 116.26–27.

133.29 Aldebaran II] Aldebaran, sixty-five light-years from Earth, is a red giant of the first magnitude and the brightest star in the constellation Taurus.

135.23 Chanel] Chanel No. 5, based on Coco Chanel's number 5 fragrance developed in 1921.

137.10 "La Paloma."] "The Dove," a Spanish song by Sebastián Iradier (composed 1860s; registered 1879) inspired by Iradier's journey to Cuba but popular for generations in Mexico, the setting of Bradbury's story. The Mexican allusions in this tale evolved from Bradbury's extended 1945 automobile trip through Mexico.

148.17 Uruapan?"] A town in the heart of the Tarascan Indian culture west of Mexico City; Bradbury stayed there to tour the newly formed Parícutin volcano during his fall 1945 trip to Mexico.

158.7 Bergson] Henri Bergson (1859–1941), French Nobel laureate whose theories of time and duration inspired Bradbury's story "Frost and Fire" (originally "The Creatures That Time Forgot," 1946).

164.4 the green lady] The Statue of Liberty (dedicated 1886) has the characteristic green patina of copper statuary exposed to the elements.

167.31–32 *Wonder Stories, Scientific Tales, Fantastic Stories.*] Bradbury began to read *Wonder Stories* in the early 1930s, and throughout the 1940s he placed his own tales in its bimonthly successor, *Thrilling Wonder Stories.* The other two magazine titles appear to be conflations of genre pulps in which Bradbury published stories in the 1940s and '50s, including *Super Science Stories*, *Famous Fantastic Mysteries*, *Fantastic Adventures*, *Fantastic*, and *Fantastic Universe.*

172.31 "California, Here I Come"] American standard composed by Buddy DeSylva (1896–1950) and Joseph Meyer (1894–1987) for the 1921 Broadway musical *Bombo*, featuring Al Jolson and recorded by Jolson in 1924.

172.36 "Oh, You Golden State"] A fictional song title.

172.39 "Santa Claus is Coming to Town,"] Composed (1934) by J. Fred Coots (1897–1985) with lyrics by Haven Gillespie (1888–1975).

173.10–11 "How Do You Do, Everybody,"] Composed by Cal DeVoll (1886–1970) from gospel song origins.

173.18–19 "For They Are Jolly Good fellows."] Originally a French folk tune used to celebrate military victories in France (Malplaquet) and England (Waterloo). Known in America in its celebratory form ("For He's a Jolly Good Fellow") since the mid-nineteenth century.

174.5 "Roll Out the Barrel."] A Czech composition (1927) by Jaromir Vejvoda (1902–1988), Americanized in the late 1930s as "Beer Barrel Polka" (lyrics by Lew Brown and Wladimir Timm).

178.27 those lever fellows] A reference to imagined machinery levers of the rockets and weapons in the 1930s and '40s pulp magazines and comics.

182.1 full of Saroyans] Armenian American writer William Saroyan (1908–1981), author of the stage play *The Time of Your Life*, which won the Pulitzer Prize for Drama in 1940. See also note 621.7.

183.6 Uncle Wiggily games] A Milton Bradley board game (subsequently marketed by Parker Brothers and Hasbro) created in 1916, based on the children's stories about Uncle Wiggily Longears written by Howard Roger Garis beginning in 1910.

183.14 Okies?] A denigrative term for the Oklahoma Dust Bowl migrants of the 1930s.

184.32 racing forms] Off-track betting sheets used to place racetrack wagers remotely from licensed gambling venues.

188.32–33 Bond Street and Melachrinos!"] Bond Street, men's cologne named for the main thoroughfare of the long-standing Bond Street shopping district in London's West End. Melachrinos, an expensive Egyptian cigarette brand.

189.22–23 'Love will fly . . . tightly.'] Cf. Bradbury, "How to Keep and Feed a Muse" (1961; collected in *Zen in the Art of Writing*, 1990). In *Zen* Bradbury credits Oscar Wilde, but the citation is unknown.

205.35 Two-bit words."] I.e., expensive words; "two bits" refers to a quarter dollar, originating with the eight reales piece, or Spanish dollar, circulating in the Americas through the mid-nineteenth century.

205.40 "A fifth column,"] Wartime resistance groups organized to assist an enemy, either openly or undercover.

206.30 p's and q's.] The origin of this caution is unknown: possibly "pints" and "quarts" (a drinker's caveat), or the mirror-image letterpress type of lowercase "p" and "q" (a printer's admonition from the hand-set type era).

THE OCTOBER COUNTRY

226.1–2 *For who else but August Derleth*] Reviews of *The October Country* in *The New York Times* and *Time* magazine revealed that some critics did not realize that most of the stories were brought forward from the earliest period of Bradbury's career. It was too late to add a clarifying note to the October 1955 hardbound issue of the first edition, but the March 1956 paperback printing included this note, which also served to replace and amplify his original dedication line to Derleth:

> Fifteen of the stories included in this collection were written before my twenty-sixth birthday and published in August Derleth's Arkham House edition of my first book *Dark Carnival.* This book has been out of print for some years and I welcome the opportunity given me by the editors of Ballantine Books to select, edit, and in some cases rewrite my favorite stories from that early work. For my later readers, *The October Country* will present a side of my writing that is probably unfamiliar to them, and a type of story that I rarely have done since 1946. Looking back on those years I cannot help but express again my gratitude to August Derleth, who was my first publisher-editor, and to my hardest working and most patient teachers, Leigh Brackett and Henry Kuttner.
>
> R. B.

229.14 hoopla rings] A fairground or carnival ring-toss game using blocks or posts as targets.

229.32 Screwy Louie's Room.] Bradbury's idea for the story was inspired by The Bug House mirror maze, built just before World War II on the famous Ocean Park Pier between Santa Monica and Venice, where Bradbury lived through much of the 1940s. "We went in the mirror maze one night, and we got back into Screwy Louie's Room, which is a room of mirrors where you made yourself fat, thin in various mirrors" (Bradbury to Eller, March 14, 2002). His friend and mentor Edmond Hamilton suggested that Bradbury write a story about a dwarf who makes himself tall.

231.15 little gink] A dismissive term for an odd or foolish man or boy.

236.28 Charlie Boyer . . . Cary Grant?"] Prominent foreign-born American actors Charles Boyer (1899–1978) and Cary Grant (Archibald Alec Leach, 1904–1986).

237.6 tambourines] In the street-corner musical appeals of the Salvation Army, the tambourine often accompanied percussion and brass instruments.

241.12 State Opera House] Teatro Juárez, in Guanajuato, also used for vaudeville and motion pictures over the years. Bradbury stayed in Guanajuato during his fall 1945 trip through northern and central Mexico; see also note 148.17.

241.13–15 *Rasputin and the Empress, . . . Mama Loves Papa*).] Hollywood films: *Rasputin and the Empress* (1932), *The Big House* (1930), *Madame Curie* (1943), *Love Affair* (1939), and *Mama Loves Papa* (1933).

241.17 box Brownie.] A box camera manufactured by Eastman Kodak Company from 1900 through the 1950s.

241.25 local Rotary's] An international service organization dedicated to supporting a wide range of causes; used here to belittle the organizers of the town's evening celebrations.

241.27 the mummies] The Guanajuato catacombs are famous for the preservation of the mummified dead, periodically disinterred from the city graveyard as families were unable to continue payment of the burial fees. Bradbury's mid-November 1945 excursion through Guanajuato's catacombs underlies this story, which he wrote "to purge my terror."

242.10–11 rebozos] A shawl-like garment.

244.6 Patzcuaro.] Bradbury had traveled through Pátzcuaro earlier in his 1945 trip; on All Hallow's Eve he embarked on a canoe ride across Lake Pátzcuaro to observe the midnight Day of the Dead (*Dia de los Muertos*) ceremonies in the island town of Janitzio.

244.8 Don Posada] Based on the Posada Don Vasco Hotel, where Bradbury stayed while exploring the *Dia de los Muertos* festivities during his 1945 visit to Pátzcuaro.

244.18 Paricutin, that's near Uruapan] A modern-day volcano west of Uruapan in the largely Indian state of Michoacán, Mexico. Parícutin formed in a farmer's field in 1943 and rapidly grew into a cinder cone volcano. By the fall of 1945, Bradbury and his driving partner, Grant Beach, were able to tour the lower slopes by horseback. Parícutin rose to nearly 1,400 feet in elevation and became dormant in 1952.

244.28 statue of Morelos] The statue honoring Miguel Hidalgo stands in Guanajuato, but the José María Morelos statue is in Pátzcuaro; both these leaders of the unsuccessful 1810 Mexican revolution were executed.

249.4 *trabajador*] Spanish: a worker or laborer.

253.27–28 an ironical book to publish.] Bradbury would eventually collaborate on *The Mummies of Guanajuato* (1978), a photographic essay of the catacombs by Archie Lieberman paired with Bradbury's story "The Next in Line."

255.26 *corazon*] Spanish: heart.

255.30 Albondigas soup] Mexican meatball soup.

257.33 Guadalajara] Mexico's third largest city and capital of the state of Jalisco. During Bradbury's November 1945 stay in the city, he was fascinated by the mummies preserved in the city's regional museum.

260.11 drum-box trees.] The ceremonial and festival drums based on the pre-Columbian Huehuetl of the Aztec and Tarascan cultures are made from hollowed-out tree trunks.

260.27–28 *Posts, Collier's, Mercury . . . Superman!*] Two of the story sales that Bradbury used to finance his fall 1945 trip to Mexico appeared in magazines mentioned here: "The Big Black and White Game" (*American Mercury*, August 1945) and "One Timeless Spring" (*Collier's*, April 13, 1946; sold July 1945).

260.39 *Farmacia Botica*] Spanish: Pharmacy or drugstore.

266.4 "Cielito Lindo."] A traditional Mexican romantic song composed in 1882 by Quirino Mendoza y Cortés (c. 1862–1957).

267.32 the Oz books] See note 14.28–32.

269.5 her one little mech] A psychological defense or avoidance mechanism.

269.35 Leon] A city west of Guanajuato; Bradbury stayed in León following his catacomb adventure in Guanajuato in November 1945.

275.1 Matisse] Henri Matisse (1869–1954), perhaps the greatest influence in modern art along with Picasso, was celebrated in salon circles during the 1920s; his mastery of line art led to celebrated designs and eventually to cut-out paper collage art in his later years.

276.36 Muggsy Spanier and Bix Beiderbecke.] Two of the Midwest's greatest jazz cornet talents, Francis Joseph "Muggsy" Spanier (1901–1967) and Leon Bismark "Bix" Beiderbecke (1903–1931). Bradbury was introduced to their music during the mid-1940s by his pulp agent Julius Schwartz, and to a broader range of jazz by Arkham House publisher August Derleth and writer Theodore Sturgeon.

277.21 Stanislavsky!"] Konstantin Sergeyevich Stanislavski (1863–1938), influential Russian and Soviet-era acting teacher, actor, and producer.

277.31–32 hillbilly "Waltz?"'"] "Tennessee Waltz" (1946), lyrics by Redd Stewart (Henry Ellis Stewart, 1923–2003) and music by Pee Wee King (Julius Kuczynski, 1914–2000), adapting King's signature "No Name Waltz" melody.

278.17–18 had crushed him in the Terribly Strange Bed] An allusion to the Procrustean Bed of Greek mythology. The ironsmith Procrustes, son of the god Poseidon, stretched or amputated the limbs of his victims to fit the dimensions of the bed he offered them.

278.34 *Nucleus.*] Possibly *Nucleus: A Little Magazine* (1953–54), an art and literature magazine published for Brown University.

278.37 *Antipurgatorio* and the *Paradiso Terrestre*] In *The Purgatory* (*Purgatorio*), the second part of *The Divine Comedy* (c. 1308–20) by Dante Aligheri (c. 1265–1321), Dante travels through Ante-purgatory, Purgatory, and Earthly Paradise (*Paradiso Terrestre*).

278.38 Cantos XV–XVIII] In *Purgatorio*, the doctrinal cantos involve Dante's passage through the third terrace of the seven deadly sins (Wrath).

279.7 *Kraft-Ebbing?*] Richard Freiherr von Krafft-Ebbing (1840–1902), German-born psychiatrist and expert on abnormal sexual behavior. His book *Psychopathia Sexualis* (1886) introduced terminologies for what was considered to be deviant sexual behavior into English psychiatric scholarship.

279.17 Elinor Glyn?] Elinor (Sutherland) Glyn (1864–1943), British novelist whose romantic fiction introduced the "It-girl" to American culture.

279.19 Milton Berle.] A popular actor and performer from silent films and vaudeville stage to radio, movies, and television, Milton Berle (Mendel Berlinger, 1908–2002) became an icon of the early golden age of television.

279.23–24 *Ma Perkins* and *John's Other Wife*.] Radio soap operas broadcast primarily by NBC in the 1930s and '40s.

279.26–27 Two Black Crows] Vaudeville blackface duo of the 1920s made up of Charles "Mack" Sellers (1888–1934) and George Moran (1881–1949). Their songs were favorites of Bradbury's childhood.

279.27 Bonnie Baker] Born Evelyn Underhill or Evelyn Nelson (1917–1990), a pop singer (as Wee Bonnie Baker) and recording artist with the Orrin Tucker Band (1939–43).

279.29 Guy Lombardo?] Gaetano Alberto "Guy" Lombardo (1902–1977), founding leader (in 1924) of the Royal Canadians dance band. Their soft big-band sound garnered more than 140 charted hits from 1927 to 1954). From 1955, Lombardo's Royal Canadians became the perennial New Year's Eve performance headliners in North America.

280.6 *Maxfield Parrish*] The professional name of American painter and illustrator Frederick Parrish (1870–1966), who had wide success as a print artist through his unique blend of neoclassical composition and idealized fantasy subjects. Parrish prints such as *Daybreak* (1922) were found in many American homes.

280.18–21 Nora Bayes, . . . Rippling Rhythm.] World War I–era singer Nora Bayes (Rachel Eleonora Goldberg, 1880–1928), subject of the film *Shine On, Harvest Moon* (1944); the Knickerbocker Quartet (sometimes as Knickerbocker Male Quartette, fl. 1908–22), known primarily for re-recording popular songs, sometimes backing artists such as Al Jolson (Asa Yoelson, 1886–1950); Jolson's "Where Did Robinson Crusoe Go with Friday on Saturday Night" charted during July 1916; bandleader Shep Fields (Saul Feldman, 1910–1981) performed with his Rippling Rhythm orchestra in the 1930s.

280.34–35 *Vic and Sade* and *Pepper Young's Family*] The short but immensely popular daily radio episodes of *Vic and Sade* (NBC, CBS, Mutual, 1934–46), written by Paul Rhymer, ran to more than 3,000 episodes. A brief television continuation followed in the late 1940s. NBC's long-running radio drama *Pepper Young's Family* (1932–59) was written by Elaine Sterne Carrington. Most of the recordings of both shows were destroyed after broadcast, prompting Bradbury to gather any recordings he could find; Bill Idelson, who played Vic and Sade's son Rush, was a longtime friend of Bradbury's.

282.4 Pluck it out, the Bible says.] Cf. Mark 9:47.

282.13 his Gallup ran low] Gallup public opinion polls, often used to determine the relative popularity of candidates or products, were developed by George Gallup (1901–1984) beginning in 1935, with the foundation of Gallup's American Institute of Public Opinion (now Gallup, Inc.).

282.31 to Leica] I.e., the popular German camera line Leica (LEI[tz] CA[mera]), produced by Leica Camera AG, founded by Ernst Leitz in 1869 and known by his name until 1986.

286.31 Dali and Fuseli.] Spanish surrealist artist Salvador Dalí (1904–1989) and the Romantic-era Swiss artist Henry Fuseli (1741–1825), known for his supernatural paintings. The first edition of Bradbury's story collection *Long After Midnight* (1976) includes a dust jacket image of Fuseli's *The Nightmare* (1781).

290.14–15 ceramics business.] Bradbury's friend Grant Beach—who had traveled with him in Mexico in 1945—worked primarily in ceramics and, like Bradbury's protagonist Harris, was also a hypochondriac.

296.11 quid] English slang term for a British pound. It may be an abbreviated form of "quid pro quo" (Latin: "something for something"), "quid" (literally "what") was an abbreviated form of "aliquid" ("something").

318.2–7 THE WAVE . . . away.] Bradbury revised the opening paragraph from its original 1945 *Weird Tales* publication:

> They cut the sky down to my size and threw it over the Michigan Lake, put some kids yelling on yellow sand with bouncing balls, a gull or two, a criticizing parent, and me breaking out of a wet wave and finding this world bleary and moist.

318.33–34 Donald and Delaus Arnold's feet] In the original 1944 magazine text, the surname is Schabold; Donald and Delose Schabold were identical twin friends of Bradbury's during his Waukegan childhood.

323.28–29 a strange woman named Margaret] The original 1944 magazine text read: "a strange awful person named Margaret . . ."

324.2 Dog ran] In the original *Dark Carnival* version (1947), the dog's name is "Torry."

324.21–22 sickness bleached him white on his bed.] Bradbury had an extended case of whooping cough in 1927 that confined him to bed during much of the fall of his second-grade year.

336.31 ninety-two degrees Fahrenheit] This concept first appeared in Bradbury's screen treatment for *It Came from Outer Space* (1953), during a heated debate between the sheriff and the protagonist astronomer late in the film.

345.2 JUST WHEN THE idea occurred] The original magazine "novella" text was divided into three chapters. The first chapter was titled "The Third Element."

351.18 In the morning] The second chapter in the original serial text began here, titled "Sound of the Heart."

352.31 sulfa] The first drug group systematically used to fight infections in the human body (patented 1935). Used during World War II to protect wounds from infection.

357.38 Then he started] The third and final chapter began at this point in the original serial text, titled "Lucifer, My Son."

360.32–33 The child is born hating.] Bradbury always maintained that he could recall neonatal and even prenatal memories; he did not recall ever reading the studies of infant birth trauma as a source of subconscious hatred by Melanie Klein, but he did read deeply on related aspects of neurosis and psychosis in the work of Sigmund Freud and in Karen Horney's *The Neurotic Personality of Our Time* (1937).

375.7 ladyfinger firecrackers] Small (.75-inch) firecrackers ignited in strings or packs, releasing multiple colors.

377.3 Picasso ladies and Dali gentlemen] The early abstract cubism of Pablo Picasso (1881–1973) is best represented in *Les Demoiselles D'Avignon* (1907); Salvador Dalí's wide range of surrealist human figures often reveal a dream world of suppressed psychological conflict.

381.38–382.2 "In the beginning . . . God Himself . . ."] Cf. Genesis 1:1–10 and 2:18–25.

391.1 *The Scythe*] The personification of death as a hooded skeleton holding a scythe emerged from the fourteenth- and fifteenth-century ravages of the bubonic plague.

391.2–392.15 QUITE SUDDENLY . . . the dead man.] In early 1943, Bradbury had great difficulty with the opening of "The Scythe"; he freely acknowledged that his friend and mentor Leigh Brackett wrote the first 500 or possibly 600 words; Bradbury was able to complete this 5,300-word tale in mid-February.

391.9 Drew Erickson] Originally Tom Joerg in the July 1943 *Weird Tales* version; the name change first appears in *Dark Carnival* (1947).

392.40 *Kyrie eléison!*] Greek: Lord have mercy! The kyrie is also an ancient Christian prayer, part of both Eastern and Western orthodox liturgies.

394.11–12 WHO WIELDS ME—WIELDS THE WORLD!] Possibly drawn from the poem "The Hand That Rocks the Cradle Is the Hand That Rules the World" (originally "What Rules the World," 1865), by William Ross Wallace (1819–1881).

405.19 London, Moscow, Tokyo.] Bradbury's submitted typescript (dated February 18, 1943) for the July 1943 issue of *Weird Tales* was composed at the time of the air war over London and the German advance toward Moscow during World War II. The *Dark Carnival* version (1946; published 1947) added the allusion to the American daytime bombing and low-altitude nighttime firebombing raids over Tokyo.

405.21–25 Belsen and Buchenwald . . . Siberian skies.] In revising for *The October Country*, Bradbury added mentions of the German concentration camps at Bergen-Belsen (Saxony, Germany, 1943–45) and Buchenwald (near Weimar, Germany, 1937–45), the first detonation of the atomic bomb (July 16, 1945) at a New Mexico desert site subsequently incorporated into the White Sands Missile Range, the American atomic bomb detonation over Hiroshima (August 6, 1945), postwar American thermonuclear tests in the Pacific at Bikini Atoll (Marshall Islands, 1946–58), and the first Soviet test of an atomic bomb (August 29, 1949) at Semipalatinsk (Kazakhstan) and the Siberian Novaya Zemlya archipelago (beginning in 1954).

405.27–28 Korea, Indo-China. . . Africa] Bradbury's final revisions for *The October Country* also added references to the Korean War (1950–53) and the early flashpoints of the mid-century postcolonial world.

407.1 *Uncle Einar*] Named for Bradbury's favorite maternal uncle, Inar Moberg (1894–1966).

408.16 Mellin Town, Illinois] One of Bradbury's fictional names for Waukegan or the smaller towns of his native Lake County, Illinois.

409.19 who wants to live in Europe these days?"] Bradbury began circulating this story in June 1946, early in Europe's slow recovery from World War II.

415.7 Allin."] The wind-hunter's original name is John Colt in the March 1943 *Weird Tales* magazine text, prior to a complete rewrite of the story for *Dark Carnival* (1947).

416.14 Valley of the Winds] Bradbury was inspired by "Child of the Winds" (*Weird Tales*, May 1936), written by his friend and mentor Edmond Hamilton.

420.5 the Celebes] Sulawesi, the third most populous island of Indonesia.

420.29 Stoddard] Perhaps an allusion to John L. Stoddard (1850–1931) and his widely published ten-volume set of travel lectures, offering an echo of the eerie journeys of Bradbury's wind hunter Allin.

432.27 crumblees] A Bradbury family idiom.

433.20 Marion Barsumian] Cf. Edgar Rice Burroughs's "Barsoom," the name for the Red Planet in his Martian novels, which Bradbury read and imitated on his dial-a-letter toy typewriter at age twelve.

438.1 *There Was an Old Woman*] English nursery rhyme first published in *Gammer Gurton's Garland* (1794). One version (*Infant institutes*, 1797) includes two closing verses about buying coffins for the children.

441.2 Harry Lauder] Sir Henry Lauder (1870–1950), internationally famous Scottish singer.

441.3 Madame Schumann-Heink] Ernestine Schumann-Heink (1861–1936), Austrian American opera and concert singer.

441.13 way off the trestle] Trestle, a closely spaced bridge support; i.e., way off course.

441.16–17 I'm too old to be made love at] Death as a seducer would soon become the focus of Bradbury's 1960 short story, "Death and the Maiden."

444.11–12 "By the Lord Harry] A mild oath; Lord Harry is perhaps a reference to the devil.

447.22 "Saint Vitus] A Roman martyr (d. c. 303) from the reign of Diocletian; venerated beginning in the fifth century.

451.15–18 cisterns . . . go everywhere and finally go down to the sea,"] The large-diameter storm drains and cisterns of Los Angeles play a role in the mystery and resolution of Bradbury's novel *Let's All Kill Constance!* (2002).

457.7–9 Genesee Avenue, . . . Ocean Side] North-south cross streets above the ocean-bound storm drains and cisterns running west beneath Los Angeles and Santa Monica.

457.13 Highway 101] Now an interstate running southeast to northwest through downtown Los Angeles before becoming the Ventura Highway.

460.9 "Uncle Einar] See note 407.1.

460.10–11 Cousin Vivian] The only child of Bradbury's uncle Inar and aunt Arthurine Moberg.

461.21–22 Bion and Leonard and Sam.] Based on Bradbury's father Leonard and uncles Bion and Captain Samuel Bradbury.

468.35–36 the Imperial Valley, . . . Beside the Salton Sea] A fifty-mile-long valley running from the Salton Sea and the city of El Centro southeastward across the Mexican border at Calexico.

476.4 Thomas Wolfe] Thomas Clayton Wolfe (1900–1938), whose highly emotional and impressionistic fiction captured Bradbury's imagination in the late 1930s, would become the subject of Bradbury's short story "Forever and the Earth" (1950).

476.37–38 Michelangelo's God creating Adam] *The Creation of Adam*, one of the most widely reproduced images from Michelangelo's fresco on the Sistine Chapel ceiling in the Vatican (1508–12).

477.9 Marley's Ghost,"] Jacob Marley, the deceased business partner of Ebenezer Scrooge, in the novella *A Christmas Carol* (1843) by Charles Dickens (1812–1870).

479.29 the Wedding Guest's eye.] The unnamed narrator of the long poem *The Rime of the Ancient Mariner* (1798), by Samuel Taylor Coleridge (1772–1834).

481.33–34 the Great Coal Sack Nebula] The Coalsack, a dark nebula first recorded by Spanish navigator Vincente Pinzón in 1499, is a large light-absorbing nebulae near the constellation Centaurus.

OTHER STORIES

489.2–12 THERE WAS THIS fence . . . rockets more.] Bradbury heavily revised the original 1943 text to form the title story of his 1962 collection *R Is for Rocke*t. His greatly expanded opening grew from this minimal original paragraph: "We were just a lot of kids. With cut fingers, lumpy heads and whining tenor voices. We liked our game of mibs as well as the next rumple-hair; but we liked the rockets more."

489.25 semantics exam] For a time, Bradbury advocated the concept of general semantics as outlined by Alfred Korzybski (1879–1950) in *Science and Sanity* (1933), a system of applied epistemology, or study of the nature of knowledge. Bradbury had come to know Korzybski's work through Robert A. Heinlein and other science fiction writers he knew in the early 1940s.

489.27–28 fog roaming in off the Atlantic] The fog from Bradbury's original setting on Southern California's foggy Pacific coast remained in the story, even after the 1962 revisions to a Florida setting.

490.11 monorail] The underground transit system of the 1943 original serial text was replaced by a monorail in the 1962 collected version, revised at a time when Bradbury had become a great proponent for overhead monorail public transit.

490.14 A guy fifteen] In the 1943 version, both boys were fourteen.

490.23 Mac Leslyn] A conflation of Anson MacDonald, an early pseudonym of Robert A. Heinlein, and the first name of Heinlein's second wife, Leslyn Heinlein Moccabi.

491.23 astronauts] Bradbury replaced the references in the original 1943 text to the space patrol and gliders with astronauts and helicopters.

492.29 mechs] See note 269.5.

493.25 formula-school] Presumably bridging the traditional "either-or" logic formulas and the general or psychological semantics of Korzybski.

495.15 ortho-station] Korzybski advocated setting up "orthological" centers based on the impact of language on thought.

505.3 McGuire's] Bradbury changed the name of Rockwell's assistant from Murphy to McGuire in the 1966 *S Is for Space* text.

512.13–14 malarial fever . . . syphilis] The malaria therapy developed in 1917 by the future Nobel Laureate Julius Wagner-Jauregg (1857–1940) relieved paralytic dementia in advanced syphilis patients. It was used until the development of penicillin made it obsolete.

512.25 He's working out his own salvation.] Cf. Philippians 2:12.

515.20–21 the only war . . . universe!] This conviction would evolve into the conclusion of Bradbury's televised statement during the Apollo 11 moon landing: "All the universe doesn't care whether we exist or not, but *we* care whether we exist . . . this is the proper war to fight."

542.25–34 The scientists worked . . . death.] The inspiration for this story, which Bradbury originally titled "Eight-Day World," came from his reading of a thought experiment by Nobel Laureate Henri Bergson (1859–1941) in *Time and Free Will* (1889), "Real Duration and Prediction." In private conversation, Bradbury later reflected, "He was talking about time, and how strange it was in very different shapes and forms. He said, 'If you lived in a world where you were born and grew up and grew old and died in nine days, how would you know it?' . . . The way you know is lack of knowledge. You wouldn't have enough time to accumulate knowledge to make changes, whereas, in our world, we have a lifetime to grow up, get knowledge, and change things" (Bradbury to Eller, March 2002).

569.25 calla lilies] A hardy perennial (Greek: "beautiful"), the calla bulb is not actually a lily, but it symbolizes rebirth and regeneration.

572.11–17 shell-like machines . . . centrifuge] From 1942 to the fall of 1947, Bradbury typed his stories in a garage that looked out onto a neighborhood electrical distribution substation in Venice, California. The far larger electrical transmission substation of "Powerhouse" was inspired in large part by this experience.

577.33 "Wope!"] A traditional western horseman's term used to start a standing horse into motion.

581.13 the new town of Salem.] A great seaport during the early decades of the nineteenth century in Massachusetts, Salem was also a center for the Puritan migration of the 1630s and is best known for the Salem witch trials of 1692. Bradbury's ancestor, Mary Bradbury, was tried and found guilty, but escaped imprisonment and survived.

581.32 that Pillar of Fire] The Israelites were led out of Egypt by a manifestation of God embodied in the form of a pillar of cloud by day and fire by night; cf. Exodus 13:21–22.

591.23 Machen and a man named Derleth] For Machen, see note 121.38–39. For Derleth, see note 5.4.

597.37 those little green toads] Possibly the Great Basin spadefoot (*Spea intermontana*), which can hibernate deep underground to survive drought conditions for five to ten years if necessary. There are many stories of living toads found buried in stone, but none has ever been authenticated.

600.27–28 Now is the time . . . their party] Often ascribed to colonial patriot and Virginia governor Patrick Henry, ending with "their country," the sentence was also used as a test line to determine the speed of an early typewriter in 1867.

600.40 Arise my love, and come away—] Cf. Song of Solomon 2:10–13.

601.3 Lazarus, come forth from the tomb . . .] Cf. John 11:43.

605.9 McClure."] The maiden name of Bradbury's wife, Marguerite McClure Bradbury.

614.34 Osiris and Bal and Set.] The ancient Egyptian god Osiris (ruling over the human life and death cycles and agriculture) and his brother-murderer Set (the desert, discord, and violence). Bal (properly Ba'al) is an ancient Semitic deity associated with storms and fertility, and the "false god" of the Old Testament, worshipped by the Phoenicians and the Canaanites.

614.34 the Necronomicon] The fictional book of magic appearing in the work of H. P. Lovecraft beginning in 1924 and periodically adapted by other horror genre writers.

614.35 the house of Usher] Setting of Edgar Allan Poe's "The Fall of the House of Usher" (1839). Roderick Usher's sister, the cataleptic Madeline, revives and claws her way out of her tomb.

614.35–36 the Red Death.] See note 118.34.

614.37 cask of Amontillado] From Edgar Allan Poe's "The Cask of Amontillado" (1846), where Fortunato is mortared into the catacomb alcove by the narrator Montressor.

615.5–6 black candle . . . inverted cross.] Symbols associated with Satanic worship.

615.7 I am Dunsany and Machen] For Dunsany, see note 125.20–21. For Machen, see note 121.38–39.

615.8–11 Legend of Sleepy Hollow . . . castle wall.] Supernatural or horror stories: "The Legend of Sleepy Hollow" (1820) by Washington Irving (1783–1859); "The Monkey's Paw" (1902) by William Wymark Jacobs (1863–1943);

"The Phantom 'Rickshaw" (1888) by Rudyard Kipling (1865–1936); stage plays "The Cat and the Canary" (1922) by John Willard (1885–1942) and *The Gorilla* (1925) by Ralph Spence (1890–1949); *The Bat* (1920), a stage play by Mary Roberts Rinehart and Avery Hopwood, adapted from Rinehart's novel *The Circular Staircase* (1908). In *Hamlet*, Hamlet's father's ghost initially appears in Act I on the walls of his castle in Denmark.

615.18 Guy Fawkes' day] In Great Britain, a national holiday celebrated with bonfires and fireworks on November 5, commemorating the capture of Guy Fawkes and others involved in the failed Gunpowder Plot designed to destroy Parliament and kill King James I and his heir.

616.15–17 the Maelstrom, . . . the Telltale Heart] Edgar Allan Poe, "The Maelstrom" (1841) and "The Telltale Heart" (1843).

616.33 *"For the love of God, Montressor!"*] See note 614.37.

617.1 *Asleep in Armageddon*] The apocalyptic battle described in Revelation 16:16 takes place at Armageddon, literally the Mount of Megiddo, site of significant battles in the Old Testament. Bradbury changed the story's title to the Shakespearean "Perchance to Dream" when it was first collected in *The Day It Rained Forever*, the British variant form of Bradbury's 1959 collection *A Medicine for Melancholy*.

620.19–20 *War and Peace*] The massive 1869 historical and philosophical Russian novel by Count Leo Tolstoy (1828–1910), set in the days of Napoleon's invasion of Russia in 1812.

621.6–7 and think how good it is to be alive . . . William Saroyan!] Cf. Saroyan's introduction to his Pulitzer Prize–winning play *The Time of Your Life* (1939). Bradbury had an abiding admiration for Saroyan's affirmation of life: "That old saying from the Bible, which was taken by William Saroyan for one of his plays, 'in the time of your life'—In the time of your life, live. Don't doom yourself."

625.9 All the world's a stage.] Shakespeare, *As You Like It*, II.vii.139.

625.36 Helen King. Remember Helen.] Possibly an allusion to Bradbury's unpublished story "Remember Helen Charles" (completed March 11, 1943), written as he was also completing his first draft of "Asleep in Armageddon."

626.25 perchance to dream.] Shakespeare, *Hamlet*, III.i.64.

627.23–24 A pox on both your houses!] Shakespeare, *Romeo and Juliet*, III.i.106.

634.31–32 Hormel Valleys] Possibly named for the internationally marketed meat-packaging giant Hormel Foods Corporation, founded by George A. Hormel in 1891.

634.36 Osseo] An Ojibwe American Indian name usually translated as "Son of the Evening Star" and subsequently used as the names of towns in Minnesota and Wisconsin.

647.4 Plandome] Bradbury's aunt Tilita Bradbury Schwab, the widow of his uncle, Captain Samuel Bradbury, remarried and settled in Plandome on Long Island. Bradbury visited her there several times during various trips to New York City.

648.25–34 Washington Street . . . Impi Johnson—"] Bradbury has transplanted memories from his own childhood in Waukegan: his Bradbury grandparents lived next door, fronting Washington Street; he attended Central School; Isabel [Skelton] was a close friend; and Impi Johnson was his fifth-grade teacher.

653.4 Eiseley's *The Star Thrower.*] Anthropologist Loren Eiseley (1907–1977), who authored "The Star Thrower," an essay featured in his 1969 collection *The Unexpected Universe*, was a longtime friend of Bradbury's. Bradbury published three reviews of Eiseley's books in the *Los Angeles Times*, including a review of *The Unexpected Universe* ("Anthropologist's Magic Vision of Nature," December 14, 1969).

655.3–4 Goodbye . . . God be with you?] The first documented usage of the contraction "godbwye" for "God be with you" is found in a 1573 letter written by the English writer Gabriel Harvey.

656.3 Central School.] See note 648.25–34.

660.39 that story by Edgar Allan Poe] The premature burial of Lady Madeline in "The Fall of the House of Usher." See note 614.35.

662.4 the *Throw-Your-Voice* book] The most likely source is *Art of Ventriloquism: How to Throw Your Voice* (1890) by George W. Callahan (1862–1894).

662.26 Princess Ommanatra] Possibly a play on Amanitore or her predecessor, Aminishakheto, queens of Kush (Nubia) buried in the Meroe pyramid complex. A great treasure of jewelry was discovered in Aminishakheto's tomb in 1834.

666.38 a *mandrake* root."] In folklore, the root of the English mandrake plant (*Bryonia alba*) was thought to give a deadly scream when uprooted, killing all who heard it.

675.21 fire and ice, fire and ice.] Cf. Robert Frost's poem "Fire and Ice" (1920). Frost was a favorite of Bradbury's by the mid-1940s.

680.21–25 Magazines and books . . . touching *them.*] Bradbury felt that the television-dominated cultural desert of "The Pedestrian" was the immediate precursor of "The Fireman," eventually expanded into *Fahrenheit 451*: "a number of months . . . later, I took that pedestrian out into the streets of the city of the future, and I wandered that pedestrian around. And along the way, I changed the sex of that pedestrian from a man to a girl named Clarisse McClellan . . . Around the corner, from another direction, comes a man smelling of kerosene, and she speaks to him, and says, 'Oh, I know who you are. I know what you do. I can tell from the smell of the kerosene on your uniform. You are a fireman. You're one of those men who goes to places to start fires'" (*Fahrenheit 451: Audio Introduction*, 1976).

680.36 "Eleven South Saint James Street."] Bradbury's actual childhood address in Waukegan.

685.13 TORQUEMADA'S] Tomás de Torquemada (1420–1498), the first Grand Inquisitor of the Spanish Inquisition.

685.39 Black Hole."] The Black Hole of Calcutta, a small guard room in Fort William, Calcutta, was used to confine British, European, and Indian survivors after the fort fell to the rebellious troops of the Bengali ruler on June 20, 1756. Two-thirds of the prisoners died before their release the next day.

686.2 Gestapos,"] The German secret state police (Geheime Staatspolizei), created in 1933 by Hermann Göring under the Nazi regime of Adolf Hitler.

688.27 Green Town] One of Bradbury's often-used settings based on his hometown of Waukegan, Illinois.

690.19 Cruikshank children] George Cruikshank (1792–1878), prominent British illustrator and caricaturist known as the nineteenth century's Hogarth. Bradbury admired (and at times collected) the early magazine and newspaper illustrations of Thomas Bewick, Hogarth, Cruikshank, and others.

690.24 thumb-screwers] Thumbscrews were an instrument of torture in use from at least the sixteenth to eighteenth centuries.

690.36 given the laying on of hands.] In Christian traditions, this phrase can refer to an anointing for the sick or to the last rites for the dying.

698.14 Musterole] A mustard-based skin irritant designed to stimulate blood circulation and reduce the pain of joint and muscle injuries as well as lung congestion.

699.31 golden salamanders] Some classical Greek and Roman sources maintained that the salamander could endure and even quench fire; the Talmud and later sources observed that the salamander was created in fire. The logo of Bradbury's firemen in *Fahrenheit 451* was the salamander.

699.33 Irish-black] See note 95.6.

700.9 If the election] The polarizing McCarthy-era presidential campaign of 1952 was heating up as Bradbury completed this story on February 1, 1952.

716.30–31 Palmer Penmanship hand.] The method of using forearm muscles in concert with finger movements to create what was considered more aesthetically pleasing and legible forms of cursive letters. Developed by Austin Palmer (1859–1927) and widely used for a century or more.

718.17 fog spunks] Possibly the whitish streaks or trails in fog.

719.36–37 Rosicrucians, . . . Sealed Book] The various sixteenth-century Rosicrucian movements evolved from Christian mysticism and esoteric Eastern traditions concerned with secret knowledge of ages past. The largest twentieth-century organization is the Ancient Mystical Order Rosae Crucis (1915), which publishes a sealed book of Rosicrucian initiation (1921).

724.11–12 *Copa de Oro*, . . . *Prometheus* and the *Icarus*] Copa de Oro, Spanish: Cup of Gold. The Titan Prometheus, the giver of fire and knowledge to humanity in Greek mythology. The mythological Icarus, who flew too close to the sun using the wings fashioned by his father Daedalus and fell to his death when the wax in the wings melted.

724.18 "'The golden apples of the sun'?"] From "The Song of Wandering Aengus" (1897) by Irish poet and playwright William Butler Yeats (1865–1939).

724.20 "'Fear no more . . . sun'?"] Shakespeare, *Cymbeline*, IV.ii.258.

724.22 "'Cup of Gold'?] *Cup of Gold: A Life of Sir Henry Morgan, Buccaneer, with Occasional References to History* (1929), by John Steinbeck (1902–1968).

724.22 'The Crock of Gold'?] *The Crock of Gold* (1912) by Irish writer James Stephens (1882–1950).

727.40–728.2 atomic bomb . . . only the sun has the secret.] The first American hydrogen bomb, a fusion weapon triggered by a fission reaction that was far more powerful than the fission-based atomic bomb, was tested in 1952, just months before Bradbury published this story.

729.23–27 *Sometimes I see . . . burning Tree . . .*] This verse is apparently original to the story.

731.1 *And the Rock Cried Out*] See "There's No Hiding Place Down Here," a traditional African American spiritual with no known composer or date of composition. First published in 1915. Cf. Revelation 6:15–17.

738.9 the gas in the glass container] Glass cylinders with graduated markings in gallons were part of automobile gasoline pumps at many service stations by the 1920s, allowing customers to see how much gas was actually being pumped during a fill-up, or to see how much gasoline remained in the pump.

741.32 Colonia] Often a generic term for an ethnic town district in Latin America.

746.7 the Butler's Ball.] A servants' ball or dance, offered in aristocratic homes in Britain and occasionally in the homes of the wealthy in America until the post–World War II era.

752.12 *carnecería.*] Spanish: meat market or butcher shop.

752.16 Juatala, Porto Bello, San Juan Clementas, or Brioconbria.] Like Colonia, these appear to be fictional names set in a Central or South American nation beyond the immediate reach of the story's nuclear holocaust. Porto Bello is a historical coastal Uruguayan town; however, Bradbury's unproduced screenplay version of this story is set in one of the Central American countries bordering the Caribbean Sea.

760.15 masks . . . in the lake town of Patzcuaro] During his fall 1945 trip through Mexico, Bradbury and his driving partner Grant Beach collected native Indian masks for the Los Angeles County Museum and for their personal collections. The masks of Sr. Benda in Pátzcuaro were Bradbury's favorites.

762.2 Paricutin volcano?"] See note 244.18.

763.2–3 a girl with long soft dark hair . . . sky blue] Bradbury created this fictional encounter from an actual experience in Zimapan during his 1945 trip: "I looked in the front door of someone's house, and there's a beautiful lady, a young girl, sitting at a blue piano playing Beethoven" (Bradbury to Eller, October 20, 2007).

765.30 zocalo] Typically a Mexican town square.

766.4 "*La Cumparsita*" and "*La Paloma Azul*,"] "La Cumparsita" (1916), a Uruguayan tango composed by Gerardo Matos Rodriguez (1897–1948) with lyrics by Pascual Contursi (1888–1932) and Enrique Pedro Maroni (1887–1957). "La Paloma Azul" ("The Blue Dove," 1940), by Mexican composer Carlos Chávez (1899–1978).

766.40–767.1 "*Ay, Jalisco.*"] "Ay, Jalisco, no te rajes!", 1941 song by Manuel Esperón (1911–2011) with lyrics by Ernesto Cortázar, Sr. (1897–1953), which romanticizes the Mexican state of Jalisco and its capital, Guadalajara. The song was composed for a popular Mexican film of the same title (1941) and supplied the melody for the Disney animated film *The Three Caballeros* (1944).

767.9 "Toreador Song."] "I Toast You" ("Votre toast, je peux vous le rendre"), by Georges Bizet (1838–1875), libretto by Henri Meilhac (1831–1897) and Ludovic Halévy (1834–1908); from the Bizet opera *Carmen* (1875).

769.29–30 "*La Golondrina*, . . . "*Luna Lunera*."] "La Golondrina" ("The Swallow") by Narciso Serradell Sevilla (1843–1910), an 1862 song for Mexican exiles under the French-imposed military intervention (1861–67). The Mexican harvest dance ritual "Danza de Los Viejitos" originated with the Tarascan culture that Bradbury experienced in the Michoacán region around Pátzcuaro. "Michoacán la Verde" may refer to the famous La Verde copper deposits and mines in the Michoacán region. "Barcarolle," originating in the gondolier songs of Venice, is a popular folk rhythm used extensively in opera. "Luna Lunera" ("Moon, Gentle Moon") is a Latino children's song or lullaby.

770.16 *The Cask of Amontillado*.] See note 614.37.

775.21–22 typewriter . . . into the river."] By November 1945, the long road trip through Mexico had led to tensions between Bradbury and his driving partner, Grant Beach. The final break came at the Rio Grande in Juárez on the way home to Los Angeles, as Bradbury recalled in a 1998 interview: "I left everything . . . left my typewriter, left my clothes. I walked up to the bus station and got on the bus and came back to L.A. on my own. And of course, on the way back to L.A., he took my typewriter and threw it in the river."

777.18 to Morelia?"] The capital of the Mexican state of Michoacán, northeast of Uruapan and Pátzcuaro. Bradbury spent time in all three cities during his fall 1945 trip through Mexico.

777.29–30 blue-colored piano, . . . "Moonlight Sonata."] The popular name for Beethoven's Piano Concerto No. 14 (1801).

786.11–15 *At midnight . . . so be deep!*] Lines from Edgar Allan Poe's poem "The Sleeper" (1831, revised 1841).

794.38 "Tom Dillon] In the prequel tale "The Whole Town's Sleeping" (1950), collected in *Dandelion Wine*, the victim (Lavinia Nebbs) and her friends are pranked by "Frank Dillon," who jumps from behind a tree and laughingly claims to be "The Lonely One."

796.5–6 Two dozen panes . . . ices.] Bradbury's grandparents, living next door during his Waukegan childhood, had a multiple-paned stained-glass window in the stairway landing.

804.4 'Genevieve, Sweet Genevieve'!"] "Sweet Genevieve" (1869), composed by Henry Tucker (1826–1882) with lyrics by George Cooper (1840–1927).

805.5 Delphic caves] The Corycian cave on Mount Parnassus, located above Delphi's oracle sanctuary complex for the worship of Apollo and Dionysus in classical Greece; the oracle of Delphi was widely sought for prophetic utterances.

806.1 *Icarus.*] See note 724.11–12.

806.25 *Montgolfier.*] The brothers Joseph-Michel (1740–1810) and Jacques-Étienne (1745–1799) Montgolfier, inventors of the globe-shaped hot air balloon first flown in piloted free flight in November 1783 outside Paris.

807.10 Wright.] Wilbur (1867–1912) and Orville (1871–1948) Wright, the inventors and pilots of the first powered aircraft raised in controlled flight, first launched from the coastal sand dunes of Kitty Hawk, North Carolina, on December 17, 1903.

811.2–7 'A wheel in a wheel . . . grace of God.'] Cf. Ezekiel 1:15–21 and the spiritual "Ezekiel Saw the Wheel," arranged by William L. Dawson (1899–1990) and recorded as early as 1920.

811.38–39 'Because it's there'?] Spoken by British mountaineer George Mallory in a 1923 *New York Times* interview, in response to a question about why Mallory felt he had to be the first to climb Mount Everest. In 1924 Mallory disappeared during his third attempt; his body was located in 1999.

812.22 strung ladyfingers] See note 375.7.

821.22–23 play in pictures or in that orchestra under the stars.] The Hollywood Bowl has hosted concerts under the stars since 1922, often performed by the Los Angeles Philharmonic Orchestra and other ensembles. Musicians from various motion picture studio orchestras have also performed there. During the 1940 and 1941 seasons, Bradbury ushered at the Hollywood Bowl.

826.3 tin lizzie] A nickname for the Model T Ford, manufactured from 1908 through 1927.

826.19–20 all nine rings of hell] In *The Inferno*, the first part of Dante's *Divine Comedy* (see also note 278.37), Dante's guide leads him through Hell, arranged in nine circles of sin: Limbo, Lust, Gluttony, Greed, Anger, Heresy, Violence, Fraud, and Betrayal.

826.28 Judas goats.] A working animal trained to lead stockyard sheep and goats to the slaughter line; the name originates in the betrayal of Jesus by Judas Iscariot in the garden of Gethsemane.

832.14 "'In Xanadu . . .'"] The subsequent passages are from "Kubla Khan: or, A Vision in a Dream: A Fragment" (1797; published 1816), by Samuel Taylor Coleridge.

836.2–3 an ancient Moon] An automobile or truck manufactured by the Moon Motor Car Company founded by Joseph W. Moon (1850–1919) and operating from 1905 through 1930.

841.5 Ketchum and Sun Valley] American writer and Nobel laureate Ernest Hemingway (1899–1961) died in his home in Ketchum, Idaho, on July 2, 1961, from a self-inflicted shotgun wound. The Hemingway Memorial (dedicated 1966) is located on a trail of the nearby Sun Valley winter resort, where Hemingway had lived for short periods during the last twenty years of his life.

842.20 the Michigan stories] Hemingway's Michigan stories, often centered on the autobiographical character of Nick Adams, drew on his memories of Windemere, his father's summer vacation home on Walloon Lake near Petoskey, on the northern tip of Michigan's lower peninsula.

847.33 my albatross,"] The source of the curse on the sailors in "The Rime of the Ancient Mariner" by Samuel Taylor Coleridge.

848.9 "January 10, 1954."] Hemingway was seriously injured in a plane crash during an aerial tour of East Africa in January 1954; he nearly died when the rescue flight also crashed. Bradbury closely followed the erroneous news reports of Hemingway's death from the United Press International office in Dublin, Ireland, where he was writing the Warner Brothers screenplay adaptation of *Moby-Dick*; he kept the UPI teletype printouts for the rest of his life.

850.5–8 on the western slope . . . at that altitude.] Almost a direct quote from Hemingway's brief prologue to his story "The Snows of Kilimanjaro" (1936).

851.7 Captain John Wilder] A principal character in two of *The Martian Chronicles* story-chapters ("—And the Moon Be Still as Bright" and "The Long Years"), though here Wilder is presented in an adventure outside of the *Chronicles* story line.

853.26 Sam Parkhill] Parkhill also figures in two of *The Martian Chronicles* story-chapters ("—And the Moon Be Still as Bright" and "The Off Season").

854.11–12 "The lion prowls . . . slaughter!"] The Lion of Judah and the lamb led forth to slaughter are both scriptural images referring to Christ.

854.18–19 "Behold the angel . . . Annunciations!"] Cf. Luke 1:26–38.

855.8 Icarus] See note 724.11–12.

864.13 "To be or not to be—"] Shakespeare, *Hamlet*, III.i.55.

869.34 rigadoon] An energetic baroque-era dance from the Provence region of France.

871.6 Curiouser and curiouser.] Alice's opening comment in chapter II, "The Pool of Tears," in *Alice's Adventures in Wonderland* (1865), by Lewis Carroll. In 1948, Harper's invited Bradbury to develop a multi-author anthology of fantasy fiction, which he titled *Curiouser and Curiouser*, but Harper's ultimately declined to publish it.

872.33 dark albatross] See note 847.33.

873.7–8 So long, Meg. Farwell. Toodleoo."] "Good-bye, so long, farewell, toodle-oo" was a Laurel and Hardy signature line in many of their films. In October 1953 Bradbury attended a Dublin farewell performance by Laurel and Hardy and eventually published three stories inspired by their film exploits.

874.17–18 Horsehead Nebula . . . Andromeda] The dark Horsehead Nebula at the eastern end of Orion's Belt, and the far larger Orion Nebula (which is not a galaxy) are both roughly 1,300 light-years from Earth. The Andromeda Galaxy was considered to be a very bright nebula until the 1920s, when Edwin Hubble and other astronomers confirmed the existence of galaxies beyond the Milky Way. Nebulae are often birthplaces of new stars.

881.1 *I Sing the Body Electric!*] A long verse celebration of the human body first published in *Leaves of Grass* (1855, 1892), by the American poet Walt

Whitman (1819–1892). The 1963 Bradbury *Twilight Zone* teleplay that aired under this title was based on this then-unpublished short story.

883.22 "Fantoccini,"] Derived from the Italian word for marionettes or puppets manipulated by human or mechanical means.

886.15–16 Balinese kite-bamboo-translucent dolls] Cotton fabric kites stretched on bamboo or plastic armatures are an important part of the cultural heritage of the Indonesian island of Bali.

888.10 Delphic caves] See note 805.5.

888.25–26 "Nefertiti," . . . The Beautiful One Is Here."] An ancient Egyptian queen consort (c. 1370–c. 1330 B.C.E.) of the Eighteenth Dynasty. "The Beautiful One Is Here" is a variant translation of the meaning of Nefertiti's name.

891.40 lapis lazuli] A deep blue semiprecious stone used on King Tutankhamun's death mask, found in the pharaoh's tomb by British archeologist Howard Carter after World War I. One of Bradbury's earliest preliterate memories was the 1924–25 syndicated newspaper photograph of the death mask, which was printed during the earliest days of color newsprint: "I saw a picture in the paper. In those days, there were very few color pictures. But I saw one color picture somewhere—God knows where it was, because I don't think I'd seen a color picture before then—a color picture of the golden mask, and I fell in love with Tutankhamun. I said to my mother, 'Who is this?' and she said, 'He's famous for being dead five thousand years.' I thought that was wonderful" (Bradbury to Eller, 2007).

892.5 ranuncula] A flowering plant family that includes buttercups.

892.33–34 daughter-of-Ra] The three daughters of the Egyptian god Ra (Bastet, Sekhmet, and Hathor) were known as the Eyes of Ra, exacting vengeance in the name of their father.

895.9–11 first morn of the lovely Garden . . . biting the apple . . .] Cf. Genesis 2:8–25, 3:6.

898.13 Abigail] An Old Testament heroine who subsequently became one of the early wives of King David (Cf. 1 Samuel 25:2–42).

902.2 Mariano] Based on Elisabetta "Nicky" Mariano (1887–1968), long-serving librarian of the Berenson Library at I Tatti outside Florence, Italy, and personal assistant to the Italian Renaissance art scholar and attributionist Bernard Berenson. Mariano was a friend of the Bradburys from their May 1954 visit to I Tatti until her death.

903.1 "Agamemnon . . ."] In Greek legend, a Mycenaean king of the late second millennium B.C.E. who led the Achaean alliance of Peloponnesian kings against Troy in the Trojan War.

903.8 Agonistes] One who triumphs over suffering, personified most famously through the play *Samson Agonistes* (1671) by the English poet John Milton (1608–1674) and the modernist poem "Sweeny Agonistes" by T. S. Eliot.

903.15 Alcibiades] Alcibiades (c. 450–404 B.C.E.) was an Athenian leader who also served Sparta and Persia before being exiled by the Athenians late in the Peloponnesian War.

905.5 Les Deux Magots] This restaurant in the Saint-Germain district of Paris, which opened in 1885, was a favorite destination for Bradbury and his wife during their many visits to Paris from the 1950s through the 1990s.

912.18–19 'Whatever you do . . . forgive you.'] Helen Flanders Dunbar, *Your Child's Mind and Body: A Practical Guide for Parents* (1949). In private conversation, Bradbury observed that "Flanders Dunbar had a phrase in there which said, 'Whatever you do, don't die—your children will never forgive you.' That's so perceptive. Because, if you suddenly go away, without leave, and you didn't say goodbye, you're suddenly dead and gone, how's your child going to adjust to that? It's all cut off, suddenly. They've got to feel resentment that you didn't at least tuck them in before you went away to the graveyard" (Bradbury to Eller, 2004).

913.10 Versailles jet] The Palace of Versailles outside of Paris, a grand lodge initially built by Louis XIII and expanded in stages by Louis XIV. The fifty fountains of the gardens of Versailles include more than six hundred water jets.

This book is set in 10 point ITC Galliard, a face designed for digital composition by Matthew Carter and based on the sixteenth-century face Granjon. The paper is acid-free lightweight opaque that will not turn yellow or brittle with age. The binding is sewn, which allows the book to open easily and lie flat. The binding board is covered in Brillianta, a woven rayon cloth made by Van Heek–Scholco Textielfabrieken, Holland.

Composition by Jordan Koluch.

Printing by Sheridan, Grand Rapids, MI.

Binding by Dekker Bookbinding, Wyoming, MI.

Designed by Bruce Campbell.